Tainted Truth

Book One of The Wolf Riders of Keldarra

Nathalie M.L. Römer

Emerentsia Publications, Sweden

ISBN-13: 9789188459800

Emerentsia Publications
Marielundsvägen 9c
711 95 Gusselby
Sweden
emerentsiabooks.com

Ordering Information:

Orders by U.S. trade bookstores and wholesalers. Please contact Ingram: One Ingram Blvd., La Vergne, TN 37086 • 615.793.5000 or visit www.ingramcontent.com.

Independently printed as a Swedish publication.

*This edition has previously been published under the title **The Stone of Truth** which has since been discontinued and been replaced by this updated and improved edition. The series name has remained the same.*

Interior design and layout by Emerentsia Publications.

Official Website:
nathaliemlromer.com

Official Facebook Page:
facebook.com/nathaliemlromer

Official Twitter Account:
twitter.com/nmlromer

Book website: nathaliemlromer.com/tainted-truth

For my loving partner Anders.

* * *

*K*eldarra, *the largest of the three ancient continents making up the world, was once a beautiful and tranquil land of peace--*

This is long forgotten by the people who live there now. Some people even say peace never existed. Others claim it existed, but some curse brought upon the world destroyed it. It's uncertain which one--peace or eternal warfare--is the truth, and which version is just rumour brought into existence because of the turmoil existing in this fragile world.

The fate of other continents is unknown. Did the Wolf Riders reach those distant shores?

The ocean between Keldarra and its neighbouring continent is too vast to breach with the small ships many seamen possess. The days of the majestic ocean-faring ships are long gone, a part of The Old Days. People now live in more close-knit communities and don't travel or venture out much. It seems most people who live in the turbulent Keldarra have grown to not care less about distant lands.

Only the Keepers of Truth know. Or so it's whispered when people think no one in authority is listening. But even the Keepers of Truth are seen by many as a retelling - the traditional Keldarran word for a story - conjured up to explain the lack of anything being done about the turmoil in the world. No person, except those started into the Order, knows the truth about them, and even fewer understand why they keep their purpose so secret.

In the city of Ruh'nar, prosperity is relatively untouched by the warfare the Wolf Riders inflict upon the land. The latest whisper, however, is of an impending incursion by the Wolf Riders, who have become more aggressive and bolder in the last few decades - a menacing reality no one can ignore --

* * *

Part One

CHAPTER ONE

Marrida shudders at the thought of the Wolf Riders, hurrying home as fast as she can. She has heard the rumours that they are coming closer to Ruh'nar; every day the people of the city grow more fearful. Some have even started to make up retellings of having encountered the Wolf Riders, and many merchants who'd normally be busying themselves in the central market square now stay away.

The city feels so empty these days.

The pain of the impending incursion, whether or not the rumours are true, is visible on the faces of those Marrida passes in the streets. Even she is feeling fear in the deepest recesses of her heart, but it's not so much fear for herself. If the Wolf Riders are going to attack, what will happen to her younger brother?

"They'll snatch you too," she'd shouted at him in her latest fit of anger when he'd again mentioned his chosen vocation to her. Her brother, in turn, had stomped off to his room, slammed the door shut, and stayed there for hours. Not even a meal would tempt him out.

Another shudder of fear runs through Marrida. It is too risky for boys to be outside these days. The Wolf Riders are renowned for snatching them to be trained in the ruined city they claimed as their own centuries earlier. No one really understands why the Wolf Riders do this. Some say it is related to their own legends – although you can hardly call the retellings of a brutish group of men 'legends'. And now these men are targeting *her* city to plunder and destroy, taking even more power for themselves.

Marrida is a young, headstrong woman, only a few years beyond her woman initiation, First Rites. She and her younger brother and sister occupy a small but luxurious house on the most north-easterly street off the central market, just a few streets past her uncle's shop which sells exquisite pottery, leather wares and stone works. The district she lives in has been notable for centuries for its artisans, but even those are fewer these days as the residents of Ruh'nar seek safety in the untouched cities on the western coast of the vast continent. Although Marrida's district is still considered among the wealthiest parts of the fast diminishing city, even grandeur can pay the ultimate price.

Marrida sincerely hopes one day to convince her uncle that they too should leave, but he is probably as stubborn as she is. He tells her the family has lived in Ruh'nar for more than nine generations since leaving their original home behind, so they will *stay* in Ruh'nar.

* * *

DEEP IN THOUGHT, Marrida passes her uncle's shop. She can hear noises from within, indicating her uncle, Joharan, and his five young apprentices are hard at work.

Years ago, she was in the shop as a young child. A group of seven cloaked women and a solitary man, who acted as their guard, entered and asked for her. With some reluctance, her uncle called her from the back room. When the women explained to him that they were looking for a stone of innocence and only a young girl could see its innocence, he agreed to the process, and let them use the room behind the storage area for privacy. Why he so readily allowed his young niece to be alone with this group of strangers is still a puzzle to Marrida.

Once they were alone, Marrida watched as the women took off their long, dark grey-blue cloaks and revealed themselves – the guard had gone outside by now. She realised from their appearance they were from the Temple – the mysterious building at the south end of the central square which only a few can enter.

The most striking thing about the group, at least in Marrida's young mind, was how wealthily dressed they were. The leader, whom she would come to know as Elder Sharriba, wore her silver-streaked hair tied back with a clasp studded with small gems, and her dress was the richest dark red. Sharriba's face was heart-shaped, and as a young woman, she must have drawn plenty of interest from men looking for a life partner. Her only piece of jewellery was a gem in the shape of a rubha apple hanging from a beaded chain around her neck, and Marrida couldn't keep her eyes off the gem however much she tried.

Sharriba's piercing green-grey eyes seemed to stare right through Marrida as she spoke to her. She told the young girl that she had observed Marrida in a dream, and like them, Marrida was destined to be a Keeper of Truth. At the time, Marrida did not understand what all this meant, but as she started her extensive training with Sharriba, she was quick to learn.

The first thing the Elder told her was that no person, not even her family, should ever know that she was a Keeper of Truth. There would be dire consequences if it was ever discovered she had revealed this information. The punishment would be severe, but Marrida was not told how it would be 'imparted', as Sharriba put it.

Was that a bit of a play on words? Marrida thinks now, chuckling at the irony of dealing with truth while lying to kith and kin about what she does in the Temple. Sometimes the humour of the situation is easier to consider than the consequences of what she's doing in secret.

Three days after the fateful day in her uncle's shop, Marrida became an initiated Acolyte. That day, her destiny altered, giving her life a new meaning. But what Marrida didn't know was that this destiny would lead her towards another.

She was so innocent back then.

* * *

MARRIDA SOON NOTICED ELDER SHARRIBA singled her out for in-depth training and discussion. After a time, the other Acolytes started to treat her differently, to the point where she sensed their resentment as soon as she entered a room. It left her with no friends at the Temple, and at times loneliness overwhelmed her. There were three slightly older Acolytes who liked picking on her whenever she was alone in a room with them.

In her private history lessons with Elder Sharriba, Marrida learnt that the First Elder created the Order nearly a thousand years ago, at a time now commonly referred to as 'The Old Days'. The First Elder possessed the rare ability to see not only into the past, but also small fragments of the future, and that Elder was instrumental in entrusting two brothers with the task of creating a force of peacekeepers who could keep the world safe. Sharriba told Marrida never to mention any of this to the others in the Temple.

These two brothers lived in a city now lying in ruins, used as a base by the Wolf Riders. Why and how they changed from being peacekeepers to the warmongers of today is something the Keepers of Truth do not understand fully. One afternoon, while they were alone, Sharriba told Marrida her family came from that ancient city, but they fled and settled on the south coast. There, many generations later, her mother started her life. As Marrida learnt what her own uncle had kept hidden from her, she realised she had a further reason to hate the Wolf Riders.

The Elder explained about Marrida's merchant father's journey south to Marridina. When he saw Marrida's mother, he asked her to become his life partner, and she agreed. They bonded in a traditional ceremony after only knowing one another a single day, and this part of her family's history moved Marrida beyond words. It brought genuine tears to her eyes – both of remembrance and sadness.

Marrida wonders if she'll ever meet someone whom she can love so genuinely, and so quickly. And whether she'll be able to learn more about her parents' traditional ceremony, as Elder Sharriba never spoke any more about it.

This ceremony forced Marrida's mother to leave her duties as a Keeper. Several months before she'd died, her mother had come to see Elder Sharriba in person and asked the older woman to initiate Marrida into the Temple. Although it went against tradition, Elder Sharriba had agreed.

When the time came for Sharriba to honour her promise to Marrida's mother, it was necessary to test the girl's skills. Untested, she wouldn't be welcome at the Temple, even if the Elder insisted upon it. Marrida's mother had made Elder Sharriba a secondary guardian for her young daughter, Marrida's uncle being her other guardian, in case anything should happen to her and her life partner. They would remain her guardians until Marrida came of age and took over the duty of care for her two siblings.

Sharriba knew little about Marrida's father. He had been an affluent merchant who journeyed far and wide, selling the wares that Ruh'nar produced. This meant his growing family could live in the wealthiest parts of the city, and his children could attend the best school the city offered.

Marrida knew from Sharriba that her parents loved one another deeply. She loved both her parents with equal devotion, and hers was a close-knit and happy family. When the news arrived that her father had been killed on his travels, her mother had taken it badly. Heavily pregnant with the couple's third child, she had gone into early labour. Marrida's younger sister, Kalisa, had been born healthy, but her mother did not survive the birthing.

The rift between her two older children started that day.

* * *

Ruh'nar is a city of about two hundred thousand people, the population swelling by more than fifty thousand on market days, such as the spring market, and even more when the annual Festival of the Rites — the initiation of youths into young adulthood — takes place. Some say the city once had over five hundred thousand residents, and at the time dwarfed the city now lying in ruins; the city whose name had been lost to the Wolf Riders. Some say that at that time, almost everyone in the two nearby provinces came to visit the city for the Festival. To Marrida, that explains the size of the Temple, which looks so large and ill-suited to Ruh'nar now.

Ruh'nar was the capital city in The Old Days. Situated in the centre of the tranquil province of Sabeya, a rich agricultural region famous for its rubha apples, Ruh'nar now feels more like an average provincial town. The smaller cities of the west coast have taken its place in size, appearance and grandeur.

Half of Sabeya is covered with dense forests of rubha apple shrubs. The shrub grows not into a tree, but into a thick rounded bush with dark green leaves. The tiny apples cover the bush, and when they ripen, they are pure white in colour and smell of honey. The citruses from the nearby Azamella province, some of which grow into fruits double the size of a man's fist, are sometimes mixed with rubha apples to make a tart spread eaten with bread. Both are harvested in the second month of the autumn season and placed into large wooden vats in readiness for the drying process that takes most of the cold winter months.

The other province is Marridina. On the coast, it is known for its delicious seafood which is brought back to Ruh'nar by merchants from the city on an almost daily basis. One such merchant was Marrida's own father, and it was on one such journey that he met Marrida's mother.

* * *

Marrida is shivering.

Either there's a chill in the air, or those Wolf Riders are making me feel edgy, she thinks, frowning. Her duty as a Keeper of Truth – even just an Acolyte – is bearing down on her more and more each day, but the rumours about the impending incursion by the Wolf Riders have got her scared for her whole family.

Today, after a long day of training, all the Acolytes were sent home for their own safety when the gong at the gatehouse struck. Marrida's uncle is only aware she works as a Temple Maiden, and prior to her First Rites, that was exactly what she did. Thus, up until the Festival, she was telling her uncle the truth.

Now we no longer speak, she thinks sadly, *so I don't have to tell him anything.*

But Marrida is someone with a guilty secret. She has been doing visions by herself, even though Sharriba expressly forbade her to do this, and recently, a dangerous plan has started forming in her mind.

Little does she know as she walks towards her house that her plans are about to alter radically. Fate will soon set her on a path that will for ever change her life.

CHAPTER TWO

MARRIDA GLANCES BACK towards the square, wondering why her uncle never told her that her mother was a Keeper. *Does my uncle even know? Why has he never explained where the family originally came from all those generations ago?*

Ruh'nar itself is divided into several districts, each with its own function. The district Marrida lives in is by far the wealthiest and best protected part of the city, home to artisans and merchants, and Marrida's uncle is one of the most powerful of them. Throughout the city and far beyond, he's recognised for his skills, and he maintains influential connections in the Council of Seven and the Office of the Merchant Clerk.

To the west side of the city is the building housing the Academy of Warfare. In days long past, this building would have been active, with hundreds of men and women training in the art of using spears and spear arrows, knife throwing, making and maintaining siege weaponry – skills required by the ancient protectors of Keldarra, who were the peacekeepers of the land and not the later menacing marauders they have become.

Now, most of the Academy of Warfare lies barren, like most buildings of the city.

Marrida remembers how she would implore her uncle to move to a city far away on the western coast, but he told her Ruh'nar is his home and he'll stay there until he's on his deathbed. She wonders whether he's so stubborn because he wants to be like his forebears in The Old Days, back in the city brought to ruins by the Wolf Riders.

What is the city called anyway? she ponders.

The Temple, where the Keepers of Truth reside, is in the largest part of the city. Many Acolytes and Keepers claim it would take from sunrise to past midday to walk from one end of the Temple garden to the other, and Marrida once stirred up a commotion by going missing for an entire morning in the garden. When she explained to Elder Sharriba on her return that she wanted to practise what she'd learnt about the Temple, the

Elder had simply nodded in acknowledgement and did not say anything further, the suggested favouritism fuelling the suspicion and hatred the other Acolytes already felt towards Marrida.

Many also suggest that if you walk around the outside of the Temple, you will see the moon rise twice before you get back to the main stairs. Marrida has vowed to test this theory in her free time. There is no equal in size to the Temple anywhere, at least not since the most ancient of cities was destroyed by the Wolf Riders, leaving the Temple there as nothing more than a place for their wolves to sleep and eat.

No one knows how many Wolf Riders exist. There is talk of a group who have split themselves off from the rest and taken up residence on the most north-westerly coast of Keldarra in a rugged region called Zehar. Some say a man often travels from the ruined city to join these Wolf Riders, but as is the nature of rumours, no one is sure if this is the truth.

Truth, truth, always the damned truth.

* * *

MARRIDA UNDERWENT FIRST RITES three years previously. Once initiated, she was permitted to become an Acolyte of Truth – essentially, the first training position for girls in the Temple before they go on to become Keepers after ten to fifteen years of hard study. At fifteen, she became the youngest Acolyte in the Temple, at least six years younger than the others had been when they entered the Order. Many older Acolytes thought Marrida was too young for the Learning, but every time they objected, Sharriba herself stopped them in their tracks.

The Acolyte training itself is split into four parts, each taking anything from a couple of years to half a decade, depending on the skill of the girl or woman receiving the training. The first part of the training took Marrida just over a year, thanks in part to the extra lessons she received from Sharriba. Marrida has repeatedly showed how strong she is in various tests, and Sharriba is certain she will finish all four levels of her training in under a decade. Marrida recognises it will be hard work, and the work will become even harder once she puts her secret plan in motion and tells her siblings about her status as an Acolyte.

Her duties at the Temple are many and endless. She's learning six forms of ancient dialect with accompanying writings, how to balance her thoughts, mathematics and the biology of animals, about plants and their various uses, and the Ancient Histories. She studies almost all day, and when she isn't studying, she is working beside Elder Sharriba, learning from her about the First Elder and the Forbidden Knowledge. The older woman possesses endless patience, and when something is unclear to Marrida, she explains until it's clear. This is knowledge no other Acolyte has, but her mother requested that Marrida be taught it.

Marrida's curiosity about her own mother is the reason why she has started to do visions by herself in secret. She has learnt about her mother's days as a Keeper and gained even more respect for her, and she now understands why her father fell in love with her mother so quickly. She has also glimpsed a woman whom she assumes to be her maternal grandmother. There was immense sadness in the woman's face, and it felt to Marrida as if the vision was trying to tell her something more. However, she isn't trained enough to see further into the past – yet.

One day I will see it, Marrida thinks, smiling inwardly.

This year it's the turn of her brother, fifteen-year-old Esbara, to participate in First Rites. As Marrida is considered, at least in name, to be his parental guardian, she has been to meet with the Council of Seven to submit his name for the ceremony. Why it's called the Council of Seven when it only consists of three people, two men and a woman, is another of the many mysteries puzzling Marrida.

After Esbara has participated in the initial preparations, he will be considered ready for First Rites, and soon he will be a young adult. Esbara's ambition is to be admitted into what remains of the Academy of Warfare. He wants to become a soldier and protect the city and his sisters from danger – an ambition which led to his most recent quarrel with Marrida. In the end, he told her that soon he'd be a man, allowed to make his own decisions.

This quarrel happened two days ago, and they hadn't spoken much since until this morning's meal. Marrida then told him that his decision was probably one of the most dangerous things he could do, but after he argued it was better than risking being snatched by the Wolf Riders without any way to defend himself, she finally relented.

Their younger sister Kalisa is still too young to understand what all the fuss is about, or why her older sister and brother are arguing almost daily. She regards Marrida as her only mother, and her uncle Joharan is so old, to her he feels more like a grandfather than an uncle. He is the older brother of their late father, and there was an age gap of almost sixteen years between the two men.

The night of Kalisa's birthing, it rained hard. Their father had been on his last journey before the long winter months and planned to arrive home in time for the birthing. Instead, his family received the sad news that he had been ambushed and killed.

It's almost twelve years ago since Papa and Mam died.

Marrida sighs. Her own memories of her mother have come from her exposure to the Stone of Truth. Elder Sharriba considers them a necessary part of her training as an Acolyte of Truth to become the Keeper she is destined to be, so she has told Marrida all she knows about her mother. Unbeknown to Sharriba, Marrida has learnt other things about her mother from the visions she has done in secret. And as she learns more about her mother, she tells her younger siblings more about her. They think she can remember their mother because she is four years older than Esbara and seven years older than Kalisa; they do not yet know the knowledge comes from the gem hanging from a pale golden chain around Marrida's neck, hidden under her outer tunic.

The Stone of Truth is a remarkably unassuming gem, only interesting in the way it reacts. While inert, it is a cloudy white, not dissimilar to a unripe rubha apple in appearance, but when it's handled by a trained Keeper of Truth and used in the rituals the Keepers guard so meticulously, the gem lights up with a pale green tint at its base. Most gems are handed down from mother to daughter – always to daughters as it is forbidden for men to use the Stone of Truth.

Keepers give their gems a nickname, often calling them 'rubha gems' when they're in the presence of the uninitiated. If they hide a gem in a basket of rubha apples, it acts as an excellent disguise. The first time Sharriba referred to a 'rubha gem', Marrida giggled. Coincidentally, rubha apples are her favourite fruit, and she always has a couple of dozen in a brown woven basket at the back of her cooking room. She often puts her gem in the basket when she is cooking or bathing, and even with it sitting there in plain sight among the fruit, her siblings never register its presence.

Some say rubha apples are fruit given by the gods, and therefore the most precious fruit in existence. Marrida believes the Stone of Truth has been cut to a similar shape to remind its user of the precious nature of the rubha apple. Elder Sharriba has told the young Acolyte some of how the First Elder discovered how to use the gem for visions, and to Marrida, the idea of the rubha apple being a gift from the gods has something to do with it.

However, sometimes she isn't so sure her visions, or being a Keeper, are such a gift. From what she's learnt in her private Ancient Histories lessons with Elder Sharriba, nothing was able to prevent the Wolf Riders from becoming an evil force in the world, even though the First Elder had the gift of seeing the future.

There's another myth about the rubha apple, so old that not even the Keepers with their Stone of Truth can access it, which says the fruit was eaten only by royalty in The Old Days. The bushes were much rarer then than they are now, and their rarity made their fruit exclusive, but when the Wolf Riders killed all the growers of the bushes, they spread around the region by themselves.

Marrida ponders the retelling her uncle told her about The Old Days. He does not know much about this part of history, but what he does know amazed her – that is, until she used the Stone of Truth for the first time. Now she can almost live this ancient past. It will take several seasons of training to become more efficient, but Marrida has abundant skill and is learning fast. She has seen images of her mother as a young woman, and something about these visions makes her want to reach further back to The Old Days, but she keeps seeing unfamiliar cities, one of them seemingly in shadow. Instinctively, she knows these cities are going to be important to her in the future, so she has made a point of remembering them in detail in case she ever visits them.

Marrida opens the front door to her house and Kalisa rushes into her embrace. She's still young, but is the sort of person everyone likes, and she is highly intelligent. Kalisa speeds into the cooking room and walks back with a bowl of soup for Marrida, which she carries towards a table in the room directly next to the entrance door of the dwelling.

She's always so considerate whenever I get home.

Before Marrida can sit down to eat the hot soup with Kalisa and Esbara, loud shouts and a commotion come from outside. Marrida goes as white as moss ash.

"Go upstairs and wait there for me," she urges her brother and sister in a hushed voice.

After they go, Esbara rather reluctantly, Marrida steps outside, and tensely watches the turmoil weaving through the streets with the speed of an approaching storm.

CHAPTER THREE

MARRIDA STANDS FOR A FEW MINUTES, her mouth agape, her mind racing with two conflicting thoughts.

Should any of the Wolf Riders come back and find the man and his wolf lying unconscious in the street, they will ransack all nearby houses as revenge, and Esbara may get snatched--

A shiver goes down her spine as she thinks more about the Wolf Rider with the black hair. Something tells her she wouldn't want to cross paths with this man. She listens, wondering if he'll return, but can only hear indistinct sounds.

Deciding it's relatively safe once more, although the word 'safe' sounds hollow during a Wolf Rider attack, Marrida turns her attention to her second thought.

What can I do for the man and his wolf so none of the city defenders will find them and kill them?

Slowly, Marrida manoeuvres herself from the crevice in which she's been hiding. The man is lying still on the ground, a pool of blood gathering under his head, and the wolf beside him is injured as well. Marrida stares long and hard towards the square and spots no one. Glancing in the direction the dark-haired Wolf Rider rode away, she tilts her head for a moment, listening for any kind of noise, whether friend or foe. Finally, she paces towards the man and his wolf.

Several houses near hers were deserted months ago, so she doesn't need to worry about nosey neighbours catching her out, but as she is touching the man's neck to feel for a pulse, a noise behind her startles her. She turns on her heels, discovering Esbara and Kalisa standing at the open door of their house, looking pale and shocked.

"What are you doing to him?" Esbara hisses at Marrida.

"I heard someone throw stones at them. I'm checking if he's alive still."

"Do you think we should take him inside?"

Marrida examines Esbara's face for a few moments, wondering why he wants to help this man, a Wolf Rider, despite his talk of becoming a soldier to defend the city against them.

"Alright, but we need to bring the wolf into the garden as well," she replies.

Esbara runs over and takes the man's left arm, Marrida takes his right arm, and Kalisa picks up his weapons from the ground. After some effort, they get him and the weapons into the guest room next to the cooking room, then it takes all three of them to drag the wolf into the garden at the back of the house.

Marrida grabs an old broom and a bucket of sawdust, usually used to clean the road of mud, and spreads several scoops of the fine dust over the bloodied part of the road, sweeping all evidence away. She then throws as many buckets of water as it takes to wash away the final few blood smears. Checking over her handiwork, after a few moments she throws some extra water onto the pavement, grabbing the bucket of sawdust and sprinkling some more on the street. The dust will dry quickly in the sun and blow away by itself.

She glances back and forth along the road one more time before hurrying into her house and bolting the door.

"No one can discover what we have done," she tells her younger siblings, who both nod solemnly. They all know the danger they will be in if the Wolf Riders come back, and if the Council of Seven, their uncle or any other people from the city find out about the Wolf Rider in their house, he will be killed.

* * *

MARRIDA LOOKS AT THE INJURED MAN lying on the bed. She understands healing practices from her training as a Temple Maiden, but she does not know whether what she has learnt, or the treatment she can administer to him, will be enough. Only time will tell if he will live or die.

Then there's the wolf. It's a female wolf in early pregnancy.

Perhaps seven or eight pups though I don't know how long gestation lasts in this breed of wolf, Marrida thinks absentmindedly. *At least, if she survives the head wound.*

Walking out into the garden, Marrida is immediately struck by the appearance of the wolf and wonders where she came from. She has never seen a wolf as large as this one. Although she has heard that the Wolf Riders' wolves can grow as high as a man's chest, like everyone else she has dismissed this as a rumour. Now one of those fabled wolves is lying in Marrida's garden, panting for every breath she can get.

The colour of the wolf is fascinating. Most wolves near Ruh'nar are dark grey or black, but this wolf possesses a beautiful silver coat with white streaks of fur running to the tip of her tail. The tail ends in white, and most of the chest of the beast is white as well. Marrida feels the animal's fur. It's remarkably soft; obviously, someone has combed her with care.

Marrida walks back into the room where the man is lying, curious about him. He appears tall and muscular, but there's melancholy on his face even though he is unconscious.

Maybe I should use the Stone of Truth and try to glean some of his past, she muses. It would be the first time she has ever used the gem in the presence of other people, and the rules forbid this while she's still an Acolyte. In fact, even as a Keeper, it would be forbidden.

But who would know?

* * *

MARRIDA SITS DOWN next to her brother, glancing first at Kalisa opposite her and then at Esbara. Both look at her with expressions that say, "What are we going to do now?" and Marrida decides she needs to tell them about the Stone of Truth. She must use her gem, and they will be watching her and wondering what she is doing.

Sighing, she says, "I have something I need to tell both of you." After some hesitation, she adds, "I'm a Keeper of Truth. Or, to be more precise, I'm being trained to be one at the Temple."

She glances at both her siblings as their expressions go from awe to disbelief before settling on admiration. Marrida takes the gem from around her neck and places it carefully in the middle of the table so both can see it.
"It looks like a rubha apple," Esbara says, chuckling.
"Yes, and we call it a 'rubha gem' because of that."
"So how do you use it?" Kalisa whispers "Can you show us?"

"I'll show you both. I need to use this gem to find out who the Wolf Rider in the next room is."

Kalisa and Esbara both nod in understanding.

"What does it do exactly?" Esbara probes hesitantly.

"It's a tool to observe events from the past," Marrida states, adding, "It can show me where the man lived before he became a Wolf Rider, whether he was snatched."

It occurs to Esbara as Marrida speaks why she is always so scared about him being in the streets, and he silently vows to stay safe from now on for her sake.

Marrida spends several hours demonstrating and explaining the use of the Stone of Truth to her siblings while dusk settles over the city and the shouting and fighting fade. With Esbara and Kalisa watching on apprehensively, she sits down on the chair beside the man. Glancing at him again and gathering her thoughts, she picks up the Stone of Truth from the low table in front of her. Esbara nods encouragingly at her, his expression one she has never seen on his face before. He appears to be both curious and annoyed, and Marrida realises that she has no right to object to his decision to become a defender of the city he grew up in when she has been keeping the importance of her own work from him.

Marrida closes her eyes and sighs deeply. She holds the Stone of Truth in her left hand with her right hand a small distance above it. Sensing the gem starting to glow in her hand, she opens her eyes, focusing on the fog-like orb appearing in front of her in mid-air. Her eyes become unfocused, and no sound other than that being emitted by the orb is heard.

Moments later, a large oval-shaped image hovers next to her. Esbara and Kalisa watch with mouths agape, now understanding that the rumours and retellings about the Keepers of Truth are all true – and their own sister is one of them.

Esbara watches Marrida. He notices her eyes go dark and opaque, and she isn't blinking anymore. He is focusing on the image which is hovering in front of him when Kalisa nudges him. The boy scrutinises his young sister and her questioning look, and an edge of fear in her eyes holds his attention. Esbara puts his arm around her, and the girl snuggles closer to him, putting her thumb in her mouth. She still does that when she is scared about something.

She is so young still. She must wonder what is going on.

Esbara focuses on the image again. He sees a boy not much older than himself. Glancing at the bed, Esbara realises it must be the Wolf Rider as a youngster.

Looking back at the image, he sees Wolf Riders. The boy is grabbed by the scruff of his neck and pulled onto a wolf in front of a stocky man with dark hair. Something about the man seems familiar, but Esbara cannot put his finger on what it is. His eyes narrow. The dark-haired man reminds him of why he wants to be a defender of the city. He needs to talk to Marrida about it later.

Kalisa is fascinated. Wondering if she could do what her sister is doing, she glances from the image to the man on the bed and back at the image. It is scary, but interesting. She cuddled up against Esbara when Marrida's eyes changed colour, becoming completely unfocused, but now she is starting to feel braver. She sits up and takes her thumb out of her mouth, eyeing Esbara. He glances at her and smiles encouragingly. She smiles back.

Marrida is confused at first about what she's seeing in the vision. Initially, she thinks the boy is her brother, but the streets and buildings around him are totally unfamiliar. She notes the presence of the stocky dark-haired man, aware that she saw him in the street moments before the man on her guest bed was injured, and she's curious to find out who he is.

Witnessing the boy being snatched, she realises how the man on her bed became a Wolf Rider. She can see the wolf she dragged to her garden and another wolf with tan fur. Both wolves appear massive, but the silver-coated one is bigger.

She views a terrace with chairs and a door leading to a room. It looks rather untidy, yet something about it indicates whoever lives there cares about their home. The same stocky dark-haired man and the man on her bed are sitting opposite each other, drinking. The two wolves are visible again, and Marrida senses that both the man on the bed and the wolf in the garden are connected to something greater than she can imagine — something that must be allowed to happen.

They both must live.

Then the image fades away, and Marrida wills her right hand to move from above the gem. Moments later she's staring at her siblings across the room.

"Some water please," she implores.

Esbara gets up, fills a nearby cup with some water from the jug on the cabinet behind him, and brings it over to his sister. He is frowning, thinking about what he has just witnessed.

"Why didn't you keep looking for more?" he enquires.

"It can be exhausting." Nodding at the unconscious man on the bed, Marrida explains, "I need to know more about him in the here and now before I can probe into his past."

She sips the water from the cup and thinks deeply.

"How much of it did you two see?" she asks, looking at Esbara and Kalisa in turn.

"We saw enough," Esbara replies, and Kalisa nods, agreeing with her brother.

"Remember, no one else can know about him," Marrida continues, again nodding in the direction of the unconscious man and adding sternly, "Neither can anyone know I showed you the Stone of Truth being used."

Esbara and Kalisa both reassure her that they understand. Marrida puts the gem back on its chain, and puts the chain around her neck, pulling her hair over it before tucking the gem away. She lets her hand rest over the lump, the Stone of Truth hidden under her tunic, and sighs again. Glancing at the man on the bed, she wonders how many more times she'll need to use the gem before she knows enough about him — who he is, and whether her guess is correct that one of the cities on the west coast was the image in the vision.

Marrida gets up slowly. "Let's eat," she states. Her siblings get up too, and all three go into the cooking room. Esbara sits on the bench beside the table to eat the soup which Kalisa returned to the cooking room before she went upstairs with him hours earlier. Kalisa, however, first runs to the window and glances into the back garden, staring with awe at the wolf lying there, still unconscious but breathing slowly and steadily.

"Kalisa!" The young girl is startled by her name being called. She turns and goes to sit beside her brother, while Marrida reheats the soup. Then Marrida sits down opposite her brother and sister.

The meal is accompanied by inconsequential chatter, mostly initiated by Kalisa who is still too young to realise the significance of what has happened to them all on this day. She is telling them both about her visit to their uncle's shop, and how Damir demonstrated stone working to her and promised to teach her to do some for herself tomorrow.

"Damir is so amusing whenever I visit the shop," she says with a big grin on her face.

Damir is almost six years older than Kalisa and became Joharan's apprentice eleven years ago. He and Kalisa are the best of friends, and Marrida and Esbara smile at each other, knowing looks in their eyes. They know Damir likes their sister a lot.

Neither Marrida nor Esbara talk much at first during the meal, but encouraged by Kalisa's endless chatter, they start to join in. By the end of the meal, everyone is chatting and laughing like it is an ordinary evening.

* * *

AFTER THE MEAL, MARRIDA TUCKS KALISA IN BED and kisses her goodnight. She then walks downstairs to the guest room with the Wolf Rider in it and is surprised to find her brother sitting on the chair beside the bed, staring at the injured man intently.

He looks up as she enters the room. "Who is he?"
"I don't know," she replies.
"How old do you think he is?"
"While he's unconscious like this, he seems younger than he may be. He could be as young as twenty or as old as thirty."

They look each other in the eyes, each with their own thoughts about the events of the day. Both are tired but are not feeling ready for bed. Marrida guesses that Esbara is probably thinking the same things as she is, and more. She is thinking about the Stone of Truth and wondering if she should try to do a vision again.

Reaching up to the bulge under her tunic, she holds her hand there while glancing at Esbara. His eyes trail down to where the Stone of Truth hangs around her neck and his facial expression answers her unspoken question.

"Use it," he states simply. "But tomorrow when you aren't tired."

After checking the injured man, both Esbara and Marrida go to their own beds, and not long afterwards, all the lights are extinguished in the house. Sleep comes slowly for Marrida, who lies awake for several hours thinking about the events of the day. From now on, her life will be different. It's almost as if her initiation as an Acolyte of Truth is happening again, except in reverse.

Now she has used the Stone of Truth around uninitiated people, she will have to be extremely careful at the Temple. Elder Sharriba will be furious if she ever finds out what Marrida has done today, downstairs in the room where an unknown man lies sleeping.

Tiredness overcomes Marrida in the end, and once she has fallen into a deep and restful sleep, the whole house settles into peace and quiet. The only sounds come from the wolf in the garden, yipping softly as she lies unconscious in a strange city.

And in the guest room on the ground floor, dreams come slowly into the man's mind too – dreams he has dreamt many times before of a girl with golden-blonde hair, a curious gem hanging on a delicate chain around her neck.

CHAPTER FOUR

KALISA IS THE FIRST TO RISE, a routine of almost seven weeks now. Before the arrival of the man in the bed downstairs, her brother or sister often needed to come into her room to wake her, but now, she's eager to climb up on her bed and glance down at the wolf below. Her window overlooks the garden behind the house, and each day the young girl watches the wolf, but the beast never moves.

Today, however, the wolf lifts her head when she hears a noise coming from above her. She sniffs the air, analysing the unfamiliar surroundings with her wolf senses.

Kalisa calls out, "Wolfie? Wolfie?"

The wolf in the garden glances around. Her nose catches the scent of her master, but where can he be? She tries to lift herself up, but slumps back down in pain.

Marrida is woken by Kalisa's voice calling for the wolf. She gets up and goes to her sister's room where Kalisa is leaning from the window, looking down. Marrida sits beside her on the bed and puts an arm around the girl in a protective manner; she doesn't like it much when her sister leans from the window, which is something Kalisa seems to be doing a lot lately.

"Is the wolf awake?" Marrida asks sleepily.
Kalisa turns around and nods.
"What are we going to do with the wolf?"
"I'm not certain yet," Marrida acknowledges. "It depends on the man downstairs."
"Possibly we need to check on him."

Marrida nods, and they descend the stairs, walking through the large cooking room Tand entering the room where the man is resting. Marrida checks his breathing and feels his forehead.

Seems his fever has finally broken, and his breathing is becoming normal again.

She has been caring for the man since the Wolf Riders' attack seven weeks earlier, giving him sleep-inducing liquids to calm his body from the occasional convulsions he's experienced as he has drifted in and out of fever from the severe wound inflicted on him by someone defending the city, but he has never once regained consciousness. Just as she thinks today will be the same and decides to leave, the man on the bed grabs her hand.

Marrida blanches and freezes in place.

"Where am I?" he rasps.

"You're in my house," she replies, motioning at Kalisa to get Esbara. Kalisa nods, turns and runs upstairs. Moments later, she returns with Esbara, dragging the somewhat sleepy boy by one hand.

Marrida inspects the man carefully as he holds her arm. The strength in his grip slowly starts to lessen. He needs to heal more.

"What's your name?" Marrida quizzes.
"My…name…is Alag--"

The man has lost consciousness again. His grip slips away, and Marrida's arm is free. She glances at Esbara and Kalisa, seeing their faces showing the same curiosity as she is feeling. They need more information about this man. They are aware of the danger he presents – a Wolf Rider in their home – but they don't know where he is from.

"I need to eat something before I start," Marrida states in answer to her siblings' unspoken question, "I'll eat here in case he wakes again."

For a few minutes, Marrida ponders whether to use the Stone of Truth once more now the man has awoken. Every time she has tried, she has failed to discern anything more than the first vision revealed.

Esbara nods and turns to get bread, butter and a honey and fruit spread from the cooking room. Kalisa pulls a chair to the window, climbs on top of it and gazes out.

"The wolf is definitely awake, Marrida," she says.

Marrida paces to the window and gazes out, marking the wolf's location in the corner of the garden. With her head held high, the wolf is turning her ears in all directions as though a sound has caught her attention.

Marrida glances back at the unconscious man on the bed, a concerned frown forming on her face. *Can the wolf hear the man's voice? What am I going to do with the beast if he dies?*

Sitting at the small table at the foot of the guest bed, Marrida eats the bread her brother has given to her. He's cut several pieces, coated each with some butter, and spread the honey and fruit mixture over the top. Marrida savours the bread slice; the spread, produced in Marridina, is a speciality of their mother's home town, a small coastal town called Ezamir. It consists of autumn honey which has been aged throughout the winter and finely chopped kima berries. When the kima bush bears its small bright purple berries in the spring, they are harvested, cooked slowly until soft, and chilled on ice slabs for a week. They are then well chopped and mixed in with the honey, giving it a blue colour and adding a slightly tart flavour to offset its sweetness. Marrida was overjoyed when she found a merchant was coming from Ezamir to Ruh'nar once every two seasons, bringing the honey and fruit mixture with him. It gave her something flavoursome to remember her mother by.

A noise coming from the bed makes Marrida stop eating, and she glances at the man. Two vivid blue eyes are staring back at her.

He's awake.

"How do you feel?"
"My head hurts," he replies.
Marrida perceives how softly spoken he is.
"You were injured."
He nods, reaching up to his head and noting an expertly wrapped bandage surrounding his scalp.
"What happened to me?"
"Do you remember attacking the city?" Esbara almost shouts at him. Marrida gives him a stare to shut him up.
"You're a Wolf Rider, aren't you?" she asks.
The injured man nods.
"Someone threw two rocks at you. One hit you, the other hit your wolf--"
"Where's Yalla?" he asks, panic in his voice.
"Who's Yalla?"
"My wolf."
"The wolf is sleeping in our garden," Kalisa speaks up this time. The man regards the young girl, who eyeballs him back with curiosity and a

touch of defiance.

She's young to have such courage, but she has confirmed the wolf is alive and well. He pierces the air with a whistle, and a grunt from outside confirms his wolf's location.

The woman said a stone injured Yalla. He reaches up to his face and rubs his hand over the advanced stubble.

"How long have I been here?" he murmurs.

"Seven weeks," Marrida replies. "Most of the time, you lay unconscious in a high fever."

A searching hand again reaches to where the pain is coming from, but when it touches the edge of the bandage, the man decides to lower it and examine the woman standing next to the bed instead. With a start, he realises why she seems so familiar — she is the woman he has seen in his dreams.

Marrida peers down at the man as he whistles for the wolf again. This more than anything confirms him as a Wolf Rider. She has heard they possess an uncanny ability to communicate with the wolves they command. But she also remembers the vision she did. Needing to talk with the man, she motions to her siblings to come with her to the cooking room.

"He may not be communicative if both of you are in the room, so I want you to stay in the cooking room, concealed near the door. Listen to what he says, but do not interfere."

Both her siblings nod. Esbara takes Kalisa's hand and leads her to the corner of the room, where they sit down on the floor. Once they are settled, he holds his finger to his mouth to warn his younger sister to stay quiet.

Marrida walks back into the room where the man is resting and waiting for her. When she enters, he glances towards her and notices she's returned alone. Marrida catches sight of his vivid blue eyes once more as she grabs a chair and puts it close to the bed, studying his face.

"What's your name?" she questions, sitting down. "You started to tell me before, but lost consciousness."
"My name is Alagur."

"And you're a Wolf Rider?" He nods again. "But you weren't a Wolf Rider all your life," she adds hesitantly, wondering how much to tell him.

He gapes at her, astounded. "I have always been a Wolf Rider."

"No," Marrida replies.

An uneasy silence follows for a few minutes, then Alagur speaks again.

"I think I've seen you in dreams," he says, his face going bright red. *Dammit*, he thinks. *What's wrong with me? Why do I go red like I'm ashamed of what I'm saying?*

Marrida nods. As a Keeper of Truth, or an Acolyte at least, she knows dreams hold importance and are tools either to put a day's events in order or to open the mind to suggestions. She needs to determine if it's the former or the latter in the case of this man.

"Do you understand who I am?" she asks. The man shakes his head. "My name is Marrida. Why do you say you see me in dreams?"

Alagur contemplates her words. She isn't mocking him, or at least, it does not seem as though she is. Something about her seems simultaneously familiar and unfamiliar. He scrutinises her thoroughly. She has long blonde hair, a slender heart-shaped face, and blue eyes with long dark lashes framing them, and she is tall and slim. She is wearing a long grey-blue dress tied at the waist with a cloth belt.

Like in my dreams, he muses. Noticing the bulge under her tunic, he wonders what it represents.

Marrida patiently waits for an answer from the man. Except for his vivid blue eyes, she doesn't see anything about this man she finds especially appealing. The fact he's a Wolf Rider, one of the brutish men who'd snatch someone like her own brother, makes him even less appealing to her. Yet there's *something* about him; something about his demeanour almost convinces her he's one of the neighbouring artisans' sons who occasionally try to court her.

She shrugs off the thought.

"I keep having dreams, and the woman appearing in them resembles *you*." His voice is almost a whisper.

"I think I need to explain something about who I am," she responds.

Reaching up and pulling a gem on a gold chain from under her tunic, she dangles it in front of her body. Alagur's eyes fly open in shock.

"The gem…in my dream--" he stammers.

"Do you know what the gem it is?"

"It's a gem you use to see things." His voice cracks under the strain of his shock as the reality of his situation dawns on him.

"It's called the Stone of Truth," Marrida says. "We use it to view the past. I can see your past with it."

Alagur is dumbfounded. All his dreams are turning out to be true.

"What are you going to do with it?" he asks.

"If you wish, I can check your past to find out more about you. But only if you wish."

Alagur stares into the space in front of him. He's aware of the woman beside him, waiting patiently for an answer.

Do I want to know more about myself?

He ponders the question long and hard, thinking about Yalla. When he whistles for her, he hears the wolf answer.

He considers the woman's words once more.

"Can my wolf be here with me when you do this?"

Marrida thinks for a moment, then she nods hesitantly.

"Esbara," she calls out.

Her brother walks into the room and waits for instructions from her. He has already guessed what she's going to ask, but remembers his sister's instructions not to interfere or give any hint that he's been listening in. As soon as she has spoken again, he leaves the room, and a few moments later, he's back. Following him is the wolf, who instantly goes to the man on the bed. Laying her head on his leg, she yips until his hand signal makes her lie down at his feet at the end of the bed.

Marrida nods approvingly while Esbara gawks at the giant wolf in awe.

Once Esbara has left the room again, Marrida scrutinises the man on the bed and then the wolf. *She is loyal to her master for sure.*

Marrida glances down at the gem, hanging from the golden chain which she is holding in her left hand. When she looks up, she sees the man looking at the gem with curiosity. Like everyone else, he has believed the Keepers of Truth to be nothing more than a myth or a rumour. Alagur knows what the Wolf Riders say about their own beginnings, how they rebelled to become pillaging warriors rather than the peacekeepers they were almost a thousand years ago. And the rumour which circulates among them is that one of those calling themselves Keepers assisted them in their rebellion.

Alagur wonders how this young woman knows of his past, or the Wolf Riders. He considers for a moment whether to tell her about the Wolf Riders' history, but recalling her brother's earlier disdain, he holds his tongue.

Marrida takes the gem off the golden chain, which she puts on the bench beside her. Alagur watches as she places the gem on her left hand, then she positions her right palm a short distance above it. His eyes grow wide as a disc-shaped image appears next to the woman.

The next image makes him go pale as he watches a familiar black-haired man grab a boy and drag him on top of a wolf. This is a man he knows as a friend.

As Alagur views his history unfolding, a flood of long-forgotten memories invades his mind. The next emotion he feels is intense anger about Samur and his trickery, followed by sadness as he spies a young girl, a few years younger than Kalisa, running after him with tears streaming down her dirty face.

Something about the girl is familiar--

My sister. What happened to her after I disappeared?

Marrida isn't aware of the emotions she is stirring in the man on the bed. She is searching for answers — answers as to who he is, where he's from, and more importantly, why he is with the Wolf Riders. In her eagerness to see more, she goes past the time of Alagur's youth, and in a flash is almost a thousand years ago.

Alagur is startled by the images he's seeing. He is familiar with the legends of the first Wolf Riders, Sey'qar and Yozan, and he realises the vision is showing him glimpses of why the Wolf Riders are as they are now. He watches the two men of the distant past plotting to bring disarray to the world for their own greed, and marks the similarity between their plans and what he and Samur were planning to do once they were both back in City of Wolves.

Feeling unexpected shame about the similarities between himself and the first Wolf Riders, Alagur tries to stop Marrida's vision. In desperation, he reaches up to grasp her hands, but instead of pulling the woman out of her trance-like state, he feels a connection between himself and the gem in her hands.

Marrida realises what is happening and forcefully snaps herself back to reality. She scowls at the man.

How dare he touch the sacred gem?

"What do you think you are doing?" she snaps at him. Her angry voice causes Yalla to growl menacingly, making her even angrier. "Shut your wolf up."

Alagur bows his head and the wolf stops growling.

"Don't you know it is forbidden for men to touch this gem?" Marrida glowers at him and Alagur shakes his head. He didn't know. He realises there's much he didn't know.

"I'm sorry," he says softly.

Marrida peers at him in silence for a few minutes, realising that she too has done many things which are forbidden when it comes to the gem. First she told her siblings about it, then let them witness her visions, and now she's allowing this man to see her work with it too.

"Do you mind if my brother and sister sit in with us?" she asks eventually, taking a breath to calm herself.

Alagur shakes his head. He doesn't mind. He admires the young girl for her courage, and Esbara reminds him of himself as a boy.

"Esbara, Kalisa, please come in here," Marrida calls out.

After a few minutes, both youngsters walk into the room, Kalisa immediately running to the wolf and snuggling up beside her. Yalla sniffs the girl's hand and leg before laying her head down. Kalisa scratches the wolf's head and smiles at the man in the bed. He smiles back at her weakly before resting his head on the pillow and closing his eyes, exhausted.

Esbara grabs a chair from the corner of the room and sits down beside his older sister, watching the man with both curiosity and dismay. He still doesn't like having a Wolf Rider in their home, but decides to keep quiet out of respect for his sister.

He glances from the corner of his eyes towards Kalisa with the wolf. *How can she not be afraid of the beast?*

All four of them are silent for a while, deep in their own thoughts about what to do next. It's Kalisa who's the first to speak.

CHAPTER FIVE

"M"ARRIDA, WHAT WERE THOSE TWO CITIES you viewed the first time you showed us how you use the Stone of Truth?"

Alagur's eyes fly open and he looks at Marrida. *Has she used the gem more than once around me?*

Before Alagur manages to say anything, Marrida speaks. "Yes, I viewed two cities. One looked a lot like the city I learnt about in Ancient Histories--"

Marrida decides to ask Alagur a crucial question, which will explain some of the visions she has done. She has noted the same city repeatedly in visions involving her mother and thinks it must be a clue, letting her know her family has a connection with it. The other city, which she first spotted seven weeks earlier, was equally unfamiliar. It was a coastal town with what must at one point have been a magnificent, well-organised harbour. She saw tiny fishing vessels dotted along the dilapidated pier, which had clearly been in a state of disrepair for some decades.

Marrida decides not to mention the other cities she has seen.

"Alagur," Marrida begins, and the man looks her straight in the face with a hint of curiosity, "where do you live now?"

Alagur is a bit startled by the question. It isn't what he expected to be asked, and he pauses to think. If he tells her something other than the truth, she'll eventually find it out anyway. He knows something of the reputation of the Keepers of Truth, even if his knowledge is sketchy.

"I live in a city located to the north-east of here. It isn't really a city anymore as most of it lies in ruins. We call it City of Wolves."

To Marrida, the revelation comes as a lightning strike on a clear day. It confirms to her that one of the cities she has perceived in her visions is where the Wolf Riders have their base.

But what are the other three cities I have seen? Could I have seen the city in which the Keepers of Truth originated as well?

Marrida is thinking so hard she doesn't realise the man is looking at her intensely. However, Esbara does notice, and he's not happy at the way the Wolf Rider is looking at his sister. But remembering his sister's earlier words of warning, he doesn't speak. Instead, he forces himself to watch Kalisa's interactions with the wolf.

Alagur continues staring at Marrida. Something deep inside him is stirring at her beauty, and it takes all his willpower to stop himself from touching this woman he has only just met. He is confused, and his confusion causes anger to well up inside him about his own behaviour.

Why am I having these feelings?

* * *

WHEN MARRIDA'S ATTENTION RETURNS TO ALAGUR, she sees him sleeping peacefully. Marrida takes her siblings to the front room so they can talk without Alagur overhearing them. They sit on the sofa covered with hand-stitched cushions that their mother sewed. Kalisa sits on the corner of the sofa, while Yalla, who unexpectedly decided to follow the girl, lies down on the floor in front of her.

Marrida thinks long and hard before speaking to her siblings, both of whom are waiting patiently for her to break the silence.

"I did *two* visions about Alagur. They had unexpected results because I also discerned a distant past."
"What did you see?" Esbara urges.
"The time when the Wolf Riders became what they are now. I think Alagur may know who the men in the vision were."
Both her siblings stare at Marrida in shock. It's Kalisa who speaks.
"You mean to say Wolf Riders didn't exist a long time ago?"

Marrida nods without saying anything further. She thinks it best for her siblings to come to their own conclusions, and then ask her for more information about the visions she has done. Strangely, both remain quiet. Even the usually talkative Kalisa is subdued, giving Marrida a chance to ponder over the recent events.

There's one more thing worrying her. The black-haired man did indeed come back into the street to search for his companion, but when he didn't find Alagur, he rode off cursing so loudly that Marrida could hear every word from behind the closed door of her dwelling. She considers whether she should ask Alagur about the stocky man, but decides against it for now. If he wants to know whether the man came looking for him, he will surely ask her.

The words spoken by the stocky man are the most worrying part of it all. They weren't spoken in any dialect that Elder Sharriba has been teaching her, yet something about them sounded familiar.

Marrida gets up and walks to the doorway to glance into the room where Alagur is. She looks him over, marking that his breathing is shallow but regular, indicating he is deep in a restful sleep, free from fever.

She turns after a few minutes and rejoins her siblings on the sofa. When she sits, it's Esbara who speaks up next, looking down at his hands in his lap as he asks the question.

"Are we going to keep both the man and the wolf here? And if not, how are we going to get them out of the city?

"And what about Uncle Joharan?" This time the question comes from Kalisa, raising a point neither of her siblings has had time to think over. It occurs to Marrida that Joharan hasn't come to check whether his kin is safe since the incursion. She looks at Esbara for a long time before answering in a voice that's almost a whisper.

"We must keep them safe, but he needs to go home."

It isn't the answer Esbara wants to hear. He looks up and stares into his sister's eyes, swallowing hard as he weighs up his reply. Marrida sees something more is bothering him.

"He can't stay here," she adds before he can speak again. "He's a Wolf Rider so he needs to go back to them."

Esbara shakes his head. He isn't going to agree.

"He may be a Wolf Rider, but in your vision, we saw someone who lost him when he was snatched."

Esbara stops talking for a moment, taking a deep breath. He looks down at Kalisa, who is gazing up at him with earnest, sincere eyes.

"Back then, the girl in the vision was younger than Kalisa. She's probably as old as you are now, Marrida. If Alagur goes back to the Wolf Riders, he'll never find out what happened to her."

Esbara stops again, seeing a glimmer of comprehension appearing on Marrida's face as she looks from him to Kalisa, then back to him.

"Please continue," she says.

"Well, what I'm thinking is if the second city you saw in the vision is real, maybe you and Alagur can travel there and find out why the Wolf Riders are doing all these things--"

"And what are these 'things', if I may ask?" an agitated, almost angry voice asks from across the room. Alagur has awoken and walked through the cooking room to the doorway of the room they're sitting in. All three siblings stare at him in shock, then Marrida gets up, walks across the room and positions herself between Alagur and the others. If he's going to be angry with anyone, he should be angry with her.

However, when she gets up, so does Esbara, then Kalisa gets up too and hides behind Esbara, staring at Alagur. Yalla arises, confused as to whether to be loyal to her master or protect her new friend Kalisa from her master's wrath. She decides to be neutral and saunters casually into the garden, lying down under the trees for shade.

The wolf's actions break the tense atmosphere in the room as Alagur glances in the direction his companion has disappeared. He's a Wolf Master and knows what Yalla's behaviour is telling him, so decides on a new tactic.

"Alright, I'm sorry I interrupted your conversation, but if you're going to talk about *my* people, shouldn't I be involved?"

Marrida ponders over his question for a few moments, then she nods curtly. A moment later, she points at a wooden chair near the fireplace, almost opposite the sofa she and her siblings were using. Alagur understands and sits down, while Marrida and her siblings return to the sofa.

"So, what do you want to know about the Wolf Riders, Esbara?" the man asks. Esbara looks back at him with an expression Marrida interprets as her brother's attempt to look like an adult. After all, the man is treating him as such by directing the question to him.

"What is it the Wolf Riders do besides attack our towns and steal boys from their homes?" Esbara asks.

Marrida looks closely at her brother. Esbara has asked the very question Alagur himself needs an answer to – why was he snatched while a girl younger than Kalisa ran after him in tears? The initial hatred Marrida felt for this man is being replaced by an overwhelming sense of sympathy for his loss and what happened to him as a child.

She glances at the man, and instead of anger, she notices a deep sadness filling his face. He's looking down at the floor, appearing to be deep in thought.

"I don't know," is the quietly spoken reply.

Esbara is genuinely surprised. He expected some sort of outburst of rage because he dared to ask the question. Instead, Alagur has resigned himself to his own fate and is no longer acting with the bravado the Wolf Riders usually present.

On cue, Yalla walks into the room as if she senses a difference in her master's behaviour. All three siblings glance at one another, not knowing what to do next, but before any of them can say another word, Alagur speaks.

"The two men you glimpsed in your visions were called Sey'qar and Yozan, if they're the men I've been told about by the Wolf Riders. They were what we Wolf Riders call the First Riders. I've heard many retellings about them, so it's almost like they lived a few years ago rather than centuries past. We were told they rebelled…they rebelled against your kind--"

Alagur stares at Marrida to see what she makes of his last five words. Instead of anger, she feels empathy. She has heard a similar retelling, or at least parts of it, and she's familiar with the two names.

"Please continue," she says.

Alagur pauses momentarily, considering what to tell the three sitting across from him and deciding to tell them everything. Esbara has asked him a valid question, and he deserves a complete answer.

Alagur directs his next words towards Marrida. "You say I was snatched as a boy. It's the way Wolf Riders enlist new blood into their ranks – forcibly. That's how they've done it for hundreds of years."

Then Alagur asks the question that has been weighing on his mind ever since he observed her vision.

"*Was* I snatched, Marrida? You figured it out in the vision. If so, where am I from?"

The latter part of the question is almost a plea, and it makes Esbara curious. Suddenly, he regrets the way he asked his question.

Marrida thinks deeply over the direction the conversation is taking and decides to give an answer as direct as her brother's initial question.

"If you were snatched, it will have happened when you were very young. What age are the boys that Wolf Riders snatch?"

Marrida glances discreetly towards Esbara, only to be met by his concerned gaze.

"Training as a Wolf Rider begins five years before Second Rites," Alagur remarks. "The snatching happens three or four years earlier."

Marrida will be ready for her Second Rites in slightly more than two seasons. Second Rites are the moment a person is considered a full adult rather than a young adult. A few weeks ago, Esbara did his First Rites and became a young adult – a phase in between childhood and adulthood, referred to more formally as the Passing. The moment the ceremony was over, her brother was able to make some of his own decisions.

This means he can decide to become the soldier he wants to be, Marrida realises. And if training for Wolf Riders starts five years before Second Rites, Esbara is now almost too old to be considered for snatching--

Alagur continues speaking, interrupting Marrida's thoughts.

"Kalisa is befriending Yalla. Not many people outside the Wolf Riders have this ability, if any at all, and certainly not without the training I've received. The Academy of Warfare would have taught the skill in the past, but no longer does--"

At the mention of her name, Kalisa sits up straighter and decides to listen more closely. She is fascinated by the wolf and hopes the man's explanation will help her to become closer to the animal.

"Yalla is a Mountain Wolf. They live in the Miza region."

Marrida feels a sudden anger well up. Her father was travelling in the Miza region when he was attacked and killed. She was in the room when the messenger conveyed this news to her mother, who went as pale as moss ash. Moments afterwards, she collapsed in the pains of an early labour. The description of how her father was killed was identified by local people as the work of the Wolf Riders. And now here is a man saying he got his wolf from the Miza region.

Alagur sees the change his words have made in the woman and wonders why she's angry. It occurs to him that he hasn't seen any sign of the three siblings' parents. Then he realises why Esbara looks so familiar.

He has his father's features, for sure.

Alagur leans forward and glances in turn at Kalisa, who seems to be around ten or eleven years old, Esbara, who has probably done his First Rites, and finally at the older girl – no, not a girl. She's a woman – or soon will be, at least. She must have done her First Rites a few years ago, especially if she is one of the Keepers of Truth.

"I think I met your father on my journey towards Miza." Nodding towards Esbara, Alagur adds, "He looks like his father."

Marrida calms down. *He said he met our father. He wouldn't have said that had he been the Wolf Rider who killed him.*

"How did you meet him?" Marrida asks, tears welling up in her eyes, overwhelmed by memories.

"He was asking me for directions to a lake," Alagur replies. "I was alone on my travels to find a wolf – to find Yalla. When I went past the lake on my way back to the city, I overheard some travellers talking about him having been killed."

Alagur stops talking and lets his head hang. He feels sadness for the woman in front of him, who obviously loved her father deeply.

He looks up again when Marrida sobs loudly.

"I know it must have been Wolf Riders who killed your father, but there are many different groups of loyalty within the ranks." Alagur is hoping he is showing some measure of compassion. "And some of them are far crueller and murderous than others."

While saying the last sentence, Alagur looks at Esbara, who simply nods to indicate he understands.

A cruel people indeed, the boy thinks, keeping his face as neutral as possible.

* * *

ALAGUR SITS UP AND STRETCHES. His back muscles ache, possibly from when he fell off Yalla in the street. He whistles, and Yalla, who had left the room during the discussion, paces slowly back in and lies down beside his chair. Alagur thinks it will be easier to tell the next part of the retelling of the Wolf Riders with his loyal companion beside him.

Glancing at Kalisa, he sees how she becomes a lot more alert whenever the wolf is in the room.

"Yalla obeys my commands not only because I want her to, but because wolves follow a leader," he explains. "However, it takes five years of training to be able to command a wolf."

Marrida, with eyes still wet from sobbing, finds herself intrigued by Alagur's words, which are filling in many blanks in the information she has gathered about the Wolf Riders through her secret visions, both the recent ones as well as many earlier one.

"One of the things Wolf Riders can do once they get to a high enough rank is to name the wolf they ride," Alagur continues. "It was during this ceremony that I gave Yalla her name."

CHAPTER SIX

Unexpectedly, Kalisa speaks up, her question startling the other three.

"What's the name of the black-haired man I spotted before you got injured?" she queries shyly, promptly burying her face behind Esbara's arm as he returns from stoking the fire some more. Marrida wanted to ask this question, and Kalisa has remembered this.

Alagur recovers first from the change of subject. "It's Samur," he answers.

"And he's the one who snatched you?"

This time the question comes from Esbara, who has decided to confront his sister's fears about him being snatched full on. If the danger exists, he wants to understand what fate will await him in City of Wolves.

"Yes."

The short softly-spoken reply comes not from Alagur, but from Marrida. Alagur stares at the woman for a moment; he didn't expect this sudden directness from Marrida. He pauses to consider how to answer as he senses the anger coming from the boy opposite him.

Marrida has stopped crying and managed to compose herself again, but her mind is racing. Her feelings about the man opposite her are conflicted. Could it be that she is starting to like him? He's showing honesty, the one thing she likes most in people.

Perhaps we could be friends.

Snapping back to reality, Marrida chides herself for even thinking such a thing.

Alagur looks at Marrida discreetly for a while. She seems different now from when he first spoke with her.

Don't be ridiculous, he says to himself. *Just because she plucked me off the street doesn't mean she likes me, or my kind. She may be healing me to deliver me to the authorities of this city.*

Alagur leans back in his chair, the hardness of it making his joints ache further. He shuts his eyes and thinks about the events of weeks ago. Seven weeks have passed since he arrived here, but to him, it seems longer. He remembers sitting with Samur on the terrace of his dwelling in City of Wolves and wonders what Samur is doing right now. Will he be looking for his 'Pack Brother'? It's possibly two years since Wolf Riders last attacked the city, and at the time, Alagur stayed back at City of Wolves, training a group of new arrivals.

If Samur isn't looking for me, where might he be?

He cannot discern the intentions of a man who has so recently been revealed to him as no more than a kidnapper of an innocent child – Alagur himself, of all people. Alagur wonders what happened to the girl he witnessed in the vision done by the mysterious woman whose face he has glimpsed in dreams, and who has now become as real as the chair below him.

All this thinking has made him tired, and despite the uncomfortable seating, Alagur falls asleep. It doesn't register with him when the three siblings tiptoe towards Esbara's sleeping room – the one furthest back in the house – to continue their conversation undisturbed and unhindered. Only the man's loyal wolf stays beside him, glancing after the fascinating young girl she has grown so fond of until she too falls asleep and dreams the kinds of dreams only a wolf can.

*　*　*

"WHAT ARE WE GOING TO DO WITH THEM?" Esbara asks as he sits down on his bed, crossing his legs and leaning against the wall behind him. Kalisa sits on the floor near the doorway, and Marrida takes the only chair in the room, thinking long and hard about the boy's question before answering.

She starts by addressing Esbara's ambitions.

"What would you do if you became a soldier and all this happened?" she asks. Before Esbara can respond, Marrida continues, "We need to do what is right."

Esbara looks at her in confusion. Marrida notices this and decides to explain what she is planning to do.

"This man, Alagur, has been snatched. The girl I identified I believe is his sister. We – no, I must do what is best for him, but also what is best for the world."

Esbara thinks over what Marrida has said. It occurs to him that she has given him a crucial clue about the Wolf Riders, and a clue as to why she suddenly seems full of compassion towards a man she would have hated a month or so earlier. Alagur has confirmed that life as a Wolf Rider is harsh, and many of those pulled into this life – particularly unwillingly – do not survive it for long. He has hinted that they die either attacking a city or from harsh treatment by other men, or they get killed as some sort of punishment. But he hasn't told them much beyond this basic information. Esbara thinks maybe the presence of Kalisa has prevented him from speaking in more detail. It seems Alagur desperately wants to spare the youngster the real horrors of life as a Wolf Rider.

Esbara, who has only received a couple of weeks of training at the Academy of Warfare, has listened to Alagur's words with the ears of a young soldier. He understands there must be a lot more to Alagur's retelling, that the man despises the life he has been forced to lead. Several times, Alagur has stopped himself from saying certain things, and he looked deeply upset while recalling the treatment he received when he arrived in City of Wolves as a young boy.

Esbara looks at Marrida with a concerned frown. "You're going to find out more about the Wolf Riders in a vision, right?" he urges her in a flat tone.

She nods. "I think I can find out a way to stop them attacking everyone, and Alagur can help me."

"Help you?" Esbara almost shouts, but instead, he speaks in a low voice. "How can he help you? Why would he want to help you anyway?"

"Because he wants to know who the girl I sighted is as much as I want to know – or you, for that matter."

Esbara's reddening face betrays the truth in Marrida's words. If the girl was a small child when Alagur was snatched, and if that happened fifteen years ago, then she'd be around Marrida's age now. And the thought has crossed Esbara's mind several times that if he asks for a posting in her city when he finishes his training, he may find her. However, he understands that trying to find an unknown girl will be like looking for a needle in a haystack — especially as he doesn't even know her name.

Marrida realises that in under two months, she has experienced probably the most eventful period of her entire life, and now she needs to go to the Temple for more training, just as she has every day for the past five weeks. Elder Sharriba knows Marrida was Esbara and Kalisa's main guardian until Esbara reached First Rites, so she had to be away from the Temple for two weeks to take care of them following the Wolf Riders' attack. Unlike her previous journey through the Temple's vast gardens, this absence from the Temple was sanctioned.

Esbara's First Rites was a sombre event with none of the usual festivities enjoyed in peaceful times. The day after the short ceremony, Esbara and Marrida visited the Academy of Warfare for his initiation there, and then he became a co-guardian to Kalisa. Any decisions about her future will now be made by both him and Marrida, until Kalisa goes through her own First Rites just over three years from now.

Marrida wonders if recent events will change things for her or her family, but dismisses the thought as her mind turns to what to do about her duties at the Temple. It's difficult. She cannot confide in anyone outside her house about Alagur and his wolf, nor about the visions she has been doing. Not only is she having to keep two secrets from the Keepers and Elder Sharriba, she also needs to act innocently around the other Acolytes.

Why don't those Acolytes like me? she muses, then smirks inwardly at a flash of insight. *It might be because I have skills I'm yet to learn, skills the Elder is teaching me to unlock.*

There's something else bothering her, something the Elder said before all the Acolytes were sent home on the day of the Wolf Riders' attack. What was it again?

"When you arrive home, make sure everyone you care for, including unexpected visitors, is kept safe."

Everyone in the room looked at one another quizzically because the statement hadn't made sense.

"What visitors?" The murmur repeated around the room, but only Marrida noted how the eyes of the Elder were fixed on her.

Did the Elder somehow know Alagur would come to my house? No, she's not capable of seeing future events, even with the gem.

It still seems strange to her that she, the youngest of all Acolytes, has been singled out for more training, and that the training includes the Forbidden Knowledge and the Knowledge of Calling. Marrida is at a loss as to what the latter may be, or why she needs to know about it. She has figured out the Forbidden Knowledge must be something only Elders are supposed to know, or those being trained to replace them.

I--replace Elder Sharriba? How and when could that happen?

Marrida shuts her eyes like she wants to block out the whole world. Esbara looks at his older sister and tries to guess what she is thinking. Something is bothering her, but he doesn't know what. He looks at Kalisa and, holding his finger to his lips, motions to her to come with him. They leave their sister alone with her thoughts, while Esbara entertains the young girl in her own room across the hallway.

Sleep finally overcomes Marrida. Tired from the day's events and conversations, she drifts off deeply. Today has been the first time since she returned to the Temple after the Wolf Riders' attack that Marrida has been missing for a whole day.

And this time, she won't be let off so lightly when she returns.

* * *

AFTER REARRANGING SEVERAL PILLOWS AS A BACKREST, Esbara sits down next to Kalisa. Questions are etched all over her face as she tries to work out in her mind what's bothering her. The girl is clearly contemplating something important, judging by the contraction and relaxation of her copper-coloured eyebrows.

Esbara can see why Damir, his friend as well as Kalisa's, has become so interested in his younger sister. She's a natural beauty, with copper tones in her blonde hair hinting at her father's darker colouring. Their mother had blonde hair, and Marrida beyond question has inherited her mother's looks. Esbara himself is brown-haired, inheriting his looks from his father just as Alagur stated.

A question from Kalisa tears Esbara from his thoughts. Somewhat agitated, the girl repeats her question.

"What is Marrida going to do with the man and the wolf?"

"She said they need to leave," Esbara replies, embracing his younger sister.

"But I *like* the wolf--can't she stay?"

"Unfortunately not. If they're discovered, there will be consequences--"

Esbara doesn't finish the sentence because he knows Kalisa is too young to understand. If soldiers come for Alagur, they'll surely kill the wolf on sight. They may kill the man too. These thoughts make Esbara question his own choice of career for the first time.

He senses Kalisa shift as she curls up in a ball beside him, her head leaning on his thigh. She's soon asleep, leaving him alone with his thoughts and memories. Esbara ponders over what Alagur said earlier in the earlier evening, the first time the man was fully coherent after lying for weeks recovering from his injuries.

Alagur said he met their father, and now the boy wonders what sort of man his father was. He knows from conversations with Marrida that he was a travelling merchant of some sort, but Joharan, their father's older brother, never wants to speak about him. Esbara finds this puzzling.

Esbara glances at his reflection in the mirror leaning against the wall on top of the chest of drawers.

"He looks like his father."

Those words have echoed through the boy's mind ever since Alagur stated them. He studies his features closely, making sure he doesn't disturb Kalisa beside him. He has pale brown hair, so his mother's blonde hair must have influenced the colour, but his eyebrows and eyes are dark brown. His face is slightly oval, and according to Marrida, their mother's face was heart-shaped like hers.

Esbara briefly looks down at the sleeping girl and realises Kalisa's face is heart-shaped too.

Remembering the sight of Alagur standing in the doorway of the front room, the boy notes that Alagur is likely as tall as his father would have been. Although the boy doesn't have many memories of his father, he does vaguely remember a tall man filling up doorways. His mother was shorter, and with Esbara being taller than Marrida by two hand widths, he may become as tall as his father.

Esbara leans his head back on the soft pillows. He is tired, but the many thoughts whirling through his mind keep him awake. After maybe an hour, he carefully shifts his leg from under Kalisa's head. She moans in her sleep but doesn't wake. He takes a blanket and covers the girl up, then walks out of the room and descends the stairway. Passing the front room, he looks for several minutes at the sleeping man and the massive wolf sprawled out on the floor, occasionally twitching her muscles as she sleeps. The boy's destination is the garden. He can sit on one of the benches there to think.

Esbara quietly opens the back door and walks outside, closing the door behind him. He looks up at the crescent of the moon, high in the sky above him. It's sometime around midnight. The boy glances around the large garden, looking eerie bathed in the moonlight, and heads for a bench with a high carved back. He remembers with a smile sitting here with his mother by his side when he was a small boy.

Esbara stretches out on the bench. After some time of thinking and remembering, sleep overcomes him too.

CHAPTER SEVEN

ALAGUR IS A TALL, MUSCULAR MAN who participated in the Second Rites ceremony years ago. Even the Wolf Riders, it seems, observe this ritual. He's now in his mid-twenties, if he's right about his age, but he can't remember anything before he became a Wolf Rider. The excursion he's about to participate in will be his last before becoming an Elder Man, and Alagur has mixed feelings about the duties this promotion will bring him.

For a Wolf Rider, it's rare to survive long enough to become an Elder Man, and Alagur understands that among his peers, he's something of a celebrity. He has already gained rank enough within the Wolf Riders to be permitted to take part in the Wolf Naming Ceremony, which happens one year before a Wolf Rider becomes an Elder Man. Alagur witnessed the ceremony which made his friend, Samur, an Elder Man just a few years previously. Until then, Samur didn't take anything too seriously, but once he became an Elder Man, his behaviour changed – some of it not to Alagur's liking. The people Samur has started to group around himself have made Alagur suspicious of the older man's motives.

* * *

ALAGUR BRUSHES THE THICK COAT of his riding wolf.

"Are you as excited as I am?" he asks the wolf he named Yalla in the Wolf Naming Ceremony. A rough nudge from Yalla acknowledges that she understands in her wolfish way and is looking forward to being part of the group going to Ruh'nar. Wolf Riders have an uncanny ability to communicate with the wolves they ride.

Most Wolf Riders prefer black Mountain Wolves from the North Ridge Canyon, but Alagur found Yalla, a rare silver-grey-and-white wolf, in the South Valley of Miza. Months before his First Rites, Alagur went to get his wolf, and on his return, even the most hardened Wolf Riders admitted his bravery exceeded that of many others. Compared to the other wolves roaming freely throughout the city, Yalla is much larger and broader – a fact which has helped Alagur rise in the ranks of the Wolf Riders. All the wolves used by Wolf Riders grow unusually large compared to ordinary wolves – often referred to by the Wolf Riders as 'wild wolves'. Having a wolf towering over all the others, Alagur gained the right to give her a name during the Wolf Naming Ceremony much more quickly than usual, although he was calling her Yalla in private long before that.

Alagur fastens the riding harness to Yalla and attaches his thrower with spear arrows to both sides of it. He's very adept with this special thrower, having learnt to use it through endless practice sessions with the stocky black-haired man called Samur soon after his initiation as a Wolf Rider.

Last night while he slept, images kept welling up in his mind which disturbed him. He saw a woman, tall and slender with pale skin and hair the colour of an ailep hound's fur. Around her neck on a gold chain was a rubha apple. No, it wasn't a rubha apple; it was a gem. In his dream, it was glistening white with a green base.

Alagur tries to shrug off the memories of the dream, but he can't stop thinking about the woman.

Who is she?

He has never paid much attention to the legends surrounding the Stone of Truth, or he wouldn't be so dismissive of the dreams. Wolf Riders concern themselves not with legends; they live for the here and now, because often they live a life of no more than a dozen years. Life starts harshly for a Wolf Rider, being wrenched away from a peaceful and safe family to be forced into a world where honour matters above all else, and those who complain are dealt with in a swift and cruel way. Alagur has been privy to dealing with 'obstacles', as Samur calls such persons, but it has never occurred to him that he may meet such a fate too.

But none of this explains why he is having dreams of a woman he has never met. He is even considering trying to find her.

"And then what?" he scolds himself. "She's hardly going to welcome you with open arms, you damned fool."

Alagur is startled from his pensive mood by a voice behind him. He recognises the voice, and Yalla's demeanour shows him that she recognises it too. Turning, he sees his Pack Brother standing close to some stairs, beaming a big grin and motioning at Alagur with a pouch. Alagur understands what is in the pouch. He and his Pack Brother often drink together before going on an excursion.

"Hail, Samur," he calls.

Samur has been his friend for as long as Alagur can recall and always seems to be nearby whenever Alagur needs someone to talk with. He does wonder at times why the older man associates with him instead of people of his own age as there is an age gap of around fourteen years between them. Pack Brothers are not brothers in the traditional sense; rather, they are two or more Wolf Riders who decide to bond by making a Life Pact together. This rite was started by the two legendary Wolf Riders Sey'qar and Yozan almost a thousand years ago, and to this day, Pack Brothers vow to remain loyal to one another without question. Betrayal of one Pack Brother by another would result in a bounty being placed on the betrayer's head.

Betrayal can take many forms, but the most common is abandonment. Other Wolf Riders then search out the betrayer, capture the man and return him to City of Wolves for a cruel end to an already brutal life – stripped naked, smeared with blood and gagged, he would be dropped into the den of wild wolves. Alagur has witnessed the process once, the wolves ripping the captured man to shreds, and he has vowed never to come into conflict with the Life Pact he's made with Samur.

However, the thoughts which are going through Alagur's mind like a midsummer dust storm of the east coast are not thoughts he wishes to share with his Pack Brother. The mysterious woman is a private matter.

It isn't clear exactly what the two original Wolf Riders, Sey'qar and Yozan, did, but the most accepted retelling is that one of them saved the life of the other. And to honour it, they made a pact to be Pack Brothers. As Wolf Riders do not, or choose not to, remember or follow the legends of Keldarra, the legend of Sey'qar and Yozan is considered by most of them to be 'The Truth'. Always simply The Truth. No one really understands why it's called this; the reasons for the name have been forgotten in the mists of time itself.

Some of the words of The Truth have been on Alagur's mind of late, and he wonders what sort of people the two men were.

> TEN THOUSAND RIDERS ROSE TO THE CALL,
> BESET ON TO THE CITY OF OLD, AND
> FALL BEFORE THEM IT WOULD.

THEY WHO RESISTED WOULD FALL, AND
AND YOUNG ONES TAKEN BY FORCE,
AND A CITY WAS LOST TO TIME AND KIN.

FOR THE BROTHERS BETRAYED TRUTH, AND
RELEASED FEAR UPON THE WORLD,
WITH WOLVES AS THEIR WEAPON.

FOR LEGEND FORETELLS OF THEIR END,
THE END THAT WILL COME FROM ONE,
A BROTHER WHO RISES TO THE CALL.

THE TRUTH WILL SHOW THE DOUBTER,
HE AND HIS WOLF WILL TRAVEL FAR,
AN AGENT OF TRUTH WILL SHOW HIM.

SHE WHOSE NAME IS UNSPOKEN,
A WOLF SHE WILL CLAIM FROM THE WILD,
AND THE MAN WILL LEARN HER SKILL.

TOGETHER THEY END THE BROKEN WORLD,
HEAL THE WORLD TO WHAT IT WAS BEFORE,
IT IS THAT DESTINY THAT IS UNSPOKEN.

The words of The Truth are believed to be the dying words of a woman who lived in the city almost a thousand years ago, murdered by Sey'qar and Yozan after she was betrayed in mysterious circumstances. But like its name, the true meaning of The Truth has also been lost to the mists of time.

Why do I keep thinking she was stuttering? Something about it seems off. Like there should be some more lines of retelling in between the beginning of it...

* * *

THE SUDDEN ARRIVAL OF SAMUR has broken Alagur's pensive mood, and he puts aside the two things which are clouding his mind – the woman from his dreams and the legend which isn't really a legend. A final thought flashes through his brain, and he wonders for a moment who the 'doubter' is.

Alagur walks over to the man waiting for him. As he approaches, he senses Yalla is following him.

She's going to greet Uzo.

He considers again the suggestion Samur made about their two wolves weeks earlier and smirks inwardly. It would make them two of the most powerful Wolf Riders, and he wonders for a few moments whether in centuries to come there will be legends of 'Samur and Alagur and their giant silver-grey wolves' going around the camps in the city. Although it's rare to let riding wolves breed together, Samur suggested, in a stupor of drunkenness, that Yalla and Uzo should mate. And they would produce the best damned pups the city has ever seen. Alagur of course laughed profusely over the idea, but now, weeks later, he's genuinely interested and is pleased to see Uzo taking a great interest in his riding wolf.

Samur follows Alagur's gaze and sees the two wolves greeting each other. When the men look at each other, both burst into raucous laughter which echoes through the nearby courtyard and beyond.

"I think in a few seasons, a new litter will arrive," Alagur says, grinning broadly.

With this litter, the two men would be able to create a Wolf Squad of their own. In the simplest terms, they would no longer be dictated to by others, but instead would be their own bosses. And the thought pleases and amuses both men, but Samur takes a lot more pleasure from the idea than his younger friend.

Alagur ascends the stairs to the terrace, the outside seating area of his small, sparsely furnished living quarters. He drops himself down on the furthest cushioned bench while Samur sits opposite him on a stool. Alagur watches as both wolves ascend the stairs too, and then settle in the shadowy part at the other end of the terrace. He smiles again; he feels so proud of Yalla.

She possesses the grace of a wild wolf.

Both men drink their rubha ale quietly, each caught up in his own thoughts. Alagur thinks about the forthcoming excursion. He's overheard retellings of the city they plan to visit; other Wolf Riders, including Samur, have told him the city possesses wealth beyond measure. It also has beautiful women for them to have their wicked ways with. And the boys from the city are said to be strong and clever, so will make successful Wolf Riders if they 'entice' a few to return with them. Although it's more kidnapping than enticing, the Wolf Riders have convinced themselves that the boys they snatch join them willingly.

Both men glance over at Yalla and Uzo occasionally. For a long while, the silence is only broken by occasional soft grunts from the wolves, the buzzing of insects – small black flies which pester any living creature in the searing heat of the late spring sun – and the faraway howls and scuffles in the central enclosure where most Wolf Riders keep their wolves.

At the moment, it's very peaceful around them. Later, when he, Samur and thousands of others ride towards Ruh'nar, it will sound like a landslide has let itself loose. Alagur hears the chirping of a blue silverwing bird in the distance, answered by a second. He smirks, thinking that when he gets back from the excursion, he may go and raid some nests for eggs to make himself steamed eggs with fish roe. The fish he will catch in the stream two streets from his dwelling.

"What are you smirking about?" Samur asks, downing the ale which remained in his cup with a fast motion of his arm.

"I was listening to those birds and planning my meal for later," Alagur replies. Samur laughs.

"Well, if you're making food of them bird eggs again, you spare me some, and I'll join you for the feast."

Samur knows Alagur cooks good food, and the duo often feast like the warlords of The Old Days. As far as Alagur understands it, Samur doesn't know who, or what, these warlords were, but they are mentioned in the legend of The Truth, and it states they ate well. Because Samur and Alagur emulate the way of life as described in The Truth, they eat well too.

Samur reaches for the pouch containing the ale. "Want me to get some more before it's time to go?" he asks Alagur, who nods. Samur gets up, signalling to Uzo to lie back down, then he jumps down the stairs in four long strides and turns around the corner of the adjoining building. Alagur distinguishes the creaking sound as a door opens, and a few moments later the same noise is followed by the door being slammed shut. He expects to see Samur coming up the stairs, but instead sees his friend talking to someone whose voice is familiar to him: a man called Raimir.

Moments later, Samur rushes up the stairs. "Well, that puts a dampener on enjoying this," he says, pointing at the pouch of ale he's placed down on the table. "Just got told by Raimir the raid is departing in under an hour, and not this evening as planned."

Alagur's half-drunken stupor promptly vanishes, and his reply to Samur is icily serious.

"We'd better get ready, then."

Alagur gets up, and as does so, the two wolves come loping over. He walks into the small room adjoining the terrace and picks up a pouch on a long leather strap that he binds to his body.

"Been ready to depart since first sunlight hit the terrace," he states to his companion.

Yalla stands beside him, and he strokes her flank. He feels the tension of excitement rolling through the wolf's muscles – the same excited tension he's feeling in his own body. He signals to the wolf to go down to the courtyard, which she does, followed closely by Uzo, then Samur, and finally Alagur himself. He glances back at his abode with an edge of concern, feeling for a moment as though he's leaving the dwelling permanently.

A large group of men and wolves are awaiting them in the western square of the ruined city. Two spires, half the size they once were, put the square in partial shade. At the left end, the Elder Men are gathering and discussing the last few details of the planned excursion. Samur walks over to them and joins in with the discussion.

Alagur looks at his friend's back with a pang of envy for a moment, but the next time such a meeting is held, he too will be privy to it. He then turns his attention to Yalla, who is bristling with excitement now. All her muscles ripple under her coat and she snorts steamy air from her nose.

"You're looking forward to today, aren't you?" the man says to his loyal wolf, giving her a final rub down. He mounts her in readiness for the trek, seeing the glances of awe from Wolf Riders around him, especially the younger folk. Alagur beckons one of them towards him, a boy named Bergas with reddish-brown hair to the nape of his neck and freckles all over his face. Though the boy is shy, he always loves it when Alagur gives him attention.

At a slow, deliberate pace, the boy walks to the man on his wolf and looks up.

CHAPTER EIGHT

"Y OU WANT TO ACCOMPANY Samur and me on this journey?" Alagur asks.

The boy nods vigorously and hurries off to fetch a wolf with a coat a few shades darker than his own hair. The boy's name fits his colouring – a bergas bush is small, mostly prevalent in the northern lands, with unusual copper-coloured leaves and tall white flowers. The flowers, when dried, are often used by Wolf Riders in smoking pipes. Legend has it that smoking them will cure almost any ailment. In other parts of Keldarra, such as Achellon, the flower is used for offerings – at least, this is what is believed to happen in the city-state on the south-eastern coast. Yet, no Wolf Rider has ever managed to infiltrate it.

Before he knew the boy better, Alagur jokingly suggested to Samur that Bergas could hide in some bergas bushes if he was too scared to go on an excursion with them. However, the opposite appears to be true of Bergas, who has shown himself to be among the bravest of the boys, despite being so shy, and Alagur has grown genuinely fond of him.

Bergas arrived after a northern excursion led by Samur when Alagur decided to remain in the once majestic city for other duties. Some of those duties were distasteful to him, but no one escapes the harshness of life in City of Wolves. The boy was singled out by bullies right away because of his appearance, and even more so because his name went with the appearance. Days after Bergas's arrival, Alagur passed a ruckus in a side street close to his dwelling. He found Bergas with a bleeding lip and a bruised eye facing up to six other boys, one of whom Alagur had noticed following Raimir around.

Almost like some runt, he thought sarcastically.

After Alagur had broken up the fighting group, all the other boys ran off, and Bergas was left alone with the man. Alagur told the boy to come with him to his dwelling and he'd sort out the cut on his lip.

Two days after their chance meeting, Alagur approached the boy and said he wanted to take him on as an apprentice. The boy nodded, but

Alagur wondered for a while if he'd made the right choice. It was during a conversation with Bergas that his own musings about his recurring dreams started, especially when the boy shyly admitted that he still dreamt of his mother, and it was after this that Alagur's dreams become more regular.

Alagur returns to pondering about the woman from his dreams. He wonders if she lives in the city he is about to invade, and if this is the case, will he be able to find her?

He shrugs his shoulders. *Regardless of what I might become, she'll not show any interest because of what I am now.*

Again, Alagur is torn from his private thoughts when he catches sight of Samur riding towards him. Nodding a sneering acknowledgement towards Bergas, Samur relays to Alagur the plans set out by the Elder Men.

"You and I are going to lead a pack through the east gate of the city. It will give us all the spoils of the wealthiest merchant quarters."

Alagur nods approval, and Bergas nods too, even though he has no say in the matter whatsoever. After a few adjustments, Samur sits atop Uzo and both men start on their way towards Ruh'nar, Bergas obligingly following Alagur. The trek towards the city is going to be long, and Bergas is still learning how to handle his wolf, so he always feels some initial hesitation whenever he mounts the animal. He can almost feel Alagur's eyes piercing him as the man silently watches his struggle with the wolf, but Alagur doesn't say anything. Any guidance would result in the boy being ridiculed by the others around them.

Bergas still dreams of a mother he misses, and when no one is looking, he cries himself to sleep. Since his father drowned at sea and Bergas has no siblings, she will be alone now. To start with, he was sure that Alagur understood and would take him home, but as the days and weeks went by, it became clear this was wishful thinking. When Bergas and Alagur were alone, the man warned him not to try to leave, although something about his faraway look told Bergas he understood the boy's pain a lot more than he was letting on.

Bergas doesn't really like Samur. Something about the man speaks of malevolence; he seems to do everything for himself, and Bergas wonders if Alagur has noticed this too. The boy wonders if he should try to leave once he is old enough and return to his mother, despite the warning

Alagur has given him, but such an act will result in a bounty being put on him, which will make him a target for capture and an unspeakable fate. When Bergas asked what the fate would be, Alagur simply pointed towards where the wild wolves are held.

"That's the fate of the betrayer."

At the time, Bergas didn't press the matter further. Instead, he wondered how Alagur had obtained his massive wolf. He knew the wolf came from the north – he spotted many such wolves on treks south-west of Azaquina in a mountain range called Northern Blades, overlooking the northern coast of the landmass which is Keldarra. It's in the ocean north of those mountains that Bergas lost his father during a bitter storm lasting many days.

＊ ＊ ＊

THE LANDS AROUND CITY OF WOLVES have become barren and desert-like over the many centuries of neglect since the Wolf Riders took up residence. The city was once known as Masharea, which in the old tongue meant 'Truth Bearer'. In The Old Days, Masharea was the central power base of the earliest Order of Truth, but after the uprising led by Sey'qar and Yozan, the city was abandoned to time and dust, and the wolves and their masters.

It is through this desolate region that the Wolf Riders start their trek, which will lead them to the lush area of Sabeya with Ruh'nar at its heart. Alagur doesn't know yet what the journey will bring him, but he hopes it will be luck and riches. A flock of blue ravens fly over the mass of men and boys on their wolves, and to some, this is an omen of luck. Blue ravens are aptly named as they possess a distinct pale blue colour, despite ravens normally being black.

Alagur thinks about the man he met on his journey to get Yalla from the northern mountains. A flock such as this had flown overhead when the two men were gazing up at the sky. Not long after this, Alagur heard of the man's passing.

It didn't bring him any luck, he thinks, sadness gnawing at his mind. *He spoke of a family and children. Luck on the day should have been his, not mine.*

Alagur glances down at the silver-grey-and-white coat of the wolf below him, her muscles rolling powerfully, and decides the flock certainly brought him luck on that day. He strokes the fur on his wolf's neck, and the action makes the animal raise her head in a nod of approval.

Bergas also spots the flock fly off, and to him, it feels like an affirmation that he should try to go back home. One day, he will see his mother again. The boy watches the birds flying north and hopes his mother will see them too, and regard them as a signal that she will soon have her beloved son back with her.

To Samur, the flock confirms that his decision to raid the rich merchant quarters of Ruh'nar is the correct one, and it makes him think that all his plans – the excursion, the new wolf pack, his own fortune and power, and his plans for Alagur – will be fulfilled. Looking around at the crowd, Samur realises many of the men are thinking similar thoughts about luck coming their way, and he smirks maliciously.

This is the sort of thing which will give me power and influence, he thinks, scowling for the briefest moment, unseen by any around him.

* * *

IT IS CLOSE TO SUNSET on the final day of their long journey when the large group of Wolf Riders stops beside a fast-flowing stream running through the landscape almost directly from the western to the eastern coast. They will camp here for the night. News of their impending arrival will certainly have reached Ruh'nar by now, but in another half day or so, they will be at its gates, and their numbers will overwhelm the guardsmen. It will be a fitting end to a journey of close to a month, which will have to be done again in reverse after the attack.

Alagur and Samur choose a high embankment on the northern side of the river, next to a small waterfall depositing its clear icy water into the dark river below. Alagur instructs Bergas to go and look for dry tinder wood and boulders from which to construct a campfire. Spying three yellow-spotted river fowl on the bank below, he downs them with his thrower and spear arrows – they will eat well tonight.

He takes the harnesses off all three wolves and signals to Yalla to roam freely for her dinner. The other two wolves, who treat her as their matriarch, follow her as she lopes away quickly. Samur goes off to get berry wine from one of the other Wolf Riders in an adjoining encampment. Alagur hears Samur's booming laughter as he returns, and for a moment is curious as to what is so funny.

"We have berry wine tonight," Samur announces, holding up a pouch in each hand.

"And we've got some roasted fowl to go along with it, when Bergas returns with the wood and stones for the fire," Alagur responds.

A few minutes later, Bergas is back with a large bundle of wood, together with a few round boulders in a leather haversack. He places the heavy bag on the ground and unties the knot at the top, taking out the stones first and placing them on the ground where Alagur points. Alagur arranges the rocks into a square shape and places the wood in a lattice above as Bergas hands him the pieces a few at a time. Both man and boy work fast, aware of Samur taking his first taste of wine.

The wood Bergas has collected is a type which burns slowly, and rather than giving off licking flames, it smoulders without actually turning into ash. In this way, the wood can burn for half a day or more, so every traveller uses it. And a few freshly caught fowl cooked on top of this fire will taste delicious. Both men and boy think of the meal awaiting them in an hour or so, their mouths watering.

Bergas picks up his bedroll and unties it, placing it near the waterfall which reminds him of home. He remembers the days after rainfall when the sun would shine again, and his mother would take him to a small waterfall on the hills above their house.

Alagur observes a faraway look shadowing the boy's face and knows what must be going through his mind. He sits downs so that Samur cannot see Bergas and decides to question the older man more about his plans before Samur has a chance to get into one of his familiar drunken stupors.

"Where are we heading to establish the wolf pack?"

"There's a region north-west of here, between Ruh'nar and the next city, bordering a large lake to the east. You know it?"

Alagur nods. It is at the northern side of the lake where he had met a traveller many years ago.

"There's a road leading west to a coastal town, and to the north-west is Chiva'na," Samur continues. "It's the city where they do those crazy things with girls."

It's also the city you said I was from originally, Alagur thinks angrily, but he doesn't speak. He occasionally thinks he has vague memories of a life before the Wolf Riders, seeming to remember a young girl running after him and calling his name.

"If we settle at the lake, we're in a perfect spot for raiding three different cities."

Samur carries on without noticing the momentary frown on Alagur's face, or at least, choosing to ignore it. Bergas sits listening in silence to the conversation, and it doesn't escape his notice when a scowl appears on Alagur's face at the mention of Chiva'na. He believes he understands Alagur a bit better now.

The boy's thoughts are interrupted when a man approaches their small camp and calls out for Samur. Bergas looks over his shoulder and sees the newcomer is Raimir, another man he dislikes. Raimir is too much like Samur in attitude – self-centred and out to please himself.

"Hail, Raimir," Samur calls out in a drunken slur. The new arrival eases himself onto the mat beside the man who greeted him and relays his reasons for visiting their camp.

"There's talk going around of some sort of militia the inhabitants of Ruh'nar have started. I think it will be good if we can kill a few of them while we're there."

Both men nod. Alagur knows Samur is a dab hand at sword fighting, and he himself is a good archer. However, he isn't sure how they'd fare against a couple of dozen or so determined defenders, even as skilled as they are.
"We're going into the wealthier merchant quarter, and if I can kill a few of them defenders, I will," Samur replies. "And if I can grab some of their young brats for sport, it's even better."
The last remark angers both Alagur and Bergas. Their mutual thoughts are reflected in their shared expressions for a moment, but soon Alagur's face becomes neutral once again and he listens further to the conversation between the other two men. He hasn't yet finalised his plans for the next day and is still trying to figure out two crucial facts – how he's going to get the boy away from all this, and how he's going to search for the woman.

It seems my every thought revolves around the woman now. Perhaps getting Bergas out of the picture is the key to sorting out how to find her.

Neither of the other men notices the quick glances passing between Alagur and the boy sitting behind them. Bergas is of little concern or value to them, so they would have ignored him even if he'd sat right in between them.

Alagur decides not to get involved in the conversation and instead returns to the matter a lot more intriguing to him – the woman from his dreams. The latest dream was last night, and he set eyes on her face as clearly as if she were a hand's length away from him.

I do wonder who she is.

By the time Raimir bids the two men farewell, the moon has reached its highest point in the sky and Bergas has long since gone to sleep. Alagur feels drained as if he hasn't slept for days. He wonders how Samur can drink so much, be so drunk, yet still be alert to what is going on around him.

As though guided by a silent command, the three wolves, with Yalla in the lead, appear out of the darkness. They all shake their bodies, spraying drops of water over the men who use their outer cloaks to dry themselves. This clears the drunken stupor from Samur's face and he laughs.

"Looks like the wolves have been bathing."
"Looks like we're sleeping in damp beds again," Alagur replies, chuckling.

The two men look at one another and, without knowing what's so funny, burst into raucous laughter, which goes echoing throughout the camp. Grunts and shouts at them to be quiet finally stop them, and they climb into their own beds, Samur thinking about the riches tomorrow will bring, and Alagur trying to form a feasible plan. Staring at the skies, he lies awake for hours, wondering if the woman he's dreamt about is also looking at the stars at that moment.

CHAPTER NINE

Tʜᴇʀᴇ's ᴏɴᴇ ʙʀɪɢʜᴛ sᴛᴀʀ which always rises about three hours before the sun. Alagur searches the sky for the star but can't find it. Long ago, people existed who understood the meaning of the skies, studying the placings of the stars, and some claimed that they could even tell the future from how the sky looked on certain days.

In City of Wolves, there's a building with a tall tower. When Alagur climbed the tower out of curiosity one night, he was amazed at what he found at the top: a ceiling filled with small glass shapes. Or they may have been some sort of crystal, he doesn't know. Later he returned with Bergas, and they both studied the room with great interest, agreeing that certain stars would be visible through the shapes, forming a pattern.

A few days before departing from the city, Alagur went to check the room again and was surprised to notice different shapes showing the stars. Alagur guessed that in The Old Days, the room was a measuring device, possibly for measuring the passage of time. There were no books in the room to give him information; they had either turned to dust a long time before, or they had been destroyed by the First Riders, Sey'qar and Yozan, and their earliest supporters, a thousand years ago. He was sure the solution to the riddle was somewhere, though, because judging by the fading artwork in the room, the building was connected to the Temple.

And before darkness overcame the landscape earlier on this night, he could have sworn he saw a similar style tower in the city which was half a day's ride from the Wolf Rider encampment.

Alagur senses Yalla lying down beside him and, as she often does, she places her head on his chest and looks up at him. The man lifts his head for a few moments, staring into the wolf's golden eyes, and smiles a tired smile. He puts his hand on her forehead and ruffles the wire-like hairs, and the wolf nudges his hand, showing she shares his feelings. One way or another, he has a loyal friend, and that friend certainly isn't Samur. Although Alagur counts Bergas as a friend, his true friendship is with a large and beautiful silver-grey-and-white wolf from the north called Yalla.

Moments later, Alagur is fast asleep. Except for grunts from the men around him, yips from many wolves, chirps and other animal sounds, and the soft hiss of fires which are slowly dying out, the whole camp now lies silent, sleeping.

Tomorrow will be the day they will enter an almost defenceless city to plunder and pillage.

* * *

THE WOLF LIES WATCHING HER MASTER for a long while before she too closes her eyes to sleep. However, one solitary boy lies silently weeping in his bed furs, his back hunched over to control his emotions which are spilling from the depths of his soul. A boy who is feeling so alone among the thousands who sleep under the open sky; who wishes he could be anywhere else but here at this moment; who wishes to be home with his mother, eating her fish soup and listening to her retellings of The Old Days in front of the fireplace.

The first light of a new day breaks through the low grey clouds which fill the skies. Bergas rises before sunrise and has already gone off to gather more wood when Alagur and Samur each sit up, yawning, in their bed furs. Alagur decides some honey tea would be good, and perhaps some of the leftover fowl to fill the knot of hunger in his stomach.

He grabs the shirt he threw off before going to sleep and puts it on, tucking it into his trousers. There's a slight chill in the shirt from the moist ground, but he figures he'll warm up as soon as the fire gets going again. He walks to the small waterfall and, using his hands as a scoop, gulps down a few mouthfuls of the icy water. Dunking his head under the fast-flowing waterfall, he quickly pulls it back and smiles.

That has woken you up.

Bergas walks back into the camp with a dozen or so wood branches, which he proceeds to place on top of the ashes of the fire from the previous evening. Alagur kneels beside him and, using his tinder kit, gets the fire smouldering in the long-burning wood. The man and boy look at each other and their faces hold the same unspoken concern, but with Samur so close, they can't talk openly about last night's conversation.

Alagur reassures the boy with a simple gesture of a hand on his shoulder and an almost imperceptible nod. Bergas has received this gentle gesture before, and he knows without the need for words what it means: Alagur has understood the impact of Samur's words on him and they will speak together later.

The two men sit opposite one another, discussing the plans for the attack. Samur is sober, which is unusual for him. Normally he likes his half jug of rubha wine, which he procures from trading favours with other Wolf Riders, and he has typically emptied it before the morning meal is cooked. But today his thoughts are intoxicating him – the wealth he is expecting to find in the city which lies half a day's ride away in the lushest valley of Sabeya.

Flanked by two high mountain ranges, the Sabeya region will today make many a man rich. Or so Samur thinks. Sabeya is waiting for him, and nothing is going to stop him from achieving the goal he has set for himself.

"So, we're entering through the eastern gate?" Alagur comments. The eastern gate leads straight into the merchant quarter of the city. Samur nods; with his mouth full of cold fowl, it is hard to speak.

Bergas glances from Alagur to Samur, and back at Alagur. He's sure Alagur is planning something different to what the older man wants to do, and he almost jumps when Alagur includes him in the conversation.

"Shall we leave Bergas outside the gates as he's still young?" Alagur asks, flicking a dew fly from his arm with a finger.

"Yes, why not. He'll only be in the way," Samur replies with a hint of a smirk on his face.

Bergas feels anger beginning to well up, but when he catches Alagur staring at him intently, he realises the man is trying to keep him safe from harm. If something goes wrong, the boy will be the first to feel Samur's wrath, and he may even end up in the pen with the wild wolves. This isn't the fate Alagur wants for Bergas.

Alagur gets up, and so does Yalla. He picks up the harness which the wolf usually wears and fastens it onto her in a few practised motions, then fixes the rolled-up sleeping furs and attaches his thrower and quiver filled with a hundred or so spear arrows either side of it. Taking a brush from the pocket of the sack which hangs against the wolf's torso behind the saddle, he brushes through her fur. Soft grunts tell him she is enjoying the experience as much as he is.

Samur hurriedly gets Uzo ready, then proceeds to help Bergas with his wolf, even though it's clear from the boy's short answers and abrupt silences that he neither wants nor needs this help. And when the man walks away, the look on Bergas's face could have set an iceberg in flames. There's so much venom in the boy's hatred for Samur, Alagur realises he must get Bergas away from him if it's the last thing he does.

Once the two men and the boy are ready, they stand staring at one another for several minutes, not saying a thing, each deep in his own thoughts. It takes them a few minutes to comprehend that when a horn bellows, it signals departure.

They mount up, and Alagur and Samur start to ride with Bergas falling in behind them. The three wolves wade through the chilled water at the higher end of the waterfall, descending the path towards the river which runs beside the remnants of the encampment. Now their route leads south-west towards Ruh'nar.

Alagur is thinking about the two things he wants to try to do. The first one, of course, is to keep the boy behind him safe, and a plan to help Bergas get away from the Wolf Riders is hatching in his mind. He realises suspicion will immediately fall on him if he succeeds, but as it will apparently be Samur's idea to leave the boy outside the city gates, that may help to divert the blame.

The second plan hatching in Alagur's mind involves looking for the mysterious woman. He dreamt about her yet again during the night, and her face was closer and clearer than any time before. He also saw a street which he is certain is where she lives. His dream showed a house with three white gables and a roof covered with dried marsh reeds. He doesn't know if this is her house, but he's sure it holds some sort of significance.

Bergas has his own thoughts. If Alagur has suggested to Samur to leave him outside Ruh'nar to help him escape, he needs to be ready, and fast. Alagur has given him a small, sharp knife, and whispered to him to use it while holding his hand over the boy's young wolf's throat. Alagur also made a fist against his stomach. The two gestures were so fast, at first Bergas was puzzled. A stern look from Alagur, first at the boy then a sideways nod at the wolf, followed by a quick point at the knife clenched in the boy's hand, led Bergas to understand what he expected from him. He nodded a shallow nod. He needs to escape, but he certainly can't arrive home as a Wolf Rider. The evidence of his escape must be disposed of by his own hand using this knife.

I will miss my older friend.

Bergas touches the hilt of the knife, now tucked between the folds of a small rucksack which hangs over the wolf's massive shoulders, then he glances at Alagur and sighs.

* * *

THE MASS OF MEN AND WOLVES started their trek early. The sun has now risen far above the eastern mountains, which are the source of the river they are following. There's shouting and singing and laughter among the group.

Samur goes back to his old habits as they trek ever closer to the sleeping city. He pulls out another pouch of berry wine and takes gulps of it, the occasional smile on his face betraying what he is thinking about – wealth, wine and women. He may also grab a boy or two if he so wishes, but it's wealth he desires the most.

Samur raises his left arm in greeting when a newcomer arrives by his side and hands over the pouch of wine. Raimir, who has decided to ride next to Samur and Alagur, takes a long, refreshing gulp of the wine before handing the pouch back, nodding at Samur in approval.

When Raimir decides to join Samur and Alagur, his three companions do the same. Now Bergas has two boys riding beside him, both a few years older than he, and a boy riding behind him, who is maybe a year or so younger. One boy he recognises as his former tormentor, but he doesn't know any of their names so simply nods half-hearted greetings at them and stays silent. He isn't in any mood for conversation, and he notes the same applies to his three new companions.

Raimir is less impressed with the silence behind him and decides to introduce his companions to Samur and Alagur.

"Don't think you've met my riders yet," he says. "The fair-haired boy next to Bergas is Kaizor, the one with the chestnut-coloured hair beside him is Melchor, and the dark-haired little one trailing them is Ebagar."

Samur turns around on his saddle and lifts his wine pouch to greet the three boys, smirking his most malicious grin when he spots Ebagar cringe. Alagur turns as well a moment later and greets the trio with a nod of his head. All the boys lift their left arms in reply. Alagur notices the sadness on Bergas's face once more and realises these three aren't potential friends to his young companion, but obstacles which may make it hard for him to escape.

Alagur turns back in his saddle and decides to hasten the plan to leave Bergas alone. If there's going to be any chance of releasing Bergas from the Wolf Riders, the moment has come. He looks down at his packs of belongings and smiles to himself. In the two packs slung over Yalla's massive shoulders are his best clothes and weapons, and it's perfectly feasible that he wouldn't want them with him when the Wolf Riders arrive in Ruh'nar.

"Samur, you keep riding. I need to get Bergas to take my belongings somewhere safe."

Samur looks at the packs on Yalla's back and nods. While he and Raimir, followed by Kaizor, Melchor and Ebagar, ride on, Alagur and Bergas dismount and walk down to the side of the river, followed by their wolves.

Samur calls out after them, "We'll wait only for as long as it takes me to empty this pouch of wine, then we attack, with or without you. *Without* you, there will be more spoils for us."

Alagur glances over his shoulder, seeing Samur disappearing over the crest of the hill. He noticed the emphasis on one word – one word that would mean there'd be hell to pay on his return to City of Wolves.

Alagur takes several packs from Yalla's back and places them on a stone outcrop under a tree. "You know what to do?" he whispers to the boy. Bergas nods, showing the man where he's hidden the small knife by lifting its shaft up a thumb's length from the rucksack. The man nods, approving of the boy's efficiency.

"Hide my belongings among the bushes around this tree when I'm gone," Alagur says through clenched teeth. "Wait until most riders have gone past, then walk north-east along this river until midday. Then you can start riding north towards your home. In this way, any riders who see you will think I sent you back to City of Wolves."

The boy nods again.

Alagur climbs back on Yalla. He glances once more at the boy, who feels almost like a younger brother to him, then he rides off at considerable speed to catch up with his companion trekking towards the city where destiny will be rewritten for him.

Bergas looks at the fast disappearing silhouette of Alagur for several minutes, then sets the man's plan in motion by hiding all the packs he has left. The name of the bush is appropriate as it's often known as a 'hidden bush', usually concealed under some big tree or larger bushes, and now Bergas is using it for hiding stuff – and himself for a while, too.

The boy quietly chuckles.

* * *

ALAGUR REJOINS THE GROUP OF MEN AND BOYS as they start to ride across the large field of last autumn's hay which lies between the river they have crossed and the road which travels westward into Ruh'nar. He thinks about the many uses of the hay, which stretches out a great distance around him, and decides one of the things he is going to look for in the city is a floor mat for his dwelling in City of Wolves. When rubbed in mud from the river, the hay produces excellent cooking pots, and it is also commonly used for making baskets and floor mats because of its sturdy but soft texture. The floor mats are cured in a mixture of honey and milk to give them a silky-soft texture.

"Bergas wouldn't have been helpful at all, and you made it back just in time. I have a few mouthfuls left in this." Samur sneers in a way that causes Alagur to feel uncomfortable. "You had a good idea. We're planning to leave Kaizor and Ebagar before we get close enough to the city, but Raimir is going to have Melchor, who's the oldest of the three, with him when he attacks the city at the north gate."

Alagur nods to show he understands the plan. Today, it's time for action, not planning.

CHAPTER TEN

T HREE MEN AND THREE BOYS RIDE for close to six hours. Ahead is the smaller lake where the younger two of the three boys will make camp.

In the distance beyond the lake, the imposing walls of the Temple of Truth, a place run by the enigmatic Keepers spoken about by a few of the Elder Men, becomes visible. Entry into this part of the city will be impossible for the Wolf Riders. Alagur wonders how the Temple in City of Wolves would have looked before it was turned into a den for wolves. What did Sey'qar and Yozan do to turn the once majestic city into a pile of rubble? They led some sort of uprising, but no one knows why or how they did it, or even what they did. And the few lines of The Truth which are recited regularly over campfires don't really offer much information as to what happened so long ago.

This doesn't matter to most Wolf Rider, but Alagur is different, and he is sure Bergas is different in the same way. When the two were alone, they talked long about the fate which befell the old city, and why no one ever came to rebuild it to the glory status it had held for two thousand years.

"People don't come anymore because of us," Alagur explained to the boy, waving his arm broadly to encompass all the city's occupants in the statement. Now for the first time in his life, Alagur sees what City of Wolves could have looked like, and he feels a deep sadness go through his heart.

What if the woman in my dreams must face a pile of rubble tomorrow?

Alagur glances at the rest of the city's structures, seeing the east gate and the peaks of many white gabled houses beyond. Two domes are visible, one on the building where boys are trained as soldiers, and the other where the city's governing group is housed. Or so Samur has told Alagur many times.

Samur seems to know the city too well--

* * *

FROM THE CITY WALLS, the few soldiers who remain on guard watch the ominous mass of wolves and men, which is swelling by the minute. One shouts a warning, and another strikes a large gong to inform the city's many inhabitants that the threat of the Wolf Riders has arrived at the gates. They then run across the walls to arm the large catapults, but the city's defenders are truly outnumbered by the crowd which is weaving closer to the walls every moment.

In a small room in the massive Temple, a woman with long blonde hair blanches when she hears the gong. She glances up at her Elder with pleading eyes. Elder Sharriba knows what the sound means and decides to send the Acolytes sitting around her to their own homes. Of all the Acolytes, Marrida has the furthest to go, and Sharriba wishes she could keep the woman with her in the Temple, but she cannot. There's an enemy attacking, and she and the other Keepers must move all the artefacts and books to a special vault below the Temple. The Acolytes and Temple Maidens are not permitted to know about this vault until they are initiated as First Rank Keepers.

Elder Sharriba watches Marrida walk out of the vestibule which separates the Temple from the world outside. At that point, she nods, and four Keepers push the two massive stone doors shut. If anyone now looks upon the place where they can usually enter the Temple, all they will see is an unbroken wall. They won't even see the seam of a door, so thoroughly precise is the fit.

As the door slams shut, Marrida glances over her shoulder, and for a few minutes, she yearns for the safety the building could have offered everyone in the city. She's convinced all two hundred thousand inhabitants could be housed in the Temple at times such as this.

Glancing back at the other females who have exited the building, she sees the faces of those who tease and bully her whenever no Keeper is there to enforce order. One woman, Sarayna, is always bossing her around whenever she has a chance, telling her how to store books on shelves and where to place jars of herbs used in healing practices. She does the same to several of the other youngsters, but tends to single Marrida out, resenting the way in which Marrida is treated differently from the other females in the Temple, despite being the youngest Acolyte of them all. Most others, including Sarayna herself, only became a Temple Maiden at the age of seventeen or eighteen, and had to wait three to five years before becoming an Acolyte, but Marrida, who has barely served a year as a Temple Maiden, is already a third-year Acolyte at just nineteen years old. And so Sarayna spends every moment she can tormenting Marrida, who takes it all in her stride. She is amazingly resilient, despite the loneliness the bullying causes her.

Now glancing at the older Acolyte, Marrida sees not a bully, but a terrified young woman. Walking over to her, she takes Sarayna's hand and holds it, smiling at her. To Marrida's surprise, the older woman starts crying; she has never seen Sarayna cry before.

"It'll be safe soon enough--"

Marrida stops speaking because she isn't sure if it is going to be so. A shallow smile on Sarayna's face shows a glimmer of gratitude for a moment, but then she abruptly tears her hand away from Marrida's, turns on her heels and strides off to the western side of the square. She lives not too far from the Temple, so she's likely to be one of the first Acolytes to get home.

Marrida looks after her for a few minutes, sighs and shrugs her shoulders. While walking home, she sees the panic engulfing the city, and she feels fear for her own family in the north-eastern merchant quarter. Strangely enough, though, she also feels today is the day she has been waiting for ever since word first spread that the Wolf Riders were planning an attack on the city.

* * *

OUTSIDE THE CITY, Alagur sits on a boulder beside the lake, looking up briefly from priming his spear arrows and frowning when he hears the gong.

They know we're here.

Raucous laughter with an edge of malice to it comes from Samur and Raimir, telling Alagur that they too have heard the gong. For a moment, Alagur's thoughts go back to Bergas. How he wishes he could simply swap places with the boy. Although Alagur usually likes being a Wolf Rider, sometimes the whole idea of being one makes him sick to the stomach, especially when it comes to Samur's attitude. A 'friend' and Pack Brother he may be, but he is also a man with many secrets, and very good at hiding his own motives.

Samur told Alagur he voluntarily joined the Wolf Riders, travelling to City of Wolves from the far south-east after hearing the legend of Sey'qar and Yozan from 'some traveller'. What became of this traveller, Samur never said, but Alagur suspects that he may well have met with an unfortunate end. Knowing Samur's temper and violent tendency, especially when he's been drinking excessively, only too well, Alagur feels that's a fair assumption.

Samur is a burly man in his late thirties, with jet black hair streaked with the first hints of grey and a heavy-set square chin, piercing black eyes, and scars from his many fights. He ranks among the most important of the Wolf Riders, and originally chose both Alagur and Raimir as his second-in-command. But when Alagur returned from the South Valley of Miza with his magnificent silver-grey-and-white wolf, it was he and not Raimir who gained favour with the older man. And now, with Samur and Alagur becoming Pack Brothers, Raimir feels left out in the cold and at times jealous of Alagur, who is a few years younger than he. Raimir now follows Samur around like some runt, which makes Alagur wonder about the other man's motives and puts him on his guard.

"Alagur?" It's Kaizor who speaks his name. "Could you tell me where you got your wolf from?"

It is simple curiosity which has drawn the boy, who is approaching his seventeenth year, towards Alagur. Kaizor is in awe of Yalla, and having earlier seen Bergas stroke the large wolf gently, he wants to do the same.

"The wolf is from Miza," Alagur replies with a smile curling his lips. "They live in the mountains there."

"She's the biggest wolf I've ever seen," Kaizor replies, awe in his voice. "She is beautiful--"

"When you're ready for your Naming Day, maybe you should get yourself such a wolf too," Raimir interjects loudly. Alagur scowls at the other man, the good feeling which was forming between him and Kaizor disappearing in an instant.

Kaizor pulls his hand away from the wolf in front of him as she turns her head to sniff the person stroking her fur, and she snorts in disapproval at the loss of the attention. The boy walks towards Raimir, who is also admiring the wolf despite his jealousy of Alagur. However, he lacks the courage to approach the wolf or the man beside her, instead briskly walking towards Samur. Kaizor can do nothing but follow his master, although the glances he shoots over his shoulder at the wolf suggest to Alagur he would like to have stayed longer.

As Alagur turns back to tending his wolf companion, he thinks about

Bergas and hopes the boy is safe and well. He also thinks about the gong he heard from the city ahead of him, and for some moments, conflicting thoughts pass through his mind.

Can I loot sufficient wealth from the city to help Samur with his plans?

As fast as the thought appears in his mind, the man shakes it off.

I'm going into the city to find the woman if she exists. And then--

Alagur isn't sure what may happen next. Perhaps he could let himself be captured and ask the guards about the woman, hoping they will recognise whom he is talking about. Or he could try to find her and speak with her.

But will she speak with me?

After fastening the last bindings and packs to the sturdy harness Yalla wears, Alagur mounts her. He feels the wolf's muscles ripple under him, demonstrating her excitement at what is to come. Alagur glances over his shoulder and sees that Samur, Raimir and Melchor have done the same with their wolves. The other two boys have settled themselves, leaning against one of the trees near the lake's edge, both staring in the direction of the city which will soon be overrun by hordes of men and wolves. Alagur sees Kaizor nudge his companion and say something to him quietly, but because of the distance between them and the murmur of noise around him, Alagur can't work out what they're talking about. But as both boys are looking in his direction, he guesses they are discussing either his wolf or him.

"Are you ready to go?" Samur asks.

Alagur nods to confirm that he is, and the three men and one boy start towards the eastern gate of the city. They're still some distance from their destination so they set their wolves into a sprint. The wolves that the Wolf Riders favour are known for their ability to sprint over longer distances than the wild wolves that roam the land could manage. As Yalla is one of the most powerful of the beasts, she can easily out-pace the rest of the pack, but Alagur has taught her to curb her speed so that she follows the pack rather than leads it. He believes it is better that way.

Now that the moment has come for the attack to commence, all the men and their wolves are focused on the task ahead. Many an unfortunate son of Ruh'nar will see his fate sealed on this day, snatched from his family and forced to become a Wolf Rider. Wealth will be amassed in great quantities, and the city will bear witness to the power of the Wolf Riders, leaving its inhabitants reeling in fear.

The first words of The Truth flash through Alagur's mind as he sets Yalla at a steady fast pace.

> TEN THOUSAND RIDERS ROSE TO THE CALL
> BESET ON TO THE CITY OF OLD, AND
> FALL BEFORE THEM IT WOULD.

Now he is part of the crowd of riders attacking a city for spoils, snatchings and more.

As the city grows ever closer, the mass of men and wolves divides itself into four groups, each large enough to take on an army. Samur, Alagur and the men and boys who accompany them have been tasked with plundering the eastern quarter and its many merchants' homes, but Alagur has given himself a different task this day. He hopes that his face doesn't betray his thoughts.

"Ready the men!" A booming voice echoes from the highest part of the wall that surrounds Ruh'nar. Some three dozen men appear on the walls with their weapons at hand. The weapons are catapults to all intents and purposes, but they have the general appearance of larger versions of the spear thrower that Alagur is now reaching for. Again, he feels Yalla's muscles rippling under his hand as he removes the weapon and the spears from the knapsack on her right flank.

The Wolf Riders have developed methods to counter attacks from a besieged city by coating the tips of their spear arrows with a substance called slurry, made from the ash of the night's campfires. The ash is mixed with an oil-like substance most commonly found where the ground splits and the fires from within come to the surface of the land, and when the arrows are shot at a weapon atop a city wall, they destroy it by setting it alight. Alagur worked for many hours showing Bergas how to make the bad-smelling substance, and then spent half a day dipping every one of his spear tips into it before placing them in the hot midday sun to dry.

The pungent smell seeps up Alagur's nostrils as he strikes a tinder near the tip of a spear arrow then places it in the thrower. It looks as though it splits the sky with a ball of fire before landing on top of one of Ruh'nar's catapults.

* * *

ALAGUR ENTERS THE LARGE SQUARE, where less than an hour before a crowd of terrified people was hurrying home. He's surrounded by three other Wolf Riders, so he suggests splitting up into two groups. He and Samur will take the large street leading away from the square towards the east, and Raimir and Melchor will go down the northerly street. The latter two are the first to ride off, and after a short discussion, Samur and Alagur ride off too – the older man in the lead, with Alagur following somewhat reluctantly. He wants to separate himself from Samur, so he can look for the woman.

* * *

HIGH ABOVE THE TWO MEN, voices are whispering.

"Wait--this is where he told us to come. From here, we cannot be seen. He won't know what's happening until it's too late. When he laughs, it's our signal."

* * *

ALAGUR RIDES THROUGH THE LONG STREET, looking at the back of Samur's head. Suddenly, the older man turns and speaks to him.

"I'm going to investigate two streets up ahead." Samur laughs loudly when Alagur frowns. "You stay here and look out for any boys we can snatch."

Unnoticed by Alagur, Samur glances up to the roofs far above him. He then rides off before Alagur can say anything in protest. But far from protesting, Alagur realises that this is his chance to look for any indication of where the woman he's dreamt about may live. He pulls at the harness to stop Yalla from pacing forward down the street, then glances around and listens. He can hear children screaming in the distance, and he understands that somewhere, boys are becoming unwilling recruits into the ranks of the Wolf Riders. To his left, Alagur sees several ornate doors, an indication that the occupants of the houses are rich.

Just as he's about to ride away, a sharp whistling noise cuts through the air, and a pain shoots through his head. Before he falls unconscious, he hears a second whistling sound followed by a thud, then everything goes dark as he slides to the ground.

CHAPTER ELEVEN

Weeks later, Alagur regains consciousness. He sees a face leaning over him and he feels a cool hand touching his forehead with some care. A woman's voice asks for his name.

"Alag--" is all he can say before he loses consciousness.

As he drifts in and out of his unconscious state, he glimpses a few of the people around him. He's in a pleasant room, but he doesn't know where the room is located, or where Yalla is right now.

Then he sees the mysterious woman do – something.

What did she do?

Alagur sinks back into unconsciousness.

* * *

Sometime later, Alagur feels like he's woken from a groggy sleep after a day of drinking too much of Samur's wine and ale. A pain throbs on the side of his head, making him grunt out loud.

Becoming aware he isn't alone, Alagur opens his eyes to see a woman looking down at him. It's almost as if he's dreaming again because she looks exactly like the woman he's seen in his mind so many times.

In a voice filled with concern, she asks him how he feels, and Alagur states that his head hurts. She tells him what happened to him, that he was attacked and injured. This time, when she asks for his name, he can answer without losing consciousness.

"Alagur."

A vague memory of the battle comes to his mind, but it's gone a moment later. Knowing the thoroughness of the Wolf Riders, he realises the battle would have lasted for days, and it makes him wonder how long he's lain on the bed in this room. How have the occupants of this house kept themselves safe during the fighting?

* * *

LATER, ALAGUR HEARS THREE YOUNG PEOPLE TALKING, and he recognises that at least one of them is still a child.

Where are the parents of these youngsters? Dead? Perhaps killed by Wolf Riders?

Thinking about this makes his head hurt even more. Where are the other Wolf Riders, and why have they left him here? A thought starts to gnaw at his mind – he's been betrayed and left for dead by those he trusts most.

At once, a surge of panic overcomes Alagur. Where's the wolf? He glances around and sees the woman beside him.
"Where is Yalla?"
"Who is Yalla?"
Alagur explains, and the young girl, who's staring at him from across the room, answers his question. He pierces the air with a sharp whistle, and a sound from the garden tells him that her words are true – the wolf is outside somewhere.

The woman's name is Marrida, and she shocks him by explaining she is a Keeper of Truth.

I thought they were just a myth.

Marrida is accompanied by two younger people: a boy, perhaps close to First Rites, and a girl of eleven or so years. The girl keeps staring at him without flinching or looking away.

She doesn't scare easily, he thinks with a smile which is close to becoming a grimace due to the pain in the side of his head.

"I could find out more about you," Marrida explains, and the man notes some hesitation in her voice.

How are these…what does she call herself again? Keepers of Truth? How are they any different to anyone else?

Then he proceeds to explain that he believes he's dreamt about

Marrida. Still reeling from the shame of having to admit that indeed, he is a Wolf Rider, he half expects the woman to ridicule the dream, but she simply nods and accepts it as fact. It makes him feel both less and more uncomfortable around her.

She intrigues him, and he studies her facial features. She, in turn, studies him. His eyes pierce right through her, stopping at a bulge under her garment. As she reveals to him the Stone of Truth, his eyes fly wide open in awe and amazement.

"I can see the past with it."

My past? he thinks. *What does she know about it? And how does the gem work anyway?*

They are now alone in the room, apart from the presence of Yalla. Marrida explains how to use the gem with a demonstration. He sees her eyes darken and become unfocused, then a shimmering image appears, playing out a scene. It looks familiar.

Alagur feels his hand slide onto the wolf's head in a subconscious gesture of affection. The man he sees in the vision is Samur.

But who is the boy? Is that me?

Alagur watches as the boy is lifted onto the wolf being ridden by the familiar dark-haired man and sees – hears – a girl call out after him.

"Alagur. Alagur."

That is my sister, Alagur thinks. *What happened to her?*

The scenery in the vision has changed. Two men huddle together, deep in a private conversation. At first, he sees himself and Samur, but then he becomes aware of the difference in the clothing and features of both the men, and it becomes obvious who they are. Alagur has heard the retellings of Sey'qar and Yozan many times since he joined the Wolf Riders and knows what they're discussing in this vision before him. And once again, he feels shame about what he is and what those men were plotting against Marrida's kind. Realising suddenly just how wrong the actions of the Wolf Riders are, he's glad he sent Bergas home.

The man glances at the woman beside him. Her eyes are jet black with fully dilated pupils which seem to see nothing but the images drifting in the air. He touches her hands and, in the process, unbalances the gem. The motion snaps the woman out of her trance-like state, and two glowering eyes filled with seething anger meet his gaze.

"What do you think you are doing?"

A growl from Yalla snaps Alagur out of his state of confusion. An apology is all he can offer Marrida, and she immediately calms down. He sees her studying him again with the intensity he noted previously. After a few moments, she asks him if it would be alright for her siblings to come back into the room while they discuss the visions. He nods his approval.

The man notes how Yalla instantly attracts the young girl's attention, and she shows no fear of the massive wolf. Alagur feels himself staring at Marrida and catches an angry glower from the boy, who is making it obvious he doesn't like the man, or the way he is looking at his sister. But Alagur detects some curiosity on the boy's face as well.

After glancing at the young girl, smiling weakly at her interaction with the wolf, Alagur closes his eyes, opening them again on hearing the girl ask a question. At a simple confirmation from him, a realisation dawns on Marrida's face, and he wishes for a few moments he could reach out and hold her hand. But he knows it would anger her again.

He shuts his eyes and falls into a dreamless sleep before he even realises how tired he still is from his injuries, unaware when Yalla, who normally sleeps with her head leaning on his legs, leaves the room to follow the young girl.

* * *

When Alagur awakes, he reaches for the familiar shape of the wolf and finds Yalla missing. Feeling groggy, the man slowly rises from the bed. He can hear the voices of the three youngsters coming from another part of the house. Feeling around until he finds his familiar shirt, he pulls it over his head, cringing somewhat when the fabric meets the tender wound on the side of his head.

Alagur steadies himself when a moment of dizziness hits him. Dismissing the thought of lying down again, he makes his way out of the room he's lain in for the past seven weeks, through the cooking room and into the hallway. Standing in the vestibule listening, he's sure the voices are coming from the front room.

It seems, in his groggy state, to take an eternity to cross the vestibule. Eventually, Alagur reaches the room, arriving just in time to hear the boy ask a question about the things Wolf Riders do.

"And what are these 'things', if I may ask?"

Glancing around the room, Alagur realises he's spoken angrily when the three youngsters all stand up in alarm. Even Yalla rises, but her next action snaps the man out of his anger – she walks from the room. Alagur knows his lupine companion well enough to tell when she isn't going to be the menacing wolf all expect her to be.

Then he finds himself staring straight into the eyes of the woman, who has positioned herself defiantly between him and her siblings. Alagur decides to appear less confrontational and suggests he too should be involved in any conversation about his people – the Wolf Riders. The woman nods at the suggestion and points at a chair for him.

This could turn out to be an interesting conversation indeed, Alagur thinks as he sits down. Glancing around the room, he decides to look the young boy squarely in the face as he explains about the Wolf Riders. *If the boy wants to know, then know it he shall.*

The question, the inevitable question, is why the Wolf Riders snatch boys. Alagur feels like he has no answer, so he decides to tell the truth – a truth he has struggled with for a long time, he admits to himself.

The origins of the Wolf Riders relating to Sey'qar and Yozan come up too, and Alagur tells the three youngsters all he knows of the legend. It occurs to him that with her skill, the woman probably knows a lot more about them than he does, and she does indeed fill in parts of the legend with the knowledge of the Ancient Histories she has been taught at the Temple. Comparing her knowledge to his own, Alagur wonders how much he still doesn't know of those ancient times.

Interestingly, the wolf re-enters the room as if on cue when the conversation turns to the ancient legend.

After some pause, Alagur decides to change the subject, and he asks Marrida about the other city he saw in her vision. He's both curious and worried about what he's seen, and several times in the conversation the word 'snatched' has cropped up.

Was I really snatched as the vision suggested?

The conversation then changes to the origins of his wolf. Alagur thinks at first that he's doing an amazing job of amusing the young girl across the room from him.

"She's from Miza," he explains, stopping suddenly when Marrida looks furious with him. Learning that the youngsters' father was travelling in the same region when Alagur went to get the wolf, he remembers meeting the man. They'd shared a fire as the night had been cold and there wasn't much wood to go around. Neither had spoken much, and both were reluctant to tell the other his name and where he'd come from, but they'd parted on good terms.

Sadly, Alagur later heard that the man had been killed, possibly at the hands of Wolf Riders.

The change in the woman is like seeing a single ray of bright sunlight breaking through angry storm clouds. She starts to sob, not the sobs of an angry person, but those of someone who has finally learnt something life-changing about herself. She seems calmer now she's learnt the fate of her father, almost like a weight has been lifted from her shoulders.

It must have been a heavy burden to carry, Alagur thinks sadly. *I guess I carry the same burden of worry about my sister.*

Alagur glances discreetly at the woman. He could grow to like her, and more importantly, she is the woman he's dreamt about. Now he's met her, he finds her even more intriguing than he ever imagined.

Alagur directs the remainder of the conversation about the wolf towards the youngest one in the room, who gapes in awe at the abilities which Wolf Riders – especially Wolf Masters, such as Alagur – have with wolves. He sees the rare bond that's growing between Yalla and the girl. Usually, when a bond forms between man and wolf, the wolf is loyal only to his or her master. And the girl is not scared of the wolf. This too is rarity. Alagur has never seen someone take to a wolf as quickly as she has. He has never seen such bravery among the newly arrived boys – or the snatched boys, as he now grudgingly admits they are – when they've been confronted by the huge figure of Yalla.

When the subject of Samur comes up, Alagur feels a pain go through his very being. A man he called 'friend' was, in fact, his abductor. And the confirmation that he was abducted by Samur hasn't come from him, but from the woman.

Marrida questions him further about Samur, and Alagur's tired but still keen perception notices from her body language that she's holding something back. Perhaps it is something she is reluctant to say in the presence of the young girl. He sees her struggle with indecision, but a brief shake of her head confirms that this isn't the right moment to talk.

Alagur glances towards the boy and sees that he has an expression on his face that matches Marrida's.

They need to learn to trust me first, and I need to know I can trust them.

Alagur leans back in his chair and feels tired. The hardness of the chair makes his joints ache. He thinks about Bergas and hopes fervently that the boy will reach his home safely.

Gradually, as Alagur thinks about what he can do next, or whether there's a way to fix all the horror and turmoil that Sey'qar and Yozan started, he feels himself nodding off into a deep sleep.

The trio gets up and leaves. Only the wolf decides to remain with her master. She glances for a few minutes at the doorway through which the intriguing young girl left, then lies down and sleeps, yipping occasionally as she dreams the dreams only a wolf can.

CHAPTER TWELVE

Tʜᴇ ʟᴀsᴛ sʜᴀFᴛ oF ᴀ FᴀᴅɪɴG sᴜɴ is shining through the window of Esbara's small room when Marrida awakes. One of his bed sheets is covering her, and for several moments, she wonders why she is in her brother's room. She glances around, but she's alone.

She recalls a long night of discussions with her brother and sister about Alagur; discussions that have become commonplace since the Wolf Riders' attack.

How many weeks have we been talking about him now?

The routine of going to the Temple and trying to pretend everything is normal has taken its toll on Marrida. She has been discovering more about the Wolf Riders' background by doing illicit visions with the Stone of Truth every day before eating her morning meal. After the meal, she's been going to the Temple and doing all that's expected of her, then in the evening, she's done more visions until the moon has reached its highest point in the sky. These visions have often been followed by endless hours of discussions with her siblings. Her brother has been urging her to sleep more, but until now, Marrida has refused to comply.

Each day, as Marrida has attended the Temple, Elder Sharriba will have noticed a difference in her. She knows her concentration has been lacking and has no doubt that worry has often been etched on her face, so she can only hope that Elder Sharriba has put both of these things down to Marrida's concern about her family. In the first days after the attack, when many Wolf Riders still lingered in the distant fields on the north side of the neighbouring lake, there was a lot of worry in Ruh'nar about repeat attacks. This is the reason Marrida would give for her uncharacteristic behaviour if Elder Sharriba were to question her.

Marrida hears the voices of her two siblings chatting and laughing downstairs, occasionally mingling with the booming laughter of a man.

What man?

For a moment, Marrida is disorientated, wondering who they're talking to. Then all the events of the previous day come flooding back – Alagur is conscious. His laughter wakes Marrida from her confusion, and as the evening sun fades completely, she stares at the window in surprise.

"It's evening!" Marrida shrieks. "The Temple! I've been missing from the Temple for two days."

Marrida hears three pairs of footsteps rushing up the stairs, and a moment later, a concerned Esbara stands in the doorway, looking at her quizzically and panting loudly.

"I heard you scream."

Before Esbara can say any more, he's joined by Kalisa, followed by Alagur who is struggling to stay upright after climbing the stairs so quickly. He isn't totally healed yet, and the effort has sapped a lot of his energy reserves.

Even he has come to see what is going on.

"I had a dream," Marrida says, reluctance evident in her voice, "about the Temple."

Esbara and Alagur look at one another. Esbara has spoken to Alagur, and the man now understands what Marrida's absence from the Temple will mean. It may cause people to come looking for her at home.

They will find me here, and then what?

"You fell asleep while we were talking yesterday, so we went downstairs to leave you to rest," Esbara explains.

Marrida leans back. She knows she has been pushing herself to her limits, and weeks of worry and little sleep have finally caught up with her. She has felt her heart skip a beat each time she's looked up and seen Elder Sharriba's gaze fixed on her in an 'I know what you're up to' way.

It's like what we tell boys who are snatched, Alagur thinks. These Keepers must be wary of others knowing what goes on inside the Temple. If one of them is missing, it can only cause problems for them. Perhaps the females at the Temple are forbidden to leave.

Alagur shudders at the thought of the massive Temple, which looked so imposing from the Wolf Riders' vantage point across the lake before the attack.

"I needed this sleep," Marrida says quietly after a few minutes of thinking and looking at her lap. Both Esbara and Alagur notice panic etched on her face. They discreetly glance at one another, confirming that they are thinking the same thing. However, neither knows about the last time Marrida went missing from the Temple. Although the Elder was calm and dismissive about it in front of the other Acolytes, when she was back in her private quarters, she gave Marrida a good scolding about her behaviour. Sharriba warned her in no uncertain terms never to be missing from the Temple again without good reason.

Marrida tries to calm herself, breathing deeply and slowly. Considering the Wolf Riders' attack was under two months ago, she may be able to explain her unexpected absence by saying she needed to help her uncle.

But what if the Elder has been to see him and asked where I am?

Marrida gets up and looks at the three faces watching her from the doorway. And she decides on a course of action which will for ever alter her life, and the lives of those around her.

"First, I'm going to see Uncle Joharan," she says. "After that, I'm going to the Temple to read some books. Specifically, I'm going to find out more about your city."

She points a slender finger at Alagur. Esbara and Kalisa both look up at the man beside them.

"It isn't exactly my city--" he protests, but Marrida stops him in his tracks by raising her hand and nodding. She has seen enough in her visions to understand the man's dreams, but her visions have only given her a few of the many clues she needs to decipher the origins of both the city he's from and the city he now lives in. Her uncle has told her some information about the latter city – which Alagur calls City of Wolves – and that their family had ties to it, but he has always been vague. Now that she's considered an adult, even if it's just a young adult, she can demand to know more.

She doesn't yet know how she's going to convince her uncle to reveal more than he has told her up to now, but somehow, she's going to do it.

Alagur and the youngsters step aside as Marrida approaches the doorway to Esbara's sleeping room. She quickly walks into her own room and grabs a warm cloak made from the wool of mountain sheep. As she runs her hand over the cloak, she recalls a retelling her uncle often told when they travelled in the region from which the mountain sheep come from.

"In The Old Days, this distance was travelled on the back of a Sabeyan mountain horse. They have become rare in recent decades, but some people in Ruh'nar still measure their travelling time by these horses' speed rather than the speed of the Wolf Riders' wolves. Marrida, the painting in your front room was created by someone who saw two men riding those rare horses."

Her uncle's retelling about the history of the majestic horses was all very interesting, but it never offered her a clue to the origins of her family. Yet, there was something achingly familiar about his words; she just couldn't figure out what it was.

Uncle Joharan's retelling reminds me of the mystery of the deserted cave just south of the city. It's silent and empty, and no bird or animal will enter it. The wind never howls inside it, not even when a storm sweeps through the land--

Marrida ties the bindings of her cloak as she turns to Alagur.
"Alagur, can you look after them while I'm gone?" she asks. "It isn't often I go out in the evening."
He nods. "How long will you be gone?" he asks, frowning.
"I should be back in maybe two, or at most three hours."
Marrida sincerely hopes her tasks are only going to take that amount of time. She expects some sort of protest, especially from Esbara, and is surprised when none comes.

The trio in the doorway follows her down the stairs, Alagur bringing up the rear of the group as his injuries slow him down. Marrida hugs Kalisa and Esbara, then looks long at Alagur. With a resolute nod, she turns and opens the front door. Stepping into the silent street, she looks to her left, and her gaze pauses for a moment on the place where the man behind her lay injured seven weeks ago. She glances up towards the roofs and frowns as the suspicion that Samur was somehow involved in the attack against Alagur worms its way into her head.

Seeing no one, not even any soldiers, she pulls the hood of her cloak over her head. After a few moments, Marrida turns right sharply and goes towards the square.

* * *

ESBARA LOOKS DOWN THE STREET UNTIL MARRIDA TURNS RIGHT once more and is gone. Then the boy steps back and shuts the door, latching two bolts in place to lock it from the inside, and looks at Alagur. Now he's alone with the man, he feels unsure of how to act. Up to now, he has acted with bravado, pretending to be adult enough to have a conversation with Alagur, but with Marrida gone, he doesn't know what to do.

Equally, Alagur doesn't know what to say to the boy. He has been left in charge of two youngsters he barely knows. For all he knows, the boy in front of him may be about to go and fetch the city soldiers, and he could end up in jail.

Unexpectedly, the man and boy are snapped out of their moods by the small hands of Kalisa dragging them into the cooking room. She sits Alagur down on the bench at the table and — rather forcefully, Alagur notes, which shows her strength — pushes Esbara onto the bench opposite him. Next, she runs to the cupboard at the back of the cooking room, grabs two large fruit loaves from the shelf and drops them on the table between her brother and Alagur. Gingerly carrying over the bread knife, she places it in between the two loaves. She climbs onto the chair that is ordinarily Marrida's seat at the table and, folding her arms sternly, looks first at Esbara and then at Alagur.

"Either you two behave, or neither of you shall eat," she states with a mischievous smirk, adding with a chuckle, "Tonight, I'm in charge."

Esbara gasps at his younger sister. Never in a million years did he expect to be spoken to in this way by her. He looks over at Alagur, who is clearly amused by the situation, and the two of them start to laugh at the same time.

"Right then," Alagur says, still laughing, "you heard the boss. We *need* to behave."

The bad feelings that Kalisa saw arising as soon as her sister left the house are dissipating. As young as she is, she has a hidden talent: the uncanny ability to sense the moods of those around her. She's the peacekeeper in the house she shares with her sister and brother. And now she's determined to stop the man, whose wolf she's grown very fond of, and the brother she adores from tearing each other's hair out.

After their laughter subsides, the man and boy eat the food that Kalisa has brought to the table. Continuing to assert her authority, she periodically looks sternly at them both. Neither of them protests any further, and to make sure they don't get a chance to argue, the girl talks about everything that comes to her mind.

"Kalisa," Alagur says with his mouth full of the moist fruit loaf, "you do realise you can be extremely bossy when you want to."

Kalisa cups her face in her palms and looks at him in the intent way typical of a youngster looking at someone older.

"I'm not being bossy," she says in mock sincerity, "but if you two are planning to be annoying, I'll make sure you're told off by Marrida when she gets home."

A second wave of booming laughter from both Alagur and Esbara gets the young girl giggling until she's holding her belly and tears are streaming down her face. Each time the three of them look at one another, they find themselves helpless with laughter again, and it takes maybe thirty minutes before they can stop. By then, none of them can remember what was so funny in the first place.

* * *

AFTER EATING THE UNUSUAL DINNER, Esbara sends a protesting Kalisa to bed.

"It's late and you need your sleep."

After Esbara has spent ten minutes talking to her about inconsequential things, Kalisa finally pulls the covers over herself and settles in her bed. Esbara dims two of the embers lighting up her room, leaving the third on for comfort, then descends the stairway and walks to the back of the house where the cooking room is located. He bends over as he passes Yalla and gives her a scratch behind one of her ears, which results in her tail thumping the floor several times.

When he enters the cooking room, he sees that Alagur has cleared the table, placed all the crockery next to the washing basin at the back and started to scrub some of the pots clean. As wounded as the man still is, he is playing his part in the duty of caring for the house as if he has lived there all his life. But at the same time, Esbara knows it's the only way

Alagur can repay the unexpected hospitality he has received from its residents. The boy wonders whether he would have been so hospitable towards Alagur if he, and not Marrida, had been the one in charge of the household.

"What do you think Marrida is going to ask Joharan?"

The question startles Esbara out of his pondering.

"I don't know," he replies after some thought. "She has told me several times that Uncle Joharan and she were close when she was very young. I think the rift between them has something to do with her work at the Temple--"

Esbara stops in the middle of his sentence, realising that until recently, he didn't know what Marrida did at the Temple either. He now wonders how much Uncle Joharan knows, if anything at all. The revelation that she's a Keeper of Truth has put Esbara's own choice of career into perspective, and she admitted to him quietly that she would never disagree with his choice again. She called it the act of an adult worthy of his First Rites to make a conscious decision about his future.

Alagur notices the distraction on the boy's face and wonders what is going through his mind. He observes Esbara for a few moments unobtrusively. When it becomes obvious to him that the boy is completely wrapped up in his own thoughts and worries, he silently and speedily finishes the process of cleaning the crockery, pans, serving bowls, eating utensils, and then the table. Esbara dries and stacks everything away almost mechanically.

Once the task is complete, Alagur walks off and lies on the bed in the small room adjoining the cooking room, listening for Esbara's footsteps to fade away upstairs. Moments later, he hears a door slam, and then the house is still. The wet nose of Yalla nuzzles him, and minutes later, he too drifts off to sleep, rubbing the familiar rough fur of the wolf.

* * *

JUST OVER AN HOUR LATER, ALAGUR WAKES UP and goes back to the cooking room. There he sits quietly, wondering what Marrida is talking about with her uncle and what she may find at the Temple. Less than half an hour later, he's joined by Esbara and a sleepy-looking Kalisa.
"She woke up thirsty. I thought I'd come down with her."

"I woke up not so long ago, too."

"She's not back yet?"

"Not yet. I guess it's taking longer than she expected. It could be for any number of reasons."

"I guess we can stay awake until she's back."

The youngsters sit down opposite Alagur. Looking at one another seriously for a moment or two, they then fall about with uncontrollable laughter.

CHAPTER THIRTEEN

Marrida stands in front of the closed door of her uncle's workshop, listening to his booming voice talking to his apprentices. For several minutes she is hesitant, wondering whether or not to go into the house. She flinches when she hears the distant echo of people shouting in another part of the city. Marrida frowns, wondering for a moment what the shouting is about, but it's too far away for her to ascertain its origin or purpose. Her best action, for now, will be to get off the street.

If only I could hear what they are shouting about. I hope it's not another attack. I wonder if the man called Samur will come back again.

Marrida organises all the information she's learnt in her mind using the skills Keepers employ to remember visions. She recalls some of the words of The Truth spoken by Alagur.

"And the city was lost to time and kin."

Marrida knows from conversations with both her uncle and Elder Sharriba that it is likely her mother and grandmother were also Keepers. And so was her uncle's grandmother. From the same lessons with Sharriba, Marrida has learnt that the tradition of becoming a Keeper of Truth is always passed to the eldest daughter, and occasionally to younger daughters too. But Marrida has started noticing inconsistencies in this retelling, which have led to her using her gem illicitly. The biggest inconsistency from her family's point of view is the lack of earlier generations with the Keeper skill. The family history stops abruptly with either her great-grandmother or her great-great-grandmother.

Is the rest of the lineage lost in the city Alagur calls City of Wolves?

After a few deep breaths, Marrida organises the precise questions she needs to ask in her mind. She knows what she needs to say to her uncle to ensure he tells her the information she's after. After that, she'll go to the Temple to seek even more information, although it's unusual for Acolytes to visit this late. She looks up at the moon to determine the time and hopes her visit to her uncle's workshop will be short.

After looking around one more time to see if anyone else is out in the streets this late, she realises she's alone. It's been two years since her last visit to her uncle, and the reason it's been so long is the very reason she's here today. Marrida is worried about Joharan's reaction to her questions, but after a final moment of hesitation, she grabs the door handle and opens the door.

The room beyond falls silent as six pairs of eyes stare at the visitor with curiosity. Joharan's eyebrows knot together when his keen eyes notice the worry etched on his niece's face. He knows Marrida well enough to recognise when something is bothering her. With a quick gesture and a sideways nod, he motions to his apprentices to leave the room.

Marrida shuffles forward almost shyly, and a moment later lowers herself onto the bench opposite her uncle. Rather than casting her gaze down, she looks at him as directly as she dares. But she hesitates before speaking, and Joharan's curiosity and concern are piqued by the conflict of emotions playing over Marrida's face. He wonders what her reason is for this unexpected visit, especially so late in the evening when the danger of further Wolf Rider attacks is still very real.

"Are Esbara and Kalisa alright?"

Marrida jumps. She didn't expect her uncle's voice to sound so gentle. It makes her even more reluctant to speak up.

"Yes, they are."

Marrida looks down and Joharan uses the opportunity to reach across the table for two wooden mugs, pouring some of the steaming rose-flower tea into them from the jug which has been abandoned by one of the boys. Joharan takes a long gulp from his mug while pushing the second one towards Marrida. Topping up his mug, he watches Marrida timidly grab hers to sip from it. It seems to settle her nerves.

Marrida drinks all the tea before she speaks. She knows that her uncle has withheld much information about the family from her; her illicit visions have started to fill the gaps in the knowledge. Now she is struggling with the fact that she too has been keeping secrets: secrets from her uncle about what is going on at the Temple; secrets from those at the Temple about what she has been doing with her gem at home; secrets about a Wolf Rider being in her house. Her uncle, because of his high standing in the city, would consider Alagur and his wolf to be enemies of Ruh'nar, and Marrida realises she may alienate everyone if she says the wrong words.

After a long, awkward silence, Marrida finally plucks up the courage to look at her uncle once more. As she does so, tears start streaming down her face. Joharan is taken aback, and he leans back in his chair for a moment, observing Marrida closely.

Something is different about her. Was the attack more traumatic for her than I realised?

The contrast between the man and the woman opposite him is great. She's young and of slender build. Joharan is a broad-shouldered man in his mid-sixties, still well-muscled because of his daily pottery crafting. His hair is silver-grey and bound with a leather thong at the nape of his neck. Contrasting with Marrida's tear-streaked heart-shaped face, he has a square clean-shaven face with deep, dark eyes — eyes which are piercing straight through Marrida at this moment.

Joharan's voice can sometimes bellow out in the heat of anger, but at other times, he whispers with gentle tenderness. The hand now reaching out to Marrida is strong, capable of manipulating raw marsh clay, and capable of soothing a sad woman whose tears are flowing freely.

With a single finger, Joharan wipes away the tears from Marrida's cheeks. He gets a weak smile as a reward.

"Uncle." Joharan raises an eyebrow when he hears the unusually fearful tremble in Marrida's voice. "Uncle, I'm here to ask something. I need to know about our family's history."

Joharan gives a short nod before replying with his own question. "What do you want to know?"

Marrida, who'd looked down expecting Joharan to tell her once again that he's told her all she needs to know, raises her head and sees a face full of concern and love. Even Joharan's usual ever so slightly patronising frown is gone. For a moment, Marrida wonders if her uncle already knows what she wants to ask.

"I need to know about our family, uncle, and I have things to tell you."

Though the words are spoken without any hesitation, Marrida gazes down again, and under the table, she is clasping and unclasping her hands. Joharan's skill of reading body language tells him immediately that a lot more is going on in her head than she has stated. He lifts her face with a gentle finger, and for several moments, they just stare at one another.

Joharan removes his hand from Marrida's chin, gets up, and listens for movement or sounds coming from the apprentices' sleeping room. After a resolute nod, he closes the door.

This discussion is only for our ears.

Joharan sits back down opposite Marrida. Before speaking, he replenishes his cup with fresh tea.

What can I tell her?

"As you know, your father was much younger than I am," he begins. "The reason I've never told you much before is that he and I don't share the same mother."

Marrida nods. She knows this from Elder Sharriba.

"I presume I don't need to repeat how your parents met," Joharan says. Marrida nods once more.

"What you may not know is that your mother was also part of the Temple of Ruh'nar when she met your father. She was--" Joharan hesitates, thinking for a few minutes before adding, "She was a Keeper."

Marrida's mouth opens in surprise. She attempts to speak, but no sound comes out. She didn't know her uncle knew anything about the Temple and the Keepers, let alone that her mother was associated with them.

"But how?" she blurts out loudly in a voice filled with shock. She turns as white as moss ash and looks at her uncle with wide-open, scared eyes.

Why would she be scared about this knowledge?

"Because, my dear Marrida--" he begins, but pauses to consider the precise words to use. "Once upon a time, your father and I had a grandmother who swore us both to secrecy when she told us--"

Joharan takes a sip from his cup of now lukewarm tea to calm his own rising nervousness. "I knew who came to the workshop that day five years ago. And why," Joharan continues. "I knew what she was doing, even if she tried to make it all into something mysterious."

Marrida gapes at her uncle. "So…so, you know about me too?" she asks.

Joharan nods a slow and deliberate yes.

"So, your grandmother was--"

Marrida stops speaking and swallows hard, taking a quick sip from her own tea.

"My grandmother was a Keeper of Truth." Joharan acknowledges her unspoken question, and Marrida notes the hint of pride and defiance with which the words are spoken. "Your father knew your mother was a Keeper. It's one reason why he asked for her to be his life partner. The other reason comes from the vision our grandmother showed us before she died."

Marrida's interest is piqued. This is a part of her family's history Joharan has never revealed to her before.

"What were you shown?"

"She showed us a vision of a young woman sitting on a wolf. In the same vision, a man with dark brown hair stood beside her. He was using that--" Joharan points at the bulge under Marrida's tunic. "My grandmother hid part of her talent well. She could see the past as Keepers can, but she could also see future events. She told your father and me never to speak of what she showed us. That is, until the time came to tell the woman in that vision."

Joharan looks down with a pensive expression on his face. He puts his cup down and crosses his arms over his chest, looking sternly up at Marrida. But at the same time, he manages to show his love for her. This is the secret that caused the chasm to come between them for so many years.

He watches for her reaction to his revelation. *The girl has become a woman and I didn't even notice it. How long is it since the passing of both her parents? Some eleven years now.*

Joharan studies Marrida even more closely. Many emotions are passing across her face: shock; disbelief; a few flashes of anger. Joharan notices how many features she shares with her late mother and a sigh of regret escapes his mouth. He's never had a life partner or children, and he knows why. To compensate, he's recruited boys to become his apprentices — surrogate sons, if you will — and over time, his two nieces and nephew have also become like his own children.

When Elder Sharriba told him that he could never ask why Marrida was chosen by her, or ask what she did at the Temple, he complied, despite knowing the truth deep down. And Sharriba knew it was so. But she gave him her orders anyway to make it appear that he was being put in his place by the most powerful person in the entire city. This warning was another reason why the loving relationship between Marrida and him has soured over the years. He simply hasn't been able to tell her anything of importance. His promise to his grandmother stopped him from telling one side of the truth, and the warning from the Elder stopped him from telling the other side of it.

He remembers the last words his grandmother spoke. *"A tainted truth isn't truth at all. Better to tell the truth than to tell part of it and forever cause her harm."*

As the years have passed, he has developed a habit of brushing off Marrida's attempts to learn the truth with harsh remarks and retellings that explain nothing. He pushed her away until one day the familiar knock no longer sounded at his door and he knew he'd lost her.

After a few minutes pondering the consequences of what he's telling Marrida, Joharan is struck by a new thought.

Something about the last Wolf Riders' attack was different. That is why Marrida has come to see me today.

He decides to wait for Marrida to volunteer the information herself.

"Can I see the gem?" Joharan nods towards Marrida when she raises her face and stares at him with a 'how dare you to ask that?' expression on her face.

Seems she's already been conditioned, just as Grandmother warned would happen--

"Do you have your mother's gem hanging around your neck?" he asks with more urgency. Marrida jumps. She hesitates, then nods ever so slightly.

"Can I see it?"

Marrida starts reaching up, then stops and stares ahead as if she's trying to remember something. Joharan sees her shrug a moment later like the memory doesn't matter.

Marrida removes the golden chain from around her neck and dangles the gem over the table. When Joharan reaches out, Marrida jerks her hand back and clasps her other hand around the gem so tightly that her knuckles go white.

"The gem belonged to my grandmother," Joharan says softly. "She gave it to your mother before she passed away, as she only had a son and two grandsons. She told your mother to give it to you later, though she never told your mother what she told us--"

Marrida lowers her hand and slowly opens it, staring at the gem lying in the middle of her palm. She never realised that the gem came from her father's family. Until now, she has assumed it came from her mother, and her grandmother before that.

"Did my mother's mother know about this?"
"I don't know. Your mother said her mother lived in the Marridina province, but I don't know if she ever knew of your mother's calling."

Marrida looks up in surprise. She's always assumed that a daughter became a Keeper because her mother was one too. Now she has discovered a truth – her mother was probably the first one with the calling on that side of the family.

So why did Mam ask for me to become a Keeper?

The more she discovers of this hidden past, the more mysteries it throws up and the fewer things make sense.

"The vision your grandmother showed you," Marrida says hesitantly, "did she tell you what it meant?"

Joharan sips from his now cold tea before he answers. His grandmother, Lya, stated that a day would come when he'd be a surrogate parent to a woman who had lost both her parents. And that she would come to him seeking answers.

But how much can I tell her?

"As I explained, her vision was about a girl sitting atop a massive brownish grey wolf. Beside her stood a tall man with dark brown hair. He was using *that* gem." After a moment, he adds, "I was there when she did the vision."

Marrida stares wide-eyed and open-mouthed at her uncle.

Was this the secret he could never tell me? And he said, "Did the vision" not "Had the vision", the correct term. Only someone who knows about the skill would know this term.

"The girl in the vision looked a lot like *you*."

Marrida looks at her gem again, remembering what her uncle said only moments ago.

My great-grandmother could see both post and future, just like Elder Sharriba said the First Elder could. Why did Sharriba tell me this? It's knowledge Acolytes only learn in their seventh year of training. Does she know more about my family than she's letting on?

And this gem belonged to Uncle Joharan's grandmother — my great-grandmother. That makes my family history date back over a century — or longer.

Or longer?

CHAPTER FOURTEEN

As THE CONVERSATION PROGRESSES, Joharan mentions Masharea. It's a name he has never spoken in front of his niece before, but Marrida knows its significance from her Ancient Histories lessons.

Did our family come from there? Were my ancestors driven from the city when the Wolf Riders took over?

Joharan stays silent, waiting for Marrida to digest each revelation before he moves on to the next. He weighs up each word with care, remembering his grandmother's warning that Marrida would need to know all aspects of the truth.

"The best way I can describe it is that a tainted truth replaced the true measure of 'truth' as I always taught you."

A frown appears on Marrida's face. Joharan gets up quietly to fetch a jug of cold milk for a refreshing drink for them both. He then leans back and waits for the next question, the whole conversation starting to feel like a game.

He doesn't need to wait long.

"Is Masharea where our family came from?"

Joharan gives a short nod.

"But how?"

Joharan raises an eyebrow and realises Marrida is starting to come to her own conclusions. This question is more complex than two simple words can convey. He only knows what was shown to him by his grandmother. Beyond that, most of it is a mystery, except--

Hmm, maybe Sharriba's been telling Marrida things too.

"I know the family was definitely living in Masharea some eight or nine hundred years ago, though I could be wrong about the timeline. I'm an old man. However, my grandmother told me many times that the bloodline stretches as far back as three thousand years in that area, and she claimed it could be even older."

Marrida listens in fascination.

"She told me that long before the Wolf Riders rose, Masharea was a wealthy place. Our family arrived hundreds of years earlier. It's been suggested to me that before, they lived in the east."

"The east?" Marrida asks, confused.

"It doesn't matter about that part. I'm not even sure if I'm right." Joharan takes another sip of milk. "My grandmother saw a land in the east in her visions. Do you know about Mycanthia?"

Marrida shakes her head.

"She only saw glimpses but was absolutely certain that the family came from there. She didn't live to explain any of those visions, but she did explain some of what happened to Masharea. She told me that it was the Wolf Riders who caused the family to leave. It was either leave or be killed--"

Joharan stops speaking when he sees Marrida go as white as moss ash.

"What is wrong?" But as he asks, he realises a possible reason for her visit.

Might she be doing visions? he wonders. Again, he studies his niece carefully, leaning forward and looking directly into her worried eyes.

Marrida's mind is racing about the 'legend' that Alagur relayed to her.

TEN THOUSAND RIDERS ROSE TO THE CALL
BESET ON TO THE CITY OF OLD, AND
FALL BEFORE THEM IT WOULD

THEY WHO RESISTED WOULD FALL, AND
AND YOUNG ONES WERE TAKEN BY FORCE
AND A CITY WAS LOST TO TIME AND KIN

Every time he recites that verse of The Truth, Alagur says 'and' twice. Why is that? Are there some words missing?

Perhaps, it isn't actually a legend at all; perhaps instead it has a literal meaning. The answer as to why her family fled the ancient city is right there. *But why is it incomplete?*

"It was either leave or be killed." Her uncle's words echo through Marrida's mind. She now knows the truth.

Joharan has the intelligence to read people's emotions from their facial expressions, a skill that helps him to stay influential in the city. From Marrida's blanching, he guesses there's more going on here than a simple conversation about their family's history. He will let her reveal her thoughts in her own time and in her own way. In the meantime, Joharan decides to tell her as much as he knows. He has two promises to keep in that respect.

"I warn you now, if anyone ever discovers the truth about our family name, the consequences for you and everyone we both hold dear will be grim, understood?"

Marrida nods, feelings worry growing deep in her mind as she stares at her uncle. One other has used similar words of warning when conveying forbidden knowledge to Marrida. And as young as she is, even naive at times, Marrida realises there is something huge at play in the world around her. The recent attack by the Wolf Riders and Alagur's retellings have proved that. But so did the cursing of the black-haired man--

"The family originates from Mycanthia, but if you believe my grandmother Lya's words, even further back they may come from a more dangerous place. She always thought that the family fled from a great danger but could never reach far back enough to see for sure. She claimed only the First Elder could do that."

He knows about the First Elder?

Marrida decides not to ask about this. Her uncle has already said he doesn't know much.

"The family lived in Masharea?" Marrida asks again.

Joharan nods.

"The First Elder too?"

Joharan wonders for a moment why she has asked this, but decides to let Marrida keep the reason private – for now. He nods once more.

Marrida pauses to think how to ask her next question without revealing the presence of the secret guests in her dwelling. She doesn't want Joharan to know she's harbouring a Wolf Rider.

"There's a legend I've been told about--" she begins, then hesitates. Joharan nods again, but in her pensive mood, Marrida doesn't notice his guarded stare and the slow lowering of his half-raised cup. "It tells about Masharea…I think. In the legend, it says the city was lost to time and kin."

Joharan frowns. *Where have I heard those words before?*

Joharan and Marrida's father, Markalo, were close despite their sizable age difference. After Joharan's mother had died, his father chose another as a life partner. When Markalo grew up, it soon became apparent the younger of the two brothers had a skill as a merchant, whereas Joharan was a skilled artisan. Whenever Markalo returned to Ruh'nar, he'd visit his older brother and they'd spend long nights drinking tea while Markalo told stories of all he'd seen and heard on his journeys. It was on one such night that Markalo told his brother about the legend the Wolf Riders told one another.

How does Marrida know about the Wolf Riders' legend? Did she learn about it at the Temple?

"Where did you hear those words?"

Marrida stares at Joharan, her bright red face betraying the shame of being caught telling a lie. It also betrays the fact that she is holding secrets back from her uncle, and Joharan notices this instantly.

"I…heard them…somewhere," Marrida stammers.
"There's only one person I've ever heard say those words before you, and that was your father over a year before your birthing, so do tell me what's going on, Marrida Kayrsan?"

The gentleness has disappeared from Joharan's voice. Marrida shakes. She has never seen her uncle this angry.

"I was told about the legend by someone--"
"Who is that someone?" A moment later, Joharan's demeanour changes. Everything is suddenly clear to him. Before Marrida can respond, he murmurs, "She'll be riding atop a wolf, and the man beside

her will be using the gem."

Joharan stares at Marrida, who's too dumbfounded to say anything, and her face tells him everything he needs to know.

"We're going to your house, now," Joharan says calmly, getting up and putting on his overcoat.

"To my house?" Marrida echoes in a whisper. Joharan nods and walks resolutely to the front door where he waits for Marrida to get ready too. She fumbles with the bindings of her cloak, almost overcome by nervousness.

If the vision his grandmother did is correct in its entirety, Joharan already knows what awaits him at Marrida's house. His actions then must be to help his niece and her visitor to exit the city safely. She will have to travel east to fulfil her destiny.

Joharan closes the front door behind them after Marrida has exited the house, somewhat hesitantly. In a subdued manner, the two follow the route which Marrida took a few hours earlier in reverse, and sooner than Marrida would have liked, they arrive at her house.

Marrida enters first, feeling terrified. She has no time to warn anyone inside. Expecting them to be asleep, she is surprised to hear laughter and talking coming from the cooking room. Marrida cringes when the front door slams shut behind her, her heart skipping a beat or two as the voices in the cooking room go silent. She hears three pairs of footsteps approach the door, one pair slower than the others.

Esbara appears first, and he goes as white as moss ash when he sees Joharan standing behind his sister. A moment later, Kalisa is standing beside him, and after what feels like a lifetime, Alagur and the wolf arrive in the doorway. Marrida sees genuine fear in Alagur's eyes when he realises she is not alone. For a moment, she can read the question in his face.

Have you brought a guardsman to take me to the city's prison?

"This is Uncle Joharan," Marrida says in a flat voice. "I thought you'd all be in bed by now."
"We couldn't sleep," replies Esbara in a similar monotone. "We were concerned about you being gone so long. This is Alagur--"

Marrida and Alagur stare at one another, each trying to draw some courage. Marrida shakes her head ever so slightly to reassure Alagur. Esbara watches Alagur and Marrida in turn, seeing an emotion pass between them.

The emotion on Alagur's face looks almost like love, not lust as Esbara had believed.

Alagur is worried. He's wondering if she's betrayed his trust.

"This is Alagur," Esbara says again, firmly this time. "A friend – a Wolf Rider we're keeping safe."

When Esbara states the man's name and what he is, Joharan looks closely at Alagur. A man ravaged by the weakness of injury, he is leaning against the doorway, panic in his eyes. Joharan then notices Alagur is flanked by a massive silver-grey-and-white wolf. The wolf doesn't growl, as one might expect her to do when encountering a stranger.

Joharan looks back at the man's face. It's covered with stubble, and his unkempt dark-brown hair shows he has recently been sleeping.

A conversation with his grandmother floods into Joharan's mind.

"You'll meet him, and you must treat him with the respect he deserves. He's a lost one, he is. He was once with a family like you are now. He'll be the key to helping the daughter who isn't yours on her task."

Joharan glances at Marrida, then at Esbara and Kalisa. *They're all my children, just as Lya said.* And now, here stands the man from Lya's vision. Is he a lost one? Joharan is sure, now more than ever before, that 'lost ones' was how Lya referred to the boys abducted by the Wolf Riders to refill their ranks with young blood.

Alagur stares back at the old man before him, both in defiance and an unspoken plea for clemency.

Is he here as a friend or foe?

Joharan walks forward, slowly so as not to startle the stranger. On reaching him, the older man holds out a hand in an act of friendship. After some hesitation, Alagur accepts the handshake and looks into a pair of eyes filled with curiosity and concern.

"I see my niece is a good host," Joharan says with a hint of a chuckle in his voice. The other man's shoulders slump as the tension leaves him. "And who is this magnificent beast?"

The reply comes full of pride. "This is Yalla."

"Marrida, where can we sit down? In the front room?" Joharan asks. As his niece stares at him in shock, he adds, "Alagur looks like he's about to collapse."

This isn't the response Marrida expected. Does her uncle's acceptance of their unusual house guests relate to his grandmother's vision? She looks at Esbara and sees amazement on his face too.

"What's going on?" he mouths at her, but she raises a hand. Esbara has seen this gesture enough times in his life to understand its meaning: they will talk about it all later.

* * *

Alagur, supported by Joharan, enters the front room. They're followed by Marrida and Esbara, but Kalisa has decided she's tired enough to go back to her bed of her own accord. She hugs the wolf before rushing up the stairs, although she stops at the top, staring back to the ground floor for a full minute, a pang of worry passing through her mind about what Alagur and Yalla's fate may be by the time her uncle has finished speaking to the man. She then runs into her sleeping room when she hears Alagur groan in the front room.

Joharan sits Alagur on the large sofa in the corner, and Esbara sits at the other end of the same sofa. Both Alagur and Esbara smile at one another weakly as Marrida sits down in her familiar chair next to the fireplace. Joharan takes the chair Alagur found so uncomfortable the previous night.

All four are silent for a time. Joharan, who ordinarily doesn't have problems talking to strangers, is tongue-tied. There are conflicting thoughts racing through his mind about the situation. He glances at the other people in the room in turn, finally settling his gaze on the man in the corner who seems to be trying to shrink into the shadows.

Alagur's self-assured confidence has abandoned him this evening. He has mixed feelings too, and most of them involve the old man who seems to be trying to stare him down. He feels like he wants to be anywhere but here. Why has the old man not called the guardsmen to arrest him? Both Esbara and Marrida are fidgeting and looking at each other, obviously not knowing what to do about the situation. Marrida is so pale it looks like she's ill with ice burn, a condition caused by being exposed to the cold for an extensive amount of time.

Joharan is the first to recover from the awkwardness of the situation. His training has taught him to gather his thoughts quickly, and he re-evaluates the long-buried conversation he had with his grandmother when he was young.

I wonder what Sharriba will make of all this when she hears about it…but I'm certain she already knows.

CHAPTER FIFTEEN

As he compares the features of the man in front of him with his grandmother's description, Joharan realises with a jolt that he's the only link between the hidden past and the events that she warned him about. He doesn't want to think about the future, so he turns his attention to Alagur.

"Marrida tells me that you came here in rather unexpected circumstances."

Alagur nods hesitantly in response, and with an almost imperceptible gesture, gets Yalla to lie down at his feet.

"How old are you?"

"I think I'm about twenty-five if the--" Alagur stops speaking, remembering what Marrida said about her skill. Can he tell her uncle how he knows that information?

"If what?" Joharan persists.

"He knows about the gem," Marrida whispers. "Our great-grandmother was a Keeper too."

Alagur and Esbara both stare at Marrida in disbelief. This isn't news either of them expected.

"Yes, my grandmother was a Keeper." Joharan picks up the conversation. "And *that* gem was hers."

This prompts Marrida to remove the gem from around her neck. She places it on the table in front of her, deciding there's no need to keep it hidden in her own home or around her family and Alagur anymore. She sighs deeply and looks down at her hands which are clasping and unclasping nervously in her lap.

That took a lot of courage, Joharan thinks.

"So, Alagur, what were you going to say?"

"If the vision she did was of my past," Alagur replies, nodding at Marrida, "I would have been a year younger than Kalisa when I was snatched. Samur claims I've been with the Wolf Riders almost fifteen years."

It's out! Alagur has admitted being a Wolf Rider. He tries to make himself as small as he can in the corner of the sofa, expecting the old man to jump up, run out to the street and shout for the guardsmen to come, now. But the man opposite stays sitting in the chair, contemplating the revelation.

Esbara's amazement grows. Is this the same stern uncle he has known all his life? Gone are the overbearing characteristics which make Joharan one of Ruh'nar's most formidable artisans and council members. Instead, a quiet air of resolute determination has come over him as if a heavy burden has been lifted from his shoulders. Esbara wonders what transpired during the conversation between his sister and uncle.

It's obvious she never made it to the Temple. If she had, he wouldn't be here now. Is he here to help, or is he just here to make sure Alagur is brought to justice?

Again, Esbara questions his chosen career. However, he remembers something else which reinforces the choice in his mind.

I overheard that other Wolf Rider, the one Alagur calls Samur, cursing. I wonder if Marrida heard him too. If he's as dangerous as Alagur suggests, he needs to be stopped. I need to stop him.

* * *

THE SLEEP HE HAD EARLIER HAS DONE ALAGUR A LOT OF GOOD. Without tiredness clouding his mind, he can remember a lot more of his life before he joined the Wolf Riders. He talked to Esbara and Kalisa while Marrida was out, telling them that his sister would likely be the same age as Marrida now. A long-buried memory surfaced then, and he told the youngsters that she was destines to become a Caller.

Whatever a Caller may be.

It was the only detail that Alagur could remember clearly, apart from a name that Esbara did recognise – Chiva'na. He was able to tell Alagur that Chiva'na is a city on the western coast, but according to rumours it has not yet been touched by the Wolf Riders. He admitted that Marrida had spoken in the past about the family moving there to be further from the danger of the Wolf Riders, but that the idea was dismissed by their uncle.

"Not much of a refuge if a son was snatched from there."

Alagur's words weigh on Esbara's mind now, which allows his

curiosity to get the better of him. He wants to know more, but he realises the retelling is going to be told at the pace set by his uncle, so he stays quiet.

"What do you call the city where you live?" Joharan questions, leaning forward in the chair and staring at Alagur.

"We call it City of Wolves. We do know its original name is Masharea."

Joharan nods to acknowledge the information. His grandmother told him the name many times, always warning him to guard the information because, as she put it, not many people remembered, and those who did were the Keepers of Truth and the lost sons living inside the city. However, she explained that the Keepers didn't know much about the ancient city since its abandonment to the ravages of the Wolf Riders, nearly a thousand years ago now. She stated that some Keepers chose to let the world forget about it.

"Marrida mentioned a legend that you told her," he continues.

Alagur nods, noting that Joharan doesn't ask to be told the words. Instead, the old man introduces a subject that brings a frown of pain back to Marrida's face. Joharan wants to know about the origin of the wolf, and so Alagur has no choice but to tell the same retelling he told the youngsters the previous day. As Alagur tells it once more, he keeps looking at Marrida, who just tightens her lips, looks down and becomes a few shades paler, but stays calm throughout. Joharan scowls when he hears how his brother died, but he too doesn't show any emotions. Not that Alagur expects any from the older man, who seems so reserved.

He must always hide his thoughts well to keep his position of influence in the city.

That Alagur was the last person to see his brother alive doesn't surprise Joharan. He has already figured out that there must be a reason why the younger man was taken in by his niece to heal, beyond him having been wounded outside her house; his conversations with his grandmother have made him into a man who sees the hand of fate in everything.

Marrida's mother, Eshara, was a Keeper, even if only for a relatively short time. Joharan looks at Esbara, who bears such a close resemblance to his own brother, wondering if the boy knows the origin of his name.

The tradition resulting in a mother naming her son with the male version of her own name is at least a thousand years old. Thanks to the scholarly knowledge of Joharan's closest friend, he knows something of the origins of the tradition, and one possible meaning of the name: something like 'bringer of peace'. He recalls a clue his grandmother gave him which hinted at why Eshara may have decided to name her son in this way.

"Truth and knowledge go hand in hand, Joharan. For this knowledge to be known, she needs to first know the truth about herself."

It's too soon. He cannot yet reveal this clue to the others around him. Instead, Joharan turns his attention back to Alagur when the man mentions someone called Bergas.

"Who is Bergas?"

"Bergas was--or *is*, I hope--a boy who came to City of Wolves a year ago. He and I met when I walked past a group of youths. Bergas was fighting them all off."

Joharan nods. "Where is Bergas now?"

"If things went to plan, he should be almost halfway back to Azaquina."

Joharan recognises the name of the fishing city located in the most northerly region of Keldarra on the shores of Bay of Whispers. His brother, Markalo, brought cutting tools back from Azaquina that Joharan still uses in his workshop.

Another name from the past.

As the night progresses, the retelling of how Alagur ended up with the Wolf Riders becomes more and more clear. One thing Joharan notes immediately is that whenever Alagur mentions Samur, he does so with a hint of disdain in his voice.

He calls Samur a 'friend', yet he obviously dislikes the man.

This doesn't escape Esbara's notice, either. And then there's the reason Alagur gave for coming to Ruh'nar in the first place. Alagur told him he'd be considered too old to be snatched, but what will happen to all the sons of their neighbours if the Wolf Riders are never stopped? This cycle of violence has existed in the world for almost a thousand years now, and the retelling Alagur is relating to Joharan shows why it all started, based on an even older legend from when the world was conquered by warlords from the north.

Esbara shakes his head at the possible consequences. That Alagur went out of his way to save a boy from the same fate as his own has completely changed Esbara's opinion of the man. He now looks at Alagur not with a scowl of hatred, but with a smile of open admiration. He just hopes the boy in the retelling did get home safely without encountering Samur or anyone like him.

Joharan stretches his shoulders. It's very late now, and he feels he has learnt enough about Alagur. He needs sleep, and to determine what he can do to get Alagur out of the city in safety, considering the wolf in those plans. Joharan's grandmother foretold many things before she died, and they're all happening now.

"Those who live in the days when the future comes to visit don't know what they are experiencing until it has happened."

But Callers know.

"I must go home for some rest," Joharan states. "Do you have enough food in the house or should I send Damir over with extra supplies?"

"I shopped for food a few days ago," Esbara answers before his sister can reply.

"Right then, I'll be back tomorrow in the afternoon," Joharan continues. "And I suggest everyone gets some sleep before then."

He points his finger at all three sitting in the room around him in turn. They nod, and then Joharan gets up, followed by Marrida. Both walk into the vestibule adjoining the front room and are greeted there by a sleepy wolf who lifts her head and whacks the floor with her tail.

"When are you planning to visit the Temple next?" Joharan speaks softly to his niece.

"I'll have to go tomorrow. That will be two days I have been missing," Marrida whispers back, bowing her head and feeling a pang of shame.

Joharan lifts Marrida's head with a gently placed forefinger under her chin and investigates the worried eyes of his young niece.

"Tomorrow we'll make plans for your journey with Alagur," he explains quietly. "There's a destiny my grandmother told me about, and it involves you…and *him*."

Marrida nods in understanding, then Joharan turns and opens the front door resolutely. After one long glance over his shoulder at his niece, who seems almost childlike at this moment, Joharan leaves the house. As he walks slowly back towards his own home through streets lit by the full moon and the embers which adorn each dwelling at night, Joharan hears the door of the house he has left being shut quietly, and the distinct sound of bolts being locked in place.

Joharan knows the next few days are going to be hard for Marrida, and the months beyond that even harder.

* * *

MARRIDA LEANS AGAINST THE FRONT DOOR. The action of bolting it feels almost mechanical because she has lost track of how often in the last couple of months – although it feels more like a year – she has entered and left her dwelling. Her uncle didn't call the guardsmen, but she knows in her heart that if they turn up now, she won't have any choice other than to let them in. She listens, imagining she can hear the many footsteps of the soldiers approaching, but everywhere is silent.

Marrida looks up with a start when she hears a sound, and she sees the concerned but tired eyes of Alagur looking back at her. Suddenly, she's overwhelmed by the tiredness she has been fighting all evening.

Alagur rushes towards Marrida when he sees her slipping down to the floor and two strong arms hold her upright. This is followed by more footsteps, and she hears the faraway voice of Alagur telling Esbara to help him. Both carry her up the stairs where she is laid on her bed. Esbara puts a blanket over his sister and leaves the room. Alagur stands to look at the woman for a few minutes before he, too, leaves the room.

"We should let her sleep," Esbara says in hushed tones.

"Do you want me to sleep in the room downstairs?" Alagur asks the boy.

"No, I've got an extra mattress in my room. If she wakes up, she may need our help." Alagur looks puzzled, and Esbara decides to explain. "The last time she was away from the Temple this long, she ended up with nightmares. And when she woke up, she was screaming and thrashing about."

The boy bows his head. Marrida asked him not to tell anyone about that frightening time, and now he feels as if he has betrayed her trust.

CHAPTER SIXTEEN

A REASSURING HAND ON HIS SHOULDER makes Esbara look up, surprised. Alagur is looking at him with concern, almost like a father would look at his son. This is the first time a man, other than Joharan, has shown concern for Esbara since his own father died, and this man is someone he hated just days ago.

"I won't mention that you have told me any of this," Alagur mutters. Esbara can only nod. His throat is tying itself into knots with the emotions he's feeling. He turns and gestures to the man to follow him.

When they enter Esbara's room, Alagur sees a sparsely decorated space which reminds him of his dwelling in City of Wolves.

Why do all men in this world have so few belongings in their sleeping rooms? he ponders, helping the boy lift a mattress out of a wooden trunk. They carry it to a low bench beside the doorway and position it there. Next, Esbara rushes back to the trunk and carries over two large rather floppy pillows which he stacks on the mattress. When Alagur lies down, his feet will be nearest to the doorway.

Alagur nods in approval. The mattress and pillows look old, but how old they are is something he isn't going to ask at that moment.

"I'll get my clothing and belongings from downstairs tomorrow," he says to Esbara, who nods and sits down on his own bed.
"The wolf can sleep here too," he suggests, smiling.
"The wolf has made the vestibule her sleeping area," Alagur responds. Esbara nods understanding, recalling how Yalla stayed downstairs as they carried Marrida up to her room. He thought this was because of instructions from Alagur, but now he realises the wolf possesses a will of her own. It makes him even more curious as to how the man controls the wolf.

Esbara extinguishes the flickering ember that sits in a small stone bowl on the table beside his bed and lies down. Alagur takes off his shirt and lays it on the floor next to his bed, then he lies down too. Both caught up in their own thoughts, they're sound asleep not long afterwards.

* * *

JOHARAN RUSHES HOME, AND ON ARRIVAL, HE WAKES DAMIR. After getting dressed, the boy sits down where hours earlier Marrida sat. Of all five apprentices, Joharan trusts this boy the most. He knows Damir looks favourably on Kalisa as a potential life partner, even as young as she is. Damir has been an apprentice for over eleven years now, and he and Kalisa have been friends for almost as long.

Joharan pours some fresh rose flower tea into a pot while he contemplates what to tell the boy opposite him. He has told Damir some of the retellings about his grandmother, things he's kept from his niece until this evening. Soon, Marrida will be setting off on a long and dangerous journey, and Esbara is too young to be in sole charge of the household. At seventeen, Damir could be placed in the household as a guardian. That this could lead to a closer bond between Damir and Kalisa doesn't escape Joharan's notice, and with a pang of regret, he thinks about his own decision never to have a life partner.

I can't have Kalisa here with just two sleeping rooms and five boys using one of them. The laws forbid boys and girls mixing above the age of ten.

Joharan knows the tradition of choosing a person as life partner stems from a time when Keldarra wasn't a free land where people could choose the person they wanted to live with in a committed relationship. Behind the backs of their oppressors, people started to call their spouses 'life partners' to hide the true nature of the relationship. The secret then became a tradition as the northern oppressors were defeated.

"I want you to pack all your belongings and stay at Marrida's house," Joharan whispers to Damir.

"Why?" the boy questions sleepily, reaching out for the cup of steaming tea the man is holding out to him.

"You remember the retelling I told you about my grandmother?"

The boy is instantly wide awake. He nods.

"You're two years younger than Marrida, and although you're not yet the age at which you can become a guardian, I want you to take up that duty in my name. If anyone asks, you were told to go there and do this."

"Do you remember the old passage that leads out of the city?"

The boy nods. He played there many times with friends before he became the primary apprentice to Joharan.

"I want you to assist someone to leave the city through it."

Now Damir's curiosity is piqued. It's clear to him that Marrida is going on some sort of journey, but he hasn't guessed there's more going on than he's been told up to now. He looks as closely as he dares at the old man opposite, masking the action by taking another long sip from his cup of tea. The eyes looking back at him, known for being stern, are filled with seriousness and a hint of concern. The boy sees it and puts his cup on the table in front of him.

For his seventeen years, Damir is a bright, intelligent boy. He's quick to understand things and fast to learn new skills. When Joharan and he encountered one another for the first time, Damir was playing near the entrance of the old passageway. Seeing a man in his fifties walking past carrying a haversack full of tools, Damir was overcome by curiosity and ran over to the man to ask what he was carrying. He then offered to carry the haversack, and although it was hard to lift it onto his back, he managed not only to carry it, but also to ask the man all sorts of questions.

A few days afterwards, the same man visited his house and asked his parents if Damir could become his apprentice. Damir's parents were not well off, and with five children to feed, they agreed to the apprenticeship, knowing it would lighten their burden somewhat. To this day, Damir travels twice a month across the vast city to his parents' house, carrying the same haversack he once carried for Joharan. The haversack is now always filled with an abundance of food as part of the payment for the boy's services.

Joharan looks at the boy opposite him. His jet-black hair reminds Joharan that he once possessed similar dark hair, but whereas Joharan has dark brown eyes, Damir has green eyes which are close to the colour of ripe rubha apples. Interestingly, they are also the same colour the gem around Marrida's neck becomes when it is being used. Because Damir most commonly works out in the backyard of the workshop, he has developed a dark tan, resembling the appearance of some of the eastern peoples of Keldarra.

"When do I need to take this person out of the city?"
"As soon as it's feasible," Joharan acknowledges. "He won't be alone."
"Is Marrida going too?"
"No," comes the short reply. After a pause, Joharan adds, "He'll have a wolf with him."
The boy looks up sharply. Joharan can read the words on his lips.
"A wolf?"
The man nods and purposefully takes a long sip from his own cup of

rose flower tea. There could be many ramifications of telling the boy this. He must trust that Damir will go to Marrida's home the next day, and not run to the nearest guardsman and pass on the news of who is currently residing there.

Damir leans back in his chair in a gesture that imitates Joharan. He's dumbfounded.

This is the last thing I expected. Or did I expect it all?

Joharan can hear the boy muttering under his breath.
"A wolf…a wolf…someone with a wolf…that means--"
The boy goes quiet and looks at Joharan with tight lips and pale face. "We were attacked by the Wolf Riders here weeks ago," he says slowly.
Joharan nods solemnly. It's best for the boy to realise what's happening in his own time.
"And one of them is at Marrida's house at this moment? Kalisa…is she alright?"
"Yes, yes, she's fine," Joharan reassures the boy, placing a finger to his lips to silence him. "In fact, she and the wolf seem to have become the best of friends."
Damir stares at the man, his mouth wide open in amazement. That, he needs to see for himself!
"So first you want me to help the man and his wolf get out of the city, then go to stay at the house while Marrida is away?"
"That's correct," the man says in response. "And the man is going to wait outside the city until Marrida is ready to depart too."
At least, Joharan hopes this is going to be the plan. He lifts the jug which holds the rose flower tea and looks inside it. Finding it empty, he puts it back down on the table.
"I guess the tea is finished, which means you and I need to go to sleep until morning."
Damir nods and gets up from the chair, then looks at Joharan.
"Joharan, can I ask something?" he says softly. The man nods and waits for the question as he too gets up and puts the mugs and the jug on the worktop behind him.
"When Marrida leaves, where's she going?"
"She's going to unmask the truth. She needs to travel to the city where the Keeper from this city lived."

The boy nods, and Joharan continues with his explanation. "Remember the retelling I told you a few years ago about the founding of this city's Temple?"
"Yes, and you said the person who founded it came from a faraway

place."

"She had an apprentice – well, actually an Acolyte – who later became the next Keeper of Truth," the man continues. "She's the one referred to as the Second Elder in the retellings of old."

"Why is that?" the boy asks, trying to prolong the time before he must go to sleep.

"It's said each of the cities would have an Elder after The Old Days," Joharan explains. "For Ruh'nar, the situation was a strange one because two Elders were in charge – the one who was appointed by the previous Elder as she became too old, and the second one who came to the city from a long distance. She also apparently possessed the gift of seeing the future – but what is this? Are you trying to keep me up for more retellings? Off to bed with you now."

With some hesitation, Damir complies with the request and climbs the stairs to the room he shares with the other apprentices. He waits at the doorway to allow his eyes to get accustomed to the darkness of the room, and then he tiptoes to the corner where his bed awaits him. There he lies awake, thinking for a long time about the conversation he has had with Joharan. The whole situation intrigues him, and he wants to help as much as he can. However, he can't shake off the fear he is feeling about who is in the house with Kalisa, and when he eventually falls asleep, his dreams are tainted by snarling wolves and seemingly endless dark tunnels through which he is running.

* * *

JOHARAN STANDS AT THE BOTTOM OF THE STAIRS, listening for the telling silence which will indicate that Damir is asleep. At first, the boy is restless and thrashing about in his bed, but an hour or so later, his breathing becomes even. That's the signal for Joharan to go to his own bed.

His stairs are opposite the ones Damir ascended. He enters the tiny room at the top, turns on one of the embers next to his bed and sits down. That he needs to involve his young charge in something as dangerous as helping a Wolf Rider to get out of the city is weighing heavily on his shoulders, and he lets his body slump over and leans both arms on his knees, thinking long and hard about the plan he's formulating for his niece.

First thing to do in the morning is to make sure Damir is packed and ready to go, then make sure that Marrida goes to the Temple, and then what? Joharan isn't sure whether it's safe for Marrida to go to the Temple now. What if the

Order of Truth discovers that she has been doing visions in secret, or that she's harbouring a Wolf Rider in her house?

Joharan sighs deeply. *I'm getting too old for all this excitement, but I have a promise to keep to my grandmother, who risked so much to tell me what she knew.*

He gets up and walks to the window, drawing back the curtain and looking up at the sky. The first streaks of orange and pink are declaring the beginning of a new day. The sun will rise soon, and the moon has almost departed from the sky. Looking down, Joharan sees the earliest risers in the street – artisans who collect wood from the forest, and stoneworkers who collect stone from the quarry for their masonry. A fruit vendor walks past the house with a cart pulled by two jet-black bovines. Joharan recognises the animals as being of western stock, which means the fruit vendor either bought them at a trading fair in Chiva'na or got them from one of the farmers in the region of that city. The stocky, muscled bodies of the animals can pull a huge burden, and at times, Joharan uses similar bovines to bring home supplies for his own work.

Looking at the city's roofs, he sees smoke still billowing from some of the buildings as the fires caused by the attacking Wolf Riders slowly burn out. From the darkness of the smoke, he notes that many of the fires were extinguished only recently.

Joharan lets the curtain drop.

Everyone in the family was perplexed when my grandmother moved to the poorest part of the city, and then insisted on blocking over the windows on the ground floor in both houses. But she knew a day would come when it would make the enemy ignore the house, so she could save him from capture for ransom or worse. I guess the wolf being wounded wasn't part of his plan...but it proves I must be cautious with the authorities here...

After stretching his back, he climbs into bed, and after a few minutes, he falls asleep.

CHAPTER SEVENTEEN

The next morning, Kalisa is the first to rise. This has become her normal routine in recent weeks, but today, Kalisa senses something is different. She listens and notes an eerie silence around her.

Climbing up on her bed, she looks down into the courtyard as she has done so often before. There's no wolf there. She looks around her room, and she can't see the wolf. Kalisa feels the chill of the air and ponders for a few minutes where Yalla could be, then she climbs off her bed and walks to the door of her room. She looks across the landing towards the doors of her brother's and sister's rooms. They're both open.

Kalisa walks silently to Marrida's room first and looks at her sleeping sister. Marrida is usually up as soon as she hears Kalisa wake up, but today, she's still fast asleep. Kalisa frowns, feeling curious now.

She tiptoes to her brother's room and looks inside. Seeing Esbara asleep with his blanket only half covering him, Kalisa is fighting the urge to tuck him in when she hears a sound coming from the other corner of the room. She's surprised to find Alagur sleeping there, half-naked.

The girl suppresses a chuckle, placing both her hands over her mouth. *But where's the wolf?* she thinks.

Kalisa walks to the stairway and glances down, sure she can see the shape of something on the floor below. The girl walks quietly down the stairs, stopping every time a tread decides to creak. Each time she looks up, expecting either sibling to appear to chastise her for going downstairs on her own so early, but no one comes, and so Kalisa tiptoes down until she steps onto the cool tiles of the vestibule.

A soft thumping noise greets her. The wolf, trained to be alert for all noises, has been aware of the girl's downward advance from the first creak. The beaming smile on Kalisa's face as she hears the greeting makes Yalla thump her tail faster. The wolf likes this girl, and it comes as no surprise to her that the girl likes her, too. Were Yalla still in her family pack, she'd be living with her pack sisters. In the absence of a pack, this girl represents the closest thing Yalla has to a pack sister.

Yalla feels Kalisa's hand stroke the muscles of her hind leg, and they ripple in response to the touch. Being friends with a girl isn't quite the same as having other wolves around, but Kalisa treats Yalla with respect and shows she cares.

Kalisa looks at the wolf more closely. It's obvious that Yalla favours the cool floor over the heat of the courtyard. Kalisa recalls Marrida saying that the wolf's belly is full of pups. She touches Yalla's belly and feels movement under her hand.

Kalisa giggles gently. "You're going to have babies soon," she declares to Yalla, not doubting that the wolf can understand her. Yalla lays her head down and lets the girl tickle and caress her. It feels good and takes her mind off the aches in her belly. That she's pregnant hasn't escaped her attention, even if she comprehends the situation in a different manner to the girl.

Kalisa is so occupied with caressing the wolf, she doesn't notice the arrival of Alagur until he kneels beside her. Yalla greets his arrival with a wet tongue rasping his face, which startles the girl.

"I didn't know if it would be alright to come and see the wolf on my own," she explains.

"Yalla likes you," Alagur acknowledges gently, smiling at Kalisa. "It's quite alright."

"Marrida says she's having babies." Kalisa points at the wolf's belly. "She thinks there are about eight of them."

"Indeed," the man says in response. "I can tell from her behaviour that she's having pups."

"How long?" the girl quizzes.

"I'd guess another season, maybe a bit longer," Alagur replies. "That's why she seeks out the coolness of this floor rather than sleeping in the heat of the summer sun."

"Why does the birthing take so long? Esbara says the birthing in wolves takes just a few months."

"It's something about the particular breed of wolf. We — the Wolf Riders in City of Wolves — don't know why they take longer than normal wolves to have pups."

"Kalisa counts the months on her fingers. "That means early winter--"

Alagur nods. "She'll need to go home to have the pups."

"So, perhaps these wolves are slow having pups because they miss their real home. No one likes being taken from their home."

Both the man and the girl stroke the wolf in silence, sharing their fondness for the powerful beast. Occasionally, the girl smiles at him and he responds in kind. However, Kalisa's words leave Alagur thoughtful. Not even the thumping of Yalla's tail can distract him. The girl is clearly highly intelligent, and she understands what's going on.

Footsteps coming down the stairs make both Alagur and Kalisa turn at the same time. A sleepy Marrida is walking down, greeting them with a smile. She feels better this morning than she has done in days. Things are different now, and because she didn't have any dreams to keep waking her up, she decides that she must have made some correct decisions the previous day. Seeing her sister and Alagur talking puts her mind at rest — she's doing the right thing by going along with her uncle's plan for her and the man to travel to seek out answers to many questions.

"Alagur says Yalla will have her babies in the winter," Kalisa says, beaming a smile at her sister.

"Well then, let me check her to make sure she's healthy," Marrida responds, smiling back at her young sibling, then giving a hint of a smile to Alagur, too.

Marrida kneels at the right side of Kalisa, closest to the protruding belly of the wolf. She carefully moves her hand over the soft downy hairs, feeling for signs of life below the skin of the animal. Yalla obligingly lifts one hind leg as if she understands that someone with medical knowledge is checking her over.

"Yes, I can feel at least eight and perhaps as many as ten pups in there," Marrida says to Alagur over Kalisa's head. He nods with a smile. "She seems in good health, and is healing well from the wound, too."

Kalisa beams again, first at Marrida and then at Alagur. Then all three turn when more footsteps come down the stairs, announcing Esbara's arrival.

"Good morning," he says sleepily.

"Good morning to you too," Marrida answers with a smile on her face. She rises from the floor, which is a signal for Alagur and Kalisa to do the same.

"I'll make the morning meal," Kalisa says, hurrying off to the cooking room. She's quickly followed by the others, including a wolf who has let curiosity win over her discomfort.

Esbara and Alagur sit down on one side of the table, and Marrida sits in her usual place after grabbing four mugs from the cupboard nearest to the doorway. Three pairs of eyes watch Kalisa as she brings a ham in from the cold room, oat buns from a basket, and a jug of milk from a shelf. Alagur watches with interest as the young girl brings more and more food over.

Is Kalisa preparing some sort of feast?

Finally, Kalisa sits down after putting a platter of small purple fruit on the table. She puts her hands resolutely under her chin and looks at every other individual.

Marrida is first to recover from her amazement. "Are we expecting more people?" she asks her sister.

"No, this is to celebrate the puppies Yalla is having." Kalisa grins broadly.

"I guess that deserves a feast," Esbara says, looking at Marrida with a grin.

"I guess so." Grabbing the meat, Marrida cuts off a thick slice of it. "This is for Yalla," she explains, handing it to Kalisa. "You can give it to her."

Kalisa climbs down from her seat and walks to Yalla, whose tail thumps wildly in anticipation.

Alagur gives a signal to Yalla, and she understands she needs to be gentle when taking the meat. When Kalisa holds it out, the wolf takes it with such care that for a few moments, it seems that she's a pup herself.

Kalisa returns to the seat and smiles at Alagur. He nods in approval at her, then looks at Marrida and smiles. She smiles back.

He cares about the safety of Kalisa, she thinks. *That makes me like him more.* Then she shrugs off the thought. She doesn't want to admit that even to herself yet.

The remainder of the ham is divided up generously, and each person helps themselves from the rest of the food on the table. The jug of milk is passed around, and the four people eat their food, not speaking. Even Kalisa, who's usually very talkative during the first meal of the day, is quiet. But she does have a happy smile on her face as she looks from person to person, who each acknowledge her gaze with a smile or a wink.

Marrida is pouring herself a second cup of cold milk when they hear a soft knock on the front door. She glances at Esbara and then Alagur. In a few strides, she's at the door, which she unbolts and opens a crack to find Damir standing outside. He's carrying a haversack over his shoulder and two large packs held together by leather thongs in his hands.

Marrida moves aside and opens the door wider without saying a word.

Damir enters the house in silence and nods a greeting at Marrida. He lowers the two large packs he is carrying onto the floor, takes the haversack off his shoulder, and places it on top of the packs. Marrida bends over the packs and lifts part of the leather covering the contents.

"What has Uncle Joharan packed in them?" she quizzes, glancing up at Damir.

"Tools, and many different wares for you to sell to get yourself a decent coin purse for the journey," Damir explains. He thinks about what else Joharan told him. Some of it relates to the man, a Wolf Rider called Alagur; other parts are instructions for Marrida; and there's information to convey to Esbara, too. Joharan insisted that Damir repeated the instructions back to him three times to ensure he understood them all.

"Joharan sent me here--" he begins, but is interrupted by a commotion as Kalisa runs into the vestibule and gives him a hug. He hugs her back with some hesitation. Kalisa looks up at Damir and smiles. She lets go of the boy and runs back into the cooking room, alerting her brother and Alagur to the boy's arrival with excited shrieks which echo back into the vestibule. Damir tries to keep his emotions neutral, but when he glances at Marrida, he goes a few shades darker for a moment, and she gives him a knowing smile in return.

"Joharan gave me a parchment with information written on it, which you need to read and then burn so no one can ever find it," Damir says in a soft tone. "I'm not sure what he wrote as he didn't let me see it before sealing it."

Marrida nods silently.

"And I need to take *him* out of the city through the old tunnels," Damir adds, nodding towards the door of the cooking room.

Esbara comes from the cooking room and catches Damir's last words.

"You know about Alagur?" he asks, and gets an affirmative nod as an answer. "It's alright, Alagur, come and greet our new guest."

Damir turns a few shades paler when he sees the wolf walk into the vestibule, accompanying the man. Alagur is tall, but the chest of the wolf still comes to his diaphragm. Damir notes the wolf is taller than Kalisa, who's standing beside her, holding her in a tender embrace. Kalisa scratches the wolf's ear, and the animal reacts with short snorts, occasionally wagging her tail, her massive pink tongue lolling from the side of her mouth.

When Joharan told Damir about the wolf, he didn't quite believe what the old man said about her size. Damir knows from Joharan that the man standing on the other side of the wolf is a Wolf Rider. He has never seen a Wolf Rider in person before because Joharan always makes sure he and the other apprentices hide in the roof storeroom of the workshop during an attack. Last night, he was concerned for Kalisa, but seeing the girl unafraid of the massive beast beside her, he swallows hard and tries to set his fears aside.

Glancing at Esbara, Damir sees his friend smiling and looking at Kalisa. The man and wolf have clearly been here long enough for them get used to the beast and understand she poses no threat to them.

Alagur sees the various emotions playing out on the new arrival's face, edging from fear to awe, and back to fear. The boy is trying to be brave, or at least act bravely, and Alagur ponders over his next actions. Damir has stated that he'll be leading Alagur, and the wolf, through tunnels, so he needs to learn to trust Yalla, even if they'll only be together for a short period. Trust, even in the smallest measures, is a good way to take the fear away. And if Alagur is to depart with the boy in the next few days, that trust needs to be earned.

Alagur decides to do as he has done many times with new arrivals in City of Wolves. Signalling to Yalla to stay silently where she is, he steps forward until he is standing next to Esbara. Esbara understands and assumes the role of introducing his friend to the man beside him: a man who in some measure is starting to become a friend, too.

"This is Alagur with his wolf, Yalla." Then, for Alagur's benefit, "This is Damir. He's Joharan's oldest apprentice." After a pause, he adds some extra information. "He likes Kalisa, and I think he wants her as his life partner."

Damir stares at his friend for a moment with a frown, his face going from pale at seeing the giant wolf to a bright red when his intentions towards the girl standing next to Yalla are made public. The man smiles as he reaches out with a hand. Damir takes it with some hesitation and shakes it.

"Do you want to greet Yalla?" Alagur enquires, looking down at the boy and trying his best not to laugh. A big grin appears on Esbara's face when Damir looks as if he's about to bolt out of the front door. It takes a few minutes for Damir to pluck up the courage to nod, and Alagur waits several more minutes to make sure the boy doesn't want to change his mind. Then Alagur moves aside, and at some hidden command, the wolf gradually steps forward until her nose is within an arm's length of the boy's belly. Kalisa walks forward with the wolf, stroking her fur in a slow motion which seems to soothe the best as she sniffs Damir.

"If you hold out your hand, she can sniff it," Kalisa says with a warm smile. Damir looks at her and thinks about what she has said for a few moments, then very hesitantly holds out his left hand. The wolf pushes her cold nose into his hand, then looks up at the boy. Damir finds himself staring into two vivid yellow eyes, full of wisdom and understanding. That the animal is gentle is evident from the way she lets Kalisa caress her fur.

As the fear drains from the boy's face, it's replaced with a wide smile. He's completely fascinated by the beast and has trouble tearing his eyes away from her gaze. Finally, she turns and walks to the corner of the vestibule where she lies down, putting her head on the cool tiles between her two large front paws. She continues watching Damir, evident from her eye movements, but the spell of her gaze has been broken. Damir feels only awe where fear had previously been in his heart.

He looks at Kalisa and she smiles at him. Suddenly, Esbara's teasing about his feelings for the girl doesn't matter anymore. He's glad she of all people showed him that he doesn't need to be afraid of the wolf. He's glad to have her as a friend and hopes that one day she will become his life partner. Only time will tell.

Alagur watches the interplay between Kalisa and Damir with interest while the wolf is introducing herself, wondering if perhaps the words of the legend are about her. Kalisa does have an uncanny way with Yalla. She has connected with the wolf in a way that many of the snatched boys take years to master.

The man shakes his head. All this thinking about the legend is annoying him and making him confused. He's currently more interested in the message the boy, Damir, has brought with him from Joharan.

Does that mean that the old man has planned something?

Alagur is torn from his thoughts when the four younger people walk into the front room. When he follows them, he notes with a wry smile that the only seat left is the one he sat on when he told the siblings about the Wolf Riders. Even though his aches have lessened, he recalls that the chair isn't the most comfortable, but he sits down without any protest or indication that he thinks it's the worst chair he has ever used.

Alagur looks around the room. Kalisa, Esbara and Damir are sitting on the sofa that he occupied the previous evening. Kalisa is sitting between her brother and Damir, and Alagur notes how she and Damir keep glancing at one another. They clearly have genuine feelings for each other.

He looks over at Marrida, who is sitting in the chair closest to the fire as she did the previous evening when her uncle visited. She has a parchment in her hands and is reading its contents with a frown on her face, but she doesn't make any comments to indicate what it says.

When she finishes reading the letter, Marrida looks up, staring intently at Alagur for a few minutes. Alagur feels uncomfortable; he can tell from her expression she's contemplating what to tell him.

"Joharan says we need to travel north to Azaquina," she says. "You might see your friend again."

Alagur nods. He doesn't know how long it will take Bergas to get to Azaquina, going partway on foot if, as instructed, he disposed of the wolf. He doesn't even know if the boy will manage to return home to his mother, although he hopes in the deepest recesses of his heart that Bergas will.

But will Alagur be greeted as friend or foe if he too arrives there in an uncertain future?

CHAPTER EIGHTEEN

Marrida is looking down at the parchment from Joharan once more. She reread several pages before speaking again.

"Uncle Joharan says you should leave first and wait outside the city for me. Then I will leave too, and we need to travel north together--"

"He told me to take you through the old tunnels under the city," Damir interjects. "They lead to a valley to the north."

Alagur nods slowly in acknowledgement.

"Damir will stay here with Esbara and Kalisa after I'm gone."

Marrida looks up from the parchment briefly. Damir and Esbara look at one another, and a smile of understanding flashes between them. Neither thinks it is a bad idea. They are genuinely good friends, and both love the young girl sitting between them.

"You're leaving us?" Kalisa says. The young girl curls her lip, showing her annoyance at the thought of being separated from her oldest sibling.

"Yes, I must," Marrida replies, speaking softly.

"Is the wolf going too?" Kalisa starts sobbing.

"She can't stay in the city. There's a way to stop the Wolf Riders from ever attacking anyone again, and Uncle Joharan says that Alagur and I can find it---"

Marrida isn't quite sure how to explain it all to her eleven-year-old sister, so she stops speaking and sighs deeply. Damir puts an arm around the sobbing girl beside him. He feels sorry for her as she's too young to understand the calamities of the world; she just wants everyone to get on with one another.

The gesture does not escape Marrida's keen eye. "I hope it won't be a long journey, and I will be back before it is time for your First Rites," she says to Kalisa, in her heart hoping it will be so. Even this time frame is a long one for the young girl to comprehend.

Marrida reads the parchment again, thinking about what she has just told her sister. Could she really stay away from her family for four years? What if it takes much longer? She doesn't even want to consider that possibility.

"It says you need to read it too," she says, walking towards Alagur and holding out the parchment. He nods then takes it from her hand, looking down at the elegant handwriting.

Part of the parchment is addressed to him. Joharan is asking Alagur to look after his niece during the dangerous journey, and he further explains Alagur's role in all that is to happen. He also says he hopes that Alagur will find his family again.

Alagur reads the parchment several times, then looks up at Marrida, who is sitting in her chair, patiently waiting for him to finish reading.

"Do you understand now what is at stake?" she asks him. He nods. "You have a decision to make," she continues. "Either you go back to your old life, or you help me create a future for them."

Marrida motions towards the others in the room. Alagur looks again at the parchment, then at the dancing flames of the fire reflecting on the wall opposite him. He thinks about Bergas and the events that led towards the boy's attempt to return home. He thinks about Samur, the man he'd called 'friend' until he saw his deception in the vision Marrida did. He wonders once more about his sister.

Can I give up my old life in City of Wolves? A life he now despises, despite all the prestige he seemingly won within the ranks of the Wolf Riders.

If he were in City of Wolves now, he'd be celebrating becoming an Elder Man. It's a hard decision to make, whichever way he looks at it. But Alagur realises that he actually relinquished his status as a Wolf Rider the moment he assisted Bergas to return to his old life as a free boy. The consequences for the boy will be dire if he's recognised and caught while travelling home. The consequences for himself will be a brutal death as he'll be considered a traitor to his kind.

But are they still 'his kind'?

Three people in this room have got to know him better, and they all treat him like he matters – not having committed some violent act, but for some other reason. What the reason may be escapes him at this moment, but he knows that if he helps the woman, he'll carve out an existence of greater importance than the existence he's experienced so far.

Alagur makes up his mind and looks Marrida in the eyes.
"I'll help you with this mission. I'm starting to see why your uncle is a

man of wisdom."

"Then you need to tell him everything you know," Marrida says.

"I will."

* * *

THE PREPARATIONS FOR THE JOURNEY STARTED THE EVENING that Joharan returned home after his first discussion with Alagur. The next morning, Joharan woke with his mind racing over everything he needed to prepare. For Marrida's mission to have any chance of success, she would need to be able to travel virtually unnoticed. For this to happen, she'd need to be self-sufficient. However, times were dangerous with most of the land under the control of the Wolf Riders, especially in the east, according to the letter Joharan had received from his closest friend.

She can pass off as a merchant if I give her goods to sell. That way, she'll need no fat coin purse. She'll already comes with her own protection. I can press Alagur to act as her guard during the journey, but whether to go or not needs to be his choice alone.

Joharan made certain that each item he packed would serve a purpose. He'd included a large stash of items for Marrida to sell to merchants in Alzamar, so he needed to be certain Marrida and Alagur would go there first. For Marrida, he retrieved two unused tinder kits and several embers for lighting them. One of them was the tinder kit he used for his own journeys in his younger years. It would serve a better purpose on this journey with Marrida than sitting on a shelf, gathering dust. A few old woollen coats would help keep Marrida warm, and would also disguise her affluent appearance from others. He checked the coats for damage from moths. There was none.

Joharan walked back to the cooking room where he rolled the clothing into tight bundles before placing them in the bottom of a pack — a specially constructed carrying case that typically could be held in one hand for easy transport of merchandise. Above the clothing, Joharan placed several selvaya leather blankets. This soft leather comes from the selvaya goat, an animal native to eastern Keldarra. The blankets had been purchased at Joharan's request by Markalo a few years before his passing, and it felt appropriate that they'd now be used by his daughter, Marrida.

Wrapping several wooden bowls, cups, and a knife in tougher leather, Joharan finalised the items for Marrida to use. The tinder kits were the last items packed before sorting various spare clothes and work tools into the pack. The work tools might serve Alagur, who seems to have the air of an artisan himself.

After an hour, Joharan looked at two full packs with satisfaction before lifting them and placing them next to the front door.

"Damir," boomed Joharan.

The boy arrived a few minutes later, fully dressed, expecting to leave immediately. He greeted Joharan, suppressing a yawn.

"Yes, Joharan?"

"Fetch my parchments and ink pen from my office, please."

Damir rushed off to fetch the items. Joharan's office was located at the back of a narrow inner courtyard which acted both as an outdoor workshop and a place for relaxation.

A few minutes passed before Damir came back. He placed the items Joharan had requested in front of the old man, who'd sat down. Damir got a nod of approval. Joharan removed a sheet of delicate parchment sheet from the leather folder.

The ink pen was inside a long pouch. After taking it out and unscrewing the cap the ink bottle, Joharan paused to think. A moment later, he dipped into the black ink. As he wrote, the colour faded into a dark blue-purple colour, caused by the ink's reaction with the parchment. Damir smiled when he remembered using the same ink to draw beautiful flowers for Kalisa, who'd sit beside him and watch, occasionally shrieking an "Ooh" and "Nice".

But this is a message that he could not know about. It was only for Marrida, and perhaps Alagur, to know Joharan's instructions.

If I don't know, I cannot cause them any danger.

Damir turned his attention to the mundane task of preparing a morning meal for himself, his master and the others in the house, wondering all the while what Joharan might tell them about the plans. He guessed Joharan had all details formulated in his mind. Damir grabbed two large loaves of honey bread that he cut into twenty-four even slices. From the cold storage, he retrieved butter and a large chunk of cheese, then he spread the butter on the bread, being more generous with own slices. He cut the cheese into thin slivers, placing them on each slice of bread which he divided up between six wooden plates. He then pulled the ale-cured ham which was sitting nearby close to him, carving thick slices from it and placing these into a deep platter that he carried to the table where Joharan was still busy writing.

Joharan looked up when Damir approached and nodded to his left, indicating that the boy should place the platter there. To the man's right, Damir saw several pages of a densely written letter. He decided not to attempt to see what it said, instead turning his attention back to the preparation of the morning meal.

When he placed the first two plates on the table, a noise from the top of the stairs alerted both him and Joharan to the arrival of the other apprentices. Joharan paused his writing and hastily placed all the parchments back into the folder, winking at Damir when he noticed the boy's attention on him.

A moment later, the other boys entered the room. Damir sat down opposite Joharan and looked around the table. He'd miss the other boys; he regarded all of them as friends.

Next to him sat Sherino, the youngest of the boys at eleven years old, who'd only been an apprentice a year. When the youngster noticed Damir looking at him, he smiled and received a smile in return. Next to Joharan was Mazino, who was a year younger than Damir but had only been an apprentice for nine years. On either end of the table sat the remaining two boys, Kumar on the left and Kelzemar on the right. Both were twelve and had each been apprentices for five years.

Yes, I'm going to miss all of them, thought Damir. *Most of all Sherino.*

Before the arrival of the other apprentices, Damir had been companionable with Marrida, and later Kalisa. But then Marrida had stopped coming to the workshop after a strange group of women had arrived and asked for her. During the visit, Damir had been sent upstairs to the sleeping room and told to shut the door. But he had sneaked to the top of the stairs and listened to the conversation. Through cracks in the floor, he'd seen the test the women had performed on Marrida — until Joharan had arrived upstairs to check on him and caught him. The boy, still a new apprentice at the time, had thought the man would become angry and send him away. Instead, Joharan sat down beside him and, in hushed whispers, told him a retelling from his own past.

"This is how my brother and I listened whenever Mother and Father were having private discussions."

Damir had smiled at the thought of the stern old man as a boy, listening to secret conversations between his own parents.

It was sometime later that Joharan had told Damir the retelling of his grandmother's warning. Then the other apprentices had started to arrive and the conversations between them had become as scarce as Marrida's visits to her uncle's house. Deep down, Damir believed there was a connection between Joharan's refusal to tell her the secrets about his grandmother and the decreasing of her visits.

Now the plan was for Damir to live at Marrida's house. Damir pondered what reason Joharan would give to the other apprentices for this. He looked across the table at Joharan and saw the man frowning in deep thought, taking bites from the bread and ham almost absentmindedly. Their eyes met a moment later, and the frown softened into a somewhat mischievous smile. Then, as fast as the smile had appeared, it had gone and the frown was back. Damir could tell from Joharan's demeanour that he was using the morning meal to mull over his plan.

I'm sure the plan involves me, Damir thought. *I know it.*

Damir was startled out of his thoughts when Joharan spoke.
"Damir is leaving us. He's going to live at Marrida's house. As you all know, Esbara has been accepted as an apprentice at the Academy of Warfare."
Damir caught Joharan staring at him sternly for a moment. He'd been the one who'd mentioned seeing Marrida and Esbara as they rushed to the Academy of Warfare a week after the Wolf Riders' attack. Less than an hour later, Joharan and Damir had been standing side by side watching the siblings rush back home. Damir guessed that his master would have discovered Esbara's apprenticeship even if he had not seen them.

The other boys listened silently as their master explained the situation.
"Because of his duties, Esbara won't always be home to take care of his sisters, so I decided Damir should stay at the house while he's training at the Academy."
Four pairs of eyes looked at Damir, and he swallowed hard to stop himself from blushing. His feelings for Kalisa were common knowledge. The two older boys smirked at him teasingly, until Joharan coughed to get the boys' attention.

"There's another matter. I've asked Marrida to go on a journey for me," he said, pausing to weigh up his next words carefully. "So, in actuality, Damir needs to take care of Kalisa, and whenever he's free from his duties, he will assist Esbara with his tasks ahead."

Damir looked down at his plate. He was certain the other boys were staring at him once more and he wished the morning meal would be over soon so the other boys would have to start working on their various projects for the day. He wished he could grab his haversack and the two packs by the door and go.

"I'll miss you," Sherino said quietly. Damir turned and smiled at him weakly. He got a compassionate smile back.

"You'd best get ready, Damir."

Damir nodded and clambers off the bench.

"And each of you should finish your morning meal and get to work," Joharan bellowed in a stern voice.

For several minutes, the room rang to the sound of benches scraping over the floor and dishes and utensils clattering. Usually, it was Damir who washed and stored the eating utensils away, but today, Joharan's commands meant all the other apprentices did the task quickly and without protest. Within minutes, the room was clean and neat, and the younger boys had departed. Sherino was the last to go, pausing at the doorway and waving goodbye to his friend, his face betraying how upset he was to see Damir go.

Damir ran up the stairs to the sleeping room and grabbed the haversack waiting just inside. After a moment of hesitation, looking around the familiar room, he descended back to the cooking room and was met by Joharan, who turned him around and put the completed scrolls of written parchment into one of the side pockets of the haversack. The man then turned Damir back to face him, holding him by the shoulders and looking long and searchingly at the boy he considered to be a son.

Damir crashed forwards into an embrace, and Joharan was taken aback for a moment. Then he returned the embrace in kind. Both realised they'd miss one another, even though they'd only be streets apart.

I guess I will make frequent visits.

Joharan smiled, then pushed Damir towards the front door. He needed to go now in order to be at Marrida's house before too many people were on the streets – people who might question where the boy was going with a haversack and two heavy packs filled with wares.

After a moment of hesitation to get used to the weight of the haversack and packs, which was more than Damir would usually carry, he nodded at the man to indicate he could manage them.

"Try not to be seen." Joharan looked at the boy sternly. Damir nodded, then nervously bit his lip when Joharan opened the door wide. He glanced over his shoulder, listening to the familiar sounds coming from the workshop, then looked around the cooking room one more time. He didn't want to say goodbye to the other boys. Feeling tears streaking his cheeks, Damir turned back towards the front door, and with that gesture, Joharan understood he was ready to depart.

Joharan stepped outside and looked in each direction, seeing the streets were empty. Many of the nearby artisans worked to later schedules than Joharan and his apprentices, relying on products he needed to produce before starting to tackle their workloads. Joharan motioned to Damir. As Damir stepped outside, he felt a rough thumb wipe both his cheeks quickly. He smiled at his master.

He was met by the slight chill of the morning air. It would take time to walk the few streets to Marrida's house, so he'd be warm by the time he arrived with his load.

"Goodbye." Sherino had decided to defy his master's instructions and had come for one final farewell. He flinched, expecting a chastising from Joharan, but none came.
"Goodbye, Sherino."

Damir turned and walked away as quickly as he could, not giving the youngster a chance to delay him. He needed to go, and that it was that.

* * *

AFTER DAMIR HAD LEFT, Joharan stood thinking in the cooking room for several minutes, wondering what to do next. He looked towards the door where Sherino had stood moments before, but the boy had slipped away quietly. Joharan listened and heard an occasional soft sob.

"Sherino."

The boy appeared at the door, looking shy. Joharan motioned him closer. He sat and let the boy lean against him while he embraced him. The sorrow of the boy made Joharan remember that once, many years ago, he'd had to do the same with Marrida and Esbara after they'd realised they had no parents anymore.

An hour later, Joharan sat at the table and looked at the list of things he had to organise: travel papers for Marrida; speak to Sharriba, even if he wasn't looking forward to that encounter; warn Marrida to be careful at the Temple until her departure; warn a distant friend that the time of change had arrived--

Even for as prominent an individual as Joharan was within the city, the situation was a dangerous one. Questions could be asked that he wouldn't want to answer. He would need to confront opponents for information about the events surrounding the attack, and there were indications things weren't as they should be within the city. Joharan had a feeling of foreboding he couldn't shake. He didn't worry easily, but since he'd discovered Alagur at Marrida's house, a worried knot had started in his stomach.

Joharan decided that he needed to take control of the situation and plead with Sharriba to use her sphere of influence to ensure Marrida's safety. Joharan had already had prior dealings with her in his life — dealings that he kept strictly private. Their shared retelling now would be that he was sending Marrida on a journey on his behalf as a merchant, and that she was going to undertake this journey with the assistance of a guide. A letter from Sharriba, together with the correct travel papers, would ensure Marrida's quick entry into cities. It wouldn't make Marrida's journey any safer, though, especially with Alagur's wolf in the picture.

CHAPTER NINETEEN

WHEN DAMIR ARRIVES AT MARRIDA'S HOUSE, he doesn't know what to expect. It has taken him a while to walk there, and he is tired by the time he places one pack on the ground and knocks on the door.

The door is opened by Marrida.

"Your uncle sent me."

She simply nods, lets him in, and bolts the door shut behind him. After a quick exchange between the two of them, a happy greeting comes in the form of Kalisa rushing towards him.

Not too long after that, he finds himself in the presence of the wolf – the biggest wolf he's ever seen. Despite the fear he feels, he is in awe of the silver-grey-and-white wolf, whose name he learns is Yalla. This wolf is unlike any he has seen before – usually the small black wolves near the large lake outside the city. However, he notes that she is passive, and she doesn't growl at him.

Damir knows the man beside Yalla is a Wolf Rider.

During the conversation in the front room, Damir cannot stop staring at the wolf, who stares back at him periodically. She is clearly assessing him as much as he is assessing her, which makes him even more curious about the Wolf Riders. He's certain Esbara will tell him more after Marrida and Alagur and the wolf have all departed on their journey.

* * *

THE NEXT FEW DAYS WENT BY AS FAST FOR DAMIR as they did for the others. And as he settled into his new life, the conversation slowly turned to planning the actual departure. Damir's role in the departure is clear--he needs to help Alagur and Yalla leave the city.

As he was organising everything Joharan came to the house for frequent visits. Damir went to sweep the road in front of the house each day to create the illusion that these visits were to keep giving his former apprentice further instruction. Occasionally, this was true, and at such times Alagur finds himself drawn to the old man discussing carving techniques with the boy. Joharan soon discovers that Alagur, too, has an affinity as an artisan, and he suggests that Alagur offers himself to merchants and craftsmen in various cities and villages as an artisan to learn further.

While Joharan and Alagur talk one morning, Damir walks off to the cooking room and on the way there, remembers how he met Joharan in the first place. Damir had been playing with friends near the old tunnels through which needed to take Alagur out of the city. Outside the city is a quarry on the northern side of the lake. He and his friends had been there to explore, knowing it to be a place where people would leave to smuggle supplies into the city without the Wolf Riders noticing it. This was how the city dwellers hold out for weeks. However, the tunnels became unstable over time, especially the deeper tunnel under the lake, and their use was abandoned. Later the Wolf Riders could gain access, and from what Joharan had said to the boy he suspected that all was not as it should be with the city's defences. The attacks from the Wolf Riders had become more brazen; the defence of the city more lacking. *"It's the weaponry the Wolf Riders use,"* Joharan had said.

It was for that reason also that Joharan always forced his apprentices to hide above the oven. The roof there was designed to withstand the excessive heat the forge below it could generate.

Joharan had walked past the boys, seemingly trying to ignore them at first, but during the second encounter with them, he'd scolded them for their recklessness. Later, though, he'd visited Damir's parents to ask for the boy as an apprentice. Now that *same* recklessness has earned the boy the task of escorting the two secret visitors from the city safely. *If those tunnels are as unstable as Joharan says they are, then there's not much safety in that route*, the boy thinks with a slight frown.

Damir knows the man and wolf need to leave via this route. The reason is obvious. The gates are heavily guarded, and the wolf would give the guardsmen a reason to detain Alagur, and perhaps kill Yalla. As he walks back into the inner courtyard garden behind Marrida's house, Damir sees the wolf standing beside Alagur, and he must admit to himself the beast is beautiful.

* * *

LATER THAT DAY, ALAGUR SITS OPPOSITE JOHARAN for further discussion. Joharan wants to find out more about the origins of various rumours and information. The fact that certain Elder Men among the Wolf Riders used to make an effort to do retellings whenever the young Alagur was present is starting to make sense to the man himself.

"I think they did it on purpose," Alagur states as an answer to a simple question – why?

"So, you think these men had a further reason for making sure you heard the retellings?

"I can't be certain, Joharan. It's tough to sort through everything in my mind."

"I may be able to help with that during our journey," Marrida says softly. "I know a way to."

Marrida stops short of explaining, causing the two men to glance at one another with a knowing look.

"Please tell me the full words of the legend, Alagur," Joharan says. Marrida frowns, realising this Joharan's way of finding out what information the Wolf Riders relay to one another. Alagur shuts his eyes, and a grimace plays over his face. He clearly hates the words he's speaking.

In a flat tone, Alagur speaks them nonetheless.

> TEN THOUSAND RIDERS ROSE TO THE CALL,
> BESET ON TO THE CITY OF OLD, AND
> FALL BEFORE THEM IT WOULD.
>
> THEY WHO RESISTED WOULD FALL, AND
> AND YOUNG ONES TAKEN BY FORCE,
> AND A CITY WAS LOST TO TIME AND KIN.
>
> FOR THE BROTHERS BETRAYED TRUTH, AND
> RELEASED FEAR UPON THE WORLD,
> WITH WOLVES AS THEIR WEAPON.
>
> FOR LEGEND FORETELLS OF THEIR END,

THE END THAT WILL COME FROM ONE,
A BROTHER WHO RISES TO THE CALL.

THE TRUTH WILL SHOW THE DOUBTER,
HE AND HIS WOLF WILL TRAVEL FAR,
AN AGENT OF TRUTH WILL SHOW HIM.

SHE WHOSE NAME IS UNSPOKEN,
A WOLF SHE WILL CLAIM FROM THE WILD,
AND THE MAN WILL LEARN HER SKILL.

TOGETHER THEY END THE BROKEN WORLD,
HEAL THE WORLD TO WHAT IT WAS BEFORE,
IT IS THAT DESTINY THAT IS UNSPOKEN.

This confirms it for Joharan. These are the *exact* words his brother stated. He nods at Marrida, who understands what he is telling her. She closes her eyes for a few moments, and then opens them to find Joharan looking at her with curiosity. But he refrains from asking why she shut her eyes when she raised her hand to the bulge under her tunic.

Joharan looks from Alagur to Marrida.

"You'll have to make this journey," Joharan says. "Damir will stay here while you're gone. I'm making the necessary arrangements to make sure your journey can go as smoothly as possible."

"I'll help Marrida with her task," Alagur said softly.

"I know you will. I will need to speak to you about matters relating to the journey that only you can know about to ensure Marrida's safety."

Marrida and Alagur look at one another silently. Neither is prepared to challenge the old man with the question each of their minds.

What matters?

* * *

WHILE JOHARAN IS TALKING TO ALAGUR AND MARRIDA, Damir goes to sweep the road in front of the house, remembering the day he and Joharan first met, when Damir was playing with his friends near the old tunnels.

* * *

"DO YOU THINK YOU CAN DO THIS?" Alagur nods at the parchment in his hand. "Can you get me through those tunnels?"

"I think so," Damir replies softly.

"When do you think is the best time to go?"

"The streets near the tunnels are always emptiest after the midnight bell has struck," Damir suggests. "We'd have to be careful because of the wolf."

Alagur nods. "How far are the tunnels from here?"

"The back alley behind this house leads directly to a field west of the tunnel entrance." Damir feels more confident talking about a subject he is so familiar with. "There are two streets to pass through, though."

"I think you'll need to wait until it's new moon," Marrida suggests.

"That's eleven days from now," Alagur says, looking pensive. "According to your uncle, we cannot wait that long."

Marrida nods to confirm she understands.

"It was a chilly morning today," Damir volunteers. "It mean there'll be a mist this evening. It would cloak Alagur and the wolf."

"Guess we're waiting for the evening to arrive, then."

There's a lull in the conversation, then Marrida speaks up.

"I need to go to the Temple. If I don't go, I'll have been away three days. They'll come looking for me for sure."

Damir looks confused. *Why is she going to the Temple?*

Alagur notices the puzzled expression on Damir's face. "You'd better explain it to him, too, Marrida."

"Explain what to me?" Damir feels annoyed. Suddenly it seems that there's yet another surprise. He cannot take many more surprises.

"She is one of the Keepers of Truth, Damir." Kalisa answers Damir's question before Marrida can, showing again how diplomatic she can be in awkward situations. Damir can't do anything but stare at Kalisa with his mouth wide open. This causes Kalisa to giggle; it amuses her to shock her friend so unexpectedly.

It takes several minutes for the impact of Kalisa's statement to sink in. Damir then stares at Marrida, who sits up straighter and lifts her chin in defiance, as if saying, "If you have got something to say to me, then say it."

Rather than a flood of questions, a smile bordering on cheeky appears on the boy's face. Helping a Wolf Rider to leave Ruh'nar is one thing, but to be privy to knowledge that not many people know anymore is quite another. Damir soon realises he's in the presence of one of the Keepers who, up to now, have been nothing but a myth to him. Everyone dismisses them with such ease, yet here's one sitting opposite him. And she's the sister of his best friend, too. Damir smiles at Marrida, now noticing the bulge of the gem because of her posture.

Marrida notices where the boy's gaze fixes itself. "Do you want to see it?" she enquires, smiling back. He nods, his curiosity written all over his face. The boy has been told about the gem by Joharan, but until now, he didn't realise the old man was talking about something that is still in the family. It passed from a dying grandmother to the young life partner of a grandson, and later Sharriba passed the gem on to Marrida.

Marrida looks at Alagur, who nods encouragingly at her. She proceeds to take the pale white and green gem, hanging on its golden chain, from around her neck and holds it up before her. The gem glints in the licking red colours of the fire, the flames giving it an eerie appearance which sends chills up the spines of all in the room, Marrida included. Even the wolf, unable to understand what the gem represents, visibly shivers. This catches Alagur's eye, making him shudder even more.

"As I've told the others in the room, no one can know about this," Marrida says in a flat, cold voice. "I've already broken many rules imposed on me by the Order of Truth, but I want this skill to be available openly, and not hidden as it is now--"

Marrida glances down. At the same time, her arm slumps, and the gem lands unceremoniously in her lap, losing its red-flamed appearance. Damir would have believed she was holding a rubha apple in her lap if she'd not told him about the gem moments earlier.

With the spell of the gem's flaming appearance broken, Alagur gets up, stretching his aching back.

"Let's check through the packs to see what Joharan has sent over."
"You and Esbara can do that," Marrida says. "I have to go to the Temple."

She gets up and looks at Alagur until he nods in agreement. He has already realised Marrida is right. If she doesn't go to the Temple, there is a risk that he and Yalla will be discovered.

I must tell them I've been running errands for Uncle Joharan, thinks Marrida. *They must believe that's the truth.* Marrida feels unsure suddenly whether she can tell Elder Sharriba, or anyone else in the Temple, anything at all. *They'll ask too many questions.*

"I can use the skill Cheryssa taught me to still my mind," Marrida mumbles under her breath, deciding not to explain to the others with her who this individual from the Temple is.

It will prevent them from asking too many questions. I cannot tell my family or Alagur about Cheryssa without breaking another promise to Sharriba.

Marrida has decided the Temple library will offer her facts that will either support or deny the information in her uncle's letter. Before leaving, she looks around and sees Joharan's letter lying on the table in the centre of the front room. She picks up the parchment, looks it over once more to imprint all it says into her long-term memory, then drops the pile of parchment into the fire. She can access the information any time she needs it using the gem.

She watches how the flames grow taller as they consume the easily burned parchment rather than the usual slow-burning wood. Only minutes pass before all trace of there ever having been a letter have turned to ash. Now the words of the letter only exist in her mind, and that of Alagur.

Marrida looks up to be met by Alagur's eyes looking intently at her. She waits for him to say something about what she has just done, but he simply nods then walks into the vestibule. He understands why she had to fulfil her uncle's request.

Marrida follows Alagur after a moment's pause, but rather than staying in the vestibule, she climbs the wooden stairs to the upper floor of the house and enters her room. She picks up her grey woollen cloak from the top of a chest of drawers near the door. Draping the cloak around her, she pauses once more.

I need to be careful for another reason. I don't think my tormentors will let me off as easily as Sharriba or Cheryssa did. They'll press until I give in and give them answers — any answers. What can I say to them?

Marrida walks from her room and descends the stairs. There she's greeted by chaos. Many objects are spread all over the floor and on top of the cabinets. Yalla, who is lying under the stairway, is pinned to the spot and whimpers slightly when she sees Marrida look at her.

Esbara is assisting Alagur in emptying the two bulky packs, and Marrida notes he is doing it without protest. She raises an eyebrow for a moment in surprise, then hears Kalisa's giggle coming from the front room in response to something Damir has said to her. Marrida is too distracted by the chaos and her forthcoming visit to the Temple to wonder at the nature of the conversation going on between the two youngsters.

Tiptoeing to the front door so as not to step on any of the items on the floor around her, Marrida ponders again what to say to Elder Sharriba and the others at the Temple.

"I'll be back later today," she says. "Not sure when, but I'll try to be back before the evening meal."

Marrida opens the front door. Both Alagur and Esbara nod in acknowledgement of her words, indicating they understand.

"Bolt the door shut behind me, Esbara, please."

* * *

MARRIDA STANDS OUTSIDE HER HOUSE FOR A FEW MOMENTS. She listens as her brother complies with her request, and a moment afterwards hears him talking to Alagur. Marrida can't distinguish the words, nor does she want to try.

If Esbara wants to talk to Alagur about things that matter to him because they're both males, that's their business.

Marrida looks around the street for a moment. It's empty – very empty. Her street only has a few houses in it, and the nearest of them – opposite hers – has stood empty since the last occupant sold it and left the city. Though it was once common for the residents of Ruh'nar to leave their doors open during the day, recent events have made Marrida more cautious about it. She glances quickly at the place where Alagur and his wolf lay, both injured by a projectile.

Marrida glances towards the northern end of the street, and in her mind, she sees the black-haired man riding off. She wonders if he made out of the city after his brief return to the place where Alagur fell, or whether he met a fate similar to Alagur's, or worse. Marrida hasn't heard of any captured Wolf Riders, so she decides he must have returned to City of Wolves – or Masharea, as it should be called.

Looking in each direction one more time, Marrida determines that the street is indeed empty. The square to her right is the closest to the Temple, but the walk still takes Marrida twenty minutes at a brisk pace.

When she arrives at the stairway in front of the Temple, she sees the doors are open. Beyond them, she sees the silhouettes of several females walking from the left side of the grand vestibule towards the right. With the sharp morning light in her eyes, Marrida can't ascertain who is inside. Her mind races to determine who of all the Temple Maidens, Acolytes and Keepers would need to visit the room housing the ancient maps, located on the right side of the grand vestibule.

Marrida hears laughter that she recognises immediately: it's her tormentor. Sarayna has spotted Marrida arriving and is waiting for her.

"So, you have come to grace us with your presence," Sarayna sneers. She and those she's chosen to be her inner circle of 'friends', all fall about with uncontrollable laughter which echoes through the vestibule.

Marrida feels anger welling up inside her. However, she keeps it in check. She doesn't have time for this behaviour.

She forces a pleasant smile onto her face. "I guess you have finally recovered from the shock that caused you to look so fearful during the Wolf Riders' attack," she says. "I recall you went home crying, didn't you?"

Without waiting for any response from her tormentors, Marrida turns and walks away. Today the tide has turned.

CHAPTER TWENTY

MARRIDA HURRIES UP TWO FLIGHTS OF STAIRS. At the top of the second one, she looks in both directions to check for the presence of any Elders. Seeing the corridor empty, she quickly turns left towards the large doors which are the entrance to the library.

It takes her a minute or so to reach the doors. Glancing back to check the corridor is still empty, Marrida dives into the library. She finds herself in a familiar large room, filled with thousands of books – some of which have been identified by Elder Sharriba as dating back to The Old Days.

Marrida looks around the room. She has visited here a few times with Elder Sharriba. In the presence of the old woman, the room has always felt smaller. But now she's alone, the room feels large and overwhelming with only a few embers lighting it up.

Marrida smiles as she remembers the first time she entered this massive room with Elder Sharriba.

"There are three groups of books here," Sharriba had said. *"The books you can learn from now, the Forbidden Knowledge books, which you can learn from once you're a third-year Acolyte, and the Hidden Knowledge books which you may only read as a Keeper."*

Marrida, in awe of the number of books in the library, had discreetly glanced around her. Unable to speak, she'd nodded to Sharriba's every question or command.

There are so many books, and I wonder where they all came from.

The Elder explained that some of the books predated the existence of the Order. Others dated from the earliest days of the Order, and they were brought here by those fleeing from Masharea and other cities. Marrida asked who or what Masharea was, but she didn't receive an answer to the question. The Elder did, however, stipulate that Marrida shouldn't go seeking out books forbidden to her, reminding Marrida of the 'consequences' she'd mentioned previously.

What consequences? Marrida thinks defiantly.

Marrida leans against the wooden door behind her. *Where would the books I require be located? I need an answer for the mysteries I uncovered.*

Marrida closes her eyes for a moment, then opens them and reaches for the ember in the container to her left. The faint light dances on the carvings on the door as Marrida moves it. After gently blowing at the ember, she holds it up, intrigued for a few moments by the carvings. The light seems to bring them to life.

She sees the shape of a woman with her hands held up either side of her head. Each hand has a green object in them, shaped like a rubha apple. Marrida moves the ember left and then right, as she sees two other gems clasped in more hands. She concludes that the pattern must represent arms.

She looks more closely, then jerks back when she's met by three pairs of eyes – all black in colour. Marrida is held in a trance by the carving for a few minutes before managing to tear herself away.

Marrida looks up at the second floor and the bookcases it houses.

Sharriba said the books there are the oldest. And she said the books with Forbidden Knowledge and Hidden Knowledge are there too.

For a moment, Marrida wonders why the Elder made a point of telling her about these books. It would have been easier to leave her uninformed rather than piquing her curiosity.

I guess I'm trying to find an excuse to disobey Elder Sharriba. Which is what I'll be doing if I read those books.

Marrida is certain she'll find the books she seeks on the second floor. She has a clear picture in her mind about the information she will need to complete her uncle's task. Moving silently through the bookcases flanking her left and right, Marrida dashes towards the stairway on the furthest left hand side of the large room and up the stairs. She is panting when she reaches the top, but without hesitation she crosses the first floor and runs up the next set of stairs. The longer she remains on the lower floors, the more she risks being discovered.

When she reaches the second floor, she backtracks to where the bookcases she needs are located.

The library has a stupid layout, Marrida thinks, frowning at the annoyance of having to walk so far across the second floor that she can see the library entrance door below her. *Why does a person have to walk haphazardly through it all to get to where the oldest books are?*

Sharriba's answer comes to Marrida's mind, and she spins around for a moment, thinking the Elder is standing behind her.

"It is to safeguard against anyone reaching the oldest treasures in the Temple. If it's difficult to reach them, they keep safer--"

In her Ancient Histories lessons, Marrida has been taught that the library design dates back at least three thousand years to a time of warfare and conquest. An unknown people came from a northern land located across a vast ocean and proceeded to conquer most of Keldarra, until a peacekeeping force stopped them. That peacekeeping force existed until a thousand years ago.

That was the time of the Warlords, long before the Wolf Riders emerged.

Alagur has told her there was a link between the Warlords and the Wolf Riders, according to the Elder Men in City of Wolves. This shocked Marrida greatly. Elder Sharriba mentioned the Warlords in passing in answer to one of Marrida's many questions, but it turns out they were more real than Marrida wants to admit.

Now Marrida is searching for more answers. A war ravaged Keldarra in the distant past, between five thousand and three thousand years ago, correlating with the time known as The Old Days. Keepers know how to access the past, but not far enough back to see these events. Delving far into history is wrought with difficulties. The images are inaccurate; the words spoken are incomprehensible. And now, fewer Keepers seem to exist.

Elder Sharriba spoke privately about this with Marrida.

"It has something to do with how we do things in the Order. I've found evidence in the Forbidden Knowledge books that indicates that the Order consisted of three forces once, one representing the past, one the present and one the future. They were meant to balance each other in a way."

Marrida thinks back to the conversation with her uncle about his grandmother.

"She had the ability to see the future as well as the past."

Marrida frowns for a moment as she reaches the bookcases, wondering about her great-grandmother.

Does her kind of skill have a name? Is there a connection between what Sharriba said and the emblem on the library door?

The books that Marrida is searching for will have to provide answers, because she's certain she won't get any from Elder Sharriba.

Holding the ember high, Marrida looks up and down one bookcase, then those flanking it. Her face lights up with recognition when she spots the book that she's been reading with the Elder recently. She places the ember on the floor and pulls the heavy book from the shelving, carrying it with some difficulty to a nearby table, then she rushes back for the ember that she places beside the book.

Her finger traces over the highly decorative cover. She's admired the cover of the book each time she's seen it during her studies with Sharriba. It shows a mixture of carved figures and shapes, and now she sees what she's missed before.

It's a man riding on a beast. Marrida bends closer. *A wolf! Did people ride wolves three thousand years ago? I thought the Wolf Riders started eight or nine hundred years ago. Sharriba claims eight hundred years, Alagur says nine hundred. Who is right? And who or what are these people?*

Marrida straightens up, straining to remember all that Elder Sharriba has spoken about.

What did she say that place was called? Quel…something? I need to remember the name. Marrida's face lights up with a broad smile a moment later. *But Queltha existed longer than three thousand years ago. Sharriba said it was an empire in the north destroyed by people from Mycanthia. How would the Wolf Riders know it?*

Marrida stares at the wall opposite her, puzzled. Then she bends over and reads the title of the book.

Sharriba has stated that the peacekeepers were created to drive away the invaders from the north.

Were these peacekeepers the Mycanthians? How do they link to the Wolf Riders?

Marrida studies the binding again. Some of the design seems to be of Mycanthanian origin, based on information from later books.

Did those people inscribe this book with their own history, adding Queltha's history? If so, how did the first Wolf Riders know this? Marrida recalls two specific names. *Ah yes, Alagur said Yozan and…errr…if I remember rightly, he called the other one Sey'qar. Neither of those names sounds like it comes from Queltha, or from Mycanthia. And according to Alagur, they lived fewer than a thousand years ago.*

Marrida studies the binding for a few more minutes.

I don't know why it looks so familiar, but something makes me feel like I should know what it's about.

She unties the binding on the side and opens the book at the first page. Again, just like when she has studied the book with Elder Sharriba at her side, Marrida gets the feeling that she recognises the letters and words. She strains to understand the words, even though Elder Sharriba has explained their meaning during Ancient Histories lessons. Then she studies the drawings in the book.

Some show wolves: large silver-grey-and-white wolves like Alagur's companion. One drawing makes Marrida feel awed. It's a drawing of a wolf, set against a sky filled with lightning. The wolf is standing atop a snow-covered mountain.

She sees drawings of bearded men wearing foreign clothing. Marrida decides they must represent men from the most ancient of days. Just as she's about to turn the page, a name jumps out at her – Masharea. Did the city exist when this book was written? It would make the city at least three thousand years old if it existed when Mycanthia and Queltha were at war.

Marrida ponders over the implications of this information.

If a link exists between the Warlords and the Wolf Riders, then where and how did these men fit in? And who exactly were the 'peacekeepers'? Alagur mentioned that the Wolf Riders once worked with the Keepers until Yozan and Sey'qar destroyed that cooperation and made them mortal enemies. Is the legend Alagur told me some sort of warning from the past for us now? Is it a message to tell us that the Wolf Riders destroyed Masharea?

Marrida puts a hand over her mouth when her own mind answers that questions with an affirmation. The book can answer many questions about that past--

"What are you doing up here?"

Marrida jumps up when a familiar voice speaks sharply behind her, unlike the mellow tone she is used to. She spins around, seeing Elder Sharriba standing there. Instead of pursuing her, it seems Marrida's tormentors have decided to exact revenge a different way.

* * *

ELDER SHARRIBA WATCHES THE GIGGLING SARAYNA AND THE FRIENDS for a while as they run off, frowning a little because she knows how they've behaved towards Marrida in the past. All they have done today is confirm the Elder's suspicion by telling her they have seen Marrida going upstairs. 'Upstairs' in Marrida's case would mean the library: a place forbidden to Acolytes without an accompanying Keeper or the Elder.

She waits for the group to move away, then departs.

Once Sharriba is in the library, it takes one glance around the large room to locate Marrida. A single bright ember in a dimly lit room is easy to spot. She frowns again when her mind realises where Marrida is exactly, and which books are held there.

She sees a movement confirming her suspicions, and then the shadow of someone leaning over an ember is cast over the high ceiling. Sharriba moves silently through the room towards the second floor, her slippers, made from the wool of mountain sheep, hiding any sound of her footsteps.

Sharriba hides a smile, when she sees Marrida's reaction. The young woman manages to blanch and go bright red at the same time. Sharriba has been watching the intensity of the young woman's study with interest, one glance confirming which book is lying open behind her. Despite this, Marrida is desperately trying to hide the evidence of what she's been doing.

Sharriba knows deep down why this day had come. She sees

Marrida's eyes darting left and right, searching for a good excuse to give her teacher.

Sharriba raises her eyebrow when Marrida speaks.
"I'm working on my Ancient Histories lessons which we were busy with before the attack."

Sharriba looks searchingly at Marrida's face, wondering why she seems so shocked.

She's not so much shocked because of my sudden appearance. She's found something out--

Sharriba decides to hold her tongue. She knows the truth will eventually make itself known.

"What sort of information are you studying?" she enquires in a neutral tone. She glances at the page that Marrida was reading before she arrived and feels curiosity wash over her. "I can assist you with your studies."
"When I was caring for Esbara, I recalled that you mentioned something about the origins of the Keepers. I wanted to find out more."
"You never told me what happened to Esbara," Sharriba comments.
"He…err…got wounded while escaping from a Wolf Rider."

She is trying to sound so confident. I'm certain something else happened really, but I'll accept that explanation for now.

Sharriba nods then pulls a chair closer to the one Marrida was using. As she sits down, Sharriba looks once more – closely this time – at the page Marrida was reading. It's a passage about the first city of the Keepers – Masharea. She glances sidelong at the younger woman, who seems oblivious to her scrutiny.

Sharriba leans back in her chair. *If she has questions, I'll wait for them to come. No need to rush her--*

After a few minutes, Marrida plucks up the courage to glance at Sharriba, but only hesitantly. She sees the old woman leaning back, a familiar placid expression plays on her face. Marrida swallows hard, sits down, and turns her attention back to the book.

When she has read twenty pages, Marrida finds the information she is looking for. She glances over her shoulder and finds she is alone. Where could the Elder be? Marrida can hear noises, so she's certain Sharriba is somewhere nearby.

I wonder what she's doing?

Glancing one more time to make sure she's truly alone, Marrida pulls an old ember and strips of parchment from two different inner pockets. The parchments come from the blank parts at the bottom of her uncle's letter that she tore off before burning the rest. In tiny letters, Marrida transcribes the content of the page in front of her, occasionally glancing over her shoulder to look out for Sharriba's return. She holds the parchment for half a minute over the flickering ember in front of her, then she breathes against the soft material. This is a skill her uncle taught her many years ago to make the words she's written more durable.

Marrida quickly puts the dead ember and parchments away when she hears distinct footsteps. Sharriba can make her imminent arrival known if she wants to. She finds Marrida reading a different book to the one she was reading when the Elder departed. Sharriba sits down, placing two cups of steaming tea on the table, and in doing so notes what book the young woman is reading.

She turns to the younger woman and gets a smile of gratitude. *Obviously for the tea.* She sees Marrida smelling the minty aroma coming from it.
"It's Kelmari mint tea, in case you have forgotten. I hope you remember that it's an eastern tea--"

The young woman next to her seems oblivious to the fact that the Elder is imparting more knowledge.

It's best that way. It can serve her later--

It won't be long before the questions come. It's obvious to Sharriba that the books in the library fascinate Marrida in many ways. She also notes that most information in the books Marrida has chosen to study relate to the Wolf Riders, specifically thirty or forty years after they were first formed. Sharriba frowns for a moment as she wonders whether Marrida has found any information about a city to the far northeast – a city where the Order first was first established. Most Keepers of Truth know it only by description and not by a specific name.

She doesn't have to wait long before her suspicions are confirmed.
"This text mentions a city," Marrida begins. "Is it an important city?"

Sharriba leans forward, looks at the text and nods curtly. "The Second Elder lived there for most of her life. Before moving here for reasons unknown to us now."

"Why is she called Second Elder?" Marrida asks. "You are Elder Sharriba. She's only ever mentioned as the Second Elder. Why's that?"

Sharriba smiles. *Now the questions come.*

"Personally, I think she contributed to the arrival of the Wolf Riders as they are now." Sharriba pauses and looks at Marrida with the patience the younger woman is familiar with. "People want to forget her original name because of that. There are events from The Old Days that we cannot see — events from those early perilous days that most Keepers don't want to see. Events that haunt our dreams--"

Sharriba's voice trails off. Marrida looks at her, puzzled.

That's not the answer I wanted or expected.

"What events?" Marrida asks, more forcefully than she intended. There's silence for several minutes, and Marrida sees that the old woman beside her is searching her mind, using a skill Marrida has only recently learnt herself.

Sharriba turns and looks directly at Marrida. "Is there more you want to tell me about why you were absent from the Temple for several days?"

Marrida looks away quickly, and nervously clasps and unclasps her hands under the table.

"I know you are here for answers to the very things you've yet to learn from me."

Marrida looks up at Sharriba. An involuntary tear appears in the corner of her left eye and she does nothing to stop it from trickling down her cheek ever so slowly. It lingers at the side of her lip for a moment before dripping to Marrida's shoulder. She is scared now.

How much does she know? How can she guess about why I'm here?

A hand, aged by time, reaches up. It gently wipes away the second tear starting to trickle from Marrida's other eye. Sharriba smiles reassuringly at Marrida.

"I would like to know about the Wolf Riders--"

"But there's more, isn't there?"

Marrida nods so slightly Sharriba wouldn't have noticed it if she wasn't an acutely observant woman.

"Maybe one day in the future you can tell me what you need to keep in your heart." Sharriba places her hand over Marrida's upper chest. "But for now, let's just make sure you get all the knowledge you seek."

Marrida feels grateful, both for the trust Sharriba has shown in her and for the Elder's understanding that some thoughts and feelings are private – even in an Order with truth at its heart.

CHAPTER TWENTY-ONE

Aт the same time as Sharriba is comforting a distraught Marrida, Alagur and Esbara are still sorting through the many belongings Joharan has provided for the journey. At first, it's just the two of them working together, but before long they're assisted in the task by Kalisa and Damir.

I need to remember exactly what I left in the care of Bergas and match it with what Joharan has packed.

Esbara carries several of the selvaya leather blankets into the front room on Alagur's instruction, draping them over one end of the sofa. Alagur sees him run his hands over the soft material, looking somewhat distracted.

I guess they remind him of his father. They must give his mind comfort. There are two similar blankets in my own pack, so they will add to our comfort while we travel in the winter months ahead.

A moment later Esbara is back in the vestibule, helping Kalisa as she lifts several carved dishes onto a woven mat. They carry the mat into the cooking room where they lift it above the table, and the siblings catch each other's eyes. Kalisa smiles at Esbara, who returns the smile in kind.

They return to the vestibule for Alagur's next task, finding him sitting at the foot of the stairway. Damir is standing beside him, holding a basket and looking at him questioningly.

"Do you have a parchment and an ink pen?" Alagur looks up at Esbara. "I need to write down everything I can remember leaving with Bergas."

Esbara nods and walks towards a door below the stairway, which Alagur hasn't noticed until now. He's only been in the house for a couple of months, but at times, things seem so familiar it's as if he's been here for years.

After a minute or so, Esbara returns with a dusty looking parchment pack and two pens.

"I'm uncertain if they'll still work — it's been years since he last used them."

Alagur looks puzzled for a moment. The realisation strikes like lightning on a hot day.

These were his father's writing tools.

Alagur gives Esbara a simple nod of understanding, accepting the items the boy is holding out to him. Before he makes use of the parchment and pens, Alagur looks them over. Despite the passage of time, they still look exquisite.

I could restore the leather covering with some of my ash oil. It would look as new then. I'll grab it from my travel pouch later.

Alagur looks over the bindings of the parchment pack. It's held shut with three leather ropes, each tied into a simple knot. Using great care, Alagur opens the pack to uncover a dozen or so high-quality parchments. He's only ever seen such quality parchment whenever the Wolf Riders returned to City of Wolves with the spoils of war. Alagur is immediately aware that the trio living in this house must be accustomed to the finer things in life. Their parents must have been wealthy, which explains why they can live independent lives away from their uncle. The parents – Esbara has told Alagur they were Markalo from Ruh'nar and Eshara from Marridina – succeeded in their goal of ensuring their children wouldn't be left in hardship if something happened to them.

I'm sure their uncle helps them too. It sounds very much like he's one of the most successful artisans in Ruh'nar. From what Marrida tells me, he's a statesman in the government of the city and assists the Council of Seven. Elder Man Belduran told me what that is while I was in City of Wolves, so I know the level of influence Joharan can exert here. He is risking much by helping me.

Alagur pulls a parchment from the pack. He places it on the opposite side of the writing area, then unrolls the pen case, lifting the ink pots until he finds one that feels like it's full. Alagur unscrews the cap and dips the delicate tip of the pen into the black liquid. Damir, leaning against the doorpost of the front room and watching, makes a mental comparison between Alagur and Joharan, each writing down their plans.

I wonder how he knows how to write. Damir shakes his head to dismiss the thought. *It's probably the same reason why I can read and write--even Wolf Riders are someone's children. They would have learnt it before they were snatched.*

"I'm writing a list of things I left with Bergas so I can compare them with all the items here." Alagur sweeps his arm in an arc around the room, pointing at the goods strewn across every surface. "We learn to write in City of Wolves."

I know who Bergas is, Damir thinks. *Kalisa told me about him when we were alone earlier. I wonder how Alagur copes with being wounded in a city that's dangerous for him and his wolf. I wonder if he's seen the visions Marrida can do. He didn't look surprised when he saw the gem earlier. I guess he has seen the visions too.*

"Most of what we take will depend on how much Marrida wants to bring along, of course." Alagur stops writing and thinks for a moment. "I can fashion two packs for Yalla to carry, but--"

Alagur stops speaking and stares into space, deep in thought. His next words make all three youngsters gape at him in amazement.

"Marrida could call a wolf for her use."

Esbara's initial curiosity is fast replaced with fear. Alagur goes on with his writing, looking up moments later when a high-pitched "How?" escapes Esbara's lips.

"It's quite simple, really." Alagur points at Kalisa with the end of the writing pen. "The skill of mastering wolves often runs in families. Unfortunately, it has led to more than one snatching." Alagur sighs deeply. This is exactly the sort of conversation he's been avoiding since he woke from his coma, but he realises now that he can't avoid it for ever. "Kalisa has an inborn affinity with Yalla. I saw this when she showed no fear around the wolf."

Kalisa's forehead forms into a knot of concentration as she listens more closely when she hears her name mentioned.

"Furthermore, she's shown mastery over the call of wolf song."

"What's that?" Kalisa jerks her head back, confused.

"You remember earlier when Damir arrived, how I commanded Yalla to stay in one place?" Kalisa nods. "You decided when Damir needed to meet the wolf. You walked to him and called Yalla to your side with soft murmuring."

Kalisa's face lights up as she makes sense of her own actions. Her face breaks into a broad smile.

"It was wolf song you used. Usually, only Wolf Riders can master it, and then only after bonding with a wolf, but--"

Alagur pauses as a new thought enters his mind.

"I wonder what information Marrida will find at the Temple. I need to compare it with something the Elder Men said whenever they thought that I and others of my age weren't near enough to hear." The Elder Men in City of Wolves taught the youngsters that only Wolf Riders can learn wolf song. Kalisa has disproved this theory by bonding with Yalla.

I'm certain that I'm right. If they're correct, then men who don't join the Wolf Riders can't have the skill, and females would never have it. They said many things which now seem inconsistent.

Alagur frowns angrily for a moment before he continues speaking. "I think the Elder Men are wrong about wolf song." Alagur winks at Kalisa and smiles at the girl. "If you have this skill, I'm sure Marrida has it too. And you as well, for that matter, Esbara."

Esbara blanches on hearing the words. Then it strikes him that the Academy where he studies is the very place the original peacekeepers of Keldarra were likely to have trained.

If Marrida is right, those peacekeepers rode wolves. It means that Alagur is confirming that fact with his words.

Esbara realises suddenly how differently things could have turned out. Either Alagur or the other man – the one named Samur – could have snatched him when they came riding into his street.

I would be in City of Wolves with the other boys who weren't as lucky as me.

Esbara felt panic when Alagur paused in front of their house, but he hasn't mentioned this to anyone yet. He was upstairs with Kalisa. After telling her to stay put, he went downstairs, driven by growing curiosity, and listened at the door.

I heard the distinct sound of stone hitting bone – not once, but twice.

He opened the door when familiar footsteps outside reminded him that Marrida was outside. She'd also seen what had happened.

I was angry when she suggested bringing a Wolf Rider into the house.

But now, Esbara looks at the man with a new perspective. Alagur is working on a task to ensure Marrida's success. Esbara remembers how the man has been behaving since he awoke from his coma and feels almost grateful for his presence. Something about Alagur's manner indicates that he's a decent man who is concerned for others, and who doesn't want to be a Wolf Rider.

He could have grown up in the city where he originated from — Chiva'na. It's the same city that Marrida suggested we move to. Esbara draws in his breath suddenly. *If Alagur was snatched from Chiva'na, the city wouldn't have been safe for us, either.*

Esbara feels regret wash over him. He regrets arguing with Marrida so many times.

I'm not going to do that anymore. I guess we'll know more when Marrida comes home. She'll be able to connect the few facts Alagur knows with what she has learnt. But when will she be home?

Alagur gets up. His list is complete and now he looks around, deciding what to do next. He realises that some of the belongings that Joharan has sent over will be redundant.

I guess we can sell those items for a fatter coin purse. It's safer to travel as a merchant with wares than a person with a fat coin purse.

He thinks back over his encounter with the father of this family.

He had no wares. He was on his way home with a fat coin purse.

He looks at the case designed to hold unused embers, like the one in his bag upstairs which is filled with fresh embers that he carved while he camped half a day's ride from the city with other Wolf Riders. Beside it lies the bedding and sheets that can be left too.

In Joharan's letter, he said to sell the items we don't need to buy extra food and secure shelter during the journey. Maybe we can take the bedding along to sell. It will be easy enough to carry, especially if we do manage to get a second wolf.

"We need to divide all this into five even loads." Alagur points around him with a wave of his hand. "One load will be the items I'm carrying with me through the tunnel. One load will be for Marrida to carry. That load will contain the lightest items. Two loads will be carried by Yalla. Whatever is in the last load will be left behind."

Damir and Esbara nod at the same time. Kalisa's face immediately takes on a quizzical look. She looks at Yalla, who is lying just outside the door leading to the inner courtyard.

"If she's pregnant, should she carry those packs?" she asks.

"Wolves like Yalla can carry a great weight, and she is larger than most others of her kind," Alagur explains. "When I went to get her, I saw wolves carrying their young on their own backs while travelling great distances over the mountains. Those young are often as large as full-grown ailep hounds."

"They're this big, Kalisa." Damir grins and holds out his hands, showing the size. "I've hunted them. They're as big as this roll of bedding and as heavy as you were at half your current age."

Damir pushes against the bedroll in front of him.

"A wolf such as Yalla can have anything from six to ten pups," Alagur continues, nodding at Damir to acknowledge his contribution. "Marrida says she felt at least eight pups. A yearling among Yalla's wolf pack would weigh the same as half of one of these packs."

Kalisa nods. She has seen Damir's drawings of ailep hounds, and in one he'd drawn Kalisa next to one to compare her size to the small wolf breed. Kalisa was around seven years old at the time. When Yalla stood up for the first time after waking up from her injuries, the wolf towered over the eleven-year-old girl.

Kalisa studies Yalla closely. She sees that the wolf's eyes are catching every movement or gesture made by the individuals present. Their eyes lock for a few moments, and again the girl notices the depth of intelligence within the yellow eyes of the wolf. A single thump on the floor conveys the emotion the wolf feels towards the girl, and makes Kalisa smile.

Kalisa's gaze moves to Alagur, and she realises he is watching her reaction to Yalla. He sits up straight – clearly the actions of the wolf fill him with pride.

* * *

Alagur recites part of The Truth in his mind.

> She whose name is unspoken
> A wolf she will claim from the wild
> And the man will learn her skill

If Marrida is the female in The Truth, am I the man?

Alagur shakes off the thought. He focuses instead on the task at hand.

"Esbara, do you have any rope I can use as extra bindings?"

Esbara nods. Stepping over Yalla, he walks to the storage cabinet situated at the far end of the courtyard. Yalla wags her tail as Esbara passes her, and he smiles down at her. He has grown fond of the wolf just like Kalisa, and will miss her too.

In the large inner courtyard where Yalla resided to recover from her wound, rows of rose bushes flank two sides of a central paved area. Walking over paving made of reddish-brown bricks and round yellow sandstone tiles with tiny white pebbles between them, Esbara remembers helping his mother tend to the roses. He gulps as a strong fragrance wafts over him with every gust of wind sweeping gently through the courtyard, evoking the memories.

Esbara lifts the heavy log of wood which is slotted across two metal prongs fastened to the storage door and places it on the ground behind him. No bolts are needed to lock the door as this building can only be accessed by the residents of the house. A soft creaking sound echoes in the courtyard when he opens one of the two wooden doors, giving him access to the room behind it. An ember sits on a shelf to his left. Using the tinder kit beside it, Esbara lights the tiny lamp in a practised motion.

Esbara lifts the stone containing the ember and looks around. Being here brings back a flood of memories.

Last time I was here, Mam was still alive. Esbara wipes away an involuntary tear with the back of his sleeve. *I was only four years old when Mam died during Kalisa's birthing. I was too young to understand what had happened.*

Esbara remembers two years later, when Marrida found him sitting at the door of the storage building, crying. She sat down next to him, telling him more about their parents as he could barely remember them. Then Kalisa, with her first tender steps, came over and made him smile when she tumbled straight into his lap.

I've doted on Kalisa ever since. It's her constant joy that has caused us to grow closer as the years have passed.

Esbara sees a loop of rope hanging from a hook in the rafters of the storage room. He puts the ember on a box near the ladder and climbs up to reach the rope. Lifting it off its hook, he takes one end of it and tugs at it to measure its strength. It's still as strong as it was when his mother used it to bind new shoots of rose bushes to make sure they grew upwards rather than sideways. The rose bushes tended to resist, so strong bindings were necessary.

Esbara drops the bundle of rope onto the floor below him, where it throws up a cloud of dust.

I must clean this place sometime. Perhaps I should start teaching Kalisa all the things Mam taught me.

Jumping off the ladder, which brings up an even larger cloud of dust, he brushes off his trousers as best he can. He then turns and extinguishes the ember with the back of the tinder kit and lifts the rope off the floor. Yalla gets up as Esbara approaches with the large bundle of rope and sidesteps to a more shaded corner of the courtyard as he walks back to the vestibule, where Alagur and Damir have already made three piles. Two are apparently the items Yalla will carry, and the other pile is the items Alagur will be carrying.

"This is the strongest rope we have got," Esbara explains. "It was what Mam used for them." Esbara points out of the window towards the rose bushes as he hands the rope to Alagur, who takes one end of it and tugs at it in much the same way as the boy did moments earlier.

Alagur nods approvingly.

CHAPTER TWENTY-TWO

MARRIDA AND SHARRIBA ARE DISCUSSING A PASSAGE from the eighth book that Marrida has dragged to the table when they hear the door of the library open below them. Sharriba looks over the bannister to find a Keeper standing below, looking up at her nervously.

"Can I help you with anything, Kashima?" Elder Sharriba asks somewhat impatiently. She's requested not to be disturbed when she is conducting lessons with Marrida, who has turned decidedly pale.

"Elder Sharriba, we have a visitor at the door who wishes to speak with you urgently." Kashima's calm, softly spoken voice echoes throughout the large library while her mannerisms betray how nervous she really is.

"Who is it?"

"He didn't say, but said he needed to speak with you."

Sharriba gets up, stretching her back for a moment. "I'll be back as soon as I can," she states to Marrida, turning and walking towards the stairway leading to the first floor of the library before Marrida can reply. Moments later, footsteps below indicate Sharriba has reached the ground floor quickly.

As the two sets of footsteps grow faint, Marrida realises she's alone once more. *I wonder who the visitor might be.* Sometimes women come to ask for a place at the Temple for a daughter, but men never visit. The Temple is forbidden to them; every man in the city knows this. Guards who accompany the Elder or Keepers when they're conducting business in the vast city always wait for them in the square in front of the Temple.

The guard who accompanied Elder Sharriba when she came to find me a few years ago was one of the city guards.

Marrida decides to go back to the books, leaving her pondering until later. She sets aside the book she is reading and pulls another one over. This book is in one of the ancient dialects she is learning; she studies the lettering on the binding for a few minutes, trying to determine if she can remember which of the six ancient dialects it is.

It seems to be one of the south-western dialects — perhaps the one from that island. Marrida tries to remember what name the island is known by, but it eludes her.

Elder Sharriba has explained to her previously that this book tells of ancient prophecies, passed down among those living on the island in the south-west. That Order there is as old, if not older, than the Keepers themselves, and its knowledge is valued by the Elders leading the Order. Sharriba has explained some of this during Ancient Histories lessons, but she's added more detail when she's alone with Marrida.

I wonder how the prophecies of these people fit in with everything I'm reading.

Marrida looks up from the book she is reading and places her hands under her chin. Staring blankly into the space before her, she tries to digest all the information she's read so far. She frowns in concentration as she processes the information she's learnt to commit it to her long-term memory.

The name Masharea is mentioned often — even more in the older books. Her mind drifts back to what Alagur told her about the first Wolf Riders. *These books are from before the Wolf Riders started their reign of terror in Keldarra.*

Marrida realises she's been in the library for a long period and wonders what is going on at her house. She looks back down at the many books on the table around her.

I think I have learnt all I can from these books.

She flicks through the book she's been reading little by little, glancing once more at the ancient words which adorn its pages, then closes it. She makes four even piles and, one by one, carries the piles of books to the shelves to place them back in their rightful positions. After fifteen minutes, she has completed the task, then she walks past the many shelves slowly. There are over three hundred bookcases on the second floor of the library alone, and Marrida is looking for books from a specific era — those likely to have been written a thousand years ago.

I know those books will give me more information about Yozan and the other first Wolf Rider — Sey'qar?

A soft spluttering sound from the ember distracts Marrida, and she realises it will cease to function soon. Embers are effective for a time, but they need replenishing with oil extracted from specific northern trees to last longer. Marrida looks around for a new ember, and she sees one at the top of the stairway to this floor. She uses her own tinder kit to light up the new ember, leaving the extinguished ember in its place and smirking at the thought of one of the current Temple Maidens having to refill it. It wasn't that long ago that the duty would have been hers.

Life was so much simpler back then. I didn't have the burden of all this knowledge--

Marrida is descending the stairway to the first floor when she spots a promising bookcase. She knows it holds books and parchments written just after the Temple of Ruh'nar was established, so most of these documents are some nine hundred years old. Placing the ember on a nearby table, she walks to the part of the bookcase that had sparked her interest.

After a minute of searching, she pulls out a thin book. It's covered by an ochre-coloured binding, held shut with a plaited cord which feels surprisingly soft to the touch. Marrida places the book on the table and looks closely at the knots.

Why would anyone use such complex knots? I can see the sheen on the knot, which I'm guessing comes from the oil in someone's fingers. This book must be used often.

Observing that the cord looks somewhat rough from so much use over time, Marrida straightens up. She's contemplating how to unfasten the knot when she hears two pairs of footsteps coming close. Glancing over her shoulder, she draws in her breath when she sees who is walking towards her.

With my uncle? Here? What's he doing inside the Temple?

The contents of the library are considered among the most prized possessions of the Keepers. It would normally be the last place Elder Sharriba would bring her uncle to find her.

"Uncle Joharan, why are you here?" Marrida splutters. A slight smile plays around the corners of Joharan's mouth.

"I told you to get supplies ready for the journey," he barks. "I knew I would find you here when you didn't return home."

"Your uncle came to explain to me that he'd asked you to get some new books for his workshop for him," Sharriba adds. "He was so insistent about seeing you that I brought him here."

Marrida glances at the older individuals, unable to say anything to either. Both are staring at her, seemingly waiting for a suitable explanation, but she can't help but notice that neither wants to ask questions in presence of the other person. Sharriba must know that Joharan could get one of his apprentices to fetch the books. Marrida is certain, from Sharriba's darting eyes, that she's considering that Marrida's presence in the library is down to something Joharan asked her to do.

Marrida starts feeling uncomfortable in the presence of her co-guardians. She looks down, feeling a lump form in her throat. It almost feels like she's been cornered by Sarayna and her friends. She wants to run away, but stands her ground.

"I'm studying," she says. "I need to catch up on my missed studies."

Joharan and Sharriba glance at one another, but Marrida, with her head still bowed, doesn't notice the interplay between them. Joharan observes the woman beside him with keen eyes, reading her mannerisms. She's the reason why he never took a life partner. Once she was a beautiful young Temple Maiden when he, in his prime, encountered her as she swept the Temple's steps.

Joharan had been walking home from his grandmother's house, located at the south end of the city, to the house in the artisan quarter that is now his home and workshop. Their eyes had locked as he walked past Sharriba, and she'd smiled alluringly at him. From that day, they'd spoken often as he passed the Temple.

One day in late autumn, he asked her the critical question. Even though she was a decade older than he, she'd given his request serious thought. However, things changed when she was called to attendance by the sitting Elder. Sharriba had been selected as her successor, and becoming an Elder had to be more important than becoming any person's life partner.

"It's too complicated for me to explain," Sharriba stated at the time. However, Joharan wasn't listening, As soon as she'd said that she didn't want to be his life partner, he walked away, angered by the decision and muttering audibly that he'd never take a life partner if he couldn't have her.

Sharriba looks up sorrowfully when the memory passes through her mind, remembering how upset she was, and she fights back the tears that want to well up. She looks away.

I wish I could take back the words he never wanted to hear then, and which still cause him to flinch with anger now.

Sharriba couldn't ever tell Joharan the real reason why she couldn't accept his offer. She'd done a vision later that fateful day, seeing the events as he arrived home. He stormed in and announced to his parents that he would never take anyone as a life partner. Then he watched from the room above as his parents argued over his decision. It was the same place where Joharan would later find Damir listening to the test on Marrida.

The day before her initiation as an Acolyte, Sharriba rushed through the streets to the workshop where Joharan was helping his father. At her request, Joharan reassured her that their love would remain a secret which he'd take to his grave.

Many years later, after his mother had died and his father's new life partner had given him another son, Joharan would often hear his father mumble, "I hope this one comes home with a life partner."

Despite his father's misgivings, pride had shone in his eyes when Joharan got accepted into the Council of Seven as part of the city's advisory council for commerce. Although Joharan stayed without a life partner as he'd vowed, he was genuinely happy for his brother Markalo when he brought the beautiful Eshara home.

Sharriba turns to Joharan and looks at him searchingly for a few moments.

I wonder what life would have been like as his life partner. I can see the worry lines on his face, and there's a constant bitterness that makes his tan look less handsome. But he still loves me. I can see that. All these years and his love for me has never wavered once.

Sharriba suddenly feels as awkward as Marrida, who is becoming more and more uncomfortable as the minutes pass. She glances up discreetly and wonders why her uncle and the Elder are looking at each other so sadly, then she looks down again, waiting nervously and plucking at the edge of the outer tunic that she wears over her light-blue dress.

When a door slams below them and half a dozen Keepers walk into the ground floor area of the library, chatting, this effectively dispels the trance silencing Joharan and Sharriba. They smile nervously at one another for a moment, then their normal expressions return to their faces, indicating that they're ready to turn their attention to Marrida once more.

"I told your uncle you were here for studies." Sharriba's voice is quiet so as not to alert the Keepers on the ground floor.

"I should take Marrida home with me." Joharan also is whispering now.

Sharriba nods.

"But my studies," Marrida protests. She places her hand instinctively on top of the thin book she found earlier.

Sharriba walks up to the table and looks at the book for a moment. It's a journal she started writing when she became an Acolyte. She smiles, knowing the information that is in the book, then glances at Marrida beside her. The young woman looks up at her with pleading eyes. A resolute nod, and then Sharriba's hand motions quickly. She knows her next actions will probably haunt her for the remainder of her life.

Bending over slightly, she unties the knot in the bindings and refastens it with a much simpler knot. Then she picks up the book and gives it to Marrida.

"You'd best take your studies with you. You'll need the information that's contained in this book."

As Marrida's face registers her surprise, Sharriba turns to the old man standing a few paces away and looks at him for a long moment.

"I'll make sure that the group below is distracted," she says firmly. "You take Marrida with you."

Not giving either of them time to respond, Sharriba walks off briskly, and moments later she has descended the stairway to the ground floor. Joharan and Marrida hear her speak sharply to the Keepers, saying, "I need you to assist me to gather several books I need for my work."

Sharriba's voice grows distant as she and the group of Keepers walk to the furthest right-hand corner of the vast library — as far away as possible from the stairway and the door leading out of the room. Joharan listens for a couple of minutes before signalling to Marrida, who grabs the thin book she's absentmindedly put back on the table. She follows her uncle without protest.

When they arrive at the library door, he opens it and scrutinises the long corridor to check for people. When he's certain the corridor is empty, he takes Marrida's slender shoulder and walks hurriedly along it, causing Marrida to struggle to keep pace with his long strides.

At the top of the large stairway, Joharan once again listens out for other people. Marrida glances down, hoping that Sarayna and her friends aren't around. When he's certain that the vestibule is empty, Joharan nods.

Marrida knows that most Acolytes will be studying in the various rooms in the vast Temple, realising that normally she'd be in the one in the far right-hand corner of the vestibule right now.

Marrida looks up at her uncle, who smiles at her.
"Are you up for a quick run?"
Marrida nods.

The pair descends the stairway, and as they approach the bottom of it, their pace increases. Marrida holds the book tightly against her body with one hand, and with her other hand she gathers up the skirt of her dress and flowing robe, holding her clothing around the book to mask it from anyone who may see her. It isn't far from the stairway to the outer door and the square beyond, but it seems odd to Marrida that her uncle leads her through the vestibule's more shaded side. It's almost as if he's familiar with it.

A few moments later, they stand in the bright mid-afternoon sun.

CHAPTER TWENTY-THREE

Marrida looks around the square, shielding her eyes from the glare of the sun, and to her surprise finds it's empty of its usual occupants.

"Let's get you back to your house."

Joharan puts his arm around Marrida's shoulders and squeezes her close to him in a gesture of affection he hasn't shown since she was very young.

The last time he did this was just before Sharriba came for me. It makes me feel good inside.

Marrida smiles suddenly. She feels totally and completely happy in that moment, as though nothing in the world could unsettle her.

Dropping her skirt and cloak, Marrida positions the book in one hand and copies her uncle's gesture, putting her arm around Joharan and looking up at him with a broad smile of gratitude. Joharan nods approval, and the duo walk back to Marrida's house. Their pace is slow, and to anyone passing them, it will seem as if they are merely enjoying a stroll through the streets, basking in the sunshine.

Marrida leans into the armpit of the old man beside her, feeling like she's twelve years younger. In those days, she would accompany her uncle whenever he went to get supplies for his workshop from various parts of the city. Marrida feels the sun's rays touch the bare skin of her face. The sunlight would give her a tan if she were to spend enough time outdoors and suddenly, Marrida wants the walk to last for hours so she can enjoy the weather.

She glances up at the azure blue sky. *Damir said that after the chilly morning, there would be mists blanketing the city this evening. There's hardly a cloud in the sky.*

Joharan sees Marrida's upward gaze and looks at the sky too, wondering what has fascinated her so much.

I wonder why Uncle Joharan and Elder Sharriba looked at each other in that way, Marrida ponders. I'm certain a lot more is going on between them then either has said. It's definitely friendship…no — it's more than simple friendship. I wonder if Elder Sharriba really was as beautiful as I imagine she was when she was young.

Could it be that her uncle thought Sharriba was beautiful too?

Marrida's mind turns to the book she found in the library.

I won't know what is written in it until I get home. Together with all the new things I learnt today, that book could give more answers. I'm surprised Sharriba was so open.

Normally only the more advanced Acolytes learn the information Sharriba has entrusted Marrida with when they are initiated as Keepers, and many only become Keepers fifteen or more years into their studies. Sharriba mentioned that Eshara, Marrida's mother, had been a Keeper for only two years when Markalo asked her to be his life partner. The Elder explained that it wasn't common for a Keeper to walk away from her calling, and Marrida noticed the sadness in the old woman's voice when she said this. In fact, Sharriba looked so sad that Marrida didn't continue the conversation, instead asking about some rituals she'd been reading about in one of the books.

Joharan and Marrida reach the end of the street where her house is located. Joharan stops walking, stands in front of his niece and holds her shoulders with his large hands, looking at her for a moment.

"You burned those letters?" he enquires quietly.

She nods. "Before I left this morning, while they were getting the things ready for the journey."

"You showed Alagur the letter too? He knows what's expected of him?"

Marrida nods once more. Despite frowning sternly, Joharan sounds like he's talking to a young child rather than a woman less than a year from her Second Rites.

Joharan points at the book in Marrida's arms. "Do you know what that book is?"

He's never seen the book himself, and he was surprised when Sharriba so readily handed it to Marrida.

I suspect Sharriba knows what's written in that book. I guess I'll find out one day, if it's appropriate.

"You had better go home now." Joharan's lips curl into a smile. He gives his niece a long hug which betrays the emotions he's feeling at this moment. After a few minutes, he pushes the young woman away from himself and places a loving kiss on her forehead – another gesture she last experienced when she was much younger.

Joharan looks at Marrida for several minutes in silence. *I'm going to miss you.* Forcing himself to let go of Marrida, he turns abruptly and walks back to his own house a few streets away.

* * *

MARRIDA WATCHES HER UNCLE'S SLOW-PACED DEPARTURE until he turns a corner and vanishes from sight. She notes from his slumped shoulders that the emotion is running deeper than the man wants to admit to her, or to himself.

He'll probably never tell me his true feelings.

Perhaps Elder Sharriba has a hand in all that has happened. Marrida attempts to convince herself that this is the case as she glances down at the book she's holding firmly against her chest – so firmly that her knuckles have gone pale and the edge of the leather is cutting into her fingers. *If what Elder Sharriba said is in fact true, then the fate I'm witnessing now wasn't set in motion a few weeks ago. It began many centuries ago with the actions of two men. The oldest books in the Temple library mentioned a faraway city almost a season's travel from here. On the back of a wolf such as Yalla, could I be back for Kalisa's First Rites?*

All at once, Marrida feels tears sting in her eyes as she realises that, for the first time ever, she won't be in Ruh'nar for the festive day to celebrate her sister's birthing day in the autumn.

Marrida paces forward a few steps, her mind turning to the city her uncle mentioned in his letter.

It's called Azaquina, but Uncle Joharan didn't say anything about it. Alagur says Bergas came from Azaquina. I wonder what sort of person Bergas is. He sounds nice, he's only the same age as Kalisa. We're making the journey with a wolf, but he's alone and on foot. I hope he will make it home. And I hope that Alagur and I will be welcome when we visit.

Marrida glances once more at the precious book she is holding in her arms as she walks almost mechanically towards her house. Each step takes her closer to a new destiny, both for her and for those inside the house.

What will this destiny be? Marrida ponders. *But I know something will happen because of what my uncle has planned.* Each step feels heavier than the last as the burden of the task ahead weighs down on Marrida. *Why am I the one to end up in this situation? Why not someone else?*

As she arrives at her front door, Marrida frowns. She stops walking and stares closely at the place where Alagur and Yalla lay, left for dead. Marrida wonders again how things would have turned out if she'd stayed indoors with her siblings.

What if the man with black hair had come back and found Alagur instead?

Marrida shudders at the thought. She's certain Samur would have sought revenge by targeting nearby houses.

His boot could have kicked our door down, and Esbara could well have been in City of Wolves now. And Alagur? What about him?

A lump forms in Marrida's throat as she realises that she didn't just save Alagur that day, she'd also saved her brother from abduction.

And Samur did come back, and he said something odd before riding off. I hope he thinks that Alagur is either a prisoner or dead.

* * *

ELSEWHERE IN THE CITY, ANOTHER PERSON IS CONTEMPLATING recent events. Before going to the Temple, Joharan walked to the street where Marrida and her siblings live. In daylight, he studies the place where Alagur and the wolf fell. Now, Joharan recalls that he intended to get travel papers for Marrida and Alagur, and perhaps find out more about the attack too.

The Council of Seven is the governing body of Ruh'nar. Each city has such a group of people who, together with others, create the laws of the city. As an official, Joharan can ask for travel papers at the Office of the Merchant Clerk; others would have to do this at the Office of Law.

Joharan was returning home, but now he diverts his route and turns left towards where the official buildings.

If Marrida is going to travel, I can make sure she can leave through the gates in the east wall without too many questions being asked.

Joharan knows he breached a taboo when he knocked on the Temple's outer door, standing in the darkest shade so as not to be seen by any passers-by. The shock etched on Kashima's face was evident. She'd opened the door only a small amount, then almost slammed it shut when she saw a man standing on the steps. When Joharan didn't leave, she turned utterly annoyed.

"I'm here as an official representative of the Council of Seven--" was the only information he gave her, then he stared her down until she let him in. He could hear her shoo away nearby girls and women before pulling the door open, and a moment later, Joharan found himself in the grand vestibule where Kashima pushed him forcefully into a small room next to the front doors.

She is a lot stronger I would have given her credit for, Joharan thinks, smirking for a moment. *That room was nothing more than a storage cupboard.*

Joharan chuckles as he recalls the speed at which Kashima rushed through the vestibule to the large white door dividing it from the Elder's private chambers. Only minutes later, the same rush of footsteps returned.

"She'll…see…you," Kashima said, severely out of breath.

Joharan was escorted to the Elder's private chambers, and as he entered the room, he noted that they weren't so different from the last time he'd been there. Forty years ago – perhaps longer – Sharriba had secretly smuggled him inside the Temple to show him the artwork in these inner chambers.

I can't recall how long ago that happened.

This time, Sharriba wasn't in her chambers when he arrived. It betrays the reason for Kashima being out of breath. He sat down and waited patiently, looking up when Sharriba arrived. After some discussion, during which Joharan pleaded with Sharriba to help with his plans, she motioned to him to follow her. He was surprised when he was guided to the first floor of the library.

Her responses were so neutral. Did I persuade her? Only time will tell. I can make certain I play my part now--

* * *

AFTER TWENTY MINUTES OF WALKING BRISKLY, Joharan arrives in front of a massive building made of dark grey stone slabs, chiselled to even sizes by stonemasons. The doorway is framed by white marble, and the entrance, several steps up from the road, consists of red granite slabs. Joharan checks each window with a keen eye for detail, mostly to ensure none are broken.

As each window is small, there are many to allow for an even amount of natural light to enter the building to reduce the need for embers. All four floors are constructed in the same uniform pattern. After a few minutes, Joharan spots four broken windows high up, showing that the building was targeted by the Wolf Riders in the recent attack. He sees curtains flapping softly each time the mid-afternoon breeze picks up, and there are marks on the outer door that could only come from the impact of heavy axes. The wood used in this door is one of the hardest that can be found, which must have been one reason for the Wolf Riders' failure to get inside the building.

Joharan stands for a few minutes, observing the familiar building with some misgivings. Why was it targeted? What were the Wolf Riders after? The Wolf Riders are attacking more frequently, the need to increase the city's security is paramount, yet nothing seems to be done about it.

Travelling freely has been curtailed significantly, and Marrida isn't a travelling merchant which means he stands less chance of getting the damned travel papers for her. Joharan sighs deeply, opens the door, and steps inside.

He is met by two clerks who bow their heads in acknowledgement. Joharan notices that his visit doesn't seem to be a surprise to them. After the recent attack, many of the government officials must have visited the Office to seek answers and offer solutions to what to do next time the Wolf Riders attack.

I guess they want me to answer questions they can't or won't answer.

Joharan looks the two men over with critical eyes, his gaze turning stern when he's met with blank stares. Joharan knows he needs to divert their attention from his real reason for being there.

"What is the status of the defences?" Joharan stares hard at a man by the name of Marguna with shoulder-length black hair, who points over his shoulder at one of the broken windows.

"We had several fires. Reports are still arriving of snatchings that happened. Three Wolf Riders and one of the wolves were killed."

Joharan notes the coldness in the man's voice. *Why would he be so harsh towards me now?* Something about the way he is speaking to the older man seems wrong. *I guess I need to be cautious what I say, especially as he mentioned the Wolf Riders so readily.*

"Did we capture any of them?"
Marguna shakes his head.
"How much damage did the fires do?"
The other clerk, Shabrua, answers. "We had a dozen or so buildings destroyed in the fires on the south side of the city."

The answer confirms Joharan's own conclusions from what he's seen from his sleeping room window. He nods to confirm he understand, then turns to look over the windows in the room adjoining the vestibule, his eyes resting on the broken window. Finding no more urgent questions he wants to ask, he turns and brings up the reason for the visit.

"May I see Albramar, please?"

The clerks look at each other for a moment questioningly, then Marguna motions towards Joharan to follow him. The two men, Marguna in the lead, walk to the end of the dark corridor beyond the vestibule. Shabrua watches them go, a puzzled frown betraying his curiosity as to why Joharan wants to see the Merchant Clerk when travel is at its most dangerous. After few moments, he shrugs his shoulders and goes back to the work he was doing before the old man's arrival.

"Joharan Kayrsan wants to meet with you, Albramar," Marguna states before leaving Joharan with the Merchant Clerk. Once they're alone, Albramar looks at the old man with curiosity etched all over his face.

CHAPTER TWENTY-FOUR

A SOFT KNOCK ON THE OUTER DOOR tells the occupants of the house that either Marrida is home, or they have another unexpected visitor. Alagur walks into the courtyard, and the youngsters notice him signalling to Yalla to stay silent.

Esbara walks to the door and listens for a moment. Another knock. He opens the door and smiles broadly, looking over his shoulder.
"It's Marrida."
"I thought she was going to be at the Temple until the evening."
Marrida frowns on hearing Kalisa's words. "I thought I was going to be too. I did talk with Elder Sharriba for most of the time, but--" Marrida stops speaking for a moment. "Can I settle down before I go into details?"

Esbara nods, staring at the book Marrida is holding as he steps aside to let her past. Marrida's attention is drawn to the five large piles of possessions stacked around the vestibule, then to Alagur who had stepped back inside from the courtyard.

"We've been a bit busy sorting things out to get both of you ready for travelling." Esbara smiles again. He is starting to enjoy guessing which questions Marrida may have in her mind, but hasn't yet voiced. Marrida, who has got used to this new side to her brother, nods in response as she places the thin leather-bound book on top of one of the piles.

She unfastens the bindings of her cloak and drapes it over a nearby chair, picks the book back up and walks silently into the front room where she sits down on the sofa. Alagur, who has been busying himself finalising the packing of food in the cooking room, rushes into the front room and, after some hesitation, sits down next to her. Damir, who's been helping Alagur in the cooking room, arrives in the front room a moment later. Of all occupants of the house, only Kalisa was upstairs when Marrida returned home. She runs into the front room too, as curious as everyone else when she sees the book Marrida is holding.

Kalisa flops down on the floor against Yalla's flank. After a moment of indecision, Esbara follows her example and sits cross-legged on the floor near his younger sister. Damir sits near the wolf on Kalisa's other side, leaning his back against a cushion partially propped up against the wall.

When everyone is seated comfortably, Marrida looks around the room for a few moments, looking last at Alagur beside her. He flashes a brief, encouraging smile at her. Marrida then glances down at the book. She doesn't even know what its content is, or how it fits in with the knowledge she's gleaned from the books she has read in the library.

"I guess this is the most important book as I was allowed to take it with me. That's unusual, by the way." Marrida considers the almost cryptic words of the Elder. "Elder Sharriba told me that this book will help me during my travels."

It suddenly occurs to Marrida that Sharriba knows she'll be travelling. Did her uncle inform the Elder?

Marrida looks at the bindings of the book once more. Sharriba loosened the bindings with ease and retied them quickly, but the bindings had been impossible to untie when Marrida tried to undo them.

It was almost like the bindings were covered in oil when I tried.

Marrida pauses for a moment and breathes out a deep sigh, then opens the book slowly. It seems so familiar, yet at the same time, the book appears unfamiliar. Marrida glances sideways at Alagur, meeting his eyes and recognising in them the same curiosity she is feeling. Chill creeps over her skin as she runs her hand slowly over the cover. It feels like very old leather.

When Marrida lifts the book, she feels the ochre-coloured rope fall to the side of her legs. Inside the book, she finds parchment covered with writing she recognises as Sharriba's hand. She looks more closely.

Strange, it's entirely written in a dialect spoken in Ruh'nar. Why would she use this dialect instead of any of the six taught in the Temple? Marrida frowns, puzzled. *This is unexpected. It's one of the books Sharriba always used to push back onto the shelf if I tried to select it, but now she has given me the book freely. The Elder gave it to me. She encouraged me to take it with me. She didn't even hide it from Uncle Joharan.*

"This is strange," Marrida mumbles under her breath.
"What is?"
Marrida looks at Alagur and thinks about how to answer the

question. "This journal was written by Elder Sharriba."

"Who's that?"

Esbara's question surprises Marrida. "I thought told you – she's the Elder in charge at the Temple. She gave me this book – or should I say journal – when Uncle Joharan came to collect me."

Damir recognises the name immediately. "Joharan has mentioned Elder Sharriba to me relating to his dealings with the Office of the Merchant Clerk--"

"You mean to say she let your uncle into the building?" Marrida is caught by the amazement in Esbara's voice. He's remembered that men are forbidden inside the building.

"Yes – he accompanied Sharriba as she returned to the library. They seem to know one another very well from somewhere."

"How?" Kalisa's voice comes out in a shriek that echoes through the room as she asks the question every individual, Marrida included, wants an answer to.

Kalisa glances at Damir and he smiles at her in delight. He notices she's a lot more confident talking about things than she used to be when she visited her uncle's workshop. He likes the newfound confidence.

"I was looking at this book, trying to see how to undo the bindings." Marrida holds up the end of one of the ropes. "They arrived – he was with her. She didn't take the book away from me like she's done before. She untied it so easily, and then tied the knots I just pulled apart. And then the others came into the library."

"What others?" Alagur's question makes Marrida jump.

"The Keepers. They came in, and Elder Sharriba made sure they didn't know my uncle and I were there. She pushed this book into my hands and told me to take it with me. Apparently, it will help me."

There's a long silence in the room when Marrida has finished her brief account of what happened at the Temple. Both Alagur and Esbara's expressions are thoughtful. In other circumstances, it would have been funny as they mirror one another so perfectly.

"Are you ever going to read that book and see why it's so important?"

Marrida smiles. *Damir's right. How else will I know if I'm right about the book?*

"Push that table closer so I can place the book on it." Marrida nods towards the dark wooden table in the centre of the room. Alagur, Damir and Esbara all get up at the same time. Between them, with some effort, they carry the table to within an arm's length of Marrida. She places the book flat on the surface, then uses her hands to pull the sofa closer to the table.

"Grab one of the benches from the cooking room so you can sit on this side of the table." Marrida points to her right where the room is clear. Alagur nods, and in a few strides leaves the room, watched by Marrida. She makes a mental note of the vast improvement in his motion.

When he returns, he places the bench next to the table with Esbara's help, then walks around to sit next to Marrida. Damir sits down to his left a moment later, while Esbara sits on the bench nearest to Marrida. Kalisa grabs the soft cushion Damir was using and props it on the bench before climbing up and kneeling on it. Leaning her folded arms on the table, she looks with growing curiosity towards the book.

The rhythmic clicking of wolf claws followed by a soft thud tells everyone in the room that Yalla has decided she is bored with the conversation and wants some sleep on the cool floor tiles of the vestibule instead. The contented yipping coming from the wolf makes all five around the table chuckle, even in the seriousness of the moment.

Marrida turns her attention to the book once more, studying the elegant writing more closely. It shows the pen strokes of a steady hand, unlike these days when there's a visible shaking in the Elder's writing, indicating that Elder Sharriba isn't in the best of health. At almost seventy-six years of age, she's nearing the end of her life. For a moment, Marrida feels her thoughts trail off, wondering if she'll ever see her mentor again in this lifetime, but as quickly as the thought enters her mind, she dismisses it. She doesn't want to think of such things.

The fading of the ink tells of age. The ink used for writing is black in appearance when it's in liquid form, but once it's on the parchment, it takes on a distinct blue-purple colour. However, time fades the colour to light blue, and many of the books and manuscripts held at the library have been transcribed onto fresh parchment with fresh ink so the knowledge won't be lost to time. The Keepers also commit important passages of text to memory, as Marrida has learnt to do herself recently. Then she recalls the quick notes she wrote on scraps of parchment and reaches into her inner pocket, pulling out the delicate bundle and placing the pile on the table near the book.

"What are those?" Esbara questions, pointing at the scraps.

"Those are notes I made when I was alone," Marrida replies. "I found a book which Elder Sharriba always forbade me to read, and when she got called away, I copied its text on them."

Alagur laughs aloud at the idea that Marrida went around the library looking at forbidden books. His laughter sets off giggles in Marrida, and soon everyone is laughing until tears are streaming down their cheeks.

"I guess Elder Sharriba wouldn't have been so accommodating if she'd known you'd done that," Alagur manages to say between waves of laughter.

"No, she wouldn't."

The mirth has broken the silent awkwardness of the moment. When Marrida has wiped away the last of her tears of laughter, she turns back to the book and, breathing deeply to control her emotion, starts reading it.

The passage was written some fifty years previously by a young Acolyte Sharriba, noting a vision she did when she used the Stone of Truth for the first time. Marrida stops reading for a moment to try to picture the Elder as just a few years older than she is now. She can almost see Sharriba as a beautiful young woman, the grey-green eyes seeming even brighter than they are now, and even more piercing than they appeared to Marrida when Sharriba was in her uncle's workshop.

Marrida continues reading without hurrying, rereading the text to commit it to memory. Then one word jumps from the page – wolf. Seemingly, Sharriba saw an unusually large silver-grey-and-white wolf in the vision. And that detail apparently puzzled and troubled the young Sharriba greatly.

This is a vision of the past, yet Yalla looks just as Sharriba describes here, Marrida thinks.

Sharriba describes how the Elder in charge became angry when the Acolyte told her about the vision. She was told never to utter a word of it to anyone.

A frown forms itself on Marrida's forehead. Now she isn't only confused, but also angry. *Why was knowing about wolves forbidden for a Keeper?*

"What were the words from the legend about a wolf, Alagur?" Marrida asks. The man speaks the words in a neutral tone.

SHE WHOSE NAME IS UNSPOKEN
A WOLF SHE WILL CLAIM FROM THE WILD
AND THE MAN WILL LEARN HER SKILL

While Alagur repeats the words, he casts a puzzled look at Marrida.

"I think there's a connection between that legend and something Elder Sharriba saw in a vision." Marrida glances at Alagur for a moment before she rereads the page once more.

"What sort of connection?" Alagur asks, placing his hand gently on Marrida's left forearm. Marrida looks up at him once more and thinks for a long moment, weighing up Sharriba's words against the words of the legend known to the Wolf Riders.

"I think the event that caused Sey'qar and Yozan to establish the Wolf Riders is known to the Keepers, and they're keeping it from the world."

Marrida's words hit Alagur like a lightning strike. He sits gaping at her, a flood of questions welling up inside him. But he doesn't want to verbalise any of them because the whole idea is so shocking.

Marrida looks intently at the man. That he's shocked by her revelation is obvious.

"How did you think the Wolf Riders started then?" she asks him coldly. "They started because someone – probably those two people you mentioned to me – was making them into a force of evil instead of what they were before."

"How do you know that?" This time the question comes from Esbara, who's as dumbfounded as Alagur about the revelations he's hearing. In answer, Marrida simply picks up the pile of torn parchments and looks through them until she finds the piece she wants.

"This is written in one of the six ancient dialects, but it tells of other people in charge many thousands of years ago," she explains. "I can't make out all the words, but there is a name and a word I did manage to translate."

She gives the parchment to Esbara, who studies it for a few moments. He has gained some basic understanding of the dialects during his training at the Academy of Warfare and recognises the name on the parchment.

"Queltha – but that land is a myth--"

"No, it isn't," Marrida interjects. "This text which Sharriba wrote contains the name Queltha, and there's more." Marrida looks at Alagur once more and pauses for a few moments. "She says here that in her vision, she saw the Wolf Riders as a force that protected this land against those who came from Queltha."

Alagur sits back on the sofa, a scowl of anger such as Marrida has never previously seen crossing his face slowly. His tanned skin becomes several shades darker and redder.
"He *lied* to me! That Samur, he lied to me!"

Marrida moves away from him, and Kalisa grabs Esbara's arm in fright. Seeing the reaction of the younger people around him, Alagur breathes deeply to restrain his outburst of emotion. When he feels calm enough, he explains.

"Do you remember the retelling about Samur, and how he chose to become a Wolf Rider?"

He directs his question towards Marrida, who nods. The retelling is still raw in her mind – surely no person could be capable of an act as vile as the one Alagur told her Samur committed.

CHAPTER TWENTY-FIVE

SAMUR SEEMS TO BE THE ONE NAME that always pops up whenever a discussion is about the beginnings of the Wolf Riders, and today's discussion seems to be the most important of them all.

"He told me about Sey'qar and Yozan. He said they made the Wolf Riders as an act of defiance against your kind. Your kind as in the Keepers of Truth who – according to Samur, at least – are the ones who caused all the upheaval in this world."

Marrida stares at Alagur. His words sting deep into her being. All her life – or, at least, the part of it she's spent at the Temple – she's been told that the Wolf Riders are the evil in the world. However, Marrida realises that Alagur's beliefs have been shaped by the actions of the people he lived with for more than half of his life. It surprises Marrida that a month can change life so much for two different people.

I'm puzzled though, about Samur, Marrida thinks, and for a moment likely feeling as angry as Alagur. *Why did Samur choose to join the Wolf Riders? Alagur says Samur is ten years older than he, so believes it.*

Marrida was relieved when Samur had not returned, at least not right away, after he rode off, leaving Alagur alone outside her door. Alagur reacted angrily at first when she told him about this. Later, she told him in almost a whisper that after she and her siblings had carried him and the wolf into the house and hastily cleaned the street of the evidence of the attack, she had heard Samur come back. She'd looked through a tiny peephole in the door and seen his angry face, but more than that, she'd heard him cursing.

Alagur's initial anger turned to shock when she had revealed Samur's exact words. *"I'm sure Alagur was eager for me to go on, so he could betray me!"*

Repeating words to Alagur was hard for Marrida, but after she'd spoken them, she reached out and placed a hand gently on his arm. She wasn't sure if she understood the impact of the words, but she sensed the hurt that Alagur felt. This small gesture turned mistrust into the beginnings of a friendship. Alagur realised from Marrida's words that she was someone with a deep inner wisdom. Until that moment, he'd seen her as an immature girl; from that moment, he saw a woman he could respect.

Marrida remembers having written down something important. Her fingers flip quickly through the small pile of parchment until they pull out one of the last pieces she transcribed, which she hands to Alagur. He gazes, confused, at the unfamiliar dialect for a moment, then looks at Marrida.

"I cannot read this."

"Proof that the Wolf Riders weren't always like they are today." Marrida looks at Alagur with a stern gaze, easily matching Joharan's familiar expression. "This," she points her slender forefinger at the parchment, "proves Wolf Riders were once helping to keep order. They even fought against an ancient oppressor in a past long forgotten now. All the way back in The Old Days, or earlier."

Esbara, listening intently to the conversation, frowns as he thinks deeply. *I need to remember what I talked about with Marrida when we argued.*

"Marrida, I need say a few things, too," he says in a neutral tone. "It may be that this is the same thing that made you wary of me wanting to be a city protector. Please, hear me out. I argued for becoming one for the same reason as the original Wolf Riders came into being. It's the right thing for me to become a city protector, just as the Wolf Riders originally did things for the right reasons, too."

"What do you mean?"

"If I understand correctly from what you just said, the Wolf Riders were like soldiers before those two men came along, right?" Esbara looks at Alagur for confirmation and continues when he meets a confused stare. "If you need to do things to make sure the Wolf Riders cannot continue as they are, I need to do them, too — my way."

Marrida stares towards the fire in the fireplace to find answers. She realises straight away how correct her brother is. *Who am I to deny him his choice of vocation when I am going into a potentially dangerous situation myself?*

Marrida acknowledges Esbara's reasoning with a curt nod. "I think you have proved yourself as an adult, as one should expect from someone who has gone through First Rites."

Esbara notices an accepting smile appears on Marrida's face when she answers the implied question in his statement. Alagur looks back and forth between the two siblings, wondering what their words mean.

I wonder how much of what I've said has influenced whatever decisions they've made. I've heard them arguing while I've been here. They argued as children, but they have resolved their differences as two adults would.

As confused as the situation makes him, both about what Marrida has said about the Wolf Riders and the somewhat cryptic conversation between the siblings, Alagur feels it's not his place to ask for clarifications. His gaze fixes on Kalisa's face, and the girl stares back with a knowing "I know something, and you do not" smile.

Alagur glances down at the parchment that's still in his hand, squinting his eyes to make sense of the unfamiliar dialect. The longer Alagur stares, the more familiar the letters feel, but where he's seen the letters before evades him. Next to him, Marrida turns a page of the book. Alagur listens absentmindedly as she reads quickly through the second page. It seems to be an account of Sharriba's encounter with her own Elder.

I can tell she feels grateful for however she's been treated by this Elder Sharriba, Alagur thinks. *I can hear it in Marrida's voice.*

"The Elder apparently selected Sharriba as her successor. It explains how the young Sharriba was torn between her mind and heart."

It seems to me that she poured all her feelings into this book. I wonder why the Keepers all those decades ago selected her for entry into the Temple. Where were they from? It's very much like what happened to me.

"Acolyte Sharriba's skill developed very fast. She was in the third period of her study after just five years in the Temple. She says here that she was visiting a market on the western side of the city – that market doesn't exist anymore, by the way – and she met our uncle there. He was still a child at the time."

"Oooh, really," Kalisa and Esbara say at the same time, glancing at one another.

I'm learning my skill just as quickly, Marrida thinks. "They met by chance again years later when Joharan was a year away from Second Rites," she adds a moment later. "Sharriba was twenty-eight years old by then. She recognised him from their earlier encounter. Feelings grew between them, but her selection as the next Elder meant she couldn't become Joharan's life partner because it would have meant leaving the Temple."

"Aww!" Kalisa blurts out.

"I guess that explains their glances at one another when they came to find me," Marrida says softly. "She mentions Joharan a few times on these pages. She mentions feeling regret for having had to make the difficult choice. I guess I understand how lucky Papa was when he asked Mam."

A thought occurs to Marrida, and she stops reading for a moment. *What if my mother asked Sharriba because she knew about her connection with Uncle Joharan?* Marrida shakes her head, dismissing the idea.

Marrida slowly tells the four individuals around her what it says in the book.

"Sharriba tells of a second vision she did when she had only just become a Keeper. It describes a city here." Marrida frowns and looks at Alagur again, but breaks into a smile when she's met with concern. She picks up another of the pieces of parchment that are scattered over the table, comparing the words against those written in Sharriba's book. Using the words in the book, Marrida translates the words on the parchment into the dialect common to Ruh'nar. After translating, she glances back at Alagur. She sees recognition on his face, a pensive stare partly masked by the still present scowl.

"The text references a town you mentioned whenever you spoke of Bergas," Marrida states gently, then pauses for a moment and waits. Noticing Alagur isn't truly listening to her, she tugs his tunic gently. "I know you are thinking about the things Samur said. I can tell it from your face."

"Huh…what?"

"I think you did something good," Marrida says gently. "You said Bergas is from Azaquina. We're going there first, right?" Alagur nods slowly. "If he reaches his home, he can help me translate local books. I hope he can--"

Alagur's scowl is gone in an instant and he flashes a smile at her. The image of a flower unfolding its petals in the sunshine after a long period of rainfall enters Marrida's mind. It's obvious from the pleading look in Alagur's eyes that he hopes that the words she has just spoken will come true.

"*When* he reaches his home," Marrida hears Alagur whisper ever so quietly. She raises her hand as a signal for the others to stay silent.

"I think that we will be welcome there," Marrida says, "as you're welcome here--"

Alagur cannot help smiling broadly at Marrida, who in turn feels some of her reservations ebb away. She smiles back at him, a warm, happy smile, while unnoticed by the two of them, Esbara, Damir and Kalisa glance at one another with knowing looks on their faces. They all keep silent, though, as none is willing to break the spell of what is happening right in front of them. None of them dares to say anything in case Marrida and Alagur shy away from expressing their feelings so publicly to one another.

After several minutes of staring at Alagur, feeling her heart beating faster because of the magnetism of his bright blue eyes, Marrida tears herself away from the moment and forces herself to continue reading the book, silently this time. She doesn't dare speak because she's certain her voice will break under the new emotions racing through her body. Months ago, Marrida had hoped to meet someone she could love as quickly as her parents fell in love with each other.

It may not happen in a day, but it happens if we spend a season together alone. Am I starting to feel love for Alagur? Is that what I'm feeling right now?

For his part, Alagur suddenly feels like hugging Marrida, but he stops himself because he's still uncertain if Esbara would approve. After all, with Marrida's impending departure, Esbara is the head of the household now. By naming him as an adult, Marrida has placed the role on his shoulders. So instead of acting on instinct and hugging Marrida, Alagur shows his gratitude by asking further questions.

"What does it say about Azaquina?"

Alagur's question tears Marrida from her thoughts and she is reluctant to look around the room, least of all at Alagur. She's certain she'll be as red as the bergas bush after which the boy is obviously named. Whenever Alagur speaks the boy's name, it is with pride in his voice.

"It...it mentions the town several times. It...it was once a powerful seafaring harbour. That...that was more than three thousand years ago."

Dammit, Marrida thinks. *Why do I stutter now of all times?*

Marrida points at the passage in the book, and Alagur, who has a rudimentary knowledge of the dialect spoken in Ruh'nar, sees he can read this text. He now understands why Bergas wanted to go home so badly. Azaquina is old, though it seems the harbour is older. Bergas said that without him there, his mother would be unlikely to be able to look after herself. The city the boy described was a destroyed shell, unlike the city Sharriba described in the book.

I wonder why the Wolf Riders even bothered going there. Or did they go there because it couldn't easily resist their vile actions? I have even more questions now, and if Azaquina can answer some of Marrida's questions, I need to start seeking my own answers there, too. I need to go with her so she gets there safely. Bergas also needs to get home safely if we're going to rely on his help while we're there.

Marrida hurries through the remainder of the book, deciding most of its contents can be explained in detail to Alagur during their journey. However, she wants her siblings and Damir to have a basic knowledge of the contents, too, so they won't be left with unanswered questions. After thirty minutes, she reaches the end of the book and stops, looking to every person around her for questions. None come.

"We need to decide exactly what we're going to do while we're travelling." Marrida looks questioningly at Alagur. He will be able to give the best suggestions. "Uncle Joharan said that those things in the vestibule are to be sold in Alzamar. Do you that town?"

Alagur nods. *I have visited that city to purchase food, disguising myself in old clothes.*

"It's the city closest to City of Wolves and is the one most often attacked." He stops short of telling the people around him that the Wolf Riders scout cities they want to attack, and often. "The city lies about seven to ten days' journey northeast of City of Wolves. It will take close to double that time to get to Azaquina on foot from there."

Marrida guesses that the man is omitting information, but she decides not to question him about it now. "What direction will Bergas travel to get home?"
"I told him to head to the South Valley of Miza, which is directly north from here. He'll then travel east. Did you know the South Valley of Miza stretches all the way from the west coast to just south of Azaquina? Just south of the city is Bay of Whispers--"
Marrida nods. She's silent for a moment to formulate her next question, but is interrupted by Esbara.
"When we talked a few days ago, you mentioned that Bergas lost his father in a storm at sea. Didn't that happen in the bay you just

mentioned?"

"Yes – Bergas mentioned that and it happened there. It happened about five years ago, if I remember rightly--"

"How are you going to get to Azaquina? I mean, you mentioned something about going through a mountain pass."

Marrida speaks before Alagur can give a reply. "If we're going over the mountains, won't it be dangerous with the winter snowfall? And what about ice burn? Though I guess travel will be slow with all the stuff we're selling..."

Alagur looks from Esbara to Marrida and back. Both raised valid points he hasn't considered.

It's the autumn season soon. I forgot how long I'd been here because this region seems always warm. The winter's breath is evident whenever I go into the courtyard, especially in the evenings.

Winter's breath is the name for the chill that goes through the South Valley of Miza in mid-winter. Travelling over the mountains when that weather pattern comes would be foolhardy. He knows he and Yalla can cope in the mountains in the winter – Yalla because she's a mountain wolf, and Alagur because he will have the wolf to warm him.

I don't know if Marrida can cope. But if we don't go through the mountains, then where and how can we travel relatively safely? We're going to need a wolf for Marrida as well.

Alagur glances down at his hands resting on the table as he contemplates their options, becoming aware of the silence around him. The others in the room are waiting for answers from him.

"Do you know of Venrasia Woods?" Alagur looks quizzically around to room, fixing his gaze on Marrida. All four individuals nod and grin at the same time. Alagur waits for someone to say something, but it seems he's become the subject of a private joke. In the end, Marrida heaves a big sigh.

"We went there as children with Uncle Joharan," she explains. "We visited it for several months about six years ago."

Alagur nods.

"We all know it as Joharan took us all there for an excursion," Damir adds. "I went along to learn more about different wood types. Marrida was there to look after her brother and sister. That was the last outing because Joharan felt too old for any more."

"Then you should know about Ribbon Lake south of it?" Alagur looks at Marrida. She nods. "We can head there first. If we follow the northern side of the lake for a few weeks, we'll pass over two ancient dried-out riverbeds. The estuaries of both once deposited their water into the bay I mentioned."

"Isn't the second riverbed close to City of Wolves?" Damir asks.

Alagur nods again. "If we follow Ribbon Lake to its end, we'll be close to City of Wolves. However, I know of a path that will divert us away. It's the route that Bergas is taking to get home. If we go that way, we can avoid both the winter weather of the mountains and encounters with Wolf Riders."

I knew we'd travel close to City of Wolves, but I didn't realise until now how close. And Bergas — I hope he does get home. A shiver goes down Alagur's spine suddenly. He looks down once more, expecting anger from the others in the room.

"We can travel north earlier, Marrida, but it would be colder." Alagur's voice is almost a whisper. "Do you think you'd cope with travelling fast without many breaks?"

Marrida looks at Alagur. *I wonder what he's planning. Could I travel like a Wolf Rider? That's what he's asking of me. We'll be sharing Yalla, and I wonder if Yalla will cope with that.*

But she's read the answer to that questions in the book in front of her — the Wolf Riders snatched boys from the cities they attacked, and that meant the wolves had to carry two people back to City of Wolves.

Part of her feels excitement about riding Yalla; part of her feels a slowly rising knot of fear. She nods an almost imperceptible answer, clenching her lips as she does so.

CHAPTER TWENTY-SIX

JOHARAN STEPS INTO THE FADING SUNSHINE OF THE LATE AFTERNOON from the Office of the Merchant Clerk. In his hand, he holds a dark pouch made from woven cloth that contains the travel papers Marrida will need. He looks up at the sky to determine the time of day and quickly lifts his left hand to shield his eyes against the glare of sunlight reflecting off windows and roofs above him.

I told Marrida I'd be back at her house two hours after sunset with these papers. Alagur and she need to be ready for when I arrive.

Joharan starts walking without any destination in mind right now. If he sets his pace at a reasonable speed and walks through the city to visit clients, he'll arrive at Marrida's house at the agreed time. As he walks, Joharan considers the plan to take Alagur out of the city. Alagur will then need to wait for Marrida at the lake where he says his own belonging are waiting for him. When Alagur explained, as politely as he could, about leaving two boys from City of Wolves near the lake before the attack on Ruh'nar, Joharan changed the plan for Marrida to join Alagur in that place.

"It will mean you have got to walk for two hours alone, Marrida."

"I'm not afraid to make that journey."

I hope the plan to get Alagur out of the city safely works well, Joharan thinks. *I'm certain he's the key to solving this crisis gripping the land.* His grip on the pouch tightens as he feels a flash of anger. *It can all be resolved, but will one person be able to succeed where so many before have failed? I wonder what Marrida will find, what Alagur will find. What can one young woman really do, even with Alagur's help? But she needs to try. We all do--*

Joharan realises what Sharriba must have given Marrida. *I'm sure it's a journal of some sort. It's good she did that.* Long after Sharriba rejected his invitation to be his life partner, she told him of the visions she'd done. At first, the conversations were hesitant, but gradually they eased into the new normal as the resentment between them faded. When she confided in him, Joharan felt comfortable enough to tell her about his grandmother's vision in return. To his surprise, Sharriba didn't show any surprise when he repeated his grandmother's words.

"You'll meet him, and you must treat him with the respect he deserves. He is a lost one, he is. He was once with a family like you are now. He'll be the key to helping the daughter who isn't yours on her task."

"They could have a deeper meaning to them that we yet need to discover," Sharriba stated.

That conversation was twenty years before Marrida's birthing when no one knew what fate would bring a happy young family years later.

* * *

Joharan walks almost mechanically towards his niece's house, stopping abruptly to think again about the puzzling words his grandmother had spoken.

"The daughter who isn't yours."

What do they really mean? Did she already know that Markalo would die in the future? Yet, she never mentioned his fate to Markalo in all the times she spoke with us. So many questions yet so few answers. And a brother lost because of so much upheaval in the world.

Joharan guesses the reason he so readily dismissed the words of his grandmother was because she never mentioned Markalo's passing. She never gave any indication that Markalo would find a life partner and have children with her before dying. Deep sadness overwhelms Joharan, causing him to lean against the wall with his hand.

After a few moments of breathing deeply, Joharan continues walking. But now as he walks, he feels the weight of responsibility weighing down on his shoulders. He reaches the end of the street where Marrida's house is located and stops again, investigating the street for a few minutes and glancing around and up.

I wonder how two stones could alter the destiny of so many so quickly. I think I know who threw them. They had such precision to them. It's knowledge I must take with me to my grave. Joharan's assumptions are based on suspicions he has about the leadership of the city. *I cannot tell anyone in Marrida's house what's on my mind to ensure their continued safety from the authorities of the city. Esbara, especially, will suffer if it becomes known that a mortal enemy of the city dwellers is being harboured in his house. He would be expelled from the prestigious Academy, and I would suffer because I would lose my status. I remember Marrida begging me to move to another town — now, if it needs to be done for the safety of myself and my nieces, nephew and apprentices, I will do it.*

Joharan kept his face neutral when Marguna told him the news of a Wolf Rider and his wolf having been killed. But he knows the very man Marguna was talking about. When the defenders didn't find any Wolf Rider or wolf, injured or otherwise, they assumed the Wolf Riders had taken the man and his wolf with them. Marguna showed more concern about getting the remaining fires put out than the two dead Wolf Riders who were found at the southern end of the city. Those Wolf Riders were buried in a mass grave, then the clerks from the Council of Seven had walked around the city to tally up the missing boys. That only a dozen boys had been snatched this time paid testament to the fact that the citizens of the vast city were becoming much more cautious whenever an attack from the Wolf Riders was imminent.

This time, Joharan thinks sarcastically, still keeping his face neutral. *That is twelve attacks too many.* For a few minutes, Joharan stares along the length of the street where Marrida lives in. *I guess those people in the house opposite hers decided to leave for the same reasons that Marrida expressed to me.*

Joharan walks forward until he reaches the front door of Marrida's house. He pauses there to stare at the place where, according to Marrida's retelling, Alagur had been lying wounded. Then Joharan's head jerks up, and he wonders anxiously about where the other Wolf Rider vanished to.

He could be a danger to Marrida and Alagur's efforts if he's as deceptive and dangerous as Alagur makes him out to be.

Joharan looks at the wooden door of the house, shared by his only family, and now also shared by Damir. Part of him hopes Damir's stay will be temporary as he really can't do without the skills the boy has been learning.

I hope Marrida's journey only takes her away for a couple of years. Deep in his heart, Joharan knows the first city they need to visit, Azaquina, lies at least two seasons away on foot. *Even if they do get a second wolf for Marrida to ride — as Grandmother predicted — it will still take almost a whole season to reach the city on the northern coast, and that's if the pair never stop for rest or food.*

Joharan feels the door handle.

The outer door is locked. I must expect that with Alagur's presence in the house.

He knocks on the door several times, waits a few moments, then knocks again a couple of times using a rhythm that Damir will recognise. It's the same rhythm Joharan uses to seek entry into the room shared by his apprentices.

He hears someone drawing back the bolts of the door. The door opens a crack, and the eyes of Damir light up when he sees his mentor. The boy sidesteps, and Joharan glances left and right along the street for any pedestrians. On seeing none, he steps into the house. There he's met by neatly stacked packs of belongings that each seem to contain some of what he sent over with Damir.

The wolf, who previously looked so intimidating to Joharan, raises her head as if to say, "Oh, it's you," before flopping it back onto the cool floor.

"They're all in the front room," Damir says quietly. Joharan nods in response.

Entering the room, Joharan sees Marrida and Alagur sitting side by side, and he notes a closeness between them which he hasn't seen before. Kalisa rushes at her uncle with a hug, and rather than picking her up, the old man stoops down to her height and lets her throw her arms around his neck and kiss him on the cheek. His evening stubble makes the girl stop and look at him.

"Aw, you're so prickly," she says with a hint of a giggle in her voice.

Joharan smiles at the young girl and runs his large hand through her hair, which provokes more giggles and half-hearted shrieks of protest from her. With a bit of effort, Joharan straightens himself up again. Holding his arms around Kalisa in a gesture of comfort, he directs his question towards Marrida, who stops reading the book and looks at him. A twinkle in her eyes tells him that she's amused at the sight of Kalisa and him greeting one another.

"Has the book been of help?" he asks. He can see her reading progress is considerable, but feels a bit puzzled by the scraps of parchment with Marrida's handwriting on them. "What are those?"

Marrida answers both questions in one exhalation of her breath. "The book is helpful, and those are some of the notes I made."

Probably while you were alone, Joharan thinks, but instead of saying anything, he simply nods understanding, walks around the table and bench, and sits in the seat nearest to the fireplace. Kalisa, who has decided that being with her uncle is fun, climbs up on Joharan's lap and settles herself in his arms, which enfold her so much she looks like she's buried in between the muscles. She feels warm and at ease and so tiredness soon overcomes her.

Damir glances at Kalisa and wishes he, rather than his mentor, was holding her closely. But then he smiles, realising that at eleven years she's still too young to be interested in his feelings of love. He's more at ease with his feelings for the girl now he's away from Joharan's house and the taunts of the other boys.

Maybe not Sherino, he thinks with a smile. The youngest of the four apprentices always encouraged him to talk more to Kalisa.

Damir's thoughts are interrupted when Joharan asks the crucial question of him.
"Are you ready to take Alagur out of the city?"
"We need to pack a few more items, and then we're ready--"
Damir stops and looks at Alagur for approval. Alagur nods; he needs to adjust two of the packs before they can leave.
"We'd better get busy with it." Alagur motions to Damir to come with him. The boy follows the man, after glancing once more at Kalisa fast asleep in Joharan's arms. A wink from Joharan indicates that he knows and understands Damir's feelings for the girl, and he smiles back somewhat nervously at being caught out showing those feelings so openly.

Damir rushes into the vestibule, almost bumping into Esbara who looks at him with a knowing smile too.

Does everyone know how I feel about her? Damir scolds himself, but then he realises these are the people closest to Kalisa who'll know her best. In his heart, he's glad Joharan has put so much trust in him, making him co-guardian for the youngest of the household. Joharan himself isn't young or at his healthiest anymore, and Esbara will soon be too busy at the Academy on the other side of the vast city.

"Damir, can you hold one end of this blanket, please?" Alagur asks. Damir nods and picks up the loops at the end of the leather blanket, designed to make it easy to lift heavy objects. Looping each hand through them, he prepares himself for whatever needs doing. Looking up, he sees Esbara standing opposite him, mirroring his own motions. The two boys grin at each other, then Alagur comes back from the cooking room with several woollen sheets. Damir recognises them from Joharan's bedding storage. Alagur obviously intends to take them for extra warmth during the night. The blanket in Damir's hands, gently tugging at his arm muscles, is warm, but it may feel somewhat uncomfortable in direct contact with skin.

The sheets will offer an extra layer of warmth, but also add a softness which the leather lacks.

Alagur places the sheets over the top of the leather blanket, overlapping them generously, tucking in the parts that drape over the sides. When Damir is almost straining under the combined weight of the sheets and the blankets, Alagur finishes folding.
"You can roll that up now slowly from either end, so the roll meets here." Alagur points to the centre of the leather. The two boys oblige, although more hurriedly than Alagur intended. Pointing to the floor where they need to place their load, Alagur puts his foot in the centre of the roll and, using the four loops, pulls the bundle so it folds in half. The two boys watch as the man expertly hooks the handles together to hold the bundle in shape and ties the thick rope which Esbara retrieved from the storage room earlier in the day, making loops that both fasten and enclose the roll. Both boys understand that this is an activity Alagur is familiar with.

Marrida, who is watching from the cooking room door, wonders what sort of punishments new boys at City of Wolves endure until they master the skill. Not wanting to dwell on unpalatable truths, Marrida walks to the stairway and ascends it slowly. Glancing once more at the trio busying themselves, she then walks the short distance to her room. Her head is pounding, and she needs some time alone before they leave.

I'm certain we're going tonight.

Sitting in her room with the door shut, silence her only companion, Marrida has time to feel pensive. She looks around the room that was once shared by her parents, glancing at a small bed covered with layers of woollen blankets in the left corner.

Marrida recalls dancing in the cooking room, teasing Esbara, who was almost three years old, with the suggestion that the baby would be a little sister when the impending birthing was revealed by their mother. Esbara, who was close to his mother, sought comfort in her arms, and she reassured him that either a boy or girl would be nice to have.

This house is so full of memories.

Marrida shuts her eyes, and she can almost hear the soft humming of her mother's beautiful singing voice. But she knows the humming is more likely to be coming from the evening bees collecting their honey from the roses outside. Marrida opens her eyes once more and glances down at the visible bulge under her over-tunic.

Dare I risk a vision with the gem? She gets up and walks to the door of her room. *We aren't travelling for another hour, so perhaps it's time to try one more vision.*

CHAPTER TWENTY-SEVEN

MARRIDA TAKES THE GEM OFF THE GOLDEN CHAIN on which it hangs. Between thumb and forefinger of her right hand, she holds it in the shafts of sunlight streaming into the room. Marrida starts to reach out with her left hand, then stops in the middle of the motion.

What vision shall I do?

After thinking for a few minutes, listening to ensure curiosity hasn't driven someone else upstairs, Marrida lifts her left hand up again. She knows the vision she wants, but she also knows after the day's events that she needs to do a different vision. Placing the gem in the middle of her left hand, Marrida makes the decision to see what happened at the time Sharriba was writing her journal.

Holding her right hand above the gem, Marrida closes her eyes and concentrates. Fifty years is a large gap to span for someone as untrained as herself, but Marrida needs to find answers.

Darkness replacing the after-image caused by the bright light of the sun tells Marrida she's at the beginning of the vision. Driven by an unknown force, her eyes open, her eyeballs black and opaque.

With eyes that are seeing previously unseen events, Marrida turns her head to orientate herself and sees she's inside the Temple. The room is unfamiliar to her, and she can hear voices coming from somewhere behind her. Without moving a muscle of her body while she sits on the edge of her bed, Marrida repositions the vision to get a view of the people she can hear speaking.

She sees two women sitting opposite one another. One she recognises as Sharriba, although a much younger version of the familiar woman. The other woman is very old and unknown to her. Marrida listens and realises their voices aren't full of joy or understanding, but bitterness and anger. In all the time she has known Elder Sharriba, she has never seen her mentor angry. But this younger version is full of anger, almost spitting at the other woman who seems to be dismissing every word she's saying.

The dialect the two women are speaking isn't a Ruh'nar dialect, but a strange one Marrida cannot decipher, however hard she tries. She hasn't learnt the skill of self-repositioning yet, which is the skill needed to decipher the spoken word whenever a vision is in one of the six ancient dialects, but her astute mind realises this dialect isn't one of the ancient dialects. Perhaps it's one native to the old woman in the vision.

Marrida positions her vision closer to the pair of women until she's almost looking over the older woman's shoulder. She can now see for herself why her uncle was interested in Sharriba all those years ago. No longer is the woman's hair silver-streaked; instead, it's a mass of rich dark-brown curls which she wears in a semi-loose bundle, draping over her firm shoulders, part-visible in the dark ochre-coloured dress she was wearing. The familiar clasp, that in later years would bundle her hair tightly together at the nape of her neck, is being used as decoration to lift it away from her face. In her youth, Sharriba's face was an even more pronounced heart shape. The same piercing grey-green eyes that looked at Marrida in her uncle's workshop are filled with fire.

There's a type of flame that Marrida's uncle used to point out when she still visited his workshop called Flame of the Underworld. This flame comes about when certain types of metals are mixed with an alloy commonly used for making a tinder kit. The alloy is one of the hardest metals in existence, and is one of the few which can fire up the slow-burning wood used to warm houses. This same hardness and fire are visible in the eyes of the woman she now knows as her mentor. Marrida's taken aback at seeing another unknown side of a woman who has always represented comfort and friendship.

Marrida moves away from the seating, where the two women continue to argue, and adjusts her vision so that she can observe more of the room they are in. On a table in the corner, she sees a familiar book. As she hovers closer, she sees a half-written page of parchment — the same parchment which an hour ago she'd been reading. Next to the book lies a gem. She recognises it as Sharriba's Stone of Truth.

Marrida frowns, puzzled. *Why would she leave her gem lying like this? Why isn't it around her neck?*

Marrida realises what the two women are arguing about all of a sudden. *Sharriba must have just told the Elder about the vision of the wolf.*

Marrida looks closely at the gem on the table. Suddenly, blackness envelops her and she isn't in the room anymore. She looks around in a panic, feeling the warmth of the gem on her palm, and she realises that this is more of the vision.

There's a table. Is it a table? No, it's a dark slab of stone. The room, or wherever I am — it feels cold. Marrida hears sounds that are alien to her. *I wonder where I am. Are they people in the distance?*

Men with dark robes are carrying large torches. Marrida hears a scream. Then silence. A deafening silence overwhelms the scene before being interrupted by several loud thuds--

* * *

"Marrida? Marrida, what happened?" Esbara shrieks at his unconscious sister, who lies motionless on the floor. He's pushed aside by Joharan, who is closely followed by Alagur. They look at one another with concern. Without saying anything, they agree the best course of action would be to get Marrida on the bed.

Looking around the room, Joharan sees the reason for the woman's condition in the furthest corner. Grabbing Alagur's forearm, he points discreetly at the gem.

"Kalisa!" Joharan calls out in a booming voice that echoes through the room.

A very sleepy-looking girl arrives in the room, immediately wide awake when she sees her sister unconscious on the bed. Taking her by the shoulders, Joharan explains to Kalisa what she needs to do.

"As you know, it's forbidden for men to touch the gem." Joharan nods towards the gem on the floor. "As we're all men here, we cannot retrieve it without causing offence to everything that's sacred to your sister."

Kalisa looks at the gem, then at Marrida on the bed. "Do you think it's safe for me to pick it up?"

"I was there when Grandmother used it," Joharan replies with a smile. "Some minutes after the user has finished a vision with it, it goes inert."

Kalisa, who doesn't know this part of her uncle's past, looks at him with awe and surprise in equal measure. She nods and walks over to the corner, kneels and looks at the innocent-looking gem, chuckling to herself.

It looks like a rubha apple for sure now!

With her forefinger, Kalisa gingerly touches the gem, and when nothing untoward happens, she picks the precious object up with two fingers.

"Place the gem on this table next to the bed," Joharan says when Kalisa looks at him questioningly. She complies solemnly. With concern etched all over her face, Kalisa then climbs onto the end of the bed where Marrida is slowly waking up, moaning as if she's in pain.

Alagur looks down at her with a deep frown of concern. It wouldn't be wise to start their journey with Marrida in this condition, but he knows the decision doesn't rest with him. It's up to Marrida to determine whether she's well enough to travel.

Marrida, who doesn't realise the scream she heard in the vision also escaped from her own lips, slowly opens her eyes to see the face of Alagur above her. She sees Joharan kneeling beside her bed, with Esbara and Damir standing side by side behind him. Looking further around, she sees Kalisa on her hands and knees, observing her.

"What happened?" Marrida's voice is groggy as if she has just awoken from a long sleep.

"We heard you scream, but the door was locked," Esbara states.

Marrida feels her forehead. "I have a headache, and I'm thirsty." Joharan grabs a cup from the table next to where the gem is lying, careful not to touch it. From the cupboard next to him, Alagur passes the jug of water to the older man, who pours some of the water into the cup. Holding Marrida's head up, he helps her as she drinks a few sips of the cool liquid.

As she lies her head down again, her hand instinctively moves from her forehead to her neck.

"Where's my gem?" she screams.

"It's on the table here," Joharan reassures her. "I got Kalisa to pick it up and put it there after it fell down."

"Fell down?"

"Yes. When you screamed, you also fell unconscious on the floor."

Gratitude fills Marrida's eyes as she looks at her uncle. It dawns on her how much he respects the importance of the gem as he made sure it was retrieved by the only other person in the house allowed, even if only in principle, to touch it. Marrida smiles at Kalisa, who interprets the smile as an unspoken gesture of thanks.

"I used the gem for a vision," Marrida almost whispers.

Joharan nods. He isn't going to press her with any questions. She closes her eyes in concentration, and Joharan puts his finger to his lips for a few moments, glancing around the room. He wants Marrida to speak without the pressure of questions from those around her, including himself, even though he's curious to know what vision she did.

Joharan is taken aback when Marrida speaks up. Her eyes are still closed to allow her to see an image etched in her mind.

"I saw Sharriba on that day – when she wrote the first page of the journal."

Joharan nods even though Marrida can't see it. She continues with her account of the events of fifty years ago as if she senses his nod anyway.

"She sat in a room with an old woman. They seemed to be arguing." Marrida opens her eyes and looks at her uncle. "She seemed upset and angry at the same time. And they were speaking in a dialect I couldn't understand."

Joharan thinks for a few moments. What was it Sharriba told him about the Elder who presided over the Order in the Temple at the time? He digs deep to long-buried memories, some of which he has chosen to forget for the intervening years.

"Describe the Elder to me, please."

Marrida describes the Elder she saw in the vision and sees a flash of anger and then pain run over her uncle's face. "That is Kyrana!" he says loudly, making Marrida jump. "She is the one who--"

Joharan stops in the middle of his sentence and looks closely at Marrida, who has half-raised herself on the bed to move away from the anger in her uncle's face. Tears stream down her face without her knowing it. Kalisa, who sees the sudden distress the outburst from their uncle has caused, crawls closer to her sister, putting a gentle hand on Marrida's forearm. Behind Marrida, Alagur does a similar thing, kneeling and placing a hand on the woman's shoulder. He gives Joharan an angry stare for a few seconds, but then he catches Esbara's eye. The boy is waving his hands frantically to warn Alagur not to say anything. Turning his attention back to Marrida, Alagur remains quiet while he holds her shoulder to settle her.

Joharan notices how his reaction has upset the youngsters around him, and he leans away from the bed. Softening his expression, he looks down. He isn't sure how much Marrida saw of the events of fifty years ago, but his gut feeling tells him to listen to everything she says without scaring her any more.

"Please continue," he whispers, speaking so quietly that at first Marrida doesn't hear him. When she remains quiet, he looks up at her imploringly.

In a soft voice, sometimes cracking under the strain of the emotion she's feeling, Marrida continues telling her companions what she saw. Everyone listens without saying a word. The room is silent apart from the words and occasional sobs coming from Marrida. If anyone dropped a hat pin on the floor, it would have been the loudest sound.

As she delves further into the events she witnessed, Marrida feels calmness return. Glancing sideways at Joharan, she sees a deep sadness on her uncle's face that makes him look decades older suddenly. It humbles her to realise how far she still needs to go in her own life — a life which, until recently, was certain and ordered.

But the events of the last few weeks have shown me it won't be orderly anymore — for any of us!

Kalisa listens in fascination to her sister. She has witnessed Marrida doing visions, and it scared her at first when she saw Marrida's eyes turn jet black. Now her sister is reciting from memory every part of an event long past as if she had been there herself fifty years ago. The girl is most curious to know how her sister can retell everything in perfect detail, and guesses it must, for the most part, be due to her training at the Temple.

I want to do this. The thought catches Kalisa by surprise. She glances surreptitiously towards Damir, but he's too focused on Marrida's retelling to notice. *What would he think if I became a Temple Maiden?* Kalisa wonders. She quickly fixes her gaze back to her sister. *She was a Temple maiden first. She said some stay as one.*

A drawing in of breath from Joharan attracts Kalisa's attention back to the conversation. "What did you say you saw?" he demands, visibly shocked.

"I saw men with torches in some sort of dark chamber with a stone slab in the middle of it." Marrida's response is almost a whisper again. She doesn't want her uncle to have another of his outbursts.

Joharan stands and paces back and forth. Damir and Esbara, who both edged closer when Marrida started talking in a quieter tone, step back to avoid the distracted Joharan bumping into them. He rubs his chin with a thumb and forefinger in a way all, except for Alagur, recognise as meaning he's thinking deeply.

Marrida slides her feet off the bed onto the floor, which forces Alagur to remove his hand from her shoulder. This unbalances him somewhat, so he stands upright. Kalisa copies her sister and sits next to Marrida with her feet dangling down, almost reaching the floor. She feels her sister's arm embrace her. The sudden warmth tells her that the embrace includes the blanket from the bed. She smiles at Marrida, who smiles back weakly.

Marrida's attention is snapped back to the discussion by a question from Joharan. "Did they wear any specific clothing you could make out?"

"All I saw was that they wore long robes. But I wonder why I heard the scream."

"What scream?" Joharan asks, and in two strides he's in front of her, kneeling and looking her directly in the eyes.

"You said I screamed, but – I heard a scream during the vision." Marrida feels a pang of fear gnawing at her mind now.

"Have you had any self-reposition training yet?" Joharan asks, sounding as stern as he does when he asks an apprentice to explain a mistake they've made. The tone makes Damir raise an eyebrow.

Marrida shakes her head rather than saying anything.

"What is self-reposition?" The question comes from Kalisa, who can't stop herself from being curious. Joharan smiles at the little girl, who looks younger than ever with her sleepy eyes and the large blanket from Marrida's bed draped around her shoulders, then he looks at Marrida.

"Shall I explain it to her? I can also tell you how I know about it." All Marrida can do is nod. Now she's curious too. "The skill of self-repositioning is a skill Marrida would have learnt if she'd progressed another three years – or is it four?"

"It's four," Marrida confirms softly. Joharan nods and continues.

"I told your sister and brother, and Alagur too, about my grandmother yesterday. You were sleeping, so you don't know the retelling. Neither does Damir, really."

Joharan stops and thinks for a few moments. Damir smirks, knowing why he has made him out to be unaware.

"My grandmother could do self-repositioning. It's a skill some Keepers never master, whereas others become highly skilled in it."

"But what is it?" Kalisa whispers.

"It's a skill where a Keeper understands the dialect spoken by another person, even if it's a foreign or ancient one." Joharan smiles. "If Marrida was able to do it properly, all that Sharriba and Kyrana said would have sounded like Ruh'nar dialect, not the strange dialect she heard."

Kalisa nods. She's quick to learn, and the explanation is sufficient for her young mind.

"Something I don't understand, Uncle Joharan," Marrida interjects. "I know with self-repositioning you can hear people talk in your own dialect. But there's something else, though — actually two things."

Joharan nods and waits patiently for the woman to continue.

"When I came to see you at your workshop, I didn't tell you everything about the visions I did to see where Alagur came from."

CHAPTER TWENTY-EIGHT

Marrida bows her head, feeling herself shake uncontrollably. She'd lied to her uncle when he asked her if she did her visions alone.

Joharan sees her distress immediately and wonders why the revelation has upset Marrida so much. He looks up at Alagur, who can only confirm her words with a simple nod. Joharan glances at Esbara and sees him nod, too.

More has happened here than she, or any of them, has told me. This has been going on for weeks, long before she came to see me. Maybe since Alagur's arrival here. I need to keep this under control.

Joharan nudges Marrida's chin, forcing her to look up at him. It's a gentle gesture, familiar from childhood. Now the same gesture reassures her troubled mind that her uncle isn't angry with her. When she looks at him, Joharan smiles encouragingly at her.

In almost a single breath, the words tumble from Marrida's lips, retelling the vision as she remembers it. "I did a vision. I saw Alagur as a young boy, a little younger than Kalisa. There was a girl in the vision too. Alagur thinks it's his sister. She was shouting his name as the man with black hair rode away with Alagur in front of him on his wolf. I saw the same man before Alagur was injured. I think he could be why I heard the girl shout."

Alagur's natural tan looks visibly paler at the revelation. Marrida has never told him that she heard the girl call out his name; she's only said she saw the girl run after the man carrying him away on the wolf. Before Alagur can comment, Joharan interjects with a question.

"What's the other thing?" He takes Marrida's hands to help her steady herself and feels how much they are shaking.

"The scream I heard in the vision earlier wasn't in Ruh'nar dialect. It was some other dialect, but I understood what it said."

This revelation leaves everyone in the room in stunned silence. Alagur is the first to recover as he voices the implications of Marrida's statement.

"I think Marrida has done self-repositioning without any training. *Twice*, it seems."

The room explodes with many voices all talking at the same time. Esbara asks Alagur once more about his sister; Alagur, again, says he doesn't know the answers. Damir talks to Kalisa about Yalla. Joharan talks to both Marrida and Alagur, asking them how far they have got with their travel preparations. The noise subsides only when Yalla makes her distress clear with short bark-like sounds from downstairs, leaving Joharan worried a neighbour or passer-by may hear her.

A booming voice echoes through the room. Joharan has decided to silence everyone.

"We'd better eat something then finish getting ready."

"I made some rubha apple porridge earlier," Kalisa says softly. "It was meant to be the dessert."

The innocence of the declaration brings smiles to the faces of everyone in the room, and Alagur can't resist laughing out loud.

"Then porridge we shall eat, young wise one," he teases. The girl giggles, then gets up and runs out of the room to go downstairs.

By the time everyone else arrives in the cooking room, Kalisa has set six deep bowls around the heavy-set table, placing an extra two dishes on the floor for the wolf. One of the dishes is filled with fresh water, and in the other, Kalisa has placed a ham which is already five days old and getting past the time when it would be fit for consumption. On the table, Kalisa has also put six mugs in a tight group around a jug of warm rubha apple tea, with several dried citrus wedges floating in the liquid for flavouring. On one end of the table sits the large cooking pot, honey-flavoured steam rising from it. Everyone in the room knows honey is added to rubha apple porridge for sweetness. On the other end of the table is a platter filled with fruits which Alagur recognises as coming from various parts of Keldarra. Next to it is a jug containing a milky substance – a sauce that is routinely poured over the porridge – and an extra dish of honey. And finally, next to this dish sits a jar of Marrida's favourite honey and berry spread, the distinct blue colour giving away its origin.

Marrida stares in amazement. She has never known how her sister prepares food so well, but tonight it seems the girl has mastered the skill of laying out a feast in record time. She does not realise that Kalisa did most of the work during the afternoon when she visited the Temple, and Marrida feels a heartfelt gratitude for the sister she has.

"I guess we're feasting once more." Alagur grins at Esbara, who's standing beside him. The boy grins back.

Marrida sits at the end of the table where she usually sits during meals. Joharan takes the other end. Alagur sits closest to the old man because he can then talk to him about the events of the evening, and in case Joharan wants to discuss the travel arrangements with him. Damir takes the place on the bench next to him, and Esbara sits opposite. That leaves one place for Kalisa, who is still bringing food from the other end of the cooking room.

After going back and forth four more times, Kalisa stops and looks at the table. Then with a resolute nod, she sits down and grins in satisfaction at everyone.

They wanted a feast, so I've made it a feast.

For a while, no one is sure who should start to serve the food out. Finally, Joharan takes matters into his own hands. He places various pieces of bread and fruit on the small platter next to the deep bowl intended for his porridge. Next, he helps himself to three ladles of the warm substance, bringing up a cloud of honey-scented steam with each scoop.

Moments after he has finished serving up food for himself, arms are flying all over the table; everyone takes their share of bread, fruit, cheese, porridge, savoury and sweet biscuits, and slices of roasted ham, as well as a mug filled to the brim with sweet-flavoured tea, each person pouring the milky sauce over their porridge to his or her own liking. Marrida's face shows exactly what she thinks of the honey and berry spread that she covers her two pieces of bread with – she savours the wonderful flavours from her mother's hometown.

The cooking room is silent for the first fifteen minutes or so of the meal because each person is deeply occupied by their own thoughts. Even the normally talkative Kalisa looks into the middle distance pensively, contemplating two different things going through her mind. She wants to learn about the Keepers of Truth. It seems an acceptable Order to be involved in. The idea that she could use the gem, which is at present hanging around Marrida's neck, to view past events – and Kalisa is sure someone said some can even see the future with it – excites the girl's mind, and she wants a similar destiny for herself.

I'm not sure how I'm going to tell anyone about my plans – if I can even call them that. I know Damir feels a certain way about me, and I don't want to do anything that would get in the way of that.

The second thing niggling at her mind is what Marrida said about seeing men with torches.

Marrida heard a scream.

Kalisa was asleep on her uncle's lap when it all happened. Rather than waking the girl, Joharan cautiously placed her on the sofa before going upstairs with everyone else. When his loud booming voice called out for the youngest member of the family a short while later, she awoke to find the front room deserted. For a moment, she thought her sister and Alagur had already left, and that something bad had happened. When the girl with her sleepy face arrived upstairs, it scared her to see her sister so distressed, and she wonders if being a Keeper of Truth is really such a fun skill to have.

I don't think I want it after all. Seeing Marrida in that way wasn't fun at all.

Setting the thoughts aside, Kalisa concentrates on the food in front of her and soon forgets all about them.

Alagur is also thinking about the events of the evening, but he has a different take on it all.

I wonder if it's such a good idea to go on this journey after all. Marrida showed how frightened she was — when I put my hand on her shoulder, she was shaking uncontrollably. I could well have been settling a youngster in City of Wolves the way I held her. She never argued against me holding her, either. It took a long time for the shaking to diminish.

It's obvious to Alagur that the second part of the vision is significant in some way. *Joharan proved he knows much more than he should.* Alagur can't help feeling a bit angry at the old man for making Marrida relive the event by asking specific questions. He glances now at Joharan, who has a distant look on his face, and picks up on the old man's body language with ease due to his acute Wolf Riders senses. Joharan is clearly fighting to stay silent.

It's obvious he wants to ask her more questions, but every time he looks at her, she looks down at her food and refuses to make eye contact with anyone around the table.

Each of the boys is also dealing with his own thoughts. Esbara keeps looking carefully at his older sister, wondering if her silence means that she's reconsidering either her position at the Temple or going on this journey.

Or perhaps both.

Damir keeps glancing discreetly at Kalisa, wondering what her troubled look is about. *I wonder if it is due to certain decisions involving me. If she changes her mind about her own life, I can't do a damned thing to prevent it.*

Joharan finally makes up his mind that it's time to speak.

"Marrida, you must go on this journey." Marrida glances up on hearing the firmness in her uncle's voice, even though the words are whispered. "It's important, and from your face, I believe *you* think so too."

Alagur raises an eyebrow. *I wonder if he possesses enhanced observation skills like the Wolf Riders. I should pay more attention to him.*

Rather than responding in anger, as Joharan was expecting, Marrida simply nods before looking back down at her plate. She picks up one of the pieces of bread with the honey and berry mixture on it, raises it to her lips, and nibbles absentmindedly at it while she contemplates the journey ahead.

Alagur looks from Marrida to the old man, and back to Marrida.

There's more going on between those two than either wants to admit. I think it may relate to Joharan's knowledge of what went on in the Temple. In part, it may relate to me, too.

The rest of the meal passes without anyone speaking. It was meant to be a feast, but ends up feeling more like a meal at a remembrance ceremony, which is customarily held in absolute silence. With her occasional yips and rolling around on the floor, Yalla tries to break the deadly silence, but not even her master Alagur can bring himself to smile at her antics. At any other time, the wolf would have had him doubled up with laughter.

When everyone is full, Kalisa gets up and moves the dishes and plates to the washing area in the cooking room. Damir helps her in her task. In silence, the other individuals walk to the vestibule to work on the last of the packing.

* * *

It's DARK OUTSIDE NOW; THE MOON IS SLOWLY RISING, and it will be filling the streets with its pale blue light in a few hours.

This time, between daytime's end and night time's moonrise, is the best time for Alagur's departure. On seeing Damir entering the vestibule after he and Kalisa have hastily cleaned up the cooking room and placed the leftover food back in the cold storage cupboard, Joharan decides to prepare him for the task ahead.

On seeing her uncle's stern face as he walks towards her and Damir, Kalisa moves out of the way. Every set of eyes is fixed on Joharan and Damir as they speak in low voices to one another. Damir is asking several questions, which are followed by the rumbling undertone of Joharan's voice as he responds, and occasionally the boy nods. Alagur keeps his face neutral so as not to alert anyone to the fact that for him, with his heightened senses, the conversation isn't so private.

After about five minutes, Joharan and Damir reach some sort of agreement about the boy's plan of action. Damir takes a dark cloak from his haversack which is still leaning against the wall near to the front door, puts it on and, after a quick glance and smile towards Kalisa, opens the door and leaves.

Some fifteen minutes pass and everyone seems to be holding their breath as they wait for the soft knock which announces the boy's return. He hurriedly enters the house after Joharan opens the door.

"There are no guards on duty yet near the tunnels," he explains as he draws in fast breaths. He ran part of the distance back to the house.

Joharan nods in response to Damir's information. "It's time for you to leave, Alagur," he says to the younger man. "Can your wolf make the journey to the tunnels in silence?"

"She will if I command her to," Alagur responds. He fastens the harness he has fashioned onto Yalla, who patiently accepts it. "Are the tunnels wide or narrow?" he asks Damir.

"They are quite broad, but low in places."

The man nods and proceeds to place two packs on either side of Yalla's broad flank, layering several of the leather packs on top of the animal.

"Can she carry all that stuff when she's expecting so many pups?" The question comes from Marrida, who is growing more and more concerned as she watches Alagur load the packs and rolls onto the harness.

"She can easily carry three times as much as this." Alagur's tone is more abrupt than he meant it to be, making the woman jump and bringing a hint of a frown to Joharan's face. The old man decides to hold his tongue because this departure needs to go well.

Alagur is the best judge of Yalla's capabilities. She seems to be waiting placidly enough for him to finish packing belongings onto her.

Damir waits until he receives a nod from Alagur to indicate he's ready to go.

Alagur looks for a long moment at Marrida as a single tear rolls down her right cheek without her even noticing. Although they should be reunited in a few hours from now, she feels for a few moments like she's seeing him for the last time. Alagur gives her a weak smile, before looking at Joharan. The initial distrust which the men felt for one another has melted away; instead, there's the beginning of a friendship.

I wonder if I'll see him again in my lifetime--I hope it will be so.

Alagur feels a momentary need to go to Joharan and embrace him, but in the pit of his stomach he knows this isn't the time or place for such an action. He lifts his left hand instead in the standard Keldarran way of saying farewell. With a wry sigh escaping his lips, Alagur realises that the last time he made this gesture to a member of this family, that person was dead days later. A similar gesture comes back from Joharan, who has noted that the younger man is hesitant to show his feelings towards him.

Alagur turns and notices that Damir has walked off silently to the rear of the courtyard garden and opened a door in the wall, which separates the garden from a back alley. Alagur gives a signal to Yalla, and the wolf paces in silence towards the opening. Halfway there, she stops briefly, looking back at the group of individuals standing in the doorway of the vestibule. Seeing the wolf stop moving, a tearful Kalisa runs towards her and gives her a final embrace. The wolf, fond of the young girl in her wolfish way, responds to the embrace by slowly licking Kalisa's cheek with a long, raspy tongue, brushing away the tears from one side of the girl's face while tears from the other cheek soak into her fur, leaving several handfuls matted in small clumps.

When the embrace continues, Esbara moves towards his sister and gently nudges her to get her attention. "Yalla needs to go before the moon is up," he reminds her gently.

Kalisa lets go of Yalla and flings her arms around her brother's shoulders instead, tears still flooding down her face. A gentle, reassuring gesture from the wolf calms Kalisa's grief somewhat when Yalla places her large head against the girl's back. When Esbara looks up, he is staring straight into the large dark-yellow eyes of the wolf – eyes which show so much wisdom that the boy wonders how much she understands what's going on. He, too, feels grief at the imminent departure of the magnificent beast. As he holds Kalisa tightly with his left arm, he reaches up and runs his right hand over the bridge of the wolf's nose. Yalla shows him one of her wolf grins in response to indicate how much pleasure the gesture gives her.

Alagur, watching the scene unfold, is amazed. It's the first time since he awoke from his coma that he has seen Esbara be so affectionate towards the wolf. Deep in the core of his being, Alagur hopes that the next time the boy and wolf meet, it will be as equal and genuine friends.

Esbara leads Kalisa back to the vestibule. The girl sobs in silence, glancing at the wolf. Yalla pauses one more time, looking towards the doorway, her sharp eyes seeing Kalisa in her uncle, brother and sister's combined embrace. A single yip, which echoes through the garden, lets the girl know that the wolf understands her grief.

And then Yalla is gone.

CHAPTER TWENTY-NINE

Damir stays in the shadow of the walls which border gardens to prevent any fires in the city from spreading as he leads man and wolf towards the end of the walkway. He listens for guards' footsteps ahead. No embers had been lit when he rushed out to investigate the streets, but he knows from experience that the guards will start their patrol of the city in about thirty minutes after the moon has risen higher in the sky.

Damir glances over his shoulder and sees Alagur's face outlined in the early moonlight. The wolf is close behind the man with her head lowered and her ears flattened. If he didn't know better, Damir would think that Yalla, even with all the packs she's carrying, was about half the size of the wolf he first encountered in the house not too long ago.

It's almost like an illusion.

Damir now understands how valuable these wolves are as companions to men such as Alagur. They can be both a vicious fighting animal, about which he has heard so many retellings, and a scouting beast, which Yalla seems to be now.

Damir glances ahead again. Seeing the light of what seems to be an ember, he holds his hand up. Alagur stops abruptly. The silence makes the boy glance back nervously, and it seems to him that both the man and wolf have merged into the shadows of the walkway. Damir smiles inwardly, then he sneaks forward carefully, trying to make him as invisible as possible to glance down the road they need to cross. He sees no one to his left, but looking right, he catches sight of the back of a guard turning into a neighbouring street.

After some minutes, the glow of the guard's ember torch is gone. Damir signals to Alagur with a frantic arm wave. A moment later, both man and boy cross the street. Damir looks around searchingly for the wolf and sees her slink past them a few minutes later.

I'm sure that Yalla caught the smell of the guard in the air and decided to check for other guardsmen.

"We're close to the tunnels now," Damir mutters under his breath. Alagur nods and, following the boy's lead, walks through what seems to be a stone quarry until they reach a dark cleft in the rock face of some sort of hill. "This is the tunnel. It leads to a field north of the lake."

Alagur nods again, and Damir hands a pouch to him. Opening it, Alagur sees it contains a tinder kit smaller than those used in Marrida's house or in the streets.

"This was mine when I played in these tunnels." Damir beams a smile of pride. "You can give it back when you return."

Alagur feels moved by the boy's unexpected gesture of trust. He takes Damir's shoulders and looks at him for a long moment. Some of Damir's behaviour reminds him so much of Bergas.

"Keep Kalisa safe, or *she* won't forgive you." Alagur nods towards the wolf standing near them. Damir looks at Yalla and is surprised to see that once again, she's as large as she was at Marrida's house.

"How does she do it?" he asks. "She seemed smaller in the alleyway."

"It's a skill all wolves learn when they bond with a Wolf Master."

With this, Alagur turns and walks into the tunnel, followed closely by the wolf, who looks up at Damir as she walks past. Minutes later, there's the sound of an ember being lit, and Damir watches two shapes noiselessly fading into the darkness of the tunnel. If the mission that Marrida and this man need to go on weren't of such importance, he'd attempt to follow them, but he's sure the wolf would sense his presence. Instead, he stands quietly at the entrance of the tunnel for several minutes, then notices an increase in ambient light. Looking up, he sees the moon in the sky. He knows he cannot be found there by guards, or they'll want to know why is visiting this dangerous tunnel so late at night.

Damir turns and walks back to Marrida's house in silence, this time in the middle of the road. If a guard sees him now, he can say that he's on some sort of errand for Joharan. That's part of the plan Joharan prepared before Damir went off with the man and wolf; the boy is carrying the travel papers in the inside pocket of his shirt which Joharan handed to him before he set off.

* * *

KALISA IS WAITING ON THE BOTTOM STEP OF THE STAIRWAY, staring at the front door. It's more than forty minutes since Damir left with Alagur and Yalla. Now she has calmed down and her tears have dried, she wants him home, so she knows he is safe.

Esbara walks into the vestibule with a mug of honey milk, which he hands to the young girl. The warm drink will settle her nerves as well as calm her from the earlier upset. He sits down next to her, puts his arm around her and looks at her with concerned eyes.

"He'll be back soon."

Kalisa nods and takes a gentle sip of her drink, pulling a face as her lips and tongue are met by liquid several degrees too hot for her liking. She places the cup on the stairway beside her to let it cool.

Esbara and Kalisa hold their breath when they hear footsteps walking the paving slabs outside the house, but as the steps fade, they realise it must have been one of the guardsmen lighting embers in the street. Some minutes later, they hear more footsteps, which stop at the front door. A single short knock tells them these footsteps are Damir's.

Esbara gets up and signals to Kalisa to stay where she is. She grabs her cup of honey milk and climbs backwards until she's almost halfway up the stairs. Joharan and Marrida, who are talking in hushed tones in the cooking room, arrive at the doorway and wait there as Esbara unbolts the door and looks at a smiling Damir. Esbara opens the door and his friend enters the vestibule.

"No one saw us," Damir says in response to the unasked question. Joharan nods approvingly.

"How long do you think it will take him to walk the length of the tunnel?" Esbara wants to know as he bolts the door shut behind Damir.

"About three hours if he's slow, but I think they'll move pretty fast through it, judging by what I saw."

Damir gives an account of how the wolf seemed smaller than normal in the alleyway.

"What *is* a Wolf Master?" He looks at Marrida for answers. "Alagur mentioned it before he walked into the tunnels."

"I don't know," Marrida replies. "It isn't something he has told me about. I can ask him when we meet, but that won't help you to know."

"He said 'seeming smaller' is something a wolf learns when it bonds with a Wolf Master."

"I think it's a special skill the oldest Wolf Riders learn, and not many of them get to the age that Alagur is."

Joharan listens in silently, contemplating this new information. He looks at his older niece for a long moment, and Marrida looks closely at her uncle's face, noticing it's purposefully blank as if he's masking additional knowledge from the youngsters around him.

"It's time for your departure, too," he whispers. "Carrying the haversack and those two sacks. You may struggle, but Alagur did say he has worked out a plan for when you meet with him."

Marrida nods. She isn't entirely sure whether she agrees with the whole plan. The guards at the east gate will have questions about her late-night departure, as well as why she's carrying so much luggage. She holds Esbara and Kalisa in an all-embracing hug, and all three siblings are silent, knowing they're saying goodbye for a long time.

"I should be back in six months--" Marrida's voice strains under the emotion she's feeling. She has never been separated from her brother and sister for any length of time; the long days at the Temple never felt like separation to her as she was able to go home every evening. But now she's going away from the two people she loves the most, and it's breaking her heart.

"You will look after them?" she asks Joharan as she approaches him for a hug.

"I will, don't worry, I will," the man replies, feeling equally sad. *My old bond with Marrida has just been mended, only for me to lose her for — how long? Six months, she said, but it may be years, possibly even decades before she returns — if ever.* That last thought puts fear into the mind of Joharan. *I'm not young anymore, and neither is Elder Sharriba. What if neither of us sees Marrida in our lifetime again?*

Marrida turns to Damir and gives the boy an embrace of genuine friendship, whispering something into his ear which makes him look quickly towards Kalisa, blush bright red, then nod. Marrida holds his shoulders for a few more moments while Kalisa looks with some puzzlement at him, wondering what her sister whispered into his ear. Then Marrida puts the large, heavy haversack over her shoulder and picks up the two packs. Looking at Damir, she nods at the heavy front door and he unbolts it.

Marrida steps into the cool breeze of the evening, looks left and right several times, then turns left. In resolute strides, she starts her walk towards the eastern gate of the city. In a small pouch, fastened cross-ways over her chest, are the travel papers that she hopes will ease her exit from the city.

* * *

Damir watches Marrida until she turns a corner and is gone from sight, then he bolts the door shut. Now there are just four of them – himself, Kalisa, Esbara and Joharan – left in the house, and soon Joharan will need to go home.

As he looks at Kalisa, he feels heat rise again to his face.

"Do the honourable act of asking Kalisa to be your life partner," Marrida said. *"You'll have to ask Uncle Joharan and Esbara for approval now I'm gone."*

Looking at Kalisa, Damir knows his heart made this choice a long time ago, but now it has come to doing the asking, he feels shyness rise in him. If Marrida was still here, he could have asked her this simple question, but now she's gone, and Kalisa's two male family members have taken it upon themselves to flank her. If Kalisa had passed her First Rites, he could simply have asked her brother. If she was past Second Rites, he could have asked her directly, just as her father asked her mother, Eshara, to be his life partner. But at just eleven years – well, almost twelve – she's too young to be asked directly, so he'll have to ask the closest family members.

Kalisa stares at Damir so intently that she would have burned a hole through him if her gaze had turned into a Flame of the Underworld. Then, as suddenly as she started, Kalisa stops staring and walks to her cup of now lukewarm honey milk, sipping the drink with a smile.

It's just right.

Esbara walks into the front room and sits down in what is usually Marrida's seat near the fire. Joharan walks into the cooking room to get some freshly brewed tea for himself. That leaves Damir alone with Kalisa in the vestibule. He walks over and hesitantly sits next to her. She acknowledges his arrival with a broad smile, then continues sipping her drink.

The two youngsters look up when Joharan walks past them into the front room, expecting him to say something, but he's too caught up in his own thoughts and either chooses to ignore them or decides other matters are more important than talking to them at this time. Esbara looks up as his uncle walks into the front room, and watches as Joharan takes the seat opposite him near the fireplace. Adding a few extra-long-burning pieces of wood to the fire, Esbara thinks for a few moments before speaking.

"I miss Marrida," he begins. "She's been gone only minutes, and I miss her so much already." A tear escapes the boy's eye.

"I miss her too," Joharan concurs in his gentlest tone of voice.

"Will she be alright?"

"With Alagur helping her, she will be." Joharan leans forward to put more emphasis on the rest of his words. "I think there's more than a bond of friendship growing between those two."

"How do you know?"

"I saw the flash of anger in Alagur's face when we were upstairs in her room after she did her vision."

The statement is as truthful as the old man can make it. He noticed Alagur's simple gesture of affection which calmed Marrida, because he made a similar gesture many decades earlier when he and Sharriba were still close. He also saw the same gesture from his brother Markalo whenever he comforted Eshara. For a man who long ago forgot the comfort of being able to show love to another person, that simple gesture was like a deeply buried memory, which surfaced when Alagur held Marrida. The anger in Alagur's eyes was like the flash of anger which Joharan felt when Sharriba turned down his invitation to be his life partner.

Esbara observes his uncle. *There's more than he's telling*. Then he glances back at the fire, which has turned into dancing flames of yellow and orange, and ponders the future. What will it bring them? Deep in his heart, he hopes for peace, but it's possible this will exact a great price from them all that no one is prepared to pay – yet. He remembers the words he listened to at the Academy: the price paid for ignorance in The Old Days was conquest by the northern invaders.

Later that same ignorance led to the birth of the Wolf Riders.

* * *

ALAGUR WALKS AT A FAST PACE FOR ABOUT AN HOUR. Damir told him that it could take between one and three hours to travel the length of the tunnel. Even though fear doesn't often enter Alagur's mind, this tunnel isn't a place he'd want to stay in for long.

A nudge on the side of his left hip tells Alagur that the wolf beside him is nervous too. Although Yalla can see considerably further than he can in the darkness of the passage, even she's starting to feel uncomfortable sensing the discomfort of her master.

About half an hour's walk away from the tunnel is the eastern gate, guarded by twelve men who are watching a slender figure approaching them. As Marrida gets closer, one of the guards recognises her, and as she places the two packs on the ground and reaches for her travel papers, he looks at her curiously.

"I'm on a journey for my uncle." Marrida pants somewhat as she speaks. "His name is Joharan Kayrsan. My name is Mar--"

The guard stops her in her tracks. "I know who you are, Acolyte Marrida Kayrsan. We were told to let you through."

"Who told you?" Marrida asks, her heart beating in panic.

"Elder Sharriba sent word to us to expect you," the guard replies. "She said you'd have travel papers, but she has vouched for you because you're on an important errand for your uncle and her."

Marrida gapes at the man. This is an unexpected turn of events. Joharan prepared her with what to say if she was questioned about her destination, but to have Elder Sharriba intervene in this way leaves her speechless.

"Elder Sharriba sent one of the Keepers here on her behalf with the message, and asked us to tell you to be cautious on your journey," a second guard adds. "She asked us to remind you *not* to tell anyone who you are in the eastern cities. It's too dangerous for them to know, and others will give you this same warning, too. Not sure what she meant, but it sounded urgent."

"I think I know," Marrida whispers softly. "If she asks, tell her I heeded her words."

"Apparently, you're meeting an escort outside the city," the first guard continues. "You'd better hurry – don't keep him waiting."

229

Part Two

CHAPTER THIRTY

Bergas listens. He kneels behind two massive boulders, leaning against each other, which serve to obscure him from the people he hears in the distance.

Alagur was right when he said I would develop better hearing as my bond with the wolf grew. No wonder he was showing me every skill possible. They have helped me so far.

These are the very skills that would have made him into yet another Wolf Rider eventually. Instead, he's been using the hiding, running, hunting skills – everything that Alagur and his own instinct taught him – to bring him closer and closer to his home.

The group of men he hears talking and shouting is some distance away, and the sound fades slowly.

They're the fifth group in this last month I've avoided. How many more of them are still out there?

Alagur stated that Wolf Riders stayed inside City of Wolves for an obvious reason, but that reason has eluded Bergas until now. As a repeated rumble starts in his stomach, it is nature that provides the answer: Wolf Riders aren't farmers. The barren fields around City of Wolves make that evident, and most are mediocre hunters. The men who claimed that they were based their boasting, for the most part, on their own delusions of grandeur.

"I want you to learn the skill of using this knife to sever the life-giving blood vessel of an animal." Alagur's voice echoes through the mind of a shivering Bergas, who is kneeling on top of a small mound of soil. He looks down and pats down the soil some more, knowing that if he is seen now, this soon after his deed, it will endanger his life even more than it already is endangered.

Bergas reaches forward with his left hand and drops a few more handfuls of soil onto the mound, staring at the cave entrance and listening once more for sounds. He then raises himself up, walks to the cave exit and waits there.

"When you're listening for the Wolf Riders, don't listen to the men. They're guided by the signals from their wolves. If they hear a wolf of their own kind — a wolf that has a master — they'll know."

Bergas lifts the small knife in his hand. It's the same knife he's used many times to sever the blood vessel of a vole or ailep hound.

If I use this fast enough, no Wolf Rider will ever know about the wolf I had.

Bergas glances back at the heap under which a dead wolf now lies, and sighs. He led the wolf into the cave more than an hour ago, and the animal's instinct was to follow his master. This wolf, who hadn't even been named yet, trusted Bergas. In the darkest part of the cave, Bergas sat for a time, the wolf lying next to him to offer his warmth instinctively to the boy. At no time did the wolf seem to feel threatened.

"Watch the wolf's body language. There are ways to read the thoughts of a wolf without even needing to be a Wolf Master. If the wolf is content, he will show it by flattening his ears back. They can point two ways. Inward, and the wolf feels distrust; outward, and they feel happy. You're looking for the latter."

Bergas had a simple task until the time came to kill the wolf: wait. He had already pulled the knife out and it was lying under his leg, out of sight of the wolf. He spent his time brushing the coat of the wolf — a coat with a distinct colour like his own hair — and waited. The wolf became mellow, and as time passed, his snorting indicated that he was dreaming wolfish dreams.

Bergas gingerly pulled out the small knife, pausing the motion every few seconds as Alagur had taught him. They'd practised the motions on a piece of dead bovine, but that didn't make them less dramatic or impactful to the boy.

I wish we could be good friends, as Alagur and Yalla are, Bergas thought, watching the wolf turn his head to nip at a fly which had landed on his flank. When the wolf turned his head, his main artery became exposed, and the boy seized the opportunity to plunge the knife exactly where Alagur had taught him. A moment afterwards, the knife was embedded.

"When you have punctured the artery, you need to wait for a few minutes before

pulling the knife out. Leaving it there dazes the wolf. He will growl, but he will weaken fast. Just move away and wait. When the wolf slumps down, you can pull the knife out. Then push his head against the ground so the blood soaks into the ground."

A low growl came from deep inside the wolf. But as Alagur had stated, his motions faltered fast. He tried to walk, slumped once, then took another laboured step and slumped without rising again. The fine sand particles below the beast clumped with the blood already pouring out in slow motion – or so it seemed to Bergas. He stepped forward with caution – a wounded beast was still dangerous – pulled the knife out and jumped back. The blood was now pouring out faster, and the shiny glint disappeared from the wolf's eyes.

The beast was dead.

Bergas knelt next to the dead wolf for a while before beginning the task of digging a hole in the sand. As he was digging, he recalled the many times Alagur made him dig holes for burying the innards of the voles and ailep hounds they'd hunted. Back then, he'd hated the task, but today it meant the difference between discovery and evasion.

After thirty minutes, the digging was complete. An hour later, the wolf had a large layer of sand covering him. To anyone finding the cave, it would seem as though a sandstorm had passed and a wounded wolf had sought shelter and perished inside it.

"When you bury a dead animal well, it will seem like you are making it obvious they're there, but nature will help you out. She'll allow the wolf's essence to sink back into the soil."

After Bergas had buried the wolf, he sat staring for a few minutes, feeling aimless and very alone. The wilderness was no place for a boy not even old enough to do First Rites, which take place at a younger age in Azaquina than they do in Ruh'nar. Suddenly, all the pent up anger and frustration overtook Bergas. He pulled at the plants and nearby trees with his hands, rushing in and out of the cave with handfuls of leaves and broken branches.

After fifteen minutes, he stopped and stared, panting loudly. He was fit, but the rage had sapped his reserves of energy.

Bergas now uses handfuls of sand to brush the knife clean of the congealing dark red blood. There are ways for a Wolf Rider to determine if blood has been on a knife, and with the right ingredients, which type.

This is why Alagur told Bergas to kill so many ailep hounds which, although similar to a wolf, could render any such test inconclusive.

I need to bury this knife, too, and far from here so no one ever realises it was used for killing that wolf.

After a final glance in every direction, listening as well as he can manage, Bergas exits the cave and busies himself with the final task Alagur taught him.

"This is a skill only ever taught when a man becomes a Wolf Rider, but it's crucial you know it. It will mean the difference between life and death. You can use it in two ways. The first method will make the place where you kill the wolf invisible to those passing it."

After another ten minutes, the entrance of the cave matches the inside. It has to appear as though one of the sandstorms that pass over this part of Keldarra during the late summer months caused the damage. Now Bergas needs to put as much distance between himself and the scene of his deed as possible. Any Wolf Rider finding him at this very moment would investigate, and what they would find would be reason enough to throw him into the pits with the wild wolves.

A sad sigh escapes his mouth as Bergas looks up to check the position of the sun. The heat is more noticeable after all the work he's been doing for most of the morning. He's been riding for a long time, but part of his journey has been on foot, running next to the wolf.

"Wolf Runners don't ride." Alagur had spoken the words with disgust dripping from each syllable. *"They run, and you will need to be as good as one by the time the wolf is dead."*

Bergas is exhausted, but he cannot afford to give in to it. Not now, not ever.

Not until I'm home.

Bergas pulls up the hood of the dark cloak which he wrapped around him almost absentmindedly as the chill in the cave became too much.

"You mustn't be recognised by anyone still out hunting, especially when you're close to City of Wolves. The reason I told you where to bury the wolf is based on deception. Wolf Riders won't suspect a betrayal that close to the city."

This is the second way Alagur taught Bergas to render a location invisible to a man's mind.

City of Wolves looms east of his location: an ominous, dark silhouette. The sun reflects off some of its highest ruins. Bergas listens to check for sounds coming from the east. No sound, other than distant bird calls and the nearer chirps of insect, fill the air. The sounds of the men he heard passing by are long gone.

The path he needs to cross, which is located ahead of him, is quite familiar to him. Alagur travelled towards Venrasia Woods using a specific route which lodged itself in the mind of his young charge. Bergas knows there's a shallow river nearby, running from north to south, directly to his west. He needs to reach it unseen.

"I'm going to teach you how to run for long distances without the need to stop for food, drink or rest. When you do need to eat, don't run again for at least four hours afterwards. Only ever drink a few mouthfuls of water at a time."

The boy looks each way, then in a practised dash, crosses the path and dives behind a bush under the tree that was opposite him moments earlier. He's now near the looming undergrowth around Venrasia Woods.

"I don't know the origin of the name Venrasia, but the parchments we found suggest it's been here for at least ten thousand years."

Bergas measures the distance between his current location and the outskirts of the ancient woodland. After glancing intently at the landscape, he spots something resembling an old riverbed with his sharp eyes.

I guess I still have the Wolf Rider skill even without a wolf.

Beyond the woodland, the outline of Northern Blades – the northern mountain range where Yalla came from – is visible.

East of that is Bay of Whispers, and east of that is home. I won't ever leave Azaquina when I'm back home.

Bergas glances towards the east where another city lies – a city he glimpsed as he travelled south to City of Wolves.

"Avoid Alzamar at all costs. I don't know how, but somehow the Wolf Riders know when to attack it, and they do it frequently. If you want to go home, head north

to South Valley of Miza. It's the safest way home for you."

Bergas recognises the name of the valley – both from Alagur's retellings about Yalla, and because his own father knew many retellings of the region. One of the retellings had been a warning about the Wolf Runners, who live somewhere in the western end of the valley. A similar warning came later from Alagur.

With his general bearings now established, Bergas looks around one more time, listening attentively to the sounds of his surroundings. He gets up and picks up the bundle he carries with him, strapping it to his back before walking towards the dried-out riverbed ahead of him. He keeps listening for sounds that may alert him to danger, but can discern none. Soon afterwards, he is engulfed by the deep shade of the ancient forest.

Bergas immediately notes the contrast in the temperature between the open landscape and the woodland. He's glad now that he put his cloak on earlier, even though he's been sweating profusely from the heat around his midriff where it's tied shut. Bergas grabs an edge of his cloak and uses it to wipe the droplets of sweat from his face and hairline, then reaches for the water pouch he filled with cool water from the river he passed over a day earlier, taking a mouthful, and then one more.

"Heat can kill," Alagur had warned, *"so keep drinking plenty of water, even when you've left the direct heat of the sun."*

After drinking the cool liquid, the boy feels more at ease, the sweaty discomfort seeming to pass.

The trees of Venrasia Woods possess thick trunks and Bergas is curious about their general appearance, stopping at a few to feel their texture. The bark feels surprisingly spongy to the touch, and Bergas decides that this relates to the age of the woodland. The landscape is different from anything he has ever seen, but remembering what his father told him long ago, he searches the bark for signs of a specific type of moss which only grows on the northern side of a tree.

"If you follow the moss trail, you'll always find your way northward."

Tentatively at first, but gradually with more confidence, Bergas walks north through the dense, old woodland. Keeping a steady pace, he grows familiar with the sounds of the birds and insects. Although the sounds of wolves and other predatory animals occasionally make him scurry for cover, after an hour of travelling, he feels safe enough in the surroundings to up his pace.

As his progress is good, Bergas recalls the events of the last few weeks. It's almost a season since Alagur rode off on his massive wolf, and the boy wonders whether Alagur ever glances towards this wood from the old walls of the city in the east, tracing the boy's journey in his mind.

I may even be home before he gets back to City of Wolves.

After Alagur had left and Bergas had placed the packs under the bergas bushes as instructed, he sat down for a good hour, thinking about the journey ahead. Bergas hoped then for a miracle, but the progress he has made is better than he ever dared to hope. The boy knows that the journey from the region outside Ruh'nar to Azaquina will take him at least a whole season, and that's if he doesn't stop or sleep. That's why Alagur's suggestion had been so clever: if the boy travelled north-east in the direction of City of Wolves for a period – only for ten days, Alagur warned – using the speed of the wolf, he could cut at least two weeks off his overall travel time. He was indeed fortunate because the wolf proved to be faster than he expected.

When Bergas arrived at the old tree stump Alagur had described to him, he steered the wolf northward, riding at the highest speed his young body could manage.

"Wolves are masters at traversing long distances when they've formed a pact with a Wolf Rider. I can teach you the skill to make certain this wolf thinks you are one, like me. The wolf's natural abilities will heighten, but so will yours. It's something that they don't do in the wild."

It took a month to travel from outside Ruh'nar to the cave south-west of City of Wolves. Another week got Bergas as far as the most southern outcrops of the ancient woodland. He then had to wait for the right time to dispose of the wolf before the later parts of the journey could commence, so the cave served its usefulness in so many ways. The journey north was frightful for someone as young as Bergas, but he is now going towards home – he hopes.

Bergas turns on his heels to climb the steep path of a slope, listening once again for voices or wolf howls. A misstep on this path would cause serious injury or even death. He frowns for a moment, reconsidering whether to attempt the climb.

"Do not ever deviate from the route I've shown you. It's the shortest route north."

Bergas never dared to ask how Alagur knew this to be true. The boy kneels down and studies the obstacle thoroughly for several minutes, then gets up and resolutely places his left foot on its surface. Before stepping up, he makes sure none of tiny chip stones are underfoot. These caused a landslide on the scree near Bay of Whispers, and the boy listens to an inner voice repeating his father's warnings to measure his footsteps.

When Bergas knows his foot is secure, he pushes up and immediately places his right foot a little higher. With a slow and steady rhythm, Bergas ascends the hill without any mishaps. At the top, he wipes away the sweat pearls that have appeared due to the effort.

A good half an hour later, Bergas stands a hundred paces further along the top of the ancient bank. He draws in his breath when he sees a vast field of grass, covered sporadically with small mounds of soil. On each grows a large bergas bush. Bergas recalls seeing a strange orange and green landscape from the western window of the highest tower still standing inside City of Wolves, and he had wondered then what he was looking at. Now he knows.

Venrasia Woods is now visible to his left. Looking back at the embankment he's just scaled, Bergas figures he's standing on what was once a deep riverbank from a time as ancient as the woodland. In those days, the river spanned from west to east as far as an ancient resident of Keldarra would have been able to see. In the west, he sees the woodland swells to a thicker mass, but the south-east end seems scraggly by comparison. He knows this side is closest to City of Wolves, and the Wolf Riders are the cause of its desolate appearance.

"Pretty much every Wolf Rider cares nothing for the woodland's glorious vastness. They're more interested in it as a continuous source of wood for the bonfires they want to burn in the city, day and night."

"I guess you came this way to get Yalla," Bergas murmurs, walking on the embankment's edge. As he does so, he increases his speed little by little. An urgent feeling in the depths of his stomach makes him want to get away from this place – now.

If I could see this landscape from the city, then anyone looking in this direction from one of the towers could possibly see me running through it.

Bergas starts to sprint without realising it. Then he stops, glancing towards City of Wolves silhouetted against the lighter limestone hills that lie beyond it. The contrast between the old buildings and the landscape would have amazed the boy at any other time, but now he squints his eyes against the glaring sunlight and looks in the direction of one specific tower, the distinct shape of which is visible even from this distance.

"I hope you're there, watching me going home, Alagur."

Bergas sighs deeply and continues running.

Had the boy looked west towards a long, narrow lake, he would have been looking towards where Alagur and Marrida would erect a small camp on their journey. But at this moment, Alagur is still in Ruh'nar, walking through an almost ruined tunnel that dates back several hundred years.

CHAPTER THIRTY-ONE

AFTER WHAT SEEMS LIKE A LONG TIME, Alagur sees moonlight at the end of the tunnel. The exit is directly north-east of Ruh'nar, and Damir explained to him that the moonlight would indicate where he is.

The musty tunnels have felt precarious to the man. In places, he has sensed rather than seen that the structure is in some state of repair, but in other places, it has felt like he's climbing over rubble. Fresh air and a shallow breeze tell Alagur he'll soon be outside. Grinning inwardly, he thinks that for all Samur seems to know about Ruh'nar, he doesn't know about these tunnels.

Or does he?

A slight nudge alerts Alagur; Yalla is advocating caution, so when the man at long last reaches the tunnel's exit, he kneels in the shadow of its overhang and glances out. To his left, he sees the shimmer of the vast lake, features surrounding it telling him this is the same lake at which the two youngest boys – Kaizor and Ebagar – were left before the attack on the city.

Looking back towards the exit of the tunnel, Alagur understands why the Wolf Riders never found it.

If you look at it without knowing what you're looking for, the exit looks like a shadow inflection in the rocky hill which flanks the city on the north side.

Alagur's inherent skill as a master tactician tells him at once it's a very good form of defence. The rock slopes are *too* steep to climb. In the eerie light of the moonlight, together with the mists cropping the tops of the hills, the scene takes on an otherworldly feeling. It sends shivers up Alagur's spine.

No wonder Joharan told Damir not to play in those tunnels.

Alagur frowns. Looking towards his right, he can make out the high crest of the nearby mountains which flank the valley in which Ruh'nar is located. He sees the footpath which Damir described.

"You need to follow it until you come to a fork in the road. There you'll find a large boulder made of white chalky stone next to which you'll wait for Marrida."

Signalling to Yalla to be cautious, the man straightens up and gradually walks towards the path ahead of him. He knows the wolf will follow his lead, but will make herself as invisible to human eyes as she can. The ash, which he rubbed over her fur while preparing her before they set off, helps to remove its sheen, which would otherwise reflect the moon's glow.

A single cloud decides to play in the man and wolf's favour, floating in front of the moon just as Alagur comes into open view on the path. Alagur rushes the length of the path and is at the boulder after just ten minutes. Here he directs Yalla to hide in the shadows of the boulder without making any sound, while he sits at the fork in the road and makes a small fire as planned. Should any person walk by, he needs to appear to be an escort waiting for someone.

Alagur takes the tinder kit from the pouch Damir gave him before setting off so he doesn't need to go to Yalla and reach for his own tinder kit, risking the wolf being discovered. Alagur sends a silent thought of gratitude towards Damir for the gesture, and vows to himself he'll make good on his promise and return with the tools one day to hand them back to the boy.

It isn't long before Alagur sees people walking along the path, coming from the north and heading towards the city. The men and women raise their left arms up in the customary greeting used by all on a journey – Alagur learnt this when travelling to find himself a good quality wolf. The group is soon out of sight and Alagur lets go of the breath he was holding in as they approached. He feels genuine relief that they merely greeted him as a waiting traveller rather than stopping and questioning his presence.

* * *

A FIGURE APPROACHES FROM THE SOUTH – from Ruh'nar. It's the slender shape of a woman carrying several packs. For a moment, Alagur thinks it's yet another traveller, but then, as the moon reappears with its pale light, he lets out an audible sigh of relief when he recognises Marrida.

She smiles when she sees him. "How long have you been waiting for me, then?" Her voice holds a hint of teasing.

"I've been here twenty minutes or so." Alagur tries to sound stern. "There were some travellers who greeted me as they walked past."

"I saw them." Marrida places the two large packs she's carrying on the ground. "Where's Yalla?" she hisses.

"She's nearby."

Marrida nods and looks up at the man in front of her. The moon reflects in his eyes, which are a dark shade of indigo-blue in the night light. His normally sun-tanned skin seems even darker, and she sees strands of his hair waving about in the soft breeze. Marrida fights an urge to reach up and tuck the hair back under his hood. Now they're alone, she feels the attraction towards him more than before, even though deep down she still feels some underlying mistrust for what he once represented.

This is a Wolf Rider, she tells herself, *he's only here because it is convenient for him.*

But Marrida also knows she needs him, and he's here by his own choice. His every action since he awoke from his coma has indicated that he doesn't want to be part of the Wolf Riders anymore, and this journey has presented him with a chance to break free from that life. Perhaps it will even present him with an opportunity to go home again.

The strands of hair, dancing back and forth in the soft night breezes, tease Marrida. As she keeps looking up, she feels her misgivings about Alagur ebb away little by little. He looks down at her without speaking and sees emotions playing over her face, but he doesn't ask her what she's thinking, instead deciding to wait for her to make up her mind what to do next. He also doesn't want to spoil the moment.

"We should go," he whispers. Marrida breaks her gaze and nods. Picking up the two packs from the ground, she starts to walk, but Alagur's hand stops her.

"Let me carry at least one of them."

Alagur doesn't wait for an answer, quietly forcing Marrida to relinquish her grasp on the pack in her left hand. Marrida doesn't respond to the gesture, but deep down she feels grateful. The weight of the packs has taken its toll. As strong as she is naturally, it's pushed her strength to its limit. She suddenly feels a wave of tiredness overcome her and she sighs deeply.

Alagur speaks up. "Joharan told me that we need to follow this road north until we find two houses opposite one another, then we turn east beyond them."

"What about the wolf?" Marrida can't mask the panic in her voice.

"She'll follow us, but she knows to stay out of sight. When we reach the small forest your uncle told me about, we can pack all this on Yalla and mount her. She'll carry us for some distance."

The duo walks for half an hour or so before they spot the two houses ahead. As they pass the wooden structures, the laughter and banter from the families within drift towards them. They see the road ahead that goes from south-west to north-east. Alagur points towards the north-east and Marrida sees waving treetops nearby. This woodland is more of a copse, one of the many that cover the fields just north of Ruh'nar, and Marrida remembers it is where she and her uncle gathered wood for his crafting when she was a child.

Alagur smiles for a moment, recalling an evening, a month before his First Rites, when one of the oldest Elder Men was doing retellings. This old man, greyed with age, had a presence that meant he was held in awe by the younger Wolf Riders. He chose that night to tell of the wolves who look like ghosts on a stormy night. The retelling impacted on the young Alagur, who immediately vowed to himself that he would get such a wolf as his chosen companion. Then a few weeks later, just days before his First Rites, he travelled to the Miza region and found the wolves which the Elder Man had described in his retellings. From behind some bushes in the valley, he observed the pack of around twenty-five to thirty wolves of various sizes and ages before making the bond with one of them. One wolf only needed to give a single command and all the other wolves would scramble towards a specific location. It was this skill which attracted him to the wolf he'd later name Yalla.

The unique bond which develops between a Wolf Rider and wolf is forged when the wolf willingly comes to the man and lies down on its belly. If the wolf doesn't rise when the man kneels in front of it and lays his hand on its forehead, they have a bond. The man knows then that the wolf will follow him when he returns to City of Wolves. Yalla, whose name means 'Mountain Ghost' in Alagur's childhood dialect, lay down in front of him within minutes of his arrival. When Alagur laid his hand on Yalla's forehead, she pushed it with her large, wet nostrils. Then as a further act of acceptance, she rolled onto her side and exposed her belly to the man – a wolf's ultimate act of trust.

Now, Yalla is showing this trust again by the way she is lying down, waiting for her master. Alagur's pace quickens as he and Marrida approach the edge of the copse. Yalla waits in silence, watching for a signal from Alagur to say she can come out of hiding. She hears Marrida's heavy breathing and knows instinctively that the woman is labouring from the effort of carrying the packs without understanding the reason why. A gentle wag betrays recognition as she catches Marrida's scent in the wind.

A few moments later, at Alagur's signal, the wolf reveals herself. Marrida is relieved to put her heavy pack down at long last. She smiles as Yalla greets her with a nudge of her nose and a raspy tongue over her hand. The same hand scratches the massive wolf's ears and forehead, which brings on delighted tail wagging in response. The wolf greets her master, and their greeting is the familiar pressing of forehead against forehead. Marrida watches the genuine and open display of affection between the man and wolf.

After the greeting, Alagur spends some time adjusting several packs on Yalla's back, using a spare piece of the rope Esbara supplied him with to fashion a harness for the two packs Marrida carried from Ruh'nar. She knows their first city stop will be Alzamar to sell the contents of the packs to local merchants there. Joharan's reputation for high quality good is widely known, and the travel papers she is carrying identify her as his representative. The additional papers from Elder Sharriba that she was given at the gates of Ruh'nar will make it easy to enter any city without being asked about her destination. No one will ask questions of someone who's travelling as the representative of the current Elder of the Order of Truth.

Alagur finishes his task and mounts the wolf. It's at this moment that Marrida sees how large Yalla really is. The man's feet are at least shin height from the ground, and the woman realises hers will be even further off the ground because she's at least a head shorter than him.

Alagur guides Yalla to a nearby fallen tree trunk and motions towards Marrida.

"If you climb up on this tree trunk, you can just lift your leg over her back and sit on her."

Marrida decides this isn't the time or place to start arguing with Alagur. She'd be happier to walk beside him as he rides on the wolf, but time is of the essence. They need to be out of Sabeya by sunrise or people will notice them. When they were finalising their plans, Alagur mentioned that he sent Bergas home via a specific route, and that apart from their visit to Alzamar, they'll follow the same route. Bergas has had almost a season's head start, and he's alone and unburdened by a heavy load, so if they want to catch up with him, they'd better travel much faster than they could manage on foot.

Marrida climbs the tree trunk, feeling very self-conscious because it means lifting her skirt up. She has always felt the need to keep her dignity and be properly dressed around Alagur, and she wishes she'd grabbed some of her brother's old trousers to travel in instead of her long dress. But then she may have had problems at the city gate as Keepers always wear long dresses, coming to a hand's length above their ankles.

She remembers, with some fondness, the time when Joharan brought her with him to these very woods. Then she wore trousers so she could climb around and get dirty, but that was more than half a lifetime ago.

Holding on to a thick branch with one hand, Marrida balances herself upright when she's on top of the tree trunk. Alagur guides Yalla next to her and holds out his left hand. Marrida is about to climb behind him when he shakes his head.

"You need to be in front. For balance."

Marrida looks at him for a moment, wondering why. But without saying a word, she decides to oblige and lifts her right leg over Yalla's broad shoulders. She momentarily draws in her breath when Alagur takes hold of her waist to help her sit down, feeling the haversack glide from her arm. The motions from behind her tell her that it has joined the one Alagur is carrying.

Looking down at the elaborate harness which is strapped over Yalla's head, she sees Alagur's hands grab hold of two leather straps, which means she's enfolded in his warm arms. It makes her feel both at ease and somewhat awkward at the same time.

"Are you comfortable?" Alagur asks from behind her. She feels his warm breath on the back of her neck and shoulders as he speaks.
"Yes," she replies quietly.
"Hold the strap in the centre of the harness."

The woman nods. "I think I'm ready now." Marrida feels a knot of fear form in her stomach as Yalla starts to walk forward at a slow pace. She can feel the rippling of the wolf's muscles below her, but she can also feel herself pressing against Alagur. This unexpectedly shoots tingles through her body. Neither speaks, and Marrida doesn't realise that the man behind her is biting his bottom lip because of the sudden surge of feelings which are welling up in him, too.

Better concentrate on getting us safely away from Ruh'nar.

Alagur forces himself to put aside his feelings for Marrida. He has liked her from the first moment he laid eyes on her, and now they're alone, he can no longer hide from these growing feelings. But he's still convinced that Marrida dislikes him, and only puts up with him for the sake of their mission.

Slowly, Yalla picks up speed, adjusting her usual pace because she's carrying two people and a lot more packs than she has carried in the past. She veers north, instinct telling her the large woodland, which is steadily coming into view, is where Alagur wants to go. Venrasia Woods, which Bergas entered for his own safety, will also give cover to a man, a woman close to Second Rites, and a large silver-grey-and-white wolf.

The instinct to go at speed takes the wolf over. Within a few minutes, Marrida feels the cold wind of predawn pushing into her nostrils and sweeping her hair back. She never thought she'd do anything like this, and it feels good. As she watches the landscape flash by through squinted eyes, she smiles in delight, and some of the discomfort of sitting so close to Alagur washes away.

The wolf is strong. I doubted whether she could cope with carrying her load and two people, but now I see how powerful she is, both in strength and endurance.

Alagur feels Marrida relax in front of him. Part of him thinks it's only because she's no longer scared of riding the wolf, but as she relaxes more, she leans back against his chest. Whether she realises she's doing this, he doesn't know. And Alagur doesn't want to break the spell of the delight that the fast pace of the journey is causing her, so he stays silent and uses his knees and legs to guide the wolf below him. He does, however, feel the same surge of emotion he felt earlier when Marrida relaxes against his chest.

The journey gives Marrida a chance to think about the days ahead, and what they may encounter. Without realising how tired she is, as she thinks she drifts into a dreamless sleep, lulled by the steady rhythm of the wolf's motion.

Yalla keeps running tirelessly, and Alagur, who senses Marrida is now asleep, urges her to greater speeds than before.

CHAPTER THIRTY-TWO

Bergas has been running for four hours since waking up. He left the grassland behind days ago, and he's now enjoying a less hasty trek through elevated areas in the landscape that are more familiar to him. He manages to climb up another steep bank marking the beginning of the higher plains of Northern Blade which he once trekked through with his father. But as he always climbed around the other side of the tall mountain range, the side bordering the ocean, this part of the region is unknown to him.

Bergas occasionally spots mountain sheep grazing in sporadic groups. From their unkempt appearance, he can tell they're the wild variety, not the type herded by the farmers in the hills and mountains. One grazing sheep looks up at the boy while chewing on the long blades of the late summer grass which dot the landscape.

Looking back, Bergas can still see the vastness of Venrasia Woods looming in the lower part of the valley. Everything looks impossibly big from here.

I can see the dim outlines of the structures in City of Wolves. The buildings there must have been huge before they were destroyed in the first revolt of the Wolf Riders — one that Alagur told me was orchestrated by Sey'qar and Yozan hundreds of years ago. I can also make out the vast desert-like plains bordering the ancient city on the other side of the forest.

Looking west, Bergas can see the true length of South Valley of Miza for the first time. Alagur told him about the region, but the boy dismissed his words as a myth. However, he now sees the true size of the region where Alagur found Yalla: it stretches to a distant blur, beyond which is a place Bergas has to avoid at all costs: Zehar. Comparing this region to the small area he saw with his father, or the small pockets of the valley he's passed on his journey, he can see that it is every bit as vast as Alagur said.

Along its southern side is the evidence that it used to be the bank of a great river in ancient times. It is likely he was standing in the dried-out bed of that river when he looked up towards the mountains in the north and the woodland to the south. The river he passed earlier was an offshoot of this greater river bed.

"I suggest you look west. You'll see a vista that has no equal in any part of Keldarra."

"You're right, Alagur."

Bergas flops down on a round boulder and just stares for a while to take in the landscape. He's certain he won't see anything like it again in his lifetime, because once he gets home, he plans to stay there and never venture out again.

In the retelling, the earliest Wolf Master came here with the two men he trusted most. All three rode off with wolves that resembled Yalla. Bergas frowns. Why am I thinking about them? Why do I feel so connected to this region and to Northern Blades all of a sudden? Could this be the special dreams Mam mentioned starting for me?

Bergas glances over his left shoulder when something wet hits his nose. He sees glistening white streaks floating just above the surface of one of the many mountain peaks.

Snow — that's the last thing I need. It's still a season before it comes down heavily, and then I'll be wading through it waist deep. I need to hurry.

Most of the ground around Bergas is still a blend of brown and yellow rock surfaces, but as he wipes away another snowflake from his face, he knows it won't be long before the high ground is covered in snow. As he watches the snowflakes fall, he's reminded of the pearls he used to help to gather with his father from a type of shellfish for the local tailors or jewel makers.

Snowflakes do resemble caranimia pearls — a large pile of them.

The memory sends a wave of emotion through the boy, and he looks forward towards the woodland instead. Glancing down at the woodland, he wonders again if Alagur is going to leave the Wolf Riders too.

It's obvious Alagur knows these lands well, probably a lot better than any of the other Wolf Riders realise. That's why he told me to go this way and not to go near Alzamar. Bergas looks east through eyes squinting against the sun's glare. *I wonder — if I travel for another four days in that direction before going up one of the mountain passes, could I shorten the journey by a week or more?*

"I need to take the risk," Bergas mumbles. "I'll be close to City of Wolves for several days — the shortest distance is about five days — so there's more chance of meeting Wolf Riders, but I can travel at night. That way I'll avoid them."

It is a risk, but he needs to get home as quickly as possible. That is his priority, and risks are worth taking when something is a priority.

Reaching down to the pack of belongings he is carrying with him, Bergas takes out a small piece of dried meat. Tearing tiny strips from it, he eats slowly, glancing again at the outline of the city on the horizon. It seems to shimmer in the sunlight one moment, then be swallowed up by clouds the next.

It was sunny like today when I arrived in the city, after travelling for weeks in front of the man who snatched me. Bergas thinks long and hard about his life in the city. *I never knew the man's name, but I will never forget his face, or how he stank.*

The journey from Azaquina to City of Wolves took maybe twenty-three days. His abductor was a man with long, dirty blond hair worn loose. Covering his head, he wore a hat made of some sort of leather. It was bleached lighter in places and stained with sweat marks and possibly blood. The wolf the man was riding was jet black, and when the boy tried to reach out to the wolf, its menacing snarls provoked a wave of laughter from the Wolf Riders and other boys alike. After that, Bergas felt afraid each time he was told to tend to the wolves, and whenever he was in the enclosures where the wolves were kept, the other boys would tease him.

This teasing continued until the early days of last autumn season. Bergas was walking back to the building where he slept at night: a stone house, which could have been the house of a merchant in a distant past. He was two streets away when a group of boys approached him. The oldest two pushed him into a side alley, and between them, they started to beat him up. Bergas fought back, and the shouts attracted the attention of one of the Wolf Riders. On seeing the tall, muscular man, closely followed by his massive silver-grey-and-white wolf, most of the attacking group ran off, but the instigator of the fight – a boy with brown hair that came down to his shoulders – was caught by the scruff of the neck. A menacing growl from the wolf caused the boy to stop struggling very quickly, but not before his flailing arms had hit the Wolf Rider on the side of his face. A red mark and swelling grew as the man escorted the boy to the Elder Men, who took it upon themselves to punish him quite severely.

"I'll look at that bruise." Bergas had been a bit surprised when he was tended to by the man he'd later come to know as Alagur – even more so

as the man seemed unconcerned about his own injury. *"You're going to sleep in that room over there from now on."*

No boy dared to tease the red-haired boy from that day, after Bergas was befriended by Alagur. The man became a mix of a brother and a friend. But Alagur had not simply chosen the boy for charitable reasons. As soon as Bergas had recovered from the blows to his head, his training started. Alagur was a hard taskmaster, though not as cruel as others.

"It's a year since I arrived there," Bergas mumbles. "It feels so much longer."

Alagur selected the wolf for Bergas either by accident or by design; Bergas never knew which. A pang of renewed sadness washes over the boy when he remembers the beast, now rotting down to be reclaimed by nature in a distant cave. He glances south for one moment before his gaze jerks back east. After selecting the wolf, Alagur started telling Bergas about Yalla and about the city. Soon afterwards, Alagur took him through the snow-covered streets to a large, deserted building, holding up a makeshift torch and pointing at the walls. Among the many legends known to the Wolf Riders, the ones he began telling with six simple words, which echoed through what would have been a grand vestibule in a distant past, sent a particular chill down Bergas's spine.

"This is where it all started."

Later that same week, Bergas returned to the building and walked around inside it, wrapping his cloak tightly around himself. The chill from the winter's day had crept into the building and snowflakes drifted through several broken windows. In a small room on the third floor of the building, he found some parchments which he and Alagur looked at later. After reading the parchments, the man became moodier and more pensive.

"You can never speak of what we saw here."

The day of departure for Ruh'nar came faster than Bergas wanted. Although Alagur seemed excited about the attack when he was with Samur and the other Wolf Riders, the boy knew better. In the week before the departure, everything the man said was a warning: a warning to exercise caution while they were in City of Wolves, and during the journey. Every action Alagur made told Bergas he was planning something.

"I never realised that the plan was to help me to leave," Bergas mumbles.

Others in City of Wolves noticed the friendship between Alagur and Bergas, particularly Samur, who subjected the boy to disparaging remarks at regular intervals.

I guess he was jealous. I heard him talk about dealing with that traveller who told him about the Wolf Riders, so I guess Alagur knew Samur was dangerous, but didn't want to talk about it. Probably the reason for his bad mood most of the time.

Bergas had witnessed the growing bad feeling between Alagur and Samur, although they were claiming to be friends, even Pack Brothers.

Alagur didn't confide much in Samur, but he did share things with me — he treated me more like a brother. One day, I hope I can tell Alagur how much I appreciated it. When I'm home, I hope that I hear a knock on the door, and when I open it, he'll be standing there.

Bergas gets up and starts walking northeast.

I'll stick to Alagur's plan. I'll show him that I trust him.

His thoughts turning to home, Bergas ponders what he may find there. *I don't want to get there and find out that the Wolf Riders returned and snatched more boys from the city. And Mam — I hope she's safe and alive.* A momentary gnaw of doubt forces a fatalistic thought into his mind. *She could be dead, and I'll have made this return journey for nothing.* Bergas shakes his head to dispel the thought. *It will only take me two or three more weeks at this pace, then I will be home.*

Bergas stops abruptly, looking around for shelter. All the thinking and running has exhausted Bergas to a limit he isn't prepared for. Glancing at the hill he's stopped beside, panting loudly despite having built up some measure of resilience over the previous few weeks of travel, he spots a ledge nestled in between two black slabs of stone, with a further small opening spacious enough for his bag. Bergas needs to get up the hill and inside the shelter.

Clambering up to the ledge, Bergas checks inside. A moment later, he slides down to where his bag lies.

Bergas looks up at the sky. His surroundings have become darker without him noticing. *It's going to be a dark night,* he thinks. *There are too many clouds for the stars to be visible.*

Shrugging his shoulders, Bergas swings the bag onto the ledge. He uses an outcrop midway between the ledge and the ground to hoist himself up with some effort. A few false starts and then a successful push up later, and he is kneeling on the ledge. He pushes the bag forward and leans down on his elbows, panting.

After his panting subsides, Bergas looks around and discovers the space is larger and deeper than he thought.

I can shelter from the wind. It's cold at night even with this cloak.

He sees a pile of small rocks in the back corner of the shelter. For a moment, he considers moving some, but remembers another of Alagur's warnings.

"Except for when you dispose of the wolf, do not alter your surroundings in any way, or a passing Wolf Rider may notice that something is different. Many of them search the landscape for…well, to be precise, they search for boys to snatch. Like the one who arrived all black and blue not long after you did."

Bergas pulls his hand back from the stones. He once again sees the Wolf Rider whipping the boy with a bundle of hardened leather strips. In his mind, the whip has just struck his hand for even thinking to disobey Alagur, though that wouldn't ever have happened. Alagur never punished him like the other Wolf Riders punished their apprentices so liberally.

I may attract the attention of anyone travelling past here if I don't leave things as they are.

But after ten minutes or so, Bergas changes his mind. With some effort, he moves three of the largest rocks to the edge of the platform, not realising that each stone he's selected resembles a rubha apple. Bergas purposely spreads the other stones randomly over the rock surface, then crawls on his hands and knees to the furthest corner of the ledge and lies down to sleep, pulling his cloak tightly around him for comfort.

A gentle breeze catches the flap of the bag above the boy so it hangs down. When he shifts his position, Bergas notices and makes the effort to anchor the flap in place with a few stones, fashioning it into a makeshift tent. He smiles at his handiwork then lies back down.

If Papa was still alive, he would have been proud.

Bergas's smile drops into a sad grimace. His father first taught him the skill of surviving in the wilderness. He taught his son many skills, included fishing, butchery, weapon making and carving, and these skills ultimately allowed the boy to survive in one of the harshest places in existence: City of Wolves.

"These skills will help you if you're ever snatched."

Bergas had looked at his father and told him he would keep safe. *"I'll hide so they won't find me."*

The first few times that Azaquina came under attack, Bergas did manage to avoid the Wolf Riders. Then a storm arrived over the bay and damaged many boats and nets. Bergas went to help repair them, as did many other boys, and stood staring at the ocean, waiting for his father to return from a fishing trip he'd gone on a few days earlier.

Mam said Papa died while he was fishing. And I was so stupid to rush to the harbour that day. And then the Wolf Riders came.

Bergas was found hiding under an overturned, partially-constructed fishing boat.

He grabs a leftover piece of bread from the open sack and takes a bite. It tastes stale. He was passing a house, and the smell of freshly baked bread led him to the back of the building where he grabbed one of the four loaves lying in the open window. Without delay, he wrapped the bread in his leather hat, then rushed away to a nearby copse to eat some of it.

Bergas glances past the overhang and sees his surroundings getting visibly darker. He listens for sounds, and the most audible are the evening birds in the nearby trees. No sound tells him that Wolf Riders may be passing, and that settles his mind.

For a time, Bergas stares into the space in front of him without seeing anything as the light gradually diminishes, first bathing everything in a red hue, and then a dark blue hue. Finally, he falls asleep.

CHAPTER THIRTY-THREE

ALAGUR SLOWS THE WOLF DOWN as the vast wilderness of Venrasia Woods comes into view. Their location is perhaps three days west of where – ten days earlier – Bergas entered the same woodland. The sunlight of early morning reflects off the leaves of several saplings edging the tree line. Alagur looks up at the trees that tower above him, recalling the first time he entered these woods on his way to find himself the biggest mountain wolf possible. That day it rained, but now the drops of moisture falling on his face are from the early morning dew.

Yalla's raspy panting catches Alagur's attention. She's tired from running; he has pushed her to the edge of her limits as he doesn't want to be in open view of anyone who may pass them. Under the cover of the woodland before the day truly starts, they are safer.

Marrida yawns and moans. "Where are we?" she asks.
"At Venrasia Woods."

Alagur is almost scared to speak, because Marrida is still leaning against him, and it feels good to be holding her so close. He's now sure his feelings for her are more than just friendship. Marrida feels the warmth of Alagur's body behind her, and it gives her a languorous feeling of comfort. She's in no hurry to wake up. At this moment, it doesn't matter to her who is behind her or what he represents. She feels happy, warm and safe leaning against the man with his arms around her.

"How far do we need to travel through this woodland?"
Alagur swallows hard before answering, then feels tongue-tied.
"Maybe three or four days if we travel directly north."

Alagur feels flustered all of a sudden. He's never felt the need to be close to any woman or lie with one, like the other Wolf Riders who'd often rape women if they were less than willing to oblige. With no women in City of Wolves, there was never a chance to learn how to handle a healthy relationship with one. Now he is sitting on his wolf with a woman in front of him, and as the minutes pass, it becomes evident that what he is feeling could be equal to whatever is causing Marrida to lean back.

I want to be a friend to her, Alagur thinks. *She needs to know that she can trust me, even considering where I came from. I could see the beginning of a friendship at her house. I cannot do anything to harm it. I swear that I'll always treat her with respect.*

In the few days since he awoke from his coma, Alagur has seen a friendship grow with Marrida and her siblings, and also with Joharan the few times that he visited.

Kalisa was always so delighted whenever she could play with Yalla. She learnt from the wolf about loyalty.

A sense of understanding has developed between himself and Marrida, even though they're essentially from completely opposite backgrounds. What if the initial essence of friendship has grown into deep-seated feelings for her too? But most importantly, living in Marrida's home has given him an understanding of what real family life means, which is something he lost when he was snatched.

Smiling as he remembers watching Kalisa, he ponders over what became of the girl in the vision who called out, "Alagur, Alagur." His sister.

While Alagur sits on the wolf, lost in his own thoughts, Marrida is also in the mood for reflection. She senses that the rigidness in Alagur's posture may be caused by him feeling uncomfortable with the situation he finds himself in. It hasn't escaped her notice that he's never mentioned any women in his descriptions of City of Wolves.

Does it mean that there are none? I wonder what he thought when I did the retelling about my parents. He raised his eyebrow when I said they met one another and committed themselves to being life partners in just a day. I know Mam was still very much in love with Papa when he died, and she died of a broken heart. I'm sure of it. Maybe Alagur doesn't want to get off the wolf now because of his feelings for me.

Marrida doesn't realise how close she is to the truth about Alagur. Her thoughts are simply the unintentional echoes of similar thoughts going through the man's mind.

In the conversations before they left Ruh'nar, Joharan mentioned the existence of Callers. Alagur isn't sure if Marrida knows the term.

What if there's a link between that ability to understand people's speech in visions and being a Caller? I don't understand how they link together, but it's obvious Joharan knows. How he knows is a mystery we'll only solve when we get back to Ruh'nar – if ever. He called it self-repositioning, and Marrida has not learnt it. It's clear Marrida doesn't know what she's capable of. I'm going to help her, whatever it takes. And I'm going to keep her safe as best as I can. I vow that on everything good that I want for this world.

Alagur did not bother to put the facts together while he still was in Marrida's house. He was too busy worrying about his safety and that of his wolf. He has not told any of the occupants that he jumped up from his bed at each sound he heard. The morning that Kalisa found him sleeping in Esbara's room was the first time he slept uninterrupted.

A hesitant finger touches Marrida's hand. Instead of pulling her hand away as she would have done at her house, Marrida lets Alagur's hand cover hers and then takes hold of it firmly. Marrida notices a drawing in of breath before the man seems to relax. She doesn't realise she is mirroring his actions.

"We need to dismount. Yalla needs some time to rest."

Marrida jerks back to the reality of the situation she's in. For a moment, she flinches when she realises she's leaning against Alagur's chest, but then she chides herself.

It's childish to behave in that way when I'm trying to show him I like him.

So, she leans back again, and even dares to rest her head against his shoulder. And after a moment of hesitation, she relaxes totally against the man's chest. This has an immediate effect on Alagur. He feels a surge of feelings well up for Marrida from the deepest reaches of his being.

Where are these feeling coming from? Alagur feels confused suddenly. But then the confusion leaves him when a singular thought enters his mind. *I've always felt this way about her, even before I knew her and she was just a glimpsed image in a dream.*

Still holding Marrida's right hand, Alagur slowly lets go of the reins with his left hand and somewhat hesitantly enfolds the woman in his muscular arm, pulling her even more tightly against him. Glancing down, he sees Marrida's head is leaning sideways against his chest. Her eyes are shut. She seems to be waiting. Alagur, good at reading body language, notices some doubt on her face.

She isn't sure what my intentions are. She feels safe, or she wouldn't have leaned back again. I guess I can prove to her now that she can always trust me.

The embrace of his powerful arm envelops Marrida like a mother would do with a child. His muscles, which can withstand riding the largest, strongest wolf in City of Wolves, hold Marrida with a tenderness that Alagur has never known in the city. The feelings he's experiencing must come from somewhere else. Deep down, he remembers sitting with his mother's arms embracing him in a similar fashion.

Marrida suddenly looks up at Alagur, and the similarity between this moment and when she looked at him at her house causes a new wave of feelings to wash over him. And it seems that Marrida feels the same way.

Marrida suddenly feels a hand push against the left side of her face, and Alagur's lips meet hers.

Yalla isn't immune to the interplay going on between her master and the woman who's become a friend. She notices when the reins are loosed by her master and instinctively starts a slow pace towards a nearby pond bordering the woodland. Her instinct tells her that is the direction Alagur would want her to go. It's only when she stops abruptly that her two riders realise what's happening between them, causing them to stop abruptly and look in opposite directions.

A moment afterwards, Marrida slides her right leg over Yalla's shoulders and drops to the ground. Walking quickly to the side of the pond, she takes several mouthfuls of the refreshing water. Somewhat unceremoniously, Alagur follows suit and gives Yalla a disapproving look. The spell of the moment is broken, so it doesn't matter what happens next as far as he's concerned. The wolf almost looks like she's teasing him with her wolf grin. He kneels a few paces away from Marrida and takes several mouthfuls of the water, scooping handfuls over his head and face, all the while not daring to look at her. He's sure she's angry about his actions.

Marrida, in turn, is torn between feelings that she can only describe as love, and feelings that still have something to do with how she regards the Wolf Riders.

Don't let those feelings get in the way of how you really feel about him, she scolds herself inwardly.

A quiet awkwardness keeps both individuals from saying anything for the next half an hour or so. Each goes about their necessary tasks in an almost mechanical fashion. Marrida checks and rechecks her haversack for items she packed in it the evening before. Alagur takes a brush from one of the pouches covering the saddle and brushes Yalla's fur in even strokes without genuinely paying attention to the wolf, or anything else. Yalla, who thinks her master is angered by her actions, keeps her head low to the ground instead of nudging him as she usually does whenever he brushes her in this fashion. She even lays her ears flat. She isn't scared of him as he has never given her any beatings, unlike many other Wolf Riders, but she senses in her own wolfish way that her actions interrupted his moment of closeness with Marrida.

Yalla is tired from the running and the discomfort of the offspring she can feel moving in her belly. The silence between Alagur and Marrida makes her feel even more uncomfortable as she has grown used to them always talking about something.

Marrida gets up and walks anticlockwise around the pond at a slow pace. She needs some time alone to think. Her hand instinctively reaches up towards the gem hanging under her travel tunic; its bulge gives her a feeling of comfort. But she knows that this isn't the time or place to do a vision because she isn't sure how Alagur could help her if something bad happened during the vision, as it did the previous evening. She looks over the lake that stretches for some distance, and the gentle play of the morning light on its surface has a soothing effect on her turbulent mind.

She notices a bush with white flowers covering it, and in front of it is a stone slab. Pausing at the stone, she looks at it for a minute or so, then decides to sit down. She stares at some undetermined point in the centre of the pond, noting how dark blue the water looks from her current position. A sudden shadow crosses the lake as a few clouds cover the sun, making the water an even darker colour, almost indigo blue. The ripples, which the gently blowing wind is causing, have the same effect as the dancing flames of a long-lit fire, and Marrida smiles. She listens and hears several morning birds tweet and chirp in response to one another, while birds further away whistle their replies.

A movement in the pond catches her eye, and she sees a fish reach from below the surface, snap at an insect with long wings and drag it under the water. Several birds, obviously disturbed by some predatory animal, fly up from a tree on the other side of the pond. Marrida wonders for a few moments what disturbed the birds, and in turn, it disturbs her own sense of peace in this place.

From her vantage point, Marrida can glance towards where Alagur is setting up their temporary camp without him noticing that she's looking at him. Without realising she's doing it, she glances half a dozen times towards him, remembering his embrace and kiss, and her heart pounds faster.

Is this love like her mother experienced?

Just as she looks at him for what feels like the umpteenth time, the man dives into the pond. For several moments, Marrida trails the motion of bubbles rising from the water, until Alagur breaks the surface close to the tree where the birds were before. In the sunlight that breaks through the clouds at that moment, she sees for the first time since the day he lay injured on a bed in her house how well-muscled he is. Strong muscles show on his back and arms as he stands in water, which comes to slightly above his waist, completely unaware he's being watched by Marrida. He saw her walk off and is assuming she went some distance along the lake's embankment.

Alagur watches the reeds along the pond. The reason he took off his shirt was to wash his upper body, but the birds flying up catch his attention. As a keen hunter, he immediately notes there's a predator skulking in the reeds. He removes the remainder of his clothing to give him a smoother swim in the darkness of the pond, and when he dives into the water, his keen eye sees a small rodent-like animal scurrying along the bank. There's likely a birds' nest there somewhere.

He swims the distance from the camp to the reeds in several fast, strong strokes, then emerges from the water. The idea is to scare away the rodent, which is a type that's unpleasant to eat, and get the eggs from the nest before the rodent or the birds return. After a few minutes wading along the pond's edge, he finds the nest with nine large waterfowl eggs lying in it and lifts it up.

I will build a small fire and place the whole nest on it to cook the eggs inside their shells. It will make a nutritious, filling meal that will give us the energy we need for the journey. We can each eat two of the eggs, and the rest of them I can give to Yalla to replenish her depleted energy reserves.

No longer feeling anger towards the wolf over her interruption of the perfect moment of tenderness, he lays the nest down on top of a rock then scratches behind her ear with a grin on his face. Not realising how his exit from the water has affected Marrida, he stands beside Yalla, lavishing affection on her.

At the other end of the lake, Marrida draws in her breath as Alagur stands dripping wet on the embankment, totally naked. Until now, Marrida has only seen him with his upper torso uncovered because she didn't feel comfortable undressing him fully. She even took care to go to her own room whenever he went to the washing room. But here, in the middle of the wilderness, she doesn't have that luxury any longer. With mouth agape, she looks at the naked man. He sends her pulse racing.

Alagur nonchalantly walks to some nearby bushes and relieves himself against them. However, when he turns, he sees Marrida looking directly at him. Her face turns a dark shade of red as she looks down, but that's nothing compared to the reaction discovering he's being watched has on the man--

CHAPTER THIRTY-FOUR

Bergas freezes in mid-motion when familiar sounds echo from the east. The shouts of men would not have alarmed him unduly, but the accompanying growls and grunts tell him that in the wilderness beyond the small ravine he's been trying to cross over for the last hour are people he must regard as an enemy. He surveys the vastness of the landscape and decides that they're further away than he first assumed.

What are Wolf Riders doing this far up the mountains, especially this late in the season? Alagur said that they wouldn't be out on excursions this late in the summer season, that they'd be back in City of Wolves before autumn.

He ducks down behind several bushes and slowly pushes the leaves aside to stare towards the mountain pass just below him. Initially, the sounds seemed to come from far away, but now they sound uncomfortably close. In fact, they seem to be coming from the very place he wants to cross.

It sounds like the men, whoever they are, are having some sort of gathering. Bergas frowns. *What can I do now? They're there, and if I try to pass them they'll discover me and will likely snatch me right back to City of Wolves, or even kill me.*

Feeling a tingle start in the lower part of his calf muscle, Bergas ignores it and grits his teeth to suppress the pain. Then he holds his breath and waits.

* * *

Bergas doesn't know how long he has been sitting in a crouched position under the dense covering of the dark green leaves of the bush when finally he sees the men mount up and ride off towards City of Wolves. Their motions are somewhat clumsy, like they are drunk.

They are acting like they don't know how to ride. And their wolves don't act like any I saw in City of Wolves.

Bergas looks south towards the city looming as a shadow on the horizon. He glances back and sees the dust trail veer off in that direction and slowly becoming less.

"Watch for the dust clouds that rise whenever Wolf Riders are riding close to you. The way our wolves run causes the dust cloud. If it trails away as it comes towards you, that means they're riding away from you."

Bergas lets go an audible breath and slumps back on the damp soil behind him, his heart beating fast. He feels a throbbing tension in his temples at the realisation he's avoided capture – or really recapture – by the Wolf Riders. Lifting one of the branches and seeing the first shades of dusk gather, he decides that perhaps sleeping under the bush is the best option available to him.

Bergas lets the branch drop and thinks long and hard. A knot of panic makes its presence felt. Bergas glances numerous times in the direction of City of Wolves to check for any riders who may be coming back his way. However, after some time, he realises that the only sounds present are the chirps of various evening birds, the snuffles of nearby mountain sheep heading towards higher plains to shelter among their cliff drops and boulders, and the first sounds of night dwellers waking up.

In the distance, a wolf howls. Bergas listens for a reply.

I guess that's likely one of the loners travelling away from a pack of wolves that has set their territory. The wolves of Yalla's kind are further west and higher in the mountain range.

Bergas isn't sure if his memory serves him well right now, but he does recall Alagur telling him this as part of the retelling of Yalla.

I miss you the most, Yalla. You taught me kindness and loyalty.

Now he is sitting, Bergas starts to feel exhausted from travelling fast and sleeping little. Hunger is also gnawing at the inside of his stomach, but he doesn't want to make a fire.

If I make a fire, I'll risk discovery by Wolf Riders.

Bergas opens his bag of dwindling supplies and searches inside it for anything to eat. He finds a package made of soft white leather. Pulling out a haunch of ham that he found in one of the bags Alagur left behind, he eats the slightly salty tasting meat at a leisurely pace. Thirsty though he is, hunger is a greater concern, and the meat tastes better than he ever remembered it to be.

While he sits there eating, he stares pensively into the distance through gaps which appear in the foliage covering him from time to time as the wind blows the large green leaves aside.

The journey is so much longer and further than I ever thought possible. Bergas frowns with concern. *There's a difference between travelling south on the back of a wolf and having to travel on foot. I thought I'd be home in a season. I can barely cope anymore, and that is making me less cautious, which could cost me my freedom.*

Bergas pulls out the small piece of wood he found a few days into the journey. He looks at the many small notches he's chipped from one side of it.

"Almost got the fifth line filled to represent the days of another month," he mumbles. "I guess I'll be on the sixth row by the time I'm home."

The travels into the mountains with his father were never this intense, but now the boy is certain that's what his father meant when he said he was 'preparing him'. Additional ramblings after his father's death had helped to prepare him further. So had the many treks with Alagur.

An immense feeling of gratitude washes over Bergas when he remembers the time he spent with his father. *I miss you, Papa, I miss you so much.* A sob escapes his lips and a tear streaks his right cheek. *I wonder if Alagur is in City of Wolves right now, sitting in his seat on the terrace of that place he calls home. I wonder how it would be for me if I was sitting there with him.* At the same as he is thinking these thoughts, though, Bergas knows deep down that Alagur wanted him gone because he was leaving himself.

How do I know that?

Bergas frowns and straightens up, staring with seething hatred towards the dark shadow representing City of Wolves. *If Alagur had gone while I was still there, Samur would probably have found a reason to throw me into the pit of wild wolves.*

Bergas turns his thoughts to his mother. *I wish she was holding me in her arms right now.* Tears stream down his face. He doesn't even bother wiping them away, instead lying down and curling himself into a tight ball on the damp ground with the bag against his stomach, crying all the tears he wanted to cry throughout the seasons he was in City of Wolves. He cries tears which express the hurt of being torn from his home. He cries because he misses his mother.

Sleep replaces the tears after some time, his dreams full of a home he misses and a mother beckoning to a boy she misses too.

* * *

MORNING WAKES BERGAS WITH A TEASE, the sun shining a bright beam of light exactly where his head is lying on the ground. The beam dances for a while over the boy's cheek, replacing the caress of his mother in his dreams with one of its own. A moment later, it hovers over the boy's eye before returning to his cheek.

The warm early autumn sun shines brightly above the bush where the boy finally let exhaustion overtake him and fell asleep. The wind plays with the leaves on the bush, tugging at them, and then tearing one leaf off. It glides slowly downward until it lands on the boy's forehead. Not to be outdone by the wind's game, the sun, now partially obscured by a few light grey clouds, takes advantage of the enlarged hole and bathes the boy's face with sunlight.

Bergas wakes up and yawns loudly. Pulling the leaf from his forehead and looking around sleepily, he notes from the position of the sun that it's mid-morning. But where the land should appear bright and sunny, it isn't; it is enveloped in a dense mist.

Bergas pulls several branches of the bush out of the way and stares. He looks up at the mountain tops, almost invisible in the mist soup that is moving about in swathes of droplets, dispersing as the wind gathered speed then moments later settling back into the dense blanket it had been moments before.

This must be why Wolf Riders don't travel here in the colder seasons of the year.

Bergas grins, digging through his sack for his last remaining food. While eating, he stares at the sack and considers leaving it behind. He has only used it to carry food as he's been wearing all the clothes he managed to salvage from the haversacks and packs Alagur left with him.

I could make some sort of weapon — a spear perhaps — but it could be problematic to trek through the mountains with a heavy spear. Bergas stares at the pouch he fashioned from cloth and leather which contains the slender knife Alagur gave him. *I could use that and some snares to lure a mountain sheep as I did with the wood voles in Venrasia Woods, then kill it like I killed the wolf.*

Bergas swallows hard at the thought of the dead wolf, and even harder when he realises he's disobeyed Alagur's command to dispose of the weapon.

He turns his thoughts to the fading memory of the dream in which he saw his mother beckoning to him. *Did I really dream that?* A moment later, Bergas sees a vivid image of his mother holding him in her arms, gently rocking him back and forth like she did whenever he awoke from a bad dream. *It feels so long ago that she last did that. I want her to do it when I get home. She can do it for as long as she wants, if only I get home safely.*

Home.

Home is right on the other side of that mountain range, and here I am wasting time while nature is lending herself as an ally. Bergas grabs his rucksack and places the bread he's been gnawing on inside it. He picks up a few small round stones lying on the ground around him.

I don't know what they'll be useful for, but they might help me in some way.

Looking around, Bergas sees some golden dew mushrooms.

"If you're ever out here alone, these mushrooms are readily available and will provide you with the nutrition you need. They will also tell you that you've reached the higher elevations of these mountains, because that's where they're the most common."

"Thanks, Papa."

Cautiously, Bergas gets up and stands in silence for several minutes within the confines of the bush. He stares towards the north, then the east, and then back north again, listening for sounds coming from either direction – most specifically those signalling the presence of men and wolves. It's silent all around; so silent that Bergas imagines that nature is holding her breath in anticipation of his next move.

I don't know what to do.

Just as Bergas is deciding whether to chance his luck, nature blankets herself with even denser mist.

I guess this is my chance.

Bergas's eyes focus on a rocky outcrop through the mist soup. *It's a long way off, but I must try to get to it.* Bursting from the bush and causing the mist to swirl in every direction, he sets off at a sprint. The thought of seeing his mother once more gives him renewed energy, which keeps him going higher up the hill and closer to his next temporary destination. He keeps going even when he feels his heart pounding painfully in his chest; when his breath feels at an end; whenever his young body wants to give up. Bergas knows the weather in the mountains during the early autumn days is fickle. It could change without any warning, and the rocky outcrop he's chosen looks like it will offer shelter if the weather does change.

One way or another, I need to reach it and get beyond it to the parts of the mountains I know on the other side. Then I can determine where I am from shadow formations, from the way plants grow, even from the location of animals.

The bleating of a startled mountain sheep stops Bergas in his tracks. He watches the animal closely as she dashes off, determining her to be a ewe by her enlarged belly. Bergas smiles at the idea of two lambs accompanying their mother down to the green pastures of the South Valley of Miza for grazing. He then smiles even more widely when he realises the direction the ewe has gone: she's shown him the mountain pass which he's been looking for over the last two days.

Looking back one more time towards City of Wolves, Bergas sends a silent thought of gratitude.

I hope you'll be alright, Alagur. Thank you for what you did for me. I hope you live your life well.

Bergas turns and climbs the slope which will lead him into the mountain pass and – he hopes – closer to home. Now that he's on the final lap of his journey, he gives himself the time to think more about his home city.

Papa always did the retelling in such a beautiful way. I hope I did him justice when I told Alagur about the city. But Mam was the one who knew how old the city is. She said two thousand years. She said it was established by merchants from far away who settled here. She never knew where they came from, but suggested it may have been the south-west.

The timing of Azaquina's establishment coincided with the last days of the occupation of Keldarra by the people from the north. It was assumed the merchants had come with mercenaries who drove the northern people away for good, then rebuilt the city.

Mam said that long ago a city stood where Azaquina now exists.

When the region was safe, Azaquina was rebuilt into a magnificent harbour which dozens of ships sailed to and from every day, bringing wealth, exotic goods and knowledge to the town.

That is until the Wolf Riders arrived, I guess.

Azaquina's wealth was used to establish the northern watchtowers and guard the lands between Azaquina and the most north-eastern coast of Keldarra, where the first Keepers came from. The watchtowers stopped the Wolf Riders' advancement from the east initially, but when the watchtowers were abandoned – Bergas isn't sure if there really were four as he's only ever seen one – those who guarded them disappeared.

"How do you know so much about them?" he'd asked his mother, but she never answered the question. After a time this gave her an air of mystery, which Bergas loved. It was her wisdom that prompted his father to ask her to be his life partner.

"She came from the east originally, but she never even told me where from," was all his father would say. Those words often go through Bergas's mind as they were part of one of the last conversations he had with his father.

"What's a Keeper?" Bergas asked his mother a few days before the Wolf Riders came. He didn't know where he'd heard the word; not once had his mother mentioned it. She simply smiled him at sadly.

"I'll tell you when you get home."

She then turned and walked off before Bergas could say more. It puzzled the boy greatly.

No longer distracted by the risk of capture, surrounded only by nature, Bergas starts analysing the meaning of his mother's cryptic words, the chill of the autumn air awakening his mind to a higher state of awareness. He ascends to the right when the path ahead splits into a fork, and after reaching the crest of the lowest hill, he looks over the landscape below. To the left, he sees a small portion of the bay where his father once fished; to his right, he sees the fading outline of the massive City of Wolves, looking like it's being swallowed whole by a blanket of mist.

Seems the mist reaches further than I thought.

Ahead, Bergas sees the closest of the watchtowers. From his vantage point, he can also see a darkened trail: the mountain pass he needs to descend to the bay commonly known as the Bay of Whispers.

I can follow the curve of the bay until I'm home.

Bergas cranes his neck to see if he can see Azaquina, but the mist around him makes his effort fruitless. The mist is blanketing most of the region.

I'm too far to see home anyway.

Bergas turns on his heels and gingerly steps onto the scree of the outcrop. His feet slide somewhat, and after a moment of rebalancing himself, he pulls his cloak closely round his body. The wind picks up and pelts him with tiny shards of ice crystals.

He stops walking for a moment when he thinks he hears the howl of a wolf from behind him, listening for an answering howl or the shouts of men to determine if it's a scouting party from City of Wolves. When neither howl nor shouts come, he starts to walk again, picking up his pace. If he can get to the mountain path at the lower elevation that he knows so well, he'll be ten days from home.

* * *

IN THE WEST, A WOLF LIFTS HER HEAD AND SMELLS THE AIR, catching a familiar scent. Grunting, she indicates to the man riding her that she's sensed something. The man stops and looks at the woman sitting in front of him on the wolf. Each of their faces asks the same question: friend or foe?

Yalla howls a long, eerie wolf song. She's recognised who's ahead, and she hopes he will remember her voice.

CHAPTER THIRTY-FIVE

THE EVENING SKY, BLANKETING THE BUSH UNDER WHICH BERGAS IS SLEEPING, gradually moves west towards where Marrida and Alagur are settling down after a long ride. They haven't moved since Marrida saw Alagur leave the pond naked and now sit on opposite sides of the campfire, feeling awkward despite the fact Alagur is now dressed, watching each other's every move. When he saw Marrida watching him earlier, he put his clothes back on hastily and mechanically with a lot of cursing under his breath.

The bird's nest with the large eggs in it is cooking on the fire, and Alagur feels relief when the rising smoke hides him from Marrida's gaze. Marrida, for her part, shuffles her left foot from side to side to give her something to focus on other than the thought repeating in her mind.

He was naked, and I saw him.

Silence.

Marrida feels her heart pounding. *No one ever prepared me for this. I didn't know I would respond to a man in this way. So yeah, I might have fallen in love with any man, and then what? Would I have reacted in this way with anyone?*

It's Alagur who finally plucks up the courage to speak first.
"Tell me more about the Stone of Truth. Where was it made?"
Marrida looks up and studies Alagur's face through the glow of the flames between them. He looks sincere.
"There are few left who know how to cut these gems. They come from the east. Do you know the Caves of Elgorra near the town Elsana?"
Alagur shakes his head; he has never travelled east with the Wolf Riders.
"Those caves are close to the coast of Achellon. There's an island group called Spires of Achellon, and the cave is on the mainland near it."
Marrida bows her head and allows herself some time to think, then she speaks again, looking at Alagur. "I think the vision I did during our last night at my house was of Achellon."
"How do you know that?"
"Because of the dialect I heard during the vision."

Marrida opens the haversack leaning against the rock next to her and lifts Sharriba's notebook from it. She places the book on her lap, flicking through twenty or so pages until she finds the page she wants. Alagur gets up and sits on the rock next to her, looking at the page which shows writing he cannot read.

Marrida continues explaining. "This is part of a vision Sharriba did about six months after she became an Acolyte. She heard words in this dialect in addition to seeing events unfold during the vision and decided to transcribe the way the words sounded phonetically."

Alagur nods to indicate he understands.

"She spent almost four years translating the wording, mostly in secret. It's now one of the dialects we learn as Acolytes in the Temple. Before Elder Sharriba, there were only four taught."

"You said there are six dialects. What is the other one?"

"The other one is Sharriba's mother tongue – Sab'ruhi."

Marrida stops to think once more.

I wonder if I'm doing the right thing in deciding to share this knowledge with Alagur. It's forbidden for men to know about Keepers of Truth. For a moment, the rebellious part of Marrida again questions why this is. *I know I'll be expelled from the Temple, or worse, if my decision is ever discovered.*

"Uncle Joharan told me that my great-grandmother was a Keeper. She possessed another skill too – my uncle referred to her as a Caller."

Alagur nods – Joharan told him this in a quiet conversation when they were alone.

"Until my uncle mentioned it, I didn't know what a Caller was, or that they even existed." Marrida blushes and jerks her gaze back down to the book, hoping the red flames of the fire will hide her blush from Alagur. She doesn't even notice Alagur staring at the ground in his own pensive mood. His words startle Marrida when he speaks.

"I recall Callers being mentioned in relation to my home city. Samur said something like, 'Those crazy things they do with the girls in Chiva'na' and I remember him telling Raimir what it involved, though I didn't really pay attention to the details. I guess the mention of the city made me angry enough to ignore them."

"Who is Raimir?"

Now it's Alagur's turn to be startled and he falls sideways onto the ground in an undignified way. It causes Marrida to giggle uncontrollably, which in turn sets Alagur off. He stares down and laughs even more when he realises how silly he looks.

When the laughter subsides, the feeling of embarrassment has left Marrida, and she slides down onto the ground next to Alagur and gives him a glorious smile.

"I guess I need to tell you more about who is who in City of Wolves for anything I say about the city to make sense to you. And you need to set aside the rumours you've heard all your life."

Marrida nods.

"Then I earn the right to ask more about that." Alagur points at Marrida's upper chest. She nods, but only after a hesitation, which Alagur decides to ignore.

"Raimir is someone I'd refer to as a runt. It's a term – not used with kindness, I should add – for those in City of Wolves who do nothing but follow the leaders around, begging for favour."

Marrida nods. *I guess that's what Sarayna's 'friends' were – they were runts.*

"Samur is one of the Elder Men. I'm unsure how he earned that rank. There're also three boys I know – Kaizor, Melchor and Ebagar."

"Who are they?"

"They are, for want of a better word, apprentices – they're learning to be Wolf Riders, just like Bergas was before I helped him get away. Those three boys follow Raimir around and he feels more important because of it."

Marrida waits silently for Alagur to continue.

"Bergas is almost like a brother to me. At least, that's how I feel now. He didn't like those other boys much. I didn't like them either because they acted like a bunch of runts. Well, maybe not Kaizor as he was genuinely interested in Yalla."

Alagur nods at the large wolf who is lying near some boulders, sheltering from the wind which has picked up since darkness engulfed the camp. The mention of her name makes Yalla lift her head and look towards the two people with golden-yellow eyes which reflect the red colour of the licking flames of their small campfire.

"Initially, I was somewhat annoyed by the questions Bergas kept asking all the time about the city. He could be very talkative when we were alone." Alagur grins broadly at Marrida.

"What did you talk about?"

"Most questions were about being a Wolf Rider. But then we started to talk about the city itself."

Alagur stops speaking and stares with a trance-like gaze at the flames in front of him, while Marrida studies him closely for a moment.

"He asked me what the biggest building there was for. I told him I didn't know so we went there to investigate. We saw old drawings on the walls and carvings on the doors that fascinated both of us. We spent a long time there, trying to work out what it all meant."

"Can you draw what they looked like?"

Alagur nods and looks for something to draw with. He sees a short, straight piece of wood near a bush at the lake's edge. Rising and collecting the wood, he then walks back to the fire to continue the retelling.

"Most of the drawings were very old and faded, but even though the door was quite damaged, the carved images have survived the passage of time."

Alagur sits down on the ground next to Marrida, thinking for a moment how to proceed. Smoothing the yellow-grey sandy soil of the lake bank in front of him, Alagur draws hesitantly.

Marrida soon recognises what the man is drawing. The first words of Alagur's 'legend' echo in her mind.

TEN THOUSAND RIDERS ROSE TO THE CALL,
BESET ON TO THE CITY OF OLD, AND
FALL BEFORE THEM IT WOULD.

The words suddenly have clarity. They tell of the events when Masharea was destroyed by the first Wolf Riders who'd started an uprising against the city's leaders – one being an Elder – and the city they'd sworn to protect.

"That's the Symbol of Unity– Sharriba told me about it. The library of the Temple of Ruh'nar has a similar emblem on its door. What is it doing in City of Wolves? Or should I say Masharea? The building must have been a Temple once."

Alagur nods and understands the implications of Marrida's words. But immediately he has a question about it.

"What does it mean?"

Marrida takes the stick which Alagur has leaned against the rock and points at the left side of the image.

"Sharriba says this side represents the Keepers. I presume the right side would be the Callers, now I know they exist." Marrida taps the top figure. "I don't know what this figure represents – or maybe I do." She looks down at the book in her lap. "I could see if this says something about the symbol. Sharriba said I might find answers to many of my questions in it."

She smiles suddenly, realising she's as talkative and inquisitive as

Bergas must have been. Despite their different environments and backgrounds, both she and Alagur seem to be in similar situations.

"Can you light an ember?" she requests.

Alagur nods and rises once more. From a small side pocket of his haversack, which is leaning against the rock overhang, he retrieves Damir's tinder kit, smiling briefly as he remembers the promise he made to return with it. He places one of the round pieces of slow-burning wood into the stone chamber, then pours over some oil, followed by a powder. He wrinkles his nose at the familiar smell of slurry – a substance the Wolf Riders use on spear arrows. Alagur strikes two small metallic stones, also retrieved from the haversack, against each other. A moment later, an orange-yellow flame sparks up, turning a darker shade of orange as it grows in intensity. He places the unused parts of the tinder kit, together with the two stones, back in their container and returns it into the side pocket.

When Alagur turns to walk back to the campfire, he sees Marrida staring towards the lake, deep in thought, with her hands resting on a page. It seems she's found the page she was looking for. Marrida turns her head as she hears Alagur approach her, smiling warmly at him.

"I found the image in the book." Marrida nods at the drawing on the ground. "Sharriba calls it 'Unity of Truth' in the journal, but there's no doubt that what you saw is this symbol."

Marrida stops speaking and waits until Alagur sits. He raises the ember above the book and watches on as her explanation continues.

"The image you drew misses the four gems. See the gems here and here?" Marrida points at the drawing. "They are the Stone of Truth and Stone of Calling."

"So, the book explains what Callers are?"

"Yes. They're my opposites in the simplest terms." Marrida sees a puzzled look appear on Alagur's face. "It says here a Caller sees future events. Like my great-grandmother, for example. This part of the image might be someone capable of both. Sharriba never told me what they're called, but she did mention that there are only a few left these days. She said the First Elder was one."

A long silence follows Marrida's explanation, giving each individual time to ponder. Alagur is struck by the significance of the Callers.

If I do originate from Chiva'na, and there are Callers there, could my sister be destined to become one? She might even be a Caller now, and if that's the case, she of all people will know of my plan to return. I was alone when Samur snatched me. My scream couldn't have been heard by her because she was in the cellar. Yet seconds after I was abducted, she was running after us, calling for me.

"Alagur, Alagur."

"Marrida...I need to ask you about the vision you did that showed my snatching."

Marrida nods at Alagur and waits for the questions. *He wants to know in more detail what I saw in the vision — perhaps also what I heard.*

Alagur sees sincerity and compassion in Marrida's eyes. He knows, thanks to Joharan's revelations, that she can tell him more about himself, but he isn't sure how much the old man told her. Several times, Joharan conveyed the importance of the journey to Alagur — and the need to keep Marrida safe. But he always added that Alagur was important in all this, too.

Whatever 'all this' is.

"When you did your vision of my childhood...abduction, you said you heard a girl call out my name."
Marrida nods silently.
"What did your uncle call it?" Alagur frowns as he tries to remember the unfamiliar term.
"You mean self-reposition?"
"Yeah, that's it. Are self-repositioning and being a Caller linked somehow? Does it say anything about self-repositioning in the book?" Alagur stares at Marrida, hoping that her ability to hear his sister in a past event by self-repositioning means his sister can see a future where he'll be reunited with her.
"I don't know if they're linked, but I can look for it in the journal."
Marrida turns her attention to the book and skims over the text of almost thirty pages before she finds something which sounds promising. When she looks up, she's smiling.
"Maybe we should visit Chiva'na after we've searched for answers in the east. If the answers about the Keepers are in the east, then the answers about the Callers lie in the west. That just leaves the third part of the emblem as a mystery to uncover."
Alagur nods. Marrida has given him hope with that one sentence.
"It seems you're much better at the skill of doing visions than either Joharan or Sharriba knew."

As Alagur's playfully teasing smile curls his lips, Marrida blanches. She didn't realise someone would notice her advanced skill — that of a fourth-year Acolyte — least of all Alagur. Marrida stares at Alagur, whose grin grows wider when he sees the shock on her face. He's an observant man and skilled in body language, and he doesn't miss much.

Marrida looks back down at the journal, more to hide her embarrassment than to read it. In that moment, her attention is caught by a corner of the left-hand page which she's ignored before. She raises the book closer to her face and squints her eyes, the edge of embarrassment all but disappearing. Someone has written text in letters so small that, to a less observant person, they'd appear as a smudge.

"Alagur, hold that ember closer, please."

Sharriba was correct in saying this book contained hidden answers, but what kind of answers? Answers to what a Caller is? Is there more?

Alagur, feeling like he may have teased Marrida too much, composes himself.

What has she found in the book? I already know it tells something about the beginning of the Wolf Riders.

He rises from the ground. Whisking up the ember container, he blows at it to make it brighter and positions himself next to Marrida, his left leg leaning against the boulder on which she sits. Using the boulder as a support, he holds the ember as close as he can to both the book and her face, noting how the flames create contrasting shades of golden yellow and deep sunset red in her hair.

She has found something, and it's important.

"I think Sharriba knew she'd found something forbidden, either in a book or in one of her visions. The vision I did was of her being chastised for that knowledge."

CHAPTER THIRTY-SIX

Sleep doesn't come easily for either Marrida or Alagur, and they only manage a few hours before they wake with the smell of morning dew in their noses. The night before, they spent many hours reading the journal, then when Marrida finally started nodding off, Alagur wrapped it in a selvaya leather sheet he'd retrieved from one of the packs. The book now lies on top of one of the haversacks, forgotten.

Marrida rolls onto her back and looks up at the sky, which is awash with the colours of early morning, ranging from yellows to pinks to azure blues to the leftover dusky purples of night. The air is filled with the warmth of early autumn. Marrida glances sideways towards Alagur, who is sleeping peacefully. She decides to take advantage of this to bathe in the lake before he wakes.

Yalla lifts her head when Marrida gets up. Marrida attempts to make sure the wolf doesn't wake Alagur, waving her hand up and down, then putting her finger to her lips as if to say, "Stay there and be quiet." Yalla looks towards Alagur and, seeing her master asleep, decides to comply with Marrida's command – for now, at least. She lays her head on her forelimbs, but from Yalla's eye motions, Marrida sees that she's being observed closely by the wolf. Again, Marrida notes the startling bright golden colour of Yalla's eyes, which matches her own hair colour.

Silently, Marrida opens one haversack then the next one, and finally finds what she's looking for: a towel made of selvaya wool. She holds the cloth against her face and moves it against her skin; it is probably the softest material she has ever felt.

After a few moments, she glances at Alagur again. He has rolled onto his side in his sleep, his back now towards her. Looking at Yalla, she again places her finger over her lips, then soundlessly walks clockwise along the lake's edge until she reaches a small green pasture just beyond where Alagur emerged naked from the lake's dark water. Marrida looks in all directions before glancing once more at the small camp, which lies three hundred paces away from her. Alagur is still asleep, but if he wakes, he'll see her bathing as he has rolled onto his left arm and now faces the lake.

Marrida spots a brown bush near the water's edge. Briskly walking to the left-hand side of it, she looks over the top at Alagur and decides the bush will offer her the privacy to bathe undisturbed. First draping the towel over the bush so the sun will warm it, Marrida unties her outer tunic, takes it off and hangs it over another part of the bush. Then she removes her outer skirt and hangs it next to the tunic. Glancing over the bush at Alagur, she sees he has stirred and rolled onto his back. Marrida freezes in mid-motion and waits for a few minutes to see if he's awake. When he rolls onto his right side, followed by the audible sound of snores, she decides he's most definitely still sleeping.

Good, I can bathe quickly, and he won't know I did it.

Marrida quickly removes the remainder of her clothes, then wades into the lake. *The water still has a night chill to it, but that will refresh me and help wake me up.* After eight paces, Marrida stops, pauses a moment, and then dives head first under the water. She's an excellent swimmer, having been taught the skill by her uncle when he became her guardian. Marrida swims in long strokes and emerges close to the other side of the lake, which is narrow, but long – hence the name Ribbon Lake. After a few minutes of drifting in the water on her back, Marrida slowly swims back towards the small pasture, only to be met by Alagur, standing there with the towel in his hands, holding it up for her. She stops swimming; she doesn't want him to see her naked.

"I'll keep my eyes shut if you want." Alagur's voice betrays his feelings for her. To show he means what he says, he looks away to the side.

Marrida hesitates for a few moments, looking at the man standing on the embankment.

"I woke up and you were gone from your bed, so I looked around and saw you swimming." Alagur's grin is firmly planted on his face as he speaks. "And you know, we're going to be travelling together, so we may see each other in 'awkward situations' more than once."

I know he's right.

Overcoming her reservations, she walks out of the water, and the last of her childhood washes away. She emerges as a young woman; Marrida is a girl no more.

Naked, she stares at Alagur on the embankment, making no attempt to reach for the towel he's holding out, his arm muscles shaking from the tension. A smile playing on her face, standing a little more than two paces away from the towel, she waits to see how long he will struggle to keep his promise to not look.

"Are you ever going to get out of the water?" Alagur looks towards the lake, only to be greeted by the sight of his companion standing naked on the bank, bathed in the light of the early morning sun. Alagur can do nothing but stare as he slowly lowers the towel. Droplets of water run slowly down different parts of her torso, her arms, her legs, only to be replaced by new droplets dripping from her hair, which is a soft copper-orange colour now it's wet. Her lips are quivering somewhat; Alagur isn't sure if it's from the cold air or apprehension. Her body is slender with firm, wiry muscles, and as she's only nineteen years old, her breasts are still those of an adolescent. He's in awe of Marrida's beauty at that moment, and he feels his heart pumping faster as a wave of emotion overcomes him.

Is this what real love feels like?

Every feeling Marrida can imagine races through her body. She walked naked from the water to test the man's resolve.

Will he rush up to me, grab me, push me to the ground and do the things he described the other Wolf Riders doing? Will he take advantage of this situation with no regard for how I may feel?

When Alagur just stands there staring, Marrida starts to feel embarrassed, then she feels like he's appraising her. She even feels empowered by the situation – the longer she can stand there with no reaction from him, the more power it gives her.

Marrida is unexpectedly interrupted from her thoughts by the soft selvaya wool towel being wrapped around her, held in place by two powerful, muscular arms. Alagur has snapped himself out of his trance-like state and decided to make sure she's warm. She looks up at two startlingly blue eyes filled with love and compassion.

If this is love, I now understand what Mam and Papa felt for each other, she thinks, the warmth of the towel around her making her feel languorous . But more than that, she feels how close Alagur is holding her. Moments later, nothing else matters when his lips reach hers and kiss her.

It seems like the kiss lasts for the longest time ever. When Alagur finally stops kissing Marrida and she looks at him once more, the pain she has seen in his eyes so many times is gone. She senses that Alagur is feeling a sense of peace deep in his heart for the first time since he was snatched by the Wolf Riders. Chance brought him to her, and chance has given him an opportunity which few among the Wolf Riders get – the opportunity to walk away.

Perhaps fate was set in motion when he helped Bergas leave the shameful lifestyle that so many boys end up in. If he helps me with my mission to bring genuine peace back to the world, that fate will give him a chance to change things for boys now growing up across Keldarra.

Alagur smiles at Marrida and is greeted with a warm smile in return. "Shall we go and bathe together?" He jerks his head towards the lake. Marrida nods approvingly.

As Alagur disrobes and places his clothes beside hers on the bush, Marrida smiles sensuously at him as she steadily lowers her towel, then removes it completely and hangs it from a low branch of the tree overhanging the pasture. They both stand naked, staring at each other for a few minutes, then Marrida steps back little by little. When she's in the lake to mid-waist, she splashes cold water at Alagur with a giggle, then turns and swims towards the centre of the lake where she waits for him to catch up.

Alagur rushes into the water and swims after her in several fast strokes. On reaching her, he takes her slippery body into his arms. As he holds her, he kisses her on her forehead, then once more on her lips. He draws her closer to himself and feels her hardened nipples touch his chest. This causes a reaction in his body, and he feels a surge of heat rising inside that he has never felt before. Despite the cold water, he feels hot, and he's feeling something more – an inexplicable sense that he wants this woman to be more than just a temporary companion. He wants to share his life with her, protect her. For a few moments, he wonders how she'd react if he asked her to be his life partner. They've only known one another for slightly more than a season.

Is that enough time to fall in love?

Alagur looks Marrida in the eyes and sees his feelings reflected in them. At that moment in time, nothing else matters – not the mission they're on; not his past with the Wolf Riders; not even the fact that she could easily go from liking him to hating him if he says or does the wrong thing.

Suddenly, the two individuals are interrupted by a nuzzle from a giant wolf, who has waded into the water and joined them. Yalla's long, wet hair gets in the way of the man and woman holding one another, and Alagur gives her a scowl that makes her whimper.

Marrida puts her arms over the wolf's broad shoulders and smiles. "Yalla wants to play with us too." She gently puts her hand against Alagur's cheek, which ebbs away his anger towards Yalla, and he gives the wolf a signal to show her she hasn't done wrong.

All three of them play and swim until the morning has gone, when exhaustion finally makes them clamber from the water and sit down in their small encampment, letting the midday sun dry them. When she's dry again, Marrida puts on her under-dress and ties it at the waist. She isn't going to sit there naked all day long; she comments to Alagur that fishermen from nearby villages could easily appear to catch some of the different fish that live in the lake. Following her example, Alagur puts his trousers back on, then sits down next to Marrida.

With a thoughtful glance towards him, she speaks. "How many days' riding until we're at Alzamar? And what direction are we heading next?"

"You see how far the lake stretches in the distance?" Alagur points towards the east as he speaks, and Marrida nods. "We should try to reach the end of the lake in the next three days. Then we're past City of Wolves and less at risk of being discovered by any of them."

His last words make Marrida's head jerk sharply towards him. Staring at an undetermined point in the distance, Alagur is thinking more about the journey ahead of them.

"We'd better get going if we want to make any progress today." Marrida notes that the man's voice sounds distracted. "I don't really fancy meeting any of those fishermen you mentioned, either, if we can help it."

Marrida gets up and helps him repack all their belongings onto the wolf. Then they mount Yalla and ride away.

CHAPTER THIRTY-SEVEN

JOHARAN SITS STARING AT THE CLOUDS ABOVE HIM, feeling pensive and withdrawn. He looks up when he hears his front door open. His remaining four apprentices are either out on errands or visiting family.

I'm not expecting any visitors.

Joharan listens to ascertain who the visitors are, only to be greeted by the familiar giggle of Kalisa. His young niece, his nephew and Damir have come to visit.

He smiles and leans back, clasping his hands together, waiting patiently for the trio to appear in the courtyard. A moment later, two arms throw themselves around his neck. Kalisa is closely followed by Esbara and Damir, carrying one of the benches from the cooking room between them.

Joharan watches on with interest. *I guess they're here with questions or news, or perhaps both.*

The youngsters sit down on the bench that the boys have placed opposite Joharan with Kalisa closest to her uncle, Damir next to her – which causes Joharan to raise an eyebrow – and Esbara at the far end. As he's tall, it seems to Joharan as though he's no further away than the others.

Joharan waits for the youngsters to speak. Although Kalisa giggled as they walked into his house, all three of them seem subdued, and the air of solemnity is telling.

They aren't here to socialise; they're here because they are concerned about Marrida.

She's been on her journey for half a season now and Kalisa is acutely aware that her sister wasn't home for her birthing celebration. She insisted on being taken to the gate through which Marrida had departed, and she stood on the uppermost floor of the gatehouse, watching the east road for any sign of her older sister. Joharan is fully aware of the promise

Marrida made on the day of her departure to be back before the girl's First Rites in just under three years from now.

I can't even tell them how long the journey might take. They're likely close to Alzamar, if I'm right about Alagur's wolf.

"Uncle, we came to talk to you about some things," Esbara says hesitantly, looking at his companions for support. Damir responds with a nod of encouragement. Esbara swallows hard and glances sideways at Kalisa, who is biting her lower lip. "We were wondering about Marrida's journey."

Joharan nods slowly. He guessed correctly when he determined they'd come here to talk about Marrida.

"All we know is she went out of the city through the gates, and Alagur went to help her, but where is she going, exactly?" The words tumble out of Kalisa's mouth, then she looks down as if she has transgressed. A reassuring hand on her head from her uncle tells her it is fine to ask.

"Damir, please lock the front door if we're going to talk about it." Joharan looks calmly but sternly at his former apprentice, an expression which is familiar to the boy. Damir gets up and almost runs to the front door to bolt it, then he draws the curtains of the window next to the door – a longstanding sign that Joharan isn't to be disturbed. If any of the other apprentices return, they will know to go to a nearby tavern for the night.

When Damir returns, he sits down between Esbara and Kalisa again, and takes Kalisa's hand, holding it momentarily in a reassuring way. Kalisa smiles weakly at him.

After waiting for a few moments to collect his thoughts, Joharan speaks slowly. "Marrida first travelled north to Venrasia Woods. You remember when I took everyone there?" The trio nods in unison. "When she arrived there, Alagur planned to go north-east to Ribbon Lake. I told Alagur they should follow it all the way to the end so Marrida would only have a day or so to travel to get to Alzamar. He agreed with me as it's the safest route he could think of to bypass City of Wolves."

"Is City of Wolves – errr – Masharea as Marrida calls it – close to the lake too? I recall Alagur telling me that."

"Yes, Esbara, it is. When Alagur told me how close it is, I told him to travel as fast as possible to get past the city."

Joharan waits for further questions only to be met by silence, and both he and the youngsters are caught up in their own thoughts for a time. Then Joharan continues speaking, but changes the subject.

"Marrida will be arriving in Alzamar soon if Alagur was correct about it taking half a season to get there. I gave her merchandise to deliver so she can earn a filled gold purse. It was too dangerous for her to leave here with a lot of money on her. She'll get the best prices for the merchandise as she'll visit those who know my work."

"Did you send word to Eldagu that Marrida will be arriving?"

Seeing Esbara and Kalisa look questioningly at Damir at the mention of an unfamiliar name, Joharan says, "He's an old friend of mine. Marrida knows him. He last visited Ruh'nar when you'd have been too young to remember him, Esbara. Damir knows him because he has had to deliver letters for Eldagu via the Office of the Merchant Clerk. I've known him since just before my Second Rites."

Esbara and Kalisa nod.

"They should soon be travelling north to Azaquina where Alagur's young friend comes from."

"Yeah, he told us about Bergas," Esbara responds.

"It gets interesting for Marrida when she gets to Azaquina as she'll discover that one of the dialects in Sharriba's journal is spoken there. If any individual can help Marrida decipher some of Sharriba's writings, it's Bergas."

"Why did she give Marrida that journal?"

The two boys look at Kalisa in surprise.

Joharan sighs deeply. "There's much history attached to the journal, and some of it involves me."

The three youngsters stare open-mouthed at the old man. They didn't expect him to admit that there's some sort of history between him and Sharriba.

Maybe it's time to tell them. It has a bearing on the whole situation anyway.

"You remember I told you about the vision my grandmother did? I told Sharriba about that vision when she and I became friends once more after--"

Joharan hesitates and wonders how much he should say.

"What I'm about to tell you is never to go beyond this house, understand?" Joharan looks at everyone in turn with his strictest frown. All three young people nod solemnly. Joharan pauses and takes a deep breath. "Maybe I need to do the whole retelling, so you can understand why Marrida needed to go on her journey."

Damir, Esbara and Kalisa look at one another, all three realising they're about to hear a retelling only a few others – if anyone – will ever hear. Joharan folds his hands and breathes deeply before speaking.

"It started some three thousand years ago, during the oppression by those from a land far to the north of Keldarra. Do you know where the name of our land comes from?"

The youngsters shake their heads.

"In one of the oldest dialects – some believe it was spoken in The Old Days – the meaning was 'Bound to Queltha'. From the old name 'Qelt'aera', we got the name we use today – Keldarra."

Joharan pauses to pour himself some water from the jug on the table next to him.

"Fundamentally, the old name meant we were enslaved to Queltha."

"Marrida mentioned Queltha." Esbara gets a nod to continue from Joharan. "She spoke the name in the context of what is written in Sharriba's journal."

The old man takes a sip from his cup and thinks about what to say next.

"The Old Days was the time long before the Wolf Riders started their reign of terror, isn't that correct?" Damir asks before Joharan can speak. The old man nods, realising the boy must know this from speaking with Alagur.

"Sharriba thinks 'The Old Days' refers to a time before we were oppressed by those from Queltha, so it's an even earlier time in our history than most realise. One of the things Sharriba told me in connection with her journal – which she wrote when she was a new Acolyte at the Temple – is that she did visions of the earliest Wolf Riders. She didn't tell me what happened precisely, but she did say the Keepers of Truth are suppressing knowledge of those days. Or, more accurately, the Elder who was in charge at the time was doing so, and Sharriba thought she wasn't the first."

Kalisa straightens up and stares at her uncle, puzzled. This is something she didn't know about the Keepers of Truth. Joharan sees the dismay on his young niece's face and nods.

"The Keepers of Truth – even now – aren't necessarily as they seem. They even call themselves the Guardians of Truth at times, but from what Sharriba told me, they're far from it. They're a fractured, authoritarian people. Not a people I'd want to mix with – and if it hadn't been for my promise to both my grandmother and your mother, I would never have let Marrida become involved with them."

The mention of their mother's involvement in the retelling makes

Esbara and Kalisa even more curious and they look at each other behind Damir's back. Damir is hunched over, listening to the old man's words closely, so he doesn't notice. Joharan, however, does notice.

He continues again after a pause. "Your mother was a Keeper at the beginning of her second year when she met your father – my brother – when he travelled to Marridina. As you both know, they made their promise to become life partners after only knowing one another for a day. I know they were very much in love, but initially, I distrusted your mother because she was a former Keeper, and therefore one of *them*."

Joharan looks down at the cup he is holding between his hands. *I was ashamed that I hated their mother in those days, even more so when I saw her die in childbirth because of what happened to Markalo. They had thirteen years of a loving relationship that should never have ended. They would be celebrating twenty years together now. But that ended the day that man killed Markalo.*

Joharan looks up when he feels a hand on each of his knees. Both Kalisa and Esbara are looking back at him with eyes filled with compassion.

"Marrida told us why you couldn't accept that she had to join the Order of Truth. She told all of us, including Damir, just before she left. It has something to do with Sharriba, right?" Esbara stares at his uncle until Joharan nods.

Joharan sips his water before continuing. "My grandmother possessed the ability to use a Stone of Truth, but I don't know if she was ever a Keeper. The gem Marrida uses once belonged to her. I was a boy, not much older than you are now, Esbara, when she told me of her visions – one of them. She told me that one day I'd have a daughter who wasn't my own, and I would need to let her become a Keeper. You showed interest in the Keepers when I talked to Marrida before she left, Kalisa. Don't make your decision until you've heard my complete retelling."

Damir glances at Kalisa as if to say, "Be careful with your decision". She has told him about her thoughts regarding the Keepers. However, Kalisa has already started to dismiss the idea of being a Keeper, realising it's more of an imposed vocation than the calling it may have been centuries ago.

"The Elder who governed the Temple when Sharriba was young told her she'd written forbidden knowledge when she wrote down the visions she'd done – visions which showed the beginnings of the Wolf Riders. I told Sharriba about my grandmother's visions. She in turn entrusted some of her journal's knowledge to me. Sharriba is about decade older than I am, and the visions were done when I was a boy just before First Rites. That would make it fifty-six years ago."

"Marrida said something about the journal being in six dialects. So, she's going to Azaquina to get one of them translated?"

Joharan nods slowly at Esbara, takes another sip, and continues. "There's a long-held belief that the damage done by the Wolf Riders can be undone. They've been the evil in this world for too long, when once they were the force that drove off the invaders from Queltha. But in those days, they had a different name."

Esbara looks at his uncle in amazement. *Alagur told me something similar, but I didn't realise Uncle Joharan would know about it, too. Now I realise why I want to be one of the Ruh'nar defenders. I want to help rid the world of the Wolf Riders, too.* But Esbara remembers something Marrida said.

"There might be a way to get the Wolf Riders to go back to their beginnings, for them to change again."

Is the answer simply that the world needs more people like Alagur who, underneath all the bravado, is a pretty decent guy who doesn't want to be a Wolf Rider? And what about Bergas, who was rescued from a life as a Wolf Rider by Alagur. How many other boys could be spared a similar fate? I was saved by the simple fact that I listened to Marrida and hid. But not Alagur. Something caused him to disobey. Or was that true? Was he targeted?

Although he never told Marrida, Esbara had heard Samur come back as well. He had heard the man curse and, like his sister, had questioned the odd dialect.

Perhaps I could help rid the world of people like Samur who want to keep the Wolf Riders going. It says in the legend that Alagur recited that there's going to be an end to the Wolf Riders. But when? Well, that is the biggest question of all.

"And do any of you know where the Stone of Truth comes from?"
Joharan has obviously been continuing his retelling, but Esbara has been so engrossed in his own thoughts that he's missed a large chunk of it. Glancing at his sibling and friend, he follows their example when he sees both shake their heads.
"There's a cave far away to the east. I don't know its name, but legend has it the first gem to be known as a Stone of Truth was found there by

chance by a young girl. She was a convicted thief who had been put into a place of servitude, and as a thief – of course – she took the gem. When she got home, she and two of her friends discovered the gem possessed some interesting properties. It's said those three became the first Keepers. Or, as Sharriba told me, one Keeper, one Caller, and one Preserver. However, Sharriba never did tell me why the other two disappeared and we only have Keepers now. The answer to that question is the 'truth' which Marrida is going to find on her journey."

Joharan takes a deep breath and a large gulp of his water. The silence from the youngsters tells him they're fascinated by the retelling, and in awe of it, too.

"So, the general idea is that Marrida goes to Alzamar to sell all the expensive goods I entrusted her with, and make enough money for her whole journey, however long it may take."

Joharan observes Kalisa, who is staring back at him. As her facial expression goes from curiosity to deep sadness, the old man realises she understands it could take a very long time indeed before her oldest sibling returns to Ruh'nar. And that's only if the journey goes as planned.

"How far does she need to go?"

Kalisa asks the question in a whisper, letting out a sob at the same time. When Joharan looks at her again, he sees a tear slowly travelling down her right cheek. Damir puts his arm around her shoulders, and Kalisa leans against him as the tears come flooding down both her cheeks. The truth of how long she'll be without her sister is out. She knows from retellings that her father travelled long distances, the longest taking three years in one stretch. After Esbara had been born, he elected to make shorter journeys, but it was this decision that ultimately cost him his life.

"Marrida is travelling to a city which lies in the far north-eastern corner of Keldarra. It will be dangerous in that region. Some say that those from Queltha still have it in their grasp. After that, she'll travel to the south-east to the island nation which lies there. This place is the origin of the vision she did. Along with the two dialects spoken in these places and the two she's learnt from Sharriba herself, there are two other dialects in the book, but I've no idea where those are spoken.

"Marrida may know enough after travelling to the island nation to come home." Joharan looks solemnly at the youngsters and adds, "We can only hope for that."

CHAPTER THIRTY-EIGHT

A GUST OF WIND TEARS MARRIDA'S HOOD OFF HER HEAD as she stands to wait for Alagur's signal that all is clear. They're now so close to City of Wolves that she can see the city by craning her neck and staring south. North of her is a rock formation that remind her of a wolf's teeth.

The wind toys with strands of her hair, so she reaches up and tries to gather it into a bundle. Marrida feels inside one of the pockets of her cloak for something to fasten her hair with and decides a length of leather ribbon will do the trick, but it takes a lot of effort in the violent gusts of wind.

A nudge on her left hip brings Marrida back to reality. She glances down and sees Yalla standing next to her with her head low in the wind. Something about the wolf's demeanour makes her pay attention. Marrida looks to the east where Alagur is waving his arm in a beckoning motion.

"I'm coming, Yalla, stop nudging me. You nearly made me fall over."

Yalla walks without hurrying along the edge of the woodland which skirts the north side of the lake, Marrida following the wolf closely. When she reaches Alagur's position, he smiles at her new hairstyle, caressing his hand over it for a few moments.

"It suits you," he says.

"It's probably easier to manage with it tied." Marrida smiles back. "I may sort it out later, so it looks neater. After all, when I get to Alzamar, I need to look like a respectable Keeper."

Alagur grins. "As long as I get to brush it first--"

* * *

STANDING ON A SMALL HILL WITH SEVERAL TREES obscuring her and Alagur, Marrida can see City of Wolves very clearly. She notices a tell-tale sign that the city was once under the control of the Keepers and points it out to Alagur. The highest tower, which shimmers in and out of the mist filling the air, has the same structural shape as the highest tower of the Temple in Ruh'nar. It is a vestige of her Order's past, and his own kind's beginning.

Marrida can't tear her eyes away from the city. Sharriba's often told her about it in private lessons, so to see it, even from a distance, makes history come alive.

"Sharriba said Masharea was once the central place of learning for all Keepers, and the two other parts of the Order. If I had time and it was safe, I would do a vision to see if I could learn more. This close to Masharea, I might pick up on its past."

Marrida looks at Alagur with pleading eyes, as if asking him for permission. Alagur thinks for a long moment, crossing his arms over his chest and scanning the skyline for any tell-tale signs that the Wolf Riders are travelling through the region.

"Can you stop a vision after a certain amount of time has elapsed?"

"I learnt a way to do that in the Temple. I could teach you how to pull me from a vision."

"What do I need to do?"

Marrida stares pensively towards City of Wolves, which causes Alagur to look at her with a familiar worry knot on his face.

"I remember Sharriba's lesson from two summers ago. I had been an Acolyte for two years at the time."

Alagur notices the hesitation in Marrida's voice as she speaks. When she stops speaking, Alagur uses his skill of reading body language to see what she is really thinking. She's trying to convince herself she's doing the right thing.

"Sharriba said there are two ways that one person can pull another person from a vision."

Absentmindedly she sits down; Alagur mirrors her actions.

It seems the city teases us with occasional glimpses of itself from this angle — I can just see the buildings from here.

"For example, now I could take my gem and put myself into a state where I can bring up a vision of Masharea." Marrida points at the city's vista. "However, I only have basic knowledge of the method because I've had fewer than three years' training. I hope you understand it's a skill you work hard to learn and not some sort of magic, right?"

Alagur nods when he sees Marrida stare at him. He's seen the effect doing a vision has on Marrida. The gem — which is, from what he's seen of it, a smoothly-cut crystal — is the conduit through which doing visions is possible.

"I think it's time for you to learn how to handle the gem too."

Marrida reaches up and undoes the gold chain from which the gem hangs. She's so abrupt and sudden with the decision that Alagur has no time to protest, and a moment later, he is sitting with the Stone of Truth in the palm of his right hand, Marrida's hand covering it. She looks at him candidly and, he notes, defiantly.

It seems she made up her mind a long time ago to defy the rules set by her Order. I guess this journey has served as a tipping point where she crosses the line from training to be a Keeper to being a woman doing things her way.

Alagur looks closely at Marrida and sees her smiling. He feels her hand lifting away slowly at the same time. Alagur glances down at the delicate white and green gem lying in the centre of his palm. It seems to glow dimly from time to time.

"Is it supposed to do that?" he whispers.

"I'm not certain." Marrida looks at the gem with renewed interest. *I've only ever seen a gem demonstrate this ebb and flow of light when a newly initiated Acolyte is introduced to it. Could Alagur learn my skill?* "Try holding your other hand over it."

Marrida cups her own hands to demonstrate the position Alagur's hands need to take. Her right hand points almost completely left and her left hand points almost completely right, forming a cross shape in front of her midriff. Alagur copies Marrida, only to have his left hand yanked up when he positions it too close to his other hand. After a few tries, he sees Marrida nod.

Expecting an explanation, he instead feels a sensation course through his entire body like lightning on a stormy day. He looks at the top of his left arm, expecting his hairs to be standing up, but they are lying flat against his well-tanned skin. A moment later, he feels warmth grow between his palms.

And then everything goes black.

* * *

MARRIDA TAKES A DAMP CLOTH AND WIPES THE SWEAT AWAY from Alagur's forehead. Yalla lies next to her master, whimpering because she doesn't know why he isn't responding anymore. The third time Marrida places the cool cloth on his forehead, Alagur reaches up and takes hold of her arm. It reminds her of the first evening he awoke from his coma nearly a season ago.

"What happened?" he enquires in a raspy voice, his mouth feeling dry.

"You did a vision, or at least a small portion of one."

Marrida's voice seems to come from a distance even though he can sense her next to him. Alagur gradually opens his eyes. Marrida is looking down at him with concern etched on her face, smiling when she sees he's conscious once more.

"The first time can be very dramatic for a new Acolyte. I'm not sure, but I think you might be able to do something with the gem as well. You were the one who brought me out of the vision when I was self-repositioning. It takes a person with Keeper skills to do that."

"Keeper skills? I'm no Keeper," Alagur protests, trying to raise himself into an upright position.

"But your sister may be."

"My sister?"

"Yes. While you lay there, I decided to read more of Sharriba's book. It mentions Chiva'na several times, as you know, and the Callers."

"Callers? What have they got to do with me being a Keeper? Or my sister, for that matter?"

"You recall the drawing you did of the emblem? Remember I said Callers were my opposite in essence?" Alagur nods. "Keepers look to the past, Callers look to the future, and what binds them is the Preservers."

"I thought you didn't know what the third woman represented."

"I didn't. Not until these last few hours, at least."

Alagur looks at Marrida with such a puzzled expression on his face, she can't resist giggling.

"You do look funny when you're totally clueless about something," Marrida snorts. Then, taking several deep breaths to let the flow of laughter subside, she continues. "What do you think happened in the last few hours?" Marrida looks up at the sky, causing Alagur to look up as well. It's well past midday.

How can so much time have elapsed without me being aware of it? Alagur looks around. First, he sees the gem lying on a piece of cloth on the ground to his right, he then sees Yalla almost in a state of panic. *What happened to me?*

Alagur returns his gaze to Marrida, who has followed his glance as he looked around. He sees a knowing smile on her face, indicating she knows something he doesn't. He frowns, but Marrida doesn't flinch, nor does her smile diminish or disappear. She keeps staring and it is starting to unnerve him, causing him to feel vulnerable.

"What happened?" he snaps. All he gets back is a broadening smile, then Marrida sighs before speaking.

Marrida thinks about how to explain the sequence of events to Alagur in such a way that he'll be able to recall his vision's content – as she's trained to do. She's not even sure if it is possible, but then, if anyone had told her before today that a man – a Wolf Rider, as well – would be able to do what she has been learning for the last few years, she would have laughed and told them they were crazy. But she's seen the proof today that it's possible.

"I think this is what Sharriba has trained me for," Marrida almost whispers. "There's so much more going on than either of us realise. You said you dreamed about me, right?" Alagur nods. "What if it was not a dream you were having, but the beginnings of a vision?"

Alagur stares at her for several minutes with his mouth wide open.

"Can a person do visions without that?" He points at the stone lying to his right.

"Yes, but with difficulty. You recall I told you that the first Stone of Truth was found in a cave in the east?" The man nods again. "I think it's connected to the ability to do visions. Before the first gem was found, no one reported being able to do visions, but afterwards, they could."

"How do you know all this?" Alagur asks.

"Because of your vision."

She said it again. I did a vision?

"Marrida, are you going to tell me exactly what happened, or are you going to leave me guessing?"

"Do you remember things going dark?"

Alagur thinks hard. Somewhere in the fogginess of his mind, he realises that everything going dark was due to something he did. Or perhaps Marrida triggered it. He looks at her sincere face.

"I do recall something," he says with some hesitation. "I'm not sure what, though. I can't recall what happened in detail."

He concedes that he needs things explaining. And so Marrida explains.

"You asked what you could do to help, so I needed you to understand what I do when I do visions. I wasn't entirely sure if it was possible, but I needed to try."

"Try *what*?"

"To see if men can do visions. It's a skill usually passed down from mother to daughter, or in my case, from an adopted mother when Elder Sharriba became my co-guardian twelve years ago."

"Why would you think men can do visions too?"

"Because of what happened at the house. Only a person with the aptitude to use the gem can pull someone out of a dangerous vision. You pulled me out of the vision I was doing alone in my room."

"But your uncle was in the room before me."

"Yes, but you pulled me out." Marrida points her slender finger at Alagur's chest.

"How?"

Marrida had watched as Alagur's eyes went dark. Then, slowly at first, a shimmery image appeared in the air next to him. As she watched, she saw Alagur being followed by a young boy with reddish-brown hair.

That must be Bergas. His hair matches the colour of the distinctive bergas bush so closely.

They'd been in a room and the boy was holding up an ember. Marrida saw paintings and carvings which gave the room away as once having belonged to an Elder – one who lived a thousand years ago when Masharea was still a stronghold run by Keepers.

"I think originally both men and women would have been destined to be Keepers. That something happened to change this destiny, which has something to do with the vision I did of the cave with the stone tablet on the floor, and the presence of wolves within it."

Alagur nods. Marrida's words fascinate him, triggering a long-buried curiosity within him, and he wants to know more.

"But you said you didn't know what Preservers were until now--"

"Yes, and now I do because you did a vision which showed me the missing information."

Alagur stares at Marrida as a smile plays on her face.

What's she saying? Did I hear her correctly? Could a man such as I be the missing link in all this? How can it be possible for me, a Wolf Rider, to do visions with the gem?

Alagur glances down at the inert gem lying to his right. He suddenly feels an urge to touch it, but fights the temptation.

I'm unsure if I'm ready for another vision — yet!

Marrida follows the man's gaze, sees him looking at the gem and smiles. *His view of what the gem can do has changed him, even if he doesn't know it yet.*

"Do you still want to know how to help me when I do visions?" she asks. "Because there will be some which will test my endurance to the limit."

CHAPTER THIRTY-NINE

* * *

Sitting side by side, Marrida and Alagur watch the bonfires of City of Wolves being lit one by one. In the shadows of the approaching night, they do not dare to light a campfire themselves for fear it may be spotted by someone within the old city.

They've spent the whole day working on Alagur's skill of doing visions with the Stone of Truth instead of travelling, and the man is worried as he stares at the city. They're a day's ride, perhaps a little further, from City of Wolves, but they really need to put several days' distance between them and it. Alagur is also worried about their next destination – Alzamar.

"It's frequented by Wolf Rider scouts," he protests. "We shouldn't even go there."

"It's where I'll fetch the best prices for the wares Uncle Joharan gave me to sell."

"I should accompany you."

"I need to go alone. It's more dangerous for you there – my travel papers and the letter from Sharriba will protect me."

The excitement of Alagur having done a vision leaves them, replaced by disagreement. They sit in silence, watching City of Wolves. Even Yalla is silent, either because she feels the animosity between her two companions, or because she knows that discovery by those in the city would mean danger. Her instinct tells her they must be upwind, because if their position was downwind, the wolves in the city would catch her smell and alert their masters.

Yalla rushes away through the low undergrowth in a northerly direction, making as little noise as she can. Hiding is her best option until she sees a signal from her master that they're going to travel further. The wolf sniffs the air once more to see if she can detect the familiar smell she caught a few days ago, but it's gone. The boy she knew so well, and in her own wolfish way loved, is too far away.

* * *

THE FOLLOWING MORNING BRINGS A STORM to the hastily assembled camp where Marrida and Alagur are sleeping in their travel beds. Woken up with a vengeance by nature, Marrida has her blanket pulled off her by the wind.

"Get the belongings together and head for that rocky overhang just north of us." Alagur's voice carries above the howling wind. Marrida does as she's told, the previous night's argument all but forgotten.

It takes them some time to get everything to the rocky outcrop. By the time Marrida slumps down on the dark green moss which covers the ground under the overhang, she's crying. Alagur puts his arms around her and holds her for a long time, then looks around for Yalla, realising the wolf isn't with them.

"I need to make us some sort of shelter. Bergas told me his father was caught in a storm while fishing, and that caused his death."

Marrida nods and wipes away her tears.

"You stay here," Alagur adds as Marrida starts to get up.

He places several round boulders in a row with another three layers on top, then takes a rope from his pack and throws it up at one of the trees, pulling its top towards the ground. Walking to one of the stalagmites, which betray the ancient nature of their shelter, he uses several loops to tie the rope to the rock formation in a practised motion.

Marrida watches as he ties six more of the nearby trees in the same fashion, noting his strength — he possesses muscle mass, which is well used to the endurance of work. A sniffling sound announces the arrival of the wolf — Yalla has come out of her hiding place to search for her master. Alagur kneels by the wolf briefly and checks her for injuries, looking into her eyes and mouth to make sure she's alright. When he has finished, he signals to her to lie down next to Marrida. As Marrida feels the warmth of the beast beside her, she realises her teeth have been chattering. She's more used to the almost tropical weather of Ruh'nar.

As she becomes sleepy, she watches Alagur create a makeshift tent from the trees and several of the hides. She feels ashamed suddenly that she ever questioned Alagur's knowledge of how to survive in the wild parts of Keldarra. It was in even colder climes in the mountains north of here that he found the wolf who's curled up next to her.

The wolf's head is lying in her lap and she's absentmindedly stroking it. Yalla's eyes watch her every movement and the now familiar thumping of her tail indicates she's content to be with Marrida. Yalla makes Marrida feel safe, and slowly her tears lessen.

Marrida looks down when Alagur crouches in front of her and feels his hand touch her forehead.

"Let's get some dry clothes for you, and I'll make a hot soup."

Marrida simply nods, responding to the gentleness in Alagur's voice.

Alagur walks to the packs which lie scattered at the back of the overhang. He pauses for a moment when he notices that someone has recently used the same overhang for shelter, wondering who it could have been, then he dismisses the thought and bends over Marrida's haversack. Pulling out a small bundle of her warmest clothing, Alagur walks over to Marrida. She undoes her clothing, but makes no attempt to take it off.

The man takes things into his own hands, swiftly and with minimal effort removing her outer clothing and setting it aside. He checks the condition of her undergarment and notes that it's still relatively dry, so he puts the thick woollen tunic on her almost limp body. When she is dressed, Alagur signals to the wolf to curl up around her again as he places her in a ball shape on the ground.

Yalla makes sure Marrida is kept warm by her thick fur. When Alagur sees Marrida is comfortable, he gives Yalla a rub down with one of the woollen towels, so she will be dry too. Next, he gets up and finishes the assembly of the tent structure. The weather needs to turn before they can travel on, however long that may take. Some storms are known to last several days, if not weeks.

The man takes several stones that are lying scattered on the moss-covered ground below the overhang and lays them in a circle not far from where the woman now lies sleeping in a peaceful heap, wrapped in the wolf's warm body. He takes Damir's tinder kit and strikes an ember with it. Getting up, he walks with the ember container in his hand towards a crack in the rock surface where he sees more evidence that someone has camped there. Holding the ember up, he looks at the remains of a small fire. He picks up some of the ash between his thumb and forefinger and holds it up to his nose and smells. It's a few weeks old, which means that whoever used this area for shelter isn't likely to return.

After a few more moments of thinking, he turns and walks to where he was starting to build a fire. Alagur sits down on the moss and looks with concern at Marrida. A single thump from the wolf alerts him to the fact she is watching him. Their eyes meet, and in the silent communication between Wolf Master and wolf, he conveys the importance of her mission to keep Marrida warm and safe. He then builds the fire. After a few minutes, the flames lick at the slow-burning wood log he has lit. Making a barrier opposite where the wolf and woman lie is his next task.

An hour after the storm's rude awakening, both humans and the wolf lie sleeping peacefully in the same place which served Bergas as a hiding place some weeks earlier.

* * *

SILENCE AND A GENTLE DARKNESS, TOGETHER WITH WARMTH from behind her, greet Marrida when she finally wakes up. There's a chill in the air, but two heat sources tell her she's in a safe place.

For a moment, she forgets where she is, and thinks that all her memories of being on a journey with a Wolf Rider are some sort of fever dream. Then a deep voice from across the dimming fire pulls her back to reality.

"How are you feeling, Marrida?"

"I think I'm alright," she replies, looking towards where the voice is coming from. She can only see the man's shape as a shadowy presence.

"Do you want some soup?"

"Yes, please."

Marrida takes her time to rise into an upright position. She leans quite heavily on the wolf beside her, who seems not to mind. Yalla even uses her snout to help push the woman up. A gentle lick on her hand makes Marrida smile at the wolf, and a thump from behind her tells her Yalla feels reassured by the attention Marrida has paid to her.

Marrida leans back against Yalla's flank as she takes the cup of steaming soup Alagur is handing to her and smiles at him too. He smiles back, feeling relief at her speedy recovery. The soup that Marrida sips is a clear broth. It tastes of some sort of meat, which has obviously been steeped overnight, and herbs, which she cannot identify yet, and the pulp of rubha apples. She even tastes a hint of honey; it's good. She's seen Alagur prepare food at her house, usually when Kalisa appropriated his services to be her cooking assistant. Marrida smiles at the memory as it was always so comical to see the tall, muscular man being told what to do by the tiny girl.

"How long are we going to be here, Alagur?" Marrida looks around at the tent structure made from the seven flexible trees.

"We should wait today until the storm dies down completely. We can ride for half a day after that. But the delay means we will need a full day of intensive riding at speed tomorrow."

Marrida listens to the explanation, then nods in acknowledgement. She sits staring at a random point of the tent structure for several minutes, savouring the hot broth and leaning against the warm wolf who's sprawled out on the moss behind her. She wants to talk about the journey into Alzamar again, but decides this isn't the place to do that, and definitely not the time.

Her thoughts turn to home. She wonders how her siblings and Damir are, and whether her uncle and Elder Sharriba are alright. Have further attacks been organised against the city in retaliation for the Wolf Riders who were killed or imprisoned?

Alagur, who's sipping his own bowl of broth unhurriedly, watches as different emotions play over the woman's face. A frown, a smile, another frown, then an expression that looks like sadness take their turn. He wonders what's on her mind, and why she's so quiet. It could be a result of the recent delay, just a day's riding distance from the most northerly encampments of the Wolf Riders outside City of Wolves. It isn't a luxury they can afford.

Alagur glances upwards and checks the condition of the weather. He can just make out the tops of several nearby trees, and by their stillness determines the wind has quietened down for now.

Alagur drinks down the last of his broth in a few quick mouthfuls, then he gets up.

"Are we going?" Marrida seems startled by the noise of him rising.

"No, not yet. I'm going to make the necessary preparations. You just stay there until I'm done."

Marrida feels the wolf's muscles ripple as she senses the impending departure. The woman reaches for her scruff and scratches it gently, which makes the wolf move her free hind leg involuntarily.

Marrida giggles. "You're so funny, Yalla," she says.

"Yeah, she does that a lot," Alagur agrees, chuckling.

He moves all the packs to the back of the overhang and unpacks the goods they've used on their journey. With practised efficiency, he repacks everything they'll need from now on and realises they now have one pack fewer than before. He lifts the haversacks in turn and notes both are lighter too.

This is good. It'll make the next part of the journey easier. If only she'd agree to me accompanying her into Alzamar.

"I think we're ready to put the packs on Yalla now," he says.

Marrida gets up from the ground and hands her bowl to Alagur, who pulls several leaves from one of the trees and rubs both of their bowls clean with them. He then packs the bowls into his haversack.

On command, Yalla rises to her feet and walks slowly to Alagur, stretching her legs as she does so. When she reaches him, she stands motionless as he places the riding harness on her, fastening the spear arrows and thrower to her side. Next, he drapes the packs over her back, then he signals to her to go right to the back of the overhang.

"You may want to join her there. What I'm about to do can be dangerous."

Marrida nods and moves to the small crack at the back of the rock formation just behind the wolf, who takes a flanking position in front of her.

One by one, Alagur releases the trees from their bindings, each one sweeping violently back and forth as the tension disappears from it. Marrida looks in awe at the spectacle. After ten minutes or so, all the trees are upright once more, their sweeping motions lessening by the minute.

"In a few hours' time, no one will know that anyone was here." Alagur sincerely hopes this will be true.

Alagur mounts Yalla. Standing on a mound, Marrida is finding mounting Yalla easier and easier. After both man and woman have glanced a few more times at their temporary shelter, Yalla starts running, carrying them at high speed eastward towards Alzamar.

CHAPTER FORTY

Wonderful aromas rising from the cooking fire makes both Marrida's and Alagur's mouth water. It's their first cooked meal in days as Alagur deemed it too dangerous to make a campfire while they were travelling past City of Wolves from the overhang that became their unexpected home for a day.

Three days of hard riding. Most Wolf Riders don't cope with that. How is Marrida coping with it?

Marrida looks at the meat skewered on six thin twigs which Alagur stripped of their bark and soaked in water for an hour. The meat came from a mountain sheep that the man killed skilfully with one of his spear arrows. Marrida can see that living off the land works well, especially when you want to move through the land without anyone knowing you're there.

I guess Samur won't be able to find us easily, or any other Wolf Rider. But why does Alagur say it's dangerous in Alzamar? It's a peaceful city.

Marrida watches small bubbles of fat well up from the meat, burst and drip onto the fire below. One drip of fat after another causes the fire to become smoky, making the meat smell even more delicious than she imagined it would when Alagur explained what he was going to cook.

I remember a story Mam told me about travelling to Ruh'nar with Papa after their joining. She told me how she'd watch Papa cook, whenever I asked about their joining. She always said that I'd know when it happened to me.

Marrida wonders why she's suddenly thinking about her parents in this way.

Will I be able to join with someone as a life partner? Alagur perhaps? No, not him. He can't be interested in me in that way. I guess I'll never hear the history of becoming a life partner as it's told during a joining ceremony.

It's obvious to Marrida that Alagur is a good cook and has been for many years. To survive in City of Wolves, this was probably a necessity.

The butchering and preparation of the sheep had been faster and more efficient than Marrida would have given Alagur credit for.

"Can you get the plates and cutlery please, Marrida?"

Alagur distracts Marrida from her thoughts just as she wants to spend more time reflecting on what her inner voice is telling her. She nods and walks to their main camp, and is back just minutes later with two wooden plates, eating knives, forks and cups, and a heavy water bag. She hoists the load back to where the food is cooking, and Alagur unloads her arms as she approaches.

"How long before the food is ready?" Marrida stares longingly at the haunches of meat on the open fire.

"Perhaps another half an hour."

Alagur has noticed how Marrida sits staring absentmindedly when she's thinking about the things she has learnt from Sharriba's journal. She always reaches for her gem as she does this, and frowns when things don't make sense to her. He can guess from her face what she may be pondering. It's something she's mentioned several times already.

"For a start, why would Sharriba be writing about a vision — and about the history of the Order of Truth — my Order — in a dialect that no one else at the Temple can understand?"

"Are you thinking about visions again?" Alagur has a hint of a chuckle in his voice.

"Actually, I was thinking about Sharriba. Something she said while we were sitting in the library of the Temple didn't make sense — at least, not until now."

"You told me she explained more to you about the information in the books than she's done on any previous occasions."

"Yes, she did. I've been wondering for most of the journey why she'd tell me things that it's forbidden for anyone but a fully trained Keeper to know. She let me look at Books of Forbidden Knowledge. You need to have been a Keeper for at least five years before you're allowed to look at them. And she willingly gave me her own journal, which she'd hidden among them. What is bothering me is why she hid the book there of all places."

Marrida sighs deeply and looks up at Alagur. He crouches in front of her and takes her face in his hands.

"I'm sure you'll find the answers when you can translate more of the journal."

Alagur observes Marrida closely and notes how worried she looks. She nods, and a flash of hope betrays that she wants the answer to be the right one. She almost looks at him like she's grateful, and Alagur is certain that she's aware she wouldn't have got far without him. Marrida suddenly throws her arms around Alagur and leans her head against his right shoulder. He responds in kind, putting his arms around her. There's still the matter of going to Alzamar to resolve, but at this moment in time, the embrace is all that matters to them both.

After a few minutes, Marrida moves away from Alagur and looks at him. "Perhaps I need to do a vision tomorrow morning," she says. "Do you remember the instructions I gave you about pulling someone out of a vision?"

Alagur nods. They've practised three times in the last three days, with Marrida having short visions and letting him attempt to pull her out. On the third occasion, he was successful, and the self-satisfied smile on his face told her he was happy to have learnt a new skill.

I hope it wasn't a coincidence and he does indeed know how to pull me out, because if he doesn't and there are other dangers nearby — such as Wolf Riders — then both of us will be at risk. I'm sure he'll be treated as a traitor by them for abandoning their cause in Ruh'nar. He'll certainly be killed in one of the gruesome ways he's described to me. I recall him saying that you'd know what the manner of a man's death would be by the motion of a fist in front of the stomach. He didn't go into details, but my medical mind can guess.

Alagur feels goose bumps under his hands and guesses what is going through Marrida's mind. She's heard about women — and girls too — being raped or killed by Wolf Riders, a rumour which was confirmed by Alagur, and she is having a hard time processing it.

I have a small knife in a pocket inside my travel boots. If any Wolf Rider comes for me, I'll slit my wrists and bleed to death rather than let them have their way with me.

Marrida reaches up and takes the thin gold chain from around her neck. She hands the gem hanging from it to Alagur, and he takes it from her by holding the chain between his thumb and forefinger.
"We need to practise the attunement one more time. We've got time before the food is ready."

Marrida's next few motions are well practised. In a moment, she has the gem dangling against the palm of her left hand, and Alagur copies her motions almost as quickly. When she's certain the pressure of Alagur's palm will hold the gem against her own, she lets go of the chain. She positions her right hand a thumb's length from Alagur's hand, and again he copies her motions.

They glance at each other, then at the gem.
"Close your eyes," Marrida instructs.
Alagur nods and complies. When his eyes are shut, Marrida does the same. Now both wait.

After a few minutes, they feel a warm glow between their hands. As it increases, their hands move closer until they are touching. A moment later, they clasp each other's hands.

Marrida is the first to open her eyes, and she sees Alagur do the same a moment later. They glance at one another, then down at their hands which glow because of the intense white light emitted by the gem.

They wait.

After about ten minutes, the bright white light becomes green, then it glows blue, and then it's gone.
"I think it was a successful attunement." Marrida smiles at Alagur. "You're ready to assist me whenever I do a vision."

He smiles back. He doubted he could learn something normally only learnt by females and cursed himself each time an attempt failed. Wondering why it has become so easy in the last few days, he asks Marrida.

"Opposites are required to become attuned. It's that which will make it all work properly. In the Temple, two girls with opposite personalities practise the skill. For example, if one girl is reticent, then the other girl will be unreserved."

Alagur frowns. *What's opposite about Marrida and me — besides us being opposite sexes, and her being a Keeper and me a Wolf Rider?* What neither individual realises at this moment is that their conflict over whether Marrida should go to Alzamar alone or accompanied by Alagur is the trigger which has allowed them to become attuned to one another.

"Tomorrow we'll do a vision," Marrida suggests softly.
Alagur grins. "Yes, and I'm sure I can pull you out of it."
"I think I'll attempt a vision of your sister once more."
Alagur nods. He is interested in seeing more of his sister's fate.
"When I did the first vision of you, I saw your sister as an infant of

around three or four years. You were perhaps eleven or twelve. This time I'll do a vision to see what happened to her when she had done her First Rites."

Alagur thinks again for a moment. When she did her First Rites, his sister would have been eleven years older than she was in the vision Marrida showed him. *If, as Marrida has stated, she was an infant at the time of my abduction, she must have been doing her First Rites when I was doing the Wolf Naming Ceremony. What was my life like back then? What was I doing back then? It wasn't that long ago. But honestly, I'm not certain anymore about my age. Maybe when I go home I'll know how old I really am. Marrida said I could be as young as First Rites and as old as thirty. I'm certain I heard her say this to her family.* Alagur closes his eyes for a moment and thinks about the memories the visions have evoked. *How different would my life have been if I hadn't been snatched?*

Something has been nagging at his mind since witnessing the first vision.

"Marrida, I have a question about the self-repositioning you experienced when you saw my sister. There's something I'm trying to remember about the day, but my mind doesn't seem to be able to reach the memory. I'm not trained to retain memories as you are."
"What about the vision?"
"You said my sister called out to me. How did she sound?"

Marrida is slightly taken aback by the question and pauses to think. She closes her eyes and pulls the memory of the vision from the depths of her mind.

Something about the voice — it didn't sound panicked or afraid. It sounded demanding.

Marrida's eyes fly open and she stares for a long moment at Alagur. "I think I know what she did. She ran out and called *before* you were snatched, not afterwards — as if she knew what was going to happen."

Alagur stares at Marrida in shock. "Marrida, based on what you saw and heard, do you think she might be a Caller?" His voice breaks under the strain of the emotions welling up inside him.
"She could be," Marrida replies, placing her hand on his cheek to reassure him. "You told me that Raimir said they do things with girls in that city, right? Well, maybe he didn't realise that there are Callers there."
"I thought that Sharriba's journal said there are few Callers left, and that the Preservers have totally disappeared."

"I thought so, too, but it seems there are clues which show both are still around."

"What clues?" the man probes, getting up. His crouching position is starting to cause a tingling pain in his legs, and it's also time to serve out their food.

"There are two clues so far. The first one is that your sister knew you were about to be snatched. The second one is your own ability to attune with me – to be the one who pulls me from visions."

"What has attunement got to do with my sister's ability?"

"I'm a Keeper. If your sister foresaw your snatching and came to call for you before you were lifted onto the wolf by the Wolf Rider, that makes her a Caller. And that would make you a Preserver, if I understand correctly what they are."

There's a long silence after the woman has finished speaking. She waits for more questions from Alagur, who's staring into the middle distance, thinking about what she's said. After ladling their food silently onto plates, handing one to Marrida and sitting down opposite her, he finally speaks.

"What gave you that idea?"

"I can only speculate about your sister, but we know I'm a Keeper – or, at least, training to be one. The reason I say you're a Preserver comes from what I saw in your vision."

There it is again. She insists I did a vision even though I cannot recall it. All I remember is that everything went black.

"Would Preservers do visions too?"

"Yes, all those who can use the Stone of Truth can do visions, although I suspect Callers and Preservers call their gems something different." Marrida pauses for a moment, smiling. "Keepers see the past, Callers see the future, and Preservers are the balance between past and future. In other words, they can attune themselves to both the Keepers and the Callers. They bind the events of the past with those which haven't yet happened – the future – and create the balance in history. This causes peace, prosperity, unity and co-operation between all the people who live in this land. At least, that's how it's supposed to be."

Alagur stops eating for a few moments and looks at her. "And you know all this how?" he questions.

"Because when you held the Stone of Truth in your hand, I had my hand over yours. The vision I saw was the beginning of the Order, and the future of it where Wolf Riders will once more be a peacekeeping force."

Alagur stares at Marrida, open-mouthed. The more he learns about the vision he did, the more fantastical everything she says sounds.

"There's more," Marrida continues, ignoring the sceptical look on his face.

"More? How much more?"

"The legend which the Wolf Riders tell each other, they've always told as if it's a retelling of their triumph over the world. But, believe it or not, it's a prophecy foretelling their downfall. Well, not literally their downfall; more the end of their reign of terror. Note the last words of it."

Alagur listens as Marrida recites the last verse of the legend.

> TOGETHER THEY END THE BROKEN WORLD,
> HEAL THE WORLD TO WHAT IT WAS BEFORE,
> IT IS THAT DESTINY THAT IS UNSPOKEN.

Marrida pauses for a few bites of her food before continuing. "What do you think those words mean?"

Alagur thinks about the words once more. Now that Marrida has told him about the Order of Truth, and about his sister possibly being a Caller, the words take on a new meaning for him.

"You mean to say that 'they' in the verse could be you and me?"

"Even more than that, about it could mean you, me, and your long-lost sister."

"How do you know?"

"Because the legend wasn't created by the Wolf Riders. It was a vision, and the Wolf Riders heard it while they were taking over control of Masharea. They changed the meaning of the vision."

"The meaning of what vision?"

"The meaning of the vision of an Elder. Someone who lived in Masharea a long time ago foresaw not only the coming of the Wolf Riders, but also their end. That someone could only have been a Preserver."

CHAPTER FORTY-ONE

Marrida grumbles under her breath when her foot slips on the muddy slope. She hears Alagur let out a curse and realises he too is finding the footpath unsteady. The climb down is tougher than she anticipated, and neither's mood is going to be improved by it.

The arguments have started again in the last few days. These arguments don't involve them shouting at one another; they're more a game of yes and no, with neither party wanting the other to win. And all the time they've spent arguing about whether or not Marrida should go into Alzamar alone has meant they haven't been discussing what really matters: the Stone of Truth, how it works, why Alagur can use the gem, and how his sister fits into the bigger picture.

We don't talk, haven't done so for four days now, except for a brief discussion this morning before we started walking in this damned rain. The evenings are so lonely without his company.

The outline of Alzamar's buildings lies ahead of them, maybe a few hours away, although the rainfall is making it seem further away than it is.

Just a bit further, Marrida thinks as she feels the muddy ground give way under her feet again. She grabs the wolf's reins to steady herself. Yalla has been commanded by her master to walk beside the woman, and she is gingerly pacing down the footpath. Her hair is matted against her body, and as Marrida reaches for her reins, she also manages to grab hold of some of the wolf's fur. A short yelp from Yalla tells her to be more careful.

Marrida frowns as she glances in the direction of Alzamar. *I wish Uncle Joharan had given me a sack full of gold coins for my travel, but I know he doesn't have that sort of money lying around. And people would have noticed if he'd tried to obtain it fast, resulting in more questions he wouldn't have wanted to answer.*

When the path bends to the right, it gives Marrida an opportunity to glance discreetly up to the higher part of the hill, seeing Alagur struggling for balance as much as she has. The slope isn't steep; it's just soaked from the rain that has been pouring down for at least three hours. At least

Marrida's cloak has kept her dry and warm.

After another two hours of carefully descending the hill, the pair and the wolf finally arrive at a flat rocky outcrop. Alagur unloads the packs from the wolf with all possible haste, then signals to the animal to hide. Yalla complies, though she struggles to make her way back up the slope. At the top, she turns right and disappears behind several thick bushes.

Marrida watches Yalla go and hopes the wolf will be alright. She sighs and looks around her, then in the direction of Alzamar. The stubborn expression on her face doesn't go unnoticed by Alagur, but she's made up her mind. She's going to the town alone, even though she's starting to regret her decision deep down.

I have just five packs to carry, not the eight packs and two haversacks we started out with. They have eaten most of their food and have already sold some of the less valuable items on the way here. Marrida now faces the prospect of brazenly picking up the goods to sell and walking away towards Alzamar.

Once I go, I cannot stop. I've grown stronger during the journey, but this rain isn't making things any easier.

Marrida walks to the packs and lifts each in turn to determine its weight. She picks up her haversack, which she dropped down soon after arriving, and uses the rope attached to it to stop it sliding off her shoulders, then tries the packs once more. When she's sure she has an even weight ratio for each arm, she lifts two packs with her right hand and the other three with her left hand. Without saying a word or even glancing at Alagur, she starts her trek into Alzamar.

* * *

ALAGUR HAS SAT DOWN ON A ROCK, more to steady himself than to rest. He sees all the body language Marrida thinks she's hiding from him, and he raises an eyebrow when she simply walks off without a word, displaying the headstrong nature she's often shown at the Temple. His eyebrows knot together from seething anger, but also from fear. Marrida is as wilful as he can be.

Alagur remembers trekking to the South Valley of Miza after hearing the retellings about the silver-grey-and-white wolves known to live there. He'd been forbidden to go as he wasn't yet initiated to own a wolf.

I was only supposed to choose a wolf after Second Rites. I know now that the Elder Men forbade us to go to prevent us from escaping from the city. I went anyway, out of curiosity. But now I wonder if I was meant to hear that retelling.

Alagur can't help feeling admiration for the strength being demonstrated by Marrida, both in her willfulness and her determination to keep going. *Not many in City of Wolves with that sort of strength, to be honest.*

The rebuke Alagur received from the Elder Men demonstrated his strength, but he never forgot the day he returned to City of Wolves with Yalla. *I could have ended up in the pens with the wild wolves, and it was only Samur's intervention that saved me.*

Samur's intervention heralded the beginning of warnings about the 'consequences' of insubordination, which were later directed towards Bergas. And Alagur has attempted to warn Marrida of the potential consequences of her going into Alzamar alone, but she clearly places no value on his words.

I need to follow her, regardless of how she may feel later.

Alagur gets up and lets out two piercing whistles. This is a signal for Yalla to stay put and not to follow him.

The wolf needs to make herself invisible, so no other wolf can sense her--if any is near.

Yalla hears the signal, and the instinct to obey Alagur as her master forces her deeper into the bushes she's been waiting under. She sniffs the airs for a specific smell. Alagur has trained her to seek out the musky scent of voles in these situations to mask her own scent adequately, especially in the rain. She gets up, and a moment later rushes through the undergrowth towards where she's noticed the scent she is searching for. Finding fresh droppings, she rolls through them, then she straightens again and at an even speed, so as not to tire herself, trots briskly to a higher elevation. Here her wild instinct takes over, and she stands on the edge of a rock and howls a short wolf song.

* * *

SHE IS SECURE, ALAGUR THINKS on hearing the wolf's signal, which he can tell is maybe a hundred and fifty paces above and to the right of him.

He nods, bending over and removing a dark cloak from his haversack. He then places the bag under the tree and covers it with stones.

No one will know I've been here. They'll just see a mudslide.

Alagur has omitted to tell Marrida there are other ways to enter the town: ways that the Wolf Riders know and employ with great effect to spy on the town before attacking it. A wall has been broken down over time, usually under the cover of darkness when the guards are at their most lax. Those who use it regularly are bands of pack brothers who want to strengthen their position within the ranks of the Wolf Rider society – if one could call it that.

Now, this same method of entry will serve Alagur as he follows Marrida, and perhaps ambushes anyone who may mean her harm. Although he isn't as familiar as others with the town, he has the advantage of having heard many retellings, and knowledge seems to remain in his active memory without him realising why. He recalls that the trade district is on the east side of the city, only a dozen streets from the broken wall.

As he starts his own trek through the rain – which seems to be diminishing as he walks – Alagur realises that there is much of the Wolf Riders' ways of doing things that he hasn't told Marrida.

I wonder why not. Is it deliberate or because we haven't had time to discuss it?

He pulls the hood of his cloak over his head and wraps the cloak around him. Walking the same route as Marrida for a time, he spots a small path after about fifteen minutes and diverts towards it. Before stepping onto the path, he glances in each direction to make certain no one is near, and if they are that they're not looking his way. Then he steps onto the path and walks on briskly.

Walking at a good pace, he follows the curve of the path as it weaves through the landscape, bending over at times to avoid low branches. After half an hour, he notes that the soil has turned to rubble, which alerts him to the fact that he is nearing his destination.

He stops and listens for several minutes. *If there are any guards up there, they need to be away from the breach in the wall before I continue.*

After listening for a moment longer, Alagur walks to the breach and steps through it. On the other side, the buzz of many voices as the population of Alzamar goes about its business greets him. The town, which is a third of the size of Ruh'nar, has almost the same number of people inhabiting its compact space. And because of the attacks by the Wolf Riders, which have damaged or destroyed many houses and buildings, this space is rapidly diminishing.

Keeping himself inconspicuous, Alagur looks around. Produce and wares seem plentiful, so clearly there has been no attack recently. But there could be an attack at any moment.

I wonder where Marrida is now.

Clear, familiar laughter echoes through the air. Alagur quickly paces past three stalls selling various vegetables, then turns left and right, and stops. He sees Marrida standing in front of a shop talking to an old man who is acting as if he knows her. Gesticulating frantically, she is telling him something, but Alagur cannot determine what.

Seems she has sold some of the goods already. Two of the packs are gone – and she has a new bag. A small, firm leather bag, which he hasn't seen before, is hanging to the side of her waist.

Marrida walks into the shop after the old man. Alagur waits, and a few minutes later, Marrida reappears.

She's sold another pack.

Alagur sees Marrida pull a notebook from a pocket inside her coat. She is writing something down with a charcoal rod encased in a leather binding.

I should get one of those too.

Marrida seems oblivious to her surroundings – Alagur included. But then she looks around for a moment before picking up the two remaining packs, gently strolling through the town towards her next destination. After almost half an hour, she stops at a building made of white and yellowish-brown stones. The door opens to reveal a girl not much older than Kalisa.

Alagur's enhanced hearing can hear every word of the conversation.

"Papa – it's Marrida Kayrsan."

Alagur raises his eyebrows. Neither Marrida nor anyone else in her family has ever told him the family name.

That name doesn't sound like it originated in Keldarra. Where did her family come from originally?

After a few minutes of aimlessly standing at the door, Marrida lifts the two packs either side of her. She's about to step inside when she stops in her tracks, glancing in each direction like something has alerted her. She looks around for a few minutes, then shrugs her shoulders and walks inside.

Why did she look around? She was almost acting like a Wolf Rider scout. Why did she feel threatened?

Alagur leans back against the wall behind him. *Did Marrida somehow sense my presence?* He looks around, then returns his gaze to the house she's entered. *If this is the home of the friend she's seeing in this town, she might be there for a while.*

* * *

WHILE ALAGUR'S ATTENTION IS FOCUSED ON MARRIDA, someone in the crowd is becoming very interested in him. Across the square, which is filled with merchants and shoppers, a pair of eyes starts paying close attention to him. The owner of the eyes has been in Alzamar in recent weeks to determine how much wealth the city has accumulated since it was last attacked by the Wolf Riders, but now he has a bigger prize in his sights.

He has recognised the mannerisms of the man across the square. He knows of the famed Wolf Rider with his magnificent and massive silver-grey-and-white wolf.

I need to report this to the Elder Men. One Elder Man in particular. The wolf must be somewhere in the hills near here if he's on foot. Samur will reward me well for bringing this news back with me.

The Wolf Rider smirks. He doesn't wait to see what Alagur is doing in the city – time is of the essence. He needs to get back to City of Wolves immediately so an attack can be organised – an attack which will include the capture of the traitor, Alagur. The Wolf Rider pulls his dark woollen cloak around him then he rushes past Alagur, but the man is too deep in thought to notice.

The Wolf Rider grins maliciously as he speeds towards the breach in the city wall. *That lapse in judgement will be your downfall, traitor!*

CHAPTER FORTY-TWO

Marrida SITS ON A LUSH DARK GREEN SOFA covered in the most exquisite satin she has ever felt. She rubs the tips of her fingers gently over the fabric.

She is waiting for her host--Eldagu--to return from upstairs. The man's daughter, Esalyn, is sitting on the sofa as well, copying Marrida's hand movements.

When Marrida looks at Esalyn, she gets a shy smile back. Marrida gives her an almost conspiratorial wink, and Esalyn giggles softly. To the girl, the woman who introduced herself as Marrida Kayrsan from Ruh'nar is a fascinating person. She is also pretty. Bit by bit, Esalyn's shyness dissipates and she reaches for the woman's shoulder-length lightly curling golden-brown hair.

"Your hair is pretty."

Marrida runs her own hand over the girl's dark reddish-brown hair, which comes tumbling down to her waist in a mass of curls.

"Yours is prettier."

"My Mam will be away for many years. She's on a journey."

Marrida is immediately reminded of her own long journey – and the fact she won't see her siblings for many years.

"I'm on a journey, too. I need to travel north when I've finished here."

"Everyone's always leaving." The girl scowls, crossing her arms and leaning back on the sofa with a soft thud.

Footsteps come down the wooden stairway and they both glance towards the doorway. Eldagu enters the room a moment later.

"What I've got to discuss with Marrida isn't for your ears, Esalyn. Off to your room with you."

Esalyn gets up, looking at Marrida once more. She smiles at the woman, then skips out of the room and runs up the stairs.

A minute later, a thud from upstairs indicates she has arrived in her room.

Eldagu sits down to Marrida's left and places a book on the table in front of them. Marrida studies the book.

It looks ancient.

"How old is this book?"
"It has been in my family for eight…no, nine generations. Esalyn will be the ninth generation to possess it."

Marrida looks at the man beside her, who she knows to be six months younger than her uncle. Unlike Joharan with his silver-grey shoulder-length hair tied at the nape of his neck, Eldagu has short, wiry curls of the darkest brown Marrida has ever seen. But in contrast to his hair and olive-brown skin, he has vivid blue eyes.

Alagur has similar eyes.

The eyes staring back at her beguile with an ageless wisdom.

I wish Papa was still alive. Joharan was a good substitute in her younger years, but Marrida still misses her father. *Esalyn is lucky to have Eldagu.*

Marrida reaches in to a pocket in her cloak and hands Eldagu a folded letter.
"This is for you from Uncle Joharan. He asks that you read it after I leave."
Eldagu takes the letter, nods and puts it into a small pocket of his housecoat, ignoring Marrida's obvious curiosity for a few moments.
"Shall we have a look at your book and compare the content to this one?"

Marrida nods. She unties the knots of her bag and lifts Elder Sharriba's journal from it. Placing it on the table next to Eldagu's book, she opens it where the text in the Alza'mai dialect starts. Marrida knows the name of the dialect from her discussions with Sharriba who had explained it was the most common dialect of the central parts of Keldarra – a region stretching from the east of the ancient city of Masharea – now City of Wolves – to a southern city called Hayzan. With this region being flanked by two mountain ranges, the dialect was prevented from spreading elsewhere.

Marrida takes out her notebook and writing implement. Eldagu moves closer.

"There are two passages I'm struggling with. This bit here. I haven't learnt enough to translate it fully."

That's written by a woman, Eldagu thinks as he carefully studies the elegant handwriting. *Whoever wrote this text possesses a good command of the dialect.*

"It's written in a much older form of the Alza'mai dialect than I've seen previously. It's even older than the text in my own book. But I'm sure I can translate it with the help of my own notes." Eldagu opens his own book to almost at the last page and points at the translations written there. "Are you familiar with Sab'ruhi?" he asks, looking sidelong at Marrida.

"That's the ancient dialect of Sabeya and Ruh'nar--not so ancient, as it happens. Elder Sharriba speaks it. She's one of the few who can, and she insisted on teaching me."

"You mean to say you know the Elder of the Temple in Ruh'nar?"

Marrida looks shocked. When she realises what she has revealed, she covers her mouth with her hand and looks away.

"I better read your uncle's letter--just in case."

Eldagu gets the letter from his pocket and opens it. In the letter, Joharan tells his friend not to repeat what it states to anyone, and to destroy it after reading it. The letter is an account of Joharan's grandmother's vision, explaining its connection to Marrida's journey. He tells his friend of the love and friendship he still feels for Sharriba, and that he's certain she's aiding Marrida's journey, too. He also says that the book Marrida has is Sharriba's old journal.

Eldagu gets up when he has finished reading, walks to the open fire and drops the letter onto it. Marrida watches the flames lick the corners of the parchment, before it crumbles into a pile of ash and soot in minutes.

Eldagu stands leaning against the fireplace, thinking.

There are implications to these revelations. I thought the Keepers were just some sort of myth to make people believe that someone exists with more power than the Wolf Riders.

He thinks about the city's own Temple, which is a mysterious building located atop a massive hill at the northern end of the busy town of Alzamar.

Its presence is a puzzle. It's obviously in use, but its inhabitants are isolated on an almost permanent basis. Where do they get their Acolytes from?

Eldagu returns to the sofa. He sits down next to Marrida, who's clasping and unclasping her hands nervously – and occasionally reaching up to something hanging around her neck – and places an arm around her shoulders.

"Let's continue with the translations," he says reassuringly.

Marrida looks up and sighs. "I've already told so many people that I'm a Keeper. Esbara and Kalisa know. Uncle Joharan knows. Damir knows. Alagur knows. So, it doesn't matter if you know, too. After all, you are Uncle Joharan's oldest friend."

Eldagu recognises most of the names. "Who are Damir and Alagur?" he asks. Marrida's face goes as white as moss ash.

Another secret I've discovered.

"Damir is Joharan's apprentice." Marrida hesitates a moment, then adds, "Alagur is a friend, guide and companion, helping me on my journey to Azaquina."

Eldagu just nods. *If Marrida needs to keep things private, I'll respect that. She's under two seasons from her Second Rites.*

Eldagu turns back to his family heirloom and again opens it at the page they were looking at before Marrida's shock announcement.

"The book the Elder gave you, how many dialects does it contain in total?"

Marrida looks at the two books. "In addition to Alza'mai and Sab'ruhi, there are four other dialects." Marrida suddenly decides to open up to Eldagu. "So, we learn six dialects at the Temple. One is Quin'zai, spoken in the north. I'm going to get help to translate from Alagur's friend in Azaquina."

Marrida stops for a moment to recall more information, not because she feels the need to hesitate. As she continues speaking, Eldagu leans back on the sofa and relaxes with his hands clasped in front of his chest, listening to her with great interest.

"There's the dialect spoken in Achellon, too. It's called Achallai. Sharriba says it is one of the most ancient dialects of Keldarra." Marrida pauses again "Sharriba hasn't taught me any of it yet, so I'm not sure what it sounds like or looks like when it's written down. According to Sharriba, it was spoken in The Old Days when Keldarra was still known by its old name."

Eldagu is fascinated. As a young scholar, he attended some of the best schools and academies, and to this day he retains the willingness and curiosity to learn new things. And the woman beside him is telling him things he doesn't know – couldn't have known. It gives him a new appreciation for the nineteen-year-old.

"The other two dialects are spoken in the west. I don't know their names without checking Sharriba's notes. But Alagur is from a city on the west coast, so when we get there we can find out more."

Eldagu nods. *Everything is learnt in its time and place.*

They're interrupted by footsteps coming down the stairs at a fast pace. Esalyn has clearly grown bored with sitting in her room. She peers shyly around the doorway of the front room.
"Papa?"
"Yes, Esalyn?"
"I would like to go and visit Roshira, please."
"Of course, but be back before supper."

A rush of footsteps, then the front door slams shut. Another rush of footsteps in the street makes Eldagu and Marrida glance at each other and smile.

As Esalyn's footfalls grow fainter, Eldagu looks once more at the journal, comparing the words written by Sharriba with words in his book. In Alza'mai there is no word for 'truth bearer', so the old name for City of Wolves – Masharea – is unknown in his dialect. Instead, in Alzamar, the ancient name is 'Roha'dea'. Both he and Marrida are puzzled as to why two different names should exist for one city.

Marrida tries to explain that the name Masharea reflects the truth by determining the past's impact on the world.
"Events from the past explain why things are as they are now."
She can see her explanation leaves the old man puzzled, so she doesn't press on, instead listening carefully as Eldagu explains the meaning of the name Roha'dea in the Alza'mai dialect.
"It's an amalgamation of two words: *rohanai*, meaning 'revelations of truth', and *dea'ai*, meaning something along the lines of 'the speaker of'."
Marrida thinks for a few moments. "So, if I understand correctly, the

name could have been 'speaker of revelations of truth'. Interesting."

"Why so?"

"Well--" Marrida is still not sure how much to tell Eldagu of her background, even though he's someone she can trust.

"Well?" Marrida looks at the man, who continues, "Long ago, around the time of our First Rites, Joharan and I developed a system of code words. We have a word to indicate dangerous situations, and we also have a code word for the Keepers."

"What is it?"

"For a start, I wasn't ever going to read the letter after you left. 'Read this after such and such has gone' alerts me to the fact that the person visiting me is the bringer of important news."

"So, Uncle Joharan's message was about me, then?" Marrida wonders why her uncle never told her any of the code words.

"Yes. When you mentioned the Elder, I knew the message was most certainly about you."

"Why did you send Esalyn to her room?" Marrida decides to satisfy a small part of her own curiosity.

"In part, I guessed as soon as I heard your name that there's a lot more going on than a simple visit to Alzamar to sell some merchandise. It's better for a child to remain a child, and not to be burdened with the realities of this world."

Marrida thinks about Kalisa. Her sister – just five months younger than Esalyn – was exposed to the realities of this world when Marrida decided to bring a Wolf Rider into her home and nurse him back to health. In that instant, Marrida feels deep shame for what she did. She bows her head and looks at her hands clasping and unclasping in her lap.

"Marrida." Eldagu speaks gently, leaning forward and clasping the woman's slender hands. "There are things in this world I often wonder about. One of them is whether my daughter will grow up feeling safe, or whether she'll grow up at all with the attacks on this town becoming more frequent. Esalyn – and Kalisa too, for that matter – deserve a world in which they can grow to the age of your uncle and me without feeling worried. My life partner is in another town. Every day, I worry I'm going to get the sort of news that your mother received the night of Kalisa's birthing."

Marrida feels tears welling up at the mention of her parents. She looks at Eldagu as she wipes away a tear with the sleeve of her tunic.

"I miss them so much, still."

Eldagu puts his arms around the young woman and holds her in a fatherly embrace. As she lets her grief spill over, the man fights his own tears. He'd known Markalo – and Eshara, too. Markalo had often visited Eldagu before his passing, so the tragic news was as hard on Eldagu as it was on Joharan. Having no brothers of his own, Eldagu had regarded Markalo as a brother.

When Marrida's sobbing subsides, Eldagu pushes her away from him gently, lifts her chin up with his forefinger and looks at her for a long moment.

"We need to continue translating, or you may need to sleep here overnight." Eldagu smiles encouragingly at Marrida. She nods, wipes the rest of her tears away, and turns her attention back to the two books on the table. Picking up her writing implement, she pulls her own notebook towards her, then looks at Eldagu.

"I'm ready."

"First write down the name I gave you for the city that you know as Masharea – I think that name will pop up more and more as you travel further east."

Marrida complies and copies the Alza'mai name of the ancient city known as Masharea in the Sab'ruhi dialect. That the people in the east of Keldarra call the city by a different name is a new puzzle to add to all the other puzzles that she's discovered. The puzzles seem to be like an endless trail of sugar used to lure certain types of small rodents out into the open.

There was a time when Marrida could have considered herself ignorant of the world she lives in. The first hint of a more dangerous world came in the form of the news of her father's passing. Now she's travelling to parts of Keldarra that even her father never dared to visit as a travelling merchant, and she wonders if she's doing the right thing.

Eldagu is pointing out another word. As she copies it into her notebook, she realises deep inside that she can never escape the fate that has already been set in motion.

CHAPTER FORTY-THREE

A COLD BREEZE ALERTS ALAGUR THAT IT'S PERHAPS TIME TO LEAVE, but he stays leaning against a wall, watching the house Marrida entered.

I wonder what is taking so long. Did I miss her leaving?

Red tints are streaking the sky. It must be an hour before sundown. He pulls his cloak back over his head and shoulders and makes his way swiftly through the crowds back to the breach.

I don't want Marrida to arrive back at the camp and find it deserted.

He disappears through the breach unnoticed and reverses his route of earlier to walk away from the town. When he gets back to the camp, he gets a campfire going. A short, sharp whistle calls Yalla to return; she positions herself under the bushes once more at a hand signal from her master.

While Yalla pretends to sleep, Alagur quickly prepares food and places it into a pan over the fire. The trek took him only forty minutes; he guesses it will take Marrida an hour. Alagur lies down on a padded leather cushion beside the wolf, who wags her tail and lifts her head to acknowledge her master's stroking.

"I know, I know. I was wrong to disagree with her decision to go to Alzamar alone."

Yalla licks Alagur's hand. She doesn't know what he is saying, but she notices the sadness in his voice.

I'll need to lie to Marrida, but she can simply do a vision to see the truth.

Wary of his own predicament, he's scared of losing the trust which has been building between him and Marrida. Most of all, he hopes he can keep her love.

He decides to apologise to her for suggesting that he should accompany her to Alzamar.

* * *

MARRIDA IS LOOKING THROUGH THE WINDOW at the dusk falling outside.

"I need to meet with my guide before nightfall."

While translating the text from Sharriba's journal, she and Eldagu have been talking, and she's told him most of what she has learnt since the Wolf Riders' attack on Ruh'nar.

"Don't mention the things you've told me to anyone else. And do not mention to anyone that you're a Keeper. There are those who'd kill you if they knew of your skill."

Marrida frowned as Eldagu told her about eastern Keldarra. She, in turn, has told Eldagu what Sharriba's journal says about the origins of the Keepers.

"There's a lot more going on than you think, much more than you are finding out about the Keepers. Those Callers you mentioned, it's the first time ever I've heard the word. And I've never heard of anyone who knows – or knew – a Preserver. There are some who say the Preservers were banished from the Order. Some say there are a few left on an island off the coast in the far south-west, but no one knows if it's true."

Marrida then asked for any information Eldagu might have about the Wolf Riders, making certain not to mention either Alagur or Bergas in the process.

"Every few weeks, they plunder Alzamar and at least a few boys are snatched."

Marrida realises now that Alagur spoke the truth about Alzamar being a dangerous place.

I must apologise to him as soon as I get back to camp. I'm never going to misjudge Alagur again.

While Marrida readies herself to leave, the front door opens and Esalyn rushes in. She skids to a halt in front of Marrida and looks up at her. Marrida smiles at the girl.

She reminds me so much of Kalisa.

"Are…you…leaving?" Esalyn gasps, still panting from running.

"Yes, I need to get going."

Esalyn throws herself against Marrida in an embrace. "I'm going to miss you. You're so nice." She pouts a little. "When will you come back for another visit?"

Esalyn looks up at her father and then at Marrida, pleading with her eyes.

"She has far to travel still," Eldagu explains.

"If I can, I'll return," Marrida adds. She leans forward and kisses Esalyn on her forehead; then she gives Eldagu an embrace, too. The man takes her face in his hands and kisses Marrida on the forehead, just as she has just done to his daughter, then smiles at her.

Marrida steps out of the house into a street bathed in the reds and oranges of a setting sun. She looks around and notices that most of the market stalls she passed earlier in the day have been cleared of their merchandise and the merchants have left. As she starts her trek from the city, the only luggage Marrida carries is a traveller's bag – an old one used by Eldagu as a young man. Within it is Sharriba's notebook along with her own, which is now filled with notes, translations, drawings and diagrams, including a full-page drawing of the emblem she saw Alagur draw in the sand on the bank of Ribbon Lake.

She walks without hurrying, unburdened because she has sold all the goods she came to sell and left the final pack of belongings, the ones Joharan included specifically for his old friend, with Eldagu. Under her long, thick cloak, she has a small, bulging coin purse.

I can now pay for food and accommodation, if we need it. I only hope Alagur isn't angry with me for walking off this morning.

With a pang of regret, Marrida wishes she could take back the day's events and start over again.

Marrida walks for just under an hour – more quickly than Alagur calculated – and her pace quickens even more as she gets further from the town. When she spots the orange-yellow flames of a cooking fire and smells a pot roast on the wind, she gathers her skirt and starts to run.

* * *

Yalla lifts her head and sniffs the air, and the short yip that follows tells Alagur who's approaching. He gets up, signals to the wolf to stay still, then hesitates a moment himself. Then he picks up his thrower and a handful of spear arrows from beside him and runs towards Marrida.

When they reach one another, she throws herself into his arms, unbalancing him. He drops the weaponry as he takes hold of her.

"I've missed you so much," she says as tears flood down her face. "I was wrong to go alone. I wish I could have introduced you to Eldagu."

"Who's Eldagu?"

"He's my uncle's oldest friend. Remember, Damir mentioned his name?"

Alagur recalls a name – he'd assumed Eldagu to be a place. He holds his tongue as he realises it must have been Eldagu's house that Marrida entered – he doesn't want to alert her to the fact that he watched her.

I will tell her sometime in the future – when it's more appropriate.

"The food smells good."

Marrida glances past Alagur at the campfire. She lets go of him and walks towards the cooking pot. He picks up his weapons and brushes off the soil which has clumped on them. Yalla – who has unusually chosen to disobey and approach – steps in beside Marrida. Marrida absentmindedly scratches the wolf over her ears and nose bridge. A snort from Yalla tells Marrida her tickles are appreciated.

When Alagur arrives at the campfire, he circles it and places his weapons against the rock. He sees Marrida stare at the tree stump he's fashioned into a seat, smoothed and layered with leather blankets and padding. She glances at Alagur then at the tree stump, asking an unspoken question.

"I fashioned it into a comfortable seat while you were gone."

Alagur smiles broadly. It is almost completely true. He did make it into a seat in the end, but at first – starting soon after her departure – he'd simply hacked at it in frustration. When he returned and saw his earlier 'handiwork', he decided to finish what he'd started and make a proper seat.

Marrida sits down and judges the stump's merits as a seat. A nod confirms it's comfortable enough.

"I can move the remaining packs behind you for a backrest – if you want."

Marrida nods again, and Alagur makes short work of the task. Marrida, her face showing how comfortable she now finds the seat, leans forward and smells the pot.

"What are you cooking?"

"I'm making a vegetable broth. When it's almost done, I'll add those pieces of dried meat."

Alagur points at a partially opened pack. Marrida recognises the meat as the tender parts of a mountain sheep that Alagur killed in the South Valley of Miza to provide them with a few weeks' worth of meat, demonstrating once more his skill with a spear arrow thrower.

Alagur watches Marrida surreptitiously, wondering what she's smiling about. For a few moments, he wants to ask her, then he changes his mind.

If we're going to talk, it will be on her terms, not mine.

Alagur leans over the cooking pot, checks its content and decides it is time to add the meat. Marrida watches as he grabs the half-unwrapped leather container, removes some of the bindings, and drops four even-sized rump steaks into the cooking pot. The sudden addition of the meat makes the stew bellow out a cloud of steam, and a sizzle comes from the cooking pot as the meat meets the hot liquid.

The food will be ready soon.

Alagur looks up to see Marrida rub her arms. *It's getting colder in the evenings now, the first hints of winter.* He retrieves a warm blanket for her, which she accepts with a grateful smile. Alagur then looks at her, masking his concern.

"We need to continue our journey tomorrow and reach Azaquina in the next few weeks, if we can. It will be almost impossible when winter comes."

Marrida nods, feeling too cold to speak. Alagur sees her glance towards the cooking pot and guesses from her facial expressions that she's hungry and wants the broth to warm her insides. He walks over to the cooking pot to check it again.

"Just serve that food up. I'm hungry and cold. It smells too good to wait."

Alagur picks up one of the bowls and places a piece of rump on it. With the ladle, he pours two spoonfuls of the broth mixture over it, then hands it to Marrida. She smiles as she takes it and places it in her lap. Accepting the utensils Alagur is handing to her, she starts to eat, savouring the meal.

It's a bit undercooked, but I'm too hungry to care.

While she chews, her mind drifts to her conversation with Eldagu.

He was so nice. I think Alagur would have liked him.

The meal and the evening go by silently, except for the occasional rustling of leaves above them as the wind gusts. After savouring the warmth of the broth and the campfire, Marrida and Alagur climb into their beds, sleeping close to one another.

* * *

When morning comes, Marrida is greeted by a beautiful sky filled with pink, orange and pale red tints. She glances sideways to be greeted by a smiling Alagur. She smiles back at him.

"I woke up and saw how peaceful you looked sleeping, so I decided to watch you until you woke. Did you sleep well?"

"Yes, I slept very well." Marrida sits upright in her bed and stretches her arm, yawning.

"Do you want some tea and fruit bread before we leave?"

She nods.

Alagur gets up and grabs two cups and a small, elongated container he filled with water earlier. It is an item Joharan originally intended for them to sell, but it has become too valuable to them for brewing fresh tea, which reminds Marrida of home. He pours extra water into the container from a pouch he's retrieved from a loop on the wolf's harness, adds a small piece of firewood to the campfire to bring it back to a high temperature, and the water in the container, which is sitting next to the campfire, begins to boil. With a leather strap, he moves the container away from the fire and places two spoonfuls of leaves in it, followed by a small piece of hardened honeycomb. With a wooden spoon, he stirs the mixture, then places the container once more near the heat of the campfire to let it steep. When the leaves have all settled – this process takes five minutes – Alagur picks up the two cups and places them near the campfire so he can pour the tea, leaving some of the water in the container to make it easier to rinse out the pulp of leaves and residue from the honeycomb.

Marrida arrives back from washing her face in the stream and sits down next to Alagur, busying herself with brushing and plaiting her hair. She fastens it with a length of ribbon, and then winds a second piece of cloth around her head to keep it warm. The effect is immediate; her shivering dissipates. A moment later, the sun breaks through the clouds in the east and bathes her in golden light just as Alagur turns to look at her.

He stares, captivated by her beauty.

While Marrida was getting washed and dressed, Alagur prepared the wolf and attached the remaining four packs to her back. With more than three-quarters of the original load gone, she will now run with relative ease. Alagur wants to get to the scree of the mountain range which overlooks the Bay of Whispers within a month to tie in with his plans for the wolf. He will then cut her loose and allow her to find her own kind for the birthing of her pups, and he and Marrida will make the remainder of the journey to Azaquina on foot. While Alagur and Marrida trek east then northeast, the wolf will travel north-west, deep into Northern Blades. When it is time for the wolf to return, the bond between her and Alagur will ensure they meet again at the scree.

Yalla must go home for the birthing. The pups will only be safe hidden by her own kind in the highest reaches of Northern Blades. Up there with Yalla's sisters, they can't be killed or captured by the Wolf Riders.

329

Part Three

CHAPTER FORTY-FOUR

"A RIDER APPROACHES."

The commotion that follows these words wakes almost everyone in City of Wolves. It's some hours before morning will arrive, but Darush has been riding hard for days. He brings news for the Wolf Riders – one of them in particular.

"I need to speak with Samur. I bring news of the traitor." *This news will be enough to earn me a handsome pay-out.*

No one asks whom he's referring to; all Wolf Riders know of the fall from grace of the man with the magnificent silver-grey-and-white wolf.

Darush circles the square a few more times, still on wolf-back. Darush is no stranger to Samur, who has selected him numerous times for scouting missions. The Elder Man with the black hair spotted him snatch a boy in Azaquina – a boy who'd been trying to hide under a partially built fishing boat – and the misfortune of the boy was the good fortune of the man. With his long, dirty blond hair, Darush can easily pass himself off as a beggar, which was exactly what he'd done in Azaquina, to blend in. Now the same trick has proved effective in Alzamar – the traitor never gave him a second glance. He was returning early because he'd spotted a bigger price in the city.

Samur is still pulling his shirt over his head as he rushes to where Darush has finally dismounted. "Where did you find that runt?" he yells.

"I saw him in Alzamar, of all places," Darush replies. "He appeared to be scouting the place himself."

The two men are surrounded by more and more Wolf Riders. Darush's news has spread quickly. Melchor, standing in the crowd with his two friends, nudges Kaizor – hard. The younger boy loses balance and falls sideways against Ebagar. They both look quizzically at their older friend.

"He's not the only one missing," Melchor hisses under his breath. "The little runt Bergas is missing too."

The younger boys nod to acknowledge his comment, although both are dismayed at the mention of Bergas, especially Ebagar. Secretly, he liked both Alagur and Bergas. He too wants to go home – a luxury which he believes will never be afforded to him.

The three boys listen to what the Elder Men are discussing, exchanging surreptitious glances of disgust when Raimir joins them. As the Elder Men argue about what to do and where Alagur may be heading next, a whisper of conscience gnaws at Ebagar's mind. He hopes fervently that they'll guess incorrectly.

"We could attack Alzamar," Raimir suggests. "There's a group of independent pack brothers to the south-east of that town. He may have joined up with them – they would prize his wolf as a valuable addition."

"No, they'd plunder Hayzan before Alzamar," Darush counters. "They know and respect that we often attack Alzamar."

"Darush is correct," Samur concurs. "If the traitor is scouting in Alzamar, he's either joined up with the Wolf Runners or one of the eastern groups." Samur's face contorts into a frown of anger. "Anything to dishonour the Life Pact we made," he snarls.

These words provoke a renewed commotion throughout the ever-growing crowd of men and boys standing around the group of Elder Men.

"Any man in Keldarra who brings me the dead body of Alagur, finds his wolf and takes the pups from her – alive – that man will get five sacks of gold as a reward, and more." Seemingly looking directly at Melchor and his two companions, Samur adds, "Any man or boy who succeeds in this quest will be lucky enough to enter into a Life Pact with me."

Although he doesn't really have the authority to call for the actions he is demanding, to him, it doesn't matter. If a person betrays him, they will pay for it with their lives.

"What about his *runt*, Bergas?" Melchor has a deep-seated hatred for Bergas for reasons he has never shared with his two friends. After Alagur took it upon himself to train Bergas as a Wolf Rider, Melchor would look with venomous anger at them both every time they passed by. When Alagur suggested Bergas should stay outside the city on the day the Wolf Riders attacked Ruh'nar, it only added to the anger, and seeing his friend Kaizor talking with Alagur about the man's wolf compounded Melchor's fury. When Raimir suggested his friends stay behind as well, Melchor scowled openly and received a massive blow across the head as a result. Once inside Ruh'nar's walls, Melchor was assigned with two other boys to check southern parts of the city. While the other boys were killed, Melchor escaped wounded, only to be severely reprimanded by Raimir for allowing it to happen.

Kaizor and Ebagar stare at Melchor, and then at one another. They step back – slowly – and Ebagar edges closer to Kaizor.

"What's Melchor doing?" he whispers.

"I don't know," Kaizor responds. "Best to wait and see what happens."

Ebagar nods.

"What about the runt?" Melchor repeats. Samur stomps angrily towards Melchor, who bravely stands his ground and stares at the man. "We haven't seen him since before we entered Ruh'nar. Alagur was the last one to see him. We haven't seen Alagur's wolf, either, and she's not a wolf you can miss."

He's right, Samur thinks, but he's not going to admit it.

"If you want to find that runt, off you go and do something about it," he retorts coldly.

Melchor goes as white as moss ash. *That's not the response I wanted*, he thinks. He'd hoped to be welcomed into Samur's fold as a hero, offered the rights of a future Elder Man. Too late, he realises that the many whispers he's heard about Samur are true: the man doesn't care for anyone but himself, and all he does is for his own gain – often at the expense of those around him.

Samur stares at Melchor with such a venomous scowl, it makes his whole face look distorted. "If you've got nothing more to add, go and stand with the other boys." Samur shouts the command right into Melchor's face, emphasising it with exaggerated gestures. The 'other boys', including Kaizor and Ebagar, are stepping further and further back as Samur's anger rises. Any disagreements between them are now forgotten.

Samur turns on his heels and stomps off, muttering. Melchor stands rigidly for a few moments, then he turns and almost runs to his companions. Kaizor and Ebagar side-step to let him pass, neither saying anything nor daring to look at him. Kaizor puts his finger to his lips a moment later to let Ebagar know that he should remain quiet.

I wish I was somewhere else, Ebagar thinks, *like home, but that's three seasons from here. Will I ever see Papa, Mam or my sisters and brother again?*

Kaizor turns to listen to the conversation going on between the Elder Men, or at least the parts of it he can hear. Samur's voice rises above the rest, and he seems angrier than ever. Kaizor sees concern on the faces of the other Elder Men, and even Raimir — who usually doesn't care about anything — seems ill at ease.

I wonder what they're worried about.

Instinctively, he turns and puts his arm around Ebagar's shoulders to lead him away from the square, but the younger boy is reluctant to move. Kaizor stops too when an audible intake of breath comes from Ebagar and several other boys, turning just in time to see Samur raise his arm and bring it down hard into the face of Elder Man Vaymaz. The fifty-year-old man stumbles under the impact of the blow, then drops to the ground, the sound of his large torch clattering across the square echoing between the buildings.

Kaizor covers Ebagar's eyes with one hand, clenching the other into a fist and biting his lip. Around him, all the boys have fallen silent. Melchor's facial expression betrays what he is thinking: the fate of the Elder Man could have been his own.

Kaizor pulls Ebagar out of the way when Samur suddenly storms past the group and disappears into the darkness.

Elder Man Vaymaz is dead.

Each boy suddenly feels his own mortality acutely. Now that Vaymaz — one of the oldest of the Elder Men — is dead, it has created a vacuum of power that Samur could fill with one of his own men. By challenging the Elder Men and killing one of them, Samur has set a precedent. He intends to command not only the Wolf Riders, but the Elder Men as well.

"Why are they not taking him somewhere?" Melchor murmurs under his breath.
"Because they can't. He was challenged by Samur, and anyone who touches his body will likely end up with the same fate," Kaizor hisses.
"We should come back later. I want to bury him."
"First we need to take Ebagar to the sleeping house."

They are among the last few people left on the square. The only light is coming from a single torch lying a few paces from the dead man's hand. The expression of pain is frozen in place on Elder Man Vaymaz's face and his eyes stare unseeing into space. It sends a shiver of fear up Kaizor's spine.

The three boys turn and walk slowly towards their sleeping house. Tears stream down Ebagar's face and he glances back towards the dead man more than once. Each time he looks, the flicker of the torch has decreased as the flame slowly dies, the pool of liquid that is gathering around the man's head reflecting the eerie light. Ebagar feels a deep sadness for the passing of the man who, on many occasions over the last season or so, has sat down next to him and told him retellings of the City of Wolves' past.

Melchor, for his part, feels a knot of guilt. *I wonder if I caused Samur to attack Elder Man Vaymaz. He might have been saying something to divert attention away from me which cost him his life.* Hardening his resolve, Melchor makes a silent vow. *I'm going to make sure Kaizor, Ebagar and I can get away from all this.*

The sleeping house that the boys share could easily have been a bakery once, but its ovens now act as latrines. Inside, they're met by a dozen or so other boys – some older and some younger than Kaizor – in the large back room of the building. The mood in the room is subdued, and some of the youngest boys are openly crying. Usually, tears would invite teasing and bullying from the older boys, but today the same boys are offering comfort instead. It is obvious that none of them have ever witnessed an event as cruel and brutal as the one they were forced to watch earlier.

One boy, Jaycan, looks up when the trio walks in. "What are they going to do with Elder Man Vaymaz?" he asks.
"I don't know," Kaizor replies.
"I want to bury him," Melchor interjects.
"You're the one who started the row between Samur and him."
"Don't blame him for it!" the usually shy Ebagar yells at the top of his lungs, surprising everyone with his outburst. It silences the room.
"He's right." Elder Man Belduran enters the room.

When Belduran first came to City of Wolves, Vaymaz had taken him under his wing, resulting in a friendship between the two men which remained strong for thirty-six years. Neither of them ever trusted the smooth-talking Samur, even though he's proved himself to be a capable warrior. He is cruel and quick to anger, and his excessive consumption of wine concerns many Elder Men – Belduran included. He also takes an unnatural delight in throwing other Wolf Riders into the pit that holds the wild wolves on the slightest of pretexts.

But most of Elder Man Belduran's mistrust stems from when Samur first arrived in the city, saying he'd come from the east after 'someone' told him about the Wolf Riders. No one knows exactly what happened to the 'someone' as Samur's answer to the inevitable question is always the same.

"I taught him the price of telling me how to get rich fast."

The same menacing laughter that accompanies this cryptic answer each time rang out across the square moments after Samur left Elder Man Vaymaz lying dead in a pool of blood.

"What happened tonight was most unfortunate," Belduran's continues. "I'll personally deal with the matter of disposing of Elder Man Vaymaz's body in an appropriate way."

The room is so silent following Elder Man Belduran's words that if you'd dropped a single embelyne pearl, the tiny sound of it shattering on the stone-paved floor would have been clear to all. No one speaks for a while, and it seems the boys are all holding their breath.

"Why did he do it?" Jaycan's voice cracks with emotion.

"Because he could," Belduran acknowledges. "But I'm not saying it's right."

"Can you stay here, Elder Man Belduran?"

"Perhaps, but I need to visit three more sleeping houses first." Belduran looks around the room silently for several minutes before turning and leaving without another word. The boys all hold their breath, listening as his footsteps fade into the distance.

"We need to do something," Jaycan says. Many boys nod in agreement, but none at that moment can think exactly what to do.

Melchor looks down at his feet as he speaks. "I'm starting to think that Alagur and Bergas are the fortunate ones. Wherever they are, they've escaped all this."

"You're the one who called Bergas a runt. I heard you, and so did most of us here."

"That was before I knew how Samur would react."

"Nonetheless, you may have caused this to happen."

* * *

WHAT *NONE* OF THE BOYS KNOW, IS THAT EARLIER IN THE DAY an argument had started between Elder Man Vaymaz and Samur. The younger man had suggested that, as he'd put it forcefully, 'certain changes needed to be made to how things were done in City of Wolves'.

"There needs to be a single leader," Samur had snapped at the older man.

"Everything has always been done by a collective decision from the Elder Men," Vaymaz had answered calmly.

"You're an old man, and mark my words, you won't be around here for long if I can help it."

* * *

SEVERAL HOURS LATER, AFTER BELDURAN HAS COLLECTED a bedroll and some blankets, he returns to the sleeping house of Kaizor, Melchor, Ebagar and the others. The boys give a collective sigh of relief when he steps into the room, his presence giving comfort to them. And Belduran realises there's less chance of something 'unfortunate' happening to him during the night in the presence of the boys. The events of earlier have caused him to re-evaluate whom he can trust in the city.

Tomorrow the excursion to the south will start, and if it fails to find Alagur, then what? Will Samur kill more Elder Men?

"Elder Man Belduran, can I ask a question?" Ebagar's quiet voice whispers around the room.

"Of course."

Belduran is glad of something to distract him from his thoughts, but Ebagar feels overwhelmed all of a sudden, especially when he notices all the boys in the room have fallen silent in anticipation of what he's about to ask. Stalling his question, he climbs onto the bed next to the Elder Man. He looks hastily at Melchor, then looks down.

"I heard about the boy called Bergas," he begins hesitantly. "It's said he's missing."

Belduran nods slowly. He had discussed the disappearance with Vaymaz a few days previously.

"He was my friend," Ebagar explains. "If Alagur helped him to go home, isn't that good?" Releasing a sudden sob of grief, he adds, "I want to go home to my mother."

Belduran can only sigh sadly and hug the boy, comforting him as well as he can. He can't change the way things are – not for Ebagar, and certainly not for himself. But in his mind, a plan starts to develop.

CHAPTER FORTY-FIVE

The dark rain clouds match the subdued and sombre mood within City of Wolves. Despite the plans made in the earliest hours of the day, to ride southeast towards Hayzan, the usual hive of activity prior to an excursion is notably absent today. The main reason for this is the fact that the boys have been ordered to stay inside their sleeping houses by the Elder Men and not to watch the preparations.

Most of the boys who witnessed the killing of the Elder Man Vaymaz are too scared to come outside anyway, and they instinctively huddle together, a tight group in the back room of their dwellings. They have overheard rumours that Vaymaz's body has gone, but apparently no one is admitting to taking it away. And an hour or so before the departure time, a light rainfall washed away the blood which remained on the old paving slabs.

Samur leads the large group of men from the city. As the crowd starts to leave through the south-eastern gate, he doesn't notice how many of the men following him bow their heads in a gesture of respect as they pass the spot where Elder Man Vaymaz fell.

Four boys have defied the command to stay away from the windows. They watch as man after man rides towards the gates, noticing how some pause momentarily at the place where the Elder Man fell and bow their heads before riding off. Even the wolves seem to do this, which amazes Kaizor, Melchor, Ebagar and Jaycan.

Belduran has decided to stay behind in the city, even if Samur's order did demand that even the Elder Men would ride. He's never cared much for plundering cities, and after the killing of his trusted friend, he cares even less. His thoughts this morning turn again to the legends – the same matters he was pondering for a long time before he went to sleep.

I wonder if The Truth is more than a retelling to scare newly arrived boys. I wonder what – and who – Samur will bring back when he returns.

"Belduran, can I speak with you?"

Elder Man Rudrig pulls Belduran from his thoughts. He turns to greet the younger man, whose almost white hair makes him seem much older than his thirties. Belduran stops walking so Rudrig can catch up with him – Rudrig walks somewhat slower than most because of a persistent limp in his right leg.

"We need to do something about Samur."

The words are spoken so softly that only Belduran, with his enhanced hearing, can hear them. He nods in agreement.

"If he doesn't find Alagur, he could become even more dangerous than he was last night." Rudrig pants more, then adds, "If he returns without Alagur, we have to convince him that a much wider search would be a good idea. And we need to do it in such a way as to make him think the idea is his own."

"Perhaps we need to send riders out towards the northern regions before he returns. Then if he wants to ride out in that direction, we can say it has already been done."

Belduran nods. "Will you can organise it, Rudrig?" Another nod confirms that the other man agrees.

Belduran watches as Rudrig walks away slowly. A moment afterwards, Belduran turns and walks along the north street towards the abandoned building which may once have been a storehouse for a stonemason. In the building lies a body wrapped in a woollen cloth, tied together with thick leather straps.

Farewell, my friend. May your death be avenged. Belduran's thought echoes through his mind as he and three other Elder Men carry Vaymaz on a stretcher made of thick, dark leather to the place intended for his burial. It's a well-rehearsed duty, but none of them can remember burying an Elder Man who has been killed by another Elder Man. Although it was admirable of the boy Melchor to offer to help, Belduran has decided the boys have endured enough.

It's a sombre procession that exits the western gate. On arrival at the designated field, the Elder Men place the stretcher on the ground and silently wait as four younger men dig a grave. Once the grave is deep enough, Belduran and his three companions pick the stretcher up and lower it into the ground. The leather and the wooden poles of the stretcher will cover the body and prevent wild animals from disturbing it.

Once the body is in position, the grave is refilled with the soil and then covered over with large stones. Then Belduran opens a bottle of fluid and pours its contents liberally over the grave. The familiar smell of the slurry commonly used on spear arrows penetrates every man's nostrils. Belduran lights an ember using the tool from his tinder kit, and once the spark takes hold, he holds it close to the slurry. A moment afterwards, the entire grave is engulfed in distinctive blue flames.

* * *

SAMUR SQUINTS AGAINST THE LIGHT OF THE SUN reflecting off the surface of a lake. He's waiting for the last of his scouts to return from the south and east. As the day is ending, they come back one after the other, shaking their heads.

"He isn't anywhere to the south."

"We checked and there's no indication of him heading east."

Samur frowns at each negative answer. Could the old man have been correct?

"Check to the north. Bergas was from the north."

Samur had found the suggestion preposterous. How could a boy influence Alagur's decision?

Samur gets up and paces back and forth for several minutes. "We're moving out," he shouts at the men around him. Climbing onto Uzo, he starts riding south without saying another word. His scowl – along with the memory of what happened to Elder Man Vaymaz – stops any of his men protesting.

Ahead of the long procession of wolves and men lies the wilderness of the Eastern Mountains of Sabeya, which create a natural border between that province and its neighbour, Zunatia. The province of Marridina, located on the most southerly coast, borders both. Samur remembers overhearing Alagur asking about the towns in Zunatia, so it seems logical to conclude he may have travelled in that direction.

As the journey progresses, the mood in the large group accompanying Samur grows more and more sombre. The usual camaraderie is missing. If any bystander were foolish enough to get too close to this group, he or she would have thought they were on their way to their own trial and execution.

* * *

BELDURAN AND HIS COMPANIONS RETURN TO CITY OF WOLVES in a hurry, then go their separate ways. No one spoke as they part.

Belduran decides to climb the highest tower in the city to see if he can spot the dust cloud of the Wolf Riders. He walks back to the central square, glancing quickly at the place where Vaymaz lay dead for several hours, then turns towards the imposing building which flanks the square.

Belduran walks through what would have once been two magnificent wooden doors – now not much more than rotting timbers hanging from rusting hinges. Inside the building, he looks up at the ceiling, which would have been covered in beautiful engravings long ago. Now, it is a soot-covered shell. Nonetheless, Belduran can appreciate the grandeur of the place, and he's noted on several occasions that the boy Bergas – and Alagur, too – share his interest in the buildings of the city as more than just places to sleep or eat. All three of them – four, if you include the late Elder Man Vaymaz – have seen this building for what it may once have been.

This is where Sey'qar and Yozan started The Pack. The name we're known by now came much later from the victims of our pillaging, those left behind whenever boys were snatched.

Crossing the entrance area, where, according to the retellings, the last Elder residing over the city died at the hands of the first men in The Pack, he ascends the stairway. Despite the abuse that the building has endured over the centuries, it still is strong and beautiful.

Whoever constructed this stairway was a worthy craftsman.

On the second floor, Belduran turns left into a long corridor. As he walks along the passage, he again gets the feeling that the place is haunted – not by people, but by memories. The hairs rise on the back of his neck and he quickens his pace, almost running to the far end of the corridor and up the stairway to the top of the tower.

On arrival, he stands looking around for several minutes. He remembers showing this room to Bergas, and later he saw the boy drag Alagur here, too. Alagur had looked pensive when he emerged from the building later.

This room likely changed Alagur. Did he realise it was occupied by someone important? Someone he learnt about from my retellings?

Belduran steps onto the southern balcony and, leaning against the stone cladding, looks south. The dark dusk cloud is just visible in the distance.

Judging by the direction of the wind, they're heading south.

Belduran knows of a natural passage in the south east, bordering the eastern end of Marridina, called Pass of the Two Bells. This region has its own long history, and Belduran can vaguely remember from retellings that it was important in the defeat of the Warlords. Some two and a half thousand years ago, this ancient enemy from the north forced the local people to build two towers, one on either end of the massive valley flanked by two mountain ranges. Each tower had a massive bell placed within it. A watchman would stand guard continually, each man being replaced by another every ten hours. If an enemy was sighted, the watchman would ring the bell – for an enemy from the east, the East Bell tolled; for one from north, the West Bell tolled.

So, no one there will know that Samur and his runts are on their way now to plunder the region.

Belduran feels sad all of a sudden, wishing that fate had been different for him. He wished he was not standing in the same place where once a woman awaited her doom.

Belduran turns when he hears voices approaching. A few moments later, he's joined by Kaizor and Ebagar.

"What are you two doing here?" Belduran looks sternly at the boys, but there's a smile playing on his lips.

"We saw you come in and wanted to keep you company up here. Or, more exactly, he wanted to." Kaizor nods towards Ebagar, who is standing behind him.

"You're both most welcome," Belduran says with a broad smile, glad of the company.

Kaizor and Ebagar walk towards the man and flank him.

"Is that them?" Ebagar asks in a subdued voice, looking south. Belduran puts his arm around Ebagar's shoulders reassuringly.

"Yes, it's them – if you mean Samur's Wolf Riders."

"Are they riding south, or are they going to head into those mountains?"

Kaizor's voice is as subdued as Ebagar's. Before Belduran can answer, they hear more footsteps approaching. All three look behind them to see who else has decided to defy the order to stay inside the sleeping houses. They all share the same surprise when they see Jaycan helping a struggling Rudrig through the doorway to the balcony.

"I knew I'd find you up here." Rudrig is panting, but he still manages to smile broadly. "This lad helped me up the stairs. There are *others* downstairs who were not brave enough to come up here. Maybe they should come up now."

Rudrig speaks the last few words in a commanding voice that echoes through the building. For several minutes, the two Elder Men, Kaizor, Ebagar and Jaycan all look towards the darkened doorway – though the boys glance at each other somewhat sheepishly at times. They're uncertain if they should speak as the Elder Men are speaking in hushed tones in a dialect none of the boys comprehend. Then the footsteps of a large group of individuals come closer, and a moment later boys from several sleeping houses come crowding onto the balcony. Belduran recognises that most of the boys present always were in contact in one way or another with Samur or his men.

They all need to be safe before he returns, he thinks bitterly.

"Let's sit inside, out of this wind." Belduran looks at the group for a moment. "And I'll tell you the retelling of the Pass of the Two Bells."

The boys rush back into the room they've just exited and find a place to sit down. They all enjoy hearing the retellings of the various Elder Men, but none of them has ever heard this particular one before.

The two Elder Men wait until all the boys are inside.

"We'll be with you shortly," Belduran calls out, then he turns to the other man and whispers, "Are the preparations made?"

"Yes. If all goes to plan, we can mount our own journey north in the morning. We may want to bring some of those boys with us, so they don't bear the brunt of his ire--if he comes back in a rage--"

Belduran nods before quietly walking into the roomful of waiting boys.

* * *

MORNING BRINGS MORE RAIN FOR THOSE STILL PRESENT in City of

Wolves. Belduran and Rudrig stand in their dark cloaks, overseeing the process of getting the Wolf Riders – selected by Rudrig – ready for their journey.

"Be sure to bypass Alzamar so any scouts loyal to Samur don't see you," Belduran says to Jymar – the lead scout – who's standing next to his wolf, a massive ebony beast with a white line of fur stretching from its forehead to its neck. The wolf is named Kiato. Jymar is the only rider not yet mounted, and the twenty-seven men with him listen as he finalises details of the plan. Rudrig tells Jymar what he needs to do and where he needs to go.

"What of Samur? What if he finds out?"

"Leave him to us to deal with," the older man replies. The Elder Men are becoming less and less comfortable with Samur.

Belduran and Rudrig don't wait to watch the men ride away from the city. It's an all too familiar sight for them now. Instead, they nod to one another and walk in opposite directions – Rudrig to the weapon-making courtyard in the north-east of the city, and Belduran to the sleeping house where he knows he'll find Ebagar and his friends. Melchor's comment about the missing Bergas has sparked a new plan – possibly the most daring of them all.

It will test their bravery.

At the doorway of the sleeping house, he's greeted by several of the boys. His loud, commanding voice echoes through the building a moment later.

"I need to speak to Melchor, Kaizor and Ebagar – alone."

CHAPTER FORTY-SIX

Ebagar SITS ON THE BENCH NEXT TO HIS TWO FRIENDS, looking up shyly at Belduran. The Elder Man is silent for several minutes while he waits for the rest of the sleeping house to empty. The sleeping house is home to eighty-seven boys, and normally at least a third of them would be inside it. The others would be either riding with excursions to other cities or working inside the city – mostly pitching the spear arrows, a process which involves coating them in the flammable materials used by the Wolf Riders. Other boys would assist with meal preparations, usually ending up being the ones to gut the mountain sheep speared by the older Wolf Riders. Some would even assist with repairs to clothing, or metalworking, or leather cutting. Then there's the boys' least favoured task – cleaning latrines.

At other times, the boys learn to control the wolves, and various Elder Men teach them the skills of writing, counting and reading. But instead of doing any of these tasks, the boys who've been ordered out of the sleeping house have free time on their hands. Most enjoy this unprecedented sense of freedom – a freedom which Belduran is now working to ensure will continue.

Belduran gets up as the last boy shuts the door behind him and bolts it, pausing to gather his thoughts. They fix themselves on the words of The Truth.

If it is a prophecy, then I need to give it a helping hand. If I take the words literally, then it tells that the Wolf Riders will end.

Belduran sits opposite the three boys and looks at them once more. He's met by three pairs of eyes, all showing curiosity and fear in equal measure.

"Do you remember the words of The Truth?" he begins.

The boys all nod. Ignoring their affirmation, Belduran recites the words deliberately and thoroughly, emphasising the last phrase of the fourth verse, as well as the whole of the last verse.

TEN THOUSAND RIDERS ROSE TO THE CALL,

> BESET ON TO THE CITY OF OLD, AND
> FALL BEFORE THEM IT WOULD.
>
> THEY WHO RESISTED WOULD FALL,
> AND YOUNG ONES TAKEN BY FORCE,
> AND A CITY WAS LOST TO TIME AND KIN.
>
> FOR THE BROTHERS BETRAYED TRUTH, AND
> RELEASED FEAR UPON THE WORLD,
> WITH WOLVES AS THEIR WEAPON.
>
> FOR LEGEND FORETELLS OF THEIR END,
> THE END THAT WILL COME FROM ONE,
> A BROTHER WHO RISES TO THE CALL.
>
> THE TRUTH WILL SHOW THE DOUBTER,
> HE AND HIS WOLF WILL TRAVEL FAR,
> AN AGENT OF TRUTH WILL SHOW HIM.
>
> SHE WHOSE NAME IS UNSPOKEN,
> A WOLF SHE WILL CLAIM FROM THE WILD,
> AND THE MAN WILL LEARN HER SKILL.
>
> TOGETHER THEY END THE BROKEN WORLD,
> HEAL THE WORLD TO WHAT IT WAS BEFORE,
> IT IS THAT DESTINY THAT IS UNSPOKEN.

The boys look at each other, "Why is he telling us this?" etched on their faces. Belduran smiles.

"I need to explain why I want to speak to you three." Belduran's neutral tone of voice catches the attention of all the boys. None of them speaks, and Belduran continues with his retelling.

"There are some among the Elder Men – myself included – who think The Truth is more than just a legend about our beginning. We think it originates from those called Keepers of Truth – or is it Callers of Truth? Never mind, it's one of those. They have great knowledge and wisdom, and one of their kind first uttered The Truth as she lay dying in the building we were in yesterday afternoon."

Melchor, Kaizor and Ebagar all look at Belduran, fascinated.

Alagur once listened to me with that much interest when I was telling him about Mountain Ghost, Belduran thinks. But Vaymaz told that retelling better.

Belduran continues, "If you look at the words of The Truth, it begins with how we came to exist and how they betrayed--" He pauses for a moment to consider his next words. "It also states that one Wolf Rider won't be one anymore. I think…that's…Alagur."

"It mentions a woman," Kaizor interjects.

"Yes, and that's the mysterious part. We don't know who, or what, it refers to."

"It says together they end the broken world," Ebagar points out quickly. He, like Alagur, always likes to listen to as many of the retellings and legends the Elder Men tell as he can manage, and it has made him perceptive.

"That's the point I'm coming to. We think The Truth is incomplete, and there was more going on than we know now."

Belduran stops speaking again to allow the boys to come up with their own conclusions.

"Why did you send more Wolf Riders to the north if you want all this to end?" Melchor swings his arm in an arc to indicate the city around him.

That boy doesn't miss much.

"We need to give the impression things are as they have always been. This is where the three of you come into the picture."

"Us?" Melchor explodes. "Why us?"

"Because of him." Belduran points at Ebagar, who goes pale.

"He wants us to do something no other Elder Man knows about, Melchor." Ebagar's voice is neutral, but his response is precise. "He means us to do something dangerous."

"He's right." Belduran's softly spoken words echo those of the previous night. He leans back on his chair and waits to allow the other boys to grasp the implications that Ebagar has already figured out.

It will make them enemies of the Wolf Riders--or, more accurately, of Samur.

Taking on the role of spokesperson, Melchor asks the crucial question. "What is it you want us to do?"

The time has come. The beginning of ending the Wolf Riders has started.

"You mentioned yesterday, in your haste to impress Samur, the name Bergas. Why was that?" Belduran's voice is gentle.

"Yesterday, I saw Samur as nothing more than an overzealous Elder Man with huge ambition, but--"

Melchor pauses.

"But?" Belduran queries.

Melchor decides to be honest with Belduran – something that hadn't been in his nature until the death of Elder Man Vaymaz.

"But then he started shouting at everyone. I thought I was stating the obvious, but he had a go at me." He stops again and glances at his two friends. They both look at him, but neither is showing the anger Melchor thought he'd face. He continues talking when the Elder Man doesn't speak.

"I didn't like what Samur did to Elder Man Vaymaz at all. He was a nice Elder Man who told great retellings." Melchor looks towards Ebagar, who's smiling at him now. "I've been thinking about what happened, and I would really like to know why he was killed."

Belduran looks closely at Melchor, who is now gazing down at his hands clasped in his lap, and weighs up not only what to say, but also how to say it.

He's being honest to me about how he feels. Belduran can tell this from Melchor's body language. But the depth of his regret for his outburst will be tested by my plan for all three of them.

"A day or so after you returned from Ruh'nar, Elder Man Vaymaz told Samur to let all the boys younger than eighteen years of age leave and go home." Belduran speaks the words slowly and deliberately, fixing his gaze on Ebagar to see how the youngest boy will react. "Elder Man Vaymaz didn't die because of what you said, Melchor. However, your outburst did remind Samur of the argument. He was killed because – besides me – he was the only man in the city who could stop Samur."

Melchor looks up at Belduran. There are tears running down both his cheeks and he makes no attempt to wipe them away or hide them. Belduran smiles gently. It is the first time since his arrival seven years earlier that the boy has cried; until now, he's expressed all his pent-up emotions as frustration and anger. Belduran could never help the boy – until now.

Perhaps he was so cruel towards Bergas – and Ebagar at times too – because he remembered how those first days were for him.

"The Truth tells of a female. Several Elder Men, me included, have wondered about this for a long time. She's another reason why I have sent the scouting party north. I believe that Alagur isn't on his journey alone."

"But don't they think they're going there to capture him?" Kaizor has been listening quietly and contemplating the implications of the retelling so far.

"That's a risk, but we have to make everything appear to be as normal. Their journey north won't take as long as Samur's journey south, regardless of whether it benefits the majority of those living here."

In truth, Belduran hopes both groups will fail.

It's rather interesting that Samur claimed the dwelling he once shared with Alagur as his own as soon as Alagur disappeared. It's as though he didn't expect his Pack Brother to return.

But each day that has passed with no news of Alagur has caused Samur's rage to escalate. It was at its peak when Darush arrived with the news of Alagur's appearance in Alzamar.

Samur had no right to offer a reward for Alagur's lifeless body and Yalla's offspring. Alagur, by rights, is an Elder Man now – entitled to start his own Wolf Pack elsewhere, if he so wishes.

"Right then, here's the plan." Elder Man Belduran speaks so softly that the boys have to lean forward to hear them. Each of them chuckles inwardly as the situation now feels like a conspiracy. "Listen carefully, each of you."

The three boys and the Elder Man discuss the plans in detail: how they should travel; whether to take wolves; how long the journey will take on foot. As the Elder Man explains how to remain unseen, Melchor and Kaizor realise that Alagur is avoiding being seen on his journey in much the same way.

* * *

THREE HOODED BOYS STAND NERVOUSLY IN A COPSE about half a day's walk south of Venrasia Woods, waiting for the smoke signal from Belduran. The signal will tell them they can start their journey east – a journey that has already been delayed by two days because of a fire in one of the sleeping houses. Fifty-three boys aged between thirteen and sixteen had to be rehoused into several other sleeping houses, including the one Melchor, Kaizor and Ebagar occupy.

Belduran has explained the boys' presence in the copse can be passed off as a hunting party. In the end, they decided they would be far less conspicuous travelling on foot, even though there's a risk that some Wolf

Riders may question why three wolves no longer have masters.

Belduran's signal comes later in the morning than expected, mostly because Rudrig wanted to discuss the matter of the sleeping house. Several bottles that were used to store pitch have been found in the burnt-out shell of the building. The sun is close to its zenith when, finally, Belduran reaches the tower and lights one of six signal fires situated at strategic locations. Belduran's signal is a continuous plume of white smoke, followed by a continuous plume of black smoke, then six puffs of black smoke. Ebagar suggested that would be 'significant', but never explained why. The other Elder Men will simply assume the signal is for one of the many scouting parties.

A nudge in the ribs alerts Melchor. He's feeling a bit sleepy and keeps fighting off his tiredness. The boys didn't sleep long during night and had to leave two hours before sunrise.

"Kaizor, it's time to leave."

Kaizor jerks awake when Melchor speaks in a loud voice. He stares at the city and sees the smoke clouds puffing into the air.
"Was that the signal we agreed?"
"Yes," Ebagar replies. "I was watching for it."
"Good lad." Melchor smiles. "You're more alert than I am."

Melchor embraces Ebagar and feels glad he's changed his mind about the boy. In fact, in the last few days Ebagar has started to feel more like a younger brother than a friend.

I now understand the camaraderie between Alagur and Bergas, and I'll apologise to Bergas if I ever see him again.

Packing their haversacks, the three boys then start walking in single file along a small path beside a stream. This path, formed over centuries of use, will lead them to Ribbon Lake. Once they reach the east end of the lake, they will travel south until they get to a river that runs parallel to the lake. After following it for a few days, they will go through the highlands north-east of Ruh'nar. Belduran knows this route has the least risk of contact with people. The boys will travel between dusk and sunrise once they have passed a rock formation resembling a clasped hand. Each boy chuckled at the description of the rock, but Belduran stated that they wouldn't laugh when they saw it.

"Is that Venrasia Woods?" Ebagar asks, pointing north.

"Yes, it is," Kaizor replies from behind him. The two older boys have decided to walk in front and behind their younger companion for his safety.

"It reaches all the way west," Melchor calls over his shoulder.

"Alagur said that northwest of it lies the valley where his wolf is from," Kaizor adds.

"His wolf is magnificent. I wish now I'd been able to touch her like you did, Kaizor." Melchor stops walking for a moment and turns to face the other boys. "I said and did a lot of things which I'm starting to regret. I'm sorry for many things, but I'm not sorry for calling both of you my friends."

Kaizor looks at Melchor for a moment, then speaks. "Maybe this journey is a way for you to redeem yourself. If Belduran is right, it will lead to redemption for us all."

"Not all. There's no redemption for Elder Man Vaymaz," Melchor counters softly, before turning and continuing to walk.

CHAPTER FORTY-SEVEN

THE JOURNEY TO THIS PLACE HAD BEEN RELATIVELY UNEVENTFUL, even peaceful, which is a new experience for Alagur. His relationship with Marrida has grown as they have travelled.

When the wolf finally stops, Alagur slides off her back. He helps Marrida down, then takes hold of her hand and leads her to a rocky outcrop. Marrida is in awe at the sight. She's never realised how massive the Bay of Whispers is.

To her left, mountains drop off into the ocean. The bay is bowl-shaped, so it could even have been a lake many thousands of years ago. It goes from the palest blue to the darkest blue she has ever seen; it's almost black.

To the right, a road leads from a sandy beach, crawling through the landscape as an endless pale ribbon. That it is the road they will follow.

"If you look to the north, you can just about see Azaquina in the distance," Alagur says, stretching out his arm and forefinger.

Marrida enjoys the lower elevation of the plains as she stares north at the vastness of the bay. The milder climate is also a surprise to her after the harsh conditions of the mountains. She stares west at the shape of the peaks. Alagur, who has just returned from collecting stones from the rocky beach, speaks.

"The local people have a name for the mountain peaks. They call them Northern Blades."

"I was just thinking they look like blades."

"Do you see the orange-tinted area further west?"

"Yes, I do."

"That's the most eastern part of South Valley of Miza."

Alagur notes the hint of hesitation in his voice as he reminds Marrida of a place that has caused her so much hurt. Marrida squints for a long time at the area that Alagur has pointed out to her. Now that she understands the cause of her father's passing better, the emotion isn't as raw anymore.

She glances sideways when she senses Alagur near her. He is kneeling in front of her, and when she looks at him, he places his right hand on her left cheek. His thumb softly caresses the upper part of her cheek, and she sees an intense love for her in his eyes. He reaches forward and kisses her lips ever so gently, and Marrida feels her heart beating faster.

They've been locked in an embrace, kissing for several minutes, when he moves away from her and looks at her once more.

"We need to get going," he says gently. "I know you are tired, but we need to reach the end of the bay before nightfall."

"Yes, I know. I'll manage."

Marrida almost whispers because she has trouble speaking with his kiss lingering on her lips. They both get up, Marrida helped by Alagur. He places the stones he's gathered into a small basket he purchased a few days ago from a passing merchant, who in turn purchased some of their surplus supplies. Alagur has suggested that their load needs to be lightened before they go on foot into Azaquina. The merchant never saw Yalla as she was lying in the undergrowth; she's been ordered to do this frequently during their journey.

"Yalla is close to birthing, and she needs to go back to Miza to be with her own kind."

Marrida is prompted by Alagur's comment to examine Yalla, and she realises how right he is. In fact, she is certain the wolf is even closer than Alagur thinks.

"The pups have turned. I've been present at the birthing of animals as part of my medical training at the Temple. This is a trait all mammals share."

Alagur nods. Interested, he asks her questions about the birthing process to fill in the blanks in his own knowledge.

They have decided on one final day of travelling before Alagur goes back with the wolf. The open planes they are now travelling through will make it easy enough.

"We can travel to the other end of the bay, then I'll ride Yalla bareback to the foot of Northern Blades on and do the Distant Bond Imprint."

Marrida decides not to ask what the term means, even though she wants to know. Instead, she stores it in her long-term memory to ask about later. Based on all the other things she's witnessed involving the wolf, she's certain it will help Yalla to know when to return to the scree to meet with Alagur weeks after the birthing.

While they make the final lap of the journey – for now, at least – Alagur reminisces about the days he spent watching Yalla's wolf pack. Marrida sees his delight as he talks, again feeling the joy he felt when an initial imprint connected his mind with Yalla's, and she does a small vision when they take a rest to see the events he has described to her. She now understands how precious his ability to bond with an animal is to him.

I hope I can do the same one day.

After resting, they ride for a time rather than walking. Alagur helps Marrida on to Yalla's back first, rather than pulling her up as he'd done in the early days of their journey, then jumps up behind her in a swift motion.

It's much easier this way, Marrida thinks.

Once Alagur is mounted, Marrida leans back against his chest without any hesitation. When she feels comfortable, she nods her head and Alagur signals to Yalla to set off at high speed. Despite her pregnancy, the remainder of the load and the people she is carrying, Yalla can still sustain a fast speed for many hours. However, now Alagur decides to let the wolf dictate when to stop running.

As it is so often, the fast ride is exhilarating to Marrida. She had never experienced the feeling of the wind in her face until she became Yalla's second passenger. In this wind, Marrida can taste the salt of the ocean to her left, and she smells the crisp scent of winter berry flowers in the air. These plants flower in the late autumn, then develop small dark green berries in the middle of winter. That's when they can be cooked with a large ladle of autumn honey for sweetness.

The trek takes longer than either of Yalla's passengers expected, and each time they need to stop, Alagur grumbles. When Yalla slows and veers off into the bushes, Alagur is initially annoyed, but as a group of six men and four women, two carrying infants, pass them, he understands the wolf's reasoning.

I need to imprint the wolf with a new command to warn me of danger when she comes back from birthing.

After this close shave, they make the remainder of the trek through the undergrowth which is becoming more prevalent along the curve of the coast. Finally, they arrive at their destination: a small grassy clearing Alagur had spotted from a distance. They quickly unpack everything from the wolf, then Alagur takes the harness off her.

"Do you think you can manage on your own here while I take Yalla to the mountains?" Alagur quizzes.

Marrida glances around the clearing. It's sheltered enough to block the cold sea winds, so she won't need a fire for warmth.

Seeing tree branches overhanging the clearing, she asks, "Can you fashion a tent out of those branches as you did before we arrived at Alzamar?"

Alagur walks over and pulls at the ends of each branch.

"I can tie them together here." He points at the place where the branches meet. "If I tie a rope to that tree there with a leather sheet hung over it, we'll have a basic dwelling."

They work silently to build the tent. First, Alagur fastens four branches together tightly with a leather thong and threads a rope through them. Pulling on the end of the rope, he fashions the branches into a fan shape and ties the rope to the sturdy tree.

Draping the large leather sheet over the branches is a task that requires them both. Alagur uses the stones he collected earlier in the day to weigh down the leather sheet, and Marrida copies his actions. After labouring hard for an hour, during which Alagur gets so sweaty he has to remove his tunic, they stand back and look over their handiwork. It's a crude tent, but it's only going to need to shelter them for a maximum of five nights.

Finally, after Alagur has disguised the tent structure with small cut-off branches, he feels happy that no one will be able to see it. Nature then becomes an unwitting ally by filling the sky with a light snowfall that gradually covers the tent more.

"Even nature thinks I'll be alright on my own."

Though Alagur is concerned about Marrida being alone, she's assured him several times that she'll be alright and that she has slept outside in the wilderness on her own before. Smiling broadly, Marrida reaches out a hand, palm up, and lets the gentle snow settle on it before it slowly melts to water. Yalla snaps at the snowflakes as they fall on her nose, and the playful gesture delights Marrida.

"I'll miss Yalla while she's gone."

She scratches the wolf's neck and the interaction causes Alagur to smile.

"She's going to miss you too, for sure," he says. Marrida places both her arms around Yalla's giant neck and holds the embrace for several minutes, then she lets go and pulls the hood of her cloak over her head for warmth.

"I should be back mid-morning of the fifth day, at the latest when the sun is at its zenith."

Alagur takes Marrida in an embrace which lasts longer than either expected. During their journey of almost three months, they have only separated once, and it was in anger. Now they're separating as lovers, and the pain of the separation is having a greater impact.

"How long will the trek home be for Yalla?" Marrida's words are almost inaudible because she dares not speak too loudly, and because she has her head buried against Alagur's chest.

"She's half a moon's cycle from birthing and needs to get home within ten days to rekindle the friendship bonds with her sisters, so they can help her during the birthing. I've seen how it's done, and you can see it in a vision in the future. When the pups are old enough, Yalla's sisters and aunts will adopt them. Bonding with a Wolf Rider causes any wolf to become a loner as they are always pulled back to their master. She'll be back at the scree in the early spring, and I will collect her then and take her into the mountains north-east of Azaquina."

Marrida is fascinated. "So, you witnessed a birthing?"

"Yes, and that's how I discovered Yalla." Alagur smiles. "She was an aunt to another wolf's litter. I was a young man at the time who wanted to be clever, so I decided not to get a wolf from the usual places. Before I realised what I was doing, I had bonded with the wolf. Yalla became bound to me and left with me for City of Wolves."

The retelling gives Marrida new insights into Alagur's earlier life. She understands better now why he bonded with this wolf rather than any other. It's also clear that the man has a curious mind.

That may be useful later on.

Marrida is quiet for a moment, then she says, "So when Yalla is ready to return, she'll do it because of the bond you have with her?"

Alagur nods.

"I wish I could have such a relationship with an animal." Marrida caresses Yalla over the bridge of her nose, which invites an involuntary snort from the beast. It makes Marrida giggle.

After Alagur has removed the harness from the wolf and put the packs, haversacks and other belongings in the tent, he watches for a moment as Marrida makes her own practised preparations. She unwinds the bed roll, then puts it on top of a criss-crossed mesh of branches she's placed against one side of the tent. It's a skill she learnt as a young girl during the camping excursions she went on with her uncle, her siblings and Joharan's apprentices. She then sits down to confirm that it has some give but will not break. An involuntary nod of approval from Alagur proves she has managed to surprise him – again.

She can easily live her for days if not weeks, Alagur thinks. *She said she went fishing in Ribbon Lake, so the nearby ocean is an endless food supply.*

Both of them have brought their own valuable survival skills with them on their journey, and Marrida isn't as helpless as she may have seemed at first.

They work on reinforcing the sides of the tent with extra stones and adding tree branches for insulation and to make it more inconspicuous. After another half an hour, both stand back and appraise their handiwork, then nod approvingly at one another.

Alagur takes Marrida's hand and holds it for several minutes, just looking at her. He leans forward and kisses her lips, letting go a moment later and mounting Yalla in a sweeping motion. He glances down at Marrida, then he rides off.

* * *

As Yalla's speed increases, Marrida watches them leave, feeling tears sting her eyes. A knot of doubt gnaws at her mind as she wonders whether she'll see Alagur again. He could easily just ride back to City of Wolves - she only has his word that Yalla really needs to go home.

After a few minutes of indecision, Marrida glances around at the small clearing that will be her home for the next few days. The wind has picked up and she pulls her cloak more tightly around herself, then leaves the tent and listens to the sound of the waves.

Seems the ocean is closer than I realised.

She smiles and walks into the tent to fetch her haversack. From a long pocket on its side, she retrieves a thin stick. After fastening six small prongs and one of her thinnest cords to it, she has a crude but serviceable fishing rod.

Marrida pushes the undergrowth aside and spots the coast just a short distance north of the clearing. She walks to a small rocky outcrop that looks like a large grinding stone, but on examining it more closely, she concludes it's of natural origin. She realises how much more curiosity she now has about the world.

While she fishes, Marrida remembers when she first learnt to fish with her uncle.

I was almost ten, Esbara was six, and Kalisa was a boisterous two-year-old. Uncle Joharan took us — his 'acquired family' — on a journey, which ended about a third of the way along Ribbon Lake, and we set up camp between it and Venrasia Woods.

Marrida smiles at the memory, and for the first time in a long time, she feels the ache of longing to be home with her siblings, her uncle just a few streets away.

A tug on her fishing rod startles Marrida from her thoughts and she smiles as she hauls in a large brown flatfish. She carries the fish back to the camp, then packs snow around it and on top of it. The chill of the snow will render the fish lifeless, and it will freeze so it won't spoil.

After piling more snow over the fish, Marrida lies down on her bed and falls asleep instantly, clearly more tired than she realised.

CHAPTER FORTY-EIGHT

Aᴌᴀɢᴜʀ sᴛᴀʀᴇs ʙᴀᴄᴋ ᴀᴛ ᴡʜᴇʀᴇ ʜᴇ's ʟᴇꜰᴛ Mᴀʀʀɪᴅᴀ to fend for herself for a few days. He's certain he can see someone moving about, and for a moment he feels tempted to turn and go back. The feeling of dread rises in him as his mind tricks him into believing he's being watched.

I hope Marrida is going to be alright on her own. I promised Joharan I would keep her safe during this journey.

Alagur doesn't understand where the dread is coming from. Yalla's demeanour is as it should be – the wolf is calm, almost placid, though her behaviour is in part due to the instinct of motherhood kicking in. She doesn't seem to sense danger, so Alagur has no logical reason for feeling as though he's being watched.

He gives Yalla a gentle nudge to signal an increase in speed. Alagur has decided to let her run at her maximum speed, but the trek back to the scree will still take half a day. On foot, the same journey took three days. A wolf's speed is on average three times faster than their bipedal companions, and without any encumbrance, Yalla can go even faster than this.

I wonder how the Wolf Runners manage to learn to run alongside their wolves. This thought has often passed through Alagur's mind before, but each time he has dismissed it with the sentiment shared by all Wolf Riders. *Those damned Wolf Runners are as vile as they come.*

Alagur has promised to return to Marrida in fewer than five days, but he isn't sure if he can do it. As he rides, his mind figures out a solution – Wolf Runners. Although he has as much aversion to the Wolf Runners as any other Wolf Rider – he has been conditioned to hate them – he's fascinated deep down by their reasoning and skill. In secret, he had started teaching himself and Bergas a similar skill.

When thoughts of Bergas enter his mind, he urges Yalla on to even faster speeds. If a watcher saw him on his wolf now, they would wonder if they'd seen an apparition. Yalla is living up to her name – she is truly like her namesake, Mountain Ghost.

Mountain Ghost was a giant white wolf who could run through the landscape at speeds unprecedented by any other animal, and for a moment Alagur wonders about the origins of her legend. Samur's assumption was that Mountain Ghost was one of the mythical beasts used by the Warlords, even though neither of them at that time could work out who or what the Warlords were. However, Alagur knows now. The Warlords were the model on which Sey'qar and Yozan created the Wolf Riders.

What a difference a couple of seasons in the presence of a Keeper of Truth makes--if I was still in City of Wolves, I would never have learnt so much more about this world or its origins.

The retelling about the two friends becoming the first Pack Brothers fills Alagur's mind for the next hour of his journey – not the version he heard from Samur, but the version he was told by Marrida as she attempted to translate Elder Sharriba's journal. In a vision Sharriba did some thirty years ago, she saw two men discussing someone she later identified as an ancient Elder. The name of the woman was the same as the name spoken in the retellings of certain Elder Men in City of Wolves – especially Elder Man Vaymaz. This Elder Man always seemed to come up with valid reasons why the Wolf Riders shouldn't exist.

Alagur feels regret wash over him at the memory of Elder Man Vaymaz. *I was one of those who'd shout him down and say he was being ridiculous.* But now, after hearing the translations and learning some of the dialect Elder Sharriba used in the journal, Alagur is wondering if Vaymaz was more correct than anyone gave him credit for. A translation that Marrida finished a few day ago was eerily similar to one of Elder Man Belduran's retellings, and he's a close friend and Pack Brother of Vaymaz. He always insisted that The Truth was a warning from the ancient Elder of – what was the name Marrida gave the city? Masharea? Belduran often said it was the earliest Wolf Riders – the two who started The Pack – who distorted it into what became known as The Truth. Essentially, they tainted the truth. Even by calling themselves Elder Men, they were distorting the truth. Alagur now realises this acutely.

Alagur recalls one of Marrida's visions. He'd told her about symbols he'd seen in a building in City of Wolves that may have been the Temple of Masharea in the past – a past that was so distant that the Keepers couldn't see it. But Alagur had been offered a means to glimpse at that past, albeit in a distorted manner.

Why are the other two groups Marrida mentioned, the Callers and Preservers, not around anymore?

Alagur suddenly feels something wet splash against his face, breaking his thought patterns and making him look round through squinted eyes. It's snowing hard now; the light flurry which fell over the temporary camp he and Marrida constructed was clearly warning of an approaching change in the weather.

He realises he has advanced a lot further than he expected. *Maybe I should have waited a few days before sending Yalla home.* Alagur dismisses the thought as soon as it enters his mind. *I can't dictate when Yalla has her pups.*

When Alagur feels Yalla slowing down, he sits up and looks around more closely. He recognises the surroundings as he travelled through them a day earlier. In front of them is a scree.

Alagur slides off the wolf and, like Marrida did before they left the camp, he embraces the beast. He feels his eyes sting with tears and he knows they aren't caused by the icy wind or snow.

"I'll miss you, my friend and loyal companion. I sincerely hope you make it home safely, and that you will return to me in the spring.

Alagur presses his face against Yalla's forehead and they stand motionless in that posture for several minutes. Yalla is the first to break the spell of the moment when she lowers her head. Alagur lets her go. She turns and paces steadily up the scree lining the mountain slope next to the path that Alagur and Marrida used days earlier to descend to the bay. After she has been climbing for five minutes, the wolf stops, turns and looks directly at the man below her. Lifting her head, she lets out her wolf song, both to say goodbye to Alagur and to alert the wolves in the mountains above her of her impending arrival.

She then starts climbing at a fast pace, and after ten minutes she's on the crest of the lower mountain elevation. Yalla stops one more time to look at the man in the distance, before turning and running towards her own kind.

* * *

It's been four hours since Alagur started his return journey.

363

He stops at a small pond and kneels to take a few mouthfuls of the chilly water to replenish what he has lost through sweat, then looks around at his surroundings, spotting what looks like a boat.

A boat — it could help me get back more quickly.

He walks over to the craft and finds it to be a well-structured vessel with two paddles in good order. He looks around in all directions to see if the boat's owner is anywhere nearby, but the landscape is deserted in every direction. Absolute silence shrouds the Bay of Whispers; it's as if no one lives here.

"I guess no one will mind if I 'borrow' this."

Alagur's voice echoes all around, but no one answers or appears, so he pushes the vessel into the ocean. It takes some effort, even for a man as strong as he is. After a good ten minutes, he manages to get it afloat. He waits for several minutes to make sure that there aren't any leaks, then climbs in. Before pushing off, again he glances round. When he's quite sure no one is watching, he pushes off using one of the paddles.

For a moment, Alagur glances towards the scree of the mountain range. He wonders if he left Yalla close enough to the mountains for her to pick up the trail of her own kind. He imagines her distinct yellow eyes, keener than those of the masters they obey, staring at him from somewhere high above. The lingering feeling of the wolf's presence is caused by the bonding.

Alagur pushes off again, checking the flow of the ocean's water. There's a current, but it is going in the wrong direction. Alagur sits down, grunting under his breath.

"I guess I'm stupid for thinking I could 'borrow' a boat." But he starts rowing eastward nonetheless — against the current. He glances over his shoulder to measure the distance between his current location and the distant undergrowth where he'd left Marrida.

Further from the shore, two contradictory forces come into play. Whereas the ocean current is going west, pulling him further from his destination, the rather brisk wind is blowing from the west-north-west. It takes some effort to persuade the boat to go north-east.

* * *

TWO BRIGHT EYES ARE INDEED WATCHING THE MAN, and as he struggles to climb into the boat. Yalla also feels pulled by the bond they share. She sniffs the air, and some of his scent drifts towards her at intervals. Then she turns and runs at a considerable speed. She has no burdens left to carry – not even her master – so nature takes hold and gives her the speed of freedom.

She runs up the side of a snowdrift-covered slope at a higher elevation, then sniffs the air again and catches the familiar scent of her sisters and aunts. She'll be with them by the evening.

Yalla has been developing her winter coat for a moon cycle already so she can cope with the winter conditions of the higher elevations. The onset of winter is more evident here than on the lower slopes and the icy wind pulls her fur in all directions. Yalla will retain this extra coat of fur once her offspring are born to cover them as they suckle. Later, her loyalty towards her master will pull at her, and it will be at that time that her sisters and aunts will adopt her offspring so she can start her journey eastward. The pups must never be found by Samur.

By the time Yalla returns to the scree slope, she'll have shed most of her winter fur, and without her master's brush, the wolf will instinctively seek out low-growing bushes to help her shed the rest. People usually refer to these bushes as 'Wolf's Brush' because they find clumps of wolf hair in them so often.

Yalla jumps over a crack in the rocky landscape with ease, then turns south. From here she can follow a lower elevation for a considerable distance. Her kind has no name for this vast region where the grass grows throughout the year; the bipeds call it South Valley of Miza. Right now, it's the colour of hay because of the late-autumn winds, but during the summer, it's the brightest green possible and covered with tiny purple flowers as far as the eye can see. Known as Mountain Sheep Sweetbloom by the locals, these flowers attract bees and other insects, as well as tempting the mountain sheep. When the sheep eat them, it causes their milk to taste sweet, almost like honey. As autumn comes, the flowers die, turning black, and small pods of seeds burst from them in the later months of autumn and the earliest days of winter.

The people of the region erect nets to catch the seeds floating in the air. These seeds are then dried for a year and used in soups and stews for a spicy flavouring. Yalla's instinct is to avoid the people she can smell in the distance.

Yalla nibbles at a few seed pods; she knows instinctively they will enrich her milk. Because of the nourishing nature of the seeds, Alagur has been feeding her handfuls every day throughout their journey.

Smelling the air for guidance, Yalla turns northward again. As she runs, the landscape is gradually bathed in the shafts of the setting sun. The wolf stops and slowly walks around, smelling droppings on the ground. She hears a howl in the distance, and she lifts her head to let out an answering howl. Three more howls respond, and after several minutes, a group of eleven wolves, almost matching Yalla in height and appearance, come thundering through a small pass that leads steeply northward up the slope.

She is home.

Yalla lowers her head instinctively as the dominant female approaches her, and she lets all the wolves smell her scent. After the various members of the group have greeted her individually, the dominant wolf grunts and starts back up the steep slope. Yalla follows the group in a submissive posture so she can re-establish her family ties before seeking out the cave where pregnant females stay when they are about to give birth. She can smell the pre-birth liquid oozing from her vaginal opening and she feels the spasms within her own body. The wolves who have greeted her can sense and smell the same, and they realise the urgent need to get her back to their own territory. She'll have had her offspring by the time darkness envelops the landscape.

Yalla enters the dark cave and is greeted by four more mothers-to-be as well as new pups, some birthed only a day or so earlier, some nearly a season old. Yalla sniffs several of the pups before moving towards a moss-covered area in the furthest left-hand corner of the cave. She lies down on her side with some effort. Her contractions are now frequent.

Maternal instinct takes over as the first pup is born. Yalla nudges the youngling towards her nipples and proceeds to clean the remains of the birth sack from the small, squalling animal. The pup is a shade darker than she is – he has some of Uzo's colouring mixed in with the white and silver-grey of his mother. Only time will tell whether the mother's or the father's colouring will become dominant.

After a relatively short period, compared to a woman's birthing process, a total of eight healthy pups lie suckling side by side from Yalla's milk-swollen nipples. After she has cleaned the pups thoroughly and eaten the afterbirth, she lies down, layers her long bushy tail over the pups, and rests.

Yalla will remain inside the den for the first four weeks of her litter's fragile lives; her sisters and aunts will bring the small prey they catch to feed her. The initial nutrients required by her offspring for their growth — as well as their resistance to the diseases which ravage even the healthiest of wolf packs at times — will come from the thick milk that oozes freely from Yalla's nipples, and the afterbirth she has devoured will further enrich this milk. When her litter is about a month old, she too will forage for small animals to kill to bring back for the pups to eat in addition to her milk. After two more months, the pups will no longer be suckling, and she'll leave them in the care of her sisters and aunts.

A month after she leaves her younglings, when the spring starts to warm up the lands, the other wolves will guide them to the higher reaches of the Northern Blades, where they'll begin their lives as hunters.

CHAPTER FORTY-NINE

Aʟᴀɢᴜʀ ᴍᴀɴᴏᴇᴜᴠʀᴇs ᴛʜᴇ ʙᴏᴀᴛ ᴛᴏᴡᴀʀᴅs ᴛʜᴇ ᴄᴏᴀsᴛ for the last lap of his sea journey. The wind has turned, so a journey that might have taken him four days has taken just two. When Alagur finally moors the boat, the first pinks and oranges of sunset are shading the western sky. He judges the distance between himself and the undergrowth, where he knows Marrida is waiting.

Tired from two days of rowing, he glances around for a resting place and spots a perfect hideaway. The hollowed-out indent in the ground may have been the den of a sea mammal, though he can't discern from the nest's condition or appearance what type. Using his foot, he judges the stability of the den's structure. If it's the entry to a larger den, the ground will collapse under the pressure of his boot.

Alagur soon ascertains that it's a small moss-covered nest and he clambers inside. He pauses for a few moments to glance around, then shifts his position so he can lie down. The sides of the hollow are high enough for the wind to bypass it and it's partially covered over.

It is warm in here--or, at least, warmer than the shore or the open space of the nearby steppe-like fields.

Once he's lying down in his makeshift bed, Alagur lets his thoughts turn to Bergas.

I wonder if Bergas made it home. I don't know what I'll do if he didn't. Perhaps, even if Bergas isn't there, his mother might still be willing to assist us with our task.

Alagur turns onto his back and looks up at the sky, which is now a palette of various oranges, yellows and pinks.

I wonder if Marrida is watching this colour dance as well. She loves watching the setting sun. I will resume my journey as soon as the ache in my arms lessens. Then I can sleep in the bedding she spread out — it'll be more comfortable than this damned den. As if to prove his point, a stone prods him in the back.

Alagur straightens up and stretches, peering through a small crack in the den's lining at the shoreline which glints in pale blues and milky whites in the dimming light as the waves advance and recede. He gets up and walks slowly to judge the condition of his muscles, then he sets off at a jog which gets faster as he travels further east. Soon, he's running at a high speed.

When he has been running for a number of hours, Alagur decides to sit down and rest for an hour. His mind drifts, and he recalls one of the last conversations he had with Samur. *A friend who was never a friend.* Perhaps it's the parting with his loyal wolf that has prompted these thoughts.

"How's your wolf's health?"

"She is well."

"She is also ready for mating. I'm considering our options and have decided we should establish our own pack."

"We can do that after the next attack. I believe we have one planned against Ruh'nar."

"We have to be careful. There are those among the Elder Men who are unwilling to accept that things are changing here."

Alagur sits up with a jerk, realising what has been gnawing at his mind all this time.

Samur is planning something against the Elder Men.

He looks east, needing to get back to Marrida as soon as possible. He needs to ask her to do a vision immediately.

Something isn't right in City of Wolves, but I don't know what.

Alagur gets up and runs as if chased by a pack of wild wolves. Fear is rising in the deepest recesses of his mind – fear of what may happen to Marrida if the warning gnawing at his brain is more than just the anxiety of having left her alone. He runs as he has never run before. Adrenaline pumping through his veins, he takes a little over two hours to reach the place where the wolf veered off the road to avoid the group of people heading their way. Alagur instinctively follows the same route that Yalla took through the undergrowth, tracing the contours of the coast.

Branches scrape against his forearms and face. Then, before he knows it, he's in the clearing.

Alagur stands staring at the tent structure for several minutes, not sure if it's real or if he's imagining it. Leaning over, he places his hands on his thighs to allow himself to catch his breath once more. A sharp ache has started in the left side of his torso, but he chooses to ignore it.

"Who's there?" a faintly panicked voice calls out from within the tent.

"It…is…me."

"Alagur? I didn't think you'd be back so soon."

Marrida appears from the tent, wrapping her warm cloak around her.

"Yalla is…faster than…I thought she could be. I ran most of the way back."

Marrida takes a cup from the haversack and picks up the jug of cold tea she'd left sitting on top of the snow. Pouring the liquid into the mug, she hands it to the man.

"Drink this, but slowly."

He takes a small sip, waits for a few moments, then takes another. Marrida observes him closely.

Something is troubling him.

Alagur's breathing gradually slows enough for him to be able to stand without getting aches in his belly. Until he recovers from his sprint, he won't be in any fit state to answer questions. When the panting has subsided, Alagur sits down on one of the two pieces of wood that they dragged close to the tent structure on their arrival.

"I've remembered something important from last winter season."

"What?"

"About Samur. I think he means to do something to cause the Wolf Riders to become even more aggressive than they are now."

Marrida's eyes widen in shock. A conversation about Samur is the last thing she wants to have.

"We'll not only need to stop the Wolf Riders, but also stop Samur before he repeats what Sey'qar and Yozan did all those centuries ago."

Marrida nods.

"And I think he intended for me to be like Yozan."

"What do you think he wants to do?" Marrida frowns, trying to remember something important. Alagur's words have jogged a memory, but she can't figure out what it is.

"I need to try and remember everything I can from my last winter in City of Wolves. Not the attacks, but what people were doing or saying. I think you can help with that."

"What can I do?"

"Your Stone of Truth – you could use it."

Marrida thinks about what Alagur has just told her. She's not sure if he's fully capable of pulling her from a vision yet, but she knows he's right – she needs to try. She reaches up and lifts the gold chain from around her neck, then looks the man directly in the eyes.

"If I'm going to use this, I need to know everything that's relevant – everyone you know, everywhere you went, the things you did, the food you may have eaten. Even things you may not want to tell me."

Alagur swallows hard for a moment, hoping Marrida doesn't notice it in the darkness of the night, then nods.

Marrida removes her gem from its gold chain and places the chain back around her neck so she knows where to find it. She looks down at the gem in her hand and chooses to ignore the worry she has noted on the man's face.

But what is troubling him?
"Are you ready?"

Alagur gets up and walks to the tent. He grabs one of the leather pads from his makeshift bed, places it on the ground in front of Marrida and drops down onto it. It's somewhat disconcerting to be sitting at a lower level to her, but it can't be helped.

"Yes, I am."

"Do you remember when I explained about anchor points?" Alagur nods. "We need to create an anchor point so that I can establish a frame of reference for the vision. It's a bit hard to explain in a few minutes what it ordinarily takes an Acolyte two seasons to learn."
Alagur thinks for a moment. "If I understand it correctly, you want me to give you names of certain people and what they might be doing now. Is that right?"
"That's right. You've already mentioned Samur, so we've got one reference point, but for this to work properly, I'll need at least half a dozen. When I did the vision back at my house when you first awoke from your coma, I used your name, the wolf's name, the fact you were a Wolf Rider, the attack on the city, and the fact that the Wolf Riders abduct boys as references. They helped me with the vision."
"Ah, right, let me see. Samur has a friend – that's Raimir, whom I mentioned before. Raimir is usually accompanied by three young boys he is training, like I was training Bergas. Their names are Kaizor, Melchor

and Ebagar."

Alagur stops, unsure how to proceed.

"Are there any others whose names may be important? Perhaps one of the Elder Men you referred to in your retellings about the city?"

"Yes, there are three prominent Elder Men. A couple of them are quite old, although not as old as your uncle. The oldest of the three is called Vaymaz. Then there's Belduran. The younger Wolf Riders were always poking fun at him because he and Vaymaz knew so much about The Old Days, and I must admit I was one of them, but Bergas admired him. No one knew how Belduran could know so much. And there's the crippled man, Rudrig."

Alagur pauses as he thinks more about the people he'd once called 'friends'.

"Of the three of them, Vaymaz has the most influence. But I'm actually really worried for all three of them."

"What about the boys?" Marrida has a knot of concern in her stomach. "You mentioned the three boys who are training with Raimir. How friendly is this Raimir, and more importantly, do any of the boys look up to him?"

"I don't think Kaizor cares much for Raimir. He sought me out when I was brushing Yalla while we were camped out. It was the morning of the attack, and he wanted to know about her. Raimir didn't like that at all. As for the other two, Ebagar is as much a victim as Bergas was. Sometimes I wish I'd been able to get him away from it all, too. Kaizor is very protective of Ebagar and treats him as a brother. They could even be Pack Brothers in the future. Melchor is the one I am wary of. He always seems to want to copy Samur's behaviour, and it was he who led the bullying on Bergas."

Marrida nods, and she's about to ask another question when the man speaks again.

"There's one other who goes by the name of Darush," he says. "He's the one who apparently found Bergas under an overturned fishing boat in Azaquina. That attack was planned by Samur, but Darush seems to know this northern region well."

"I think I've got enough information to do a vision." Marrida decides to start before Alagur has a chance to speak again. In a practised motion, she lifts her left hand and places the gem in the centre of her palm with the tips of the thumb and forefinger of her other hand. She closes her eyes and positions her right hand in the air above the gem, then waits.

For Alagur, watching the woman go into a vision still feels eerie. He looks up at her face as the muscles become relaxed, and any hint of expression falls away. He doesn't have to wait long before she gradually opens her eyes – unseeing but seeing all – and he stares at the blackness where before her irises were blue.

Progressively an image comes into focus to his left – her right – and he moves his attention to it instead of looking at her. Various events play out from the days before the attack on Ruh'nar, and he smiles at the image of Yalla and the other wolves shaking themselves off and spraying him and other Wolf Riders with water from the lake. Then he frowns as he hears once more Samur's remark about Chiva'na.

Then the image changes. It shows a city full of people, and Alagur is shocked when he recognises one of the people as Marrida – and he is another. But then he sees someone else he recognises, and he wonders why he didn't pay greater attention to his surroundings in Alzamar as the man brushes past him with an evil smirk on his face.

The scene changes again.

It's night time. Alagur sees a large group of people, among them Samur. There seems to be some sort of argument going on. Samur strikes one of the Elder Men, then strikes him once more. The man falls to the ground, and from the blood spreading around his head, it's evident to Alagur that he's fatally injured.

Alagur realises with a shock it's the very man he was worrying about during his trek back to Marrida. Elder Man Vaymaz is dead.

CHAPTER FIFTY

Marrida starts to sob uncontrollably. She has never been prepared by the Elder for the more gruesome visions she might experience. Slumping down from the tree trunk, she falls into the arms of Alagur, who tentatively puts his arms around her. Even Alagur – as battle hardened as he is – is shocked to the core by what he has witnessed. From his own eyes, the tears flow as freely as they do from hers, but he doesn't notice them. He's concerned about Marrida. He curses himself inwardly for suggesting that she do a vision, but the deed is done and can never be undone.

How many is it now that Samur has killed by his own hand?

He feels the woman's sobbing lessen, and slowly he removes his arms from around her. When he lets go, she lifts herself away from his chest and looks at him.

"You said you didn't follow me."

"I'm sorry."

"Why did you do it?"

"I needed to make sure you were safe. It's a town which often gets attacked by the Wolf Riders--"

"I think you were right."

Alagur jerks his head up in surprise. "Why?" he enquires.

"Because I think the man who walked past you and looked at you so menacingly is one of the Wolf Riders. Who is he?"

"That's Darush." Alagur's answer is spoken in a flat voice.

"He's the one who found Bergas in Azaquina, right?"

"Yes, that's right."

It's finally out in the open that he followed Marrida into Alzamar. He closes his eyes, trying to imprint the things he saw there into his memory as Marrida has taught him to do.

Marrida watches his efforts with a hint of a smile which has both a bemused and teasing edge to it. "Alagur?" she says.

Alagur opens his eyes slowly on hearing his name. There's a faraway expression on his face, and from this Marrida knows he has successfully managed to put the imagery into his long-term memory. After having done so many visions, she can complete the process almost instantaneously.

It takes Alagur some effort to focus on her, and he looks at her questioningly.

"Alagur," she says with more urgency.

"Yes?"

"We need to reach Azaquina as fast as possible, don't you agree?"

He nods.

As they get up, both feel the distinctive after-effects of the vision. Marrida feels weak, while Alagur is still struggling with the effort of imprinting the powerful images from the vision into his mind. He now understands why Marrida always feels thirsty after doing a vision.

"We can do a vision again tomorrow, before we leave." Marrida speaks softly as she leads him by the hand into the tent. As she lies against Alagur's chest with his arm around her, Marrida thinks long and hard about what she saw in the vision. Even after the man beside her has fallen asleep, she lies awake.

He said he didn't follow me into the town, but he did. Marrida is surprised that she feels no anger about it, until she remembers one of her conversations with Elder Sharriba.

"Sometimes you'll find out a truth during your visions which will hurt you. But as a Keeper, you need to rise above it and not let the emotion cloud your mind."

"But what if I discover that a person has lied to me? What then?"

"Truth always comes back to the reality of life. If you forgive the transgressor, you actually grow stronger as a Keeper."

Did Sharriba mean that by forgiving Alagur tonight, I have ensured my skill as a Keeper will become stronger? Marrida feels the urge to test the theory, but as she has promised Alagur they'll do another vision tomorrow, she cannot answer his transgression with one of her own. What her mind decides to omit at this point is that she has been transgressing from the first time she lifted the gem from her neck in her sleeping room – with the door shut and locked for privacy – and attempted to do a vision.

Marrida looks over at the man when he grunts in his sleep. After watching him for several minutes, she then goes back to her own thoughts. Looking around, she focuses on a single star which she can see between the edges of the leather sheets hanging above her. The star is playing a game with her, seeming to wink at her at intervals.

Marrida fixes her gaze on the star and thinks about her Ancient Histories lessons. Thousands of years ago, there were people who watched the skies and measured the positions of the stars they could see. Back then, some claimed to be able to tell the future from the stars.

I wonder what could have happened to alter the world so much that these skills were lost.

Her hand reaches up to the bulge under her tunic. She is instantly struck by a thought.

What if they stopped looking at the skies because of this gem?

Marrida sighs. The sky watching skill existed in The Old Days. Keeper Erythmia was the most knowledgeable in the Temple of Ruh'nar about this subject – even more so than Elder Sharriba. Marrida recalls some of the Keeper's words.

"The invaders came from the north, destroying all the ancient knowledge of the time and killing those who possessed such knowledge, thereby controlling access to it."

I wonder if there's a link between those events and the emergence of the Order of Truth. It didn't emerge among the rulers or wealthy members of Keldarra's society but was discovered – if the retellings are to be believed – by a thief convicted into servitude.

Marrida's mind drifts and she thinks about home. Just five days from now it will be Kalisa's birthing celebration. Tears sting her eyes as she compares three girls whose fate she has in her hands.

Kalisa always has been optimistic about life. In a few short months, she has encountered many things that most people avoid until adulthood. Esalyn remains innocent, protected by Eldagu from the horrors the Wolf Riders inflict on the world. Then there's Alagur's mysterious sister who witnessed her brother being abducted, lost to her and her family.

Marrida wonders how her own life compares to theirs. She too has been protected to some degree by the Temple, but she has also been exposed to similar things as Alagur's sister.

However, I haven't had to deal with my brother's snatching.

Then she thinks about the boys she saw in the earlier vision. Now that she has committed the vision's content to memory, she's able to avoid feeling the horror of the moment when she sees the murder, instead concentrating on the crowds. Her mind focuses on three boys in particular.

Those three seem important. Why?

Then her mind turns to the group of older men.

I assume that they're the Elder Men Alagur was talking about. One of the men comes into focus. Something about him seems familiar; something about his mannerisms. Particularly way he stares down those around him.

A stirring from next to her breaks Marrida's concentration. She decides to recall the images again when she has a moment alone.

Perhaps I can do it while Alagur is fishing.

She suppresses a giggle when she remembers that outside – under a mound of snow – lies the flatfish she caught. She didn't know when Alagur would be back, so she decided to make a small campfire and cook the fish soon after his departure. The next morning, she went fishing for a fresh one, forgetting to eat the remainder of the one she'd caught and cooked the previous day.

Marrida looks up once more. The single star has been joined by another celestial body, the soft glow of a high moon almost drowning out its light. Marrida smiles. She imagines that in a distant part of Keldarra, her sister and brother, and many others she is yet to meet, are looking up at the same sky and sharing in its beauty. And she imagines that a long time ago, another girl with dreams and hopes was also looking up at it.

* * *

SOMEONE ELSE IS INDEED LOOKING UP AT THE SKY. About two days' travel from Marrida's position is Azaquina, and on a slope east of the ancient seafaring city is a house. Outside the house, two people are defying the cold of the northern wind to sit side by side and watch the sky together.

Bergas awoke from a restless sleep earlier, and an hour or so later, his mother awoke too. Looking around, she finally found him sitting on the porch in front of the long, low house. She joined him — bringing with her two steaming cups of hot broth left over from the evening's meal. Side by side, they have been sitting there for hours, watching as the stars gradually travel along the sky.

The same star which caught Marrida's eye also holds the boy's attention. He stares at it until the first morning light slowly fades it from view.

* * *

FURTHER WEST, THE SAME STAR IS AT ITS ZENITH. Ebagar, lying snugly underneath the bushes known as bergas, is thinking about a boy of the same name — a boy who has given him and the two older boys who are now his closest friends the courage to keep going on towards a city called Ruh'nar.

Ebagar sees the star arrive in the sky and it evokes memories of home, where his father and he would have climbed onto the roof of one of the storage buildings — the highest building in their small village — to watch the night sky. Much like the people of The Old Days, he asks the forces which govern the star's motion through the sky to give him a future where he'll be reunited again with those he loves the most — his father, mother, and the three older sisters and brother he left behind when he was snatched.

On that fateful day, Ebagar had defied his father, who'd stated plainly that it was too dangerous to go fishing. The boy had slipped out via an open window in the storeroom at the back of the house. Before anyone had even noticed his disappearance, the boy was walking along the river, throwing small stones into the water and smiling each time one disturbed a fish or other river-dwelling creature.

Not paying attention to where he was going, Ebagar had arrived at the small encampment of the two men, one wearing a hooded cloak, the other with a bare torso. Seeing their two wolves, one jet black, the other grey, he had tried to run away. Sneering, the two men had chased after him and the taller one with the hooded cloak had grabbed him. Struggling with all his might, despite being small for his age, Ebagar had managed to bite the man's hand quite hard and received a blow across his face from the other man for his troubles. As he'd never been treated so roughly in his life, this blow was enough to daze the boy.

When Ebagar eventually awoke from the blow to his head, he was lying with hands and feet tied together on something which could hardly pass as a bed. The same star he's looking at now caught his attention then, and ever since, that star has given him hope. And he'll take any glimmer of hope that one day he'll get back home again.

There's a season's ride between Marrida and Ebagar, and between Ebagar and the other boy who's looking up at the sky. But distance is insignificant to the star which holds the attention of so many this night, its presence acting as a measure of reassurance for them all. And nine hundred years earlier – in a small room at the top of Masharea's highest tower above an imposing white building – a woman stood looking at the same star, using the old measurements of sky watching and divination to try to make sense of the dreams which had been plaguing her for weeks. In those dreams, she saw men on wolves entering the Temple – her domain. She saw herself lying on the floor in a pool of blood, dying from a stab wound while two men stood sneering at her.

CHAPTER FIFTY-ONE

MARRIDA'S NOSTRILS FILL THEMSELVES WITH DELICIOUS SMELLING FOOD. She reaches over and finds the bed platform next to her empty. Lifting her head, she looks around the small tent structure. It too is empty.

She hears the gentle footsteps of someone walking through crisp, fresh snow, attempting to stay silent. A shadow casts itself across the entrance of the tent.

"Are you awake?" Alagur murmurs.

"Yes, I am," Marrida mumbles, yawning. "What's cooking?"

"Well, when I got up, I looked around for something to make for our morning meal and found a fish half-buried in the snow outside." Alagur chuckles softly. "It seems some small rodent tried to get away with it, but instead froze itself into a block of ice."

"I forgot about the fish when you turned up so suddenly."

"What's left of it I'm warming over a fire now. The rodent only managed to chew through the tail."

Marrida gets up and grabs the warm cloak she'd dropped down on the floor beside the bed the previous evening. The chill in the air tells her winter is soon to settle on the land. After wrapping the cloak around her, fastening the bindings at the front of the garment, she walks out of the tent.

Alagur is by the campfire, throwing a few extra pieces of slow-burning wood onto it. He has clearly started the preparations for their departure, and from the advancement of the cooking progress and the fact Alagur is fully dressed in fresh travel clothes, Marrida gathers he has been awake for some time. He hands her a steaming cup of tea, and after she's taken a tentative sip from the hot liquid, she nods in approval. The tea has an unfamiliar flavour, but it tastes good and she makes a mental note to ask Alagur what is in it.

The fish is lying in the fire, covered in a thick layer of what, to her sleepy mind, looks like either young reeds or old grass. But because she has explored her surroundings, she knows neither grows nearby. Reeds usually grow next to still ponds and smaller lakes, and the tall grasses need the much warmer southern climate. Even in the south, they only grow in the early summer months.

Alagur notices the puzzled stare on Marrida's face and decides to explain. "I saw Sweet Vine when I went collecting wood." When this response results in a frown and a questioning look, he adds, "It's a plant which grows in these parts of Keldarra. It'll give the fish a tangy, slightly sour taste, which you may like."

"I never saw such a plant before."
"Of course not. It only grows near oceans in the colder parts of Keldarra." Alagur nods towards Marrida, then adds, "The tea you're drinking has some of its sap in it for flavour."

Marrida takes another mouthful of the liquid and holds it in her mouth for a minute to let the flavour penetrate her tongue. It is a technique she learnt in the Temple during her medical training, usually to recognise poisonous saps from plants.

It has a slightly sour taste to it, but it's sweet at the same time.

She gazes again at the fish, looking forward to eating it.
"I saw a container of green berries in the tent but did not know what you planned to do with them, so I placed them near the fire."
Alagur nods at a container sitting partly sitting a pool of half-melted snow.
"Add cold water until the container is half filled and put it on the fire. It'll make a delicious accompaniment to the fish. Those are winter berries, which I recognised when we arrived here."
They smile at one another when they realise each had managed a food that they recognised.

Both individuals sit staring silently at the campfire as they savour their hot drinks. After a few minutes, Marrida speaks up.
"How far is it from here to Azaquina? And how did you get back here so fast? You said it would take you five days to return."
"I found a boat along the coast."
"So, when you go back for Yalla, the journey back may take longer?"
"Perhaps. The fastest part of the journey was when I rode Yalla to the mountain slope. It may not take long on her back from those mountains to the ones beyond where Bergas lives."
Marrida thinks for a while, then changes the subject. "Before we go, we should do the vision I suggested."
"Before we do anything of the kind, I think we should eat this fish."

"Of course. I can't do a vision on an empty stomach--"

Marrida's voice trails off as she gets absorbed in her thoughts. Alagur looks at her curiously, but decides not to disturb whatever it is she's thinking about. She takes the plate he hands her, but her mind is undeniably on other things now.

I hope it doesn't include me having visited Alzamar.

"Tell me more about Darush. What do you know about him?"
"Are you going to tell me what you've been mulling over once I've told you?" Alagur's words come out more aggressively than he intended, which makes Marrida look up sharply for a moment. However, it's almost as if she can sense Elder Sharriba standing next to her, whispering in her ear.

"Truth always comes back to the reality of life. If you forgive the transgressor, you actually grow stronger as a Keeper."

Alagur decides to reply to Marrida's question.
"In some ways, the boy Melchor – whom I have mentioned before – reminds me of Darush, even though they came from different parts of Keldarra. I think Melchor came from Alzamar."
Marrida frowns when she hears the name of the town that caused them so much grief for many days.
"Darush is the one who claimed to have captured Bergas. And Bergas pointed him out to me as the one who snatched him."
Marrida nods.

"Darush said he came from the south-east, but none of us ever knew where exactly. It seemed that Samur favoured him after he captured Bergas." Alagur pauses to think, then continues explaining. "In the vision, he was hooded. So you can recognise him if we ever encounter him somewhere, I need to describe him to you. He's a tall man with dirty blond hair. He has the same colour eyes as I do and a scar above his right eyebrow." Alagur shows on his own smooth forehead where Darush's scar would be. "Samur made him a scout after he found Bergas in Azaquina. Admittedly, he makes a better scout than I do." Alagur gives a wry smile, stopping once more to think. "I seem to recall he and Samur travelled to the south somewhere once. Or was it the east?"

To Marrida, it's obvious that Alagur is trying to access long forgotten snippets of memory. The techniques he has learnt from her to commit new scenes to long-term memory are also designed to make it easier for a person to access forgotten memories. In a way, he's becoming her acolyte.

Alagur stops his reminiscing to collect a few more pieces of wood for the campfire. When he returns, he stokes the fire, then continues.

"In the vision you showed me--"

Alagur stops again, unsure of the woman's reaction.

"You can continue, Alagur. I'm not angry about it. In fact, I think your visit to Alzamar *may* have given us a glimpse of what Samur is up to."

"Why do you think that?"

"Tell me what you were going to say."

"In the vision, Darush wasn't just scouting. He was searching something out."

"Don't you mean someone?"

"Yes, he saw me," Alagur responds, frowning. "I may have caused our plans to become more dangerous. I'm sorry for what I did."

Alagur looks down at his cup.

"Alagur, you may have been seen, but something Eldagu said to me makes me think the town is being scouted for a lot more than just an attack."

Alagur looks up at the woman. "Why do you say that?" he quizzes.

"Remember when you told me Samur is making plans to establish his own wolf squad?"

Alagur nods. It was one of the first conversations they'd had alone when he'd told Marrida more about the sort of person Samur was – after she'd told him that she'd heard Samur accusing Alagur of betrayal.

"You said – if I've got the information correct – he's going to establish a region for himself which would stretch from north of Ruh'nar to Chiva'na, and all along Ribbon Lake. If that's the case, he'd need to establish Alzamar as a place to attack so he would be strong enough to separate from the Wolf Riders in City of Wolves."

Marrida stops and looks at Alagur, who gradually shows comprehension.

"Do you think I was driven to Alzamar by fate to set certain events in motion?"

"Yes, I do. Even more so now I've committed all I saw in the vision to memory. I reviewed the events prior to the attack." Marrida sighs deeply before concluding her explanation. "There's something familiar about the one you call Elder Man Belduran. I'm not entirely sure yet how and why he's important, but I've realised something which I overlooked because of the murder."

"What did you overlook?"

"He signalled to the boys to move away from the scene. The signal he used went unnoticed by Samur, even though he was standing next to Belduran."

Alagur looks puzzled. Seeing the man's expression, Marrida continues explaining.

"You told me about the three boys. Were any of them in the vision of the event?"

"Yes. The one who shouted out about Bergas is Melchor, and the two standing beside him are Kaizor and Ebagar."

"Good. Now I have faces for them, it may make it easier to do other visions that will show some me where they're from. But I digress. Belduran was definitely signalling to the boys."

"You keep mentioning this signal, but I cannot remember seeing any signal from him. What signal, Marrida? Tell me, please."

His voice becomes several pitches higher as he speaks. It makes Marrida chuckle softly.

"He did this." Marrida shapes her hands into what appears to be an embrace followed by the posture of someone sleeping. She places her finger to her lips, then makes a circular motion in the air. She does it twice slowly, then in one fluid motion.

"I don't think Kaizor – who was looking directly at the Elder Man for guidance – was even aware of the motion. He turned and pulled Ebagar with him, but he'll probably be wondering why he turned before Elder Man Vaymaz was killed. Just like you'll likely wonder for a long time to come why you looked down as Darush passed you and not around at your surroundings. And I'm left with my own puzzle as Elder Man Belduran used a signal that is only known by Keepers in my Order."

Alagur stares at the woman with mouth agape. This isn't what he expected to hear.

"Elder Sharriba says that truth and the realities of life are linked, because one event never goes by without causing another event to happen. They're also linked because if you want to change the future, you have to know what came before. Essentially, that means that the emblem you saw in Masharea's old Temple and the same emblem in Ruh'nar are symbols of the connection that truth causes. Truth starts in the past, we are its recipients in the present, and we have to give caution to it for the events of tomorrow."

If Sharriba had been sitting in the encampment with Alagur and Marrida, she would have been proud. The recitation is a word-perfect retelling of what she explained to Marrida almost two years earlier. Back then, Marrida didn't understand what it meant, but as she has started to witness how events which are happening now have been caused by events of the past and influence events of the future, she understands it a lot better.

She decides not to share the other thought that plagued her during the night.

What if Alagur's discovery by Darush in Alzamar means the Wolf Riders will now set out to capture him? And do unimaginable things to me in the process?

While they talk, the feeling of foreboding grows inside Marrida's mind. She glances discreetly at Alagur, whose expression is mirroring her own concern. Neither wants to say what they're thinking – Darush's presence in Alzamar can only mean danger lies ahead of them.

Marrida closes her eyes and listens to the ocean waves breaking on the shore near them. This small spot in the middle of an unfamiliar landscape possesses at this moment a feeling of peace, even tranquillity. Alagur has told her the ocean can be a torrent of violent storms at times, but her thoughts settle on its name – Bay of Whispers. This must mean that on a windless day, the ocean is so still that the immediate surroundings would almost be silent.

Then her mind fixes on the name of the legend. It's called The Truth for a reason, and this takes on a new meaning for her now.

CHAPTER FIFTY-TWO

Alagur and Marrida have been journeying throughout the day, and their mood is filled with banter and laughter. Though they have to stop when Marrida becomes tired, the delays don't lessen their feeling of joy which has replaced the foreboding that started the day.

The wind picked up somewhat as they walked along the sandy beach, but now they're sitting down, it has settled. Marrida looks at the landscape around her. Although it's nearly winter, the hills they're approaching are green. She asks Alagur why this may be, and he suggests it could be due to the area being sheltered compared to the exposed beach they were travelling along earlier in the day.

Marrida glances west towards Northern Blades. A mist has settled around them and only the tips can be seen now, reminding her of Yalla's teeth.
"Don't the peaks look like a wolf's teeth?"
Alagur smiles.

After Marrida and Alagur have drunk some tea and eaten the last of the honey bread which Alagur found by chance in his haversack, they pick up their haversacks, fasten them to their backs, and distribute the remaining packs between them, Marrida carrying the two lightest. They had a chance to sell some of their remaining merchandise during the day when they passed a travelling merchant, which gave Marrida an idea of what life might have been for her father.

I'm a travelling merchant of sorts, at least until we sell all the goods we need to sell.

"I'll make you a harness." Marrida guesses from the sudden statement that Alagur does mean for her to have a wolf too.

An hour later, Alagur decides they should stop, even though it's not evening yet. "If we get to sleep early tonight, we can leave for Azaquina two hours before sunrise. This way we'll avoid most of the people who live in the town."

Marrida, tired to the bone from the lengthy trek, just nods in agreement.

Not long afterwards, having climbed up a hill, they stand on a ledge, and for the first time Marrida gets to see what the ancient seafaring city looks like. She's been told about it by Alagur and she has also seen images of it in the books she's been reading in the library, but she's never seen it for real before.

And tomorrow, all being well, she'll be there at long last.

Marrida decides to figure out how long it has taken to get to this city. She counts, tapping her fingers against the side of her leg.

It was a week before summer's end when we left, and now it's nearly the winter season. Kalisa will be heartbroken when I don't arrive back home after six months as I promised. I wonder how she's doing. I'm going to miss her birthing celebration, and she's three years from First Rites, too. I'm not even a quarter of the way through my travels.

Marrida is so deep in thought, she doesn't notice Alagur approach her. He's been calling out to her to come and sit under the small rocky overhang he spotted moments earlier, and when Marrida didn't answer, he turned and saw her still standing in the place where they looked over Azaquina together. When he reaches Marrida, he sees the sadness on her face.

Marrida is pulled from her thoughts when Alagur's hand gently caresses her cheeks. "What are you thinking about, Marrida?" he enquires.
"About home – about Kalisa."

Marrida leans her face against Alagur's chest, and he puts his arms around the woman he loves and holds her close to him. She doesn't cry – perhaps all the joy and laughter of the earlier part of the day has made her feel like she doesn't need to cry. She just stands there, letting the feeling of being loved by someone who really cares wash over her. It gradually takes away the sadness she was feeling.
"You'll see Kalisa again, I promise." Alagur's voice is very quiet, almost inaudible above the soft breeze. He sounds sad, too, and Marrida assumes that he is also missing the girl who found her way into his heart.

After they've stood together for twenty minutes, Marrida lifts her face from Alagur's chest and looks up at him. When some of her golden-blonde hair escapes its binding and plays over her face in the wind, he tucks the strands back behind her ear and she smiles at him. He then bends over and kisses her on her forehead, takes her hand, and without hurrying, leads her to the rocky overhang. When he points out a white slab of stone at the back of the overhang, Marrida sits down on it.

The gentleness of his kiss didn't escape Marrida's attention. She sits watching him with a languorous smile on her face, feeling happy. It occurs to her that their friendship and feelings for one another have grown even stronger since they awoke this day.

When I see Sharriba once more, I'll have to thank her for the wisdom she gave me that I could pass on to him. Perhaps, I'll return to her as his life partner--

* * *

BERGAS WALKS UP THE HILL TOWARDS HIS HOME. His mother insisted that she needs new supplies of vegetables and grains, and after a lot of hesitation, the boy went down to the city. He's been nervous about leaving the valley where their house is located ever since he arrived back home fewer than two weeks ago.

The boy puts the leather bag he's been using to carry the food back to the house on the ground for a few moments and looks all around him. Ever since he watched the star in the sky with his mother, he has had a feeling he can't shake. He glances back towards the Bay of Whispers, and then towards the city, looking south for any tell-tale dust clouds which would indicate the imminent arrival of Wolf Riders

Having been with them has given me one benefit — the ability to tell when they're coming.

His mother worries constantly about the possibility of the Wolf Riders returning and taking her son away from her again, even though Bergas has assured her that he evaded capture several times while journeying back home.

Bergas lifts the bag back up. Using the handles, he fashions it into a makeshift rucksack. As his home is located in a depression in the landscape, he only needs to walk another hundred paces or so up the gentle slope and he'll be able to see the rooftop.

As he walks, he hums one of the songs his mother has taught him since he returned home. The tune originates in the east, which is where she came from originally. When he pressed her for more details, she merely smiled.

"I'll tell the retelling when it's the right time."

* * *

"ALAGUR, CAN YOU GRAB MY HAIRBRUSH FROM MY HAVERSACK, PLEASE?" Marrida unwinds the cloth she uses to keep her hair off her face.
"Whereabouts is it?"
"It's in the second pocket on the left."

Alagur is busy writing notes in the notebook which Marrida purchased in Alzamar. He places it and the writing implement – which he still finds ingenious – on the stone next to where he's sitting, then reaches over to his left and, with the strength of one arm, lifts the bag towards him. He opens the pocket and takes out the brush, then gets up and sits next to the woman.

"I'll brush your hair today," he says softly.

Marrida nods and turns ninety degrees so she's facing away from Alagur, who takes her hair – which has grown even longer since they started their journey – in his hands. With slow motions, he runs the brush through it in the same way as he has often seen her do.

"When you are finished, I'll do the vision."
"What event are you going to use for it?"
"I need to do one about Ebagar."
"Why Ebagar?" Alagur stops brushing the woman's hair for a moment and glances at her over her left shoulder. She looks at him before speaking.
"It's a feeling I have. He seems to be the one that Belduran cares about." After a pause, she adds, "Otherwise, Belduran wouldn't have signalled to the other boy to move Ebagar away from what was about to happen to Vaymaz."
Alagur nods and turns his attention back to brushing Marrida's hair. He thinks for a while before asking his next question.
"Are you going to try to find out where he's from? I don't know, because he wasn't brought to the city with any raiding party."
"I know."
"How?"
"Because of the way Belduran tried to shield him from those who did

bring him to the city."

"Who was that?" But Alagur already knows the answer deep within his mind.

"It was Samur."

* * *

IT'S AN HOUR BEFORE ALAGUR LETS MARRIDA DO THE VISION, after making sure she has eaten well and has had plenty to drink. He reluctantly leaves her in the camp, but only after she promises not to do anything while he's gone, and descends to the shore that lies some fifty or sixty paces below. Using Marrida's makeshift fishing rod, he catches several small red-coloured fish.

Back at the camp, he quickly constructs a small camp fire and decides to cook the six fish whole. While they wait for the fish to roast over the camp fire, Marrida quizzes Alagur for everything he knows about Ebagar. Because the fish are small, they don't take long to finish cooking, and not long afterwards, they sit eating quietly.

Marrida waits for the food to settle in her belly before she attempts to do the vision. While she waits, she sits next to Alagur with her head on his shoulder, watching the play of colour from the setting sun. The skies this far north often display richer colours than those in the region in which Ruh'nar is located. Looking for the star she'd watched while she lay in the tent the previous night, she can't see it.

Perhaps it rises late in the evening.

Alagur uses the moment to enjoy Marrida's company. He reaches for her hand and takes hold of it. Glancing at her, he sees Marrida smile warmly at him.

I wish she didn't need to do the vision. But if we're going to start finding answers, they'll be found in her visions. At least until she translates more of Sharriba's journal.

He nods and follows the woman's example when she gets up. They walk in single file to the back of the overhang where Alagur has prepared a makeshift sofa from a bedroll on top of the stone slab. Marrida sits down on it and watches as Alagur drops to the ground in front of her. It now feels familiar when he does this as he watches her prepare for the vision.

I still can't believe that such a small crystal can evoke such a powerful change in a person. I wonder if anyone could do a vision without a gem--

Marrida has told him that the gem came from a cave in the eastern part of Keldarra, near a city called Achellon. He stares a little longer at it before turning his attention to the opaqueness of the woman's eyes, then the vision unfolding itself to his left. He sees a small boy skipping along the bank of a river, throwing stones into the water and laughing. The boy stops suddenly and starts to back away. Then a hand grabs the child as menacing laughter rings out.

The laughter is so very familiar to Alagur.

CHAPTER FIFTY-THREE

Bᴇʀɢᴀѕ ᴛᴜʀɴѕ ᴀѕ ᴡʜɪᴛᴇ ᴀѕ ᴍᴏѕѕ ᴀѕʜ when he hears a knock on the front door as he sits on the sofa, reading a book. He listens carefully. A few more knocks sound on the outer door. Bergas frowns now, recognising the rhythm of the knocks.

It can't be him.

Emelyse, Bergas's mother, walks into the front room. She's heard the knocking from the cooking room, and she finds her son looking distressed and obviously scared.

Is it friend or foe?

Emelyse nods once towards the door and Bergas gets up with some hesitation. After looking at his mother, he walks towards the door slowly and moves the bolt aside, hesitating once more before opening the door. Looking outside, he goes even paler when he sees the visitor.

"What are you doing here?"
"I told you I would come to find you if you made it home. I'm not here alone."

As Alagur speaks the words, a woman emerges from the half dark of the morning. Expecting another Wolf Rider, Bergas feels his eyes fly open in surprise. Alagur stands still, beckoning the woman closer. Carrying a haversack, light-footed, she is obviously not a Wolf Rider. She smiles at the boy, and after a moment of hesitation, he copies her greeting.

She is the most beautiful woman he has ever seen.
"This is Marrida Kayrsan." Alagur gestures at the woman, then says to her, "I'm sure you already know who this is."
The woman nods. "I'm so happy to finally meet you, Bergas." Her melodic voice adds to the boyish smile on Bergas's face.

"Who is it, Bergas?"

The edge of panic in his mother's voice snaps the boy from his trance-like state. "It's alright, Mam. It's my friend, Alagur, with his companion, Marrida Kayrsan."

A moment later, a woman of about forty stands next to her son. She looks both visitors over, judging their intentions, then nods once, steps aside, and opens the front door wider.

"They should come in before anyone sees they're here. They're the reason I've waited to tell you more about where I'm from and who I was before I met your father, Bergas." Turning to Marrida and Alagur, she adds, "And my name is Emelyse."

The two guests glance at one another questioningly. But they step inside nonetheless. Once they're in, Emelyse bolts the door shut, then she turns to appraise the visitors once more.

"I know who you are, Alagur. Bergas has told me you helped him to get home. I thank you for the life of my son." Alagur smiles at the woman. "But you, Marrida, are something of a mystery to me. I knew that one day I'd meet the man who'd helped my son, but I never thought I'd meet another of my kind in these parts of Keldarra."

* * *

The moon is at its zenith before the two residents and their two guests sit down for the broth that Emelyse and Marrida had been preparing. Emelyse suggests that Marrida helps her in the cooking room in order to let Alagur and Bergas talk alone.

"They need it," she says plainly.

Bergas leads Alagur to the other end of the house where he's fashioned a workshop since arriving home. He points at the haversack he's been constructing. The man looks it over, then praises the boy for his ingenuity.

After a time, their conversation turns to the period of separation.

"So, you say you saw a group of Wolf Riders east of Venrasia Woods?"

Bergas nods. "They seemed to be in some sort of hurry. I didn't see much as I was trying to make sure they didn't see me. I even used the vole droppings the wolves usually roll in to mask their smell."

"That was a good call."

"Then twice, I'm sure I heard a wolf in the distance, but it seemed to be some sort of loner."

Alagur thinks back to his own journey. He'd not heard a lone wolf's song.

"I don't think it was a loner. It may have been Yalla sensing you in the distance."

"When did you start your journey?"

"We started our journey towards the end of the summer season, two months after the attack on Ruh'nar, once I'd recovered."

"Recovered? From what?"

"In Ruh'nar, I was struck by a thrown stone, as was Yalla." Alagur points at the scar left by the wound on the left-hand side of his skull. "Marrida found us in the street and pulled us into her house with the assistance of her two siblings. I wouldn't be alive if it was not for her and her family."

"She didn't hand you in to the authorities?"

"She didn't. There are things about Ruh'nar that not even Samur is aware of, and I'd like to keep it that way, so I'm not going to go into details."

Such knowledge is for Alagur to share or keep to himself as he sees fit. Bergas just hopes that one day, the man will tell him.

"With the help of Yalla, we probably ended up just weeks behind you. Did you do with the wolf as I said?"

"Yes." Bergas whispers the reply, and Alagur notes the raw emotion in his voice. "I was fond of the wolf because he had the same colour hair as mine. I always thought you chose him for me for that reason."

"Yes, I did."

"I made sure I stayed away from any town where Wolf Riders could be," Bergas continues. "I travelled in the Northern Blades for part of the journey, too, following the movement of the mountain sheep as Papa taught me." There was pride in Bergas's voice when he mentioned his father.

"I'm sure your father would be proud of you if he were here." Alagur smiles at the boy.

"I miss him." Bergas bows his head. Alagur leans forward and, using his forefinger, lifts the boy's head.

"You're now a man because of what happened to *you*. You're the man in this house. Don't ever forget it. It's your duty to take care of your mother."

Bergas nods slowly and feels Alagur's finger wipe a tear from his cheek. Then they both glance up when they hear Emelyse call for them.

"The very late evening meal is now served."

They both stand up at the same time, and on the spur of the moment, Bergas gives Alagur a hug.

This is my brother, Alagur thinks, hugging the boy back. *And I care for him.*

✳ ✳ ✳

ALAGUR AND BERGAS WALK INTO THE COOKING ROOM where the two women are already sitting down, chatting. They're clearly comfortable with one another already. He sits to Marrida's left, and Bergas takes the seat opposite him.

Once everyone is seated, Emelyse lifts the lid from the cooking pot with a thick woollen cloth and places it to her left on the unused part of the table. Then she picks up a wooden serving ladle and hands it to Marrida.

"You and Alagur go first. It's a tradition in this region that guests get the first servings from a meal."

Emelyse smiles at them both in turn, and Marrida nods. She ladles out two spoonfuls of the broth for herself, sending up a cloud of steam as she does so, and recognises the smell of some of the herbs in the mixture. Alagur decides to ladle out three spoonfuls – the last spoonful only after an encouraging nod from Bergas. Then it's the turn of Bergas who, like Alagur, takes three helpings of broth. Emelyse serves up one whole spoonful and one partial one for herself, then places the ladle into the pot and covers it with the lid to keep its contents warm. When she lifts her spoon, so do the others around the table.

Marrida takes a spoonful of the thick mixture from her bowl and puts it in her mouth. She holds it there for a few moments and chews it without hurrying, instantly liking the mixture. She tastes something meaty and wonders what it is. And she notices various vegetables which come floating to the surface as she takes more spoonfuls of the mixture.

I need to ask for the recipe before I leave so I can pass it on to Kalisa once I'm home again.

"Is the food to your liking, Marrida?"
"It's delicious. What's the meat I can taste?"
"That's the meat of local bovines."
"It tastes good."

Alagur also savours the meal. *If I was in City of Wolves, I might have cooked a meal such as this. I wonder if Bergas has cooked one of the meals we had there for his mother.*

"Can I ask you a question, Emelyse?"

Alagur looks at Marrida sharply, noticing the hesitation and shyness in her voice.

"Ask me whatever is on your mind. That's what brought you to this part of Keldarra, after all."

Alagur's gaze now turns to Emelyse, whose voice is filled with the reassurance of a mother talking to a daughter.

"You said something about me being 'one of your kind'. What did you mean by that?"

Emelyse looks from Alagur to her son before answering the question.

"I told Bergas that the day would come when I'd explain to him who I am, and today is that day. Like your parents, Marrida, I too met my life partner and started a new life with him very quickly."

Marrida sits staring at the other woman with her mouth open, too dumbfounded to speak. It's Alagur who asks the obvious question.

"How do you know about her parents?" His voice is a higher pitch than normal. And looking at Bergas, the man sees that he's shocked, too. Emelyse has made such a simple statement, but it has had a huge impact on the three younger people around the table.

"I will explain more, but not now."

* * *

MARRIDA WALKS SOME DISTANCE FROM THE HOUSE. She stares down at the landscape below her without really seeing it. Her mind is racing. Is it possible that Emelyse can see what will happen in the future?

Her thoughts are further confused by what Bergas whispered to her and Alagur after his mother had retired to her room. Before his snatching, she'd said to him, "I'll answer your question when you are home again."

"She said this just hours before the Wolf Riders came and took me to City of Wolves. She didn't even forbid me to go to the harbour. It was almost like she knew I'd come home one day."

Before he went to bed, Bergas added, *"She always told me she came from somewhere in the east, and that she left because it was dangerous there for her--"*

In a familiar motion, a warm blanket is draped over Marrida's shoulders, and she instinctively reaches up to hold the hand that has placed it there. Alagur realises from this that she wants his company, and he puts both his arms around her and holds her close to him. She leans her head against his chest, and they watch the city below, the moon reflecting in the ocean. There's a serenity to the landscape, and it feels for a moment like they're on a leisurely journey instead of a dangerous mission.

"I wonder what she meant."

Alagur feels Marrida's head tilt as she looks up at him. "Me too. And what Bergas said about the day he was snatched – I never knew that until now."

"I read something in the library at the Temple. Although now I can't recall exactly what it was, it's related to all this. Then there's the warning from Eldagu. I really want to know what's so terrible that I'll have to hide my calling."

Alagur glances down, noticing the familiar bulge is missing from the top of her tunic. Seeing the direction of his stare, she looks down too.

"It's safe. I keep it in the inner pocket of my over-skirt now."

"When did you take it off?"

"I didn't put it around my neck when I finished yesterday's vision." Marrida's voice is at its softest as she replies.

Both individuals are silent for a while.

"Alagur?" Marrida's voice is hesitant.

"Yes?"

"You know I have to visit the library in the town tomorrow. But I've been thinking."

"Thinking about what?"

"Well, after what happened in Alzamar." She stops again, swallowing hard. "I actually don't want to go into town alone, especially if there's the danger Eldagu warned me about."

Alagur nods and pulls the woman closer to him.

"I'll go with you, if it's what you want," he whispers, leaning over and kissing her on the forehead. "But now I'm getting a chill. Let's go inside."

They walk back to the house, holding hands. Once inside, Alagur carefully bolts the front door shut, then follows Marrida to the small sleeping room Emelyse has designated as theirs for as long as they are guests in her house. The man noiselessly shuts the door, and when he turns, he's greeted by Marrida's languorous smile.

"It's a bed! After all these months of travel, we get a decent bed."

"It's a warm bed, and we're going to need it in these parts when winter truly settles over the land," Alagur replies. "Some days, it can get so cold in this part of Keldarra that the snow turns to ice as hard as rock. If that happens, we'll have to chisel out a path from the front door to the road below. Otherwise we'll be stuck here, unable to go anywhere."

Marrida stares with wide eyes at the man. This is unexpected. "How can I get to the library if that happens?" she asks.

"Simple. I plan to bring the library here."

CHAPTER FIFTY-FOUR

Marrida's eyes open ever so slowly. She yawns aloud, and then stretches. The warm bed makes her feel lazy, like it doesn't matter that she's taking her time getting out of it.

She looks around and sees the room is still cloaked in the early morning darkness. She looks towards where Alagur would normally be lying beside her. Today he's out, helping Bergas collect more wood in the nearby hills for the fire. Their supplies have steadily dwindled over the preceding month.

Then, she hears Alagur's laughter coming from outside, followed by the laughter of Bergas. She immediately wants to know why they're laughing, so she swings her feet out of the bed and reaches for the clothing on the chair next to her. She pulls the thick woollen tunic which Emelyse gave her over her head, then grabs her outer skirt and pulls it on too.

After tying her boots, she rushes outside. Alagur and Bergas are throwing snowballs at one another. They haven't seen her yet, so she grabs some snow, compacts it into a fist-sized ball, and throws it at Alagur just after Bergas has thrown a snowball at him. She bends down to make another one ready for the boy, but by now she's attracted their attention. They rapidly make more snowballs and pelt her with them. Before long, the scene in front of the house is a flurry of white projectiles, flying in every direction. Alagur, Marrida and Bergas are all laughing so loudly, their voices echo from the hills surrounding them.

Fifteen minutes or so later, each person is covered from head to toe in snow. Their faces are bright red, and they're all grinning widely and panting from the effort.

"I think we can eat the morning meal now Marrida is up," Alagur says breathlessly.

"Yeah, that bit of fun has made me hungry," Bergas adds.

"I think I heard Emelyse getting up too, just before I came outside." Marrida's panting so much, she's having trouble speaking. All three smile at one another again before brushing the snow from their hair and clothes and stomping it off their boots.

* * *

THE SNOW THAT SURROUNDS THE HOUSE with a knee-deep layer of white fluff has come down heavily over the last three days. The roof is so thickly covered by the snow, it looks almost as though the house is buried in the ground. As Alagur, Marrida and Bergas enter the house, they're followed by a trail of snow which Bergas hastily brushes away. After they've hung their outer clothing up to dry, they walk into the kitchen in single file.

"I could hear you laughing out there." Emelyse smiles as her son enters the cooking room. "Are you hungry?"

"Yes, I am." Bergas rushes to the cooking pot to see what his mother is preparing. Before Marrida can follow the boy, Alagur grabs her by the waist and pulls her closer to him. He gives her a long, lingering kiss, then looks at her, smiling warmly.

"That's for the snowballs you threw at me."

Marrida just smiles back at him warmly. She remembers with longing the days when she played with her siblings, and as snowfall is rare in and around Ruh'nar, she wishes they were here with her now.

Alagur lets Marrida go and they walk into the cooking room. On entering, they're met by the aroma of Emelyse's steamed ham and freshly baked bread. A large pitcher of warm milk sits centrally on the table, too. They sit down side by side opposite Bergas, who has already started to eat the food. Emelyse sits close to Marrida, and the two women smile at each other.

"Are you planning to visit the library today with all this snowfall, Marrida?"

"I have to. I've almost finished the last few pages I need to translate. Besides, Alagur can come with me to help me get through the snow."

"I first need to help Bergas with his latest project," Alagur interjects.

"What are you making now?" Marrida asks the boy.

"I decided to experiment with making baskets, when I saw yours."

"Which one of my baskets?"

"You know, the one you keep all your writing implements in."

The basket in question is a small one divided up into narrow compartments, each of which can hold one of Marrida's thin writing implements in an upright position. It's deceptively simple, appearing to be made of wood, but the sturdy sides are actually made of brushed selvaya wool. As soon as he learnt this detail, Bergas grabbed a large armful of wool from a container in the workshop and started to experiment with it, Alagur watching the boy's efforts with interest.

"You look like you want to reinvent all the innovations of The Old Days by yourself."

Bergas's first four or five attempts resulted in failures, but Alagur was more amused by the fact that his own attempts were even less successful. Alagur had then promised to help the boy, but he now found himself in something of a quandary: either delay Marrida's departure to the library in the city or renege on his promise to help the boy.

"I can comfortably go on my own," Marrida says. "You help Bergas, and if you're done early enough, you can join me."

The morning meal is eaten hastily, then all four individuals assist in clearing the cooking room and table, washing the crockery, cooking pots and utensils. After this task is completed, Marrida prepares to leave. Just as she thinks she's ready to go, Emelyse walks into the room with something draped over her arms.

"If you wear this, you'll be much warmer. It's one of my old coats. Your cloak is fine, but it is unsuitable for this weather and will gain you unnecessary attention."

Marrida removes her familiar cloak, which she places on the bed. Then she takes the coat the older woman is handing to her and puts it on. Emelyse helps her to fasten it.

"If you want to wear it closed, you tie these cords together," Emelyse says. "This belt will keep the garment from flapping about."

Marrida stands in front of the mirror in the corner of the room and looks herself over. *Now I look like one of the locals.* After hugging Emelyse in gratitude, making the older woman somewhat embarrassed, Marrida picks up the slender leather bag in which she carries her notebooks. She pulls the bag crosswise over her body and secures it with bindings on the opposite side.

Emelyse leaves the sleeping room first, followed by the younger woman. Alagur smiles approvingly at the alteration in Marrida's appearance.

"There's the hat which goes with the coat." Emelyse points at a narrow-brimmed hat sitting on a shelf near the front door. "It can be worn over the cloth you wrap around your hair."

Marrida reaches for the hat and puts it on. She looks in the tiny mirror which hangs near the shelf and smiles. Now she could pass for one of the merchant women near the city's harbour at the bottom of the hill.

"I think I'll be able to come and find you in the library in a couple of hours," Alagur calls out as Marrida is about to leave.

"I'll be careful," she calls back reassuringly.

She departs without delay, walking slowly over the snow towards the road. Once there, she turns right and walks downhill. While she walks, she looks more closely at the buildings around her, only glancing at her feet occasionally when she steps on some ice.

Marrida recalls the vision she did of Alzamar in which she saw a Wolf Rider scout disguised as a beggar, and she decides to keep a lookout for ruffians. Alagur has assured her several times over the last few weeks that the Wolf Riders don't venture far beyond City of Wolves in the winter months, but he's never totally managed to reassure her. She can't help feeling Alagur is keeping certain information about the Wolf Riders from her, but she has refrained from actually accusing him of this.

After walking for about forty minutes, Marrida arrives at a fork in the road which is becoming increasingly familiar to her. When she asked Bergas where the right-hand fork led, the boy looked sad. After some hesitation, he answered.

"It leads to the part of the harbour where I was busy helping when the Wolf Riders came."

Marrida stops for a moment and glances towards the hive of activity at the bottom of the road. Then she turns left and takes the road that leads to the oldest part of the town, and her destination. As she gets closer to the heart of the city, the number of people walking past her increases. However, unlike previous visits, no one even glances at her.

Marrida looks up at the small building, which has also become familiar to her in the last month. It's slightly larger than her own dwelling. Most of the library is on the second floor, which is reached by climbing two steep staircases. She glances up at the three windows, beside which she'll sit and read the books she retrieves from the various bookcases. Then Marrida opens the door and walks inside. She climbs the stairway, and at the top is greeted by Jarryca.

Jarryca has a mellow smile, but her eyes betray an active mind. At the age of almost ninety-nine, she's probably the oldest woman Marrida has ever met. Her behaviour and mannerisms sometimes remind Marrida of

Sharriba, whose piercing green eyes often seemed to stare right into her inner being. Jarryca makes Marrida aware of how much she misses her mentor.

During her previous visit, Marrida asked Jarryca about several books, and when she arrives at the top of stairway, she's greeted by four neatly stacked piles on the table next to the banister. She quickly carries them over to the table at which she plans to work.

"Those are the books you wanted, right?" Jarryca calls out from the small room adjoining the library. Her clear voice could easily belong to someone half her age.

"Yes, thank you," Marrida answers.

"I only heard one pair of footsteps coming up the stairs. Is your man friend not with you today?"

"No, he's meeting me here later. He had other things to do." Marrida doesn't want to tell the old woman where she and Alagur are staying, in case it causes unwelcome attention for her hostess.

"Never mind," Jarryca says, smiling at the young woman as she approaches with a cup of steaming tea. Marrida takes the cup from her and tastes the rubha apple tea she's been served each time she has visited. Jarryca turns and fetches her own cup of tea, then both women sit near the windows, placing their cups on the large wooden table so simultaneously that anyone watching them would think they were playing a game of mimicry.

Marrida looks at the four piles of books.

"Is there a particular topic you are going to research today?" Jarryca asks.

"I want to check the retellings you told me about this city some more."

"I think you'll find the fifth book in the pile on the right helpful."

Jarryca takes several sips from her cup as Marrida reaches for the book, pulling it carefully from the stack without causing the four books above it to topple. Marrida places the book in front of her and studies it closely. It looks very old. She reaches into her bag and pulls out her notebook, placing it next to the book.

"If you turn to page twenty-eight, you'll find some information which may serve you well in the future." The old woman's voice is now almost conspiratorial, then she smiles at the puzzled look on Marrida's face. "I've lived a long life, seen many things, and read all these books so many times, I think I can guess which information someone needs from them. When someone comes to visit this library, that is. And not many do anymore."

"Why not?"

Before Jarryca can answer, the two women hear footsteps on the stairway. They look over to see who is about to arrive on the second floor. Marrida smiles when it is Alagur.

"There's your man friend now."

Jarryca gets up to fetch Alagur a cup of rubha apple tea.

"I forgot how to get here. I almost missed the building--"

"Don't worry, Alagur." Jarryca approaches the man with his drink and hands it to him. "Most in this city don't seem to remember this building exists."

* * *

A MONTH EARLIER, BERGAS ESCORTED HIS TWO FRIENDS to the building and – rather shyly – introduced them to Jarryca. Marrida immediately took a liking to the woman.

"If things here were different, she could have been an Elder like Sharriba," she whispered to Alagur later that day as they lay side by side.

Marrida and Alagur's tentative explorations of the city have revealed blackened ruins on the coast which no one has bothered to rebuild. When they asked Emelyse about them, the woman looked sad and said the ruins had been there for as long as she'd lived in the city. She arrived about four years before Bergas was born, and he's now almost twelve years old. Emelyse's statement provoked a reminder from Bergas that she'd promised to tell him more about where she came from, but as usual, her response was cryptic.

"I'll tell you before it's time for Alagur to go to get his companion."

Like Emelyse, the woman now sitting opposite Marrida and Alagur also displays an uncanny ability which Marrida can only describe as foresight.

Were some people here Callers? Was the building which now lies in ruins once some sort of Temple? If someone destroyed the building, why did it happen? Even more significantly, who did it?

Marrida checks the records for the city – the few that the residents of Azaquina have bothered keeping – and finds indications that it wasn't the Wolf Riders. There have been two recent Wolf Rider attacks – the one just over a year ago which resulted in Bergas being snatched, and one around ten years earlier. Before that, the last attack by the Wolf Riders had happened two centuries earlier.

However, the building was destroyed fifty years ago. Marrida now turns her attention to the book Jarryca has told her to read in a bid to find out more.

CHAPTER FIFTY-FIVE

Marrida and Alagur are walking back towards Emelyse's house in the half-dark of the dusk that has settled over the city. They stayed in Jarryca's library much longer than they'd planned as she told them about the destruction of Azaquina's Temple, and have left with heads filled with as many questions as answers. As the daylight started to fade, it was Jarryca who ushered them from the library. Her parting words were a warning about the eastern region of Keldarra, which left them wondering how much the old woman knows about who they really are.

"I want to go home," Marrida says. She sits down, in part because she's tired from labouring through the knee-deep snow, on a small rock that appears to have been cleared of snow for that very purpose. Alagur kneels in front of her and takes hold of her hand. She stares at him with sad eyes.

"I miss Kalisa and Esbara."

"I know you do," he answers. "I miss them both too. But don't you want to be able to arrive back home knowing that nothing can harm them anymore?"

"I do, but it all feels so wrong around here," Marrida replies, waving her hand to point at the city below them. "The destruction of the Temple wasn't at the hands of the Wolf Riders. It was destroyed by someone else."

"Who do you think it was?"

"If we're going to talk about this, I would rather get back to Emelyse's house first."

Marrida gets up so abruptly that Alagur is left in a kneeling position for a few moments. Then he gets up too and rushes to catch up with her. Marrida is walking at such a fast pace, even his longer legs have trouble keeping up. Anyone watching them would probably think they had just argued. And this is exactly the impression Marrida wants to convey; she doesn't know who is watching them and speculating on their comings and goings in the city.

It takes them less than half an hour to reach Emelyse's house. Marrida rushes in and goes straight to the guest room. Emelyse and her son glance at one another questioningly, and when Alagur rushes by too a moment later, Emelyse is certain that something has unsettled them. She motions Bergas towards his sleeping room.

If something bad has happened, I don't want him to hear of it. He has suffered enough.

She gets up and walks towards the door of the sleeping room, behind which she can hear the muffled sound of Marrida sobbing. Emelyse taps softly on the wooden surround of the doorway, listening out for a reaction from inside the room. After a moment, the door is opened wide by Alagur, and Emelyse sees Marrida sitting on the edge of the bed. Tears are streaming down her face, but Marrida makes no attempt to wipe them away.

Emelyse stares hard at Alagur, but sees a deep sadness in his eyes, too. He's biting his lip as though trying to curb his own emotions.

Something has happened, and I need to find out what, and perhaps why.

Emelyse enters the room and closes the door behind her – for the most part to prevent Bergas from overhearing what she's going to discuss with the couple. Silently, Emelyse nods towards the chair, and Alagur picks it up and brings it over to her.

She takes the chair and places it in front of Marrida, looking closely at the younger woman who has now bowed her head. An occasional hiccup indicates that she continues to cry. Emelyse takes a cloth out of the pocket of her skirt and, reaching forward, gently wipes the tears from the other woman's face. She has grown to love Marrida, whom she sees as the daughter she never had, and never will have. The younger woman leans forward against Emelyse's shoulder and Emelyse puts her arms around Marrida, glancing up at Alagur who's looking on helplessly.

He's crying now, too. Whatever has happened is very serious indeed.

"Marrida," Emelyse says gently.

Marrida raises her head from the other woman's shoulder and looks at her. Emelyse promptly reaches up and wipes Marrida's tear-streaked face with the corner of the apron she's still wearing from cooking an hour earlier. "Tell me, what has happened?"

"I am just so sad," Marrida explains. "When Jarryca told me about the destruction of the Temple here, I started to miss home so much."

Emelyse looks at the younger woman for several minutes. "You don't know who Jarryca is?" she says finally. "She hasn't told you?"

Marrida stares at Emelyse with open mouth. "Told me what?" she manages to blurt out.

"That at one time, she was one like you."

"Like me? You mean she was a Keeper?"

"Yes. But she's not actually a Keeper – she's a Caller."

"A Caller?" Marrida and Alagur's response is so synchronised that Emelyse looks at them both in turn, smiling.

"If you clean up a bit, Marrida, then both of you can come into the front room. I'll get Bergas as well. It's time for me to tell you exactly what happened here fifty years ago, and more about my origins. Then you will know what awaits you when you get to the end of your journey."

Emelyse gets up and rushes from the room. As soon as she has departed, Alagur walks to the wash basin and dips a cloth in cold water. After wringing the cloth thoroughly, he gives it to Marrida, who uses it to wash her face and neck and soothe her reddened eyes.

"What do you think that is all about?" Alagur quizzes.

"I don't know, but I'm sure – now more than ever – that something terrible happened here. Perhaps the Order of Truth has a hand in it, and perhaps others, too."

Marrida gets up and Alagur immediately takes her in an embrace. "We need to know more. If then you think it would be better for you to go back to Ruh'nar, I'll help you get home safely."

Marrida nods, feeling grateful for the man's consideration.

When they enter the front room, they find Emelyse and Bergas sitting on one of the two sofas near the fireplace. The fire has been stoked up, and on a small, low table between the sofas, four large mugs of steaming tea are standing. Marrida can smell the rubha apple that Emelyse always puts in tea as she comes closer to the seating. She glances at Bergas, who looks worried. He's aimlessly playing with his fingers in his lap and keeps looking from person to person.

When the man and woman are sitting down, Emelyse looks at each person in turn before speaking.

"It's slightly more than sixteen years since I arrived in Azaquina. It was two years after I met Bergas's father – by chance." Emelyse lets out a deep sigh, then looks for a few moments at Bergas. He stares back in a thoughtful way that surprises her. "He saw me walking near the beach. It's the beach to the west along which you arrived. I was looking for a place I'd heard about, but I couldn't find it, so Jerid – that's Bergas's father – took me in. Not even six months later, he asked me to be his life partner." Emelyse smiles at Bergas. Then she continues, "As you know, Bergas lost his father a year or so before he was gone from me – and it hurt him a lot."

"It still hurts every day," Bergas interjects. Emelyse nods and puts her arm around the boy.

"The day the Wolf Riders came was probably the worst day of all for Bergas, because I had promised to tell him more about myself. It was my own sadness at losing Jerid that kept causing me to put it off. But that isn't the whole truth, I must admit now."

Emelyse pauses, reaches forward and picks up her mug. The others follow her lead, and all silently drink the tea for a while. Then Emelyse speaks again.

"I met Jarryca for the first time perhaps a year after Bergas was born. She's the one who finally showed me the ruins of the Temple – the building I'd been searching for when I first arrived in the city."

"What happened there?" Marrida's voice is almost a whisper.

"She was there when it happened." Emelyse stops again, and sighs.

Alagur glances at Marrida, who's sitting staring at the fireplace with the mug between her hands. He noticed when she asked her question, her voice was a monotone.

"It was the day when Unity was broken."

Alagur, who's still looking at Marrida, sees her usually placid face contort into a grimace of pain, anger, disgust, and perhaps even disbelief at Emelyse's words.

"Did Jarryca tell you who she is?" Emelyse asks again.

Alagur and Marrida both shake their heads. Their conversation with the old woman was all about the destruction of the building, explaining the contents of various books. Never once did Jarryca say anything about herself. As Marrida deals with the implications of Unity being broken, she decides to voice her thoughts.

"She reminds me of Elder Sharriba."

"Was she in charge when the Temple burnt down?" The question comes from the intelligent and perceptive Bergas.

"Yes, she was. There are perhaps only four or five others who know this, and all those who know are sworn to secrecy. Because I keep her secret, she chooses to keep mine." Emelyse takes another sip from her drink, then continues. "Has anyone ever warned you to be careful of revealing your vocation, and never to display the gem you carry, Marrida?"

Alagur and Bergas both look from Marrida to Emelyse and back. Marrida stares at the floor, her face as white as moss ash, her body language showing that she doesn't know if she'll be able to control her emotions at that moment. She sits perfectly still, hoping that the older woman will simply continue with the retelling of past events.

To cover the growing awkwardness of the situation, Alagur answers in Marrida's place. "She was warned by a friend of her uncle, a man called Eldagu who lives in Alzamar, that Keepers aren't looked upon in a favourable way. And yes, she has a gem. She keeps it in a hidden pocket in her tunic." Marrida jerks her head up and stares at Alagur. He smiles encouragingly at her. "Marrida, it's alright to tell her. I've got a feeling there's a reason she asked."

"In this you are correct, Alagur." Emelyse pauses, sighs deeply again, then speaks in a monotone not too dissimilar to Marrida's. "I came here just over sixteen years ago from the east to find the Temple. I wanted no part in the travesty which replaced the original Temple where I come from. I won't tell you the name of the city as the mere mention of it will put you in danger. Perhaps you should heed Eldagu's words and turn back. Go home--"

"Is it really that dangerous there?" Alagur asks. "Danger from what, or whom?"

"All I know are my mother's last words as she told me to travel west. It took me two years to get here on foot. You can't miss the road that leads there – it goes past the ancient watchtowers, some of which are said to date from when the Warlords came from the north."

Alagur looks at Bergas, who nods in an "I told you so" manner. Alagur decides to hold his tongue.

"My mother knew I'd be selected for the Temple – not that it deserves that title anymore. When selected, you must enter, but no one who goes inside ever comes out again." Emelyse's voice is almost a whisper and tears are rolling freely from her eyes. "If anyone in that city discovers your skill, you'll be in danger, Marrida."

Alagur thinks about the implications of what the woman is telling them. If danger lies ahead and danger lies behind from the Wolf Riders, they'll have two threats to deal with.

He's torn from his thoughts when Marrida speaks. Her voice is calm now.

"You still have not said how the Temple here was destroyed."

"I know I haven't, but before I do, I'll tell you more about Jarryca," Emelyse responds with a hint of a smile. "Jarryca is very perceptive. It won't be by chance that she has selected specific books for you to read whenever you've visited her over the last month, Marrida. Be sure she knows, or at least suspects, you're a Keeper, and with her the secret will be as safe as it is with me."

"So, who is she?"

"Before I tell you, Alagur, you must promise never to mention this to anyone else. This goes for all of you. Especially you, Bergas."

The words 'I promise' are spoken in unison by the younger people in the room, and only then does Emelyse continue.

"She was the Temple's leader. Someone you would call an Elder in your Temple, Marrida." Emelyse doesn't add how she knows Marrida is from a Temple. "And there's more. When I came to the city, I happened to walk into the library where she works and ask about the Temple. Bergas must have been a three-year-old at the time, so he won't remember the conversation, but he remembers going to the library. That's why he took you there to introduce you to Jarryca."

Bergas smiles at the mention of his good memory.

"Bergas has always regarded Jarryca as a grandmother of sorts. She taught him reading, writing and counting skills. But had the Temple still been standing, she would have done more than that – as a Caller."

Emelyse looks directly at Marrida before she speaks once more.

"And the Temple is where I would have gone…to be a Caller too."

CHAPTER FIFTY-SIX

There's a deafening silence in the room after Emelyse has finished speaking. The revelation has even impacted Bergas, who is staring at the floor with a frown on his face. Now all the mysterious statements and comments his mother has made are starting to make sense.

He glances at Marrida, who looks even paler than before. Emelyse's revelation has serious implications for her.

Emelyse speaks again. "It was a cold morning when they came. Jarryca said they brought with them weapons they'd taken from an enemy, and in visions, she saw the origins of the weapons. When I tell you that you possess such a weapon, Alagur, you'll know the enemy of whom I speak--"

Emelyse looks at Alagur directly. "I do know," Alagur replies rather coldly.

"I will only remember that you made sure my son could come home. All you did beforehand doesn't matter, just as it won't matter to your sister."

This statement confirms it – Emelyse is telling the truth when she says she's a Caller.

"Keepers came from a city far to the south to destroy the Temple here. It was the last Temple which still stood as a message that once there were three in the Order who worked together."

"The Symbol of Unity," Marrida whispers.

"Yes. It can still be seen in many places, but its meaning is lost to the world now. Just like the meaning of peace was lost to Keldarra, to my son when the Wolf Riders snatched him, and you, Alagur, when the same happened to you--"

"So, the books Jarryca has are from the Temple she once served?" Marrida quizzes.

"Yes, most are, but some are from the eastern city I come from. Jarryca says some of her books are as old as the Order itself, rescued from the place where it all started--"

"Alagur, I need to go to that city."

"Why?" Alagur is surprised at the sudden clarity and calmness in

Marrida's voice

"So I can find out more about why all this happened. I think I understand what Emelyse is saying. She and I should be able to do our calling side by side in the open. In the east, she shouldn't have had to hide who and what she is – and nor should I, for that matter."

"She is right." Emelyse directs her next question at the man. "Alagur, where were you from initially, before you became a Wolf Rider?"

"From Chiva'na. Marrida saw it in a vision she did while I lay injured at her house."

"Do you know what the city was known for in the past?"

"No."

Bergas is listening with growing interest. He already knows some aspects of what's being discussed from conversations with Alagur, but other things are new to him. He feels genuine surprise that his mother has permitted him to stay and listen to something this important, something that could have an impact on the whole world. When Alagur answers negatively, he frowns in dismay.

He does know!

"Alagur, don't you remember Samur's comment when he said, 'The city where they do those crazy things with girls'? He believed they do something which involved a ritual with a stone of some sort. I was there – I heard you and him talking, and you didn't look happy when he said it."

Using skills learnt from Marrida, Alagur starts to retrieve the information from his mind. However, he's interrupted by Emelyse's next words.

"It seems you didn't adhere to the rules of your Temple, Marrida."

Alagur and Marrida look at one another in shock and both turn bright red. How has the older woman recognised the skill Marrida has taught to the man? Seeing them so embarrassed, Bergas starts laughing in a way only boys of almost twelve can laugh, making the two of them even more embarrassed.

"No need to feel ashamed of what you did." Emelyse smiles warmly. "If the times and circumstances were different, you'd become a Keeper too, Alagur. Or perhaps a Caller, if you're indeed from Chiva'na. And if you are from there, you have someone here you can talk to about the city. Jarryca is originally from Chiva'na too."

"She is?" Alagur smiles back at Emelyse just as warmly.

"She won't be able to tell you much about recent years, but she can tell you about the city as it was when she was only a little older than you,

Alagur. She arrived in Azaquina when she was almost thirty, after travelling for close to four years to get here. I think she said she stopped at Ruh'nar, too, but you can ask her about it yourself when you see her next."

Emelyse realises that Marrida is using the recall skills she's learnt as a Keeper. She seems to be counting back, but Marrida is the only one who knows she's counting back years.

If Jarryca is almost ninety-nine now, she got to this city sixty-eight years ago. Sharriba is now seventy-six, which would mean when Jarryca arrived at the Temple, she was just a child.
Marrida shakes her head. This theory doesn't make sense.
It doesn't solve who I saw in the vision. I thought it was Sharriba as an Acolyte, but Jarryca also possesses a heart-shaped face and green eyes. Marrida sighs. *What if the woman I saw wasn't Sharriba, but Jarryca? What if she was crying because she'd just heard something terrible?* Marrida shakes her head again. *It's all getting too confusing. I need to do a vision to sort out all the facts.*

Marrida is so absorbed in her thoughts, she doesn't notice the silence in the room, or how three pairs of eyes are watching her intently. Alagur stays quiet. Because he has become used to her actions, he knows she's sorting through her stored memories of events she's seen in visions. Emelyse keeps quiet, too, because she's observing how the younger woman will react to all the information and revelations. She stops her son from speaking, placing her finger over her lips and smiling at him in a conspiratorial way.

Marrida is about to dismiss the memories and go back to asking Emelyse questions when one catches her attention. In one of the first visions she'd conducted by herself, she'd seen an event which related to her mother. But as the vision progressed, she'd seen another woman – a woman who looked sad. She'd always assumed the woman to be her maternal grandmother, but now she looks at the vision in her mind's eye once more, and…

Marrida's hand flies over her mouth in shock and she stares wide-eyed at Emelyse. "I think I did a vision of Jarryca when I first became an Acolyte."
"When was that?"
"Just after my First Rites."
Emelyse frowns for a moment. "Isn't that young to become an Acolyte?"
"Elder Sharriba didn't think so, but if you think it was--"

"I didn't mean to question your ability," Emelyse replies in a softer tone. "I'm just surprised girls that young are accepted into the Order now. These days, they're usually eighteen or nineteen. It was more common to be accepted into the Order at the age of twelve or thirteen when Jarryca was young. She became an Acolyte in Chiva'na's Temple aged twelve."

"Twelve?" Alagur and Marrida say simultaneously, staring at Emelyse in disbelief.

"At the Temple, the other Acolytes never seemed to like me," Marrida adds in a whisper, bowing her head. "Especially not Sarayna."

"Who's Sarayna?"

"She's another Acolyte at the Temple. She's now probably doing Second Rites. She joined three years before I did, but became a first rank Acolyte only last year, when I'd already been one for three years. I'd be a fourth year now if I hadn't gone on this journey."

Marrida feels Alagur's finger softly wiping her cheek and notices tears have started to flow as she talks.

"Marrida, Elder Sharriba meant to prepare you for this journey. She knew it would come." Marrida nods, and Emelyse continues. "But now there's another subject I wish to discuss. And that's you, Alagur. I think you too have a role in all this, and you set that in motion when you helped Bergas to get home. But something I don't understand is why you specifically looked for Marrida in Ruh'nar."

Alagur looks at Bergas, who squirms in all directions under his gaze. The boy had promised not to discuss the Wolf Riders with anyone, but when he was quizzed by his mother, he told her what Alagur had said about how he was rescued by Marrida.

Emelyse sees the man staring at her son. "Yes, he told me," she says pointedly. "Did you think I'd let a man stay in my house without knowing more about him? And please remember this. If ever you send anyone you meet on your travels in the east my way, Alagur, make sure you send them with a letter so I know they're someone I can trust." She pauses and continues in a softer tone. "I asked because of a comment Marrida made. She said you were looking at the houses in her street, and after she rescued you, you told her you were looking for her. How did you know which houses to look at? And more specifically, why her?"

Alagur looks at Marrida, then at Emelyse, then at the ground, then at Marrida again. Marrida speaks up to encourage him.

"Tell her about your dreams, Alagur. Tell her what you told me when you woke from unconsciousness."

Alagur takes a deep breath. "I started having these dreams, and in them I saw a young woman who bore a strong resemblance to Marrida. Then I woke up and saw her."

Bergas sits staring at the man with his mouth open in disbelief. He'd known Alagur for two seasons – perhaps a little longer – while he'd lived in City of Wolves, but nothing the man said had ever given any indication he was having 'these dreams', as Alagur put it.

If Alagur was having dreams he didn't understand and wanted to investigate, that's why he warned me not to do anything to anger Samur, and why he helped me to get home. He knew I would be in danger from Samur if he left to find the woman in his dreams.

"Why do you think you were having the dreams?" Emelyse asks.

"I don't know. They just kept recurring. I had the last dream the night before the attack on Ruh'nar, and I haven't had any since."

"They weren't simple dreams you were having, Alagur," Emelyse responds. "They were the beginnings of your Awakening."

"My Awakening? What do you mean? What Awakening?"

"Callers refer to the first few times a person gets visions of the future as the Awakening."

"Was the vision I did of Jarryca such an event, too?" Marrida asks.

"Perhaps, but you'd need to use your Stone of Truth to do the vision again and show it to me to confirm it. And you can also tell me when you decided to teach the Keeper skills to Alagur."

"How did you know I used her skills?"

"Because they're the skills Callers learn, too. I've been taught the same skill by Jarryca."

"Mam?" Bergas startles his mother. She's immediately unsettled by the tone of his voice, so it takes her a few moments to regain her composure.

"Yes, Bergas?"

"I may have been having similar dreams to Alagur."

Emelyse looks at her son closely. The boy seems worried, almost panicked. She puts one arm around him and rests the other on his shoulder, looking him in the eyes.

"Tell me more about the dreams you have been having."

"They started a week or so after I got home. In them, I'm walking somewhere." Bergas swallows hard before continuing. "I arrive in this room where I see all these people gathered. There are perhaps as many as fifty or sixty people there. Around them, it's all dark, but they stand there as if they're waiting for something--"

Bergas stops for a moment, then continues.

"They looked so strange, Mam. They're wearing these masks, and all are silent. But even though they're silent, it feels like they're telling me something. I can never figure out what."

By the time Bergas has finished explaining his dreams, he has tears streaming down his face. He leans forward and buries his face against his mother's chest, and she can do nothing but put her arms around him and hold him close to her.

Emelyse looks first at Marrida, and then at Alagur, pleading with them for answers. But they can only shake their heads to indicate they don't recognise what the boy has described. Neither has ever seen anything which matches it, and Emelyse sees sweat pearls appear on Marrida's face as the younger woman tries to recall a vision's content which may help. In the end, she can only concede defeat.

For a moment, Marrida thinks Emelyse has soothed Bergas to sleep, but then he raises his head and looks almost imploringly at her.

"I'm wondering if you've inherited the skill of foresight that your mother has suggested Alagur possesses," she says. "I'm certain of one thing, though. If you dreamt of those people, Bergas, they're somewhere, and we'll meet them in the future."

Emelyse nods. She has come to a similar conclusion.

Bergas looks at the two women incredulously for several minutes, shifting his gaze from one to the other. "You mean to say I've got the same skill as you, Mam?"

"Yes, son, you do. I'm sure of it."

CHAPTER FIFTY-SEVEN

A SOFT BREEZE BLOWS, AND THE MODERATE WARMTH OF THE SUN lightens the mood around Alagur and Marrida as he holds her close in an embrace before setting off on his journey west to collect Yalla. Alagur has been delaying the journey for as long as possible, but the pull of the Distant Bond Imprint is becoming too strong to fight. He must leave today as the consequences of not going will be unbearable.

Seeing the grimace of pain flashing over Alagur's face more and more often in recent days, Bergas finally understands why he had to dispose of his wolf so quickly. *If I had waited, I'd have bonded with the beast, and I would now be in pain like him.*

Marrida is going through her own pain. Ever since the day in the middle of winter when Jarryca and then Emelyse revealed the darker side of the Order of Truth's history, she's been subdued, even withdrawn. She's refused to participate in any further snowball fights with Alagur and Bergas, and most evenings after dinner, she's sat alone near the fireplace, staring intently into the yellow and orange flames. Alagur has heard her mumbling the same words over and over.

"It's a tainted truth."

One evening, as Alagur was walking towards Marrida to check on her, Emelyse stopped him in his tracks.

"She needs time to process all she has learnt. She was sent on her journey for this reason."

Alagur nodded, then beckoned to Bergas to come with him to the workshop. By the time he'd left the workshop, Marrida had decided — either by herself or cajoled by Emelyse — to go to bed. But thinking about Marrida's murmured words, Alagur found himself getting more and more worried about what lies ahead of them.

When Alagur entered their sleeping room that night, he'd watched Marrida sleep for almost an hour. Then, as he still wasn't sleepy, he'd decided to go and sit on the porch of the house — now six paces longer and three paces wider since he and Bergas enlarged it. He sensed a restlessness in his mind, and it wasn't just due to his worry about Marrida.

It'll soon be time for me to travel west, back to the screes.

When Alagur announced his need to the other occupants of the house, Bergas understood immediately, but Marrida's reaction was bordering on unreasonable. She started crying and kept repeating that she'd never see him again and he was going to leave her at Emelyse's house. Not even Emelyse could reassure Marrida, so in the end, Emelyse suggested that Alagur should just pack up and go when the call of the Distant Bond Imprint meant he couldn't delay his departure any longer.

"Give Marrida one last hug, then turn and go. I'll deal with whatever is bothering her."

And so the day has come. Alagur gently pushes Marrida away and looks down at her. She looks up with sad eyes.

"I'll be back soon, although this journey will take me longer than last time. The return journey will be faster as I'll have Yalla, but I'll have to hide her in the mountains above us before I can come back here. No one in Azaquina can see her. As I'll be travelling at night, you can look up at the night sky and imagine we are looking at the same stars."

Marrida nods solemnly.

Alagur turns to Bergas and gives the boy a hug too. In the season since he arrived with Marrida in Azaquina, Alagur has got to know the boy better than he had a chance to in City of Wolves, and he is fonder of him than ever.

"Take care of Marrida and your mother, little brother," he says, smiling widely.

He and Bergas have done a ceremony together – watched by the women – in which they pledged themselves as Pack Brothers. It wasn't as elaborate as the ceremonies in City of Wolves, but it felt more genuine to the man. Since that day, he has taken to calling Bergas 'little brother'.

One evening, after Bergas had gone to bed, Emelyse held Alagur by the shoulders and told him she felt like she had gained not just a daughter in Marrida, but another son, too. It moved Alagur so much that tears were rolling down his cheeks.

He hugs Emelyse next. She smiles encouragingly at him, then he turns and starts his journey. He doesn't take the route by which he and

Marrida arrived through the outskirts of the city. Bergas has shown him paths up into the mountains and alternative routes to the Bay of Whispers that the boy was shown by his father. After walking over the southern field, Alagur finds the trail he needs and glances back one more time. Marrida is standing with Emelyse's arms around her on one side, Bergas leaning against her on the other side, his arms around her waist.

When the boy sees Alagur looking, he waves at him. Alagur waves back, then turns and continues walking, slowly picking up the pace. It feels strange to be on his own again. The journey reminds him a little of when he went to find Yalla in the first place, except this time he'll be meeting a wolf already bonded to him.

He has missed his loyal wolf companion.

* * *

At the same time as Alagur is setting off on his journey, a wolf is pacing back and forth at the entrance to a darkened cave. Around her, eight lively pups are playing. Pushing the pups aside whenever they try to suckle from her nipples, the wolf awaits the arrival of the pack matriarch, who'll assign an adoptive mother to the pups by instinct. That adoptive mother will then journey further west, where the pups will learn to hunt, starting with the earliest lambs of the mountain sheep who haven't yet descended to the South Valley of Miza for their spring grazing.

Yalla smells the air, and then releases her wolf song. It's time for her to leave; her bond with her master is calling her east towards him. But until her pups are securely in the custody of their adoptive mother, she cannot go.

When a dark shadow appears above Yalla, she knows the time has come. An answering howl from the top of the large rock flanking the cave which serves as the pack's nursery confirms this. Moments later, Yalla is surrounded by six wolves. Each wolf sniffs her pups, who greet their aunts with an enthusiast wagging of tails. Then, the matriarch descends from the higher elevation, and Yalla bows her head in deference. She paces backwards until her litter is between herself and the matriarch.

Two sharp barks echo through the tiny valley, and then a dark grey wolf with light orange stripes over her fur steps slowly forward from the six wolves who greeted the litter. She lies down on the ground and lifts her hind leg, and in an act of acceptance lets each of the eight half-grown wolves take hold of a nipple and suckle for several minutes. She then gets up, and after a few short grunts, trots away, followed by the pups. They in turn are followed by the other aunts, and after just five minutes, Yalla is alone with the matriarch.

The matriarch circles her several times, then she too starts walking away, stopping after some thirty paces and letting out a final wolf song to allow Yalla to leave the pack. Yalla doesn't answer. Instead, she simply turns eastward and starts running. She senses her master closing the gap between them even now.

* * *

ALAGUR WALKS FOR FOUR HOURS AND FINALLY REACHES THE END of the mountain path Bergas pointed out to him. He glances around the landscape and finds himself at a point much further east than he'd anticipated, realising why the boy sent him this way. Ahead of him lies the coastal path which leads past the Bay of Whispers all the way to the mountains.

The man glances towards the mountains known as the Northern Blades, which Marrida suggested look like a wolf's teeth. He tries to measure the distance from his current position to the mountains to work out how quickly he can do the journey.

I wish I could just journey on east with Marrida.

Alagur again feels the respect that surged through his mind when he listened to Emelyse's retelling of her journey to Azaquina, though he has a nagging feeling she's holding something back.

She did the journey alone without much food, and she was in constant danger from those from whom she was fleeing. I wonder what Marrida's journey would have been like if she had done it on her own. She would likely have had to stop every few days at a farm, a village, a town. She might even have wintered with Eldagu. She wouldn't have met Emelyse, though I think, eventually, she would have met Jarryca. But if she had arrived alone, their meetings would have been different.

As the morning progresses, Alagur becomes more and more reflective. He looks inwardly at how life has changed so quickly for him. Now, he is able to enjoy the weather becoming warming. He watches insects buzzing around the earliest flowers, listens and mimics some of the nearby birds, and appreciates the changes happening to nature. Life with the two women who share a mystical vocation, although from opposite perspectives, has changed Alagur's outlook on life more than he has realised up to now.

* * *

AFTER ALAGUR'S DEPARTURE, THE TWO WOMEN AND THE BOY stand looking at the horizon for a long time before returning to the porch. Marrida sits down on one of the chairs there, leaning back and closing her eyes. She tries to distract herself from the sorrow she's feeling by imagining the man and the wolf reuniting at the screes. The mountains are visible for the first time in weeks as the early spring sunshine warms up the air and burns away the mist which settled over the bay as winter advanced.

I've missed Yalla, with her intelligent golden eyes and her beautiful silver-grey-and-white fur.

Marrida could do a vision to track the progress of Alagur or Yalla, or both, but she dares not try. In her mind, images are forming of the wolf lying dead somewhere, or Alagur riding Yalla back to City of Wolves. She shudders over the worst possibility: them both being killed by the Wolf Riders who are out looking for them.

Marrida senses someone sitting silently beside her and opens her eyes. Bergas is to her right, smiling shyly.
"I hope I'm not disturbing you."
"It's alright, I'm just thinking about the things which have happened to me over the last year."
"I drew the people I saw in the dream for you." Bergas hands Marrida a piece of ochre-coloured parchment. She looks at it with interest to distract her from her own thoughts.

He's extremely good at drawing.

"My sister has a close friend who draws as well as you do." Marrida smiles at Bergas. "His name is Damir."
"Tell me about Damir." Bergas sounds genuinely interested, and inside the house, Emelyse nods approvingly as she walks to the cooking room.

That's the way to help her get over the sorrow.

"He wants my sister Kalisa as his life partner. He is almost eighteen now."

"I hope they'll be happy together." Bergas smiles at Marrida again. "I've not told Mam yet, but there's a girl who lives near here. I wouldn't mind having her as a life partner."

"Does the girl know?"

"Yes, I asked her last week…because I saw how close you and Alagur are." The boy pauses for a moment, then continues before Marrida can respond. "I think Alagur wants you as his life partner, but he's too shy to ask you."

Marrida's blush tells Bergas that the feelings are mutual and his smile becomes broader.

"How do you know?"

"He told me about what happened in Alzamar. He blushed when I asked him if he followed you because he cares for you. He did it because he loves you, not because he wanted to go against your wishes."

"Did he actually say that?"

"No, I worked it out from talking to him. And today, both Mam and I saw how he held you before he left. He held you for so long, it is obvious there's love between you."

"How can you be twelve years old yet so wise?"

"Alagur says I'm now a man, and with it comes the responsibility of showing wisdom," Bergas responds seriously. "Besides, I regard both him and you as friends, and I want you to be happy."

Marrida's mind is racing, *If Bergas is right, then it means that Alagur will return to me. And I know I love him. I'm going to do what Alagur suggested and look up at the stars each night, imagining him doing the same.*

Marrida looks southward in the direction the man left. He's getting further away from her every moment, and she wishes now more than ever that he'd reappear over the crest of the nearby hills.

Bergas notices Marrida's expression turn from sad to wistful and he leans himself against her arm, looking south too. They sit there – side by side – for several hours without saying much, each absorbed in their own thoughts, until Emelyse walks out of the house to tell them the midday meal is ready in the cooking room.

* * *

ALAGUR PULLS THE STOPPER FROM THE WATER CONTAINER which

423

Emelyse gave him to use on his journey. She also gave him a coat which belonged to Jerid, explaining he'd then appear to be just another local resident.

Alagur has based his calculations of the time the journey will take on following the precise contours of the Bay of Whispers, but the path Bergas has directed him to is in fact a much straighter route than he'd anticipated. Glancing behind him, then on towards where he's going, he calculates he could easily shorten the journey by a day or two.

Even more so if I cut westward each time the road meanders south.

Something about the road reminds Alagur of a riverbed. It must be one of the many dried out riverbeds which criss-cross the Keldarran landscape. But as this ancient riverbed is shallow, Alagur concludes the ocean's waves must have eroded its banks on one side, and the winds which blow over the landscape must have eroded it from the other side.

Alagur goes past the undergrowth – the final stopping off point for Marrida and him before they entered the city – wondering if luck will be on his side and he'll find the boat he used before. He glances up for a moment to look for any flocks of blue ravens flying over, but then realises he won't be able to use it even if it is still lying on the beach. Bergas told him that during the early months of the year, the direction of flow in the bay turns.

"If you attempt to use the boat, you'll be going against both the ocean's current and the wind blowing down from the mountains flanking the bay."

"It was at this time of year that Bergas's father drowned," Emelyse added in a whisper.

And that was what made Alagur promise not to attempt to travel by sea.

CHAPTER FIFTY-EIGHT

Alagur cautiously approaches the rocky outcrop next to the scree where he'd watched Yalla climb upward to her former home high in the mountains. The shadows caused by the diminishing daylight make the landscape feel eerie, even dangerous. It's an hour before sunset, and he needed to arrive here before the daylight disappeared to be certain no one was waiting to ambush him.

Alagur had received an unexpected bonus on his journey. A passing merchant had offered him a ride in his cart pulled by bovines, which was a faster method of transport than even the fastest sprint. This allowed Alagur a half day or so to rest while he sat on the back of the cart.

In conversations, it transpired the merchant's ultimate destination was Ruh'nar. Posing as one of Joharan's apprentices, Alagur enquired whether the merchant knew the artisan, and found out that he was actually on his way to deliver supplies to Joharan. Alagur then asked if he could take a message to the old man. As he didn't want the merchant to discover too much if he were to read the message, Alagur decided on a code that only Joharan would understand. He still had Damir's kindling kit, so he used it as the message, asking the merchant to return it to its rightful owner so 'the apprentices could use it for exploring the tunnels again'.

When the merchant wasn't looking, Alagur wrote another short message on a parchment scrap which he hid in the lower compartment of the kindling kit. He hoped the merchant wouldn't attempt to use it.

The kindling kit should arrive with Joharan in the summer, and I'm sure the old man will be clever enough to realise the message has a deeper meaning than simply being the babbling of 'some madman' that the merchant met on a road in the northern lands.

Alagur whistles sharply, then again.

I won't need to wait too long — at least, I hope not.

He walks around, examining the area closely, necessity triggering his scouting skills. Alagur wants to be certain that no Wolf Rider is awaiting him. He places his hand over the sheath which holds the hunting knife he'd obtained in Azaquina just to be on the safe side — carrying his spear arrows and thrower would have identified him as a Wolf Rider and put him at even greater risk.

Alagur squints towards the western sky to see the placing of the setting sun. It'll be another forty minutes before it's dark enough to travel unseen on the back of the wolf. Then he hears a grunting noise and turns. In the dark shadow of a boulder, he sees an animal. With his hand once more on the sheath, he paces forward slowly, but a moment later, he realises he is in no danger from this creature. A rush of movement followed by the familiar pushing of a furry face against his tells him that Yalla has returned to him.

The wolf lies down on her belly and Alagur kneels before her. He notes from her slender contours she's no longer carrying any pups.

I wonder how Samur will react when he discovers the pups are out of reach of him now. Then Alagur's smirk disappears. *Samur would probably kill me for losing him the opportunity of having those pups as the first in his new wolf squad.*

Alagur leans against the wolf's forehead to touch it with his own. He holds the pose for perhaps five minutes, the restless feeling of urgency gradually ebbing away from him. When he sits up straight again, the wolf looks up at him.

The ritual which separated us is now reversed, and the bond is as it was before.

Alagur hastily picks up the small rucksack he has been using during his journey. First, he removes the few clothes he's brought with him, then he retrieves the harness from the bottom to fasten onto the wolf. The brushing against the right side of his body tells Alagur that the wolf has recognised it, and she has placed herself ready at his side. The motion of strapping the harness onto the wolf is so familiar, it's become mechanical, and Alagur chuckles when he realises he's looking around for his spear arrows and thrower to fasten to the wolf's side. Instead, he fastens the small rucksack to her harness.

We'll ride until two hours before sunrise, then we'll stop and sleep in the undergrowth or an abandoned den, or under those flat rocks I inspected on my way here.

Alagur stands holding the wolf's massive head in his arms for several moments. Stroking Yalla's nose bridge, he chuckles when it makes the wolf snort. He recalls the growing friendship between Yalla and Marrida. The woman went out of her way to greet the wolf in this way each time they were separated.

"You miss Marrida doing that, don't you?"

Although the wolf doesn't understand his words, the inflection of Marrida's name makes her raise her ears in recognition, and she glances around as if looking for the familiar woman.

Alagur climbs on Yalla's back and signals for the animal to set off at a fast pace. The experience of being on top of his wolf again makes the man feel exhilarated. He remembers the first time he rode on her back, when he was just coming up to his First Rites, days after he found her in the South Valley of Miza. The bonding ritual with her was accidental, but Alagur has never regretted getting this wolf. Yalla is loyal; she is fast; she is the largest among her kind; she has an inherent intelligence. And above all, she is Alagur's trusted friend.

Alagur was a loyal Wolf Rider for more than half his life, not realising the true origins of what's believed to be a legend by the Wolf Riders. The dying words of a woman foretold not only the demise of the Wolf Riders, but also that this demise would come about by the actions of a man and a woman. The last Elder of Masharea said the man would learn the woman's skill, and she'd learn his. And Alagur believes Yalla in her own way will assist to bring about that end too – by giving birth.

Alagur slows the wolf down. He wants Yalla to have some rest before continuing. Taking the last piece of bread from the small rucksack Bergas used for his travel home, he recalls the boy's words.

"Once you no longer have a use for the rucksack, please destroy it or bury it. I don't want it around as a reminder of my life with the Wolf Riders."

Alagur looks at the nearby surroundings and sees what looks like the entrance to a den. Glancing down at the rucksack he's holding, he then pushes it as far as he can reach into the hole with his long arm.

Bergas will have a chuckle when I tell him this rucksack has become the bedding of a rodent, he muses.

He walks back to where he was sitting and the wolf tilts her head, as if questioning his sanity.

"I'm allowed some moments of madness," Alagur says as he

approaches her. "I'm alone with you, and I miss Marrida. I hope she's coping on her own – but she isn't really on her own, is she?"

Alagur signals to Yalla, who gets up from the ground. She stretches her muscles, then notices her master's attention on her and wags her tail several times. Alagur mounts her, looking for the correct direction to go in. After some hesitation, he admits to himself he's lost. He glances down at the wolf below him, then he has a sudden idea.

"Yalla, go to Marrida," he says to the wolf. "You remember Marrida, don't you? Find Marrida's scent. Follow Marr-id-a."

He ends the sentence by saying the woman's name unhurriedly. The wolf's ears prick up in recognition of the name, and she raises her head to smell the air. As she does so, Alagur looks up at the skies above him. In an instant, he recalls how he told Marrida to look up at the stars, and he'd be looking at them too.

The wolf starts pacing slowly, first to the left, then she stops. She paces to the right and stops again. Yalla can obviously smell something, and he feels the animal's pace increase steadily. Within minutes, the wolf is running at her top speed, with Alagur bending over her back to make them more aerodynamic.

At the sound of waves breaking on the shore, the man realises the wolf has caught the scent of the journey he and Marrida made along the shoreline a season earlier. He laughs suddenly when he realises that they'll soon pass the boat, if it's still where he abandoned it.

If Yalla keeps up this pace, we'll make it to the encampment that Marrida and I built for ourselves faster than expected. When we get there, we'll stop and rest until it's night time again.

The journey feels good. Alagur knows that every stride of the wolf underneath him brings him closer to the woman he loves.

I can be in the mountains beyond Emelyse's house within days. He motions to the wolf to go faster, but as her speed decreases rather than increases, he realises she's nearing the limit of her endurance. When Alagur looks up, he sees hints of orange and red which signal the coming of day. Daytime brings with it the risk of being seen by travellers, so he glances around for somewhere suitable to use as shelter. When he sees a tree trunk, he directs his wolf to it. Arriving at it, he looks it over and smiles when he sees it has partially rotted away into deadwood. He knocks his boot against the deadwood and reveals a hollow space within.

Alagur motions towards the entrance. Going into enclosed spaces, except for the safe delivery of pups, isn't in a wolf's nature, and there is some hesitation in Yalla's motions. The wolf briefly sniffs, then clambers inside. It smells musty and rotten – the man catches a whiff of it, even with his less developed sense of smell.

"It'll be fine in there." Alagur speaks in a gentle voice. Once inside, Yalla settles into a ball on what appears to be a mixture of sand, leaves and bark chips, then Alagur climbs inside too, settling himself near to the entrance. He wants to be aware of the surroundings in case anyone comes near.

Alagur glances up at the sky where the stars are fading away little by little. He suddenly feels an overwhelming sadness. Glancing around, he wishes he was side by side with Marrida at that very moment.

He strokes Yalla's head absentmindedly as she whimpers softly. "I know this is uncomfortable," he whispers, "but it's safer than out there." A wet, raspy tongue licks over the back of his hand in response to his voice. Yalla lays her head down, but she doesn't sleep. The motion of her eyes shows she's watching every movement her master makes. She senses a difference in him which she can't figure out just yet. In the time they've been apart, Alagur has changed.

Alagur leans against the tree trunk's opening, watching the sky gradually getting lighter as the rising sun casts its familiar oranges, reds, pinks and yellows over the landscape. He reaches up to the left-hand side of his face where three seasons earlier, he was wounded by a well-aimed stone. Marrida's medical skills are excellent because he can hardly feel any scarring. Alagur smiles at the thought of how he reacted when he awoke after weeks of unconsciousness and reached for her hand to find she was real, not an illusion or a dream.

He glances sideways when he hears soft puffs coming from the wolf. She's sleeping peacefully now. Alagur smiles broadly. Soon he'll be at Emelyse's house and he'll be reunited with Marrida. He recalls his last conversation with Bergas, and the boy's words of wisdom.

"When you are home, tell her how you feel. Tell her you want her as your life partner. She wants this too."

The question is--does she really?

CHAPTER FIFTY-NINE

Emelyse and Marrida are walking side by side, as a mother and her daughter would, towards the central part of the ancient seafaring city. Marrida's face, although placid, is still somewhat sad. But Emelyse has a smile playing on her face that she fights to keep in check.

"Where are we going?"

Emelyse glances at the younger woman as they turn into a street that's unfamiliar to Marrida.
"There's something we're going to do together."
"Alright."
Emelyse ignores the flat tone in which Marrida speaks. She's acting like a sulky girl and not an Acolyte.

They arrive at a one-storey building and Marrida looks up. She's drawn by the house's obvious resemblance to Emelyse's house.
"This is where Jarryca lives these days," Emelyse whispers. "It used to belong to Jerid's parents, when they were still alive. Jerid gave it to Jarryca fifteen years ago."

Emelyse knocks on the wooden door.
"Come in, the door is open," the familiar voice of Jarryca calls out. Emelyse opens the door and nods at Marrida to enter first. The younger woman does as she is instructed and walks inside. Moments afterwards, Emelyse follows her. The distinct sound of bolts slamming in place comes from behind her and startles Marrida. It takes her a moment to get used to the shadowy interior of the house after the brightness of the early spring day.

Marrida sees two figures standing side by side at the end of the long room.
"This is Hadukin. He's here to help. He's someone I trust." Jarryca's voice drifts softly across the room, and Marrida frowns.

What is going on?

Behind her, she feels Emelyse prodding her to move closer to the two older individuals. She reluctantly does as she's told.

As Marrida steps forward, she notices a table with seven unlit embers sitting on it at intervals. She feels Emelyse's hand pulling at her and finds herself positioned at the end of the table with Emelyse to her right, and her mind gradually starts to make sense of what she sees around her. Her hunch is confirmed when Hadukin stands to her left, and he and Emelyse each take one of her hands.

She looks at the table where one by one the embers are being lit by Jarryca, who starts a monotone hum. It too sounds familiar.

"Did you organise a Second Rites ritual for me?" she asks.
"We did indeed," comes the softly spoken reply from her right.

Marrida smiles broadly, first at Emelyse, then at Jarryca, and then somewhat shyly at Hadukin, who smiles back and winks at her.

Suddenly, Marrida realises something profound. The two women, with their Caller skills, have probably known for a long time that she – a Keeper – would come to the city seeking answers. They may be her opposites, but perhaps they still understand the knowledge that was lost with the Preservers. They know that their skill and that of Marrida balance each other.

The day when the Wolf Riders attacked Ruh'nar – three seasons ago – coincided with it being three seasons until my Second Rites. When I started my journey, I promised to be back for my sister's First Rites in three years' time, but in reality, I hoped I would be back for my own Second Rites.

As the day of her Second Rites came ever closer, Marrida started to panic, realising she was in a foreign city with none of her relatives nearby. She had no one and nowhere to do her Second Rites. When a month earlier, Bergas did his First Rites, which happen at the age of twelve in Azaquina and not fifteen as they do in Ruh'nar, it sent her head spinning, and she'd rushed from the house and slumped down in the corner of the porch.

Emelyse had listened to Marrida closely that day, and after the tears had ended, she suggested that perhaps Marrida should go and lie down on her bed for a while. Emelyse then set in motion the events which led to this moment.

First, Emelyse wrote a note to Jarryca, explaining to the old woman that she needed to see her, and she sent Bergas to deliver it as fast as he could run. A note in return confirmed that Jarryca would be available for Emelyse to come and talk to her whenever she needed to. In response to that note, Emelyse went into town immediately. In a soft voice, Emelyse explained to the old woman that it was time for Marrida's Second Rites. She also told Jarryca she'd overheard Marrida confess to Bergas that she loved Alagur and hoped to have him as a life partner.

"She cannot choose him as a life partner if she hasn't done her Second Rites," Jarryca stated.

"I know that. She told me her parents are both dead. So, she requires her uncle to be present for Second Rites. However, I regard her as a daughter, so I could stand in."

"Indeed you could, if it's what you wish."

The two women discussed the correct procedures. Jarryca, who'd visited Ruh'nar as a young woman, remembered seeing a Second Rites in the Temple there.

"In Ruh'nar, an Acolyte who reaches the age of twenty will be summoned to a small building adjoining the Temple. There she will be met by the Elder and a male relative, such as her father or uncle. She is escorted there either by one of the Keepers of the Temple, or by her mother. Once she is in the building, she stands at the longest side of a table with the Keeper or her mother to her right and the male relative to her left. If no male relative is available or alive, then a trusted representative of the city can stand in."

For Marrida on this day, Emelyse has taken the place of her mother, and Hadukin – as the last living relative of Jerid – is acting as the male relative. The ceremony is almost completely accurate in reproduction, because essentially Emelyse is Jarryca's Acolyte.

Marrida feels tears well up as she watches each ember being lit in turn. *I wish that Alagur and Bergas could be here too.*

A cloth is draped over Marrida's head and she realises exactly what is happening. *They're doing the ritual in the way it would have been done by Elder Sharriba. Jarryca must have spoken the truth when she said she visited the Temple all those decades ago. Today, I end my life as a young adult. Tomorrow, I'll wake as a woman in the proper sense. And tomorrow, Alagur might ask me to be his life partner.*

Marrida smiles at the thought, and her smile brings knowing glances from the two older women.

Marrida feels something sliding over the slick cloth which is covering her head, and when she looks down, she sees her Stone of Truth on its gold chain. For a moment, she panics.

"If we're going to do Second Rites for you as a Keeper, then you should wear this." Marrida hears Jarryca murmur the words in a soothing voice, and it settles her mind. She glances at Hadukin on her left and wonders what the man is thinking. "He has known all his life about me, Marrida. I said he can be trusted. He won't tell anyone in this city about you, just as he has never told anyone about me."

Marrida lets out an audible sigh and realises she has been holding her breath since the gem was placed around her neck. Her reaction brings a smile to the faces of the three older people.

Hadukin glances at the young woman beside him. *I wonder how a twenty-year-old can already be skilled enough to be inducted as a Keeper. In the fifty years since that fateful day, I've never heard Jarryca speak as she does about this woman.* Hadukin had been drafted to search the ruined Temple for survivors. He was then the same age as Marrida is now. *It was just after my own Second Rites.* Jarryca was one of the few survivors he found that day. She'd been hiding for days inside a cupboard, and he took pity on her and allowed her to stay in his home while she recovered from the injuries she'd endured during the attack on her sanctuary. *I'm still amazed she came away with only a broken arm, a massive bruise on her lower leg, and a black eye. Almost everyone else present in the Temple either died in the attack or perished soon afterwards from injuries too grave to heal. And here I am now, the only living relative of Bergas and his mother. I wonder if I was there that day to rescue Jarryca so that this day could happen.*

After her recovery, Jarryca had to change her direction in life and she became a quirky, eccentric librarian. Despite her eccentricity, though, she soon became known as a skilled librarian, and she taught skills such as histories, science, art, reading and counting to children. However Hadukin, and later Emelyse, knew who she really was and where she came from.

I won't ever tell another person this information, Hadukin thinks. *But it's strange that she's inducting Marrida as a Keeper. Were they not the ones who attacked her Temple so long ago?* Jarryca was able to show him the events at the Temple, which has caused him confusion to this very day. *As a Caller, how could she show me something from the past? She used a gem like the one she put around Marrida's neck.*

Hadukin glances at Jarryca questioningly as she walks past him, and when she turns and looks at the trio, he frowns and nods towards Marrida. Jarryca either doesn't see his questioning look or chooses to ignore it, so Hadukin decides instead to concentrate on the role he's performing. From his pocket, he takes a white cord, then he raises Marrida's left hand to chest height and ties the cord around her wrist, wrapping it round twice. He glances towards Jarryca hastily and she nods slightly, indicating the action is correct. Hadukin then watches from the corner of his eye as Emelyse removes a bright red cord from her pocket and ties it to Marrida's right wrist.

Jarryca walks slowly to their end of the table, and as she does so, she extinguishes each ember except for the last one. A murmuring sound comes from her in an unfamiliar dialect. Glancing at Marrida, Hadukin notices that she recognises the words the old woman is chanting.

On arriving at the end of the table, Jarryca hands Marrida a small oval-shaped spoon which she has used to extinguish the first six embers, and watches as Marrida lowers it over the final ember, taking her time to extinguish it. After this, Jarryca moves around the trio until she's standing behind Marrida. She turns the woman clockwise until Marrida is facing her, then takes hold of each cord. In a single motion, she loosens them, letting them drop on the floor. Neither she nor the others attempt to pick the cords up off the floor.

Jarryca lifts the cloth from Marrida's head and looks for several minutes at the woman's face. Marrida has stopped crying, but the evidence of her tears is still visible in the matting together of her eyelashes and the slight streaks trailing her face.

"When I step aside, you will leave this building as a woman," Jarryca says, slowly and deliberately. "When you enter the world outside, you will accept the responsibilities that come with being in the world. When you step into the world, you will become the person everyone expects you to be: responsible, caring, truthful, honourable and helping. Those who were present for your Second Rites will guide you for the first fifteen days as you learn the new responsibilities. After that time has passed, you can call yourself a woman."

By instinct, Marrida knows the words Jarryca is speaking. They're the First Words of Acceptance: the words which not only declare a girl to be a full adult, but also declare her to be a Keeper. The simplicity of the ceremony is designed to give powerful meaning to the words.

I am a Keeper of Truth now.

She sees Jarryca step aside to the left to stand behind Hadukin, as tradition dictates.

I cannot be seen by the male participant as a Keeper, and the motion is symbolic to ensure that from this moment, my vocation is forever hidden from his view. Although in practice, Marrida realises Hadukin would have known she was an Acolyte, and therefore must know she is now a Keeper.

There's a slight hesitation in her step as Marrida moves forward. *I wonder about Elder Sharriba. Would she approve of me having been initiated into adulthood by someone like Jarryca? Would she approve of me being made a Keeper by a Caller?* Jarryca notices the hesitation but says nothing.

For a moment, Marrida panics, wondering if it were Keepers from Ruh'nar under the guidance of the previous Elder – a woman named Kyrana – who were responsible for the destruction of Jarryca's Temple. But she pushes the thought aside and steps forward. On reaching the front door, Marrida glances back towards the table where the three older people are still standing in their respective positions, none of them speaking or moving.

Marrida undoes the bolts on the door and steps outside. The brightness of the daylight unsettles her for a few moments. Realising her gem is still hanging visibly around her neck, she quickly tucks it under her tunic, glancing around for anyone who may have seen it. The street is totally empty.

She walks slowly away from the house, taking the same route as she and Emelyse took earlier. In Ruh'nar, after the ceremony, she'd take her symbolic walk home to start the fifteen days of guidance there, only returning to the Temple on the last day. Her journey back to Emelyse's house is symbolic in much the same way.

She glances back momentarily and sees she's alone. The journey home is the first responsibility a person who has just finished their Second Rites ceremony faces. Emelyse will wait until she's sure Marrida has finished her journey before setting off for home herself.

The whole ceremony was as the walk home is – short, simple, and to the point.

CHAPTER SIXTY

Bᴇʀɢᴀs ɪs sɪᴛᴛɪɴɢ ᴏɴ ᴛʜᴇ ᴘᴏʀᴄʜ ʀᴇᴀᴅɪɴɢ ᴀ ʙᴏᴏᴋ when he sees Marrida approaching. He waves at her, and Marrida waves back.

She looks happier now, he muses.

When Marrida steps onto the porch, Bergas rushes over to give her a hug.
"How did it go?"
"How did you know about it?" Marrida counters, smiling widely.

Bergas looks down for a moment and shuffles his feet. "I looked at the note from Mam," he confesses after some hesitation. Marrida rubs her hand through Bergas's reddish-brown hair, which is already becoming lighter in the springtime sun. "Are you hungry? I made some stew so Mam doesn't need to do it when she gets home. Where is she, by the way?" Bergas looks at the road beyond Marrida as he asks this but sees no one walking along it.
"She needs to wait until I'm home."
"Why?"
"Because we did my Seconds Rites as we do it in Ruh'nar." Now Marrida looks around, examining her surroundings thoroughly. "I guess Alagur hasn't arrived yet?" she comments dreamily.
"I can go up into the hills and see if he's there, if you want."
"You can if you wish."
The moment Bergas hears that, he rushes off up the hill. Marrida stands watching him for several moments, then she walks into the house. He said there's stew, and she is very hungry indeed.

Once she's inside the house, Marrida takes off her coat and hangs it on the hook to her right. She feels the bulge under her tunic, and for a moment considers whether to put the gem back into the pocket of her haversack where she usually keeps it.

I wonder how Emelyse knew where the gem was. I guess she probably knows a lot more than she ever lets on.

Marrida smiles, realising she does in fact regard the woman as a surrogate mother. In some ways, Emelyse reminds her of her own mother, Eshara.

Marrida walks into the cooking room. Using a thick woollen cloth, she lifts the lid from the cooking pot which is hanging over the fire. She inhales deeply and savours the aromas coming from the food.

Bergas is as good at cooking as Kalisa; it smells delicious.

Marrida puts the lid on the top of the cutting table to the left of the fireplace and walks to the cabinet on the opposite side of the cooking room to retrieve one of the deep bowls from the middle shelf. She walks back to the cooking pot and, using the ladle to the right of it, scoops herself three helpings of the steaming stew. After placing the dish on the table, she walks back to the cooking pot and replaces the lid. Marrida then sits down and once more inhales the aromas. She can feel her tummy rumbling, so she picks up one of the spoons lying on the table and starts to eat.

While she eats, she tries to work out how long Alagur has been away. He said the outbound journey should take seven days and the return will take only five because he'll be riding on Yalla. Three more days and he should be back. The thought of seeing the beautiful wolf brings another smile to the woman's face, which becomes gloriously broad when she thinks about Alagur.

She hears the front door open and a disappointed Bergas walks into the cooking room, panting loudly.
"I didn't see him anywhere. Perhaps he'll be here tomorrow."
"Perhaps." Marrida smiles at the boy. "And by the way, this stew is delicious."
"I'm glad you like it. I hope Mam likes it too."
They both glance up expectantly when they hear the front door open and close a moment later. Marrida's shoulders slump when she sees the new arrival is Emelyse, not Alagur.

Bergas rushes to his mother and hugs her. "Do you want some of my stew, Mam?" the boy enquires, smiling in delight.
"Yes, sure, when did you make it?"
Bergas rushes off to get a bowl and brings it to the cutting table next to the fireplace. He carefully removes the lid from the cooking pot and ladles two scoops of the mixture of meat, vegetables and grains into the bowl, then he brings it to his mother. Emelyse sits down opposite Marrida.

"It's delicious," Marrida says in between mouthfuls of the meal. Emelyse nods. Both women eat in silence, while Bergas makes a point of rushing outside every five minutes or so. When he rushes back into the cooking room, Emelyse frowns and stares at him.

"Why do you keep rushing outside like that?"

"To see if Alagur is home yet. She wants to know."

Bergas smiles broadly at his mother and points at Marrida. Marrida blushes at the remark, which brings a knowing smile to Emelyse's face. She attempts to hide it by placing more food in her mouth, but she's curious to know how the younger woman will react once the man is back.

It will be telling if he returns early. His timing will show how he really feels about her.

Once Marrida has finished eating, Bergas rushes in and takes her bowl from her, making a point of washing it. He then sits on the stool at the end of the table and waits there until his mother has also finished eating, cleaning her bowl too, along with the utensils and work surfaces he used for food preparation.

Emelyse walks to the cooking pot and looks inside it. "Why did you make so much?" she asks.

"I made enough for two days," Bergas replies. "And enough for Alagur and his wolf if they arrive today or tomorrow."

"Why for the wolf?"

"Because the wolf is special."

"In what way?"

"Because--"

Bergas doesn't really know why he made enough to feed the wolf.

"Well?" Emelyse says sharply.

"I think he means to say the wolf is another who helped him to return home," Marrida interjects, seeing the boy struggling to give a reason for his love for Yalla. "When you see the wolf and how she is towards everyone, you'll know why she's special enough to get cooked food too."

Emelyse looks at Marrida. "Have you been with the wolf much?"

"Yes. Alagur and I did most of our journey on her back, as it happens. Her name is Yalla."

Bergas looks at Marrida with grateful eyes.

"I drew pictures of Yalla, Mam. Do you want to see them?"

"Of course. Bring them to me," Emelyse replies, smiling at her son. She can't stay angry with him for long.

"Emelyse, Alagur told me about when he helped Bergas leave," Marrida says softly to the older woman. "The wolves the Wolf Riders use have a specific wolf song to alert the other wolves to an unauthorised departure. Yalla never used this specific wolf song, which showed her loyalty towards Bergas. Alagur also thinks that during our journey, the wolf sensed Bergas ahead of us at times. She made Alagur aware that someone was there, but again, she never sang the wolf song that would alert the Wolf Riders."

Emelyse listens attentively to the other woman's words, which explain a lot. She recalls Bergas waking up one night – perhaps three days after his return – screaming and thrashing about. He explained he'd been dreaming of a wolf – the wolf he'd needed to rid himself of. With a face wet with tears, he told his mother how Alagur had told him to kill the wolf before he arrived home. The man said he mustn't get home as a Wolf Rider.

Emelyse is starting to understand that the ties between a Wolf Rider and his wolf are greater than she realised.

"What happens if Yalla is no longer alive?" she asks Marrida in an urgent whisper. "What will happen to Alagur if his bond with his wolf is broken?"

"I don't know--"

Both stop talking when they hear footsteps coming closer, and they smile encouragingly at Bergas when he steps into the cooking room holding four pieces of parchment.

"Let's sit down in the front room by the large window," Emelyse says.

In single file, they walk from the cooking room to the front room, with Bergas in the lead, followed closely by Marrida. Emelyse follows them after making sure the lid is firmly back on the cooking pot.

In the front room, a narrow table and bench sit under the large window, where Bergas often reads or draws. It's also the place where he's been watching the landscape for signs of Alagur ever since the man departed. The three individuals sit down and automatically look at the downward slope leading away from the house in case Alagur happens to come into view. When he doesn't, they turn their attention to the drawings which Bergas has fetched.

He first places in front of the women a drawing of a wolf lying down with her head between her paws. The wolf's eyes are so lifelike, it almost seems as if she'll jump from the parchment into their midst. The next drawing is of Yalla's face, which makes Marrida smile because it shows the wolf grin that appears whenever something pleases her, such as a good scratching over her ears, or a rubbing of her neck fur. Marrida has seen this expression often enough on Yalla's face to recognise it, and it speaks volumes about how much time the boy spent with the animal while he resided in City of Wolves. The next image Bergas shows is an impression of how Yalla might look with her pack. It fits the description Alagur gave of when he went to get Yalla as his personal riding wolf, so both women guess the boy used his retelling for inspiration.

The last image makes Marrida go as pale as moss ash and fills her mind with shock. Even Emelyse blanches. It depicts Alagur, drawn so accurately that his features are instantly recognisable, sitting on top of Yalla. The wolf is standing at the top of a greyish-black rock. Next to Yalla, another wolf sits on its hind legs, looking straight at them. The wolf has a mixture of greyish-brown and dark grey stripes, which Emelyse recognises as being typical of the wolves living in the Upper Plains. But the most striking part of the image is the depiction of Marrida. She's kneeling on the ground in front of Alagur, Yalla, and the other wolf. Marrida sees immediately the position her hands are in, and that her eyes are depicted as two black shapes. Then she sees the floating image Yalla seems to be looking at. In the picture, Alagur is looking at it too.

How does the boy know what it looks like when a Keeper does a vision?

Both Marrida and Emelyse stare at Bergas, who starts to squirm under their scrutiny. After looking down with growing shyness for a minute, he looks up at them directly.

"If you want to know, I dreamt that image a few nights ago," he says in a placid, almost emotionless tone of voice.

"I think you experienced an Awakening." Emelyse frowns for a moment, then glances at Marrida.

"Is this something from the future?" Marrida's voice rises a few pitches above its normal level.

"Yes," Emelyse replies. "And do you remember telling me about the dream you experienced of what looked like people in a cave?"

Marrida nods.

"I think it was your Awakening. Just as my son may be a Caller like me, you may have inherited your great-grandmother's skill of seeing the future as well as the past. It means in another time, you would have been a Preserver--"

Suddenly something Marrida read in Sharriba's journal makes sense. *Preservers are the balance between past and future.* Marrida stares blankly out of the window, thinking.

With Elder Sharriba being a Keeper and Jarryca being a Caller, could it mean that my interaction with both has unlocked this skill in me? Am I in fact a Preserver of Truth? Let's think here. If I did see the future, then what future was it I saw, and where? My great-grandmother saw the future, and she apparently saw me in it. So, my vision of the cave is the future. And I saw Jarryca, too, but I thought she was my maternal grandmother, until I met her. So, how does all this tie together? And when will what Bergas has drawn happen?

Marrida is so absorbed in her thoughts, she doesn't notice Bergas frantically nudging his mother and pointing to the north-east. Emelyse places her finger over her lips, motioning to Bergas to come with her. They get up quietly, tiptoe to the front door, and Emelyse opens it, making as little noise as possible.

Once outside, Emelyse walks to the end of the porch and places her finger over her lips again the moment Alagur notices her. He frowns for a moment, wondering why the woman is telling him to be silent, then he sees Marrida sitting at the window. From her facial expression, he can tell she's deep in thought. He has seen that expression often enough to realise that, at this moment, the world outside her own mind doesn't exist.

He walks onto the porch and hugs Emelyse, then gives Bergas an even longer hug.

"Go inside and sit next to her," Emelyse whispers. "And look at Bergas's drawings. They'll explain why she's busy with her Keeper exercises. Once she's done, it will be a wonderful surprise for her to find you beside her. We'll sit here until it's time for us to go inside again."

Before Bergas can protest, Emelyse takes him by the arm and, with the hidden strength which comes from being a boy's mother, drags him to the furthest end of the porch. There, she pushes him down onto the seat, hissing at him to stay silent.

Alagur looks after them for a moment, then he enters the house and sits down at the table as instructed. The drawings of Yalla surprise and shock him in equal measure, but he smiles when he realises the wolf and boy were a lot closer than he ever gave them credit for.

Then he looks down at the drawing of himself, Yalla, Marrida and the second wolf with a frown, feeling a knot of worry form in his stomach. *It seems the boy has drawn an event which hasn't yet happened. What has been going on since my departure? And when did the boy draw these images? The depiction of Yalla among her own pack is uncanny in its accuracy, too.*

He glances at Marrida beside him, seeing the trance-like state dissipating gradually. He leans back so she'll have to turn her head completely to her left to see him, and waits.

Marrida reaches up to her face a moment later and shakes her head, as if to wake herself.

She must have been using the deeper form of organising thoughts. Coming out of that takes some effort.

Alagur sees Marrida glance around slowly – for a moment not seeing any of her surroundings – then she rubs her eyes and looks again. The man holds his breath.

"Alagur, you're back!" she squeals. "When did you come back?" She throws herself at the man beside her and puts her arms around his neck. He responds in kind and adds a lingering kiss on her lips.

They're locked in this embrace for several minutes, then Marrida moves away from him slightly.

"When did you come back?" she asks again.

"I arrived minutes ago. Emelyse and Bergas saw me, and they ensured I could surprise you."

Emelyse and Bergas walk back inside the house. Bergas runs to the cooking room and places four ladles of the stew into a bowl, which he carries gingerly to the front room. Alagur is sitting on the sofa near the fireplace with Marrida beside him, leaning against him.

"Where's Yalla?" Bergas asks as he places the bowl in front of the man.

"She's in the cave north-east of here," Alagur replies.

Bergas rushes out of the house.

"You need to explain to me what has happened here in my absence," Alagur mumbles between spoonfuls of the stew.

"Alagur," Marrida replies slowly, "it's looking like I may be a Preserver."

CHAPTER SIXTY-ONE

Aʟᴀɢᴜʀ ꜱʜᴀᴋᴇꜱ ʜɪꜱ ʜᴇᴀᴅ ɪɴ ᴅɪꜱʙᴇʟɪᴇꜰ.

"But why do you think you're a Preserver, Marrida? And how?"

"There are two things pointing to this conclusion," Emelyse explains placidly. "Marrida joined the Temple of Ruh'nar, where she was inducted into the Order of Truth to train as a Keeper. She told us about her great-grandmother telling her uncle about a future, which included Marrida. The words she used to him were 'A daughter who will not be your own'. Is that right, Marrida?"

Marrida nods.

"She foresaw Marrida's birth. According to what Marrida explained to me, she also saw past events, so it's clear she was a Preserver. And she kept this secret from everyone around her.

"When Marrida was born, her mother insisted that Sharriba take her in when something happened to her. I have just realised the significance of the fact that in your retelling, your mother always said 'when' and never 'if' or 'perhaps', Marrida. It puzzled me for a long time."

"How is it significant?" Alagur feels a knot of worry forming in his stomach.

"I think Marrida's father was a latent Caller," Emelyse concludes. "And therefore, it may not have been chance he asked your mother to be his life partner, Marrida."

"Why?"

"Because of all that happened. Explain to me again, in minute detail, what your uncle was told by his grandmother, and when."

Marrida thinks pensively for several minutes. She closes her eyes to access as much information as she can reach in her stored memories, then opens her eyes once more and speaks.

"He said he was there when my great-grandmother did her vision. It seemed to show me as a young adult, because Uncle Joharan told me I now look exactly as I was in the vision. He said to me he became distant towards me to protect me; he didn't want anyone to realise he already knew my destiny." She pauses and sighs deeply before continuing. "Apparently, Sharriba too was fully aware of my skill, but she made it appear as if she regarded me as just another potential Temple Maiden when she came to Joharan's house to do the Test."

"Do you actually know what the Test is?" Emelyse asks.

Marrida shakes her head. It's something that Elder Sharriba has never explained to her. Emelyse is clearly going to tell her another of the many secrets of the Order that she probably won't like, but she forces herself to listen anyway.

"It started being used seven hundred years ago when the Order fractured. At this time, all the Preservers began to disappear. Some say a few of them managed to leave the Order and start their own Order somewhere else, but no one knows where, or even if it's true or not. What Jarryca told me was that the Preservers were regarded as a threat by those who wanted to block the world from knowing about the end of the Wolf Riders. She said to me the Preservers understood how to interpret events of the past, and they could take events shown by Callers and help shape the world towards peace. But to this day, some in the east do not want peace, which is why it's dangerous to be a Preserver now.

"Then Jarryca told me there were some in the west who wanted the world to be blind to the way the future could be shaped, so the Keepers started to go after the Callers--"

Emelyse stops again and stares for a while into the fireplace. No one speaks, allowing the woman time to gather her thoughts.

"The Temple here was run by the last Callers to conduct their vocation openly. When the Keepers came, they took with them the writings and books which foretold the end of the Wolf Riders and made them Forbidden Knowledge. I think your Elder Sharriba came across those writings and recorded them in her private journal."

"She seems to have done visions too--"

"Yes, and I'm sure Kyrana will have punished her heavily for it."

Marrida stares at the woman. *How does Emelyse know about Kyrana? I've never mentioned that Elder's name to her.*

"Don't be surprised. I heard about Kyrana from Jarryca." Emelyse breathes deeply to regain her composure. "Jarryca visited the Temple of Ruh'nar when she was twenty-six and she was there for nearly four years. She told me the rest of her retelling — and the rest of the history of the Temple of Azaquina — before I came back home today, which is why I took so long to get here."

She smiles at Bergas to say sorry, then continues.

"How old is Elder Sharriba now?"

"She's seventy-six now. No, almost seventy-seven," Marrida answers.

"So when Jarryca arrived in Ruh'nar, Sharriba was around four. Too young to have known about the altercation which occurred between Kyrana and Jarryca one evening — around a month before Jarryca was banished from the Temple."

"Banished?" Marrida splutters.

"Yes. Didn't you know that in the time of Kyrana, you could get banished from the Temple?"

Marrida shakes her head.

"It happened to Jarryca, which is why she travelled here. From something Jarryca heard perhaps twenty-five years later, it seems it almost happened to Sharriba too, although Jarryca could never find out exactly what happened."

Marrida frowns. She thinks about the vision she did of Sharriba together with an older woman, where Sharriba was extremely upset.

I had assumed up to now that she'd been chastised for suggesting that her Elder should heed the warning her vision of Wolf Riders gave. Now, in the context of Emelyse's information about Callers and Preservers, it's starting to make more sense. What if Sharriba, too, is either a Caller or a Preserver, and Kyrana somehow discovered it? And what if Kyrana was a less benevolent Keeper than Sharriba has always striven to be? Could it be that the things Kyrana did are the reason Sharriba behaves as she does as an Elder?

"How was Jarryca banished?"

Emelyse thinks for a few minutes. "She said to me something happened during an attack by the Wolf Riders which caused her to do a vision. In it, she saw a man being injured in the street. She said to Kyrana that the man she saw would learn to be a Caller. Kyrana wasn't too impressed to find out she had a Caller at her Temple, so she banished Jarryca."

Emelyse smiles. "Jarryca saw you in the vision, Alagur. She has known for many years that one day she'd meet the two of you in person. She said it's good that, for the first time in many centuries, a man is being taught the vocation too. She knew you were a Preserver to all intents and purposes, Marrida, rather than the Keeper you were trained to be, the moment you walked into the library for the first time."

Marrida and Alagur look at one another, then at Emelyse, then back at each other.

"Doesn't The Truth say that he will learn her skill? And she his? And no, don't look accusingly at my son. He has never told me of the legend the Wolf Riders tell one another – the legend actually being the words of the last Elder to be a Preserver." Emelyse pauses, then continues. "But I was going to tell you how Jarryca got banished. It happened because she challenged Kyrana about the lack of a Second Elder. When Jarryca arrived at the Temple here, she rose quickly through the ranks, and perhaps in Ruh'nar she could have become the Elder instead of Sharriba. But she was exposed as a Caller, who were much maligned by then, and the warning from her vision was the last thing she told Kyrana before she was marched from the building and out of the city by soldiers. Yes, Kyrana let men inside the building."

"*Second* Elder?" Marrida asks, her eyes widening in disbelief. Everything the older woman is relating sounds more like a fictional retelling told by entertainers than actual events.

"The last time there was a Second Elder in Ruh'nar was about seven hundred years ago, and that's when the fracturing started, caused by events in Roha'dea. Or Masharea, as you know it. The last Preserver to be an Elder in her own right uttered the words known as The Truth, and because of this, Keepers started to destroy the Order as it should truly exist. Jarryca is convinced there should be three Elders for true balance. Also, Jarryca says to remember these words: 'stolen truth'. She didn't say what they mean, but she says they are important and will help guide you to the truth about the fracturing."

Emelyse pauses for a moment and sees Marrida nod, then close her eyes to add the information to her stored memory. The older woman is amazed when Alagur copies the action.

"For three thousand years, the ability to do visions has existed, but only in the last seven hundred years have they been done with the Stone of Truth. Some say the Test was created to prevent entry by Callers or Preservers into the Order, and its orchestrator was Kyrana. And that she followed the example of one who lived in a distant past."

Emelyse stops talking abruptly, uncertain how much to explain.

"The Stone of Truth originated from a cave in the east. Its discovery wasn't by anyone with power, but by those who lusted for the power it offered them."

"Is it the cave you mentioned to me that Emelyse is talking about?"

"Yes, Alagur, the cave where a young girl obtained the Stone by thievery to tap into the skill we possess."

"Did Sharriba ever tell you anything about the Books of Forbidden Knowledge?"

"She let me read them."

"But do you know how old they are, and where they are from? Jarryca told me this. She said they originated two thousand years ago."

"Sharriba never told me anything about their origins, or how old they are."

"You need to seek out more of these books when you go east. I can't tell you where to find them because I never travelled around the city much. My mother even kept its name from me, saying that if I were to mention it here, the mere name would endanger my life. I've told you all that either Jarryca or I can tell you, Marrida, but Jarryca wants you to spend as much time as possible studying in the library before you leave."

Marrida nods. She has learnt so much in the conversations she has had with both Emelyse and Jarryca, and it's causing her head to spin. She needs time to digest everything.

"I need some time — alone. Can you tell me where Yalla is, so I can go and greet her?" she asks Alagur.

"She's in a cave north-east of here. Let Bergas show you the way." Alagur understands why the woman needs time alone; he's having a hard time digesting the information too.

Marrida gets up, and so does Bergas. They walk to the front door, and Alagur and Emelyse listen as their footsteps diminish. After several minutes, one pair of footsteps becomes louder again, and Bergas walks back into the room alone. He sits down next to his mother.

"I think she's crying. She tried to make sure I didn't notice."

Hearing that, Alagur bites his lip. He hoped his return would be more festive, and his eyes are now stinging because of the sorrow he feels for what Marrida is going through. *She loved her life as a Keeper, and the recent revelations, though necessary, have thrown everything she believed into disarray.* He wonders how he can help her but realises the best help will come from a wolf. Yalla will listen without casting any judgements on her.

Alagur is so deep in thought, he doesn't notice the woman opposite him observing him. Neither does he see the sympathy on Bergas's face as the boy realises that Alagur is suffering as much from the revelations as Marrida. Bergas looks up at his mother, and she smiles at him for a moment, but the emotion of the retelling has been hard on her, too. He can see her eyes glistening. Bergas now understands why she was so secretive about her origins, and he vows to keep everything she has told him safe.

Emelyse feels the emotion of the moment starting to affect her. She wants to take Marrida in her arms as a daughter and reassure her that everything will be alright, but she realises why Jarryca was so insistent that once she was home, she must tell Marrida everything. During Marrida's fifteen days, she must learn her responsibilities. And the greatest responsibility of all is the knowledge of who and what the Order of Truth is.

Jarryca said it's important to let things develop by themselves, because in the end, the knowledge will help Marrida with some of the most difficult choices she'll have to make in her entire life.

Emelyse looks again at Alagur. His greatest tests are yet to come. He could lose the woman he loves because of the Wolf Riders. He could also lose her because of what some in the Order of Truth will do to keep themselves safe. When Emelyse told Jarryca about the vision Marrida spoke of, in which she saw a darkened cave with a white stone slab, Jarryca turned as white as moss ash and clasped her chest but refused to say what had upset her so.

And then there is the chance Marrida will need to choose between her feelings for Alagur and the Order she loves so much. But after today's revelations, will she still love the Order? Emelyse stares at the fire. *How can one woman who is barely a woman and a man with a past which most would hate change the world?*

* * *

MARRIDA SEES THE CAVE BERGAS DESCRIBED TO HER. As she approaches, she looks for signs of the wolf. She can hear Yalla grunting as if she's in a playful mood, perhaps enjoying the warmth of the sun.

"Yalla, Yalla," she calls out, then she waits. The grunting stops. "Yalla." Marrida sees movement to her right, and moments later she feels a raspy, wet tongue lick her face. The distinct sound of Yalla's tail wagging breaks the silence of the landscape around her.

"Did you miss me?" Marrida scratches the wolf's head as she did so often during the early part of the journey. She then looks around and sees a flattened piece of rock. She walks towards it, closely followed by the wolf, then stops for a moment, trying to figure out how to get on top of the rock. When she sees a small footpath, she ascends with Yalla following. From the top, she can see over much of the landscape. It's breathtakingly beautiful. She's sure Bergas must have spent many hours in these hills.

The woman kicks her shoes off to her left and sits down, letting her legs hang over the edge of the rock, swinging them back and forth in turn like a child. Hearing a thump, she glances sideways and sees the wolf has settled herself close by. When Marrida looks at Yalla, the animal instinctively lifts her head and looks back, her yellow eyes filled with wisdom. It makes the woman smile.

"You seem to have no care in the world," she says to the wolf.

But deep in her heart, Marrida knows this isn't true. There was a time when this animal was marked as an enemy, and a stone was thrown at her which injured her seriously. A small lump still remains where the stone struck Yalla three seasons earlier.

Marrida looks around, wondering if these mountains on the east side of Azaquina have a name. She's sure Emelyse mentioned a name, but she is having a hard time remembering it now. Her thoughts then turn to her ceremony of womanhood.

"When you enter the world outside, you accept the responsibilities that come with being in the world."

She does have responsibilities. She has known it from the day she left the Temple of Ruh'nar.

CHAPTER SIXTY-TWO

Marrida wakes up suddenly and tries to look around her. It's as black as pitch. She moves her hand around to determine where she's lying and feels penetrating coldness below her. How did she get to her current location? Her head is still spinning from the vivid dreams that were whirling through her mind until she woke up.

One hand finds the thick fur of the wolf, who has stayed with her all afternoon and evening, keeping guard as she slept. Marrida realises she's lying in a ball on the ground, and Yalla has settled herself around her to keep her as warm as possible, like the wolf might have done with her pups.

"Thank you, Yalla."

After some searching, Marrida finds the boots she kicked off earlier and puts them on. Her feet are icy cold, and the dampness of her clothing causes her teeth to chatter.

Why is it so dark, and why does it have to be so cold?

Marrida glances around in all directions, once more trying to make sense of the darkened surroundings, and realises she likely fell asleep at the top of the hill after watching the sun set and the moon rise.

Why has no one come to find me?

She gets herself into an upright position and feels momentarily dizzy. Lack of food must be the cause of this – she hasn't eaten anything since midday. As she tries to get up, the wolf rises ever so slightly to make sure that she is alright.

It takes perhaps fifteen minutes before Marrida can stand up, and she notices how Yalla instantly steps in front of her. The wolf realise that, somewhere in the pitch darkness ahead of her, is a drop of thirty or so paces – an elevation that gave Marrida such a fine view of the landscape earlier.

Marrida reaches out for the wolf and finds powerful neck muscles under her hand a moment later. "Do you think I can get on top of you on my own, Yalla? Will you let me climb on you?"

She leans forward and attempts to reach her right leg over the back of the wolf, but she isn't tall enough to climb up unaided. Yalla senses what the woman wants to do and lowers herself down to the ground. Once Yalla is lying down, Marrida swings her leg over the body of the animal, and when Yalla lifts herself off the ground, Marrida leans forward and holds her neck for support. She's on top of Yalla without any harness, and without Alagur for support, and she feels momentarily terrified.

Marrida can feel her heart beating hard inside her chest, the beating accompanied by the life-giving pulse in the side of her neck. She holds on too tightly to the hair on Yalla's neck, the wolf's occasional yelps telling her that it hurts.

"Do you think you can find where the house is?" Marrida says to Yalla. "Find Alagur for me. Find Alagur." She feels Yalla's head rise and hears a faint snorting sound come from the beast. "Find Alagur. Go to Alagur for me."

The wolf, sensing her current rider isn't as proficient as her master, starts at a slow pace down the side of the hill. A low-hanging branch hits Marrida in the face.

"Ow! Watch out, Yalla, please."

Yalla moves to the right, and the leaves and tree branches that were scraping and hitting Marrida's face and upper body thin out. After a while, they disappear completely. Marrida guesses that they're walking over the large meadow that she crossed before reaching the wolf. The ground under them levels out, and this allows Marrida to sit more upright. She looks up to check if she can see any stars or the moon, but the sky is covered with a thick layer of clouds. Looking around herself once more, she sees some lights in the distance to her right, guessing that they are embers lighting up the streets of the city below.

She feels the wolf slow and stop.

"Go on, get to Alagur," Marrida urges. Yalla starts to walk again, and Marrida guesses that the experience of carrying someone other than her master is a bit confusing for her.

She sees a faint light ahead of her, and as if by a hidden command, the wolf increases her speed. Soon Yalla is running fast, but she curbs her speed a little. After about ten minutes, the wolf slows, and Marrida almost slides off in panic when Yalla calls out a wolf song.

The sound of several running footsteps comes from within the house in front of them, and a moment later, the front door flies open.

"Marrida!" Alagur calls out. "You're back!"

"And she's not alone," Bergas points out. "Mam, that's Yalla."

Emelyse stands in awe of the wolf who is unhurriedly pacing onto the porch. She's so great in size that there are only two arms' lengths between Marrida's head and the ceiling of the porch. The wolf looks at Emelyse curiously, smelling the familiarity of her scent because of her relationship to Bergas. Bergas at once approaches the wolf and wraps his arms around her neck. Alagur notices the similarity between Bergas's action, and those of Kalisa three seasons earlier.

Emelyse has to admit that the beast is majestic, immensely beautiful and, from how Yalla reacts to both man and boy, more loyal than most people. She now understands fully why her son wanted to give some of the stew to Yalla.

"If you get off Yalla and we all go inside, she can come and lie in the front room with us." Emelyse's statement makes the younger individuals smile gratefully. "We need to get Marrida inside, because she looks like she has caught the mountain chill up there."

It soon becomes apparent that the front room furniture will need rearranging to allow the wolf to enter. Yalla is much larger than Emelyse imagined, and the room looks somewhat smaller than usual in comparison. While Alagur and Bergas set to the task of making space in the room, Marrida dismounts and introduces the wolf to Emelyse in the same way that Kalisa once introduced her to Damir. However, whereas Damir was fearful initially, Emelyse seems to feel comfortable around the animal, and she's soon scratching Yalla everywhere that brings snorts of pleasure from the wolf.

Emelyse goes into the house when she sees Marrida rubbing her arms, and brings out a warm woollen blanket, which she drapes around the other woman's shoulders. Marrida pulls the blanket closely around her and smiles gratefully.

Bergas appears at the front door. "I think Yalla can lie down in the front room now, Mam."

"I'll whistle from inside, so she knows where to go," Alagur adds, turning and walking back to the front room. A moment later, he gives a sharp whistle, then another. Yalla gradually moves forward, but hesitates on the threshold. After a minute or so, she continues walking and steps through the front door, sniffing the air. Alagur's whistle comes again and the wolf walks further into the house, turns right and enters the front room. The two women follow step by step as Yalla walks towards the man, who's crouching down next to a thick leather blanket that Emelyse doesn't recognise.

A moment later, Emelyse realises she hasn't shut the front door. She's about to go and do it when she hears the distinct sound of bolts being drawn. A moment later, Bergas is at her side, leaning against her hip.

"Why don't you find a large container of some sort to put the stew in that you promised Yalla?" Emelyse looks at the boy next to her and sees a grateful smile on his face.

Bergas rushes off to the workshop where there's an old trough that his father used for feeding the few mountain sheep he and Emelyse possessed when Bergas was very young. It's a cumbersome item to handle, but Bergas is sure Yalla will appreciate it.

Emelyse's eyes fly open in surprise about five minutes later when Bergas walks back into the front room carrying the trough under his arm. The container is so unwieldy that the boy almost has to walk sideways like an elderly man who has lost his walking stick. She steps aside to let the boy pass. Once Bergas is in the room, the much stronger Alagur takes the trough from him and places it to the left of the wolf, who immediately smells the air.

The man signals to the wolf, and she gets up off the leather blanket and paces the short distance to where the food is served. It's not so much pacing as turning in a circle, like she does before settling down to sleep. Emelyse cringes when the wolf's tail almost hits a large pot standing against the wall. Bergas notices and drags the pot out of the way.

Emelyse smiles at her son and mouths, "Thank you". The pot is one of the only items of Jerid's that Emelyse still possesses.

"Where did you go?" Alagur's voice indicates that he's been worrying about Marrida all evening, but every time he suggested he should go and look for her, Emelyse said he should wait.

"I needed time to think and process all the things I have learnt," Marrida answers. "I'm alright now. The information still disturbs me, but

I'm prepared for what I may find out during the rest of our journey." She smiles at Alagur; it's the warm, happy smile he has grown to love. "Tomorrow, I'm going to the library again," she continues. "Emelyse said something about us leaving in three weeks' time. Is there a reason why?"

"It's the earliest time in the year that the mountain pass leading east will be accessible," Emelyse explains. "Alagur said Yalla can travel a lot faster than I could. And my journey took so long because I stopped at each watchtower. If you only stop at the fourth watchtower along the route, you can be at your destination in a fraction of the time."

"What's so special about the fourth watchtower?" Alagur frowns as he asks.

"I'll leave that for the two of you to discover." Emelyse looks at Bergas in a conspiratorial way, then states, "Bergas knows because he travelled that far with his father the summer before Jerid died."

Bergas smiles broadly as it occurs to him what he saw.

"It'll be worth your while." Bergas confirms his mother's statement without revealing what it is the man and woman will see. Alagur and Marrida look at each other, curiosity etched on their faces.

"I think we should all go to bed," Emelyse suggests. "If you're going to the library tomorrow, Marrida, it's better to do it with a fresh mind."

Marrida nods and gets up. A moment later, Alagur gets up too, signalling to the wolf to stay where she is.

"Is it alright for Yalla to sleep here?" he asks.

"Yes. Yalla can be a guardian for us until you leave. I like her a lot." Yalla thumps her tail at the mention of her name and the warmth in Emelyse's voice. "Off to bed with you, too, Bergas," Emelyse adds sternly.

Somewhat reluctantly, and with a glance which suggests he would rather sleep next to the wolf, Bergas walks the length of the house to his room. Emelyse cringes when he slams shut the door to his sleeping room harder than usual.

Marrida gives Emelyse a hug before the older woman walks to her own sleeping room. Then Marrida and Alagur are alone in the front room. Before going to bed, they decide to pay attention to the wolf who's lying on the floor, taking up a third of the available space with her legs stretched out.

"Did you truly sort out what was bothering you?" Alagur murmurs as they scratch every place they know will give Yalla pleasure.

"Yeah, I think so," Marrida replies. On seeing some doubt on Alagur's face, she adds, "I'm really sure now."

Alagur runs his hand over Marrida's cheek and looks at the woman with loving eyes. "I'm glad you're back."

"I missed you while you were gone, too," Marrida replies.

There's an awkward silence for several minutes while they pay extra attention to the wolf.

"Marrida," Alagur says eventually, "I want to ask you something."

"Yes?" Marrida mumbles, looking down at the wolf, not wanting to meet Alagur's eyes.

"I've been thinking--"

Should I really ask her this question now? Alagur chides himself for a moment, then dismisses the thought.

"I want you as a life partner," he blurts out, his face going bright red.

Silence again.

He asked me to be his life partner. He asked me! Marrida's head is spinning with emotion. *He loves me enough to want to be with me for the rest of our lives.* Her mouth is dry, she's not sure whether she can speak.

For Alagur, the wait is agonising. He imagines the woman next to him jumping up and shouting at him to leave and never come back. He even wonders for a moment if she heard what he said.

"Alagur--" Marrida begins hesitantly. "I've loved you for a long time, but--"

Oh no, here it comes. Alagur prepares himself for rejection. *I don't want that. I love her too much. I have loved her from the moment I first laid eyes on her.*

"But we need to wait until we are safe. Then we can do the ceremony. I love you too. Not at first, but then the things you said and did convinced me that it would be possible." She pauses for a moment. "Yes, I want to be your life partner very much."

Alagur feels like his heart will explode in his chest when he hears the woman's response.

She loves me! She wants to bond with me!

Alagur feels Marrida's hand stroke his lower jaw, making him look up towards her. She has glistening eyes, but there's a happy smile on her face.

"It's an hour into a new day, and today I can give you that answer myself," she says softly.

"What do you mean?"

"Yesterday, Emelyse and Jarryca — with the help of a man called Hadukin, a person Jarryca trusts a lot — did the Seconds Rites ceremony for me." Marrida reaches up and gives the man a gentle kiss on his lips before continuing. "I reached full womanhood yesterday. I can make decisions about myself in my own right, which means I can choose my life partner myself…and I choose you."

Alagur looks at her with his mouth wide open, and his expression makes her giggle.

"I always like it when I can surprise you."

Alagur's expression of surprise turns into a broad smile. "I love to be surprised by you," he replies. He leans forward and kisses the woman slowly and passionately on her lips, finding her a willing participant.

"Let's sleep," he says. "If you're going to the library tomorrow, you need your sleep." Alagur gets up, then holds out his arms to help the woman up. He then lets go of one hand and leads Marrida towards their sleeping room by the other. Once inside, he leans towards her again and kisses her once more. He decides, however, that kissing will be the extent of their passion. He respects Marrida too much to take advantage of the situation and force himself on her before she's ready. He remembers when she walked from Ribbon Lake naked, and realises it was her way of letting him know she felt the same for him as he does for her.

They lie down on the bed and Alagur stretches his arm out so Marrida can lean her head against his chest.

"Tomorrow we'll tell the others about us," she whispers, before closing her eyes and falling into a dreamless sleep.

CHAPTER SIXTY-THREE

Marrida looks out of the window at the four small fishing vessels that are slowly coming closer to the city, craning her neck to see the harbour. As the second floor of the library is at a higher elevation than most of the houses around it, the window offers her a good view of the activities in the city.

Marrida turns her head away from the window when Jarryca sits down next to her. The old woman hands her a cup, and Marrida is surprised to taste a refreshing cold beverage containing rubha apples — and something else. She looks at the old woman questioningly.

"It's made from rubha apples and the sap from a local tree," Jarryca clarifies.

"It tastes good," Marrida comments. "Is there any honey in it too?"

"No, it would spoil the flavour. The sap is collected just as winter ends, before the tree begins its spring growth. It provides all the sweetness needed."

Marrida nods and sips from the drink, which is unlike anything she has ever tasted before. She then turns her attention back to the scene in the harbour. Four men are pulling one of the boats closer to a stone wall which stands in the water.

"What are they doing there?"

Jarryca squints to see what the other woman is pointing at. On seeing the boats, she smiles.

"The fourth boat is owned by Hadukin," she answers. "They'll have travelled to the north side of the Northern Blades, several days from here. There's a cave there where a certain type of shellfish lives. They've caught it for the upcoming spring celebration."

"When is the celebration?" Marrida asks, hoping she'll not have gone on her journey by then.

"It starts in four days from now, and it lasts for two whole days."

Marrida smiles and lets out a relieved sigh: *A celebration just before Alagur and I leave will be a good omen.*

"Are you going to the celebration?" she asks the old woman.

"Yes, of course. And Hadukin will be my escort."

Marrida frowns and looks at the woman, puzzled. "Why do you need an escort?" she quizzes.

"Well, as I'm old, I don't really need one, but Hadukin likes to spoil me each year, so I make a claim on him as my escort for the festivities. Being young, you'll need an escort if you want to go."

"I need an escort? Why?"

"The only women who do not need an escort are mothers with a son who has done First Rites. This means Bergas will accompany Emelyse. But you – who will your escort be?" Jarryca smiles mischievously. "It needs to be someone who is special to you. Do you know such a person?"

Marrida and Alagur's intention to tell everyone that they have vowed to become life partners didn't go according to plan. Whenever they went to speak up, they felt uncharacteristically shy all of a sudden. As a result, two weeks later, they still haven't told Emelyse, Bergas or Jarryca.

Two days after Emelyse allowed the wolf into her house, Alagur decided the cave in the hills was perhaps a better place for Yalla, and he and Marrida accompanied her back. During the walk, they discussed the general details of where, when, and how they'd do the ceremony which would make them life partners. Their plans were perfect, except for one crucial detail – they'd not told them to anyone else. Emelyse and Bergas have been giving each other knowing looks, each suspecting something has changed between their two visitors, but neither knows for sure.

I don't even know what a ceremony to become life partners entails, Marrida thinks now. *I'm just basing my suggestions to Alagur on my idea of how it was for Mam and Papa. I hope someone will tell me.*

Marrida realised that Jarryca is suggesting Alagur should accompany her to the upcoming festivities – the city's most important celebration. The young woman blushes at the prospect. Jarryca is wise enough to realise she has discovered the young woman's feelings towards Alagur. It amuses her to see Marrida so uncommonly shy.

Jarryca smiles, and makes it appear that she hasn't noticed Marrida's embarrassment by watching the boats in the old harbour. They are now all tightly secured to the tall stone posts dotted along it. She counts the number of containers coming from each boat to determine the success of the fishermen while Marrida squirms next to her, unsure what to say to the old woman.

If I want to go, I need an escort. Is Alagur the right sort of escort?

Marrida frowns. Several times, she attempts to ask the woman next to her for advice, but every time she glances round, she sees the enigmatic woman smiling and smiling – still smiling. It seems to Marrida that Jarryca is playing with her discomfort, which is growing by the minute.

"Alagur asked me to be his life partner," she finally blurts out.

"So, you *do* have someone to escort you to the celebration, then," Jarryca replies, smiles generously.

They hear footsteps coming up the stairway at that moment, and both turn to see Alagur and Bergas arriving on the second floor. Jarryca decides to carry on with her teasing and speaks up when she sees who has arrived.

"And here comes your escort now."

Bergas guesses what the old woman is talking about and joins in the teasing.

"But I'm escorting Mam to the celebration," he says with a grin. "Who's escorting Marrida?"

As Marrida blushes all over again, Bergas looks from her to Alagur and back again. Jarryca winks at him, and Bergas's grin broadens.

Alagur wonders what's going on. He sees Marrida blushing and the boy beside him grinning – no, almost smirking.

"What you do you mean by 'escorting'? Who's being escorted, and where?" A hint of panic sets in to Alagur's mind as he wonders if something bad has happened.

Bergas starts to laugh. "I think Jarryca has found you out – both of you."

"Huh, what?" Alagur looks at Marrida again to find she's looking back at him. The moment he catches her eye, she blushes again and looks down.

"Don't worry, Alagur. I've seen so many life partners pair up in my lifetime, I can recognise when two people want to join."

"Did you tell her, Marrida?"

"Yes, kind of."

"She told me, but I'd already guessed from how she has been behaving each time you've arrived in recent days."

"But what's the stuff about an escort?" Alagur wants to know.

"It's time soon for the spring celebration," Bergas explains. "And it's traditional for a woman to go with a man she loves. Mam can go with me. She's been alone since my father died, but now I've done First Rites, I can take on the role of escorting her. You can go with Marrida because she's special to you."

Bergas smiles first at Alagur, and then at Marrida. She smiles back at him.

Jarryca's face clouds over somewhat before she speaks. "The festival takes places in four days from now, so you can attend before you leave. Marrida told me you're leaving in a week from now. I'll miss both of you a lot."

Suddenly the reality that their journey will commence soon hits both Marrida and Alagur hard. They look at each other, reading each other's emotions. They'll miss Jarryca, who has become a surrogate grandmother to both of them, and to Marrida something like an Elder too.

Jarryca gets up and walks to the table on which the large pitcher containing the cold beverage is standing. She fills two mugs and hands one each to Alagur and Bergas.
"The drink will refresh you after the walk here."

Alagur takes a large sip from the drink and is as surprised by its flavour as Marrida was. He watches as Bergas drinks down all the liquid in the mug and walks to the table to help himself to more. It's evident the boy has tasted it often before.

Alagur sits next to Marrida and looks at the harbour too. It's becoming busier by the minute as more fishing vessels arrive, and he can understand why Marrida has selected this vantage point in the library. He glances around at the houses which stand between the library and the harbour. Each house is reflecting the sunlight, and the effect makes the city appear as though someone has scattered a bag of gems on a table and brushed them around with their hand.

Marrida too looks more closely at the surroundings now she knows she'll soon be leaving them behind. Maybe it will only be for a while, but it'll more likely be for ever.

Jarryca has been teaching Marrida the Quin'zai dialect – a dialect spoken in Azaquina until nine hundred years ago – to help Marrida with her translations. There's one particular book in the library, written in that dialect, which has taught her more about the origins of the city, when it was one of the Seven Cities. Jarryca, who was as surprised as Marrida at this revelation, and she have been spending hours today searching for more information. When Jarryca clutched her chest, Marrida became concerned and suggested they rest. And it was during the resting period that Bergas and Alagur arrived.

The notebook which Marrida purchased in Alzamar is now full of the many notes she has taken from the books she has been reading, as well as notes relating to recalled visions. When Jarryca saw how full the notebook was, she offered Marrida one of her own, and the gesture earnt her an embrace from the younger woman. Jarryca felt moved by the love shown to her by Marrida.

Azaquina was established as one of the mysterious Seven Cities around fifteen hundred years ago on the ruins of an even older harbour city, according to the oldest book in the library. By Jarryca's calculations, the city originated from a time three or four hundred years after the Great Resistance started. When Marrida asked what this was, the old woman explained it was the time when those from Mycanthia established the Wolf Masters to drive the northern invaders from the lands. She also told Marrida that the last two cities to be in the hands of the northern invaders were Azaquina and the city to which Marrida and Alagur will travel next, but no one knows if that city was ever freed from their influence. The Wolf Riders took over before they could find out. Marrida has learnt that Azaquina's location was chosen because it was flanked in the west by the Northern Blades, and to the east by the Upper Plains.

Bergas has also been coming to listen to the lessons from the old woman. Like Marrida, he wants to learn more about the city he's growing up in. The old woman suggested that the bay formed itself in ancient times, before the lands were taken from the animals which had roamed their surface, and that it could have been formed when the sea breached parts of the mountain.

"If you and Bergas visit west of where the Temple once stood, Marrida, he can show you the Eye of Waves." Jarryca smiles conspiratorially towards the boy, and Bergas grins back at her on hearing the name. He knows exactly what the old woman is referring to.

Jarryca goes on to explain to Marrida and Alagur the origin of the name for the massive bay.

"In ancient times – when the mountains were one long barrier – there was a cave here. It's said the cave was connected to a river that ran past the south side of the mountains. As time went by, the river enlarged the cave, and it became so large that it could no longer support the mountains above it. The mountain collapsed, and the massive rocks eroded to become the outcrop of land that Azaquina is built on. The Bay of Whispers is all that's left of the ancient cave that once existed, and we think its name refers to the sound that echoed through that cave."

Marrida finds the history lessons with Jarryca fascinating. The old woman knows much about the earliest history of Keldarra, and Marrida suspects that the many books in this library are hundreds of years older than the oldest books in the library of the Temple of Ruh'nar. And when she looks at the role Azaquina played in the defeat of the northern invaders, the emergence of the Order of Truth, and the subsequent uprising of the Wolf Riders, and compares all this to what she has seen and knows of Ruh'nar, she starts to make sense of the decline of the cities dotted all over Keldarra. Had she lived nearly two millennia ago, she would have seen Keldarra as a flourishing nation, recovering itself towards the ancient power base it was more than three thousand years ago. That recovery was halted only because a new enemy emerged, this time from within. And the nation had been unprepared for this to happen.

Further studies have revealed that Masharea was indeed the final power base for the ancient version of the Order of Truth, but Marrida was surprised to learn that it originated in the east.

"Do you think Masharea was one of the Seven Cities?" she asked Jarryca earlier that day.

"Yes, and Ruh'nar was too, as was Chiva'na," the old woman replied. "But Masharea – or Roha'dea – was the first one."

Marrida listened to the woman with interest, learning things she'd never contemplated until now. She and Jarryca speculated about the city's name changing from Roha'dea to Masharea, working out that it came about because of the Keepers – who were the strongest within the Order. The original name has a more eastern origin, and Marrida suggested it might have been the city's name when the Order was still new.

Jarryca agreed, then surprised Marrida further by telling her that her family name – Kayrsan – almost certainly originated from the ancient days when the Seven Cities were established. Marrida made a point of storing that information away, vowing to find out more about her family's true origins.

Marrida watches over the city that once seemed imposing and alien to her. With Alagur by her side, she now feels connected with it, even if she can't explain why or how. Jarryca might have an influence on how she feels about the city, but she senses she's more likely to discover the answer when she sees her uncle again.

When the time comes to go home, Bergas makes a point of inviting Jarryca to the house. She accepts, and an hour later, she's walking slowly up the gentle slope, leaning on both Bergas and Alagur for support. Marrida walks ahead to forewarn Emelyse of the additional guest. She is now glad that Alagur insisted on returning the wolf to the cave, because she isn't entirely sure if the old woman would be able to cope with Yalla's presence. Jarryca has hinted that something isn't quite right with her health, and Marrida's medical mind is already analysing the symptoms she has noticed.

Marrida walks into the house and Emelyse comes from the cooking room to greet her. She's surprised that Marrida has returned alone, even more so when she learns Jarryca is on her way. The two women set to work to clean the house of any evidence of the wolf, but they don't have long before the trio arrives.

"It seems your boy wants me to continue retelling the past," Jarryca says to Emelyse as she enters the house. "I'm quite alright with that."

Jarryca sits at the cooking room table, looking around Emelyse's house with curious eyes. This is the first time the old woman has visited. Bergas sits next to Jarryca, and she puts her arm around the boy's shoulders and allows him to lean against her. He grew up without knowing anyone to call Grandfather or Grandmother, so Jarryca is the closest he has to a grandparent.

"So, what is it you want me to tell you about, Bergas?" Jarryca asks gently.

CHAPTER SIXTY-FOUR

A WONDERFUL AROMA GREETS MARRIDA as she enters the cooking room. She woke early, feeling excited at the prospect of the upcoming spring celebration which is due to commence later in the day.

Leaning over the cooking pot, Marrida glances over her shoulder as Emelyse arrives back in the cooking room with four baskets.

"You can taste it, if you want," Emelyse says.

Marrida rushes towards Emelyse to assist with carrying the baskets. She almost feels like a ten-year-old again as she watches Emelyse retrieve a small bowl from a shelf and ladle a spoonful of the thick liquid into it. Marrida sits down with the bowl, then takes the spoon Emelyse is holding out to her.

Emelyse smiles at Marrida's eagerness. "Before you try it, dip some of this bread into the liquid. It brings out the flavour."

Marrida takes the dark-coloured bread from the older woman. It's still slightly warm, and she can tell it was baked recently. Its texture is like no other bread Marrida has eaten before, and the aroma rising from the slice is of winter berries and something citrusy.

She dips the bread into the liquid until it's almost entirely covered. The mixture in her bowl has a much thicker consistency than she expected. Marrida places the bread in her mouth, and her expression becomes one of wonder. It reminds her of the berry and honey mixture she loved so much while she was still at home.

"It tastes so good," Marrida blurts out, forgetting for a moment it's bad manners to speak with food in her mouth.

Emelyse smiles. "It's something we eat at the celebration," she explains. "Every family brings a cooking pot, together with ten or twelve loaves of bread, to the festivities."

Marrida decides that if this is a taste of the good food that will be served at the festival, celebrating the coming of spring with those she has grown to love will be even more enjoyable than she'd anticipated.

Alagur has been carrying his and Marrida's belongings to Yalla's cave, together with their haversacks and three carrying bags he has constructed with Bergas. The sound of stomping feet announces they have arrived back down from the mountain. In the last three days, they've been coming back with snow clinging to their boots. Winter hasn't yet completely relinquished its grip on the higher reaches of the eastern mountain range where Alagur and Marrida will soon be travelling.

Marrida, who is from southern climes, would have preferred to wait another month before setting off, but Emelyse explained that the later they leave their departure, the more likely it is that they'll be caught out by hot weather. In the cooler spring and early summer weather, travelling will be far easier.

"I think we have everything ready now," Alagur says as he enters the cooking room, followed by Bergas. "My little brother here made a suggestion to make things somewhat easier." Alagur smiles towards Bergas and adds, "We only need to bring one haversack containing your belongings up the mountain on the morning of our departure, Marrida."

The belongings Alagur is referring to are the few clothes Marrida still has on the shelf in their sleeping room, her three notebooks with their accompanying writing implements, the packs of food Emelyse prepared a few days earlier that is now lying in the cold room, and an old coat Emelyse gave Alagur to replace the cloak he intends to leave behind for Bergas.

Alagur sits down opposite Marrida and smiles at her. "That smells good to a man with a rumbling stomach."

"If you eat it with this bread, it tastes really good." Marrida points at the dark loaf lying close to them. Alagur nods and helps himself to two slices of the bread. A moment later, he too is given a small bowl of the liquid, as is Bergas, who's sitting next to him.

"Don't eat too much otherwise you won't have an appetite for all the food at the spring celebrations," Emelyse says.

"Are you looking forward to the celebrations?" Marrida asks Bergas.

"Yes, I am," Bergas says, nodding. "I missed one when I lived in City of Wolves."

All three adults notice the sadness in his voice.

* * *

As the day progresses, Marrida, Alagur and Bergas start to become restless. More than once, Emelyse has to tell them that they'll depart for the festivities three hours after midday, and they need to be patient. Excitement permeates the air, and the trio play games of guessing and chance to pass the time.

An hour after midday, Marrida decides to try an experiment. She sits opposite Bergas.

"Bergas, hold out your hand." When Bergas does so, Marrida drops the Stone of Truth into it. Emelyse draws in her breath, but she keeps quiet and observes. "I want you to try to do a vision. The way you need to do it is by holding this gem in a specific way."

Bergas stares at the gem, not wanting to know whether his mother is looking on in approval or disapproval. He watches as Marrida positions his hands with the assuredness of someone who knows what she's doing.

"Try it now." Marrida points at the gem. Bergas gives it a go, then looks up questioningly. Marrida nods, but repeats the exercise.

"Do it again."

Bergas practises until his motions are as smooth as the woman's. As she watches on, Emelyse recalls doing similar exercises with her own mother. For Alagur, it's fascinating to watch the interaction between Marrida and Bergas. For Emelyse, the realisation is that Marrida is doing something that Jarryca predicted. The old woman has stated more than once that men are as capable of doing visions as women. As she recalls the words spoken by her mentor – her secret mentor – Emelyse reaches up to her chest just like Marrida does so often. Alagur notices, and the gesture prompts a thought.

Does she have her own Stone of Truth?

Alagur recalls the shock he felt when Marrida revealed to him that the blackout he thought he'd experienced was in fact a vision. For him, the experience was traumatic; for Bergas, in contrast, it seems almost peaceful.

I wonder why I had to go through that. Was it necessary for me to have my skills awakened as soon as possible?

He thinks about how Emelyse has always kept her sleeping room off limits to the others in the house – even her own son.

She says she uses it to think and to remember Jerid. But now, it's obvious that she has a secret she hides from the world.

One moment later, Emelyse notices Alagur's observations, and her hand jerks down into her lap. She then clasps and unclasps her hands to regain her composure.

Alagur turns his attention back to Bergas, and Marrida beside him, as the boy closes his eyes. It appears Bergas is asleep, but from the relaxation of his facial muscles, Alagur can tell he is in reality attempting the trance-like state which precedes a vision.

"Keep yourself relaxed." Marrida's voice is so quiet that even with his enhanced hearing, Alagur has trouble catching the words.

Bergas has been attempting to do a vision for several minutes, but his eyes have stayed shut. Alagur half expects the boy to open his eyes once more, stating that the exercise is too hard and he wants to stop. He glances again at Emelyse, this time unobtrusively.

She's surprised and shocked — her amazement is evident. It's obvious she has never seen her son act in this way — but I have, when we lived in City of Wolves.

Bergas opens his eyes, and Alagur imagines his own eyes becoming similarly unseeing and jet-black when he sat opposite Marrida near City of Wolves. He sees the floating image a moment later. Alagur feels somewhat annoyed, although he's unsure why.

A vision shows itself, but it doesn't last long. It's over in seconds, but that's long enough for Alagur to realise what he saw. And the audible drawing in of breath from Emelyse confirms this. When Alagur snaps his face towards her, she is as white as moss ash and tears are streaming down her face.

Bergas has shown the image of the final embrace between him and his father on the morning Jerid went off to go fishing. Later in the day, a storm hit the Bay of Whispers and most of the coast and northern oceans, and Jerid was later found dead near the scree where Alagur and Yalla parted ways at the beginning of the winter season. His body was bruised. He'd drowned at sea without any chance of surviving the massive storm.

Emelyse had no chance to recover from the shock of seeing her son doing a vision before this scene presented itself in the disc shape. What she saw was the boy's most treasured memory, but then he also showed the drowning. Both caused Emelyse to cry uncontrollably. In the years since the unfortunate accident, Emelyse has always kept her emotions in check for the sake of her son. She has never allowed him to see her upset. But every unshed tear, every stored emotion, now comes welling up.

Alagur sees her expression a moment before Emelyse chokes with grief and slumps forward. He gets up quickly and takes her in his arms, allowing Emelyse to cry on his shoulder.

Bergas and Marrida notice something is wrong. Bergas frowns, and Marrida wonders what has brought on Emelyse's outpouring of emotion. She glances at Bergas, who hands her Stone of Truth back to her and gets up. As he approaches his mother, Alagur gently lets go of Emelyse. Sensing that her son is beside her, she puts her arms around his shoulders, continuing to cry in loud sobs.

Alagur stands and motions to Marrida to follow him. He takes her by the hand and leads her outside. Once there, he explains.

"She started crying when she saw the image of Bergas with a man I suspect was his father on their last day together." He pauses. "There's more. Emelyse did this." Alagur does a perfect imitation of Marrida reaching up towards her own Stone of Truth. Marrida immediately understands the implications of his gesture and glances towards the front door, behind which she can still hear Emelyse's sobbing – Emelyse, who's both a friend and a surrogate mother to her. When Marrida makes a move to go back inside, Alagur takes her by the shoulders to stop her.

"They need some time alone to grieve. I'm guessing they've never done this before." As he speaks, Alagur pulls Marrida to him and embraces her. She needs comforting too. "It's the same as the grieving you needed to do when you heard about your father from me."

As he kisses Marrida on the top of her head, she remembers how she felt when he told her of her father's fate. This time, rather than feeling the anger she felt that day, she's overcome with grief. She lets herself slump into Alagur's arms and buries her head against his chest.

"But this is supposed to be the start of the celebrations," she says after a few moments. "How can we celebrate with Emelyse feeling so sad?"

"I don't think she'll be sad for long," Alagur replies. "I think she's taking her son to see whatever it is she keeps hidden from him in her room."

Marrida listens to the sounds coming from within the house, hearing fading footsteps and a door opening. This is followed by the murmur of two people talking. From this, she guesses mother and son are having a similar conversation to the one she herself had with her uncle before she departed on her journey.

Alagur and Marrida let go of one another when they hear two sets of footsteps walking towards the front door. A moment later, a shyly smiling Emelyse walks outside. She's closely followed by Bergas, who smiles at them both warmly.

"Bergas and I have finally managed to talk about his father. I'm going to start teaching him my skills. You've shown me I shouldn't shield him from my own heritage."

Emelyse walks towards Marrida and Alagur, embracing them both warmly.

"Alagur, you feel like a son to me, and you, Marrida, feel like the daughter I've always longed for. Perhaps one day soon, if it's not too late for me, I'll meet someone who'll be a good father to my son, and who'll grant me that wish."

Emelyse lets go and they all look at each other. Emelyse's eyes are glistening with renewed emotion, but she manages to stop herself from crying again.

"We should make the final preparations, or we may miss the start of the festivities, and that would be a shame."

The mention of the celebration causes Marrida to feel excited again. Her excitement spills over into her facial expression, and she looks like a young girl for a moment. This in turn heightens the excitement of her companions.

Before following Emelyse and Bergas into the house, Alagur grabs Marrida around her waist in a playful gesture. "I like it best when you are happy," he murmurs in her ear, before kissing her forehead. She smiles at him.

"Are the two of you actually going to help us?" Emelyse calls from inside the house. Marrida giggles when she sees the mock-disappointment appear on Alagur's face.

"We'll have all the time in the world to be close when we're on our way." Marrida smiles mischievously at Alagur, then rushes into the house before he can respond, giggling loudly and leaving him gaping. Shaking his head at her ability to tease him so effectively, Alagur finally steps inside too.

CHAPTER SIXTY-FIVE

T HE SPRING CELEBRATION IS TAKING PLACE ON A GREEN PASTURE at the south-western end of the city. For Alagur, the route feels familiar. It includes the first part of the path Bergas pointed out to him when Alagur travelled to the main road which runs parallel with the bay's shore to fetch Yalla.

This time, at the second fork where Bergas told Alagur to turn left, Emelyse and her son lead the party right. A short distance further on, they turn right again, and can now see the field where the celebrations are being held in the distance. They are met by a group of six others — a man, three women, and two girls. One of the girls rushes to Bergas and makes a point of walking next to him for the remainder of the journey.

"That's the girl he mentioned to you," Emelyse whispers to Marrida over her shoulder. The *aah* from Marrida confirms that she remembers the conversation she had with Bergas about the girl he would like to become his life partner one day.

At the final turning, the paths which lead to the field start to become crowded. Marrida can now see how many people live in the city. She waves when she spots Jarryca and Hadukin coming towards them from the right, and Alagur, who has also made friends in the city over the winter months, raises his left arm in greeting when one of these friends approaches.

"Marrida, meet Jerabor. He's the toolmaker I visit before joining you in the library."

Jerabor is close enough to hear himself being introduced to one of the prettiest women he has ever seen, and he baffles Marrida by embracing her.

"It's customary for a man to embrace a woman when he's introduced to her by her escort," Jarryca murmurs in her ear.

Marrida smiles at the man now she understands.

As time goes by, the crowds swell. The whole city seems to have turned out for the celebrations. Azaquina is about the same size as Ruh'nar, but it has only half as many residents. The voices of people greeting one another, talking and exchanging pleasantries fill the air, sounding to Marrida like the buzz from a beehive – if anyone were brave enough to put their ear against one to listen.

I've never heard a sound like this in Ruh'nar, thinks Marrida, *even when the population is double its normal size during the First and Second Rites ceremonies. I guess that people in Ruh'nar are more reserved than those in Azaquina. Perhaps the attacks on Ruh'nar have altered how we behave.*

Marrida hears something which, at first, sounds like the whistling of a bird. The sound increases as more whistling starts up, and gradually the crowd falls silent until the air is filled only with the sound of the whistling.

Marrida then hears a soft rhythmic thudding. This is joined a moment later by someone playing a string instrument. The blend of the two sounds makes Marrida feel like she wants to dance and she starts clapping. Moments later, everyone around her is clapping along to the rhythm of the music, too.

Marrida feels a hand take hers and she looks up. As Alagur leads her into a dance, she forgets all her worries.

Marrida looks around for a fleeting moment to find most people paired up for the dance. The style of dance doesn't seem to matter; everyone is dancing differently. Some are dancing slowly to allow themselves to absorb the rhythm of the drum, while others dance at a fast pace – like Marrida and Alagur. It feels exciting and relaxing at the same time. The music seems to be endless, and the thuds of the many feet on the grass take on a musical rhythm of their own.

Marrida smiles broadly as Alagur lifts her up by the waist and swirls her through the air. When she lands on her feet, her arms find themselves around Alagur's neck, which causes him to slow down until they're dancing to the slowest beat possible. She feels so happy at this moment in the arms of the man she loves – the man who'll become her life partner. There's only one wistful thought tempering her happiness.

I wish Esbara, Kalisa, Uncle Joharan, Damir, and even Elder Sharriba could be here to celebrate with me.

As Alagur's lips touch hers for a kiss, the thought is forgotten.

Marrida dances. She dances at a whirlwind pace, then slows down. She doesn't know how much time has passed before the beat slows and everyone calms down. When the music finally stops, a roar of applause and yelling announces that the dance has been a good one. It almost sounds like Marrida is standing under a huge waterfall, and she winces momentarily. But after a few minutes, the roar settles back into the buzzing which reminds her of bees in their hive and calms her mind.

* * *

Jarryca takes her by the hand.

"Let me take you to where the food is served and explain to you all that is on offer."

Jarryca strides off with Marrida, followed by Emelyse and Alagur. Then come Hadukin and Bergas, and several of the people Emelyse's guests have been introduced to. Jerabor follows, interested in the visiting pair.

As Jarryca leads her through the crowd, Marrida notices people side-stepping to let the two women pass. Each time she looks at those who have side-stepped, she gets a nod and a formal raised left arm greeting from them. Because Jarryca is holding her left arm — and rather firmly, Marrida notices — she can only nod greetings in return.

I wonder if I'm disrespecting some sort of local custom. But I'll be gone in three days, so it doesn't really matter if I'm seen as a rude outsider.

Emelyse and Hadukin follow on, attempting to explain that Marrida is a guest. "She asked us to greet everyone on her behalf," they repeat over and over again.

Bergas and Elennia, the girl who is walking by his side, fall about in giggles, snorting with laughter each time his mother and Hadukin speak these words. They find it even funnier that Jarryca is throwing custom to the wind and marching Marrida towards the food so forcefully. They imitate the old woman for a moment, giggling helplessly.

It's obvious Jarryca doesn't care, Bergas thinks. *And I think I understand why.* Jarryca is shunned by most in the city because of her ties to the burned-out building that stands as a mark of shame near the Eye of Waves. Not one of them came to help when the building was burning brightly against the night sky fifty years ago. Except one man — Hadukin. Jarryca was one of the few survivors of the attack by her 'own kind', and she has nightmares about it still. Now she's teaching the townsfolk not to dwell on the past, but to let it go in the truest sense. She's telling them to give her a place in their midst.

Hadukin looks closely at the townsfolk. He expects to see angry faces, but he sees none. He sees shame. He also sees many nodding their approval of what the old woman is doing.

She's causing a change to happen here this year to help the future.

Jarryca and Marrida reach the place where all the food is laid out on top of eight long tables. Marrida's eyes fly open in surprise.

I've never seen so much food in one place in my entire life.

"There you go, I wanted you to see this before it gets eaten." Jarryca's voice is forceful and strong – filled with the authority of the Elder she once was. "This is what you're working towards, Marrida. This could happen in every one of the Seven Cities – and beyond." She smiles at Marrida conspiratorially before speaking again, this time quietly. "This is what life will be like every day once there are no Wolf Riders to ruin the festivities."

Alagur hears her last statement and frowns momentarily. Then he sees the food too and realises that Jarryca is showing the value of what Marrida and he are doing. The old woman knew precisely what she was doing when she pushed through the crowds with Marrida in tow.

She's a Caller. Has she already seen the success of our mission?

Jarryca is standing with her hands on her hips, looking defiant. Beyond the old woman, Marrida sees nods of approval pass from person to person as her words make their impact. The people of Azaquina have just witnessed the true skill of a Caller, and it was demonstrated out in the open.

I wonder who these people are who are nodding. Perhaps they're family members of the Callers who were lost in the destruction of the building.

Marrida glances over the crowd at the silhouette of the ruin against the late afternoon sun. She smiles at Alagur when he catches up with her.

"I think we should give the guests in our city the first choice of our best food," a loud voice calls out. It seems Jarryca has achieved what she set out to do. Her townspeople now know that Marrida and Alagur have come to assist them in overcoming the problem the Wolf Riders pose, and that Jarryca considers them people worthy of her trust. Steadily, Marrida and Alagur are surrounded by people introducing themselves and pointing to the foods they prepared. Slowly, any lingering distrust and disapproval ebb away.

When voices call out for more music, it starts up at an even faster tempo than before. After a second impromptu dance, Marrida then sits down at a table to eat from the food. Several large pitchers are passed around, and when Marrida tastes the liquid they contain, she realises it's the same refreshing drink she enjoyed at Jarryca's library. Even children are drinking it – no alcohol is served at this festival.

Various people sitting at the same table ask Marrida and Alagur questions about where they're from.

"He is distant kin of Jarryca," Emelyse replies on Alagur's behalf. Marrida notes that Emelyse simply says he comes from the west without specifying where exactly.

"It's possibly best you don't mention the city you come from," Emelyse whispers into Marrida's ear. "People think 'they' came from 'there' – you know what I mean." Marrida nods, realising that many in the city likely lost daughters, aunts and even mothers in the fire caused by the Keepers of fifty years ago.

It will cause issues if I mention Ruh'nar.

"I come from Marridina. I was named after it."
Several women nod approvingly.
"How are you two connected?"
"Are you sister and brother, or something else?"
Alagur answers in a booming voice. "This beautiful woman gave me her answer just over two weeks ago. She'll become my life partner." He gets an equally booming cheer from the crowd, and many people walk over to congratulate them.

When Emelyse gets up to fetch food for herself and Bergas, Jerabor takes the opportunity to sit next to Marrida. Looking at both visitors thoughtfully, while they regard him with similar curiosity, he removes a small package from an inside pocket of his coat.

"If you hadn't promised yourself to Alagur as his future life partner, I would have asked you myself." Jerabor winks mischievously at Marrida. "But as you're promised to him, I have got something I wish both of you to have as a gift."

Jerabor hands the package to Marrida. She can sense every person at the table craning their necks to see what she's been given. Emelyse arrives back with food. Giving Bergas his plate, she decides to stand and eat while watching Marrida open the package.

Marrida places the package on the table, noting from the soft thud that its contents are made from a hard material. She undoes the thong holding the package shut and moves the soft leather material out of the way, drawing in her breath when the object is revealed. It's a small statue of a woman with folded arms made of white stone. But what causes Marrida to draw in her breath isn't the beauty of the figure; it's the posture.

Behind Marrida, Emelyse's eyes fly open when she sees the statue. She glances up and her eyes meet Jarryca's. The old woman is in an equal state of shock.

"She is so beautiful," Marrida whispers.

"I will tell you why I'm giving you this," Jerabor explains. "Jarryca has proved to us today that the animosity we hold towards what she was should stop. Yes, most of us know who you are, Jarryca, but we didn't want to admit it to ourselves, so we excluded you. Perhaps we did it to punish ourselves for what happened fifty years ago, or to pretend that you somehow caused the destruction of your Temple."

Jerabor looks searchingly at Marrida for a moment before speaking again.

"My sister was in the Temple. She went back early that evening to study. And then they came."

The silence around Marrida increases. There's solemnity in the air – without the earlier feeling of disapproval.

This is a moment of grieving for them all, even Jarryca.

She glances back at Jerabor when he continues his explanation.

"This carving was done by my sister. She told me it's a statue of the woman who will return unity to the city. She'll bring a man with her, and they'll both bring hope back. I'm not going to hide what they were in the Temple anymore. My sister was a Caller; Jarryca is still a Caller. My sister always said that one day, two people would celebrate with us before leaving on a journey. Jarryca tells me you and Alagur are leaving in three days from now, Marrida."

Jerabor pauses and lets his words sink in.

"Tomorrow we start to rebuild the Temple for a new generation of Callers."

The roar which explodes at that moment – a roar showing support for the idea – is so loud, it leaves Marrida feeling stunned. She glances down at the mysterious carving to distract herself from the noise. It's made of white stone, but the hair has an almost golden colour to it. Jerabor's sister must have used plant pigments to achieve the effect. The figure's left hand is below the right hand, and a small object that looks like a rubha apple rests between them. The figure's eyes are black.

Marrida glances up instinctively and her eyes meet those of Jarryca. The old woman is watching her with interest, leaning her chin on her clasped hands. Nothing in her demeanour or expression gives away what she's feeling or thinking.

If she's shocked by the outcome of her actions, she isn't showing it now.

Marrida gives Jarryca a fleeting smile, and the old woman winks at her. This gives Marrida the impression that Jarryca had foreseen the events of this day, and – perhaps – Marrida and Alagur's arrival in Azaquina in the first place.

I hope I have a chance to visit the library before I leave. I'm certain she'll only tell me more when we're alone.

Jerabor walks off to talk to others at the festival – in particular the town's stonemasons – and Emelyse takes her chance to sit down next to Marrida again.
"If I want more food, I'm sending Bergas to get it so no one else can sit here and give us all another…surprise. But yes, that statue is beautiful." Marrida ignores the older woman's grumble and re-wraps the statue carefully.

For a while, Marrida talks privately to Alagur using the Sab'ruhi dialect. Then she notes that Emelyse and Jarryca are also having a private conversation.

What dialect are they using? Emelyse seems more fluent, so it must be her mother tongue.

She glances around discreetly and notices that no one seems to be paying attention to the two women talking. Her mind races as she talks more with Alagur, all the while analysing the dialect the women are using.

Yes, certain words and inflections sound familiar.

Marrida's attention intensifies as she hears a name: Roha'dea. The other name Emelyse says so quickly that Marrida only discerns the first and last letters: a D and an A. She drinks down her beverage, then nods at Alagur to pass her the pitcher for more, allowing her to position herself behind it so she can glance at Jarryca.

Hopefully, she won't notice me observing her.

Marrida makes a point of refilling Emelyse's half-filled mug, giving her a sideways glance. Using a skill Sharriba taught her in private, Marrida observes what is going on around her at the festival. With heightened curiosity, she listens very carefully to what Jarryca and Emelyse are saying – especially since Emelyse mentioned the mysterious name.

I'm certain that's a dialect Sharriba taught me. Why are they talking in a dialect spoken in Achellon?

CHAPTER SIXTY-SIX

Alagur gently pulls the blanket over Marrida, who is lying flat on her back, almost rigidly, and wonders for a moment if he is causing her discomfort. He straightens up, walks across the room and begins to undress to get ready for bed too. In mid-motion, he stops and pulls the curtain covering the window aside, glancing outside. It's still night time, but his enhanced Wolf Rider eyesight perceives a hint of daylight in the sky above him.

He glances to the south of the bay and sees from the distant orange glow that the celebration is still ongoing. Letting the curtain drop, he then turns to look at Marrida. She is lying on her side now, staring at him with wide-awake eyes.

I wonder what she's thinking about. She seemed happy with the gift from Jerabor, but now she seems withdrawn. She wanted to come home from the celebration because she was tired. Now she doesn't look tired at all. Is she using her skill to store the knowledge we learnt today into her long-term memory? Or is she just thinking about something?

Alagur realises that from the moment they left the festivities, she hasn't said a word. He kneels next to the bed and looks at her more closely, running his hand through her hair and caressing her cheek.

"What's wrong, Marrida?" he quizzes. "Are you unhappy you're leaving? Or worried about the journey?"

She shakes her head.

"What then? Is it the gift? Because Jerabor did tell me privately that you could return it to him if you were uncomfortable about having it."

Again, Marrida shakes her head, then she bites her lip like she's making an effort not to cry. Her subdued demeanour seems strange after all the laughter and fun of the dancing earlier.

"Marrida, is it me? Did you not like it when I told them about us?" He wonders if she is reconsidering her decision. When Marrida shakes her head again, he heaves an audible sigh of relief and his body slumps.

Marrida doesn't notice. "I want to go on the journey later today," she says suddenly.

"Why?" Alagur frowns at her.

"Because of what Emelyse and Jarryca were saying."

"What were they saying? I could hear them talking, but couldn't understand any of it."

"They were talking in Achallai, the dialect of Achellon."

"How do you know?"

"I know five of the six dialects we learn at the Temple very well, but the sixth one has always eluded me," Marrida explains. "I started lessons last year, but Sharriba explained it as…how did she put it again? 'Some dialect from the east'. I recognised it, especially when they said the name Roha'dea."

"Isn't that the other name for Masharea?" Alagur enquires.

"It is." The reply comes out in a whisper.

Marrida stops talking abruptly when the front door opens and two pairs of footsteps tread softly through the house. It's clear their hosts want to make as little noise as possible. They hear two doors open and shut softly moments later.

After the faint sound of people readying themselves for bed has subsided and the house has gone quiet again, Marrida continues.

"Emelyse spoke the dialect with the fluency of someone who was brought up speaking it. Jarryca could also speak it, but as a learnt dialect." She pauses for a moment before adding, "They were talking about the city Emelyse is from. I couldn't make out the name of the city, but it starts with a D and ends with an A. I get the impression something is going on there which neither of them has told me about. They seemed worried about the fact we're going there.

"After this, Jarryca told Emelyse about a vision she did. All I could understand was, 'There's a cloud of smoke I see on the horizon, and the sound of a wolf growling'. It's making me worried, Alagur."

Marrida stops and sighs deeply.

"We need to go soon if we're going to avoid whatever Jarryca saw. That's why I want to go today. I would go now, if it was possible."

Alagur frowns and looks down at the shirt he is clutching. He straightens up, turns Marrida's words over in his mind for a moment, then puts the shirt back on.

"I have a plan, but you must stay here in bed – please."

Marrida watches as Alagur quietly leaves the room. She hears him gather all their possessions from the other parts of the house, including the food from the cooking room, and then he returns to pack them all at the end of the bed, leaving a few travel clothes for each of them.

"I'll be back soon."

Once again, Alagur opens the door of the sleeping room, then Marrida hears the front door open and close a few moments later. She listens for footsteps outside, but soon realises Alagur is too good at travelling unnoticed to be overheard by her – or anyone else.

She lies motionless on the bed, listening for anything that will alert her to the man returning. After perhaps forty minutes, she hears the quiet sound of him re-entering the house. A moment later, he is back in the room. She sits up on the bed and looks at him questioningly.

"If you want to leave now, we can. Yalla is ready for the journey and waiting for us in the copse near here. But we'll need to hurry if we want to be gone before first light."

"I'll leave a short note for Emelyse and Bergas to find when they wake, so they'll know we're sorry about leaving without telling them."

Alagur nods, but Marrida senses that he wants her to hurry with the task. She writes a short note, saying she'll send word later to let Emelyse and Bergas know that they're alright, then she places the note on the small table next to the door and leaves the unlit ember on top of it. She returns to the bed to put on her shoes, but Alagur stops her.

"I'm not wearing my shoes. Carry them, and once we're some distance from here, we can put them on."

She nods and ties the laces together, putting the shoes around her neck. Taking hold of Alagur's hand, she leaves the house by his side, listening out for sounds coming from the sleeping rooms of their hosts. They have just reached the end of the porch when a voice speaks from one of the windows, freezing them in place.

"I guess they spooked you with their conversation if you want to leave in the middle of the night."

Alagur and Marrida glance to their right to see Bergas leaning out of his window, his arms on the sill.

"They don't realise how much I understand when they talk in that dialect. Is it Mam's real dialect?"

Marrida nods.

"I won't tell her I saw you leave. I won't tell any of them."

Marrida tiptoes to Bergas and gives him a hug. She notices his cheeks are wet with tears. Alagur gives the boy a hug too.

"Look after your mother, little brother."

"And you look after her." Bergas nods at Marrida. "I'm going to miss both of you a lot."

Bergas closes the window of his sleeping room silently. After a few moments, Alagur and Marrida take hold of each other's hands again and walk away from the house towards the northern side of the copse. Here they're greeted by a gentle snort from Yalla, who pushes her head against Alagur as he approaches her. The familiar greeting feels good to him. Marrida then greets the wolf by scratching the bridge of her nose, bringing a second snort from the animal.

Alagur lifts Marrida up onto the wolf, then he hoists himself up behind her. Marrida glances back at him and smiles. He smiles back, then leans forward and kisses her.

"Are you ready?" he murmurs.

"Yes," Marrida replies.

Alagur signals to the wolf, and Yalla starts at a fast pace up the side of a slope. After perhaps fifteen minutes, Marrida sees a familiar feature in the landscape.

"Alagur, can you direct Yalla over there, please?" Marrida points at a flat rock slab. Alagur turns the wolf, and after a few minutes they're standing on top of the rock.

Alagur stares at the vista, understanding now why Marrida stayed away for as long as she did. It is peaceful, and the air around them is quiet. After a few minutes while Marrida and he absorb their final view of Azaquina below them, he turns the wolf and signals for her to travel to a higher elevation. Bergas has shown him the route over the preceding month to get to the ancient mountain road which will lead them east towards whatever awaits them there.

* * *

IT TAKES SOME HOURS TO GET TO THE PEAK OF THE MOUNTAIN, but it soon becomes evident the Upper Plains are a mere shadow of their counterparts across the bay. Northern Blades, the coldest and highest parts of this mountain range, are possibly two or three times higher. There is evidence of erosion from rain which leaves the terrain looking like a badly cooked cake. Pockets of ice and snow are still visible, showing that at these higher elevations, nature does not let one season become effortlessly dominant over another. At this height, spring takes longer to impact on the landscape, and the alternation between winter weather and warm spring weather can cause the rocks to crack under the pressure of the ice forming within. Then newly formed melted water carries some of the smaller particles to lower areas. The next time it's cold enough for the process to happen again, the water penetrates the recently exposed rock surfaces. It's a process which caused the mountains of the Upper Plains to flatten themselves many thousands of years ago.

"Stop for a moment, please." Marrida's request is sudden and Alagur frowns. "Can you help me off? I want to look down there."

Alagur climbs off the wolf and helps Marrida down. She immediately walks to the western side of the small hill they have arrived at.

"I think that must be the Eye of Waves." She points at the coastline below them, flanking the city as a yellow-white ribbon. Alagur looks towards where Marrida is pointing and gapes in awe at the natural structure, which reminds him of a cave, standing at the entrance of the bay. A wave rises from the ocean beyond the structure, explaining by its action where the name originates from.

The man and woman stand watching the play of the waves against the structure for ten minutes before they turn, remount the wolf, and set off at a fast pace eastward.

Alagur tries to calculate how far away the watchtowers they've been told about are from their current location, and how far they are from Azaquina. That it took two years for Emelyse to travel the Upper Plains has left him puzzled. The woman seems strong, and she was more than capable of keeping up a fast pace when they walked to the festivities.

The other puzzle occupying his mind is what she said about the watchtowers.

"You'll know you've arrived at them. Pay attention to the fourth one as it's significant."

He wonders why.

Alagur puts his arm tightly around the woman's waist as a feeling of foreboding washes over him, even though there's nothing about the surroundings that indicates danger. In fact, it's a beautiful spring day. Alagur slows the wolf momentarily and glances first behind them, then to the southern valleys and the horizon beyond. He sees no one. But it doesn't diminish the feeling of foreboding, which fills his heart and mind.

Alagur realises a moment later that Marrida has fallen asleep and it brings a momentary smile to his face as he recalls his first evening's fast ride with her in his arms. He urges the wolf to the highest speed she can manage, and Yalla complies, seemingly picking up on her master's sense of danger. She has renewed her reserves of energy during her time nursing her pups, and she's now at the peak of her strength. Had circumstances been different, she'd probably be heading out in an attack as she did nearly a year earlier. Alagur glances down at his wolf and hopes that the effort she's putting into the journey will not be in vain. His mind keeps trying to convince him that Marrida will wake up saying she regrets leaving so soon.

If we're forced to go back, we'll face danger from the people of Azaquina. Why is he thinking of them as dangerous all of a sudden? *The mysteries are stacking up. How many will there be by the time we're in the east?*

Alagur's mind turns to Bergas. Adulthood will come to the boy in fewer than eight years' time, and after he has done his Second Rites, he can make decisions about his own future. The journey that took Bergas home, part of it on the back of a wolf, took him over a season and part of the next one. The same journey on foot would have taken him twice as long.

I wonder how long the journey that Marrida and I are taking will last? Marrida said she wants to see the caves where her gem originates from after we've been to the city in the east. Not sure how long that will take. I want to go to Chiva'na at some point, but I'm not sure if she'll want to travel from the eastern coast to the western coast without visiting Ruh'nar.

Alagur realises that it's impossible to figure out how long the journey will take, so he focuses on the landscape ahead of him to dispel the thoughts from his mind. It takes him several minutes to register what he can see in the distance.

"Marrida, wake up!" he hisses. "Wake up, and look!"

"W…what?" Marrida's sleepy voice mumbles vaguely, then she sees the same thing as Alagur and leans forward suddenly. Ahead of them is the silhouette of a building. It's high — from the small windows Alagur can count, it could be four or five floors high.

If this is one of the smaller watchtowers, then the fourth one — the one we need to investigate — could be at least double the size of this one.

Marrida is looking the building over in awe. Alagur recalls her telling him about her impromptu walk through the massive garden of the Temple of Ruh'nar.

I guess she's comparing them in her mind, he thinks as Marrida leans back and rests her head against his shoulder.

As the wolf comes closer to the building, Alagur slows her down and finally stops her. They all hold their breath as they listen for any signs of life from within the massive building.

When Marrida speaks, it's clear to Alagur that she's getting the same sense of foreboding from the surroundings as he was earlier.

It's like someone is trying to warn us off. I can sense the violent past of this area, and that building feels out of place.

"Please ride on, Alagur."

Marrida's words are spoken quietly, yet they seem amplified by the building. The panic in her voice sends ripples of fear through both the man and the wolf.

Part Four

CHAPTER SIXTY-SEVEN

As they ride past the second of the watchtowers, Alagur starts to wonder if it's really such a good idea to take the route over the mountains. Both he and Marrida keep feeling the ominous sense of danger that seems to blanket the landscape.

"I'm wondering what these buildings are for." Marrida cranes her neck to peer past Alagur at the dark shadow behind them. Though distant, it still casts its presence over the landscape. "Why would Emelyse have suggested this route to us?"

"I'm not entirely sure, but perhaps it was her way of preparing us for whatever we'll find in the city she came from. And remember what I noted when you got Bergas to do a vision? There's more to what she's said — or not said — but I'm still trying to figure it out, so I'll wait before I share it with you, alright?"

Marrida nods silently, then looks forward. Alagur isn't certain if she's angry or trying to figure the clues out too.

Surreptitiously, Alagur slows the wolf down to half her speed.

I'm not certain if I want to get to that city in the east any time soon — or to the fourth watchtower, for that matter. I can sense something wrong about these watchtowers. Whoever built them must have meant them to be a warning. They're old, and their architecture doesn't match any I've seen in my travels as a Wolf Rider.

* * *

The next few days go by rather repetitively, then finally the third watchtower comes into view on the horizon. Alagur is surprised by the suggestion that comes from Marrida.

"Alagur, maybe stop at this one so we can look inside it."
He glances down at her and notes she's leaning closer to him.
"Are you sure you want to?" Alagur's quite prepared to keep riding on without stopping; he has a feeling he can't shake off, and it's growing as they progress further east. The distance between the second and third

watchtower is greater than the distance between the first two.

And then he spots a depression to their right that has an unnatural appearance to it.

"What do you think happened here?"

Alagur brings the wolf to a halt, noticing that Yalla is uncommonly nervous too. She's clearly picking up on the feelings of the man and woman on her back. Alagur is trying to settle the wolf when Marrida places her hand on his arm and points to an area a hundred paces below them.

"Wolves!"

Alagur now realises why Yalla is so nervous – she can smell the pack below them. He gets off her back and helps Marrida down, signalling to Yalla to stay where she is. He and Marrida then walk step by step down the slope of the depression until they're perhaps forty paces from the group of animals.

Alagur looks in all directions for any signs to indicate the pack belongs to a scouting party, but the air is filled with an eerie silence which makes the hairs on his neck stand up. He glances at the woman next to him and sees her jaw is clenched, her expression determined. She has a self-assuredness about her that he has never seen in her before as she stares unflinchingly at the wolves milling about below them.

When he looks back at the wolves, Alagur realises three are standing still, staring directly back at them. The scene has an odd familiarity to it which he can't quite grasp right away.

Marrida veers off to the right, away from Alagur, and one of the wolves gradually moves forward in her direction. He pales when he notices the colouring of the animal, which bears a striking resemblance to a drawing by Bergas. The wolf, who's pacing unhurriedly towards Marrida, is grey-brown with a hint of dark stripes running through her fur. As she reaches Marrida, the man holds his breath. If anyone had told him the events he's now witnessing when he was still in City of Wolves, sitting on the terrace of the place he used to call home, he would have laughed loudly and said that person must have been drinking too much wine. But as Marrida's hand rises little by little towards the snout of the wolf, the words from The Truth flash through Alagur's mind.

SHE WHOSE NAME IS UNSPOKEN,
A WOLF SHE WILL CLAIM FROM THE WILD,
AND THE MAN WILL LEARN HER SKILL.

I have indeed learnt her skill. Is she capable of learning mine? Am I seeing the prophecy coming true right in front of me?

A sound penetrates Alagur's mind. He realises Marrida is humming in a monotone, and he recognises it as a sound he has often heard Jarryca make. She is holding her hand still each time the animal hesitates.

Alagur watches the other wolves closely, then he reaches to his side and lets out an involuntary curse under his breath when he realises he's forgotten to bring his spear arrows and thrower with him. If the wolves mean to attack, he'll have a hard time defending the woman – and himself – against the pack.

Alagur cringes as the wolf near Marrida lets out a wolf song, but then he sees the other wolves backing off, hesitantly at first. After perhaps fifteen minutes, the only beings near to Marrida and the wolf are Alagur and Yalla – whose presence Alagur can feel behind him on the hill.

He frowns when he realises Yalla hasn't answered the wolf song with her own. He turns his head little by little so as not to startle the wolf, who's still interacting with Marrida, to his presence – although he knows the animal is likely as aware of him as he is of her. Seeing a bonding between a wolf and a person as an outsider is a fascinating event. Alagur hopes Marrida and this wolf are indeed bonding. The woman seems to be in a trance-like state, as she is when doing one of her visions, and Alagur decides this must be her method of achieving the state of mind which is second nature to him.

Alagur's jaw drops when he sees the familiar head-to-head touching between the woman and the wolf. He has often explained to Marrida how he bonded with Yalla, but he was never sure whether she had fully understood it. He looks around. All the other wolves have disappeared into the undergrowth which surrounds the unnatural depression in the landscape.

Alagur's heart jumps when Marrida's voice suddenly echoes throughout the surroundings.

"I'm calling her Lya."

He looks at the woman. She is standing in a familiar pose, her arm outstretched towards the wolf — at least, it would be familiar if the wolf standing next to her were Yalla.

Has she been able to bond with the animal in the way I did with Yalla? I need to see how the wolf will behave now.

"Walk up the hill without guiding her," he tells Marrida.

He gives a low-pitched whistle and a rustling sound moves away on the hill above, disappearing after several minutes. Then he nods at the woman. Marrida climbs up the hill one step at a time, fighting the urge to look behind her for the wolf. As a result, she doesn't see the wolf hesitate, then start to follow her. But the man does.

When the wolf's pace quickens, he smiles. Marrida has succeeded.

After the wolf has disappeared over the crest of the hill, Alagur hears sounds of pleasure and encouragement coming from Marrida. He climbs the slope too, in a few fast strides. At the top, he's met by a scene which reminds him so much of the day Yalla bonded with him, he smiles generously.
"You've made a new friend, for sure."
Marrida beams a happy smile as she looks up at him, making his heart beat faster with love for her.
"Marrida, get up for a moment. I need Yalla here, as this wolf must accept her as the matriarch before we can be sure she can come with us." When Alagur sees disappointment flash over the woman's face, he explains, "Until Yalla accepts her, the bonding isn't complete. Once it is, you'll get a feeling…it's hard to describe. It makes you feel like the wolf's mind is inside your own."

Marrida nods and lifts herself off the ground. Alagur must have gone through this same scenario hundreds, or even thousands of times with boys in City of Wolves.

Alagur sees her close her eyes for several moments and open them again. "I don't feel any different from how I felt before we found the wolves. Perhaps you're right." Alagur grins, guessing she's just playing with him.

Alagur whistles a long, sharp-sounding whistle, then a shorter, lower one. The man and woman, the wolf she has already named Lya standing nervously near them, wait a few minutes, then Yalla appears, taking her time to walk towards them. When she stops, Alagur takes the harness and all their belongings from her back.

Yalla looks at the new arrival. After the man has removed her bindings, her stance changes.

"What is she doing?" Marrida whispers.

Alagur replies by placing his finger over his lips. She nods and watches.

Yalla stands, tall and proud, with head held high, her ears erect and forward. Lya, who's a third shorter in height, comes forward slowly with her head lowered. When she reaches Yalla, the larger wolf moves forward so slowly that Marrida wonders if she's imagining the motion.

Marrida holds her breath, seeing a change in Lya occurring at the same slow pace as Yalla's walk. The wolf lowers her head even more, and her ears move backwards. In this posture, the brown-grey wolf allows Yalla to lick her, and Marrida suppresses a giggle when she sees Lya lick Yalla's face in return. Then Lya drops onto her side, and as Yalla sniffs the reproductive region of the smaller wolf, Marrida feels a sensation wash over her. It feels like nothing she has ever experienced…

Two strong arms catch Marrida as she's about to collapse. She looks up at Alagur for a moment, not knowing what has happened to her. Alagur smiles at her. Then she feels a raspy, wet tongue lick her face and she looks in its direction, expecting to see Yalla's golden eyes looking at her. Instead, she sees a pair of deep, dark brown eyes, and she recognises, both inside and outside herself, that it's Lya looking at her.

"You were successful," Alagur says as he helps the woman steady herself into an upright posture. His voice has an edge of amazement to it.

"You mean Lya is bonded with me like Yalla is bonded with you?"

"Yes. And even more than before, I now believe The Truth is a foretelling, like Emelyse and Jarryca said it was," he replies. "Bergas gave me his wolf's harness when we first arrived in Azaquina. He told me he kept it because he felt I might need it. Guess he was right."

"Elennia is going to be lucky to have him as her life partner."

"Is that her name?" Alagur quizzes. "No one really told me about her."

"Bergas told me about her the day before I did my Second Rites." Marrida smiles at the memory.

Alagur unpacks the old harness and hands it to Marrida. Somewhat hesitantly, she takes the device, and opens it out to see its full size. She looks at the wolf.

"What if she won't let me?"

"She will. You're bonded with her. See how she's looking at you and standing still? She's waiting for you."

Marrida nods and swallows hard.

"Watch me first," Alagur suggests. "I'll put the harness on Yalla, take it off, then repeat the process step by step so you can copy me."

Using motions which are a lot slower than usual, Alagur fastens the harness on Yalla, who stands patiently waiting for him. Then he removes the harness and repeats the process two more times.

It feels like I'm teaching a new arrival in City of Wolves rather than Marrida.

"Now watch me and repeat each motion. And stand on the wolf's left side as it makes the process simpler, and quicker."

Marrida does as she's told. She sees the man drape the harness on top of Yalla, and she copies the action with Lya. Silently, he shows her one specific strap and takes hold of it in his right hand. He leans forward, and reaches with his left hand across Yalla's neck, holding the strap's counterpart from the other side. The process continues until Lya is similarly encased in her harness, and the man stands smiling at Marrida encouragingly.

"We'll repeat the process many times while we travel east, so both you and the wolf will get used to it. Now you need to get on top of her."

Marrida looks at him, wide-eyed. She didn't realise she'd be expected to ride the wolf this soon.

Alagur's next words give the request a more ominous context. "In City of Wolves, if a boy cannot ride a wolf within an hour of being given one, he can end up in the pit of wild wolves."

Marrida remembers his retelling of the things that went on in the city, and she goes as white as moss ash when she realises that in another life, another gender, this would have been the moment to seal her fate. She'd have lived as a Wolf Rider on one wolf or died torn apart by the teeth of many.

"What's the easiest way to get up?" she enquires hesitantly.

"How did you climb on top of Yalla when she brought you down from the mountain?"

Marrida thinks for a moment and remembers how Yalla lay down to let her climb up.

"How do I make Lya lie down?"
"Stand in front of her and do this with your hand."

Alagur demonstrates a motion which immediately makes Yalla lie down on the ground. Marrida repeats the motion a few times without success, and is about to give up when Lya too lies down. She moves to Lya's side and tentatively swings her leg over the wolf's body in the same way as she did with Yalla. When she is in a central position, balanced on top of the wolf, to her surprise, Lya lifts herself off the ground until she's standing on all four legs.
"Did I do that too?"
"It seems you did. I guess being with Yalla that night gave you an added advantage."
Alagur smiles at the woman.
"I need to get her moving now, don't I?"

She catches on faster than most boys in City of Wolves. That's a good sign.

"Yes," he answers. "And that's something you have to figure out by yourself. When you do, we can continue our journey."
Marrida nods, somewhat hesitantly.

I don't want the wolf to go fast yet, Marrida thinks, and her mind says, "Slowly." Although Marrida doesn't know how she has managed it, she feels the wolf move forward. First one step, then another. Marrida is concentrating so deeply on the task, she doesn't notice Alagur rapidly fastening all the packs onto Yalla's harness once more and climbing onto his own wolf. After a few strides, Yalla catches up with the smaller wolf, and Alagur signals wordlessly for her to keep to the side and slightly behind Lya.

It takes a while for Marrida to realise she's riding a wolf, and when she does, she calls out to Alagur to celebrate her success. She's surprised to find him next to her, astride his wolf, and Yalla pacing unhurriedly beside Lya. Marrida glances back and sees all their belongings on top of Yalla's harness.

When did Alagur and Yalla catch up with me?

Then Marrida sees the distance they've travelled since she mounted her wolf. *My wolf? I have a wolf of my own now?* She glances forward at Lya below her and sees the wolf's strong neck muscles rolling with every step she takes. *If Elder Sharriba could see me now, she'd very likely think she's having a hallucination.*

Marrida smiles. "Let's try to go faster."

Before Alagur can protest, a prophecy becomes reality in front of his very eyes.

Marrida feels free. She smiles broadly, and as she encourages the wolf – her wolf – to a faster speed, it doesn't matter to her anymore that the watchtower ahead is imposing. She wants to reach it and find out what secrets it holds within.

Yalla speeds up too, and Alagur notices she has done this without him signalling. Gradually, Yalla overtakes the other wolf and assumes the dominant position as lead wolf in their miniature pack. Alagur hears a distant wolf song and thinks it must be coming from the pack of wolves he and Marrida discovered. He doesn't notice Yalla's ears prick up as she recognises the sound, nor does he realise it's the reason for her increase in speed.

* * *

Some distance away – in a valley south of the Upper Plains – a group of men notices two dozen or so wolves run off in a southerly direction.

"I think those wolves found him," a booming voice calls. And with that, all the men mount their wolves and start the slow journey to the top of the mountain.

CHAPTER SIXTY-EIGHT

A BIRD FLIES UP OUT OF THE DERELICT BUILDING as Alagur and Marrida quietly walk through it. They can't make out how the animal has exited when they glance up to track its movements. A pile of ruins lies in the middle of the central tower, and the two staircases, which could have allowed the man and woman access to the upper floors, are broken to such an extent that Alagur has decided it is unsafe even to try. They move instead to the only room that feels relatively safe.

Much later in the day, Marrida is sitting on a makeshift chair – a rock which, in a distant past, has been chiselled into a square. She discovered the remnants of two drawings as they explored the ruin, and she wants to copy as much as she can make out of them into her notebook for future reference. Alagur stands by her, assisting her by holding two embers above her, one being his own ember, the other one she has given to him for safekeeping.

"I think this line needs to be a bit longer." Alagur puts both embers in one hand and points at part of the parchment on Marrida's lap. She looks and agrees. Over the months of their journey, he's become as good at drawing the things they observe around them as she is.

While Marrida is drawing the images, they discuss the watchtowers.

"I think there were once five buildings," Alagur suggests. Once again, Marrida agrees.

* * *

AFTER LEAVING THE THIRD WATCHTOWER, a completely derelict building, they ride for a month, finally arriving at a deep ravine. In the past, a bridge had spanned it, but the bridge now lies at the bottom of the ravine. The blackened soot that still cakes the base of one of the bridge's supports indicates that someone must have destroyed the structure deliberately.

"I can't tell if it was destroyed to prevent people reaching the northeast, or to prevent people from there having easy access to the rest of the continent," Alagur says.

The destruction throughout the landscape is becoming clearer as they close in on the fourth watchtower, and Alagur's feeling of foreboding is gradually increasing. He often feels tempted to look back towards where they have come from.

I sense something, and whatever it is, it's not giving me a good feeling.

As they explore the ravine's edge to find a way over it, Marrida spots a trail. They descend it, finding themselves on a somewhat slippery path. As it becomes steeper, Alagur improvises by lowering their belongings down on a rope. He then climbs down and guides Marrida's descent. After struggling in her own clothes, Marrida reaches into one of Alagur's bags and pulls out a pair of his trousers, leaving Alagur laughing loud at her mutterings.

"It's easier to do all this as a man!"

Alagur teases Marrida mercilessly until he slips and slides across the mud for fifteen paces, causing Marrida to laugh. Then she slips too. Moments later, they lie laughing in the mud. Both wolves, who have followed them by jumping over rocks and cracks in the landscape, stand looking at them, tilting their heads sideways as if to say, "What are you doing down there?"

When their laughter has subsided a little, they attempt to get up. It is then that Marrida touches Alagur's arm and he looks in the direction she is pointing. What he sees causes them both to burst out laughing again.
"If anyone came down that stairway now, they'd think we were crazy," Alagur splutters.
"I wonder why we didn't see the stairs before. And there's a set on the other side, too."
"Perhaps they were built in such a way as to make it impossible for them to be seen. But we'll never know why they're there, just like we'll never know who destroyed the bridge, or why."

It takes them an hour to reach the lower end of the western stairway. The chance finding of a small pond near the stairway allows them to wash off the mud which is clinging on to their clothing. Marrida repacks her bag, fitting her skirt into the haversack so she can retrieve it easily if it becomes necessary for her to be clothed in the customary manner for women. Alagur can't help but notice that his trousers show off Marrida's slender frame, and to him she appears even more beautiful than before.

Alagur whistles once and signals to Yalla to wait for him on the other side of the ravine. Lya follows the great wolf obediently. He hoists the haversack onto Marrida's back and she picks up the lightest two of the four packs they are carrying with them. He then places his own haversack on his back and picks up the other two packs.

They discover the path that connects the two stairways and follow it step by step. Finding the path level, they increase their speed slowly. On reaching the stairway on the eastern side of the ravine, they discuss how to ascend it and decide Alagur will go up first. He'll place his haversacks and packs somewhere above, and the wolves will guard them while he descends to take the belongings Marrida is carrying. Then she'll follow him up, fastened to him by a rope for safety.

The actual ascent takes them the remainder of the day. Once they are at the top, they make a point of walking back to the bridge's remains to compare them to those on the other side.

"Now we're this side, we can get a better perspective on how deep and wide the ravine is," Alagur says, frowning.

"It was definitely destroyed from that end," Marrida adds. "I think those responsible for the destruction wanted to prevent access to the west. It makes me wonder why the watchtowers were built, and by whom."

"The fourth watchtower is that way." Alagur points eastwards. "It will probably take us a month to travel over this terrain to get there, but by then we'll be well over halfway through our journey. Perhaps then you can go through all the drawings you've done during this part of the journey and compare them to the things Emelyse and Jarryca told us."

And perhaps I can do a vision to see the past of these buildings and the bridge. Marrida decides to refrain from mentioning this thought to Alagur.

Alagur glances back towards the western side of the bridge. How could Emelyse have made it through the massive ravine unaided and uninjured? It has been enough of a struggle for Marrida.

Maybe she lied about how long she travelled.

Alagur whistles twice sharply and waits for first Yalla and, shortly after her, Lya to come into view from the crevices which scar the landscape on this side of the mountains. For this part of their journey, they will need to go at a slower pace.

Alagur glances over his shoulder to find Marrida already busying herself attaching the harness to her wolf. She's learnt the task extremely quickly, and in some ways has become more proficient at handling her wolf than many young Wolf Riders are, even after training for three or four years. Her extensive – and intensive – training at the Temple of Ruh'nar has certainly assisted her in this, her mind having been moulded by hours of lectures and discussion.

The knowledge people used to possess of how the learning centre of their mind works has been lost, buried in a time known to all as The Old Days. Even the Keepers of Truth, who have an exceptional ability to recollect and access past events, have no way of reaching that far back in time. And some say this limitation is of their own doing.

When Alagur looks over at Marrida again, she is sitting astride her mount, and she smiles at him. She looks happy, and he can't help but smile back. That feeling, which he can only explain as love, courses through his body again, and he wishes they could be somewhere safe where he could hold her and kiss her.

When Alagur approaches Marrida, she speaks up.
"How long do you think it will take us to get to the watchtower?"
"We've been travelling for more than a month now since leaving Azaquina, and we've not even reached it. I think it will take another month to get to it. The landscape here is not as hospitable as the mountains west of the ravine."

Marrida nods, but Alagur notices sadness flash across her face for a moment. He wonders if the emotion relates to how long it will take them to get to the watchtower, or whether it was brought on by her memories of Azaquina and the people they met there.

The mood is subdued as Alagur and Marrida start riding again, with Alagur leading the way. He occasionally glances back at the woman and sees she's deep in her own thoughts.

What was the unnatural indentation near the second watchtower? Did another watchtower stand there in the past? Alagur isn't sure, but its discovery led them to a pack of wolves.

The bonding with Lya has caused a change in Marrida. She has lost all the fear of the journey and what it could bring them, proving her bonding with the wolf has been successful.
"Could we make camp soon? If we rest now, we can ride faster than this tomorrow."
Alagur has to admit she's correct. Yalla is walking slowly, tired out after travelling through the mountainous terrain surrounding the ravine.

"Look for a cave or overhanging rock," he calls over his shoulder. "It will make it easier to shelter."

Marrida smiles, happy at this suggestion.

I guess she's more tired than she wants to admit.

It takes them more than an hour to find somewhere to make their overnight camp, by which time the skies above are displaying the blue and purple hues of night. As Marrida looks up, she can see the earliest stars have appeared. She looks in every direction to find somewhere to camp.

"There." Alagur is pointing at an overhang which reminds her of a hand cupping over the Stone of Truth as a Keeper starts a vision. She grins at the comparison.

"Perhaps I could roll one of those round stones under it, and colour it with white and green pigments."

Alagur chuckles at the idea. "I wonder what the next person to pass this place would make of it."

The pair dismount and lead the two wolves to the overhang. The animals settle down on the left side of it, where the overhang covers less of the area below it. Alagur places several stones in a small circle towards the back and right of the covered over area.

"You can place your haversack where the wolves are lying."

Marrida complies, and with some effort manages to do the same with Alagur's haversack. He lifts all the packs in both his hands and carries them to a slightly raised platform next to the haversacks, placing them in a row.

"We can make a bed behind these packs for shelter. It will get cold here as we're much higher up than the mountain range on the other side of the ravine. I suggest you put on your skirt over those trousers for added warmth."

Alagur removes his tinder kit from his haversack. He realises all of a sudden that a year ago, he was sitting on a terrace with Samur, enjoying good wine. He glances up when he remembers Samur, and something makes him look west. After gazing for several minutes in the direction he and the woman have come from without seeing anything, he turns his attention to preparing the bedding for them both.

Alagur doesn't notice Marrida is still staring west. When she saw him look in that direction with a hint of worry on his face, she wondered if he sensed some sort of danger approaching. She wishes she could do a vision to ascertain the origin of his concern, but she's too tired.

"Do you want food, or do you want to go to sleep immediately?"

Alagur's question makes her jump, and for a moment she's confused. When Alagur repeats the question, she finally realises what he's asked.
"I'm hungry," she replies.
"Alright, I'll make a quick soup then."

Alagur sets about producing a soup from some dried meat and their last remaining supplies of root vegetables from Emelyse. He cuts strips from the two haunches of dried leg meat. After stripping the bones of all the meat suitable for their own consumption, he walks to the two wolves and hands each of them a bone. They can gnaw on them, and later they'll be able to drink whatever is left of the soup.

Conversation during the meal turns to Ruh'nar, with Alagur asking Marrida more about the Academy of Warfare. He is interested to find out it once served as a place for young people to learn to ride wolves, but more than a thousand years has passed since this happened last.

Perhaps one day soon it will serve that function again.

When they've finished eating, Alagur and Marrida lie down on their makeshift bed, but sleep doesn't come easily for either of them. Alagur, who is lying closest to the exit of the overhang, keeps looking up and listening. Marrida turns onto her right side, and every time the man looks out at the darkened landscape beyond the faint flickers of the small campfire, she glances through her lashes at the back of his head. She is now getting seriously concerned about whatever is bothering him. She thinks he's checking for something out there, but she can't work out what it is. It is hard to make out any sounds, beyond the snorting and grunting from the two wolves.

Alagur hears a far-off sound which seems familiar for a moment, but then the wind changes and it is gone. A thought enters his mind, telling him that he and Marrida should reach the fourth watchtower as soon as possible for their own safety.

But safety from what? Or from whom?

They haven't passed anyone on their journey so far, and all the buildings seem abandoned. However, the small knot of worry, which started to manifest itself soon after the encounter with the wolves, has grown to a full-blown feeling of foreboding.

When Marrida hears the man make an unfamiliar sound, something like the hiss of water reaching boiling point, and she sees Yalla and Lya get up, she realises that danger lies not just ahead of them, but also somewhere behind them.

Now she knows she has to do a vision to find out what it is.

CHAPTER SIXTY-NINE

Belduran had chosen his men well to scout the northern regions for the missing Alagur. Jymar is a reasonable man. Like Belduran, he believes the Wolf Riders can't continue to snatch boys from the cities they attack. Belduran only really wants to know where Alagur is heading so he'll have the upper hand when Samur returns.

Jymar knows that if he was alone at this point, he could easily have followed Alagur and found out where he was going. He could then have gone back and reported this information to Belduran in private. But he isn't alone, so he has sent out three of the men accompanying him to scout the region. Jymar stands waiting as they approach him on the backs of their wolves.

"It appears they passed over the ravine with the old bridge," the leading rider calls out as he slows his wolf to a stop. "I saw their tracks going down, and they may have used the old thief's stairs to climb back up. I think they have a lead of a month on us now."

Jymar nods and rubs his chin as he thinks about what to do.

"Are we going after him or not?" Jervis, one of the three scouts, queries.

"Yes, mount up," Jymar replies. "We'll follow this road east before we head up into the mountains. This way we'll bypass the ravine."

Once he's sure all the men have mounted their wolves, Jymar sets his wolf eastward. As the pace of the group of men quickens, the wolves they are riding are alarmed by a small pack of wild wolves. This is the same pack of wolves that crossed the path of the scouting party a month earlier, and Jymar's keen eye notes that one wolf is now missing.

* * *

Alagur and Marrida hear a wolf song, and their wolves respond to it. But it is the man who understands the sound. It is a warning from kin to kin that danger is close. Lya doesn't simply increase her speed because she's being urged on by Marrida, but also because of the warning from her sisters and aunts. She's communicated the warning to the greater wolf — now her matriarch — who also starts to run faster.

* * *

JYMAR CURSES AS DELGRUN, THE SCOUT SENT UP TO THE CLIFFS high above them, comes back shaking his head.

"Alagur has left. All I found is an abandoned camp. However, I did find something interesting."

Delgrun takes a small package from the makeshift bag he's created using the twigs from trees. He opens the package and lifts two large bones from within. Throwing the bag into the bushes, he gives the bones to Jymar.

"These are a wolf's teeth marks," Jymar remarks.

"I found them in a camp, perhaps a day's ride past the ravine," Delgrun tells him. "It seems they weren't there long. I saw the marks of two wolves."

"Two wolves?"

"Yes. The prints of the smaller one are similar to the prints left by the wild pack we saw."

Jymar frowns. He wonders who could be riding with Alagur, then recalls the mention of a boy by the name of Bergas.

That's the name shouted out by the boy called Melchor. I wonder if we're chasing after two missing Wolf Riders rather than just one.

The man observes the mountain range above them. He fixes his gaze on the third watchtower and studies it closely. From what he can see, it has suffered a great deal of damage. Looking back along the length of the mountain range, he determines Alagur will need to rest his wolf soon. And the fourth watchtower will be ideal for this purpose.

"We're going to the fourth watchtower," he booms. "If we find him there, we'll capture him and his runt."

"What if they manage to get away?" Jervis wants to know.

"Then we follow them to see where their journey leads. After finding out, we'll go back to City of Wolves to get everyone ready for an attack."

* * *

HALF A CONTINENT AWAY FROM THE SCOUTING PARTY, three boys are currently hiding in the undergrowth at the most southerly end of Venrasia Woods. Here the woodland lies close to the mountain range that flanks Ruh'nar on its northern side.

"Do you think the guards are gone?" Melchor hisses under his breath.

"We've been here for almost an hour, and no one has come back along the road," Kaizor whispers.

"How far are we from the city?" Ebagar enquires.

"I think it's about two days on foot. According to Belduran, there are hidden tunnels leading into the city."

"Why don't we all go into the city?" Kaizor suggests. "I don't plan to go back to City of Wolves, not if Samur is likely to come back even angrier than when he left."

The three boys are silent for a while, each wondering what they can do. Could they really get into the city?

Melchor, Kaizor and Ebagar have been travelling for two seasons, swapping retellings about their origins. Ebagar was the first to tell the two older boys how he came to be in City of Wolves, and the retelling put into perspective how different each of their lives could have been.

"Maybe our destiny can change in this city." Melchor nods south in the direction of Ruh'nar. "Belduran said to try to find someone there who'd be able to help us. And the other boys in City of Wolves, too."

"How are we going to do that?" Ebagar asks. "If the Wolf Riders find Alagur and Bergas, they'll be killed for sure, and if Samur gets to be the leader, he'll make it all even worse than it is now."

"You remember what Belduran told us about The Truth?" Kaizor says gently. "He told us it's a forewarning of some sort, perhaps even a prophecy. If it is, then there's someone around who can help us all. We should at least try to find someone in this city we can trust."

The three boys are silent again for a while. Neither of the older boys has had the heart to mention to Ebagar that the mission they're on is probably going to be a fruitless one. Perhaps it will even end up in their deaths, and those of Alagur and Bergas, Belduran, and probably many others if Samur has his way.

"Hey, you there!" a loud voice calls out, making the three boys jump up in shock. They stare as a man climbs off the cart he's driving, pulled by a couple of bovines. "Yes, you there, under the trees." The man waves his hand to beckon the boys towards him.

Melchor walks forward slowly, followed closely by the other two boys. They decide to be cautious until they know the man's intentions. His pale skin betrays the fact that he's almost certainly from a northern region.

"I've travelled since the end of last autumn to get here, and now I'm in need of a few strong lads to assist me at the market with unloading. Would the three of you like to earn yourselves a few gold coins?"

Melchor, Kaizor and Ebagar glance at one another. They won't be presented with a better opportunity than this to enter Ruh'nar, so they nod simultaneously.

"Hop into the cart with your rucksacks. My name is Mardun. I'm here for the spring market, but also to deliver a message from a fellow traveller in the north."

The mention of the north makes the boys exchange glances.

"We're here to visit a cousin," Melchor blurts out.

"Ah, good. I'll be useful to you too – I can gain you easier passage into the city. You need to have valid papers these days to get in and out. Didn't you know that?"

The three boys shake their heads.

As the eastern gate looms closer, they get more and more nervous. There's a chance that Melchor will be recognised by the guardsmen as belonging to the Wolf Riders. But the exchange of formalities turns out to be an uneventful, almost mundane affair, and the three boys sigh with relief as the cart rolls into Ruh'nar.

It's the first time Ebagar and Kaizor have seen the inside of the city, and even to the oldest boy, it feels like it's his first time here. When the city isn't under attack by Wolf Riders, it appears almost tranquil, with people busying themselves getting on with life.

The spring market Mardun plans to visit is a month-long affair, where various merchants sell their wares, perhaps also purchasing items to sell on wherever they come from. Mardun wants to purchase the leather blankets Ruh'nar is renowned for, and he has already located two suppliers to approach.

But most of all, the conversation he had with the strange man he met at the Bay of Whispers has made him curious, and Mardun wants to meet Joharan.

He stops his cart next to a large market stall which is his to use at each spring market, jumps down, and motions to the boys sitting in the cart. They jump down too.

"If you unload all the merchandise I've got in the cart, I'll give you your gold coins, but I need you to do something else for me. Can I trust you to do what I ask of you?"

The boys nod. They're only in the city thanks to the man's assistance. Not one of them wants to spoil their chances now by upsetting Mardun in case he calls for a guard to arrest them.

The man opens a pocket in a leather bag he's taken from below his seat on the cart and pulls out a package. He unwinds the cord holding the package together and reveals a tinder kit.

"This needs to be returned to someone by the name of Joharan, who lives in this city," he explains. "I want all three of you to go and find that man, and relay the strange message I was given."

"What is the message?" Melchor asks.

"The message is for someone this Joharan knows personally," Mardun replies. "It says, 'Tell him that he can use this in the tunnels as I used it once'."

Mardun repacks the tinder kit and places it in his pocket.

"First, you need to do what I asked of you, then you can deliver the message, and after that – well, that's up to you. If you really have a cousin here as you said, you can visit him. And if not, it's your business, and not mine. When you see Joharan, tell him a man by the name of Mardun plans to visit him tomorrow. You can deliver that message at the same time as the tinder kit."

Driven by curiosity as to why someone would deliver such a mysterious message from somewhere far to the north of City of Wolves to a person living in Ruh'nar, the boys make light work of their task. After an hour, they've unpacked all the merchant's wares, and each receives three gold coins from Mardun. Then he hands the package containing the tinder kit to Melchor, and repeats the message.

As they walk away from the merchant, Melchor soon realises Mardun hasn't told them where to find Joharan. *Perhaps he is testing our ingenuity.*

"Pull your hoods up," he says to his companions. "We want to look like one of them." By 'one of them', he means the many merchants who are busying themselves preparing their market stalls.

Ebagar pulls Melchor's sleeve. "I've got an idea how to find out where Joharan lives." He points at the front steps of the imposing Temple of Ruh'nar.

"Why do you think they might know?"

"They'll know who's in charge of the merchants here," Ebagar states, ignoring the older boy's irritable tone.

"Why?" Melchor and Kaizor ask at the same time.

"Because I remember something from home." Ebagar looks at the ground and shuffles his foot. Both older boys kneel to look up into his face.

"What do you remember?" Melchor asks in a gentler tone.

"I remember going to a similar building with my father and older sister, and my father telling me the people who live in it know everyone in the city."

"Good point," Kaizor says. "Let's try that."

Melchor and Kaizor get up, and all three boys walk towards the door of the Temple. After looking at the doors hesitantly for a while, they stand waiting. Finally, they see a woman approaching from within the building, which makes each boy wonder how she knew they wanted to speak to someone inside.

As chance – or otherwise – would have it, it's Elder Sharriba who walks to the entrance of the Temple. She raises an eyebrow when she sees the three boys standing shyly on the steps of the building.

"You do know this isn't a place for men or boys?" she says pointedly.

"We know, he told us." Melchor points at Ebagar.

"Why are you here? Have you got family within?"

"No."

"So how can I help you?"

"Where I come from, my father and sister always went to a building which looked like this. And my father told me when you don't know anyone in a town, you can find out where a person lives by asking here. He said the people in this sort of building know everyone in charge of a town."

Ebagar looks down, unsure whether he should have spoken to the woman. Melchor and Kaizor just stare at their younger companion.

Elder Sharriba looks at each boy in turn. "Have you come far?" she questions in a softer tone.

"We came with Mardun." Melchor points over his shoulder. Sharriba raises her eyebrow again and glances towards the corner of the square, where she knows the man's market stall is located.

This is the first time Mardun has come into the city accompanied by anyone.

"So, you want to know if I know the person you're searching for, is that it?" All three boys nod. "Then tell me the name so I can send you on your way. It seems to me that Mardun is having a laugh at my expense."

At the next words from Melchor, the woman draws in her breath so sharply, the boys all look at one another with genuine concern.

"I know that man," she says softly. "He's the uncle of one of my… students."

Ebagar frowns when he hears this. He knows those within the Temple are more than just students, but he decides to keep quiet on this point.

"Follow that street there and walk for six hundred paces, then turn left and immediately right again. After another left turn, you get to Joharan's house. It's on the left and has a dark red door."

Sharriba turns, closes the Temple door and walks quickly towards her private chambers before anyone can see how pale the boys' message has made her.

CHAPTER SEVENTY

"S HE TOLD US TO TURN LEFT HERE." Kaizor blocks Melchor's way when the older boy wants to go right. They've arrived at the final junction of the street that will bring them to their destination.

"Are you sure?"

"Yes, I am."

The boys turn into the street to the left, and after a short distance come to a dark red door.

"This must be it," Ebagar notes. "We should knock first."

Melchor knocks twice on the door and waits. He hears fast-paced footsteps, and a boy of perhaps twelve years old opens the door.

"Can I help you?" Curiosity is evident in the boy's voice.

Melchor, Kaizor and Ebagar glance at one another, not entirely sure what to say now.

"Is there someone at the door, Sherino?" a loud, booming voice calls from within the house. The boy's face disappears as he answers the question.

"Yes, there are three boys at the door, but they won't tell me what they're here for, Joharan."

"It's him," Kaizor hisses at Melchor, prodding his friend in the ribs. The boy who answered the door hears the comment and sticks his head around the door once more.

"It's him – *who*?" he asks. "Are you after someone?"

"Yes," Kaizor replies. "We've got a message for someone by the name of Joharan."

"Joharan, they say they're here with a message for you," the boy at the door calls.

"Show them in, Sherino. Tell them to wait in the cooking room for me."

Sherino opens the door wide and motions to the boys to come inside. "You can sit there to wait for him." He points at the cooking room table.

Melchor, Kaizor and Ebagar sit down on a bench on one side of the long table – the same side where, three seasons earlier, a tearful Marrida sat while she told her uncle about her unexpected visitor. They wait. Finally, footsteps descending a stairway announce the arrival of the master of the house, and a moment or so later, Joharan enters the cooking room.

"I'm told you've got a message for me." He looks questioningly at the three boys, who are staring at him, wide-eyed. When he wants to, Joharan can cut an imposing figure.

"We were told by a merchant to come and look for you--"

"First tell me your names."

"My name is Melchor, this here is Kaizor, and the young one there is Ebagar."

"And what is the message you bring me?"

He doesn't waste time with small talk, Melchor thinks before speaking again.

"Actually, we have two messages. One of them is from a man called Mardun."

Joharan raises an eyebrow for a moment. He knows the man the boy speaks of, but says nothing and allows Melchor to continue at his own pace.

"The other message is a bit odd," the boy reveals. "But where I come from, odd messages can actually be very important."

He pauses for a moment to recall the full message, then continues talking.

"Mardun says he met a man on his travels, before he met us. And this man gave him an object and a few words to tell you. Or, more correctly, to tell someone you know."

Melchor opens the pocket of his tunic in which he's stashed the small package containing the tinder kit, and places it on the table an arm's length from himself.

"The man told Mardun to say to whomever the message is meant for, 'You can use it again in the tunnels as I used it once'. Mardun made us repeat the words several times to make sure we got them right."

"Did Mardun tell you where he met the sender of the message?" Joharan asks.

"Yes, somewhere in the north. He said the man was walking eastwards, while he was travelling west."

Joharan thinks for a few minutes. "Come with me," he declares sternly, getting up and wrapping the cloak he's grabbed from a hook next to the front door around his shoulders. He opens the door, then waits for the three boys to scramble up from the table and walk outside, single file.

"I'm going to be at Esbara's house for a while. Close up the workshop and have some free time," Joharan shouts out, then he steps out of his house and shuts the door behind him. "Follow me," he commands, signalling towards the boys. As he walks past them, Melchor notices Joharan is holding the package they brought with them tightly in his hand.

It doesn't take long before the four of them arrive at another house in another street. All three boys look surprised when the man simply opens the door without knocking.

"Come inside," Joharan whispers, then he calls out in a booming voice which reminds the boys of Belduran on a day when you wouldn't want to cross him. But this man's voice has no anger in it.

"Uncle Joharan, what are you doing here?" a voice calls out, and in a flurry of activity, a young girl flies into a welcoming embrace from the man.

"Is Esbara home?"

"No, he and Damir have gone to buy supplies at the market. They should be back soon." The girl glances at the boys, and asks, "Who are they?"

"They're here with a message from Marrida and Alagur," Joharan says. The statement makes the three boys look at one another in shock.

How do these people know Alagur?

"This is Kalisa," Joharan says. "She's Marrida's sister, and Damir's promised one."

"Melchor."

"Kaizor."

"I'm Ebagar."

"They can sit in the front room," Kalisa says, smiling at the boys.

"You heard her. Go in there, and sit on the sofa." Joharan adds, "We'll be there shortly."

The three boys walk into a well-decorated, spacious room where a fire is burning. It's obvious that those who occupy the house are well-to-do. Somewhat hesitantly, the boys sit down and look around.

"How do they know Alagur?" Melchor mouths discreetly to his two companions.

"I don't know," Kaizor mutters. "But if they do, maybe that message came from him."

"We definitely can't go back to City of Wolves now. We could put him in danger if we did," Ebagar whispers.

"I don't think Belduran meant for us to return anyway. He wanted us safe from Samur's temper."

"I wonder where Alagur was going when Mardun met him."

"He said the man was walking, so where was Yalla at the time?"

"And who is this Marrida? And why did the old man refer to them both?"

"Marrida is my niece," a deep voice says. Melchor, Kaizor and Ebagar were so deeply involved in their discussion, they didn't notice Joharan and Kalisa enter the room, and they almost jump up when the man speaks. "Who is this Belduran you mentioned?"

"He sent us here," Melchor replies simply.

"To save you from Samur?"

The boys nod.

Joharan looks at Kalisa for a moment. "You'd better go and find Esbara and Damir, and tell them to come home right away," he commands. "If they ask, say that there are more unexpected guests waiting at Marrida's house."

Kalisa nods, and without saying another word, she puts on a cloak and leaves the house, slamming the front door in her hurry to find her brother and friend.

Joharan sits down on a chair opposite the boys and observes them each in turn. *They don't look like they're well-fed or in good health.*

"I think I need to explain what's going on. It may explain why this Belduran sent you here, too."

The boys nod.

"I presume you came from the same city as Alagur and his friend, Bergas?"

The boys' shocked expressions as they glance at one another tell the man the answer – yes, they did.

"Alagur was a guest in this house, which is owned by my niece Marrida and her two siblings, one of whom you've already met. He was wounded in the Wolf Riders' attack here last year."

The man looks more closely at the three boys. The oldest one bears a striking resemblance to the description of a boy who escaped when his two companions were killed.

"You were here that day, weren't you?" he asks sharply, looking directly at Melchor. The boy frowns, and for a moment his expression says, "How do you know?" But then he remembers the vow he made after Elder Man Vaymaz's death to make sure he and his two younger companions would get away from City of Wolves safely, and he softens his expression.

"Yes, I was here," he confesses, looking down and going bright red. Kaizor and Ebagar look surprised when they notice how ashamed he is.

"It's good that none of the city's defenders recognised you," Joharan says. "And don't worry, I'm not about to deliver people who are here with a message from Marrida and Alagur into their hands."

The boys' shoulders slump as they hear the words. The tension which has been gripping them from the moment they knocked on Joharan's door leaves them now, and Joharan sees it.

Sounds from the vestibule announce Kalisa's return, and the discussion pauses. The breathless way the girl is talking to her companions indicates that she ran as fast as she could into the city to search for them. She even went into the Temple to ask if her brother was on guard duty for the Keepers, noting that Elder Sharriba looked pale and withdrawn. Then she spotted the two boys in a side street, where they'd just left a shop selling metalwork.

Kalisa and the two new arrivals walk into the front room and lower themselves onto the bench which Esbara and Alagur carried through from the cooking room the previous year. It has never made its way back to its rightful place. Then a battle of wills ensues as the young people stare at each other.

It's the visitors who look down first.
"I have already introduced Kalisa to you." Joharan smiles.
"Hi," Kalisa says.
"And this is Esbara, who's Marrida's brother, and Damir, who's going to be Kalisa's life partner."
The boys each lift their left arm up in a formal greeting when the man speaks their name.
"You need to reintroduce yourselves as I can't remember who's who," Joharan says to the three young visitors.
"I'm Melchor, this is Kaizor, and this is Ebagar."
Joharan nods, then reaches into a pocket of his tunic and pulls out the small wrapped package.
"Let's find out what the message is. Can you repeat the words Mardun told you, Melchor?"
"He said the man stated that the person could use this in the tunnels 'as I once did'."
Damir frowns momentarily.
"I think this message is meant for you, Damir. You'd better unwrap this and see what it contains."

Damir gets up and kneels next to the table where Joharan has placed the package. He looks at the old man and gets an encouraging nod in response, then he unwraps the package. He's surprised to find his own tinder kit within it.

"I gave this to Alagur just before he went out of the city through the old tunnels."

The news makes the three visitors look at one another again. How did Belduran know about the existence of the tunnels? They'd doubted the man, but now they have confirmation that the tunnel exist. And why has Belduran never told anyone in City of Wolves about them?

"There's a parchment lodged inside the inner chamber," Damir states, arousing everyone's curiosity. He pulls out a tightly-folded parchment from the tinder kit.

"What does it say?"

Damir looks closely at the text on the parchment. It's certainly Alagur's handwriting. "He tells us where he was. He says Marrida visited Eldagu, and it went well. They've travelled to the Bay of Whispers and will soon be at Azaquina for wintering. Then the plan is to travel east from the city. That's all it says."

"I guess he didn't have a great deal of time to write more than that," Joharan responds.

"Oh, and on the back, it says, 'Tell Kalisa Yalla is off to have her babies', and it shows a small drawing of the wolf too."

"Ha! That means Samur won't have his wolf squad then," Melchor blurts out. Six pairs of eyes turn to stare at him at the same time.

"What you mean?" Ebagar asks.

"Don't you remember his ranting in the city? He said he wanted Alagur killed, and Yalla's offspring brought to him."

Melchor still remembers the way Samur shouted at him. His previous admiration – misguided as it was – has been replaced during the boys' months of travelling by an ice-cold hatred for the man who so callously murdered Elder Man Vaymaz.

"You're from City of Wolves too?" Kalisa is starting to understand how their three visitors know Alagur.

"Yes, we are."

There's a long silence after Melchor's confirmation. It makes the visitors even more aware that they'll probably be killed by Samur if he ever gets his hands on them.

Melchor speaks again, very softly.

"I don't want any of us to go back. Belduran told us to deliver Ebagar here so he could find help for us all, but when Mardun asked us to help him out, we took our chances and all came into the city with him." He pauses before continuing. "I think Belduran wants things in City of Wolves to end. It's getting increasingly dangerous there, especially since Samur killed Elder Man Vaymaz in cold blood. Belduran and Vaymaz told Samur to let all the boys younger than eighteen leave. It would have meant Kaizor and Ebagar could have gone home, but not me as I'm already eighteen."

Melchor looks at Joharan and pleads with his eyes before continuing.

"I was horrible to Bergas when he was in City of Wolves, but now I just want to have what they've got." He points at Esbara and Damir, who are sitting across the room from him. The two boys look at one another. "I want a normal life with my family. I want to see my sister growing up, like Kalisa is--"

Melchor starts crying uncontrollably. Joharan, Kalisa, Esbara and Damir look at one another silently for several moments, considering between themselves what they can do for the three visitors.

"I think they should stay here," Esbara states. "They can use the room that Alagur used before." As he's the one in charge of the household while Marrida is on her journey, it's for him to decide whether the three boys will be guests or not. Kalisa and Damir nod to agree with the suggestion.

"It seems you have a place to start your normal life," Joharan says. "And I'll help you in any way I can."

There's an audible sigh from each of the visitors when they realise that their chance for redemption is in front of them.

CHAPTER SEVENTY-ONE

Aᴌᴀɢᴜʀ ᴀɴᴅ Mᴀʀʀɪᴅᴀ ᴅɪsᴍᴏᴜɴᴛ and pat their wolf companions to reward the animals for their efforts. They've been travelling hard without any pauses for the greater part of the day, only slowing an hour or so before they reached the fourth watchtower.

"It's so massive when you stand right next to it." Marrida cranes her neck to get a grasp on the height of the building.

"I can count at least seven windows above us, so it's as high as four or five houses." Alagur is also straining to see the upper storeys of the building.

"I can see daylight coming through the top four windows, so I don't think the building is totally intact."

"You're right. We need to be careful as we enter."

Marrida nods.

Alagur removes his spear arrows and thrower from Yalla's harness, and two embers from the haversack he has placed on the ground. He hooks the haversack over the saddle part of the harness and sees Marrida copying his actions with her own haversack. His weapons he places in a halter over his left shoulder.

He checks Marrida's readiness and she gives a nod. Alagur then gives Yalla a signal, and with a short grunt, the wolf moves to the nearby undergrowth, followed by Lya.

"If it's too broken up in there, we'll need to forgo staying here and continue travelling."

Marrida nods again.

They look around for the entrance to the building and see an opening on the western side. They pass the wolves as they approach the doorway, and Alagur signals once more for them to stay put. Using his thrower to determine the stability of the doorway, he steps through it, closely followed by Marrida.

Inside, they're met by a massive space, which in a time long past could have been a grand vestibule. Its size dwarfs the vestibule in the Temple of Ruh'nar, and Marrida mentions this to Alagur.

"Maybe they started building the Temples larger later on."

Marrida looks up and confirms that the upper floors are missing from the building. However, a staircase leads to two floors which are partially intact. There's another entrance one level up from where they are that must have been put in to accommodate the gentle slope in the landscape.

Alagur looks around him too with a feeling of awe, wondering what the building was used for.

"Maybe we can check out those two floors at least," Marrida suggests softly. When the man looks at her, she pleads with her eyes.

"I think we can if we're careful," he acknowledges, smiling.

Holding Marrida's hand, and the ember he has lit in his other hand, Alagur gradually ascends the stairs, testing each one with a foot before stepping onto it; there's no banister to hold on to. The pair look to the side of the stairway and see what could have been a banister in the distant past, before the building was abandoned.

They arrive at a platform where the alternative entrance is located, and after a short discussion decide to continue up to investigate the second floor. The landing there is more intact than the one on the floor below it, and a doorway leads into a large room. It seems it was once some sort of library, but now the books stored there crumble when either of them tries to pick one up.

An opening on their immediate left reveals the clearest clue as to what happened to the building, and inside it, during its destruction. The man and woman each take a turn looking out of the gaping hole, and the darkened smudge on the outside of the building tells them the damage wasn't done naturally. Someone used a powerful weapon of destruction against those who once used the building.

"Who do you think could have done all this?"

"I don't know. The damage seems very old, and similar to what happened to the bridge." Alagur frowns as he speaks.

"We could stay in this room to rest from the journey," Marrida suggests. "This opening is perfect for Yalla and Lya to come and go."

Alagur nods.

"I suggest we stay here rather than trying to explore the rest of the building. I'm not sure how stable it is. And once we're ready to leave, we can use this opening here as an exit."

Alagur whistles twice, and the wolves come loping towards them moments later. The man leads each animal up a pile of rubble to allow them entry into the building. The wolves sniff the floor, or what is left of it, for several minutes, then they settle down near the opening. Alagur gets each wolf to lift themselves from the floor in turn so he can remove the packs, which he places against the wall to the right of the opening. He's about to take off Yalla's harness when he changes his mind, leaving the device on her. He does the same with Lya, which surprises Marrida. But then she recalls how, weeks earlier, Alagur had been restless while they slept under an overhang.

She turns and goes to find somewhere to settle down for a bit of relaxation. Picking up her haversack, she carries it to the north-eastern corner of the room, where she places it next to a stone similar to the one she sat on in the third watchtower. She sits down, then looks around her.

I wonder who built this. It feels oddly familiar.

She decides to record what she's seeing here before they have to leave.

"Alagur, how long can we stay here?" she calls out to the man across the large room.

"I would guess we can stay for two or three weeks."

Marrida gives him a radiant smile.

** * **

ALAGUR HAS HIS BACK TO MARRIDA. HE'S HARD AT WORK, giving Yalla's coat a good brushing, showing why he has the bulk of his muscles in his upper arms. Marrida has tried several times to do the same with Lya, but each time she has to stop after five minutes or so. Alagur can brush one wolf for an hour or more without his actions diminishing. And then, he'll start on the other wolf.

It has almost become a tradition that when Alagur brushes the wolves, Marrida will do some of her own activities. Most days, Marrida has Sharriba's journal open to study the sixth dialect. She knows two or three hundred words now.

Marrida has started to copy what Sharriba wrote in her younger years, transcribing the verbal part of any self-repositioning she'd encountered during visions. While she's busy with the translations, she also recalls from her memory what she heard Emelyse and Jarryca say, writing the wording in her journal phonetically. She's been doing this for more than a week now, and her understanding of the dialect has increased considerably in that time.

But today, she wants to draw various aspects of the mysterious building they're staying in. Or, more accurately, she wants to copy several of the wall images that are still visible, and perhaps a depiction of the vestibule. Earlier she examined an image just outside the door which leads into the ruined library, and she has made up her mind to draw that first.

Marrida sits down on the second tread of the ancient stairway. Once she's sure the structure is safe enough to hold her weight, she looks up at the artwork on the wall above her. The pigments which were used for the work have either faded away or flaked off the wall. However, part of the image is still visible, and it fascinates her. She has never seen any artwork like this, and she wonders what the meaning of the image is.

She takes out her writing implement and opens her second notebook: the one she uses for drawings. Looking carefully at the wall, she copies what she can make out of the image.

Slowly a picture appears, and it causes her to worry. The image reveals men on wolves, but their clothing is foreign, and thousands of years older than what people commonly wear today.

"How's the drawing going?" Alagur asks as he appears through the doorway onto the stairway. He frowns when he sees Marrida's face.

"I don't know. This image is puzzling me," she answers slowly. "Why would people draw an image of men on wolves in a building?"

"Men on wolves?" Alagur exclaims. "Let me see the drawing, please."

Marrida hands the notebook to the man, and he studies the image, comparing it with the one on the wall.

"I recall reading in one of the books in Jarryca's library about ancient weaponry," he comments, lowering the notebook. "This weapon looks like one described in that book. Wait here, I'll get my notes."

Alagur hands the notebook back to Marrida, who places it on her lap to add more detail to the drawing from the image on the wall. She soon realises she has copied everything already.

She looks up when Alagur returns after a few minutes with a small stack of parchment.

"I only copied it because I was curious about it. I wanted to attempt to make one of the weapons in the future, if I had an opportunity."

"Why is this weapon so interesting?" Marrida asks.

"Because no one has made it for almost fifteen hundred years. It was probably used by the northern invaders we were told about. Because of this drawing, I'm starting to think this building was used by them in the past."

"I think you're wrong."

"Why?"

"Since we arrived here, I've felt as though the building is familiar. The feeling intensified when we entered this room." Marrida points at the doorway next to them. "I think this building once housed the Order."

"You mean this was once a place for the Keepers of Truth?" Alagur looks around more closely for any clues he may have missed.

"No, I said it housed the Order, not the Keepers of Truth." Alagur looks at her with such a puzzled expression on his face that Marrida starts to laugh. "You don't get it." She chuckles even more. "Listen to what I said – it belonged to the Order."

"Ooh – right," Alagur says finally. "So, does this mean we're getting closer to the original form of the Order of Truth the further east we go?"

"I think so, but I keep remembering the warning Emelyse gave. She was sent away from something her mother didn't want her exposed to, so we need to be cautious. I may also have worked out the last three letters of the city we're travelling towards. D and A are visible there on the wall, with an H, I and A further along. I'm missing just four more letters, then I'll know the name Emelyse said to Jarryca."

Alagur smiles. He knows Marrida has been working hard to translate the journal and solve the many mysteries they are discovering wherever they go.

"I'll go and hunt for something to cook for a meal. Please be careful if you plan to go anywhere else." Alagur gets up.

"I will. I'm going to compare this drawing's composition with what I read in Jarryca's books to see if I noted down anything useful."

Marrida gets up too and walks back into the large room which is acting as their temporary dwelling. Alagur picks up his spear arrows and thrower. After whistling a command to Yalla to indicate the animal should stay with Marrida, he climbs over the rubble by the opening on the side of the building. Pausing momentarily to listen for animals to track, he turns in a north-easterly direction.

* * *

Marrida listens until Alagur's footsteps have faded away, then she decides to see what she can see from the windows in the room. At the fifth window, the sight which greets her makes her draw in her breath.

There's a steep slope to the south, and beyond it lies a bright green valley telling of good rainfall at the right time of the year. It's probably the most beautiful place Marrida has ever seen in her life.

Could this have been one reason why an ancient people chose this location for the building?

The valley is surrounded by a few hills and higher mountain slopes, and a river makes its way through its centre as a glistening trail of sparkles. A distant orange hue tells Marrida that she can see rubha apple shrubberies in blossom.

They'll come into harvest two seasons from now.

A long waterfall on the east side of the valley betrays the height of the surrounding mountains. She wonders where the water thundering down in an endless whirl of foam originates from and, more importantly, whether it will offer invigorating bathing.

Marrida leans her head against the window frame, which lost its glass many centuries earlier. The peacefulness of the region relaxes her, and she would happily spend the whole summer here, if she could convince Alagur it would be a good idea.

However, Marrida knows her task dictates her destiny, so she only has the next two or three weeks to look out over this valley. She opens her notebook and absentmindedly draws the general features of the landscape, knowing later she can draw a more complete image of what she's seeing from her memory.

Marrida glances down when she notices the wolves are sitting next to her. Looking first into Yalla's intelligent yellow eyes, and then into the liquid brown eyes of Lya, Marrida gives each wolf a scratching. In response, they thump their tails on the floor, bringing up a cloud of dust.
"You'd better go and lie over there." Marrida coughs and points towards the floor in the middle of the room. The wolves look at her a moment longer, then they obey her command. Marrida smiles when she realises she can command the wolves as well as Alagur, and she decides it might help to practise the whistling too.

Marrida glances at her notebook and sees dust has settled on the page she was drawing on. She raises it and blows on it gently. A small dust cloud lifts, and then she can finalise the image in a few strokes.

She closes the book and looks up once more, frowning when she sees someone has spoilt the beauty of the landscape with smoke from a campfire. What her mind doesn't register is that the dark column rising in the distance could be something other than smoke.

CHAPTER SEVENTY-TWO

Mᴀʀʀɪᴅᴀ ᴅɪᴠᴇs ᴜɴᴅᴇʀ ᴛʜᴇ ᴡᴀᴛᴇʀ and swims across the small lake in a few even strokes. Alagur follows her lead, and a moment after she rises out of the water, so does he. The wolves are having their own fun, rolling through the mud which lines the bank of the lake.

Alagur found the lake during his trek north the previous evening when he went out hunting for an animal to butcher for their meal. When he woke up that morning, he lay beside the woman, watching her sleep. When she stirred, he leaned over and kissed her.

"Would you like to come with me? I've got a surprise in store for you."

Marrida nodded and smiled. They trekked for perhaps fifteen minutes until they arrived at the 'surprise' – the small lake in which they're now bathing naked. It reminds Marrida of when she was swimming early one morning the previous summer, when Alagur walked over to hold her towel up for her.

This time, it doesn't matter that we're both naked. This time, we're swimming as people who'll become life partners in the near future--

Marrida drifts on her back in the cool water, looking up at the branches of the trees waving softly above her. She feels Alagur's hand slide under her back, and she responds by putting her arm around his shoulders. She looks at Alagur and smiles at him. He smiles back and leans forward to kiss her.

"Do you want me to carry you back?" he murmurs. She nods.

Alagur walks from the water. As they approach their clothing, which is hanging from one of the bushes shadowing the lake, he stops to allow the woman in his arms to retrieve it. They only partially dressed that morning and walked to the lake without wearing any shoes.

Once Marrida has taken all the clothes and draped them over herself, Alagur walks steadily from the lake to the building. Once they're inside, he lays Marrida on the bed they constructed in the most unspoiled corner of their temporary home.

Alagur pulls a towel from his haversack. Marrida lies still as his hands move the towel over her body. The sensation of his touch sends an unfamiliar feeling of heat through her, which makes her want him close to her. She breathes with her mouth open and closes her eyes when his hand travels to the lower parts of her body, ending up resting just below her belly button. Marrida feels disappointed when the hand travels up again, then she draws in a breath when it rests on one of her breasts.

Alagur watches the play of emotions crossing the woman's face and he suspects the feelings she's having are new to her. Unlike other Wolf Riders, who made a game of raping as many women as they could, he refrained from the activity, which meant he'd entered adulthood celibate. For the past eight years of his life, he has grown accustomed to being on his own. He feels his love for Marrida welling up, almost overwhelming him, but he decides on restraint, so he spends his time caressing her, watching with increasing amusement as he leaves her almost gasping for air.

After perhaps half an hour, Alagur notices Marrida is rubbing her arms as if she is getting cold, so he pulls a few clean clothes from her haversack and places them on the floor next to her side of the bed. She sits upright and smiles at him, and Alagur notices a glimpse of gratitude in her eyes. He realises his restraint has increased her trust in him.

He leans forward and kisses her lips, and finds her a willing recipient. After a few minutes, he moves away and looks at her once more, seeing how much she has matured in the three seasons they've been travelling.

They get dressed, then work on preparing something which resembles a morning meal. Once it's cooked, they walk to the stairway and sit on the tread where Marrida was sitting to copy the wall image. For a while, they eat without speaking, observing the wall in more detail.

"What do you think that is?" Alagur asks, swallowing the last piece of meat from his plate. He points up at a small object in the corner of the image. Marrida frowns and studies it for a while.

"It almost looks like some sort of crown. I learnt nothing about a crown in my studies at the Temple, or from the books which Jarryca gave me to read. It looks ancient."

"I wonder why those three women are holding it over a flame."

Marrida is wondering that too, but she doesn't respond to the man's comment for a while.

"Perhaps we need to look in other parts of the building," she says finally, then adds before Alagur can protest, "And yes, we'll do it carefully."

"We can look on the lowest floor. I noticed another drawing there," Alagur suggests. "I'll get your other notebook."

He gets up and takes Marrida's empty plate, together with his own, to the area he has turned into a makeshift cooking room. He puts the plates on the floor and signals to the wolves to lick them clean before he places them into a container of boiling water.

Alagur picks up the second notebook and the writing implement lying next to it, then walks back to the stairway. He sees Marrida has got up and is leaning over the edge of the stairway, trying to peer down at the artwork on the lowest floor.

"If you walk close to the wall, you can use it as a support," he suggests, giving the notebook and writing implement to her. Marrida nods and gradually makes her way down in the manner he's suggested, but she still grabs the man's hand when a small stone rolls away underfoot.

After ten minutes, they're at the bottom of the stairway. Both glance up when they hear the wolves softly yelping. After a signal from Alagur, both animals disappear, and a soft thud, followed by a second one, tells them that their lupine companions are lying down once more.

Alagur pulls out his tinder kit and a spare ember and lights the small lamp to illuminate the shadier parts of the lower floor. They look around closely and see a doorway in the shadows he hadn't previously noticed.

"I don't think it's safe to go in there."

Marrida nods, hiding her disappointment. She wants some sense of adventure from all this exploring. As she turns her head, her eyes rest on the image of a woman in the shadow.

"Alagur, look," she whispers.

Alagur looks in the direction Marrida is pointing, and he too is struck by the beauty of the image.

"She's wearing the crown we saw depicted upstairs. I wonder who she is."

"She looks sad," Alagur replies.

Instinctively, both of them look to the wall opposite the woman's portrait and see there the image of a man. And to Marrida, his eyes have the menace of someone born evil.

"Who could he be?" Marrida's voice is now trembling. She feels almost as if the man could step out of the portrait and strike her down. Alagur glances at Marrida, frowning for a moment as he notices the fear in her voice. He then looks back at the image and studies it closely, frowning even more.

The portraits they have found both possess a regal quality, but whereas the woman's portrait fills him with awe, the man's portrait gives him a feeling of foreboding – the same foreboding he's felt many times during their journey. Even he, battle hardened though he is, feels the menace emanating from the image. Both images seem to be as old as the building itself, but there's something odd about the man's image.

"That man could almost be Samur," Alagur mumbles under his breath. Marrida goes as white as moss ash.

"Why do you say that?"

Alagur almost jumps at the question. He didn't realise that he'd spoken aloud.

"Because Samur looks like him. If I didn't know better, this man could be Samur's ancestor."

Marrida studies the portrait closely, mostly to imprint the image into her mind. "Didn't you say Samur was from somewhere in the eastern parts of Keldarra?"

"Yes, but no one in City of Wolves knows exactly where. He has never told us. Remember how I told you that he got information about the Wolf Riders from someone who he then killed?"

Marrida nods and swallows hard. That part of the life of the Wolf Riders is something she still can't cope with. When Alagur sees the emotion his words have evoked, he runs the back of his left hand over the woman's right cheek. He feels no tears, but he does feel that she's trembling.

"Do you want to go back up?"

"No, I'm alright," Marrida replies. "I'll draw them both."

* * *

IT TAKES MARRIDA A FEW HOURS TO COPY THE PORTRAITS. As Alagur watches her work, he notices that she copies the man's portrait less carefully than the woman's and assumes this is because Marrida doesn't want to keep looking at the man. Alagur walks off to get them a drink, and as he returns to the area where the portraits are hanging, he gets the unsettling feeling that the man's eyes are following him around.

For a while, there's silence, but then Marrida asks a question.

"You mentioned that one of the boys you knew in City of Wolves came from the east too. Which one?"

"Ebagar is from somewhere in the east, but perhaps not as far east as Samur," Alagur answers. "Why do you ask?"

"Can you tell me what Ebagar looks like? Has he got dark hair too?"

Alagur thinks for a moment before answering. "Now you mention it, he has."

"Do all the boys snatched from the east have dark hair?" Marrida looks up from her work at the man.

"Yes, most seem to."

"Eldagu has dark hair too, and dark skin. His hair is densely curly, to be precise." Marrida demonstrates an approximation of the man's hair, then continues speaking. "He is originally from east of Alzamar. And you say Ebagar is from the east. Eldagu mentioned his life partner is visiting a town called Hayzan. I wonder if that's where Ebagar originates from."

"What has all this to do with Samur? Or this man, for that matter?"

"The further east we go, the further we get into the part of Keldarra which suffered the longest under the influence of the northern invaders. I don't think it was by chance that Samur ended up with the Wolf Riders. He knew the history of the northern invaders before he came to look for the Wolf Riders, and all his actions — or at least the ones we know about — point to him wanting to be like them."

"You mean to say Samur wants the Wolf Riders to be like those northern invaders?"

"Yes, and most specifically like that man." Marrida points at the portrait over her shoulder. "It would be best if Samur never knows that exists."

Alagur shakes his head, wondering how Marrida comes up with her theories seemingly from nowhere.

I guess she's been thinking about what she learnt from Jarryca's books and has worked out what the old woman and Emelyse were talking about.

"I'm done here. Can we look around a bit more?"

Alagur nods and leads the way to a corridor just beyond the woman's portrait. Alagur then agrees to look inside the room he earlier deemed to be unsafe for a short period, which seems like it could have belonged to the man in the portrait. It doesn't take long before they both feel the need to get back to the second floor and their temporary home — urgently.

Marrida gets Sharriba's journal out and turns to a page halfway through the book. She has decided to continue with a translation in the Sab'ruhi dialect which she's now fluent in. She'd set it aside three weeks ago in favour of translating Achellon's dialect.

She frowns at the passage she reads, then rereads it and sees the anomaly in the wording.

Why was Sharriba writing every few words in a different dialect? Is there a hidden message within the text?

"I think I've found it," Marrida calls out.

"You've found what?"

"The message about the vision Sharriba did. She didn't just write a simple message about a vision of the Wolf Riders, but wrote cryptically to hide the other vision she also did – perhaps the one that Kyrana didn't want the world to know about. The one for which she punished Sharriba so severely."

"Was that punishment in the vision you did at your house before we departed?"

"Yes. I think Sharriba did certain things intentionally that day to lead anyone watching the event in a vision to this message." Marrida points at the journal. "I need to access that vision again so I can find the means of translating this dialect."

"Are you sure you want to do it? Last time, you ended up seeing that dark cave." Alagur walks to where the woman is sitting and kneels in front of her. "I can help you by pulling you out if necessary. But only if you want me to."

"You can help." Marrida smiles. "Remember that I'm stronger now with my skill, so I can avoid going back to that place. You can also help by creating somewhere comfortable for me to sit."

Alagur gets up and works silently to make a seat from a layer of blankets which he places on the floor. He then puts a pack in front of a block of stone to create a backrest. Marrida sits down on the seat and nods her approval.

It feels so comfortable. Perhaps I can convince him to sit with me after I've done the vision.

But as her mind clears itself in readiness for the vision, a less pleasant thought fills her mind. Marrida keeps thinking that she has overlooked a crucial detail – something she has seen.

What was it again?

CHAPTER SEVENTY-THREE

T HE TWO WOMEN ARE SITTING OPPOSITE ONE ANOTHER, but they don't seem as imposing as the first time that Marrida saw them three seasons earlier. She looks again for a moment at the younger version of her mentor, blocking out the women's conversation as irrelevant.

Marrida moves across the room to where Sharriba's partially-written journal lies. As she approaches it, she hesitates, wondering if it was the trigger that pulled her to the time and place of the cave.

"The closer you get to the day and time of the event you see in an Awakening, the less chance there is of it manifesting itself."

Jarryca's voice echoes in her mind. Marrida's surroundings move until she is hovering over the journal. She waits, and when nothing in the vision changes, she starts to read the text.

Meanwhile, Alagur quietly picks up Marrida's journal and opens it at a blank page. Rather than simply being there to pull Marrida out of the vision if it proves necessary, Alagur has decided to make himself even more useful by writing down what she is seeing in her vision. He hopes it will make her task easier later on. As Marrida's eyes read the text in the vision, Alagur views the shimmering disc which displays the unfolding event.

Marrida realises she's reading text not in Sab'ruhi, as she thought it was in the earlier vision stored in her memory, but in the Achallai dialect. Is it possible that was Keldarra's original dialect?

She hears a voice – younger, but still familiar – saying, "The land was once called Keltana--"

A whirling mass disorientates Marrida as blackness envelops her, and two strong hands pull her up. For a moment, Marrida thinks she has blacked out after her vision and it's Alagur pulling her up, but when she looks around, she sees an ornately decorated room. It is foreign in appearance, yet has a familiar feeling to it. She can't see who caused her to feel as though she was being pulled up, though.

Blackness overcomes her again and her mind is pulled in another direction. She looks around and sees a crowd of men, cheering and shouting. One man in their midst raises something in the air above his head…

It is gone.

Panic sets in. *Why is Alagur not pulling me out of this? Where is he?* Her mind screams to be freed from this turmoil. She doesn't even know whether her thoughts are her own, or those of people who are long dead.

Marrida feels like she's being pulled into the future. She sees a stone slab and panics, thinking it's the vision of the cave again. But this time, the stone slab is bathed in a white light.

She moves towards the stone, and sees four gems lying there. Someone has placed four Stones of Truth side by side with the length of two paces between them. Marrida reaches up to her neck and feels her own Stone of Truth is there.

Why am I wearing my gem and not using it?

Her mind is pulled again, and she sees three women standing side by side. They're doing something, but what?

Is that a Stone of Truth in her hands?

Then suddenly, the middle woman is gone, and something tells Marrida this is wrong. For a while, she senses the two remaining women are attempting to keep the balance between themselves.

Her vision changes again, and she sees a building in flames. Her mind screams as she realises she's hearing the voices of many people crying out in pain. She watches in horror as women in cloaks – those worn by Keepers – fasten something over the doors of the building, and she sees arms reaching from inside, pleading to be rescued. The sky is red from the flames, and Marrida's mind can almost smell the smoke.

Then the calmness of the room where the young Sharriba is still speaking to the older woman snaps back into place, causing Marrida to jerk her head forward. Alagur sees this, and finally realises something is terribly wrong with the vision Marrida is doing. He looks from her to the disc-shaped projection, and back. The projection shows her looking at the book, yet her face betrays her terror.

Alagur throws the notebook aside, and a few pages come loose. He hastily gathers together as many as he can, then starts the process of pulling Marrida out of her vision.

It takes him more than thirty minutes to succeed. He only knows the vision has ended when her limp body slumps down onto the makeshift seat.

But she hasn't been completely released from the vision.

* * *

MARRIDA FEELS STRANGE. She can sense Alagur nearby, but her mind feels like it's outside her body.

This is the final stage of her Awakening.

She now understands why the process is called this. Emelyse told her about Bergas thrashing and screaming in his sleep while dreaming of a future in which Marrida would bond with a wolf, but his young mind interpreted the process in a different way to hers. He wasn't conditioned by the training Marrida has received as a Keeper, which causes the mind of a person to meld with the effects of the Stone of Truth, depending on their calling. Once the process is complete, the brain chemistry of such a person becomes different to that of an untrained person. The balance that the Preservers brought to the process made it possible for the chemistry of a Keeper's mind and that of a Caller to co-exist in the same person. But as fewer and fewer Preservers existed, this balance became lost.

Or so it seemed.

Although Marrida's mind should feel extremely confused, in actual fact she now understands. Her great-grandmother was an enigma – a rare person who could naturally balance the skill of a Keeper with that of a Caller – and it seems that Marrida also possesses this natural ability. Marrida somehow knows that in her vision, she observed both the ancient past of her Order and its future.

* * *

ALAGUR WATCHES MARRIDA CLOSELY. Her breathing is shallow, but the greyness which had settled on her face seems to have lessened and some of the colour is reappearing in her skin. Her eyes are moving like she's dreaming, and a moment later, they open. They're without the blackness that accompanies a vision.

Alagur lets go of the breath he wasn't aware he'd been holding in.

"Are you alright?" he enquires nervously. "I wasn't sure if I did the pulling out on time, or in the right way."

"I'm alright," Marrida replies softly, reaching up to her head to steady her mind more. Then her hand reaches to her neck and she panics. "Where's my gem?"

"Your gem? It's there, where you put it while you were still in your vision. You seemed to fall over."

"I saw it," Marrida whispers.

Alagur looks surprised. "What did you see?"

"I saw the past and the future."

"Of what?"

"Of us."

"You saw you and me?"

"No, I saw the beginning of the Order, and its future too." Marrida shakes her head. "It was strange, almost as if both were happening at the same time."

"You're confusing me now. In the image I saw, you read a book which looked like Sharriba's journal. Nothing else happened."

"You're wrong. Everything happened. It happened so fast, I couldn't work out what was what at first."

"Did you figure it out in the end?"

"Yes, and I think I saw what caused it all. I saw the past of this building. Something terrible happened here – a woman was killed. But it wasn't clear who the woman was, or why she was killed. I saw men cheering on the man who killed her."

Alagur frowns and thinks for a moment. Some of what Marrida is saying is familiar to him.

"Marrida." He speaks her name slowly. "I'm not sure if I ever told you about Eduzan. Am I right?"

"Who is that?" the woman queries.

"He's the reason why the Wolf Riders exist."

Alagur recites the retelling of a man he'd always assumed to be a character from a fairy tale. Marrida is quiet until Alagur has finished talking. It seems she was indeed seeing events from thousands of years in the past.

But I've always believed it's impossible for any Keeper to see that far back in time. Most Keepers are only capable of seeing events up to eight hundred years in the past. Again, I am getting the feeling there's something I've forgotten.

Marrida searches her memories for an explanation, and shakes her head when it fails to surface.

"Do you want something to drink? Or eat?" Alagur asks.

"Some tea would be nice."

After a moment's hesitation, Alagur gets up and walks to the cooking area to prepare the tea. He stands near the campfire, thinking over the events of the afternoon. The feeling of foreboding he's been experiencing has returned with a vengeance.

He sees a questioning look from Marrida as he starts to pack everything into the packs and haversacks, and bring them all to the opening in the wall, but he gives her a mug of tea without explaining his actions.

Marrida closes her eyes as she drinks from her mug of tea, using the moment to search her mind for what she has forgotten. It seems so important that she should remember. She then opens her eyes and glances at the gem, which is lying on the leather sheet beside her.

I could do another vision – a short one to retrieve that memory. I'm not sure how Alagur would react to it, though.

She glances up towards Alagur, who has walked to the opening in the wall and is observing the darkened landscape beyond.

When did it turn to night? Was the vision that long?

Marrida puts the mug down at her left side and glances again at the Stone of Truth lying on the floor, then towards Alagur. He's gone from the opening, and Marrida can't see him anywhere. The rebellious part of her mind takes hold, and little by little, she moves her right hand towards the gem.

Moments before her hand reaches it, she looks up again to search for Alagur. When she sees she's truly alone, she takes hold of the gem. Looking up once more, Marrida sees two yellow eyes shining in the darkness, reflecting the light from the nearby campfire.

Yalla has noticed the woman reaching for the gem. Because Marrida has placed the gem beside her so often after visions in the past, the wolf has grown accustomed to the significance of the motion — even if she doesn't understand it. Her ears prick up, and the muscles in her body tense as they always do when Marrida makes this motion. Her master has taught her to assist him with pulling the woman from a vision if his own actions don't succeed.

Woman and wolf stare at one another for several minutes, then Marrida takes the stone and starts the vision. She doesn't notice the wolf's attention turn away from her, and she doesn't hear the deep, rumbling growl which permeates the air.

* * *

ALAGUR IS LEANING AGAINST THE WALL when he hears a sound that immediately has all his senses on high alert. The growl from Yalla can mean only one thing — Wolf Riders are near. He rushes to the path beside the building and looks in each direction. It's too dark to see anything. If he wants to know who is coming and from where, he needs his wolf by his side.

Alagur whistles, and Yalla's sharp ears hear her master's call. She gets up from the floor, and a grunt from her tells her younger companion to stay where she is. Yalla walks across the room, glancing at Marrida periodically, and sees the woman is sitting motionless. Instinct tells the wolf that danger is heading their way. Yalla regards Marrida as part of her pack, and a wolf's loyalty to her pack is paramount.

The wolf clambers over the rubble piled in the opening. As soon as she is outside, she again picks up the smell of wolves in the air, and this time she's certain of what she's smelling. And what she's hearing, too. In the distance — far beyond her master's hearing range — she hears the specific song of wolves alerting their masters to the presence of one of their own.

Yalla's stance changes. She raises her tail high, her neck arches, and her hair stands on end. A low, rumbling growl emanates from deep within her body. Her original instinct, which was to regard the wolves around her in City of Wolves as her allies, has been replaced by a new instinct which tells her these wolves — and those who ride on them — are her enemies, and therefore the enemies of her master.

Her warning galvanises the man into action. He whistles sharply, and Lya rushes to him too. Alagur feels glad he trusted his instinct and left the wolves' harnesses on. He gets all the packs and both haversacks mounted on Yalla, then gives her two short whistles and she sets off to the east.

Lya is prepared. She stands waiting as Alagur goes to get Marrida and the few belongings lying around her. As he approaches the woman, Alagur wonders why she has started another vision, but their time is too limited to pull her from it. Instead, he carefully pushes Marrida down and places her – bedding and all – on Lya's back.

Alagur rushes back to pack anything he can find into a rucksack. After hastily shutting it, he hooks it on the harness. He then climbs onto the wolf. Although Lya isn't bonded to him, she senses that something is wrong with Marrida and she responds to Alagur's commands.

Ahead of her, she hears Yalla's wolf song calling her to the east.

Lya departs just in time. She and her two passengers disappear over the crest of the hill just as a massive dust cloud appears to the west – heralding the arrival of Wolf Riders.

Jymar and his entourage have finally caught up with the two riders and their wolves.

CHAPTER SEVENTY-FOUR

ALAGUR FRANTICALLY SHAKES MARRIDA IN AN ATTEMPT to get her out of the vision. It takes a while before he sees the tell-tale signs she's conscious again.

Marrida looks around her, confused.

Where are we?

"What happened?" she asks.

"You were doing a vision when the Wolf Riders almost discovered us," Alagur answers. The anger in his voice snaps Marrida to full reality. A moment later, the vision's message trickles into her mind, and she places a hand over her mouth. She has remembered what she'd forgotten earlier.

Then she speaks softly. "I think I saw them."
"Saw them?" Alagur retorts. "Why does it matter that you saw them in the vision? If Yalla wasn't trained to warn me of danger, you'd be dead now, and I'd be either dead or on my way back to Masharea." In his anger, Alagur inadvertently uses the city's old name.
"No, Alagur, that isn't what I'm talking about. I saw them when I looked out of one of the windows. I didn't know it was a dust cloud; I thought I'd seen someone's campfire ruining the beauty of the valley. I even drew how the cloud looked in a second image. Look in my notebook."
Marrida's own anger rises as she speaks, and so does the pitch of her voice. Suddenly, she feels Alagur's hand over her mouth, silencing her attempt to explain herself.

"I believe you, but please be quiet. Sound can carry far this high in the mountains." Alagur's whispered words have lost all traces of anger.

"Are we safe?" Marrida asks in hushed tones as she looks around her once more.
"Yes, we're safe. I signalled to the animals to disguise themselves. Can't you smell it?"
Marrida smells a distinct scent. "Is that vole spore?"

"Yes, and we're covered in it too. It will throw the wolves off our scent." Alagur grins broadly when he sees Marrida sniff him and screw her nose up in disgust.

"It smells awful! I hope it washes off."

"We can bathe in a few days' time when we've ridden far enough. They can follow us, but with Yalla pushing Lya to faster speeds, they won't catch us. They'll know we've gone east, and they'll probably guess we're heading to the city on the north-eastern coast, but once we're there, we'll be safe for a while. They won't be able to do anything other than turn and go back to City of Wolves, looking like a pack of runts."

Marrida grins at the use of the term. Alagur has explained its meaning to her before, and in this case it seems highly appropriate.

"Do you think you can ride by yourself?"

Marrida nods, then speaks up. "First, I need some water to drink. I'm thirsty."

* * *

Although those around Jymar want to capture the former Wolf Rider, he doesn't. The more he thinks about what Belduran told him about The Truth, and the reasons the Elder Man gave for believing the Wolf Riders need to end, the more it makes sense to Jymar that a life such as theirs is downright useless. For the first time in a very long time, he starts to wonder how his life would have turned out if he'd never been snatched.

This thought causes him to slow his wolf ever so slightly. Is this because he wants to stop chasing Alagur and return to City of Wolves empty-handed? A part of his mind knows where Alagur is heading. He recalls a journey he made through these mountains almost fifteen years earlier, when he met a woman walking from the east.

"When he is being chased, you need to stop."

Now the words of the mysterious woman are echoing through his mind as he rides towards the east.

"There's a mountain north of here where we can see the whole landscape," he bellows. "You know none of us can chase Alagur's wolf, she's too fast."

The group of men steer their wolves towards the north, and after about half an hour, they reach the mountainside. They all dismount, then Jymar signals for two of the men with him to follow him. The trio climb, and after an hour they reach the highest point.

Jymar looks towards the east. Some distance away, he can see a diminishing dust cloud. Two wolves are being ridden. He wonders who the second rider is.

Whoever it is has long, flowing hair.

Not the length at which a man would keep his hair.

Then, with a start, he understands what he's looking at.

The second rider is a woman! How can a woman ride a wolf?

The words of The Truth echo through Jymar's mind:

> SHE WHOSE NAME IS UNSPOKEN,
> A WOLF SHE WILL CLAIM FROM THE WILD

The words are familiar to him – and to those who've ascended the mountain with him. Jymar can hear them whispering 'A wolf she will claim from the wild' and 'It's true what the Elder Men are saying' over and over.

"Let them go!" Jymar says solemnly to his two companions. "We go back to City of Wolves and tell Belduran what we saw."

There are no objections.

* * *

ALAGUR AND MARRIDA DISMOUNT and once again look for the distinctive dust cloud, but this time there's none.

"We need to wait and see what they're going to do next. Let's sit down and have something to eat and drink."

Marrida nods. The hasty ride has shown her, more than any retelling could, what life as a Wolf Rider is like. They've had to ride like this to escape capture by those who have turned Alagur from friend into traitor by a simple action. And she's sure she won't be any safer than he is if they catch up with them.

I wonder if Uncle Joharan would have let me leave with Alagur had he known this could happen.

"They've mounted up again, Marrida," Alagur calls out. "I'll see if they're heading here. I can tell by the direction the dust cloud rises."

Marrida drinks the remainder of the water she poured into her mug, and puts the mug back into her haversack, hooking the water container onto her harness. She then climbs on Lya and caresses the animal's head. Lya is nervous as she isn't yet conditioned to the existence of a wolf in the service of a Wolf Rider.

Marrida also watches the cloud. She wants to learn how to read from the direction it's rising what the Wolf Riders are doing.

Are they advancing or retreating?

She looks for a moment at Alagur and sees tension in his face. Now she understands better what has made him the man he is.

He's a soldier essentially.

"They're riding west."

Marrida sees the man is right. The dust cloud seems to be diminishing. Now the question going through her mind is, why?

Marrida and Alagur turn their wolves to the east and start to ride again. For now, at least, they've evaded capture. Alagur wonders why the leader of the scouting party has turned back to City of Wolves. Then another thought invades his mind.

I know the name the Wolf Riders give to the city we're heading towards, and I've heard many retellings, some more embellished than others, about it. It has always evaded attack by the Wolf Riders. I wonder if we are about to change that.

He glances over his shoulder towards Marrida to make sure she's alright.
"Can you manage a faster pace?"
"I think so," she replies.

They urge their wolves on. As they ride, Alagur realises that, for the first time in his life, he has seen the Wolf Riders fail to capture the people they're pursuing. He wonders if the men were sent after him by Samur. But surely Samur's men wouldn't stop until Alagur was either killed or captured?

* * *

JYMAR GLANCES OVER HIS SHOULDER ONCE AS HE RIDES AWAY. He isn't leading the group this time; they all know which direction City of Wolves lies in. If they hurry, he hopes they'll reach it before Samur returns from his own excursion. Then they can talk to Belduran and leave it up to the older man to determine what to do next.

If he is still alive--

Everything seems to be different now. The man they're after is moving further out of their reach with every passing minute.

Delgrun pulls his wolf next to Jymar's, and the men nod towards each other.

"What do you plan to tell them in City of Wolves about today?" Delgrun questions.

"To be honest, I don't know."

"I think we saw a woman riding on that wolf."

"I think so too," Jymar concurs. "It could be that Belduran and the others are correct. It means Vaymaz died for nothing, and we need to help rid the city of Samur."

"You do realise he's got that runt Raimir — and Darush too — under his thumb. If they find out where Alagur's heading, they'll round up the whole City of Wolves in an attack against that place."

"If we hurry, perhaps we can prevent it." This comment comes from Jervis, who has overheard the other men talking and decided to join in with the discussion. "I think we need to stop somewhere to discuss this matter more closely. The men are restless. Most of them now believe The Truth is in fact a prophecy from a distant past."

"We can stop at the building we located them in," Delgrun suggests.

"Sounds like a fair plan." Jymar then adds in a booming voice, "We ride to the abandoned building for rest."

The group increases its speed, but it still takes them until the sun is at its zenith before they reach the building. They don't want to be seen, so all the men lead their wolves inside through the opening in the wall.

Jymar looks around. Alagur was efficient in clearing away all the belongings he and the woman are carrying with them, but not as efficient as he would have hoped. A single sheet of parchment lies on the floor. It looks so out of place against the ruins, Jymar feels compelled to walk over and pick it up.

The man smiles when he sees what he's looking at. The image on the parchment is of Yalla's face. The wolf is so distinctive, and so famous, it's rare to meet a Wolf Rider who doesn't know her – either by sight or by description. Jymar often encountered the wolf as she paced through the city, and he would watch her in awe. He's always admired Alagur privately, and the wolf is the reason why.

He folds the parchment tightly. Sure that Alagur and his companion didn't mean to leave this drawing behind, he vows to return it to its rightful owner, if he gets the chance in the future. He places it into one of the inner pockets of his tunic before returning to where his men sit. None of them will question him about what he's picked up.

Jymar sits down on one of the large chiselled stones and listens for a while to the discussion the men around him are having. They all now know what he saw – a woman sitting on a wolf, and exercising command over the beast. And they are wondering what this means for themselves, and for those still in City of Wolves.

Jymar knows Samur will likely call for an army to march east as soon as he finds out where Alagur is.

He'll risk everything to succeed in what the Wolf Riders have failed to do for nine hundred years.

"We need to decide who we'll accept as our leaders," Jymar says out loud. "We know how Samur turned up in the city, telling us he'd heard about the Wolf Riders from a man he likely killed." The silence around him tells Jymar that he commands the complete attention of every man there, and they all look at him directly. "We need to decide which is the greater goal for us," he continues. "Obviously, Samur will call for an army of ten thousand to march east. And the likelihood is we'll be expected to follow him. So, our goal is to do this without really helping him. Is everyone here agreed on this?"

Every man nods approval. Jymar waits a few moments, then continues.

"I'll tell you why Belduran sent us on this journey. But each of you must swear your allegiance to him, and to all that Vaymaz stood for."

"Samur killed that old man for no reason!" The words are shouted by more than half a dozen of the men.

"I agree with you. I admired Vaymaz myself," Jymar replies. "And it was he who said the situation in City of Wolves needed to end. I believe this end is what Alagur, and the woman with him, are working towards, too."

Jymar sees more nods of approval. *I'm going to tell some lies now, and I hope no one realises it.*

"I'm sure some of you have brothers left behind where you came from. I have two older brothers myself, and I've not seen either of them for more than two decades. I don't even know if they, or my father, are still alive."

"I've got a young brother I haven't seen for five years," Delgrun adds. "And I don't want him snatched."

Jymar nods. "Bergas is lucky to call Alagur his friend," he admits. "I believe his disappearance was Alagur's doing as well."

"Seems Bergas is a better friend to Alagur than his own pack brother," a voice calls out. All the men know who the pack brother in question is.

"I'm not even going to try to find Bergas. If he got home, we'll let him stay there. But we need to make sure our kin are safe from now on, and that means no more snatchings. And it can only happen with Samur out of the way, along with the runts who follow him around."

* * *

AND THERE ARE OTHERS WAITING FOR THE DAY when Keldarra will be free from the Wolf Riders; waiting for the one they've seen hidden in the shadows of their minds. In another time, they'd be proclaimed as Callers, but the name they're known by now is beating through Marrida's mind like an endless drum as she rides east. She doesn't dare say the name out loud in case the mere mention of it erases the content of the visions she did hours earlier.

If they really exist, destiny will bring us to them. If they really exist, the end of the Wolf Riders begins.

CHAPTER SEVENTY-FIVE

TWENTY-EIGHT TIRED MEN RIDE SLOWLY towards the northern gates of the massive, ancient city they call City of Wolves. The group's arrival feels more like a funeral march than a triumphant return.

Jymar looks around him with a frown on his face, searching the surroundings for evidence that Samur has returned. And he looks for Belduran. He hopes to see the latter first. Secretly, he hopes to hear the news that Samur has been killed by soldiers, or perhaps others within this city.

Jymar raises his hand, and the group of riders with him halt their advance. It would have been pointless trying to get back into the city without being seen as the defences are too good, and too many. It makes sense that Alagur abandoned the Wolf Riders when he was away on an excursion, and not while he was here.

Jymar looks towards the square where, in another season, a man lay on the ground, bleeding from two blows which ultimately killed him. All evidence of the occurrence has long been washed away by the spring showers. Around Jymar, the city feels subdued. The lively banter which existed before the murder has been replaced by sombreness.

He feels a hand on his shoulder and sees Delgrun and Jervis standing near him. Most of the group who accompanied him are still behind them. By and large, a scouting party would disperse back into the city's life as soon as the men returned.

Jymar runs his hand over the black fur of Kiato's neck and hears the beast snort with pleasure from the attention. A smile flashes over his face for a moment when he realises his own actions have made the animal nervous. Customarily, the beast would have been freed of the burden of his harness as soon as his master arrived in the city, but not this time.

Delgrun taps Jymar's arm and nods in a westerly direction. When Jymar turns, he sees Belduran and Rudrig coming his way, Rudrig limping as usual. Jymar folds his arms and silently waits for both men to arrive.

Belduran raises an eyebrow when he sees Jymar is making no attempt to order the men around him to disperse. The Elder Man looks him over questioningly.

Jymar speaks when Belduran arrives beside him. "These men have sworn loyalty to me. Anything we speak of, they can know about."

A hint of a smile plays on Belduran's face for a moment, then he looks stern once more. Having more men who have sworn allegiance to someone other than Samur plays right into his hands, and the hands of the other Elder Men in agreement with him. The beginning of a revolution has started within the ranks of the Wolf Riders. And interestingly enough, it matches the original prophecy exactly.

The first thing Jymar wants to convey to the older man standing in front of him concerns the events which took place when he and his men were almost close enough to capture the fugitive. He thinks once more about what he saw — a woman dismounting from the back of a wolf with more ease than most Wolf Riders are capable of. While he and his men were on their way back to City of Wolves, Jymar calculated the time it must have taken the woman to learn this skill.

How long has she been riding the wolf?

For half a season, they'd tracked one wolf, but then one set of footprints became two.

"You're right about The Truth being a prophecy," Jymar begins. "I stopped doubting you the day we saw them."
"Saw *them?* You saw Alagur and Yalla?"

Belduran looks around him, but sees no evidence of a man's capture. And none of the men present make the motion of hitting their own stomach with a clenched fist, which is normal to indicate a traitor has been found and killed. This can only mean that Jymar has allowed the man to escape alive. Belduran wonders what occurred during their travels for the men to abandon their pursuit and form themselves into a cohesive wolf squad — rare for scouting groups.

"I didn't say we found Alagur and Yalla," Jymar says. "I meant to say we found him…with a woman beside him. On a wolf."
Belduran sees all the men around Jymar nodding in agreement.
"I also saw her reaching up like this." Jymar indicates the upper part of his chest, just below his throat. "She acted like she's some sort of

Keeper."

Belduran looks sharply at the younger man. If what he's saying is correct, it means the last days of the Wolf Riders have arrived. Belduran recognises the gesture, too, and it stirs within him a memory of a woman from long ago.

"She arrived here with you, and each time she looked at you, her hand reached up."

Belduran thinks for a moment.

It's evident now that Alagur is possibly beyond the reaches of the Wolf Riders.

"I also noted from Yalla's slender frame that she's no longer with young," Jervis states. "She would have gone to her own kind for delivery."

The comment brings a smirk to Rudrig's face. "Samur can't claim the pups for his wolf squad any longer."

"Did you see any sign of the boy?" Belduran asks.

"No, I think he's long gone. Probably back home with his parents."

"I think he only has his mother," a voice calls from the group.

"That's right," Delgrun adds. "He said he missed his mother, but he only mentioned his father in the past tense."

"I think we should make sure no more excursions are sent to his city," Rudrig suggests.

"How can we do that?" Belduran asks. "You know there are still Elder Men loyal to Samur, and others who only swear allegiance to their own goals."

"In a way, it's interesting that Samur is trying to become the only leader here. He'll make people more united."

"Yes, but for all the wrong reasons."

Jymar and the men around him glance at one another. They've never witnessed disagreements between individual Elder Men before. Only a few weeks earlier, if Belduran and Rudrig had disagreed, they would have moved out of earshot and discussed the matter in hushed tones. The public discussion with the scouting party is attracting attention, and when neither of the Elder Men makes any attempt to move the group to a more secluded part of the city, Jymar starts to worry.

"What if Samur turns up?" he hisses at Belduran. "If he hears what we're saying, he'll try to claim leadership over whatever mission to the north-east you've got planned."

"Let him!"

"So you want him to go after Alagur?" Jervis asks.

"Yes, because he will be going to the city that has always evaded our attacks. And even if he is by some chance successful, I believe Alagur will see the attack coming from ten thousand paces, and he'll make sure he's long gone before the first Wolf Rider steps into the city."

Jymar grins. He can tell that the Elder Man has a plan to undermine Samur. When Belduran whispers to him a moment later, Jymar nods his head in agreement.

"When Samur gets back — and he's expected to return any day now — someone will no doubt feel compelled to tell him of this discussion. And it will urge him into action. A normal attack, such as the one executed against Ruh'nar last year, would only require three or four dozen wolf squads to be successful. This won't be the situation for the city in the north-east."

All those around Belduran know the name of the city he means is unknown to outsiders. The Wolf Riders themselves just refer to it as 'North City'.

Belduran suggests that if Samur draws the masses from City of Wolves against their nemesis in the north-east, this will leave the defences in the city sufficiently depleted to enable its recapture by invaders from Ruh'nar, if the three boys he's sent there have found an individual influential enough to organise such an attack.

"The last reckoning will come when Samur's squads return from the north and find themselves on the wrong side of the defences."

Jymar laughs out loud at the plan, which on the surface seems almost simplistic. He's already looking forward to seeing the shadow of defeat cast over Samur's face as he deals with not just one failure brought about by his own actions, but two. All Jymar and Elder Man Belduran must do is make their 'discussion' appear so important, Samur won't be able to resist sticking his nose in.

"You'd better go back to your dwellings, Rudrig," Belduran says. "I know you want to be here, but your leg will slow you if something goes wrong. And if I fail, you can finish what I've begun."

Rudrig nods and turns, watched not just by the people standing in the central part of the square, but also by the three dozen or so bystanders who've gradually appeared — half of them curious boys.

There's a lull in the conversation. Everyone seems to be straining their ears to hear the distinctive horn which will signal the arrival of Samur, Raimir, Darush, and the masses who've followed them in their pointless trek. All are curious to know the outcome of what Samur deemed to be the 'right choice', and some of the boys who are standing on the outskirts of the square are already discussing whether any new boys will arrive because of the excursion.

A boy of about ten rushes towards Belduran. "My friend told me he saw a dust cloud on the horizon," he says, breathing loudly.

Belduran and Jymar both nod.

"Go to your sleeping house," Belduran urges. The boy runs towards the eastern side of the square, and a few minutes later is gone from sight.

"Ready your men," Belduran says softly to Jymar.

"In what way?"

"Take your water bags and pour some water over yourselves to make it appear you only arrived back in the last few minutes." Then in a louder voice, Belduran adds, "Go and get your friends, and come back here in thirty minutes. Go *now*!"

Belduran doesn't have to repeat his command. Most present understand the implications of what the men have been discussing. If it means stopping Samur from gaining more power, it's something they all want to assist with.

It's as if the city is holding its breath when Samur finally rides into the square.

CHAPTER SEVENTY-SIX

SAMUR COMES TO A HALT NEXT TO THE GROUP OF MEN standing on the square. It's obvious that they've been out scouting. Immediately, his anger rises. If they've been successful, it will mean less prestige for him. If it becomes common knowledge that he's led a useless excursion south, it could even cost him his position among the Elder Men.

He glowers at Jymar, who makes a point of ignoring him. The men around him do the same.

Samur doesn't like failure. If a man fails, usually Samur is the first to deal out punishment. He sees betrayal as failure too. But his journey south was chaotic.

Those following Samur soon discovered why many among the Elder Men distrust him. Every day, the man's anger rose, but he promised those around him more and more sacks of gold to cover up his frustrations. Even his attempts to plunder small towns and villages played against him. Most people had gone to Ruh'nar for the spring market, and Samur's group was too small to attempt an attack on the city. In addition, more defence forces from the southern cities are now patrolling the eastern regions of Sabeya.

Luck deserted Samur the moment he exited City of Wolves. Even the flocks of blue ravens he kept seeing seemed to be mocking his bad luck with their song, which sounded to him like scornful laughter. At the ancient Pass of the Two Bells, the chance escape of the two youngest boys in the group left the men demanding a return to City of Wolves.

So, they turned and trekked back.

Belduran has connections with the Pass of the Two Bells, and with the southern part of Sabeya. He lived there as a boy with his adopted mother, who told him that he had been delivered to her by someone important and wealthy. Whenever he was sad, his adopted mother entertained him with retellings of the heroics of those who once defended the nearby pass. Who his real mother is remains a mystery to this day, though. But for some reason, an image of a woman with a heart-shaped face, wearing a shining gem hanging from a beautiful necklace, has stayed with him throughout his life.

Samur first arrived in City of Wolves from the east. It is said that a city there is built on stalagmite formations so large that houses are attached to the sides of them rather than being built on top. The city is rumoured to be ruled with an iron grip to protect it from attack by the Wolf Riders. If Samur is from that city, it would make him even more dangerous if he were to return there with knowledge of the Wolf Riders and City of Wolves.

As Samur approaches him, Belduran is on his guard. A quick glance around tells him fewer have returned with Samur than departed.

"What is this I heard as I entered the city?" Samur barks. "You dared go behind my back, and send them out to scout for Alagur?"

"I did indeed," Belduran replies icily.

"And what did you think you would achieve?" Samur's voice echoes between the buildings, achieving the result Belduran hoped for. On cue, the boys who'd been standing watching him and Jymar talk over the scouts' mission come back to the square, bringing other boys with them from the sleeping houses.

"Jymar has just told me his mission was successful." Belduran deliberately puts extra emphasis on the word 'successful'. As Samur's expression turns murderous, hinting that he would like to repeat the atrocity he inflicted on Vaymaz, Jymar steps forward and stands beside Belduran. He's closely followed by his men, and even the wolves pace forward with deep, menacing growls.

Samur looks around him and lowers his arm in mid-swing. He steps back a few paces.

"Not so easy to strike out when there are many against you, is it?" Jymar's voice is low and menacing. "Not so easy to be the man who wants to strike down his allies."

"You wanted to find Alagur, isn't that correct?" Jervis asks Samur.

"You know he's the traitor here," Samur bellows. "Why do you treat me as one?"

"We rode north-east and we know where he is," Jymar continues. "But we'll let you lead us there."

"So, if you fail – again – everyone in this city will know," Jervis adds.

The two men move forward in slow motion as they taunt Samur, causing him to move back. The boys who have gathered round watch on, seeing for themselves that Samur is nothing more than a bully who uses accepted standards within the city for his own gain.

Samur's face goes purple when he realises the men are goading him like he's a new arrival, freshly snatched from an unfortunate house.

"Don't you want to find Alagur?" he shrieks. "Don't you want him dealt with? He's the one who betrayed us all here, not me."

"You're the one who struck out against one of your own," Delgrun says coldly.

"That Vaymaz came up with the preposterous idea that the boys – those boys there, and there, and there too – could all go home."

"And where do you call home, Samur?" Jervis asks. "You've never really told us where you came from."

Samur ignores the question.

"You said you saw him in the north-east, right? Has he gone by chance to North City?"

"Yes."

Suddenly, Samur notices the absolute silence around him. Not a man, nor a boy speaks. Everyone in the city is staring at him unflinchingly, even when he casts his seething gaze on them individually. Not even the youngest boy looks away. He can see their anger etched in the clench of their jaws. His mind warns him that he won't walk away from here alive if he doesn't come up with an acceptable plan. He can promise everyone wealth beyond their wildest dreams, but for the first time in his life, Samur feels the promise will only be met with scepticism and derision.

"I'm leading the fight to take North City," he screams. "If you're braver than Jymar's men, go and get your wolf and your weapons and come back here." Samur stares at the men he's attempted to insult. "As an Elder Man, I order every man and every boy in the city to follow me into battle. Anyone who doesn't follow me will be killed when I return."

He ends his sentence by staring directly at Belduran, who stares back impassively – apart from a slight smirk.

Samur turns and walks back to Darush and Raimir, both of whom have been watching the events in front of them but not offering any support. After an angry glare at Raimir, whom Samur now regards as his second-in-command, he pulls out the man's water pouch and drinks down most of the water it holds. Raimir and Darush glance at one another in surprise. Neither has ever known Samur to be sober for any length of time, let alone before departing on an excursion. However, he has taken his own warning seriously, and is clever enough to know that sober he can defend himself from a surprise attack. When drunk, he'd be dead before he even had time to realise someone was near.

Samur throws the water container back at Raimir, who catches it in a reflex action. He then looks at both men in turn and laughs menacingly.

"You look like someone chased you from your beds with the stink of a vole."

Neither man speaks. They know the wrong remark at that moment will earn them a blow to the head from Samur. Deep down, Darush is wishing he could be standing with Belduran and Jymar's men, who are still staring in their direction. Darush looks at Jymar, who catches his glance and smirks. It amuses Jymar that those who've sided with Samur in the past are now feeling the weight of uncertainty on their shoulders. He doesn't plan to offer them any sympathy or support.

But the words of Samur – spoken as an Elder Man – mean that Jymar must go with him or face the death penalty he threatened.

Jymar turns and looks at Belduran with a frown of concern. "Will you still be here when we return from North City?" he asks softly.

"I have to stay to make sure the youngest people – those who can't go with Samur – are gone by the time he comes back," Belduran replies, just as quietly.

"If he comes back." Jymar pauses, then adds, "I'll make sure his campaign is unsuccessful, one way or another. We all will." He nods towards his newly formed squad, still standing around him.

"If he comes back as a defeated man, I doubt he'll find anyone here who'll assist him with his threat," Jervis says. "A single well-aimed spear arrow will guarantee it."

"I think he knows it, too," Jymar replies. "He'll probably attempt to ensure that anyone willing to fire it doesn't return."

"Those two runts who follow him around look like they're too afraid to speak to him now," Delgrun adds. "They looked like they were about to run off when we were confronting Samur. I don't trust either of them."

Jymar glances over his shoulder. Both Darush and Raimir are standing silently near the group of riders who stayed grouped together after Samur had started his confrontation. But whereas most of them are now asking questions, which Samur is answering as shortly as possible, the two men, one of whom is supposed to be his second-in-command, are making no attempt to speak to him.

Jymar turns back to the others in his group, smirking. "It seems you're right about them being runts. They're even acting like runts now."

A boy rushes up to a man called Kaydran. A moment later, Kaydran comes walking over.

"It seems things didn't go well at all for them in the south," he announces quietly. "Two boys managed to escape during an attack, which resulted in four dead Wolf Riders. One of the dead was the brother of the boy who spoke to me just then."

"He's a brave one," Jymar comments. "He could end up in trouble if Samur discovers what he told you."

"I'll make sure he's one of the first to leave," Belduran remarks. "He's from the same sleeping house as Melchor and his friends, so I'll send him to join them. When he arrives, they'll be able to vouch for him. I can get him to pass on news to the people of the city, too."

Jymar turns to watch Samur, deciding to study the man as much as possible before they depart. He has to discover a way to break the hold Samur still has over those who believe in him.

CHAPTER SEVENTY-SEVEN

Samur's promise of a battle substantial enough to match the one The Truth speaks of isn't an easy promise to keep. And it becomes increasingly difficult when the more experienced Elder Men refuse to offer a hand with the strategy. The Elder Men know they cannot dictate the way the events are to play out, but after a while they notice the boys in City of Wolves, even the very youngest, are assisting Belduran of their own volition.

It starts when one boy is asked to fetch something as simple as a bucket of water. What would have taken no time at all suddenly takes the boy three or four times longer than usual, but Belduran notices that the Elder Man who set the task makes no attempt to chastise the boy for disobedience. Then Jymar sees that boys who would once have fought each other are now sitting and talking together quietly with no signs of animosity. When Jymar mentions his observations to Belduran, the Elder Man realises that Samur too may notice the boys' behaviour. Jymar promises to observe the boys when Samur is near, and what he sees surprises him.

When the man comes into view, on a signal, the boys become rowdy and argumentative. Then as soon as Samur is out of earshot, they return to their quiet conversations. It amuses Jymar to see this hidden rebellion the youngsters have instigated against Samur. Clearly when Samur demanded leadership, he'd gained it in name only.

The journey to the place where Jymar and his men almost managed to capture Alagur took them along a route south of the Upper Plains in the milder part of the land. It took Jymar and his squad the rest of the spring and some of the summer to return to City of Wolves, and he calculates that any journey undertaken to North City will take at least a month longer. This means that Samur's excursion will take place through the hottest days of the summer season, and the return trip will see them still in the Upper Plains when the cold weather starts to blanket the land. Ice burn is Jymar's greatest concern, especially for the oldest and youngest of the forcibly assembled army.

If Alagur can do what no Wolf Rider has done before and enter North City, he can find out what secrets it has, Jymar thinks. *But I doubt he will come back here to share that information.*

Like Alagur, Jymar originally came from the west coast, although his own arrival in City of Wolves took place twelve years earlier than Alagur's. When Alagur arrived in the city, Jymar often spoke to him about Chiva'na. This, however, doesn't explain why Alagur is travelling to the most north-easterly city of the Keldarran continent. Jymar knows the continent stretches to such vast distances that a journey on foot from east to west would take five years. Travel by cart drawn by bovines would decrease the journey by perhaps a year, but by far the fastest mode of transport would be on wolf back.

"Rudrig," Jymar calls out when he sees the familiar man turn the corner and come into view. Rudrig stops and partially turns when he hears his name, waiting for the slightly older Jymar to catch up, which takes only a dozen strides. "You know to be on your guard now?"

Rudrig smiles at Jymar, appreciating his concern. "Yes, yes, I know, but I need my exercises, or this leg gets so stiff I can't even leave my bed."

"Are you heading anywhere in particular?"

"I'm heading to the sleeping house in the next street over. Would you lend a shoulder for me to lean on?"

"Of course."

Rudrig puts his arm over Jymar's shoulders and they walk unhurriedly, talking in quiet tones.

"It seems Belduran and you have made an impression on the young folk," Rudrig says. "I've never answered so many questions from the boys about warfare. Seems most of them want to leave, as Belduran predicted."

"Yes, I know, and I'm concerned about that too," Jymar responds. "I hope that Belduran can send everyone who doesn't travel with us away from here while we're gone."

"So, you are going, then."

For a while, the two men walk silently, each deep in their own thoughts. When Rudrig speaks once more, it shows the direction his thoughts have taken.

"You said you saw a woman with Alagur. Have you any idea who she is?"

"We were too far away to see her clearly, but I did see her reach up to her chest and hold her hand there."

"Just as I thought. She's a Keeper."

"Why do you think that?"

"Because Belduran's mother was a Keeper, too," Rudrig replies. "And so was mine."

Before Jymar can respond, Rudrig lets go of his arm and enters a house. The sounds from within indicate the boys inside are happy to see him.

Jymar stands for a moment, looking at the doorway and wondering about Rudrig's curious statement. Then he shrugs his shoulders and walks on towards his original destination. In a city filled with those who are still loyal to Samur, finding somewhere to discuss Belduran's plans for the boys is tough. Even tougher is talking about how they can remove Samur from the equation.

* * *

SAMUR SITS IN A CHAIR ON THE TERRACE where once he'd have shared a bottle of wine with a man he used to call a friend. Uzo paces back and forth, but each time he tries to come close to his master, all he gets is a rough hand pushing him away. When the wolf has finally had enough of the abuse, he growls at the man then walks away from the terrace. Slowly he walks down the stairs to settle among his own kind.

Samur is so absorbed in his thoughts, he doesn't notice the actions of his wolf, and probably doesn't care either. He's sitting down now after having searched the dwelling once used by Alagur to see if he could find anything of value inside. But Alagur owned little, so Samur only found a few baskets filled with stale bread, a couple of bottles of wine he plans to drink on his return, a few items of furniture and an empty wooden box.

Samur looks up at the sky. The weather has been getting warmer, but now the sky is filled with dark grey clouds which cast a dullness over everything. Samur would like to have ridden out of the city as soon as he'd ordered the attack against North City, but reality isn't as simple as this. A massive convoy will take many days of planning and organising, and he's certainly not the best strategist in the city, although he's a capable fighter. But planning and fighting are two different matters.

Sitting on the terrace, Samur contemplates everything he wants to do to make Alagur's last hours as painful as possible. He looks up when he hears footsteps coming up the stairs, and for a moment feels surprised when Raimir arrives. The man has managed to do everything possible to avoid contact with him since their return to from the south.

"I've been sent here to tell you that the preparations for the battle are nearly ready." Raimir makes sure he stands more than twenty paces from the other man. "They say we can depart tomorrow after the midday meal."

"And why should 'they' even bother themselves with a meal? Why are 'they' delaying the journey so much, huh?"

Raimir finds himself comparing the man speaking to him now with the man he'd once known, and he thinks about a comment one of the boys made earlier.

"Samur seems to have turned from a wolf mastered by a Wolf Rider into a wild wolf."

The observation is uncannily accurate. The man scowling at Raimir has lost all his charm and joviality. This Samur doesn't have friends or loyal pack brothers. This Samur doesn't care about how those around him feel, and Raimir thinks this is probably the *real* Samur.

If Samur had managed to get hold of Yalla's offspring, I wonder how long afterwards Alagur would have lived. Did Alagur see through Samur? Is that the real reason he left the Wolf Riders?

Raimir shudders and turns to leave. The menacing tone of Samur's laughter echoes between the buildings as he watches Raimir go.

He's even more of a runt than either Alagur or Bergas. Perhaps he can be one of the first casualties at North City.

* * *

"He's walking back to his dwelling," Jaycan calls out to the rest of the boys who used to share their sleeping house with Melchor, Kaizor and Ebagar. They're all curious about the comings and goings of those they have identified as 'the runts'.

"Did you hear what the boys from the other sleeping house said?" one of the boys comments. "Samur has turned into some sort of wild wolf."

"Belduran is making sure most of the boys stay here," another interjects. "Samur's not going to like it."

"Belduran said we've got to be ready to go west to Venrasia Woods," Jaycan says. "He says going to any city isn't safe for us."

"Allegedly, he sent Melchor and his two friends to Ruh'nar, and they're not coming back," a voice calls out from another part of the room.

"If they're not coming back, could they have been captured?" a second voice shouts.

"Shush, everyone! You know Samur's men walk the streets," Jaycan snaps. "I think the plan is for them to work with the soldiers of Ruh'nar."

"Why do you think Raimir acts like some sort of runt?"

"I overheard two Elder Men talking yesterday," Jaycan replies conspiratorially. "I think they mean to kill Samur for what he did to Vaymaz."

"What has that got to do with Melchor being in Ruh'nar?" a boy asks as he watches for passers-by in the alleyway behind their sleeping house.

"I think they want Samur to fail, so on his return, they can kill him for the stupidity of this mission. The plan is for us to be gone from here, so when invaders come from Ruh'nar they can easily take the city. With most boys gone, even when the Wolf Riders return, they won't find it easy to defend the city from an outside attack. But the Wolf Riders will never be totally defeated as long as Samur lives."

Jaycan isn't far from the truth. Without the organised leadership of the Elder Men, it will be hard to maintain the status quo in City of Wolves. The reason the Wolf Riders have always branched out into autonomous squads is purely to divide them up into manageable groups. Belduran knows it, Jymar knows it, but Samur doesn't have a clue. He's only ever thought about the wealth he can grab from an attack and has never bothered to study the intricacies of the political systems which regulate it.

* * *

THE MORNING OF THE WOLF RIDERS' DEPARTURE is gloriously sunny without a cloud in the sky. And as the morning progresses, the sun decides to pump the air full of the thirst-inducing swelter of summer. The air is thick with pollen, and the many men and wolves end up being caked in the fluff of the nearby rubha apple blossom, which is bursting open to allow bees and other insects access to its inner chamber of life-giving nectar.

Samur paces from one part of the city to another, never giving himself a moment's rest, even when sweat pearls appear on his forehead. His neck stings from the heat of the hot sun, but his mind is on the impending departure, and he wants to be on his way.

"How much longer do we need to stand around?" he barks.

"The men are almost ready for departure," Jymar informs him coldly.

"Tell them to prepare faster."

Samur walks off and whistles for his wolf. Uzo comes towards the man more slowly than normal, unable to forget the recent abuse. He acts like he doesn't know his master; like the bonding between man and wolf has been broken. All the men standing nearby see the wolf's behaviour and wonder.

The departure happens an hour later, and it happens swiftly. No one comes to see the men off as they depart. Every boy has been ordered to stay indoors, and today they make sure they do as they're told. None of the men who exit the eastern gate knows whether they'll return to City of Wolves, and some hope they never will. Among them are those plotting to kill Samur when – not if – this journey fails.

And other eyes are watching their departure with interest – eyes that belong to those with their own plans for the Wolf Riders.

CHAPTER SEVENTY-EIGHT

MARRIDA IS BREATHING HARD when she finally climbs off the back of the wolf. Alagur insisted they should keep riding until the dust cloud caused by the Wolf Riders had totally left the landscape. He wanted to put as much distance between them and the wolf squad as possible.

"They won't bring reinforcements?" Marrida queries, panting.

"I think they know we're heading to that city." Alagur points at the dark shadow in the distance. "Once we're there, they won't be able to take us without making a huge effort."

"Why is that?"

"Because the Wolf Riders have been trying for as long as they've existed to get inside. But someone in the city is much stronger than they are, and because of this, we've…they've never succeeded."

Marrida looks at the man sharply when she hears his slip of the tongue. They're now so rare, they hardly happen at all.

The journey has been gruelling for them both. Each has taken turns to sleep, and they've eaten while riding. The taxing journey has had an impact on the two wolves, too; they're now standing side by side with their heads hanging low and their tongues out to cool themselves.

"I think we need to stop for a bit," Marrida suggests once her breathing has returned to normal. "The wolves can't last much longer at this pace."

"We'll need to send them into the wilderness soon anyway," Alagur replies. "We're getting closer to the city and there may be merchants about, or even soldiers."

Marrida shades her eyes from the glaring sun, which is steadily rising above them. She's surprised at how hot it is in the open fields which they've descended to since riding down from the Upper Plains. The heat is greater than it ever seems to be in Ruh'nar, which itself is in the tropical regions of the land. Marrida decides nature is playing a trick on them and can easily make it cold again without any warning.

She looks again at the shimmering dark shadow of the city they're heading towards.

"Do the Wolf Riders have a name for it?"

"They call it North City."

Marrida shivers and rubs her arms.

"You can't be cold in this heat," Alagur says.

"No, I'm feeling uncomfortable looking at the city. Something about it seems wrong."

"In what way?"

"I don't know. I just feel like I don't belong there." Marrida looks up at Alagur. A tear rolls down her left cheek, then another appears from her right eye. Alagur uses a finger to wipe away each tear in turn. He looks at her with concern and love.

"If you don't want to go, just say so, and we can head south instead."

Marrida shakes her head. "I'm too curious about this place to turn away now. Hearing Emelyse and Jarryca talking piqued my interest."

"So, we're going?"

"Yes."

* * *

ALAGUR GUIDES THE WOLVES TO A GROUP OF TREES and drapes a blanket over the two lowest branches of one. Marrida follows him slowly on foot. The sandy soil below the tree is so soft in texture, it almost feels like she's dropping down onto a soft cushion.

Alagur hands her the water container, which she takes gratefully and drinks from to quench the growing thirst which has been annoying her for the last two hours.

"Alagur, can you get the blankets out and lay them over here so I can lie down to sleep?"

He nods and does as she asks. He can see how tired Marrida is, and it's giving him some concern. The rush of escaping capture has taken its toll on her.

As soon as Marrida lies on the blankets, she can't keep her eyes open. Alagur watches her sleep for a while, then decides to work on readying their belongings. By the time they arrived at the fourth watchtower, their food supplies had dwindled to almost nothing, but they can't really arrive in the city with many belongings from Emelyse's house. He decides they will only take one pack in.

First, though, the wolves need to hide somewhere. Alagur takes Marrida's notebook and writes on the corner of the first page that he'll be back soon. He then climbs on the back of Yalla and rides fast towards the east. After half an hour, Alagur can hear gushing water. For moment, he thinks he's hallucinating, but once past a rock, he sees he isn't.

He quickly gets off his wolf and signals to Yalla to go down to the small oasis below. He doesn't even wait to see where Yalla and Lya will end up, instead turning around and starting his return trip to Marrida at a brisk pace.

Dusk has descended on the landscape, giving it an eerie feeling of being disconnected from the rest of the vast continent, by the time Alagur arrives back at the camp. He finds Marrida awake and stirring something in a pot over a campfire.

"I found your note when I woke up an hour ago." Marrida smiles at him. "For some reason, now it's dark and I can't see North City, I feel much calmer. No, that's not the right word – it seems that whatever was causing me to feel like I was being watched isn't watching me now."

Marrida continues working on their meal. Alagur asks what it is, but she replies with an enigmatic smile and a "You'll know soon enough". The goods he unpacked before trekking east with the wolves are still where he left them, so he decides to organise the haversacks and packs.

Marrida times the meal perfectly to coincide with him placing the final few items in the pack. Alagur sits down, and Marrida passes him a steaming bowl of thick broth. The man's face lights up when he recognises the flavour of the broth he ate at her house on the day she overslept and missed out on attending the Temple.

"I didn't know we'd got all the ingredients for this," he says with his mouth full.

"We're missing three of the ingredients, but the berries I found nearby are a good substitute," Marrida replies, feeling happy that she's managed to surprise the man with the delicious meal. Marrida and Alagur grin at each other. Nothing else matters except how they feel when they're in each other's company – content.

Sometime after they've eaten their dinner, they are lying side by side on the bedding, and Alagur is telling Marrida some of the comical retellings he heard in City of Wolves.

"And he went to the trenches and fell into the pile of manure." Alagur wipes tears of laughter from his face. "And we told him it wasn't just any manure, but that it came from the wild wolves."

Marrida lies on her back, holding her stomach from laughing too much. "Oh dear, what did he do?"

"Nothing. He got up and walked back to the sleeping house in as dignified a manner as he could. I think everyone still calls him 'The Wolfman' because of it."

Both roll around laughing once more.

"Does anything funny happen at the Temple?" Alagur asks. "Or are they all oh-so-serious there?"

Marrida laughs again when Alagur completes the sentence in an imitation of Joharan. She's sure her uncle would have frowned if he'd heard Alagur, but she doesn't care now. She's having fun.

But then she stops laughing for a moment and tells him about Sarayna and her friends, and how they'd do everything possible to make the Keepers and Elder find fault with her.

"I think they're the ones who told Elder Sharriba that I'd arrived at the Temple and was in the library," she explains. Then she tells him about one instance when she and Sarayna been told to tidy up herbs, mimicking her former nemesis. "'You need to put that there, and that one there, and this there, there, there, there'."

"I think you missed your calling," Alagur snorts, letting out a hiccup of laughter. "You should have worked as an entertainer, you would have been good at it."

"So, would you! You're good at doing retellings."

They look at one another, trying to keep straight faces, but failing. Lying side by side, they keep laughing for no apparent reason, glancing at each other, which sets them off again.

The moon is past its highest point in the sky by the time they finally stop laughing. Looking up at it, and the many stars twinkling back at them, they're silent for quite some time before Marrida speaks.

"I wonder how things are at home – I miss them so much--"

"If we find all the answers here, we can start our journey back." Alagur moves his arm so the woman can lie with her head on his right shoulder. With his right hand, he caresses her right arm.

"I hope we do. But will we need to go back by a longer route in case the Wolf Riders come back?"

I'm sure we're safe from them." Alagur tries to sound convincing, even though he's constantly looking to the west for any signs of the dust cloud. It is gone for now, and with it the immediate threat of anyone coming after them. He also keeps glancing through the darkness of the night towards the city. It, too, feels like a threat, although he isn't sure why.

Marrida is tired. She's pretending to be alright so the man doesn't pick up on her fear, but she thinks her earlier feeling of being watched may have been a warning sign of some sort. She can't do a vision when she's in this frame of mind. Although she's stronger now compared to a year ago, she hasn't yet mastered the techniques to shield herself from the elements of danger within a vision. If she does a vision in which a violent event is replayed, the part of her which felt the foreboding earlier could shut her mind down, causing her to collapse. It's this, more than anything, that's making her avoid visions which could give her the most answers.

"Alagur?"

"Hmmm?" The man was almost asleep, but he wakes up when Marrida speaks.

"I think we should keep travelling after we're finished here."

"Which way do you want to go?"

"South, like you suggested a few days ago. And afterwards, we could visit Marridina before going home."

"Isn't that the region you're named after?" Alagur glances sideways at the woman, kissing her forehead.

"It is. I want to go there to see if I can find out more about my mother. We could travel after that to Chiva'na to do the same for you."

Alagur smiles. His greatest desire is to find his sister again, and each time Marrida suggests going to Chiva'na, it gives him a feeling of hope — as if things really are going to turn out alright.

"And after we've found my sister, we'll go back to Ruh'nar, so you can see your sister do her Second Rites." Alagur knows, with the best will in the world, it will take them at least three years to return to Ruh'nar. Neither of them knows how long it will take them to do everything they need to do to find the answers which lie in North City.

He glances over to Marrida, and sees her eyes are shut. She has managed to drift off to sleep quietly, and he didn't even notice.

Alagur looks again at the sky and watches the clouds gently drifting in front of the moon, then moving away. He thinks about his sister, and as he falls asleep, his mind is filled with dreams of his distant home.

* * *

WHILE MARRIDA AND ALAGUR SLEEP PEACEFULLY, the first light creeps over the eastern coast, and bit by bit bathes both of them — and the city beyond. At the same time, a man in that city is walking reluctantly towards a dark building, holding his daughter's hand and glancing towards the outer walls.

One day, someone will come, and when they do, I'll make sure that they know what's going on here.

With a heavy heart, the man pushes his daughter through a blackened door, then turns and walks away as quickly as he can.

CHAPTER SEVENTY-NINE

A GENTLE BREEZE STEADILY BLOWS away the previous day's heat while Alagur and Marrida wash themselves in a small pond. Marrida wants to wash off the sweat which is caking her hair into ribbons, otherwise she's sure the people in the city will be able to smell them coming.

She splashes water over her face and head. The water refreshes her and takes away the feeling of nausea she has had all morning. She even refused the piece of fruit bread Alagur offered her during the morning meal, despite his suggestion that it would make her stomach feel better. The water also soothes away the headache she woke up with.

Marrida smiles, then takes the man's hand.
"I'm blessed to have met you," she murmurs softly.
"Although a few times you have been angry with things I have said or done."
"I know, but--"
Marrida stops talking and stares with narrowed eyes towards the city.
"What's wrong?" Alagur mutters.
"I don't know. But the feeling I'm being watched is back. Something is definitely happening in the city during the daytime which my Keeper skills are picking up on."
"Even without using your Stone of Truth?"
"The skill is amplified by the crystal, but those who possess it always feel its underlying presence, even if they're not aware of it."

Alagur is surprised every time Marrida teaches him something new about the Order of Truth and her gem. He wonders if the sensations of dread he's been feeling could be his own abilities leaking from his mind without the Stone of Truth – *her* Stone of Truth, he reminds himself – channelling them.

Marrida and Alagur walk towards the massive city. With each step they take, it seems the city is growing, although Marrida reassures herself it's an illusion caused by the strange effects of the atmosphere around her. It seems that the city was built in this location deliberately, and she wonders who built it originally.

She squints at the buildings, the features of which are just about visible each time a cloud covers the glare of the sun.

"Alagur." Marrida stops walking. "What are your impressions of the buildings?"

The man stops walking too. They lower the pack they're carrying between them, and after straightening up, they place both their hands above their eyes to shield them from the sunlight. Then Alagur answers.

"Some of the architecture is like the fourth watchtower."

"You're right. When Elder Sharriba talked of a city which is older than the Order, she was possibly talking about this one."

"Did she say anything else about it?"

Marrida thinks for a moment, then answers, "No. But she did say almost all Keepers have trouble seeing the past of this city."

"So, Wolf Riders aren't the only ones who have trouble here," Alagur says sarcastically.

"It may stem back to a time before we had an Order," Marrida adds. "And there's something going on. How did Emelyse put it again? She said 'They need two to keep the northern invaders away', or something like that. I'm too exhausted now to search my mind for the exact wording."

"I'm still wondering what she really meant when she said there were two Elders in Ruh'nar in the distant past, and Jarryca challenged Kyrana about the lack of the Second Elder when she visited. What if there are two of them here?"

Alagur nods towards the massive city. Marrida looks up at it again and thinks about the conversation between Emelyse and Jarryca. It offered clues to the precise identity of the city, but Marrida won't have a point of reference until she's inside it and has heard its dialect.

"If there are two Elders here, we'll find out about it soon enough. But we need to be cautious. Remember what Emelyse said about me? No one in the eastern parts of Keldarra should know who or what I am."

"You mean about you being a--"

"Shush!" Marrida says quickly. "We don't know how far sound travels here."

Alagur blushes. He'd forgotten for a moment that he should approach everything as if he's scouting for the Wolf Riders.

Marrida giggles when she sees his red face. "I'm sure you didn't mean to say it. Perhaps we should refrain from mentioning Emelyse's name over here too."

Alagur still can't quite grasp how much Marrida has changed. A year ago, she seemed so uncertain, but now she is really finding her self-confidence. As they stand looking at the city for a while, Alagur realises that next to him is an adult woman – his future life partner. Then they quietly pick up the pack and start to walk again, somewhat slowly this time as if to delay their inevitable arrival at the dark city.

Marrida speaks once more. "There seem to be two types of architecture."

Alagur looks up again, and he frowns. *I can't see any difference in the buildings.*

"You see the somewhat lighter buildings at the top there?" Marrida points to a position north-east of where they are walking. "And now look at the ones there." Her slender finger moves to an area on the western side of the city.

Alagur nods. He now sees what she means. "Which is the older part, do you think?" he asks.

"Unfortunately, until we're inside the city, I won't know," Marrida says. "But the spire over there on the eastern side could relate to my kind."

Alagur glances at the woman next to him, noticing she is avoiding making a specific reference to what she is.

They stop again when several carts come towards them, and Marrida observes the people in the carts discreetly. One thing she's learnt from her days in the Temple is to be observant of the people around her. She remembers how she and Elder Sharriba would walk through Ruh'nar wearing dark cloaks which hid who they were. They'd sit on a bench close to the Academy of Warfare while Marrida watched her brother and others practise their spear throwing skills with varying degrees of success. From these observations, she'd noted that Esbara became one of the best after an impromptu lesson with Alagur in their inner courtyard garden, using an old tree stump as their target.

"Do you see how they interact?" Sharriba had stated. "They behave with bravado when their trainer is near, and show their uncertainty when he's gone."

"Why is it important to know about that?"

"It's important, because how people act can teach you whether they're sad, happy, angry, even in love."

"So, if I want to know if somewhere I visit is a good place or a bad place, I need to watch the people?"

"It isn't quite that simple. It comes with responsibility. You must never use your observations against a person, but always make sure they benefit from them."

"Is this the reason you brought me here to watch Esbara?"

"Yes. Watching your own kin is the greatest test of this skill. If you learn what you need to know from this, later it will help you when you need to figure out the mysteries surrounding you."

As Marrida watches the procession pass by, she becomes aware of how she was so conveniently prepared by Elder Sharriba for just such a situation as this. With a start, Marrida realises she observed Emelyse and Jarryca with the skill learnt from her mentor, and for a moment, she wonders if the two women were aware of what she did.

"They seem to be fleeing from something."

Marrida hears Alagur's whispered conclusion. She frowns. In the process of making her observations, she forgot Alagur — as a military man — would have had his own training for situations such as this. He observes those around him not with the eyes of a Keeper, but as a soldier.

"With a combination of your observational skills and mine, we can learn a lot here," she whispers back. "Not just from books in the library, but by watching and talking to people."

"How do you know there's a library in there?" Alagur nods towards the city.

"Because the spire tells me so," Marrida hisses. "It's the way a library is marked by the Order."

"Shush!" Alagur says in a perfect imitation of Marrida earlier, then he laughs. Marrida stares at the man in amazement. "Well, you did tell me not to talk of it, didn't you? I couldn't help but point out your slip of the tongue."

"I guess you're right," Marrida replies with a chuckle. "What else did you observe about them, Alagur?" she adds, nodding towards the carts, which are fading from view to the south.

"Some were young people, barely old enough to have done First Rites," he answers. "Others were elderly. The old woman in the second cart looked at me, and I got the feeling she was pleading with me for help."

"There was a baby in one of the carts too. The mother was doing her best to keep the child from crying. I'm really worried about what we might find in the city now. It feels like there's more going on than even Emelyse knew about."

"I suggest we're very cautious. We should wait until dusk before we arrive at the gate."

"How far are we from the gatehouse?"

"I'd say another four or five hours of walking."

"Why don't we stop just here for a rest? We can sit there."

Alagur looks towards where the woman is pointing and sees a stone slab. He grins when an image pops up in his mind.

"What's so funny?"

"I could image someone using that slab as the foundation stone of a house."

Marrida looks closely at the stone and sees its potential. "If I didn't have other things to do, I would build a house there." She chuckles softly. "And then I could live in it with my chosen life partner."

Marrida smiles warmly at the man. He smiles back at her.

They walk to the stone slab and sit down. After a while, Marrida decides she wants the fruit bread Alagur offered to her earlier, and she savours it while she looks more closely at the city.

From this distance, it doesn't look that bad. But Marrida is trying to convince herself that the new wave of foreboding she's feeling is just a side effect of seeing the people in their carts.

Once Marrida has eaten the bread, she drinks down about a quarter of the water in her container. After this, she lies down on the stone and looks up at the clouds in the sky, doing anything she can to dispel the feeling of foreboding from her mind. Alagur lies down beside her, and they start comparing the clouds to various real objects. One cloud in particular catches their attention. They agree it looks like the head of a wolf – similar to the one Bergas drew for them. Marrida smiles at the memory of the red-haired boy.

I'll get the parchment from the haversack later to look at it more closely.

Then she sees a cloud which startles her. It could almost be a Stone of Truth, except the cloud is completely white.

Marrida closes her eyes and organises her thoughts, pondering her memories of the preceding year. Something she saw, or perhaps heard, is the simple clue that has been eluding her.

Her eyes fly open.

The man – the leader of the Wolf Rider squad that pursued us – was folding a parchment in the vision that I was doing before we left the fourth watchtower. And it was a familiar parchment. I need to check the haversack, because if that drawing is missing, it means Bergas forewarned us of things to come. And the drawing will serve as a catalyst for these events.

She remembers Bergas's quiet whisper.

"A man will find it. And you will know to trust him when the time come."

"We need to go," she says to Alagur suddenly. "We've to get there."

They both walk briskly towards the city, Marrida trying to evade every attempt by Alagur to find out what's bothering her all of a sudden.

In the end, she replies, "I think I know what's going on. And we need to help."

An ominous feeling of dread rises in Marrida's heart as she looks upon the gates of the city they're approaching. This city is so old that her visions cannot clarify its hidden history. All she knows as she looks at the man by her side is that her own feelings are echoed by the concern in his eyes.

Alagur takes Marrida's hand and brings it to his lips. At this moment, he finally lets his heart speak the truth – he loves Marrida unconditionally. The simple gesture shows Marrida that she can be sure Alagur will do all he can to keep her safe.

As she turns to him, she smiles, and Alagur kisses her lips. Hand in hand, they pull their hoods over their heads and enter the city where the perils of the world began.

The End

573

**Marrida and Alagur's journey continues in the next instalment
in the book series THE WOLF RIDERS OF KELDARRA**

Book Two

STOLEN TRUTH

ORDER THE BOOK AT AMAZON
or your preferred bookstore

Here is the link to the book at Amazon:

https://www.amazon.com/gp/product/B088Q3SJ9P

Here's how to keep in touch with me!

Official website **nathaliemlromer.com**

Twitter   twitter.com/nmlromer
Facebook   facebook.com/nathaliemlromer
Blog   nathaliemlromer.blog
GoodReads   goodreads.com/nathaliemlromer
Bookbub   bookbub.com/authors/nathalie-m-l-romer

ABOUT THE AUTHOR

Nathalie was born in the Netherlands, lived there during her childhood before moving to Curaçao as a teenager. From there, she moved to Britain to live there for over two decades. She has lived in Sweden since early 2015 where she lives with her partner Anders.

From childhood, Nathalie has always loved to read novels. As a child, she would visit her local library and often borrow "adult audience" science fiction and fantasy novels, and as the bookworm, that she was (and still is) she'd read them all in a few days--and go back for more, often. The genres that interest Nathalie the most is science fiction, fantasy and historical novels. Her favourite authors, that include various science fiction, fantasy and historical authors are, but are not limited to) Isaac Asimov, Richard A. Knaak, Jean M. Auel, and Christie Golden. In addition to reading books, the other interests Nathalie pursues include needlework and crafts, archaeology, reading about various science topics, home cooking, photography, web design, and playing MMO games.

About the wolves in this novel!

Some aspects of how wolves behave in this story, have been fictionalised to fit in with the fantasy setting of the novel, however I've done much research into how these beautiful animals behave in their natural environment as well as around humans, and drawing on past experiences as a dog owner, to create Yalla--who is the primary wolf to feature in the story.

Please support one of the various wolf sanctuary charities that exist to give this misunderstood animal the credit it deserves!